FOOL ME TWICE

IN ALL JEST
BOOK TWO

D.E. KING

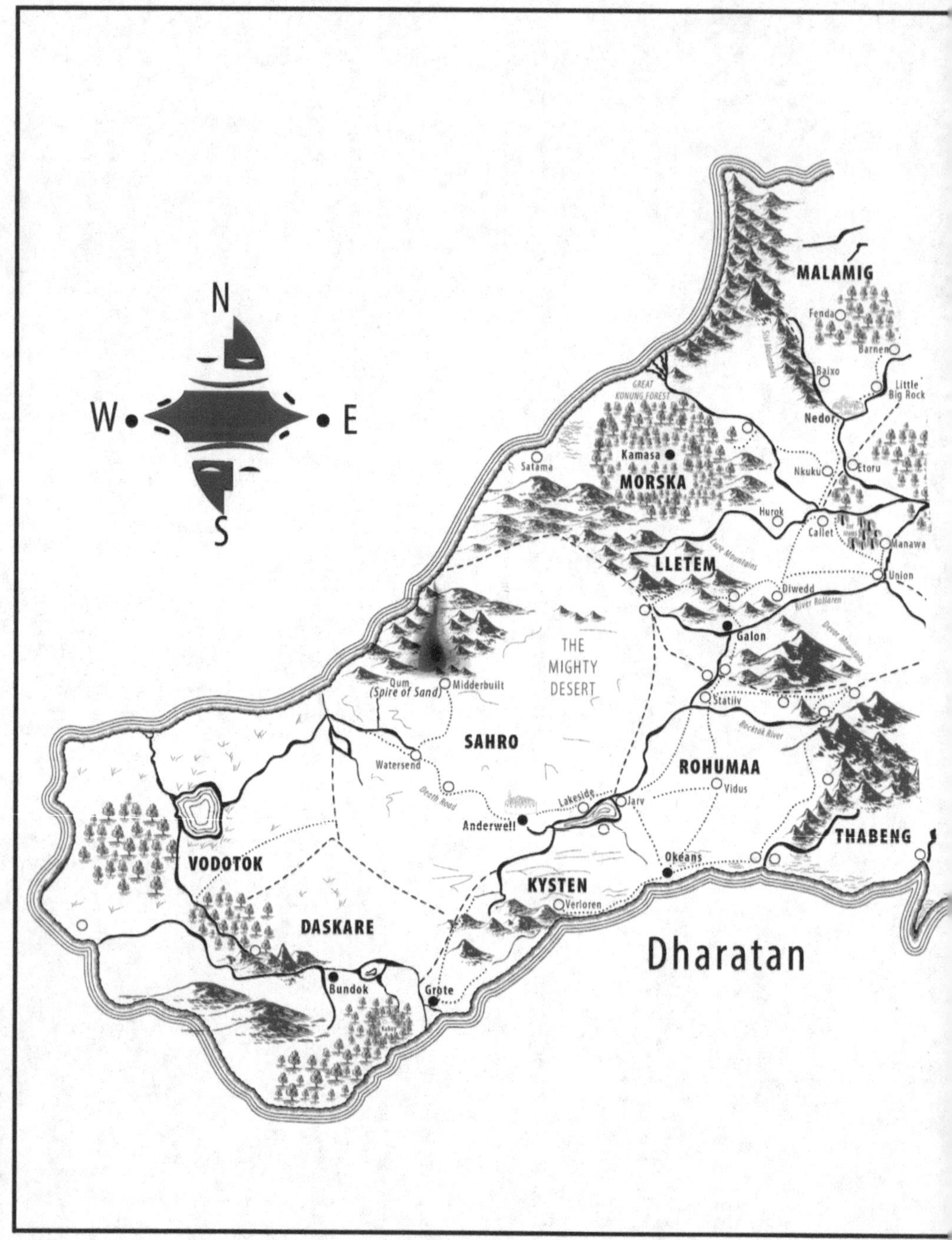

N
W
E
S
MALAMIG
Fenda
Barnen
Baixo
Little Big Rock
Nedor
Satama
GREAT KONUNG FOREST
Kamasa
Nkuku
Etoru
MORSKA
Hurok
Callet
Manawa
LLETEM
Union
Diwedd
River Rollaren
Galon
THE MIGHTY DESERT
Statilv
Qum (Spire of Sand)
Midderbuilt
Bocktok River
SAHRO
ROHUMAA
Watersend
Vidus
Death Road
Lakeside
Jarv
THABENG
Anderwell
VODOTOK
Okeans
KYSTEN
DASKARE
Verloren
Dharatan
Bundok
Grote

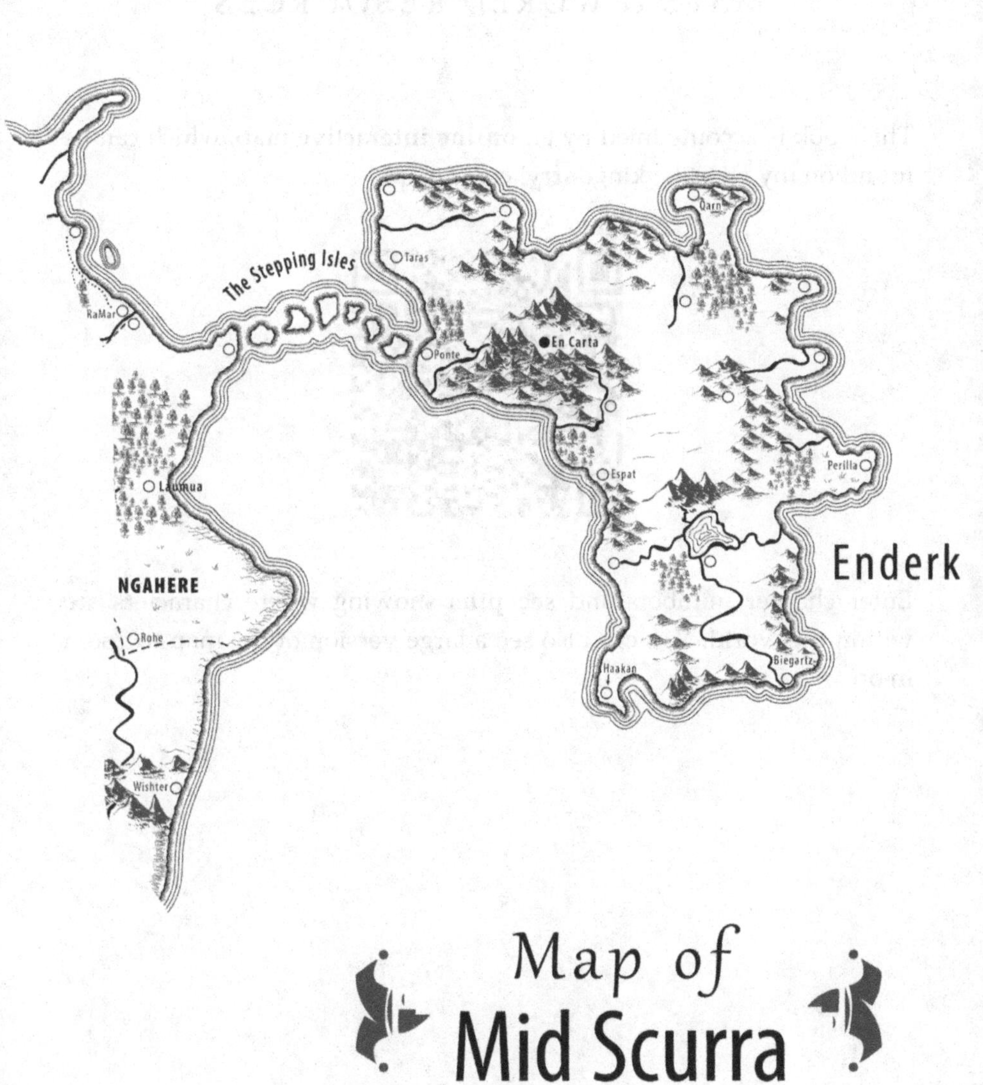

Map of
Mid Scurra

MAPS & WORLD RESOURCES

This book is accompanied by an **online interactive map**, which can be found on my website: kingdarryl.com/maps.

Enter chapter numbers and **see pins** showing where characters are within the world. You can also see a large version of the map to zoom in on.

PROLOGUE

$\mathcal{B}$etween the world of people and the place where he and the other gods called home was what the Jesters called the Void. It wasn't a void. A void is an emptiness, an absence of anything. There was plenty in this place. The word that best described it to him was the Flux.

He had thought about explaining that to the members of the Court, but they were comfortable with the Void. And explaining why it wasn't a void might mean giving away more than he wanted to. More than he and his siblings had chosen to give.

While the world had been under control there seemed little point to mete out more than was needed. People weren't always reliable and with too much knowledge they could just as easily do harm as good.

That was the paradox of the relationship between the gods and the people. They needed each other. Without people there was no way to achieve the goals that Revas had set out for them. People wanted the care and help of the gods, they wanted to know that their place in the world was favored.

Little did they know that without their worshipers the gods could not come to the land of people and help them. The larger their following the longer the Flux allowed the gods to be on land in a phys-

1

ical form. The duration of their stay wasn't an exact thing. He could never predict when his time would be up, but as it approached the pull was clear.

Without followers they couldn't do their work. Like this visit, he had to balance his time between being godly to his people and finding out what was causing the Occultation to break. If it wasn't for him and Thenis intervening to push people in the right direction, he doubted the chosen few would even understand what they did.

Thenis was able to stay within the world of people much longer because she had become almost a default deity in Dharatan. The devotion and recognition sustained her where others struggled. Mukazi, for instance, hadn't been on the world of Scurra in such a long time, and her following was so small, almost non-existent, that she rarely left their home.

Mukazi had allowed her influence on land to dwindle as she stayed by the shield and maintained it. Not just to protect her followers but all people. No one would ever know that or follow her because of it. And her numbers were dwindling, to the point he hadn't found anyone recently that worshipped or even named her.

He wanted to use the Flux to travel across the land and continue his work, but he had so little power left now, he wouldn't be able to do that. Once he crossed into it, he would be drawn back to their home where he would have to wait to regain the strength he needed to exist again on the physical plane.

Every time when it got to this point he regretted not dedicating more time to growing his own following so he could stay longer. But he became so fixated on the problem of the amulets and the hunt for them that he put it off until it was too late.

When your time was up even the most adored, Thenis, had to return, or you weaken to the point where you could never return, and your power was completely gone. That should have happened to their sister, Yantarnaya, but for some unknown reason she was still active.

He didn't know how or why, and for a very long time, she had been busy in Enderk. Again on this trip he had sensed her, or a very thin trace of her, but she was still alive and still had power. Soon he would need to dedicate his time to solving that riddle. How had she outlasted the time limit?

Had he done enough this trip to keep everyone safe for a little longer? He couldn't tell, it was out of his control for now. The few levers he could pull he had pulled, and the amulet was important to whatever Yantarnaya's plans were.

Mukazi had been right all that time ago. It had been her idea to freeze the rulers and their amulets in time, hiding them from the world, while they tried to understand what was happening. It had seemed a good plan at the time, until they had to maintain it.

The amulets still contained power, and they had been unable to learn how to control them. All but the one from Schevenal was suspended in the vacuum, which they called the Cell, as were the ancient rulers they had been gifted to. Each of the orange gemstones still exuded a level of power. They were a threat to them all, to the Citadel Stone, and until they could find a way to destroy them, they needed to keep them away from Scurra.

It was critical that Lani got the amulet she held to the Jesters, people they could trust to protect it and hide it from the Vrah, and anyone else that the Debrua Stone would send for it.

He walked into the Flux. That was the other difference from what the Jesters could do. He moved into it. It was in the Flux that he could travel from one place to the other, it was here that he could seek answers and his siblings. And it was here he could...

There it was, the draw. He couldn't stop it now it had begun. He could feel himself being pulled, like water down a drain, and he flowed towards it, towards their home.

Immediately he felt lighter. The weight of being physical was gone. He felt whole and new. Although new was an odd way to describe it, there was nothing 'old' about him here, despite his length of existence. He just was. There was no physicalness, even though he had a form.

When he moved it wasn't walking, nor floating. He just moved. He moved to a place, a spot and he was there. How it might appear to people he wasn't sure, and in truth he didn't care.

As he came to the place where the dome existed he saw that Thenis wasn't here. It had been a slim hope.

"You're back, Hembleth."

"Yes, Mukazi. How fares the shield?"

"It holds but the tearing continues. Little rips here and there." She used her head to nod at the others while keeping her hands on the transparent dome they stood around.

"We repair them as quickly as we can, but it seems to take us longer to do now, and more are forming all the time. Where once we were able to stop them, now we're only just holding on. I fear we'll lose the race soon enough."

"That would explain it."

"Explain what?"

"More knowledge is appearing in the land of people. You can sense it coming."

Mukazi looked back at the dome, her eyes closed for a period.

"There is something else."

Hembleth waited.

"We lost one of the amulets."

"Lost?"

"Several cracks happened together. We were fixing them, but it seems one of them was related to the Cell. There were not enough of us here, and by the time it was fixed we noticed that one of the men from the Cell was gone."

"What does that mean?"

"I'm not entirely sure."

"This doesn't bode well."

"The vacuum we suspended them in protected their bodies from the passing of time. Now that he's free it will catch up to him. He won't survive."

"But the amulet?"

She shook her head. It had been so long since she had been down there, she had no sense of space or time like he did. He looked around at the others.

"Why so few of us?"

"Whether they know why or not, people are calling out for our help more and more. The call to go back is growing more quickly than ever. It is only me that can avoid it."

"We should speak of that, your following is almost gone completely."

She shrugged. "Someone must stay. We need more here, if we are to keep it intact…"

He already knew what she was trying to say. The more people on Dharatan needed them, the less time they stayed here. Then they would be drawn back again to their home, and it would begin again. If there were fewer of them here, the sustenance of the shield diminished. What had been named the Occultation could not hold forever. At least, not as they had hoped.

Maybe that was a good thing, Hembleth thought. All of them standing here for so long had done nothing to stop it, only delayed it. Maybe there were better things for them to be doing.

What of the other worlds, the people that needed more from them than just a passing glance? What of places where he wasn't known as Hembleth?

It was too much to ponder now. He placed his hands on the dome and added strength to it. What was done was done, he would help hold on to it a little longer.

❧

Seerbols wiped sweat from his brow with the sleeve of his tatty robe. He was well past noticing the sand mixed in with it and little scratches formed on his forehead as he did so. Living as a desert pirate wasn't a life for the soft.

It was a way of life few chose deliberately, but once begun it was very hard to leave.

Day on day you survived the relentless sun, spending your time looking across the sea of sand to spot traveling caravans while staying out of their sight. Raids always happened at night but positioning yourself was done during daylight.

You needed to be close enough to launch your attack without too much effort, but not so close that a wayward noise from your team or camels would alert the guards of the caravan. And there were always guards of some sort.

The large distances between cities meant there were never patrolling guards which meant traders had to bring their own. Being a guard wasn't much better an existence than Seerbols's, and they often had limited career choices.

Those who had that role came in one of two types: ruthless, caused by a meanness about the injustice of their life, or lazy, because they had fallen into this work through a poor attitude and usually a reluctance to do any hard work or fighting. Seerbols always tried to avoid those who looked like the first type. He only had a three-man crew, him and his two sons. No potential reward was worth the loss of one of his boys.

Lazy guards on less rewarding caravans were good enough for them. Their needs were simple. No need to be greedy. Seerbols had seen the bones of many who had become too ambitious and attempted to raid a caravan stocked with highly trained mercenary guards.

He was smarter than that. Mostly. He knew he wasn't that smart or he'd never have ended up doing this, and dragging his sons into it.

The late afternoon shimmer was at full strength, the worst time of the day. Despite the small shade cover they lay under, their bodies were hot and weary. Rationing water to survive for days on end meant that by late afternoon you began to see things which weren't there.

Seerbols shook his head and rubbed his eyes, looking east across the rolling dunes, seeing wisps of sand flowing like silken robes in a light wind.

"Da!"

Seerbols turned to look at the younger of his two boys, Mopteb. "What is it?" Already he was turning to where his son pointed.

"A twister?" he asked no one in particular.

"Out here, Da?"

Seerbols didn't know what to make of it. The wind wasn't that strong but it looked like the air was twisting. The air looked different, you couldn't see through it entirely but they were too far away to detect why.

"Shall we investigate, Da?" the eldest boy asked.

Seerbols shook his head. "Never show yourself if you have no need, you know my rules."

They all lay still watching to see what the desert was about to do. The spot they stared at didn't come closer to them, or change at all, but it was very different to the air around it. To the left and right of it Seerbols could see sand and sky as he expected. All except this thick shimmer about the width of two men and fifty feet high.

"What on Sahro..." his voice trailed off.

A man stumbled from the shimmer and fell forward into the sand. He struggled to get back to his feet before turning to look back at where he had come from, backing away from it, holding an arm out as if to protect himself from it.

He wore a long robe, and even from this distance Seerbols could tell it was of high quality. This man was a noble of some sort. A small grin formed on his dirty face. A wealthy target appearing right in front of them was a great blessing. Seth the desert god was honoring them.

The man turned away from where he had come and took several more steps. Unaccustomed to walking on the sand he sank and fell several times. He didn't appear to see them and Seerbols waited. They had a distinct advantage.

As if the man's appearance out of the strange shimmer wasn't enough, the three pirates' eyes were transfixed by what happened next. At first his hair and beard were a rich black and full, but they changed quickly as if every step was like a year passing.

Before them his beard turned grey and most of his hair fell out, his clothing became sloppy as his body lost weight and he fell more often. Rising out of the sand became almost impossible for the man.

He called out a pained "No!" before falling for the final time.

None of the three men watching moved at all. It was only when the shimmering air disappeared that Seerbols was game enough to rise from their blind, his curved sword held out in front of him. His sons followed even more slowly behind him.

When they reached the man, Seerbols prodded him with his foot. "You alright?"

The body lay inert before him.

"Help me turn him over, boys!"

It took little effort to do so, and they all jumped back as the pile flipped over. A skeleton lay before them, wrapped in the clothing that had walked across the sand.

"Sweet Seth, what is this, Da?" Mopteb's voice almost squeaked.

"Trouble, is about all I can tell you, boys. There can't be no good that this brings, for sure."

Seerbols could feel a coolness trickle down his spine, slowly, almost painfully. In his head, he could hear his thoughts trying to tell him to turn and take the boys. To get away from here and never mention it to anyone.

But something else made him want to know more. Something drew him to kneel down and search the man.

"What are you doing, Da?"

"What we always do, profit from others' misfortunes."

He had been right about the robe, it was a fine material, not some typical cloak worn by townsfolk. He patted for pockets but didn't feel anything through the sides and untied the clasp near the skull, letting it fall open.

"Oh Seth indeed!" he gasped.

"Whoah," Mopteb exclaimed as well.

Hanging on a gold chain before them was the most beautiful amulet Seerbols had ever seen. It twinkled in the remaining sunlight, and the man sensed what he could only explain as a smile coming from it. The gem set in a dark metal seemed to be soaking up the sunlight and gleaming, as if free from a darkness.

"What stone is that, Da?"

Seerbols had to shake his head clear. He couldn't believe the size of it. The chain alone would give him a huge pay day, but this amulet was something else.

"I've only ever seen one which was anything like it. And that was the forbidden amber."

"Forbidden?"

"As long as anyone's ever known, amber is a forbidden gem, not just here either, but in all the neighboring states. The crew that tried to sell some small amber ring ended up hung, somewhere on the border near Mugan, is about all I know."

"So that's not worth anything then?"

"Ha! Oh it's worth plenty. Just because something's forbidden doesn't mean there aren't those who want it. They pay double or more for something forbidden. You should know that by now. And something like this, we'd not be needing to pirate another day in our lives."

"Really?"

"We'd live like kings for sure, mark my words."

"Shall I wrap it up then?" Mopteb asked.

"No!" Seerbols snapped, reaching his hands out to stop the boy. "That's my job, leave it to me."

"What we going to do with him?"

"I'll finish searching him then we'll cover him in sand, and get as far away from here as we can, and fast. Whatever he came out of I don't want to see again. We've just found our mother lode and I want to cash it in as soon as I can."

By the time the three men were long gone from the location of their blind, the winds had already hidden the spot where they had left the bones. They had stripped him of his fancy clothing, boots and the other jewelry he had on him. Seerbols was concerned about the signet ring he had borne on his right hand — the bear etched into it looked remarkably like the Skarian symbol.

Who was the man? And what was he doing out there?

He had no answers but he could feel a warmth coming from the amulet that hung under his tunic against his chest. He already felt like he owned it, and part of him wasn't so sure he needed to sell it. He could just sell the chain and live off that for a while.

"Where we heading, Da? Why are you taking us south, that's not normal."

"Why are you questioning me? Haven't I always made the decisions for us all?"

"Ya."

"Then enough of that attitude. Things are different now, we're going to be able to live differently. I need to find somewhere to cash in what we found, and then we'll decide what comes next after that."

Neither of the boys said anything else, they went back to following their father through the sands.

Where will I cash it in? Surely that signet is the answer. The most value for something like that has to be Daskare. That's where I feel drawn to go, I don't know why, but it seems to make the most sense. If that man was from there, then it's likely his things will fetch a healthy price from one of his compatriots. Or a reward, if he was important. Wasn't like we harmed him. I need to give Seth a sacrifice, to thank him for this gift. I don't want to turn his anger against us, not now, not with such a prize.

Seerbols plodded on, his mind spinning as he tried to imagine all the ways his life was about to change.

KARPENMOR

*B*eing alive had always seemed so pointless to Karpenmor. He stood on the balcony of his room, looking back towards the mountains. He felt like a mountain. Solid, but lifeless. Mountains existed, they were significant, but to what purpose?

What was his purpose? Everything in his life seemed to be pointless. He knew that should have changed once his father had died, being heir to ruling Enderk, but it hadn't. If anything it had made it even worse. Now he was truly alone.

The silence was almost complete, the only sounds he heard came from far across the walls, out in the city that he rarely saw. Even then they were muted, it was as if he was on a remote island, alone except for all the servants. And Uksod of course.

Uksod was the only one he saw constantly, his surrogate father. The priest told him what to do, when to do it, and what was going on. His real father, when he was still alive, had sat on his own in the Amber Room, living in whatever world it was he had ventured to.

He wished he could go and visit his father again. The stupidity of it was, he visited so few times when the old man was still alive but now he yearned for the chance every day.

It occurred to him that it was whenever he was out here on the balcony, in the fresh air, he remembered his father, as if there was some significance to the place. Each morning the thought renewed itself and he intended to do it, but as the day wore on he had forgotten it.

Why was that?

There hadn't been much point to the visits with his father, he knew, nothing was ever said, his father never even looked at him. Another pointless exercise. He had no mother; the shell of his father had been all that was left of his parents. And so, while nothing ever came of it, he had made it matter. He went despite the feelings of futility inside.

Karpenmor paced around the large balcony, stopping at the balustrade to watch some of the servants rushing about down in the grounds below. He couldn't remember the last time he'd been down there on his own. Probably when he was very small, he guessed. There was a time when he ran free and careless around the palace and its grounds. He could remember the feeling if not the actual memories.

The memories he did have were of him wandering the palace. He had lived inside here his whole life, and he knew almost every nook and cranny but he rarely ventured outside. And when he did, he was always accompanied by guards, and an escort — one of Uksod's priests, always there, always making small comments, pulling Karpenmor back into line.

The voice startled him. "There you are, Your Highness."

Karpenmor turned quickly, but recognizing the voice he wasn't afraid. He didn't feel much at all towards the man, except perhaps a little dread now that his peace had been disturbed. "Yes, Uksod, here I am."

"What are you doing?"

For as long as Karpenmor could remember Uksod had told him what to do, where to go, how to feel. Recently, though, Karpenmor had felt something stirring inside. He had begun to become annoyed by Uksod's constant questioning.

"What does it look like I'm doing, Uksod?" He surprised even himself in speaking what he was feeling. Just being asked what he was doing by Uksod angered him. Not much, but enough that he noticed it. He felt something, and he was intrigued by it.

"Excuse me?"

Karpenmor felt uncomfortable now. He had spoken without thinking and now his guardian was staring at him with a touch of anger in his eyes. It wasn't often that the anger came to the surface so readily, but someone would suffer because of it. The priest would find an errant servant or one of his own to vent his frustrations on, that Karpenmor knew. It was something he couldn't stop, not yet anyway. His acceptance of what would be was already replacing that tiny sliver of rebellion.

"I asked what you were doing, I didn't expect such rudeness." Uksod walked towards him. "Perhaps we haven't been keeping you busy enough with your preparations. That can be fixed."

Karpenmor turned away from him back to the mountains. He knew the man would fill his days with meetings and lessons about what his role was. None of it really mattered to him; he would be ruler at some point after his birthday, and at that point he'd do what he needed to do.

Most of the time he complied with what Uksod wanted him to do, but out here, in the mornings, it was different. There were times when he could see that soon he would be in charge, and that their relationship would be different. But then the activities of the day began and he was lost in the business of being the heir.

Karpenmor wasn't even sure he knew what it was he thought would change, it was merely an idea that flittered on the edge of his mind, never quite within reach. In reality he had no idea what he really wanted at all. Mostly he was just going through the motions that Uksod laid out for him.

"What is the matter?" Uksod sounded a little less officious, as though he had tried to give his voice a touch of empathy.

"Nothing's the matter. I'm not particularly interested today."

That was the truth of it, he wasn't interested. He wasn't interested in much that happened around him, and yet he knew he should be. All of this was essentially his to rule. Now that his father had died, he would be High Prince. That should interest him, but he was soaked in apathy, and didn't care. He was bored.

"This will not do. Today of all days, your lack of presence will cause us all turmoil." Uksod put his hand on his upper arm to lead him. "Can you come inside, please?"

They went back into Karpenmor's room, Uksod closing the balcony door behind them.

Inside Karpenmor could see his manservant Bwindy was waiting for him. Clothes were laid out across the bed, and other staff were coming through the room ready to prepare him.

"What's this all for, Uksod?"

Uksod sighed. "Don't you remember anything? I've told you this every day for the last two weeks. Your birthday is upon us within days and today the Imperial families are presenting their gifts."

"Why, if it's not my birthday, are we doing this today?"

"It's the way it's done, Karpenmor. Can we not have this discussion?" He paused before adding, "Again!"

"I know none of them, why would they want to give me gifts? Why do I even care? I have more than I need, I don't even use everything that's already here."

"It's what happens when you are the ruler, Lord. I've told you that."

"It's stupid is what it is. Fawning after someone they don't even know. None of them ever cared about Father, none ever came to see him."

"That's because they were told he was unwell."

"He was still the High Prince." Karpenmor felt a little more alive when he spoke of his father. This time he looked at Uksod, his meaning clear.

"Yes, he was, but in his condition the less the other families saw of him the better. What good would come of the competitive families seeing their High Prince the way he really was? There would be uproar. It was best that he was known to be aging and aloof, and that business carried on as usual. None of that matters anymore anyway. It's on your shoulders now."

Karpenmor felt offended by the way Uksod brushed over his father's death. It had only been a matter of weeks.

Perhaps seeing his face change, Uksod, softened his tone. "You are to be seen, Lord. That's the very purpose of today and what will come in future weeks."

Karpenmor shrugged. He knew it didn't matter what happened, now or today. His path here was set. He could understand now what his father might have felt, like a heavy blanket you always wore, dragging you down. It pulled at your heart and soul and left little to breathe with.

Getting through every day felt like walking through deep mud. Just walking to another room seemed too much effort. How on Enderk would he ever be able to rule properly?

"So, what now?"

"Now, Lord, we get you ready to meet everyone. I've fixed you a drink which I think will help you last through the day. You need to be alive and vibrant when you receive these guests, we want them to see in you their leader."

"You've been their leader, Uksod, not me."

"Was, My Lord. You know this. After this birthday I will no longer be Regent." Uksod paused and swallowed. "You as the heir will become the High Prince. It is your right."

Karpenmor shook his head. "I don't want this; I have no wish to rule this place. I don't even know anything outside of this palace."

Uksod pulled him back to look at him, quickly looking around the room at the servants. "You must never say such things in front of others, Karpenmor. You know not what you have just done. Enough! Drink this."

He saw Uksod nod to one of the guards standing by the doors. The man nodded, albeit only just, back in response, and looked around at each of the servants, as if noting who they were, before continuing his vigil.

Karpenmor took the tall skinny vessel, like chiseled stone, and tipped the contents into his mouth. The sweet amber liquid slid down his throat easily. Everything around him seemed to soften, edges grew blurred. He was there, he could see normally, but then he could feel and hear something else, a voice that was coming through him but not of his making.

"He'll be fine, Uksod. I'll be fine now. Let's get on with this."

"Ah there we are, now we can make some progress."

Karpenmor observed what was happening to him, the servants

washing him, his hair and immature beard trimmed and tidied. He was dressed in new garments he'd never worn before. The softest silk, all white, that caressed his skin. The voice that spoke on his behalf. He was a passenger inside himself as the process continued.

Once he was done, he stood back and looked into the mirror glass at himself, stunned by who he saw. Whatever he had drunk made him seem in command, tall and alive, regal in the fine clothes.

Uksod came over to him. "Now there's the leader we need."

"You know that they cannot stay after what they heard?" The voice spoke through Karpenmor.

"I know! The Vrah will take care of it. His guards wait outside, the three of them will be removed."

Inside, Karpenmor struggled to understand what they were talking about. A nugget of fear sat inside him. He wanted to understand it, to care about what was happening outside but everything was dulled, and he couldn't fight it.

There there, boy. Don't bother with that. Know that when you say things, they have consequences. The voice spoke to him in his head without saying anything out loud.

Karpenmor wasn't sure what consequences she meant, what it was he had said that had consequences. A sliver of his mind wanted to know what the voice meant, he tried to keep it alive in his mind. But his control over it slipped away and he lost sight of it.

2

KARPENMOR

A massive glass dome covered the entire grand hall of the palace, allowing sunlight to reach the furthest corners of the vast space. An orange hue filled the room as the light bounced off the myriad amber ornaments and jewels throughout the hall giving the space a feeling of warmth.

As Karpenmor entered the room, he saw guards lining the outside of the hall, in bigger numbers than he had seen in a long time. Their black uniforms stood in contrast to the color throughout the room.

The floor was a speckled grey stone as were the pillars holding up the vast structure above. Inset into the pillars were a mass of amber gems that draped the room in color. He climbed several steps towards the large seat placed for him. On the level above and behind him sat his father's throne. As he looked at it, an emotion tried to escape whatever had hold of him, but it was quelled before he could grasp it.

That will be your throne, once there's the official ceremony. But enough, boy, let us receive our guests.

The procession of people coming to celebrate his birthday began. They came with gifts and words which he hardly noticed. Whoever it was controlling him did the speaking for him, acknowledging their presence.

17

Karpenmor watched on like a detached observer as the guests came and went. On the floor in front of him tables became filled with gifts of many sizes, with servants quickly sliding in new tables as required. He heard mention of some gifts that could not be brought into the hall; the finest horses, and one even brought a camel, a creature he had never heard of before.

In a way Karpenmor was glad of the fact it wasn't him that was speaking. Early on he was able to almost drift off into a dream state, but as the day wore on, he became more and more present.

I've shown you what you need to do, now finish the work.

The feeling behind the voice disappeared and he felt himself fully in his own body for the first time since this morning, when he had been given the drink in his room. There was a connection there, something he needed to understand better.

A cough beside him brought his focus back to the people in the hall. He looked briefly at Uksod who was staring ahead down at the next of the guests.

One by one they approached the bottom step, but only when Uksod had nodded to them. Karpenmor had become aware of the subtle inclination of his head each time, and realized how much the priest controlled everything around him.

The line of people seemed endless still. Holding forth their package they would wish him a happy birthday and coming of age before turning and placing the gift on the table.

Taking his cue from what he had seen all day, Karpenmor nodded, smiled or muttered his thanks, but in each case only a small acknowledgement. There had been some individuals that the voice and Uksod had given more attention to, the leaders of the Imperial families. So far seven of the eight had been.

"Not long, Karpenmor." Uksod stood behind him and whispered in his ear. "We are almost there. What you can see is the last of the guests, the outer doors are now closed."

"Thank Yantarnaya for that," he muttered back under his breath.

The latest presenter Karpenmor paid more attention to. She was an elderly woman, which always intrigued Karpenmor the few times he saw her. Apart from his father, everyone around him was young or of the middle adult age. She was the eighth of the family heads.

"Lady Natillian, My Lord." Uksod formally introduced her.

"From our family to yours we wish you a long and fruitful life." She raised her eyes at this point and looked directly at him, causing him to shiver.

"From our family estate we have brought five barrels of our finest aged wine, of which I present one carafe, for your convenience. Five of our finest mares each pregnant from our lead stallion, and..." She turned to her servant behind her. Taking a sheathed sword from him, she turned and held it in both hands. "...five swords, each hand-crafted by Dominiter, the finest smith in all of the world, one of my brothers. The most exquisite blades befitting our Lord."

Karpenmor looked down at her, intrigued by her age and the list of gifts she had provided.

"She wants you to take it, Lord," Uksod whispered to him.

Karpenmor stood, which took some effort, the hours of sitting here with the amber liquid running through his veins had left his body inert. Unsteadily he stepped down to the level above her. "Lady Natillian," a small nod of his head, "this is most kind of you."

He took the blade from her, surprised at how heavy it felt. She had lifted it as if it were nothing more than a stick. He thought he almost saw a tiny smirk at the edges of her mouth. He looked up at the remaining presenters and guards and held the sword aloft. "A most generous gift from the Lady of The Five."

"Live long, Lord, and we hope more visibly than your father," Lady Natillian said just loud enough for only him to hear before she turned and retreated with her servants who placed the remaining swords and carafe of wine on the long table.

Karpenmor stared after her. The voice in his head was gone, and only he had heard her comment, which bothered him. What did she know? Or was she meaning something else?

Her family, The Five, was the most powerful of the Imperial families outside of his own, or so Uksod had educated him. He'd always been taught to be wary of The Five family.

A cough from behind him caused him to turn and Uksod, who was standing beside his chair, beckoned him back with his eyes. Karpenmor wasn't sure what to do with the sword so carried it back to the chair.

"Take that from our lord," Uksod directed a servant, who hurried over and waited for Karpenmor to give it to him.

"What did she say?"

"Something about living long and being seen more than Father."

"Oh, did she now?" Uksod looked down the hall to where Lady Natillian was about to leave the chamber. She turned at the last, looked directly at Uksod and bowed mockingly before leaving.

The room remained still after her departure. Karpenmor looked to the next presenter, who did not move. This time it was he who made a small cough, breaking Uksod out of whatever had trapped his attention.

A quick nod followed, and the presenter moved forward. Karpenmor could see the embarrassment plastered over the face of the man. Having to follow the last of the Imperial family heads with his small gifts was an unenviable position to be in. Karpenmor made sure to smile a little wider and nod to the man.

Karpenmor's clearer head couldn't stop thinking about Lady Natillian, despite the people before him. There was a challenge in her manner and words, even if it were only slight, and Uksod had been triggered by it. That Uksod wasn't necessarily as all-powerful as he'd thought was enough to interest Karpenmor.

Now he waited to see if any other interesting guests might turn up. The later presenters were from smaller families or organizations of lesser importance. Not only was it noticeable in the value of the gifts presented but also in the appearance of the presenter.

He was disappointed but thankful there were only a few left before the hall was empty of visitors.

Uksod broke the silence. "I was concerned with how you might handle today but you did well, Highness."

"That was most tedious. I still don't understand why they wish to gift so much; I mean look at it."

Karpenmor stood and looked down at the copious items along the tables, the length of the room.

"We will take care of it all, Highness, there's no need to worry yourself over it. Will you return to your rooms now? "

He turned to Uksod and looked at him. Again a small resentment towards the priest simmered.

"No, I think I want to inspect some of these things more closely, that at least will be fun."

"Very well, when you're done the servants will clean it all up." Uksod turned and left.

Karpenmor smiled honestly for the first time that day. It seemed childish, but not doing what Uksod told him to do had become more and more enjoyable this last year.

There wasn't actually anything he wanted to look at, it had been purely to spite Uksod, and counter whatever it was he had suggested. He first went to look at the swords that Lady Natillian had gifted; each was much the same as the other. The wine bottle he unstoppered and smelt, and the deep red aroma wafted out, a rich fruity nose. He wasn't game to drink it; she had a look that worried him, and he'd have a servant taste it before he tried it.

With little interest in the other items spread out before him he wandered off to his rooms, finally alone again.

3

CARNUS

His world was amongst the trees. That was the choice he had made almost six years ago, and it still felt like the right decision. The Tombs were sacred to all Ngaherians and to qualify to guard them was the reward for all his efforts.

Carnus knew he was one of the most accomplished warriors in the guards of Manawa. He had won the annual competition to find the strongest amongst them, held in the capital Laumua. His prize was a choice between entering the Tombs or his pick of stations around Ngahere.

As long as Carnus could remember, no one had ever chosen to not enter the Tombs, the honor of it meant much for their families. It was a conscious choice to leave behind day-to-day life amongst the people and spend the rest of your days never setting foot outside of the Tombs.

Ngaherians didn't believe in religions like others, they were outlawed throughout the realm, but that didn't mean they didn't have beliefs. There was a spiritual connection to the trees, something tied deeply to the psyche of their race, known as the Wooden Path.

Before he had entered the Tombs, he knew nothing of the wood people either, and it was information never to be shared with those outside.

These woods were sacred. The bodies of all who died were brought here and hung from the treetops, forever entombed in the air. No one outside knew what happened to them once they were hung there, but the Protectors learned once they entered.

It had taken him some time to come to terms with this, but now he accepted it. It was one of the reasons others were not allowed into the Tombs. This knowledge of the trees feeding off of the corpses was not be known elsewhere.

The Wooden Path linked the trees and the people of Ngahere together and there could never be any corruption of that connection. Maintaining that purity of the Tombs was why the Protectors roamed the borders and removed anyone that entered them. Such bodies were never allowed to remain within.

Only Ngaherian bodies fed the trees within the Tombs. Only Ngaherians could ever know about the Father Tree deep within the woods, and the sacred figs throughout the forest.

Being a Protector meant giving your life to ensure the Wooden Path at the core of your people was always safe and continued on forever. Carnus was honored he could live out the rest of his life this way, and had never understood how anyone could reject it.

Being a Protector of the Tombs and the Wooden Path was the ultimate service to Ngahere. Carnus still remembered the face of his mother when he had chosen this life. It held a tinge of sadness at losing her second child, but overwhelmingly pride that he had achieved what so few ever could. For her remaining years she would be treated like royalty amongst their people.

It was the least he could do for her. She had brought life to him, suffered at the hands of his father, and loved his elder sister despite what she had done to them. That shame had been erased when he had become a Tomb Protector.

That his sister had taken up a religion and tried to convert others as followers had been bad enough. To then escape from custody and leave Ngahere without facing judgment, and certain death, was worse.

Honor was what held all Ngaherians together. There was no grey in rules and the price of breaking them.

It didn't bother Carnus the way their society operated, but his sister thought very differently. Carnus's father, as cruel as he could be, took her punishment instead, to erase some of the shame to their family. At least in that way he had done good for them but the looks had never truly disappeared.

Some things were simply harder for his mother and him, at least until he had grown into his size. Then something of an impasse had occurred. No one would deliberately take umbrage with his mother, from fear of him, but neither did they fully accept her back into the social networks.

When he became a Protector, that all changed. His mother was now one of the honored, and all of her past forgotten. She lived in a special community built for the families of those who served the realm like he did.

A smile crossed his face, wiping away the grimace that had been there from thinking about his sister. Knowing his mother was living out her last years so well, touched something deep inside. He was content. He had served his mother, and honored her, the way that all Ngaherians should honor their country.

Women ruled Ngahere, and were to be honored, always. Carnus shook his head at how his father had treated his mother. Had he done enough to remove the harm done by both of them? Had his father's sacrifice been enough to cleanse their fate? He would never know.

He walked into the gathering spot, a place central to the Tombs, near to the Father Tree. With much time on their hands, the Protectors learned how to craft exquisite objects from the sacred timbers and other things more mundane, like benches to sit on and forks to eat with.

Everyone else was here. Each new moon they gathered once as an entire group. It was a check to ensure nothing ill had become of any of them, or the worst fate of all, that one had become a Runner. They were never allowed back to live amongst the rest of their society, and Carnus understood why: so much knowledge was bestowed on the Protectors that it couldn't be shared outside.

That didn't mean no one ever left. In their history there had been several Runners, those who couldn't accept what they had learned and chose to abandon their post and leave the forest. There was only one place to do that, the southern border, which led to the neighboring realm, Lletem.

Once they left, word would have to be sent back to the outpost that sat on the northeastern edge of the Tombs, and a team of warriors would be sent to hunt them down. The chase was relentless, and would not stop until they were caught, which is why they were known as Runners.

None ever survived the hunt and the bodies were never returned to the Tombs. It was the second deadly shame after running, that they were not buried with their ancestors. Carnus shook his head. He couldn't really understand why anyone would want to leave here. He was at peace here, and there were none of the politics or petty dramas that filled city life.

"Everyone accounted for?"

His second in command nodded to him from his spot leaning against the trunk of a tree.

"Does anyone have anything to discuss?"

Heads shook but no one spoke. Speech wasn't required here, many of the Protectors had stopped talking years before. There was little mandatory interaction between them all.

"I'm changing the southern patrol. Team four can take over that, and all other teams rotate your posts to the north accordingly."

"The south? No one ever comes through there, why do we have so many men down there?" Zelf, one of the newest members, spoke shocking most of the people around the circle.

"It's our weakest point, and the longest. No other reason is required. And I have not served there in a while, I wish to spend some time there. Is that good enough?"

The man shrugged in response.

"If a procession arrives, send messengers. Otherwise we meet again on the next full moon."

He started heading south; the others would follow in good time. Zelf was right, there had been little to be worried about for the whole time Carnus had been a Protector, but still he never let his guard down. They had a job to do, and while he was their leader he would do it his way.

4

FULING

*H*is full head of hair always made him smile. For someone of his age it was rare. Fuling finished brushing it in the mirror, and adjusted his dark blue robe. It was freshly cleaned and he loved the feel of it against his bare skin underneath.

A knock on his door caused him to turn.

"Come."

His manservant half-entered the room.

"Yes, Ventra?"

"The King requests your presence. I was told to inform you it is most urgent."

"Oh really? Is he having one of his turns?"

"I am not sure, Eminence, I was simply informed."

Fuling nodded. "Where is he?"

"The main hall. Can I assist you in any way?"

"No, Ventra, I believe everything is as it should be. Lead the way."

Fuling enjoyed having people at his beck and call. It was one of the many pleasures his status and position afforded him. The only sound was the slap of his leather sandals along the dark corridors that joined the wing he resided in to the central buildings of the octagon that was the heart of the King's palace.

A chill lingered most of the year within the dark stone, so far south on Dharatan. Even when summer brushed over the structure it barely made a difference to the inside temperature. Fires burned for all but a few months of the year, a taint of smoke lingering everywhere.

It was why incense held such allure for him. He sprinkled it in every fire, and ensured it was burned throughout anywhere he frequented.

One must not smell like a common blacksmith, must one?

He could hear more noise than normal coming from the main hall, and his curiosity was piqued, as was his cautious side. It wasn't often that he was left out of King Ahn's deliberations. Maybe he'd removed the amber necklace that Fuling had given him.

The last time he'd done that, the man had begun to alter their plans a little. It had taken all of Fuling's guile to get the King to wear it again. Things were difficult enough trying to find their goal, with little to no information. If King Ahn slipped out of the amber's influence it would make it near impossible.

"Finally!" The King was behind his throne, pacing anxiously.

"Your Highness, I came as soon as the message arrived. What's the problem?"

"Problem?" He stared at Fuling blankly for just a moment before grabbing hold of his train of thought, and turning back to the room.

Fuling put his left hand into the pocket in his robe, and slipped the ring hidden there onto his middle finger. Immediately he felt the touch of the amber, and sought out the necklace worn by the King. It had taken him a year of practice to be able to do it as easily as Uksod had told him it should be. He was able to hold a tiny connection in a corner of his mind, while he behaved like normal to others around him.

"These three men were caught trying to get into the palace. They said they had to see me, they had a gift for me."

"These three?" Fuling had moved alongside the throne, where Ahn now sat. The three men were filthy, their skin baked by harsh sun, and the older of the three had a cunning look to his eyes.

"Yes."

"What is the gift?"

"I have not asked, yet. I waited for you, for your opinion." The man stuttered a little as he spoke.

"I appreciate it, Your Highness." Fuling looked at the three men again, and the guards holding them. "Let him approach," he said indicating the older of the three.

The man shook his arm after the guard let go his grasp, and took several steps forward before dropping to a knee and bowing before King Ahn.

"Your Highness, I come only to offer you the finest of gifts."

"What gift is this?" Fuling spoke before the King replied. "What gift could men such as you have for our King?"

The man didn't reply quickly. He stared at Fuling, in a way the priest didn't like, and then looked to the King. He slowly went to a pouch tied to his waist and fumbled in it for something small he pulled out.

Looking at the King and not Fuling he held it out in the palm of his hand. "Your Highness, I believe this probably belongs to you?"

King Ahn stood, before Fuling could intercept, and moved forward. The guards in the room were all on edge now, Fuling could see many hands reach for the hilts of swords.

When the King reached the man, he plucked what appeared to be a ring from the man's palm and stood up, holding the object close to his ailing eyes.

"A ring! It's the royal signet, if I'm not mistaken. Here, Fuling." He turned, extending his arm to Fuling.

Taking the ring, he inspected it and had to agree with the King. Had he lost his? As if reading his mind, the King held up his right hand, and showed his own signet to Fuling.

"It's the same, is it not?"

"It is, Your Highness. Though, I don't understand."

"Where did you get this?" The King had turned back to face the man still kneeling before him.

"The desert, Your Highness."

"What desert?"

"In Sahro, roughly between Watersend and Midderbuilt."

The King shook his head. "What in Jolothos's name is a royal Skarian signet doing in Sahro? Those thieving camel-lovers!"

Fuling didn't quite understand the significance, or why Ahn was so agitated, but he enjoyed how this would help him push Ahn to do what they'd planned for.

"What's your name, man?" The King's voice was sharp.

"Seerbols, Your Highness."

"This is your gift?"

"No, Your Highness, but I believed it of great significance. I too could not believe how such a thing would be in the desert."

"How did you come by it?"

"Well, that's a story all in itself."

"Your Highness, whose ring is it?"

King Ahn turned to face Fuling, his eyes hard and lucid. "There's only one signet missing, Fuling, that of my grandfather, King Unx. We'll discuss that later."

He turned back to the man whose face seemed to be grinning, ever so slightly to Fuling's mind.

"I'm not so sure you should trust this man so quickly, Highness. He strikes me as some sort of thief, or dark trader if not much else."

The eyes of the man who'd called himself Seerbols slid sideways to look at Fuling. Any grin that he might have worn before was well hidden now.

"I'm nothing much, Eminence, Your Highness. Me and my two boys, we are truly traders. But I'm not looking to trade nothing at all here. Nothing at all. I am a man of my word, if nothing else, and I promised you I had a gift. A gift like none I've ever seen."

"If this gift is so precious, Seerbols, why not keep it for yourself? Why not trade it," — Fuling sneered as he said the words — "for your own benefit?"

"'Tis a good question, Eminence. Truth be, when I first found it, that's what I did intend to do." He turned to look at both his boys, who were scowling at their father. "Did I not, boys?"

Both gave small nods but said nothing.

"But it is meant for you. That's what it tells me."

"Tells you?" the King queried.

"Ah, yes. I get a feeling like that. I'm not a clever man, I just know somehow it's yours, or it's for you. Here!" He reached into the pouch again and pulled out a larger piece of jewelry.

King Ahn stepped forward again and picked the item up, turning it over as he did so. "Oh, my!"

Fuling couldn't stop himself gasping. In King Ahn's hand was an amulet, with a large amber stone set in it. The silver work was exquisite, and what light there was in the hall seemed to focus on the stone.

Could this be? How can this be?

"This is most beautiful, Seerbols." King Ahn was captivated by it.

"Like I said…"

"Ahhhh!" The King stumbled backward, dropping into his throne, a grimace on his face. He reached out with his left hand and grasped at his right forearm. The amber stone seemed to be shining brightly, sucking in all the light it could find.

A guard rushed forward and grabbed Seerbols. "Stop what you're doing!"

"I'm… I'm doing nothing."

As soon as it had begun, the stone stopped shining and the light in the room returned to normal. The King shook his head and pulled the tunic up on his right arm. "There's nothing there."

"What was it?" Fuling asked.

"It felt like my arm was being burned, I can't really explain it."

"Are you alright?"

"I'm fine, Fuling. What of these men?"

He leaned forward and whispered to the King. "As true as he's said, these are fine gifts, but I'm a little suspicious of their motivations, and what just happened. I suggest we keep them here as guests until we can uncover a little more about what they know."

"Yes, a good idea."

Fuling turned back to face the men. "You have brought great treasures to share, Seerbols and sons. I'm not sure what just happened there, but I think you should remain as our guests for a few days and we'll discuss this further."

"There's no need…" Seerbols began to argue.

"Oh but there is." He looked at one of the guards. "Captain, find them some suitable quarters, and make sure they're protected. Very well protected, we wouldn't want any harm to come to them, now would we?"

Fuling could see Seerbols's eyes narrow, but he didn't fight the guards as they led them away.

"Clear the hall!" Fuling commanded to everyone else.

"This is most interesting, Fuling."

"Isn't it? I did tell you of the prizes waiting for us up there, did I not?"

"You did. I must admit I was a little reluctant to be so bold, but the ring... and this..." He stopped mid–sentence, his eyes captivated by the amulet.

"What bothered you about the ring so much?"

"That ring, it's been lost since before I was born. My father talked of it, a lot. It pained him that they'd needed to make a new one for him. He never stopped seeking answers to what had happened."

"And now it is returned, assuming it is not a fake."

"No one could fake that ring, not like that. It's even inscribed on the inside, as my father told me, which was not common knowledge."

"That's great news for your family, is it not?"

"It is, but I want answers even more now. What with that and this jewel, I think I'm ready to move forward with our plans."

Fuling's eyes brightened, and he tried to mask the smile forming on his face.

"Wise timing I think, Your Highness. So we're to prepare the forces for the northern border?"

"Yes, Fuling. I want our forces there, and whatever else is needed in place. Quickly!"

"Of course, Your Highness."

LANI

Why me?

That was the question that had bounced around in Lani's head all night. She had been able to snatch sleep in small bursts. Enough for some rest, but never enough to stop her head from thinking.

Ever since Lani had found Ashantha dying outside Barnen, she had been in what felt like a crazy dream. And now she was in Callet, a city she previously didn't even know existed.

Ashantha hadn't been telling her the truth and he'd used her to get the amulet to his colleagues. But that was all for nothing. She couldn't give it up even when she wanted to, nor his ring, which was still stuck on her finger.

The one person Lani had hoped would be able to solve it all was now dead. If it hadn't been for Henri, and the sacrifice he had made for her, Lani knew it probably would have been her that was dead.

None of it made sense. Even after her dream had encouraged her to put the mask back on, and she'd read Ashantha's journal again, she still struggled to understand it all.

She could understand that Ashantha's last written words weren't as well thought out as they could have been. He was in a bad way when she had found him, and had died shortly after. Composing his story wouldn't have been easy.

She stood up and paced around the room. The dark wood replica of Ash's face lay on the table and she couldn't help but see it. Lani shivered thinking about how it had peeled off of his body, and dropped beside him. It wasn't a memory she would forget easily.

He'd warned her about the amulet affecting your mind, but he'd never mentioned it could bond to you. Maybe he didn't know. She looked at the pouch on the table which covered the amulet. Ash had said he'd worn it as a glove to hide his ring from others, but Lani wasn't sure what that meant.

It was clearly a special cloth — why would he need it to hide his ring? It didn't make a lot of sense to her. If the risk of exposing the amulet wasn't so high, Lani would have tried it on her own hand to see what it might do.

What was he doing in Enderk, anyway? What she had read didn't explain it, maybe there was more to read about why he was there. He had said he had stumbled across the amulet by accident, so that wasn't the reason.

And the Vrah, the men in black who had been hunting it since she had first met him, weren't after her really either. They just wanted the amulet. Ashantha wrote that they could track it if it was out of the pouch. Lani had a sense that was true, but now she knew. Taking it out meant bringing them to her.

She had seen the colored tendrils snaking away from it when she had exposed it. Now she knew what they were doing. Ash had said it called to you, tempting you. Lani had felt that as well.

That feeling had become much more prevalent since the amulet stung her forearm and linked to her.

Or maybe it was the longer she had been around it? Either way it was as if there was a tiny connection deep in the back of her head to it, that had slowly begun speaking to her. Not that there were actually words but still it seemed to be calling to her. That's the only way she could explain it.

Part of her wanted to reject everything that Ashantha had told her, both back in the cave near Barnen, and what she could now read in his book. He had lied to her back then, he'd told her she'd get her answers in Callet and she just needed to hand his things over.

But now she knew that wasn't true at all, and because Henri couldn't handle the amulet, and it seemed no one else could either, she was still at Ash's mercy. Even dead, he was manipulating her to do his work for her. He had lied, everyone had lied.

She'd been nearly killed multiple times, held captive and even had to kill someone herself. None of this was what she had wanted, all she wanted was a future that didn't involve hiding from guards and scraping enough food together.

Not this. Not these lies, and stories of magic and evil. Now she was expected to believe what was written down, to do more to help him and his people.

What for? And what did he mean about her mother, that she had given something up for me? That makes no sense.

The words, 'Even in her last moments she protected you,' made no sense to Lani. When she tried to focus on the words she could feel pressure in her head, as if one of her headaches was forming.

That's all I need.

Without thinking she reached for the small brooch that she always wore pinned in the inside pocket of her tunic. She ran her fingers over it, a comforting habit she'd had as far back as she could remember, except for the time it had been taken from her. And then Kyro had returned it to her and told her to always keep it hidden and safe.

Even Kyro had lied to me. What else did he know that he never told me?

Lani unpinned the brooch and pulled it out. That last memory, about always keeping it hidden and safe, she'd not recalled in a very long time. She didn't understand it at all. What did the brooch matter? He'd made it seem like it was the only thing of value she had, but there was clearly more to it than that.

The blue stone had always seemed beautiful to Lani, even as it had changed over the years. She was sure it had been a deep dark blue when she was small, whereas now it was much lighter. Maybe her memory wasn't true. She stared at it as she had many times before.

Why do you matter? What is the link between you and my past?

Her head ached again, as she peered at the stone in the brooch. She closed her eyes and gently shook her head, wishing the pain away.

It's gone!

The connection in her mind to the amulet wasn't there. She walked back over to the table and stared at the pouch, reaching out to feel it. The amulet was still in there, she could feel it with her hand, but she couldn't feel it in her head.

How odd.

She walked away and put the brooch on the bed, and then moved back part way across the room and waited. Sure enough the weird spot in the back of her mind was there again, as if the amulet was connected to her.

Stepping back closer to the bed she tried to see if it felt any different, but nothing changed. Not until she picked up the brooch, then the connection was gone.

Lani kept the brooch in her hand and walked back over to the amulet, and picked up the pouch. Still it was as if the brooch blocked it. She put the brooch on the table, and waited. Sure enough the sensation in her mind slowly returned.

She dropped the amulet quickly back on the table and picked up the brooch.

It's shielding me from the amulet. All this magic I don't understand, why is it all happening to me?

Whatever protection the brooch gave her was small, and localized. Lani would need to make sure that she kept the brooch close to her. It helped while the amulet was inside the pouch, but she couldn't risk testing it with the orange stone out.

If the Vrah really could track the amulet, it had to stay hidden. She wasn't sure how injured the man she had called Goatee was, and if he had more men close by, but she knew he wasn't going to give up. They had killed Ashantha for it, and tracked her all the way here. Lani doubted they were done chasing her, and she wasn't going to help them out.

What do I do now?

The answers were most likely in the journal, and she had only read the back of it. Lani knew she needed to spend more time reading it.

That in itself almost lifted her mood, the fact she had been able to read. When she allowed the mask to attach to her face it gave her Ash's ability to read, something she couldn't do on her own.

The thought of putting the mask on again creeped her out, but she knew there was no other way. She picked it up, his face in her palm, and took a deep breath before bringing it up to her face. The now familiar clicking sound as it joined with her face was followed by the coolness that spread across her head.

Lani knew that if she looked in a mirror, she'd see his face and not hers, and everything about that caused her body to want it off. She took a minute to breathe and settle into the strange feelings it gave her, before getting back to her task.

She opened the journal and began to flick through parts of it. It told much of Ashantha's life story, where he had been and what he thought. Lani became lost in the world of his notes, flicking through pages trying to find something that related to her.

The college in Anderwell interested her. He had been trained there, and lived there for a long time, before heading back out across Dharatan.

He had met Mother Folly at a traveling circus and asked how he could become an entertainer. He didn't know why but he had been drawn to the circus, and to the tall woman as if it was his destiny. At least that's what his journal said.

She read of many of the people he was around, including the man Goran. The way Ashantha had written about him in the past, Lani found it hard to believe that he would not trust him, but she had re-read the last pages several times and it was clear what his instructions were.

"Trust no one but Henri and Mother."

Lani kept hunting for more about her own mother, but despite the journal looking small there were more than thirty years of notes contained in its few pages. However, the magic worked, concealing the book's contents and size perfectly. No one would suspect it was any more than just a simple journal.

Trying to isolate information in it was difficult. She was reading them as him, and yet she wasn't. It was hard to focus on any one thing.

She would read from different sections of the book and be pulled into different times and places, reliving them in her mind as if she had been there.

Rainbow showed up several times in the passages she read. Ashantha had noted how odd each occurrence was. The old man was up to something, Ash had known that, and that he was a very different character. In the last meeting Rainbow had implored Ash to undertake something.

Ashantha had been quite suspicious but the story he kept telling him had never changed. Lani knew it was about her, and the mention of her in an abstract way was hard to read.

The girl must be kept safe, there is knowledge she doesn't have right now, but you must guard her from those that seek to harm her. She needs to be reconnected with knowledge of her family and who she is.

Ashantha kept trying to get more from him, but his answers were always cryptic and unclear apart from the single line she had just read, that froze her:

Your mother will know the story of her mother. It must be told.

Lani couldn't breathe. She re-read the sentence multiple times to see if anything else came out of it or the surrounding notes, but there was nothing else.

She felt for the ridge of the mask on her forehead and unclipped it, the unmistakeable click allowing her to relax a little. She left the mask and book on the table and slumped down on the bed, rubbing at the brooch.

It's all connected, somehow. This brooch, Rainbow, Ash, my mother. But how?

There was so much she needed to know, including why the strange man, Rainbow, had not told her any of this when they had met. What was he up to? Was there any way to find him?

6

LANI

Who was Rainbow? He was mentioned in those last words of Ashantha's. If he wasn't one of Ash's colleagues, then who was he? He knew things, but he'd chosen not to share them with Lani.

Why was he even around her? He'd shown up twice since this all began. In Barnen, then in Little Big Rock. Now as she recalled meeting him at the markets in Little Big Rock there had been something that had unnerved her.

He'd seemed to know who she was and what she was doing. That had unsettled her and Lani had slipped away from him in the end.

Of course he did. He knew exactly who I was. Why hadn't he helped me more, he could have protected me?

She would have to ask him the next time she came across him. Would he even tell her now? He'd not told her back then. What had he said to her...?

"Trust yourself and you'll be safe." Something like that.

Safe, she'd not felt safe at all, not then and definitely not now. Maybe all Rainbow was, was more like the seer she'd met in Nkuku. The boy with no eyes, that they had called The Eyes. Such a cruel joke.

What was his name? Cideep, that's it.

He told her she couldn't leave the amulet, and had proven that to Watcher and her. But he had been confused by the lock on her mind. That's what he had called it: a lock. It had stopped Cideep from probing her mind, which she was happy about.

Cideep had linked her to the Jesters. Told her that she was linked to their ring, and the amulet. But he couldn't see any more. He'd said he would have to speak to his mistress to understand more. Maybe Watcher would have held her prisoner until he came back, but that all changed when the Vrah attacked where they were holding her.

Lani couldn't go all the way back to find Cideep, that was way too far to go, and she'd as likely run into more Vrah than not. Despite feeling manipulated, right now she didn't seem to have many choices. She would either have to always be running and hiding from those who sought the amulet, or she needed to head to Anderwell and see if this mother could help remove it. And tell her more about her past.

Unless… unless another seer can help?

It was a new option she hadn't considered before. What if another seer could do better than Cideep? Maybe he was too young and she just needed to find someone more experienced. She felt more hopeful already. At least she might learn something else, not just what she'd been fed by Ashantha.

Lani laughed. Not that long ago she had been frightened out of her wits at the threat from the Barnen guards, that a seer was coming to town to find her. Now she was thinking of seeking one out.

She knew she would have to be extremely cautious. The man she'd called Goatee was still alive as best she knew. Yes, he was injured but he would have others to help him, that she didn't doubt. And Henri's colleagues, they would be looking for whoever killed him.

It wasn't safe in Callet but before she left, she needed at least another option to consider. The amulet had to stay in the pouch, and she had to think like a thief. Stay out of sight and keep her wits about her. She rubbed her thumb over the brooch as she thought about everything. The comfort from it helped her relax slightly.

Where to find a seer?

The keeper was her best bet, but she wasn't game to ask directly. Her next best option then was a priest.

"You leaving?" the keeper asked as she walked down to the front desk.

"Yes. Where would I find a church of Thenis in Callet?"

The keeper looked at her a little strangely. "That's an odd request in this city."

Lani felt a little silly, her face heated up as she blushed.

"Most people come here to be ungodly." He laughed. "On the east wall, there's a few churches, huddled together. I think you'll find one there."

"Thanks."

Lani also got directions to the best place to get a ride out of town before leaving. Taking a longer route, she weaved along narrow, mostly empty lanes, avoiding the busy roads, until she found the right section of the city.

Huddled was the correct way of describing how the churches looked. All in one small section of the city, they seemed to be dwarfed by what was around them. None of them was a large, proud building to attract visitors. Here in Callet, they couldn't compete with the types of attraction this city held.

The Church of Thenis wasn't any more inspiring than the others, but she saw an elderly man wiping grime off its front doors. He wore the traditional grey robe that even Despring wore back in Barnen.

He turned around as she made her way up the path to the doors.

"Hello there." His wrinkled face shone with a warm smile, setting Lani more at ease.

"Hi."

"With that red skin of yours and the dark hair, I'd guess you're a Mal?"

"I am."

"You're a long way from home. What brings you to the church?"

Lani was hesitant, it was a strange request. "I have something to ask."

"Come in then, this cleaning has made me thirsty and I'll see if I can help."

The church was quite small on the inside, seemingly smaller than the one in Barnen. There were only a handful of pews. The only window was high at the back of the hall, all of the light came from lanterns along the walls and the bank of candles beside the pulpit.

She followed the priest into a side room. He beckoned her to sit at the table, while he gathered two goblets and headed towards a small fire in the side wall. A pot hung off to the side, away from the flame, and he ladled wine from it into the goblets.

"Here try this, it's got a unique mix of spices I learned from some traveling Dotokians many years ago." He sat and raised his goblet towards her. "In Thenis's name bless this wine, and let me be of service."

Lani wasn't sure what to do but raised hers along with him.

"Do you get many people in here?"

He chuckled. "No, dear, not really. A posting here is only for the eternally hopeful. Those that come are usually in so much trouble a priest is the last thing they really need."

"So, why…"

"I was told to serve here."

"By whom?"

"Thenis of course. She spoke to me and told me this was where I needed to be."

"She?"

"Yes." He chuckled again. "Another that thinks all the gods are men, I see."

"I… I just never even thought about it. The few priests I've seen are men, so I…" Lani shrugged.

"It's okay, you're not the first, nor will you be the last. It's one of her many quirks."

"What is?"

"That she doesn't show her face often to her people. Maybe because she works so much in the background, she doesn't want to. To be honest, I don't think too much on it, I just serve."

"Did she tell you why you had to be here?"

"Oh no, dear, That's not how it works. I got the message, I arrived here, just in time it seemed. The priest before me had passed on the day before I arrived. It seemed pretty obvious that's why I was here, but I haven't asked."

"Would she answer if you did?"

"You're very inquisitive for someone I suspect doesn't spend a lot of time following her way."

Lani felt awkward. She wasn't sure why she'd asked so many questions, he seemed to be so easy to talk to they almost fell out of her mouth. "Sorry."

"Don't be. Now, I don't think you were here to ask me about Thenis, were you? So what is it that you wanted to ask me?"

It took Lani a minute to compose her question. In the end it came out the simplest way she could put it.

"Do you know about the Eyes?"

"The Eyes?"

"Yes, they are seers or something."

"Or something, indeed. Yes, I know of them. Why would you be wanting to know about such people?"

"I need to find one."

"What in Thenis's name for?"

"I'd rather not say."

He looked at her for a while, sipped his wine and seemed to be evaluating her. "It's an odd request that's for sure. My colleagues would like try to save your soul, but here... you can do much worse things than seek a seer."

"You don't approve?"

"I'm not so sure I trust them, lass. But don't let an old man's biases worry you. You won't find one around Callet."

"Oh."

"Not much here for their type. Few that come to Callet seek knowledge other than how to win at the next card game, or other forms of luck." He shook his head disapprovingly. "Your best bet is Union."

"What?"

"There's one of them in Union. At least there was when I last passed through there."

"When was that?"

"Five years at least. They don't change location much. Unless his time has come, he'll still be there."

"Where's Union?"

The priest lightened up a bit and chuckled again. "East mostly, south somewhat, but mostly east. If you follow the border with Ngahere, which you can't miss, it's all forest, you end up in Union."

"Is it near Diwedd?"

"You can go to Diwedd via Union, but Diwedd's much further south. There's a quicker way to get there than through Union."

"Thank you, I'll think about whether it's worth the journey."

"Be careful, that's all I can advise."

Lani nodded and walked back out the way she had come. The priest watched her from the doorway of his room, but didn't follow her. As she approached the outer doors she looked up at the statue perched on a wooden stand in the back left corner of the hallway, and stopped in her tracks.

"What is it, lass?"

Lani stared at the statue of a woman, sure she knew the face. "The statue, who is that?"

"That's my mistress, lass. Thenis. Rare as she is to have her face shown, it's what makes this church so special."

"Why's that?"

"Only a few actually see what she looks like, here's the only church I know. Strange, considering how popular she is. Why did you stop?"

"She looks just like someone I knew."

"Then you've been blessed, lass. She's looking over you if you think you've seen her before."

Lani shivered as he spoke, and took one last look up at the statue.

I must be imagining it. My memory must be playing tricks but she looks a dead ringer for that grocer lady, what on Dharatan was her name?

She hadn't exactly gotten the answers she sought, but at least she had an option. She could head to Union anyway, and still head south if she got no joy there. That was good enough for her. She let the door bang behind her as she left the church.

7

LANI

The afternoon sun was shining directly into Lani's eyes as she stepped out onto the street, causing her to blink. Bringing her arm up as a shield she looked up the street, thinking about what to do next.

As brief as her meeting with the priest had been, it had confirmed that she should be leaving Callet. Union was as good a place as any to head to, and was on the way south. With a little luck she might glean something else from the journal while on the road.

There was enough light in the day left for her to seek out an agent and hopefully a ride for tomorrow. Then she could find a room, and pass the time. The money she'd taken from the Safe House would see her through for the time being.

I should have asked that priest for better directions.

Out on the main road, Lani looked left and right to determine the best direction to find the area for all the shipping out of the city. The keeper had mentioned something about a clock tower and that being where she should turn.

Off to her right she could see what looked like one, poking above several buildings. There were plenty of people moving down the road, including horses and the odd carriage. Lani merged with the flow of people, still very cautious but trying to use the bodies to stay hidden.

Two blocks from the clock tower she stepped off the road and into a lane dark with shadows. With plenty of time to get to an inn, she decided she needed to be as cautious as possible. After a short wait she walked back out and merged with more people heading along.

Everyone was hustling along, focused only on their business. The buildings were all mainly storage warehouses or similar. There were few shops open and the overall appearance was grimy and tired.

As the road curved to the west Lani switched sides of the road so she was in the shade. She saw what looked like an inn up ahead, across the road, that looked large enough to have rooms for rent.

She needed to walk past it to reach the corner with the clock tower on it, but decided she'd come back to secure a room once she'd found out about rides. Lani doubted there'd be anything going this late in the day but she wasn't going to waste her money needlessly.

As she got closer to the inn a tall man walked out of the entrance who made her stop in her tracks.

Lani shook her head to shake the recognition free, as another carriage whizzed by. As it passed a gap opened in the crowded road, which she could easily cross through, but the man had turned and was looking down the road following the carriage with his eyes.

It can't be.

Unless her eyes deceived her it was Captain Kyro. She stopped dead in her tracks.

What on Dharatan is he doing here? Why?

"Watch out!" a voice behind her called out as they clipped her from behind.

The man stumbled out from the covered roof into the road, turned and cursed at her before moving on. Kyro had turned to see what the issue was and looked straight at her. He seemed to struggle to recognize her, or it was disbelief.

Only briefly though, before he started walking her way, raising his hand.

Lani didn't know what to do. She didn't want to be caught by him, but she also wanted to know how and why he was here. Why did he care that much about Harsop's death to follow her all the way here?

Not now!

Lani turned and ran, she needed to get away from him. She took a turn into an alley on her right and sprinted down it.

She pushed the bag around onto her back to stop it slapping on her hip and reached another intersection. She turned and looked back down the way she'd run to see Kyro turn into it.

"Lani," he shouted.

She didn't wait to hear any more but took a left and raced toward the main street. She crossed several smaller lanes and could see the road she'd walked up this morning in the distance. Hoping she could merge into the crowd down there and escape Kyro was the best she could hope for now. She knew she was fast enough to outrun someone his age.

Up ahead a figure walked across the exit of the alley. He turned as he heard her running and Lani slid to a stop. His familiar beard and black clothing stood out despite the light being behind him. Goatee now blocked her escape.

Her feet slid to a stop. While she'd been concerned about being caught by Kyro, she was totally scared of this man. She'd seen what they had done.

Lani turned and ran back the way she'd come. Ahead, Kyro reached the original intersection that had brought her into this road. He stopped and she could see the confusion on his face. Then he looked past her and his hand went to his sword.

She turned into an alley on her left and stopped dead.

Fussleguts.

The end was blocked by the back of a building two stories high. She spotted a door and ran to it, hoping it would be open. Her heart sank as soon as she twisted the handle, it was barred from inside.

Turning around, Lani could see Goatee had reached the laneway first. He was now coming toward her, his face cold and focused.

"Do not make this more difficult than it needs to be." He spoke evenly, despite having chased her.

Behind him another man in black reached the intersection, a sword out in front of him. Then the sudden sound of blades clashing caused Goatee to turn. Lani could see what looked like Kyro fighting the man in black.

A noise came from behind her, and she turned to see the door in the building swinging open. She immediately rushed to it and yanked it wide. A woman came flying out, her hand still on the door, and Lani skipped around her into the back of the building.

Inside the wide warehouse were racks of goods in parallel lines, some rows of barrels and stacks of what looked like hay. Lani didn't wait but sprinted through toward the part of the building with the most light. She could hear footsteps behind her and pushed across the main floor toward the open double doors.

A big wagon was being backed through the doors and she almost collided with it as she approached. She turned to look for other options just as a hand grabbed the back of her tunic and shoved her into the wall, her forehead banging hard against the wood.

"Ahhhhh!"

"I warned you to not make it harder, girl."

What felt like a foot kicked the back of her leg causing her knee to buckle, and she slid down the wall falling, hard onto her knees. Tears welled in her eyes. Her forehead was stinging, and her knees now burned as well.

"Get your hands off her, vermin!"

Lani could make out the sound of Kyro's voice, one she'd know anywhere.

"Be smart, stranger, and leave with your life while you have a chance."

"I've already put your mate to the sword, and you'll be next."

Lani had twisted around on the ground and could see Kyro through the legs of Goatee. With no warning Goatee moved sideways as fast as she'd ever seen a man move. A curved blade slid out of the sheath on his back as he moved, and was in front of him as he came around on Kyro.

Kyro was no fool and backed off, lifting his own sword, his eyes locked on Goatee. They parried and feinted, the clash of blades ringing around the warehouse. Others had come into the space now. There was shouting at the fight, but no one was game to approach them.

Goatee feinted in and backed off which drew a lunge from Kyro. It missed as Goatee spun completely around on his heel and swiped his curved blade across Kyro's chest, slicing through his coat and tunic, drawing blood. Kyro's training came to the fore. As he flinched, he pulled back the butt of his sword and then flicked the blade around, catching Goatee high on the man's shoulder.

The thinner material opened easily and even though it was a light contact the sharp sword cut through the skin, opening a wide wound.

Goatee didn't react to the cut at all. He backed off, turned around and before Kyro was fully set to face him ran straight at him. In a seamless move, he lowered his body and slid across the dirt on one side, sliding under the sword swing. As he passed under Kyro's guard, he leaped upward, his sword plunging into Kyro's midriff.

Lani shrieked as she saw the pain and surprise on Kyro's face. Goatee pushed Kyro off the blade, and he toppled over backward, his sword flying free as his elbow hit the ground. Blood gurgled in his mouth and dribbled down his cheek. He turned to look at Lani, horror written across his face.

The crowd was making a lot of noise now, Goatee turned on them and waved his sword at them, challenging anyone to come forward. The men backed away. He didn't wait for them to change their minds and ran to Lani. She tried to stand up, but he swung in his sword toward her and she stared in fright. Before it made contact, he turned his hand, and the butt of the handle cracked the side of her head with all the force he had.

Everything went black and as she slid down, all she could see in her mind was Kyro's face at the end.

8

GORAN

Goran's chest was gripped with anxiety. The worry he felt was threatening to take him over completely. Watching Henri was the main cause of it. He'd sat beside the injured man for hours, unable to leave his bedside. He felt hopeless, unable to do a thing for his colleague, waiting for Brando to return with Zeresse.

The bandages wrapped tightly around Henri weren't able to completely stop the bleeding. It still leaked out and the bedding was covered in blood. Even with the hunch in his back, the older man usually was so tall and robust-looking. Goran couldn't believe how frail he seemed now.

He lay unmoving on the bed, air wheezing in through his nose, his face colorless.

Goran wasn't the praying type, but even he found himself uttering words in his head, pleading with Thenis, Hembleth, even Seth for anything to help save their friend.

Praying now, fool? No god will save him now, he's another of your failures.

That was all he needed, Zoran showing up inside his head. *Go away!*

Or what? You'll kill me too? You can only kill by your mistakes, you're not able to harm me.

The laughter bounced around in his head as it faded into the background.

Maybe Zeresse can help me get rid of him as well?

Goran hoped Brando would return with Zeresse soon. While any healer would be better than none, their strange friend was his best hope.

Was she a friend? Goran didn't really know, Zeresse didn't fit into any box. She wasn't a direct part of the Circuit or Court. Brando and Goran had met her many years before and helped her get out of some trouble. Since that time, they'd all called on her when they needed her help and likewise, she'd asked for favors again when she needed them.

A practical relationship is the best way Goran could describe it. His mind wandered to the college. He tried to imagine how much Zeresse could teach the students there. Perhaps they should be training more healers and not just the Entertainers?

The door opened, startling him from his daydreaming.

"There you are."

"Brando, you frightened the soul out of me."

"Like you have one." Brando winked as he said it.

Goran could see he looked tired. "No luck?"

"Yes and no. I found someone to get her a message, but how long that will take I can't tell you. How is he?"

"I don't like his chances, especially if she doesn't get here soon."

Brando raised his hands and shrugged. "I've done what I can for now. Here, you can't achieve anything staring at him, let's get ourselves something to eat. You're going to need it, somehow I think we're in for a few challenges."

Goran followed him out into the main room. They left the door to Henri's room open, in case he made any sound, although that seemed a fanciful idea. Brando sat across from him and had one of his staff bring them food and drink.

"You look how I feel, Brando."

"Yeah, well the thought of losing Henri is sitting poorly on me, Goran."

"He's not gone yet."

Neither of them spoke. The whole inn had a heavy air about it. There was no making light of the situation, everyone there knew Henri. The food that was brought out got little attention. Goran picked at it, but his thoughts lay elsewhere.

The young woman Lani had brought this on Henri, whether she knew it or not. The men in black had come with her to Callet. He knew that meant he was as much to blame as her. If he'd captured her in Nedor or Nkuku, then none of this would have happened. Goran squeezed his eyes closed, letting the pain of his failure grip him. Once again, he'd let their side down.

Told you! Zoran wasn't going away completely.

What was worse was, Goran knew it was true. He'd let harm come to their family, by not capturing her earlier. Or wiping her mind. That was originally part of the plan. She couldn't know what she knew about them and continue.

They weren't allowed to kill others, unless in self-defense. They all knew the story of one of their earlier colleagues, who hadn't stuck to the rules. The consequence had left her without any memory of her life before, and she'd been banished from their family forever.

That's what he'd been told to do to this girl, use the mask so she would have no memory. The difference was that it would leave her mindless, unable to think correctly. But then Beantic had changed that and told him to make sure he got her safely back to Anderwell.

Except he no longer wanted to go along with that instruction. He wanted Lani to pay for what had happened to Henri. He could feel his blood heating up.

Or am I just feeling guilty for letting it happen?

Leave her to me, I'll take care of it and solve everyone's problems.

SHUT UP!

Chasing this young woman was tiring on him. No one had explained why she was such a threat, apart from her having Ash's things. That wasn't good, Goran knew that, but there was something else they weren't telling him. He could feel it.

Equally concerning were the Derks following her. It wasn't just Henri they'd hurt; they were leaving a trail of bodies throughout

Dharatan. How was he going to best them if it came down to it?. While he could hold his own in a sword fight, he never chose one if he could avoid it. But how to stop them without killing them?

Even Brando was concerned about them. He'd set up guards on the inn, both outside and inside. Neither of them thought they were after Henri, or would come hunting for him, but it was best to take no chances.

Goran realized he'd finished the food in front of him without even noticing. His mind was all over the place right now. The sound of feet running down the street brought him and Brando to their feet. One of the guards called out a warning to whoever it was. Together they hurried to the foyer of the inn.

"What do you want, boy?" he could hear one of the guards calling out.

"I need Master Goran." The boy was still gasping for breath, his voice weak.

Goran stepped out the door to where the youngster was being blocked by the two large guardsmen.

"It's okay, I know him. Come here."

One of the guards took a step to his left leaving just enough space for the boy to wearily walk through.

"I forget your name, lad. What is it?"

"Minto, Master Goran. Leola, she tell me you need to come, come now. There's a man hurt in Furton's warehouse and your girl she was there. Foreign men sliced him up and took her."

Goran turned and looked at Brando. "We'd best go, he might know something!"

"Let me arm up first," Brando replied and headed back inside.

"You can go, lad," Goran said, handing him a small coin. "Tell Leola my thanks."

He watched the boy turn and run off as he waited for Brando to come back.

"Let's go," he said as the keeper hurried out the front door of Follies, a sword and belt in his hand.

Brando moved quickly despite his size, and Goran with his gimp leg struggled to keep up. The keeper told him that Furton was one of the larger merchant companies that handled wholesale supplies.

When they arrived, there was a large crowd milling around the street and building. Several of the city guard were there already and were trying to keep everyone out. The pair waited until they were distracted then slipped inside.

A smaller gathering stood around a man who had been propped up against a rack. A trail of blood led back to where he'd been injured. His own sword lay beside him, and his eyes were closed. It was hard to tell if he was still breathing.

A woman with a shawl wrapped about her head and neck walked toward Goran. He recognized Leola by her arm first and her face second. She leaned in close to him, speaking quietly.

"From what I have gathered your girl was in this fight. She was taken by one of the men in black."

"One?"

"There's another one dead out the back in the alley, probably from this one." She hooked her thumb at Kyro lying on the floor.

"Where did they go?"

"I've got people looking but few want to speak about what they know, whoever he was he frightened everyone. They say this one was a good swordsman but the man in black made it look easy."

"Understood. Let me know what you find out." Goran looked back at the man on the ground. "Is he still alive?"

"For now, but that's a nasty wound. I'd not count on him lasting long unless you can get him cared for."

"Do you know the lead guardsmen here?"

Leola nodded and winked.

"Tell him we will look after this injured one and they can come find him at Follies. They don't need more bodies and they aren't going to save him at the gaol."

"He might not like that," Leola responded.

Goran handed her several gold coins. "Convince him!"

Leola left his side and moved around to the front doors. She waited for the right opportunity and stepped forward, getting the attention of one of the guardsmen. The discussion that followed went as expected, with some resistance before she appeared to put something in his hand.

She turned to Goran and nodded.

"We'll take him with us, Brando. He's involved somehow or other and anything we can find out might help me."

"Like a bloody hospital we'll be. Come on then."

Brando suddenly started talking out loud as if he knew the man. "Cousin Frilden, what has happened to you, oh poor cousin."

Together they grabbed the limp man, lifting him up onto his feet. Brando kept up some nonsensical banter while they inspected the man's wounds.

Taking off his own cloak, Goran wrapped it tightly around the man's stomach, hoping to stop some of the blood.

Brando squatted down a little and put his right arm under the legs of the man and picked him up like he was just a child. With both arms out in front of himself he carried the man in a cradle style. Still muttering nonsense about Frilden he walked out the back way to avoid the crowd.

Goran grabbed what he thought must have been the man's sword and hat and hurried out after him. Out the back of the building Goran could see the other body lying in the alley. He stopped to look over it.

"You go on, Brando. I'll catch up or see you at Follies."

"Make sure you keep that sword handy then, I'm not sure I like the sound of this lot."

"Don't worry about me. Get him back to the inn and see what we can do about keeping him alive. If he was fighting to save her, he's either just an unlucky Samaritan, or he knows something. More to the point, unless my eyes deceive me, he's also a Mal. Which could well mean he's following our girl."

Brando nodded before turning and walking away.

There was little to find on the dead Derk. He wore black clothing, of some ultra-thin fabric. The man's sword lay on the ground, and Goran looked at the unique curved blade attached to a black pommel with an amber stone set in it. He ran his hands over the rest of the man's clothing and found an empty pocket.

On one of the man's arms, he found the tattoo which he'd been warned about. At least now he knew what it looked like. He could see it was also etched into the blade. The only other item of note was the ring on the man's left hand. The black band had an amber stone set in it, much like the amber on the sword. He tried to remember the information about the amulet; it too was amber, he was sure they'd told him. Was that significant? He didn't know, but he knew any information could be useful to them.

He pulled the ring off the man's finger. Already his skin was going cold, making Goran's skin creep. He pocketed it and picked up the sword, wrapping it in his coat before heading off after Brando.

This was more bad news for them, not just this man being hurt but Lani having been captured. She had Ashantha's things, and that was bad enough, but they were now in the possession of these Derks.

You're screwed, Goran. You'll never catch her now.

Goran banged the bottoms of his palms against the side of his head, trying to shut Zoran up, as he took off after Brando.

9

TILLANDRA

Stepping into the dark map room was a relief to Tillandra's eyes. She had been on the road enduring the desert sun for weeks now and tiredness, as well as the constant glare, always took a toll on her.

A coolness welcomed her in the underground room, as did peace and quiet. She knew that wouldn't last, particularly once she told her colleagues all her news, but for these few moments she soaked it up.

As she always did, she looked up at Ninarto's mask and felt the longing for her mentor and friend.

I wish you were here now Narty, I'm not sure how I can manage all of this.

The sparkling lights hovering over the table in the center of the room drew her attention and she checked all their locations. The density around Callet answered her question about where Lani and Goran were. She wondered if he had finally caught up to her and that part of the mission was resolved. Beantic would be able to answer that, soon enough.

What she wouldn't be able to answer was what the relationship between Lani and Ashantha was. Tillandra's hope that Tingfurlew would have been able to solve the question of how Lani could wear one of their rings, hadn't borne fruit. Instead he'd answered with an option that she thought was nonsensical.

She knew Ashantha, they had been close all these past years. If he had a child, she would have known. Tillandra was sure of it. If she was wrong then what else didn't she know?

Shaking her head, she focused back on the other thought she'd had in her office. If Lani could wear the ring, then did she had to have a mask on? That's what they understood, but when she'd viewed through Ashantha's mask it was not on her.

Unless she wore a mask of her own, or the rules of the Audition weren't as complete as they were taught. But Tingfurlew had confirmed that the ring was connected to the mask. It made no sense, no sense at all.

Her doubts about her ability to lead crept back in. Tillandra wasn't going to be able to provide her colleagues with answers. Her whole journey had been a fool's errand. She'd wasted time seeking one answer, but ended up with more questions than when she had set out.

Tillandra suddenly felt faint, her head swimming and her eyes losing focus. She gripped onto the edge of the table steadying herself, breathing as deeply as she could. The room seemed to go completely dark and then an image of a shelf of books filled her eyes. The room seemed familiar. She could see a hand reaching forward to grab a book — it was her hand.

She recognized the room, it was the one in which she had found the book she kept hidden in her study. The shelf was in the library in Okeans. The image seemed frozen, as if something was stuck. Her hand was trying to grab it but the book wouldn't move. She was engrossed in the vision now, trying to pull at the book.

The book slowly slid back into the shelf, no matter how hard she pulled against it. Her brow was sweating with effort, she wanted that book. She had to have that book, it was needed, she needed to learn its secrets. She was certain of it.

Around her hand a crimson light began to shine, as if her hand was alight. Tillandra couldn't help but stare at it, her attention captured. Slowly it began to dissipate, slipping back from her hand and wrapping around several books. It took Tillandra a moment to grasp what was happening.

Three books were covered in a transparent reddish light, the one she still held was in the middle. She began to look at the other books, the titles fading from her view. The vision began to recede, becoming a bubble of an image before fading out.

Tillandra toppled forward and banged her elbow on the table.

"Mother!" Lionel shouted as he rushed into the room. "What's wrong?"

Her sight clearing, Tillandra was able to right herself and take in where she was. She held up her hand to him as he rushed to her.

"It's alright, Lionel. It was just a vision that hit me. They don't normally come to me like that."

"Perhaps you should have rested before you called this meeting?"

She looked at him, feeling the weariness of her journey back from Watersend.

"I'll be fine. This is important."

I just wasn't expecting it. Now I think I know what's been behind my inkling to head back to Okeans. There's more books.

Toolet and Junther arrived shortly after, the last to arrive was Beantic. As soon as she walked into the room, Junther closed the door and barred it.

Even in the dim light, Tillandra could see Beantic looked ragged and worn out.

"Are you all right, Bea?"

The woman nodded. "I've just come from speaking with Goran, I'm exhausted is all."

"I'm sorry."

"It's okay, Mother. This is important. You don't look so bright yourself."

"She just had one of her visions, standing upright. I think she's overdone it, and needs some rest." Lionel's voice was firm.

"I'll be fine. Let's just get on with it." Tillandra went to her seat and filled her cup, sipping the wine as she settled herself.

"What was in it?" Toolet asked.

"Let's get to everything else. I think it relates to what we need to talk about, I just need to digest it first."

Everyone sat waiting for her, staying unusually quiet.

"Maybe Beantic can tell us what Goran had to share, while I gather my thoughts?"

"Sure. As you can see by the lights, the girl, Lani is in Callet. So is he."

"He's caught her?" Junther seemed surprised.

Beantic shook her head. "No. She's very elusive, but there's more. Henri was hurt badly trying to defend her."

A collective, "What?" sounded around the room.

"I was equally upset when he told me. The details are a little sketchy, but this girl was with Henri, and he fought to protect her. That's what it seems."

"Why in Seth's name?" Junther's voice was higher than usual.

"He was able to mutter several things to Goran before he passed out."

"What?"

"They were attacked by Derks, it seems. Henri fought to save her but suffered for it. Goran believes she got away."

"Why do they want her, does he know?"

"Henri told him that they wanted an amulet she had. That's all he told him."

"An amulet?" Tillandra cut in.

"Yes, Mother. That's what Goran says."

"What does that mean, Tillandra?" Junther asked.

"A lot, I'd say. It's far too coincidental that everything I've been learning was to do with amber amulets, and here's some Derks hunting an amulet."

"You'll need to slow down, I'm confused."

"Of course, I haven't told you what I learned. Let's finish what Beantic is telling us first. How bad is Henri?"

"Bad!" Beantic was quick to reply. "There's more. Another man was hurt by these Derks."

"Does Goran know who he is?"

She shook her head. "No, but he said he's a Mal, quite definitely, and appeared to be a soldier. It was a separate event to Henri's. Whether he was trying to help Lani or capture her, Goran doesn't know."

"So the Derks got her?"

"It appears so, Mother." Bea's twitch had worsened, her head flicking.

"Anything else?"

"Only that he got to inspect a body of one of these Derks. He was very concerned. They wear a tattoo on their wrist, dress in a strange black cloth, and carry little else. He described them as assassins."

Tillandra shook her head. "None of this is good news. It gives us a little more information than what we had before, but there are still too many pieces missing."

"Perhaps you'd best fill us in on what you did learn now, Mother?" Lionel sounded impatient.

"Things didn't exactly go to plan. The mother stone is recharged and back in the tower, but there is no new ring. It seems this Lani is somehow interfering with how that process works."

"That's concerning. Why did he think that was?"

"He couldn't really say, but the only thing that resonated to him was that she was somehow related to Ashantha."

"Related? In what way?" Toolet's eyes bore into Tillandra.

"The only clue he had was something from his past, about 'the line of one,' but he had little insight more than that. He was grasping even to the point of suggesting she might be Ashantha's daughter."

Wine burst from Lionel's mouth. "He said what?" He wiped up his mess with his sleeve, muttering, "Sorry."

"What did he mean about 'the line of one?'" Junther asked.

"It's to do with the rules he makes the rings by. It's one of the conditions."

Tillandra summarized what he had told her of her past.

"And you believe him?" Toolet asked.

"Why would I not? Yes, I believe him, as fanciful as it sounds. And what I'd already started to uncover about what is called the Occultation…"

Junther cut in. "This is the part to do with blocking the past, correct?"

"Yes. I was told to ask him about it, and he told me what he could."

"Who told you?"

Tillandra wasn't sure how much she was meant to share. She hesitated.

"You seem to be holding back on us, Mother. I thought we were equals?" Lionel grumbled from across the table.

"I didn't know enough to tell, Lionel. The book has been so difficult to read, and I wasn't sure what it all meant."

"Book?"

"I thought I had mentioned it." Her head was aching from trying to hold it all together as well as think through what the vision was about.

"I found a book in Okeans that I've had in my study. I've been trying to unravel what it says. It was written from about the same time as what Ting told me."

"So you have been hiding stuff from us?"

"Not deliberately, Lionel. I was researching. Surely you don't share everything you read with us?"

He raised his hands up in submission. "You're right, sorry. It's just..."

"I know. I know. Let me tell you and we'll debate what we need to after."

She explained her vision with the lady in the Citadel Stone and the instruction to ask Tingfurlew about the Occultation. They listened intently as she retold what he had explained to her about the Great Fair, and the battle that followed.

"That's where things are crossing over."

"What things?" Beantic's voice sounded a little recovered.

"The Occultation was related to seven amulets given by the High Prince of Enderk to the rulers at the time. That's when all the trouble started, and what the veil seems to be about. The amulets were mentioned in the book as well. Now we find that Lani has an amulet, which some Derk assassins are chasing her for, and killing people over. That's no coincidence."

"Why has this all been hidden from us? From everyone?"

"Only the gods would know that, Beantic." Tillandra's mouth was dry from all the talking. She stopped and took another drink.

"Let's back up. If Lani has an amulet, then it's most likely she got it, or took it from Ash. Does anyone else agree?"

"Maybe, Junther. Maybe he brought it back from Enderk, or maybe he found her with it. That's no clearer from what I've learned, but the amulet is important."

"And now the Derks have her, and it."

"So it seems." Tillandra's anxiety had grown the more they talked this through. She'd hoped they'd ease her concerns but it wasn't helping.

"Goran has to stop them. It's as simple as that." Lionel's voice was very firm.

10

TILLANDRA

The knock on the map room door surprised them all. Very few people even knew the room existed below the college.

"Milfred?" Beantic asked.

"Let me check." Junther stood and walked over to the door.

He unbarred the door and opened it cautiously. "It is, I'll find out what's the matter."

Junther went out through the door, closing it behind him.

"That's most unusual."

"It is, Bea, and bodes poorly I'd suggest." Tillandra was worried about why Milfred would be interrupting their meeting.

Junther barred the door again when he stepped back in.

"Well?" Lionel queried.

"He brought this." He held a message tube in his hand. "He said the courier was most insistent it be delivered quickly."

"Best you read it then, Junther," Tillandra said.

Moving toward the light near his seat he pulled out the cork stopper and tapped the scroll out into his hand. He read it over quickly before sitting down and looking at Mother.

"It's from Temger, in Bundok."

"Remind me who that is?" she asked him.

"She's newish, in Daskare. She's been working as a booking agent for entertainers. We don't have anyone in Ahn's court, but we've been placing others to at least have eyes on things going on down there."

"Ah. And?"

"I'll summarize. Large numbers of knights were gathering outside Bundok. They've generated quite a stir in how many have amassed, but then they've headed north, toward the Sahro border."

"That doesn't sound good," Toolet exclaimed.

"Any reasons as to why?" Tillandra asked.

"She's clear in here to say she's only heard gossip, nothing absolute from a credible source. What she heard was they're coming for Watersend."

"What on Dharatan?" Now Toolet was agitated, standing up in her chair, rocking from foot to foot.

"So it's escalated then." Tillandra's voice was much calmer than her colleagues'.

"What's escalated, Mother?"

"The other part of what happened while I was away."

Tillandra explained what had happened on her trip to Midderbuilt — the knights on the outbound leg, the envoy in Watersend, and the other knights she'd avoided at Midderbuilt.

"I essentially expelled the envoy when I returned to Watersend. Which might have triggered this, although it seems an overreaction."

"Sounds like you had little choice. What of Pravat?"

"He seems to be as involved with it as well, though how much he knew is hard to tell. The envoy was feeding his depravities with young girls he'd brought from Daskare. Gimbden was at his wits' end trying to control him. Pravat did appear to be encouraging the idea of the road from Daskare, and it being manned by their knights."

"What was he thinking?" Lionel's tone hadn't improved.

"I'm not sure he's thinking of anything. He seemed in the envoy's power but I couldn't tell how. He seemed quite different to what I remember of him."

"So he's got to go?"

Tillandra nodded. "I thought so when I left, but now even more so. He seemed troublesome to leave there but I think it's more than that."

"What does King Ahn think he's doing?"

"That's an excellent question, Junther. I wish we had someone in his court, because this isn't good. There's been no conflict between nations since the Occultation began, that's been one of our primary functions. For them to be targeting us is even more concerning."

"If that's breaking like you said, then perhaps the old issues are coming back with it?" Lionel added.

"That makes a lot of sense, Lionel," Junther replied. "The question is then what to do about it?"

"We don't have much choice. We need to make sure we have enough forces nearby to quash any ideas they have. I'd already advised Pravat to set up a border camp so we had troops in their way. I wasn't expecting it to be this much of a threat though, we will need to increase the size of our force on the border." Tillandra's face wore a deep frown.

"Fighting, from us?" Beantic seemed to shiver as she said it.

"Unless you've a better idea, Bea?"

"Should someone go see him, at least?"

"I'm a bit worried about that. I was thinking I could do that when I went to the Carver, but the open hostility his knights showed to me here in Sahro concerns me. I think they'd have no qualms about taking a prisoner in their own lands."

"They wouldn't!" Toolet's high-pitched tone made them all turn to look at her.

"I think they would, Toolet."

"But another realm's ruler?"

"They only know the council rules here, Toolet. And I don't think they feel particularly threatened by us, otherwise they'd not be doing what they are." Tillandra shook her head as she replied.

"I guess that's what our cavalry is for. I just never thought we'd be using it." Lionel also shook his head.

"Gimbden will have to coordinate getting them in place. He'll need to stay in Watersend at least for the time being. Do you all agree?"

They all nodded to her.

"Decided then. So Gimbden will need to find us a new Mayor, coordinate the forces and keep us informed of developments. That's at least one thing settled."

The room fell quiet for a moment, all except the occupants shuffling in their seats.

"That's one issue resolved. Or is it two? Goran has to catch Lani, aren't we all agreed on that?"

"Can we go back a step?" Beantic asked.

"To what?" Tillandra asked.

"I know I'm a bit tired, but did I miss the resolution of what Tingfurlew said about the ring being only for the line of one?"

"No, I think we got sidetracked."

"So what does that mean? She's related to him and so she can wear the ring?"

"That's kind of the gist of it," Tillandra answered. "He couldn't explain it any other way. He asked me if she could be Ash's daughter."

Lionel shook his head. "So let me get this clear, Tingfurlew is suggesting that Ashantha had a daughter, whom none of us ever found out about, and just as he gets killed, she happens to be there and was able to take up his ring. That's what you're saying?"

Tillandra nodded.

"I can't see it. We're talking the better part of twenty years he kept this from everyone." Junther had stood up behind his chair, gripping the top of it firmly.

"I'm not saying I believe it either but that's the only thing that Tingfurlew could find that explained any of it. I don't have the answer to it but there's a little more to it than just that she wears the ring."

"Are we sure that she is wearing the ring?"

"If the ring had changed into a coin, it wouldn't show as blue on the map. It's still blue right?" Tillandra pointed to the lights hovering over where Callet was on the map.

"So, what of the Audition?" Junther sounded very concerned. "Is that time clock still running for us to replace Ash?"

"I don't have an absolute answer. I don't believe so, Junther, but Ting couldn't give me absolute proof of that."

Tillandra paused and stretched her neck. She could feel all the tension in the room knotting in her muscles.

"Whatever has allowed Lani to wear the ring, means the ring is still active, so I'm interpreting that as meaning there's no clock. Right now, this Lani is considered one of us for all intents and purposes."

"I hope you're right, Mother." Toolet had sat back into her pile of cushions. "For all of our sakes. I don't want us to lose one of our number."

The group went silent, contemplating what Toolet had said.

"Which is more important? Worrying about an Audition, or getting Ash's things and this amulet back?" Lionel's bluntness kept the mood sombre.

"Unless we know for sure there's an Audition then I think we have to focus on getting her and those things back." Junther responded.

"I was planning to go to the Carver to see if they could answer that for us."

"Surely not with what you just told us, Mother?" Junther replied. "You can't just duck into Daskare."

"I know, I'm just putting it all out there."

"The Audition will have to wait, essentially we're all in Goran's hands."

"Seth forbid!"

"We all know how you feel, Junther. Maybe if you leaned more toward Thenis you'd be more forgiving." Lionel turned to stare at the other man.

"There's another complication." Toolet spoke up.

"What's that?"

"With Henri injured, or worse, we need to man the Safe House, otherwise our funds will be at risk. And who knows if the knowledge of it has been compromised?"

"Good point, Toolet." Beantic added her support.

Tillandra shook her head. "Our main focus still has to be Ash's things and the amulet. If he had the amulet, then his journal potentially has answers we need."

"If it doesn't?" Lionel asked.

"Then I have to hope the girl does. Either way we need all of them here."

"Still the Safe House."

"Yes, Toolet, I understand. Surely Goran can assign someone, he's there. Quickly though, he has to chase these Derks."

"Are we sure we want Goran chasing these Derks?"

"Junther, I know your feelings toward him..."

"Hold on, let me finish," Junther raised his hand as he spoke over the top of Tillandra. "What I was trying to say, is that so far multiple people, all more capable than him, have been badly hurt, and others killed. These Derks appear to be very dangerous, so do we want to risk sending one man against them? Can we afford to lose another one of us?"

"You're right, Junther, sorry. Thoughts, people? "

"If my memory serves me correctly, isn't that keeper in Callet, Brando, an ex-soldier? He's a right brute I seem to recall."

No one spoke for a short while; the seriousness of the matter could be seen on all their faces. Tillandra broke the silence.

"I believe Junther is right. I propose we tell Goran to take Brando with him, and set someone else to watch over Follies."

Everyone nodded and spoke their agreement with her.

"Decided."

"It all falls on Goran then. He's got to free her and bring her here. One way or another." She rubbed the back of her neck. "I still need to do another journey."

"What for?" Junther asked.

"That vision I had confirmed something that's been plucking at the back of my mind. There's another book, or books, in Okeans. It's related, and there's enough time for me to get there and back, before Goran can do what he needs to do."

"Is it wise?" Beantic asked.

"I need to get us better answers about this Occultation and the amulets. I can't do anything to help Gimbden or Goran right now. It's what I need to do."

"When will you leave?"

"In the next two days. Time is of the essence, I believe."

The mood of the room was grim as the meeting ended, everyone contemplating what they'd all just learned.

11

UKSOD

The tapping on the inside of his head broke Uksod's concentration.

"Not now!"

He brushed his left hand over his bald head feeling the gold headpiece. Stopping at the amber stone set in it over his forehead, he covered it briefly as if that would block her from him. Yantarnaya had stopped using words to request a visit, now all she did was this tapping. Right behind where the stone was.

She didn't do any more than that, just the tapping. It was a reminder to Uksod that she was forever attached to him, and could reach him whenever she wanted. That was the price he'd paid. He hadn't expected her to use the gem in the circlet against him, but she had.

While she'd not attacked him again as severely as she had when the amulet had been stolen, she wasn't a patient individual. He couldn't call her a person, she wasn't that. She was his goddess, and despite her appearance he had to remember she wasn't like him.

Why she wanted him to visit her in person he never understood. She could talk to him anywhere courtesy of the stone set in the circlet on his head, and yet she expected him to traipse down to her.

He was grateful for what she'd granted him for his service. It was more than he'd ever hoped for when he'd become a young acolyte. But the time it took to get to her, and the physical toll on him was what caused him angst.

While she'd given him his extended life, she'd not thought to make him young enough to enjoy it more. As an older man he suffered the pains and aches like anyone. He never got older but he also never got younger.

He looked around his private shrine, a room he never used. It was more for show than anything else; when the goddess you worshipped was connected to you directly, a shrine served little purpose, except to show others your devotion.

Not that many ever came anywhere near the shrine. Uksod closed the door that connected his office to the shrine and bolted it from the inside. It was one thing for others to know of his shrine, perhaps even see it from his office, but only he and Yantarnaya knew its true purpose.

He crossed the small room and moved aside the orange curtain to his left. He lifted his right hand and turned it so the stone on the ring worn on his middle finger fit into a small oval hole in the wall.

A faint glimmer of orange light outlined where the stone was placed, and a click sounded in the otherwise quiet room. He removed his hand and pulled open what was a hidden door. He took a big breath of relatively fresh air before he stepped through, quickly pulling the door closed behind him.

If nothing else, he didn't want the acrid smell of the caves below to seep into his shrine.

Despite all his years within the caves, it still offended his senses when he first entered. There was no real way to accept it but thankfully he knew within minutes his body would adjust and he wouldn't notice it.

He was aware it came from the hundreds of thousands of bats that frequented the caves. The smell of the urine and feces made deep breathing difficult, but the scarf he wore over his mouth and nose aided in coping with it.

There was no point rushing down the multitude of steps, the only thing that could happen from that would be slipping and falling. While he didn't want to make her wait, he still wanted to get there in one piece.

Not only were they steep but they weren't maintained like the rest of the caves. Only his ring granted access, and there was no reason for anyone else to know the truth of her plight.

Throughout the main caves, servants and acolytes were charged with keeping the caves and walkways they used clean and clear of debris. It was a never-ending task, just not in this secret passage.

Many a time Uksod had thought about what these caves would be like without any bats in them, what a grand underground city he could build. It was just an idle dream. The bats weren't going anywhere and nothing got rid of the stench.

The path he followed was invisible from the rest of the caves. On his left was the outer wall of the main cave under the city, and on his right a partial wall that was as tall as he was. Along the top of it were gaps and spaces that allowed a faint light and air into what felt almost like a tunnel.

No one could see into it from within the cave network, and he could not see out. Who had carved the steps or made this he couldn't say. The main caves had been altered and changed to suit their needs over time, but this stairwell had been made long before that.

Bringing his focus back to his steps he was thankful for the light that allowed him to see. Small speckles of amber, stuck against the rock where each step met the wall, glowing enough to let him navigate safely down.

Stopping every so often to rest his calves, it took Uksod most of an hour to reach the layer where she lived. Or perhaps it was best described as her prison. That was what only he knew. Not that it would matter to her followers, but it mattered to her. She had always demanded that no one else know of her plight.

And so Uksod did her bidding, and kept her company, while she worked on getting free.

The floor here felt like it was the lowest part of the whole cave network, but even Uksod didn't know that for sure. This mountain was huge, and any sense of depth was lost once you were underground.

En Carta backed up to it, and to the residents of the city it was a protecting rock behind them, not a mini city of its own, alive with beast and man.

The cavern reached up hundreds of feet above them. Thousands of steps back up. Uksod wiped sweat off his brow using the sleeve of his cassock and approached the massive amber stone that filled much of the base of this cavern.

It was conical in shape, and the point was out of sight from the bottom. There were layers up in the caves where you could see the top, and the followers often prayed within sight of the Debrua Stone. That was its name, and it was her prison. For now.

Being so close to it was a life-changing feeling. It flooded your senses and captured your attention, all Uksod could think about was himself and his own desires.

He stared into the stone. The rich orange center of the stone appeared to have flecks of other shapes of color floating within it, lighter specks like yellow, auburn and brown. He was able to almost lose himself in the dream of being the one priest, ruling over all of Scurra, Dharatan included.

Despite its size it was almost transparent, or that's how it appeared. Deep within it stood his goddess, Yantarnaya, stuck like an insect within amber. She was as if frozen in place, unable to move, awaiting the time when she could be freed.

Despite the thickness of the barrier her voice could reach him without her talking through her mouth, the circlet around his head, set with amber stones, a direct conduit to his mind.

"I wondered when you would come. How long you'd make me wait."

"I have much I need to do, mistress, but it takes time to walk all the way down here."

"Perhaps I should have chosen me a younger man to fulfill your role? Someone more spritely."

Uksod looked at her, the words angering him.

"Come now, Uksod, I jest. I sense your anger. You were the only one who was brave enough to follow my instructions. I had been trying for so very long."

"And I am grateful for what you have given me, mistress. I do still feel old, nonetheless."

She said nothing for a moment. *"Perhaps I could find a way to help in that, too."*

Uksod felt a bubble of hope forming inside. "Really?"

"We'll see, Uksod. I'm feeling generous right now, but that might not last."

"How can I serve, mistress?"

"There's another amulet, Uksod!"

"Another? What do you mean, another?"

"One of the other amulets is free. I had worried that they no longer existed, but one has surfaced."

"Can you tell where?"

"I had some trouble detecting it, it is weak."

"Weak?"

"Yes, I told you once already. They have limited power, they need to be recharged, that's the best way I can describe it. They have been gone so long, that it's very weak, the connection is patchy."

"Have you learned anything?"

"Only that it is to the south. Somewhere near that desert."

"That is most encouraging. If another is free then perhaps more will soon follow."

"We still need the first one back, Uksod, don't think it absolves you of that."

"Of course, goddess. It is still good news, is it not?"

"It's excellent news, Uksod. Hence I am feeling somewhat magnanimous. But you need to get them all back here, we can't let them float around, without owners. I do not know what will happen if they lose their charge altogether, I never got to use them for very long."

"Perhaps Fuling might have some news. I will have to speak to him after I leave here."

"Perhaps that man might be able to be more useful than he has been. Gifting him a ring was meant to be of benefit to us, Uksod!"

"It takes time with such small objects, and with those unused to what we do. He has been making progress, but King Ahn, while old and doddery, still has other influencers that challenge the direction Fuling is pushing for."

"Take care of it, Uksod. I don't need excuses, just results. We still need to find where the Citadel Stone is, and he has the best force to help us hunt."

"I will, mistress. I will."

"What of the boy, Uksod? I sense something different with him. He's changed recently, and I'm not sure why."

"His father's death seems to have hit him hard. Which is strange, given how little they had to do with each other. That and his impending birthday and all it means."

"He needs to be one with us, Uksod, you know that."

"He's also still young, goddess. He will follow along, one way or another, but he's going through some changes."

"Changes?"

"It happens when people get to a certain age, mistress. He's still to grow into his body and mind."

"He needs to be on our side! I haven't waited this long for the lad to be feckless."

"He'll be fine, once he takes control. I've been working on him since he was born."

"Your confidence in your parenting skills is admirable, let's see if it's warranted. And what if he finds out."

"Finds out?"

"Who killed his father, Uksod."

"He'll never find that out. I was careful."

"Get his amulet back and I'll be able to control him. Then none of the rest of it matters! Once it's leashed to him, then I can control him."

By the time he had returned to his shrine, Uksod's heart was pounding, and he was dripping in sweat. The fetid and heavy air made breathing difficult, and the climb for a man no longer young was taxing.

He moved into his office and perched on his desk while he regained his composure. He needed to reach out and seek answers, from Fuling and Ninety-three. He needed more good news, results, but everything seemed harder when you couldn't do it yourself.

Relying on others like this, without direct communication about progress, made him agitated. He much preferred to do the heavy lifting himself. One of his weaknesses he knew, and not one he could follow in this case.

He was unable to be away from Karpenmor, at least until he was leashed to the amulet. Then Yantarnaya could sway him, and free up Uksod's time to get more hands-on. It was time he visited Fuling and pressed for him to be more proactive.

The priest was useful, and so far had done well, spreading their tendrils across Dharatan under the cover of the Church of Jolothos. By the time the church was revealed as one of Yantarnaya's it wouldn't matter to the dopes that lived there. All would be under his control by then. A grin formed on his face.

Filling his goblet and quenching his thirst helped a little. He would need to eat, and prepare for the process. He picked up the bell that sat on his desk and rang it loud enough to catch the attention of whoever was his attendant this day.

The door opened and Trorn stepped into the room. "Eminence?"

"Can you acquire me some subjects, Trorn? I have some work I need attending to."

"Will two be enough?"

"Yes."

"When do you need them for?"

"If you can arrange something for me to eat, then I'll need to do it soon after. Things are most urgent."

The priest left the room without further words. It was the thing Uksod liked most about him, he wasted little time on superfluous talk. And he rarely asked more than he needed to know.

THE TWO CONNECTIONS TO REACH NINETY-THREE AND THEN FULING HAD wiped out Uksod's energy. He lay slumped across the still body of the second man he had used.

All of it was good news. He wanted to inform Yantarnaya immediately but he was completely wiped out. She would have to wait. He slipped down the side of the bench, until he was propped on the floor, between both of them.

Someone will come to find me, they'll take care of it all. His head swam, but he didn't pass out straight away. The spurt of energy he had from hearing the news that Ninety-three had captured the amulet was good enough, but Fuling's news was the best.

They had it, the second amulet was already theirs. All he had to do now was get it back to En Carta and perhaps Yantarnaya could trace the others.

It's so close to happening now, I can feel it.

He passed out, smiling for the first time in months.

GORAN

The pain behind his eyes let Goran know he was alive, despite a preference for the alternative. Last night he desperately wanted to smoke some weed and lose himself into a fog of mindlessness. To block out the voice. But he knew he couldn't, so he'd resorted to wine.

A lot of wine.

While it worked to keep the voice at bay most of the time, it meant he suffered for it. He couldn't afford to be wiped out for days on end. He should have spoken to one of his colleagues last night, but he couldn't with Zoran bugging him.

Each step down toward the main room sent shudders through his head, amplifying the pounding already there. For now, the wine would have to do. It meant he'd be sluggish for a few hours, but it didn't dull his senses like zongleweed did.

Brando's chuckle didn't make matters any better.

"I thought you'd look like this after how much you drank last night." The keeper was standing behind the bar and pushed a tankard of ale across the top. "Here, this might help."

Goran took a good drink of it, closing his eyes from the light while he did.

"Thanks. Better that than the taste that was there before."

"No doubt you'll need more than one to get you on track."

Goran sat on a stool and took another long drink of the ale. "How fare our guests?"

"I've only checked the once this morning."

"And?"

"They both still live, is about the sum of it all."

"That grim?"

"To be honest, all things considered, I think that's a positive, Goran. Both were badly wounded and lost a lot of blood."

"You're right, I'm just not in a positive mood at the moment. None of us want to lose Henri, he's been part of our family since before most of us came on board."

"I know, Goran, but it's out of our hands. And if I'm not mistaken, you're the most senior person in Callet now. You can't be sliding into one of your funks."

Goran looked across the counter at Brando. He wanted to tell him to mind his own business, but he knew what he told him was true. It was why he'd stuck to the wine. He gave him a small nod.

"You think you can stomach something to eat? There's eggs and bread."

"I'll try."

While he waited, Goran felt the touch from one of his colleagues. He ignored it initially, thinking it was just the after-effects of the Vodotokian Red he had drunk, but it persisted. He made his way back up to his room gingerly.

This will be fun.

As he settled into the pattern of breathing he used to center himself, his head cleared a little and he pushed into the Void.

"In All Jest, Goran."

"In All Jest, Bea."

"Is that a hangover clouding your thoughts?"

"A small one. I'm fine, I needed to relieve the matters of the last few days."

She made no comment for a short while.

"There's a lot to take care of, Goran. You'll need to curb your inclinations."

"You too?"

"Sorry?"

"Brando was just lecturing me." He sensed a small chuckle from her.

"I like him even more. Enough from me on the matter."

"So, what's to be told, Bea?"

"Firstly, how fares Henri?"

"Poorly. Brando was just bringing me up to date on his status. He's alive, is about the total of it all."

"Grim news."

"Indeed."

"And the stranger?"

"No better."

"Any idea who he is?"

"No, he's not been conscious since we brought him in. I expect the city guard will come looking for him today, perhaps they will know more."

"Keep me informed as soon as you learn anything."

"Sure."

"What are your plans?"

"I need to find the girl. I assume nothing has changed there now?"

"No, the amulet you mentioned has come up more than once."

She filled him in on what they'd all been told by Tillandra.

"That's a lot to take in."

"Don't let them get her away, Goran. It's too important!"

"Do you know if she's left Callet?"

"Yes, she's heading south. It's hard to tell where exactly but they're following the border so far."

"I'll plan to leave."

"We decided you need to take Brando with you."

Goran felt attacked. "What for?"

"These Derks. Both Henri and this other man have been well bested by them, as well as others across Malamig. They're trained fighters,

Goran. We can't lose you; we want you to have help. You're too important to us."

Goran was surprised by the sentiment. He choked up a little at her words. If Beantic noticed, she didn't say a thing.

"I realize this might be a surprise, but remember he was a soldier before he was a keeper. Of anyone close by, he'll be your best company. There's safety in numbers, Goran."

It took him a moment to accept what she was saying.

"Okay, I can see the logic. I'm not so keen to confront them on my own either. I just didn't see any option before. Thanks. What of Follies then?"

"He has other helpers there; he needs to leave them in charge. It's far easier to replace a keeper than a jester."

There was little else to say about it. He had worried what would happen if he had to face the men in black himself. While he preferred his own company best when traveling, Brando would be the best choice if he had to have someone with him.

"One more thing."

"Oh?"

"You need to assign someone to the Safe House."

"I should have thought about that."

"It was Toolet that reminded us all. Put a courier in charge, they should know enough for now. Let's hope Henri recovers, then it won't be an issue."

"Let's hope."

They finished up and Goran gently brought himself back into the here and now. He peered around the room. His headache had gone, and his mind was clearer than when he started.

Interesting, I've not noticed that before.

He got up and went back downstairs.

"Where did you go? The eggs are cold now."

"I had to take care of something. Cold will do me fine. There's news."

"Oh. You look a lot better than before, did Zeresse give you a tonic?"

"No," he laughed. "Is she here?"

"Yes, she's looking in on Henri now."

Goran began shoveling food into his mouth.

"What news, before you kill yourself with food?"

Speaking through a full mouth, Goran told him of Bea's instructions.

"I better ready myself for leaving then. Yenrk will be fine to run things while we're gone."

"He's capable?"

"Yes, more than capable. I'll get us some extra horses and supplies. We're behind already we'll need to push hard."

"Even your cold eggs are tasty, Brando. What on Scurra do you put in them?"

"It's that peppercorn. Rare as amber it is, but not forbidden. I have a supplier from Satama that I can get a small supply from."

"And you'll tell me who they are?"

"Just as soon as you give up ale for life!"

Goran shook his head, not feeling any of the pains he had earlier.

They both laughed.

"Right, I better find out what Zeresse has to say." Goran got up from the stool and headed to the back rooms.

The smell of incense filled the hallway to the back of the inn. Not fresh burning incense smoke, but the sweet and sweaty odor of it that Zeresse carried with her. Her clothes were soaked in it and her very skin seemed to ooze the smell.

Goran didn't mind it, but others found her very overpowering to the nose. She was kneeling beside Henri's bed. The contents of her bag were spread out to her side.

"Zeresse, how do you fare?"

She turned her head to take him in, a vacant look in her brown eyes. Dark circles surrounded the eyes and her jet-black hair gave her a look that frightened many.

"Goran! Let me finish."

He waited while she turned back to Henri and focused on him. One hand was set on his forehead and another over his chest. Goran could hear her breathing deeply and muttering as she exhaled.

When she had finished, she picked through some small vials on the floor, pulling a stopper out of one and tipping several drops into Henri's mouth. She pulled everything into her bag messily and stood up.

"What do you think?"

She walked over to him and wrapped him in a hug. Her long arms seemed to circle him twice. She crushed him with the strength of a working man and nuzzled his neck. He hugged her back and waited. When she was done, she took a step back and looked deep into his eyes.

"I see the struggle still continues."

Goran looked to the floor. "It does."

She patted his shoulder.

"Henri is on the edge. I cannot tell if he will live. He's very close to the Void but maybe you got him back in time. Your work might yet save him, Goran."

He looked back up. "Thank you. What can we do for him?"

"Rest, and something I will brew for him. Now, there is another?"

"Yes. Someone we don't know - but someone we need to know about."

"Tell me more."

"Let me take you to him first. We can talk later. He's as bad as Henri."

13

LANI

ani woke to the sickening feeling of a bouncing motion. Her head was pounding the same as it always did after a bad head knock, and her stomach felt queasy. She tried to move but her hands and feet were bound.

She realized that she was lying over a horse, her head facing downward inside some sort of sack. Normally being in the dark helped her when she opened her eyes, but the way her head was banging against the saddle just made everything feel worse.

The air inside the sack was stale, and there was little room to spare. Lani just hoped she wasn't sick, she couldn't take that as well.

She tried to clear her head enough to think but the rocking around made it impossible and eventually she passed out with the pain.

When she woke again the pace of the horse had slowed as had the severity of the headache. Lani was able to hold her head firm against the saddle which felt almost like someone was rubbing her head.

The crack of thunder caused her to buck against her bindings, the suddenness of the sound frightening her. It took all her will to concentrate on what was happening. She was clearly a prisoner of someone, but she struggled to bring back any memories. She'd been in Callet, that was it.

Slowly it began to come back to her. The priest, leaving the church and heading for somewhere to stay. Then seeing Kyro before turning and running from him.

Lani gasped and tears ran down her cheek. She saw an image of him being cut down and the look on his face as he crumpled down on the ground bleeding.

Why was he in Callet? Why was he chasing me?

She tried to think through why he was there. It was so far from Barnen, why would he have followed her there over the death of the stranger in Barnen? Did he still think she had been responsible for Harsop as well? Or had he found out she'd looted the bodies? Even so, why chase her this far?

None of it made any sense. And now another death, another person killed because of her. Because of the stupid amulet and Ashantha.

The more she felt her head clearing the angrier she got. Of all the feelings she hated the most, Lani didn't like feeling out of control, and being a victim of others. Despite her lowly status in Barnen, she had chosen how she lived.

Lani had run into trouble ever since she had found Ashantha, and this was no different. Crying wasn't going to get her out of it, and she needed to have her wits about her. She grimaced inside the hood as her head throbbed again.

Her horse slowed abruptly, as if its reins had been pulled sharply. For the first time Lani could hear muffled voices but couldn't make out what was being said. She sensed the wind picking up as it swirled around her body, a chill cutting through her clothing.

The horse stopped completely and she could hear the voices better.

"It's coming fast."

"...take shelter."

"But where?"

Something muttered she couldn't make out.

"Isn't that what we've been warned about?"

"...better idea? Are you scared ..." Lani heard some sort of number but didn't understand what it meant.

"No, leader. As you say."

Lani could feel her horse being pulled left and it slowly began walking. More thunder boomed, closer now, and she could feel large drops of rain hitting her back and legs.

Great, now I'm going to get soaked.

The horse eventually stopped, followed by the sound of people dismounting and then footsteps close to her. Strong hands worked on whatever bound her to the horse. Once free, she was pulled backward and landed roughly on her feet.

Lani hadn't been prepared for it and fell forward. A sudden yank from the rope binding her hands behind her back pulled her upright, rotating her shoulders awkwardly and causing a sharp pain below her neck.

Another hand grasped her left shoulder, and she was marched to her right. The person walking her pushed their hand into the middle of her back to keep her moving.

A hand suddenly pushed down on her head and Lani's feet were swept out from underneath her. She fell heavily and her back slammed into what felt like a tree trunk, causing her to grunt in pain. Thankfully Lani had kept her head forward, so she didn't bang the tender spot at the back.

She was being treated like an animal and the despair came rushing back. No matter how brave she worked herself up to be she was at their mercy. She tried to compose herself, but without sight everything felt worse, and she struggled to breathe, a hollow feeling growing in her chest.

Something tugged at the hands behind her back. Without warning the hood on her head was ripped away. Lani had to blink to adjust her vision even though the light was dull. A tall man stood before her. He had very pale skin and his head was hairless.

"Stay!" he spat at her, before heading to join his colleagues.

Lani's captors had found a very small clearing amongst the thick bush that surrounded it to her right. Even that was dense enough up high to stop most of the rain getting through. A flash of lightning to her left highlighted open ground not much more than twenty yards away.

No one would see them in here, not in the dark and when the storm hit. With the light she'd confirmed what she already knew, that she was being held by three members of the Vrah. The man who had removed her hood was tending to the horses, putting feed bags over their heads.

She could see Goatee sat to her right, nursing what seemed to be a wound. It was a small relief to Lani that at least Kyro had struck some worthy blows to the Derk before he had been killed.

Good. I hope you die, Goatee.

As if he could hear her thoughts, he turned to look at her, his face covered in a cold scowl. He stood, grasping at his midriff as he did, then approached her.

He stood over her. "Where is it?"

Lani looked up at him. "What?"

"The amulet!"

"I don't know what…"

She screamed as he slapped her across the face, her head beginning to throb again.

"That's just the beginning! I'm happy to find it myself, but I won't be gentle about it. Where is it?"

Lani tried to wriggle a hand free, but they were bound tightly behind her.

"You're not getting out of there." He let out a nasty short laugh.

As much as she wanted to hide the amulet from him, there was little she could do. Lani decided she'd be better off if he was exposed to it, she could let it harm him for her. She'd need her hands untied though, it wouldn't do her any good to be tied up when he got it.

"I… I'll get it out for you. You don't want to touch it."

"Where?"

She tilted her head down to her chest.

Goatee looked at her, pulled out his blade and pointed it at her. "Don't do anything stupid." He untied one of her hands. "Get it out."

Lani fumbled around in her tunic until she felt the two objects in the pocket. She made sure the brooch was at the bottom and pulled the pouch containing the amulet out, showing it in her upturned palm to him.

"Open it!"

Using her teeth and fingers she started to pull the pouch open.

Immediately she could sense the stone within, the space in the cloth letting the tendrils creep out. Her mind began to think differently and it was as if she could see more clearly in the dark.

Goatee stood up and swayed on his feet a little. He turned to the bald one and waved him over.

"Watch her, I feel Uksod trying to reach me."

He walked away from her and sat with his back against a tree, and closed his eyes. Lani wasn't sure what was happening. She could see his lips moving, but couldn't hear any sound. The amulet was just visible in her palm with the pouch still open. She went to move it toward her mouth but the bald one waved his sword at her.

"Don't move."

A few minutes passed and Goatee opened his eyes. The bald one moved a few steps closer to him.

"What news?"

"He was happy, One-seventy-seven. Very happy, that we have found the amulet."

"What did he say to do with her? Bring her back as a plaything for the princeling?" His laugh was full of malice.

"Prince Karpenmor needs nothing from a barbarian. She has no purpose, the amulet is what we needed to find."

"Understood." The bald one turned to look back at her briefly. "Finish it now?"

Goatee was about to reply when the sound of a stick cracking underfoot stopped him. He leaped up quickly using the tree to brace himself, before turning to his left, his blade out in front of his body, his arm half extended.

Bald one moved away from her toward the sound, and the third one, still wearing a hood on his head, came from the other side closer to Goatee.

Lani's heart sped up again, and she quietly moved her head side to side trying to see if anything was close by. She felt exposed, tied up away from the others and unable to defend herself. If it was a wolf or bear she was an easy target for them.

The amulet still dragged at her focus and as much as she wanted to, she couldn't put it away.

An uneasy quiet settled over the Vrah as they all stood in wariness looking out into the dark.

"Animal maybe?" the hooded one said finally.

"Maybe," Goatee agreed hoarsely.

The thud of the arrow hitting the hooded one in the chest changed everything. His body dropped hard to the ground with a thud. Lani could hear his gurgling last breaths and fell forward in fright, losing the pouch as she did so.

Goatee and the other man had dropped out of sight, their black clothes helping in the dark forest. It went oddly quiet, the only sound was the horses snorting. Lani could hear them bucking and pulling against their ropes.

Whoever was out there had spooked the animals. She twisted around to see if she could reach where the rope was tied with her free hand. Footsteps rushed by and Lani saw the blur of someone moving, but couldn't tell if it was one of her captors or their attackers.

A scream off to her left briefly halted her progress untying the knot. Once the rope was loosened enough to squeeze her left fist through she pulled as hard as she could against it, ripping the skin surface as she did so.

Once free she located the pouch. It lay on the ground just ahead of her and she could almost see it in the dark, as if the amulet directed her to it. Picking it up and stuffing it back into her tunic, Lani focused on where the horses were, crawling toward where she could hear them stomping anxiously.

Another lighting flash and thunder crash startled her and she could see the horses bucking furiously ahead of her. The sounds of blades clashing was somewhere to her right, far enough, she hoped, to allow her to slip away. She needed her satchel and ideally a horse, if she could settle one enough to lead away, and the storm might give her enough cover to escape whoever was hunting them in here. She reached the small pile of things the men had taken from the horses. Her satchel was there, and she slipped the strap over her shoulder before reaching in to feel what was inside.

The journal and pouch of coins were easy enough to feel, as was the mask.

I don't need that ring, I just need to get away.
Lani stood cautiously and took a step toward the nearest horse. "Sshhhh," she said, trying to calm it down.

A shape appeared to her right from beside a tree. "Where do you think you're going?"

The man grabbed her by the back of the tunic, easily flinging her around in front of him. "Don't bother fighting, you'll only die quicker."

14

LANI

Lani struggled to see who it was that had her, but she could feel how strong he was. He was able to walk her in front of himself with little effort, lifting her up and down. At the edge of her vision she could see a dark-colored blade of some sort.

Flicking her head back and upward she tried to get a glimpse of who it was. He didn't sound like the Vrah who had caught her before. "Let me go, I'm not with them!"

"Quiet! Stop fighting or I'll make it easier on myself."

Lani stopped her wriggling and let him move her like a doll, anger welling up inside her. Suddenly he let go of her and she fell face first to the ground. She rolled to her side, and saw him facing off with a man she could hardly see.

As their blades swung and connected, Lani shuffled on her backside away from them, frightened. As lightning flashed through the trees she caught a glimpse of the man who had been carrying her.

He wore nothing on his upper body, and his skin was completely covered in tattoos. She'd never seen anyone as tall, broad and muscular as him. The light disappeared as quickly as it had come, the man entirely focused on his opponent.

While the fighting continued, she rose into a crouch and moved back to where the horse was. Caring little about the horse's state, she untied it from its tether and dragged it away from the sounds of fighting.

Once free of the trees the horse stopped resisting her and she was able to mount up. Lani didn't wait and kicked it hard, leaping forward and up toward a roadway.

By the time the storm had run its course and dawn flickered ahead on the horizon, Lani and the horse were both exhausted. They'd both lumbered along through the night, she never wanting to stop, the only cover the forest to her left. She wasn't going back in there, not for anything.

Through nothing but luck the tired horse had managed to keep itself safe, not stepping into anything that would harm it. Now with the orange hues flowing over the horizon she could see the plains around them spread out in all directions. Her basic knowledge of the position of the sun confirmed she was heading east and south. That was good enough for her. For now.

Despite staying awake throughout the night Lani hadn't thought too much about what was happening around her. She'd become so accustomed to people wanting to harm her, it almost seemed normal. She wanted to stop and curl up in a ball and feel sorry for herself, but the thought of who might be behind her forced her to keep moving.

Off to her left she spotted a small creek near a thin line of trees. She let the horse drink first and once it had taken its fill, she tied it off near some grass and returned to dunk her head under the water.

It wasn't icy fresh like the northern rivers, but it refreshed her anyway, and helped quench her thirst. Lani had no idea where she was, or how far they had covered, all she could hope for was to come across a village or farms before long.

Lani checked her satchel. It looked as though everything was still there. She patted her chest out of habit, though she already knew the two pieces of jewelry were there. Not that anyone could easily take the amulet from her. She would have been glad to see the end of it if someone could steal it from her. But that didn't seem possible.

Was that why the person who Goatee had called Uksod had told him to kill her?

That's what he meant, I have no purpose. They didn't need me, they would have killed me so they could take it.

She didn't know why everyone wanted the amulet. *Who is Prince Karpenmor, and why does he want it? Everyone wants it but me, and I can't get rid of it.*

So many people had died already because of it. She thought about Henri and sadness returned. He had been one person who had tried to help her, giving up his life for her.

If the woman he called Mother, in Anderwell, was anything like him, then Lani would seek her out. Whoever this Karpenmor was, his men, the Vrah, were not people she wanted to be anywhere near.

As she watched the horse chewing on the grass, she thought more about what had just happened. She recalled the priest she'd met in Callet.

Where did he say there was a seer? Union, that's it.

That was an option. She still had the coin pouch and could pay for somewhere to stay and eat. If she had to pay for help from the seer she could do that as well. It was as good an option as any.

I better keep moving, no matter what happens. Who knows who will be following?

She stood and tried to stretch out the pain she felt. Most of her chest and middle were bruised from when she had been slung over the saddle. Now the top of her legs felt achy as well. Lani knew she needed to keep moving before it hurt too much to do so.

Even the horse was reluctant to move. She had to tug hard to get it to follow her. They both drank more water from the creek then headed back to the road, walking toward the sun. Eventually the horse allowed her get back on and she let it set the pace. She didn't know if Goatee had survived or not, but if he had she knew he wouldn't rest until he caught her.

Close enough to middle day Lani rode into a small village. It was made up of half a dozen buildings, the longest of which had smoke rising from the chimney and looked to be an inn of sorts. She tied her horse up under a small shelter and was surprised by a young girl who came out to tend to it.

Lani walked in the door and heard the familiar sounds of a tavern.

The main room was smaller than she expected. The space didn't go the length of the building — her best guess was the keeper lived in the other section.

"Help you?" a tall man with a thin covering of short grey hair asked from behind the counter.

"If you have something to eat and some thin ale then you most certainly can."

"Only bread, cheese and some dried meat at this time of the day, lass."

"That will do me just fine."

"I'll bring it to you, not much else happening."

He brought her the ale first, a wooden tankard which Lani quickly took sips from, savoring the taste. When he returned with a cloth and the food, he stood back and looked her over.

"Traveling by yourself, then?"

Lani looked up quickly, suspicious of his question. "This leg I am. Why do you ask?"

"No reason, lass, you just don't see a woman out on her own like this real often. You heading to Union?"

Lani nodded, remembering it was better to say little and let the man do the talking.

"How's your horse holding up?"

"It's tired. We're not setting a great pace."

"You'll want to settle at Gwenith, it's the next town. You'll know it by the crossroads."

"Crossroads?"

"Yeah, there's a road that runs south, it's the short run to Diwedd. A smaller one runs north into Ngahere."

"A short run to Diwedd? I thought you had to go through Union?"

He chuckled. "Not if you don't need to. It's the same distance either way once you reach the crossroads. A couple of days to Union, or a couple to Diwedd, no reason to go east if you're heading to Diwedd."

"Right. I'm going there after Union."

"In that case when you leave Union, you'll follow the river south, same distance again. Anyway I need to check on tonight's dinner."

He walked away into the back of the inn. Lani stewed over her choice. Maybe there was more information in the journal but she couldn't check that now. Either way she needed to get to the town he'd told her of, and get a room there.

Lani finished off the rest of the food and left the inn. Her horse looked like it had been wiped down and had been eating from a small bucket of oats. The young girl was nowhere to be seen to thank. Lani untied the horse and headed out to the road.

I need to give you a name.

15

LEO

Mistress Wenthern was boring him to death. Leo hated her classes, they were so tedious, and she told the same story so many times he could repeat it verbatim. Looking out the window he could see the clear blue sky and wished he was outside.

The gentle sound like water rushing that he heard when he drifted off, intrigued him. He had only begun to hear it since he'd arrived in Anderwell. He hadn't though much more about it, except for how strange it was here in the desert to hear water.

Vaguely he thought he could hear his name bubbling up through the rushing water.

"PEGGLE! Are you with us?"

Turning suddenly, his face flushed as he realized she had called out his name. "Miss?"

"Yes, missing what I'm saying is the truth."

"Did you say something new, miss?" A spurt of giggles spread quickly around the room.

"Excuse me? What did you say?"

"I asked if you said something new, miss, because most classes you repeat exactly the same thing, and I've heard it so much it puts me to sleep."

A silence fell over the room, but Leo didn't care. If this was what school was about, he was done with it. The crusty old minds telling him mundane information wasn't of any interest to him.

"You're a genius now, you have no need for learning? I knew you weren't bright, boy, but I didn't take you for such a rude little sod. Well, that's good, because I have no time to waste on those without the inclination to learn."

"You taught us something new then?"

"What?"

"Well, you're berating me and calling me stupid because I wasn't listening to you, but what exactly was it you taught them I missed?"

"We were discussing the incidence of infection in wounds, and one specific example. If you must know."

"Which was the story of when you came across a caravan in Thabeng, and they had been attacked by raiders and three of them had been cut by swords." Leo went on to repeat word for word the story for another minute. "Was that what you were saying? Did I miss anything?"

Miss Wenthern stood at the front of the class, flustered, and her face a bright red. She looked down at her desk and grabbed a piece of parchment then hurriedly scribbled a note on it.

"You're done here, Peggle. I have no need for such rudeness in my classes." She held the note out for him.

"And I have no need to waste my time with stories repeated daily because you have nothing new to share. If this is learning, then I'll gladly leave it behind."

Leo picked up his things, slipped them into the open tote which he slung over his shoulder and marched to the front of the room.

Miss Wenthern wiggled the note as he approached. "Take this to the main office, and I hope they put you out on the street where your type belongs."

Leo stopped abruptly. "My type?" He stared defiantly at her.

"Yes, your type. Ignorant midgets who have such massive chips on their shoulders."

"There it is, you bigot. Look at you! Supposedly this is a place of safety for everyone and yet here's the bigoted old cripple as prejudiced as everyone else."

Leo walked over and had to jump to reach the note she deliberately held high, pulled it from her hand, and stomped out of the class. He could hear her lecturing the class about their sniggering and to get back to their books as he slammed the door behind him.

"They're all the same. Why I thought this would be any different I've no idea. It's just hidden here, that's the difference." He wasn't sure who he was talking to, but he was angry.

He headed to the main staircase and used the small steps built into the inside path to walk down to the ground level. At the bottom the main doors stood before him, and he stopped looking out at the square outside. A layer of dust always lined the tiles in this foyer, from the desert sands that blew across the city for most of the year.

Was there any point in going to the office? He would be thrown out, no doubt. His type was always treated poorly, he'd been a fool to come here and think that anything good would come of it. He should have escaped the Fool's Cart and the Driver, Kooka, when he had the chance.

It was over two years since he'd settled here in the college, but the last few months had been the worst. He was bored. The life they'd been given seemed good on the surface, but it felt like he was a prisoner here. He'd been on his own for most of his life, why change now? He didn't want to be told what to do.

Leaving the college meant going back out on the street, he knew that. That would take some getting used to again. They'd softened him and made him think that was a bad thing, but when he'd been on his own, he felt alive. Sure, some days he got hurt but they were rarer as he had gotten stronger, and smarter. Was he better off here? He did have meals every day and a room of his own, that was true. But at what cost?

He went down toward the office. At least he should let them know what was going on. He would tell them what she'd said, let them deal with the stupid old crone.

As he entered the office, he ran into a woman similar in height to him but nearly as old as Miss Wenthern. She bounced off him and landed on her backside.

"I'm so sorry," he said as he went to help her up.

She burst out laughing.

"What's so funny?"

"Oh, I laugh at the silliest of things, lad, I'm well known for it. Here, help me up."

She stood up then bent over again and picked up the book she had dropped. "So, who are you busting in here like the world was ending?"

"Leo Peggle, miss."

"I'm no miss, Peggle. I'm old enough to be your grandmother. What's all the rush, is the desert on fire?" She winked at him as she said it.

She was very disarming the way she had reacted and in her manner of speaking. He found the anger he had minutes before was completely gone now.

"I've been causing trouble." He held up the note he still had in his hand.

The woman walked to him and pulled it from his hand. "Oh lord, that windbag. What did you do?"

Leo didn't feel his normal brashness around this woman and looked down at the ground.

"Come on, surely it can't be that bad. What did you do?"

"It was what I said. I wasn't paying attention; I was staring out the window. When she yelled at me about not paying attention, I asked her if she'd taught us anything new."

The woman burst out laughing again. "Oh lordy, that's brilliant. I bet she fired up at that?"

"She wasn't too impressed. I doubled down and told her I'd rather not waste my time if she was just going to repeat the same stories every day. She gave me that."

"So, you know everything she's got to teach?"

Leo could feel his usual sharpness returning. "How would I know, all she tells us is the same ten stories in different lights. I even repeated the story she was telling word for word but that made it worse."

"Hmm. Indeed. I've been meaning to check in on our lecturers and see what we're teaching. Maybe I've left it too long."

"Sorry, miss, who are you?"

"I told you already I'm no miss. I'll let you off this time though, given you don't know my name. Toolet. You say it `Too Lay`."

"Sorry, Toolet. I didn't know."

"I'm one of the Court. We're the people that oversee the running of things around here. I have to teach students as well."

"I've not seen you in any of my classes."

"Maybe I haven't been giving enough of them, or maybe you've been taking the wrong ones." She giggled again for no real reason. "I also look after the city and its finances. Perhaps I've not been paying enough attention to what's being taught. I'll have to have a word with Mother Folly about that."

"Why do you believe me over her?"

"Because I've been in one of her classes before. She's not the most inspiring, but she does know a lot about the healing of the body. Maybe she needs some new material."

"I'm supposed to hand this to the office, it's probably my last chance. I've been in trouble a lot lately."

"Really? Why's that, Peggle?"

"People like her. They don't like our type. Always treating me like I don't belong. She even called me a midget."

"Well, that is what they call us."

"I thought it would be different here."

"Why's that?"

"I don't know, I just thought it would be. What with all the different types of people, many with differences, I just thought everyone would be more understanding."

"Then you don't know people, son. Just because they have their own difference doesn't mean they'll treat you better. People is people, and they've been brought up like you were, suffering from one person or another. We all pick up our prejudices, and sometimes it's the only thing that helps us survive when you're also caught in amongst it."

"I didn't expect it. It's been bothering me a lot."

"There's a difference between people having a prejudice and

how they act out on it. You're so used to people acting out on it, you're probably expecting the same from them. Everyone here is learning to let go of their lives beforehand, but change takes time."

"I guess."

Toolet looked at him strangely, her dark brown eyes boring into his, making him feel very uncomfortable. They seemed to go cloudy and he was locked staring at them, unable to move. It was like she was reaching inside his head.

He could almost feel fingers inside his mind, pushing through his thoughts, and pushed against them. It wasn't truly conscious what he did, but he pushed out through the inside of his head, tightening everything inside as if it was his fists.

Her laugh broke his concentration.

"Well how very interesting, Leo. And to think you don't even know what you were doing. Very interesting indeed."

Leo's forehead was covered in sweat, and he had to wipe at it to stop it dripping into his eyes.

"What were you doing to me?"

"Why don't I ask you what you thought I was doing?"

He didn't want to look at her anymore, he wasn't letting her trap his eyes like she had. Instead he stared at her feet.

"I won't, Leo."

"Won't what?"

"Trap your eyes."

He looked up and she had a friendly smile on her face.

"How did you know what I was thinking?"

"For now, let's say I'm good at reading people. Now what did you think I was doing?"

Leo shuffled on his feet a bit and he could feel his face redden, but he couldn't not say it. "Like you were in my head. It felt like fingers plucking through papers, inside my head, looking at everything I know."

Toolet's face lit up and her head nodded gently.

"That is quite a unique way to describe it, Leo. And what was it you did when you were concentrating so much?"

"I was scrunching everything up ready to fight whatever it was you were doing. Trying to push back."

She looked at him carefully, not saying a word for over a minute. Leo still didn't look directly at her eyes more than for a brief moment.

"I can see why you're bored senseless in the classes you've been attending. That can stop. I think I might need to take a direct hand in your learning. A new program, shall we say."

"A new program?"

"Yes. There are other courses here than just the ones you've been on. It's about time I took on another student. You're it, boy, unless you'd rather go back to her tales?"

"Ah, that's a no!" For some unknown reason, he stammered his way through the answer. "Thank you."

"I'll see you at sunup, right here. Don't be late, my bite is way worse than my bark!"

GIMBDEN

Getting rid of Nion Pravat wasn't going to bother Gimbden at all. His contempt for the man was at an all-time high, and even after Tillandra's visit and threats, the man's compulsions still got the better of him. There was no way they could leave such a sexual predator in power.

Having to spend days in his company, often in complete silence, only gave Gimbden hours to dream up ways for harm to come to Pravat. None of which he could actually bring to fruition, but the daydreaming was amusing if nothing else.

He particularly liked the idea of him being dragged along behind the fast-moving horses of the Skarian knights, but then they were gone from Watersend. For now, at least.

Climbing the stairs to his room in the western tower tired him. He often felt that Pravat had placed him here on purpose but for that to have happened he would have needed to have known about his condition.

Bracing against the wall he rested and let his breathing catch up. He didn't know the wording for it, whatever convoluted term the physicks had told him when he first arrived in Anderwell. Less air was what he understood. His chest didn't work like other people's, which had made him a weak and sickly child.

Despite the complete lack of care from his parents, he had lived through it. The people of their town on the coast, north of Cengel, in southwestern Vodotok, had little affection for him either. Culturally the term was 'crippled and useless' which was used of those with more obvious ailments. He was lucky in his own mind that he had all his limbs, he never had to face the sneers and blatant hate that others did.

Few of the broken survived in Cengel, it had taken all Gimbden's will to scrape out enough food to keep himself alive. When the Fool's Cart had arrived in town it took little encouragement for him to hitch a ride.

The Driver back then had been Ruport, a strange man, clearly of Ngaherian descent, but who didn't follow the path of their males. No one bothered him when he passed through towns and cities, due to his size, even if he wasn't muscular like a typical Ngaherian warrior. His build was a lot 'puffier' but in Gimbden's mind he had still been huge.

Overnight Gimbden had confirmed who the best target was for the plan Mother had suggested. He liked it for its simplicity and consequences. In Watersend, and of course Midderbuilt, gems and jewelry were rated higher than anything. In fact, it was likely they were worth more than a person's life.

Anyone found to be stealing, which in truth was very rare, spent a very long time buried in the underground prison that was infamous throughout the realm.

In Sahro the practice of cutting off hands or the like was prohibited. It made little sense to support the maiming of people when Anderwell was the home for those who had natural disabilities.

~

WHILE THERE WAS SOME EMPATHY FOR THE OUTCOME THAT WOULD BEFALL Pravat, the way the man treated girls was abhorrent to Gimbden and he was glad that would be at an end. This was the first practical way he could intervene. He had found many ways to place obstacles in

Pravat's way but ultimately the man was so desperate to fulfill his desires he always worked around them.

There was something else at play as well. Often Pravat had managed to meet with the Envoy, without Gimbden present. All he could hope was that this put an end to those plans as well.

The black outfit Gimbden typically wore when working was ideal for his task this evening. And once he reached his room, he changed into that clothing. He had acquired some charcoals from the central kitchen and wrapped them in a cloth — he would smear his face with them when he needed to.

It was thankfully an almost completely moonless night due to some heavy cloud. All the omens were in his favor to fulfill the assignment, as long as his body didn't let him down. For him to pull this off it would take all his strength and physical capabilities, which were limited.

He wished there was another option, but he couldn't delegate this particular mission to anyone. A more unscrupulous person would have assigned it to a trusted crew member and then disposed of them immediately after to remove the chance of anyone finding out the truth. That option was not allowed for the Jesters. They were only allowed to kill others in self-defense. If they did otherwise the punishment was immediate.

Their memory was wiped, the ring came loose and they lost their sight. They then had to live without the support of the Court and make their way in a harsh world. It had only happened twice in the history of the Court and the tales told of it were hard to listen to.

They all knew that one of their exiles still lived and wandered the world even if none of them had ever met them. He couldn't think of anything worse than knowing you had lost all this.

Gimbden took a vial from a hidden compartment in the wall behind some books and placed it in his pocket. It held some bitter, foul-smelling, concoction that Zeresse had given him several years ago when he'd spent time in Callet. It helped his breathing for a short time and made him feel almost normal.

The exit he chose tonight was a little-used one that ran under the council chambers in Watersend. At one time it probably had been for servants to get to and from certain sections without being noticed. While it was serviceable, it had been filled with many leftover items including old furniture and scraps. The narrow tunnels were crammed with obstacles and stank.

He knew about it because it was the best place for him to find rats when he needed them. Otherwise, it was only a very game person that used it, the odor and dangers down here weren't worth the risks. A small, dampened lantern lit the way. It was a risk he was willing to take for the middle section of the tunnels, but he left it behind long before he exited.

The door he used opened into the end of a long alley. Anyone that might have walked all the way down to the end of the alley against the wall would have been lucky to notice the doorway, it was so well cut into the building.

After climbing up the steps and pushing the door open, Gimbden was breathless again. He closed the door and rested, hating the hopelessness of his body. It didn't matter how grateful he felt for his life and the opportunities he had, he still struggled with the dislike of how his body let him down. He knew that was pointless, nothing would change it, and he shouldn't judge himself that way. But knowing something and living with it were two different things.

When he was close to his destination Gimbden rested again in a recess of a doorway, at the front of a shop. The road was generally quiet down this side of the large compound. It had a high wall which removed the need for any guards on the back and sides. They would be stationed inside the gate on the northern side.

He had only been into the compound once or twice and knew how well guarded the gates where.

Gimbden also knew the storage vaults for Master Vendren's jewels were placed near the wall he now looked at, but not right up against it. He had deliberately not built against the wall so no one could simply remove bricks and be inside the vaults.

Vendren was one of Watersend's preeminent gem dealers. He didn't produce many pieces of jewelry, recognizing that his skills were in the finding and trading of the right gems. His other problem was that he too had a predilection for young girls and spent a lot of time in Pravat's company.

On one of their many drinking and whoring sessions Gimbden had accompanied Pravat to the compound acting as a servant. He tried his best to shield the other servants from the man's behavior.

While he had hated the whole thing, he was happy he had seen what he had. That knowledge would serve him well in what he aimed to do.

Getting over the wall was the biggest problem, but one that he had a plan for.

The sound of boots walking down the road caused him to press further back into the recess. Coming from his right, two men were marching side-by-side. As they passed him on the far side of the road, Gimbden held his breath. He couldn't be spotted here dressed as he was — that would be far too difficult to explain.

They passed without noticing him, but both were clearly working and armed. It seemed that Vendren didn't take his security as lightly as Gimbden had first thought. If he wasn't mistaken these were guards doing rounds of the compound and neighboring streets.

That changes things, a lot.

As soon as they passed, Gimbden started counting in his mind, step by step until they finally showed again. This time, he started counting when they turned into the road he was watching them on. That was the first point he would be visible to them, and would tell him how long he would have to get over the wall.

17

GIMBDEN

$\mathcal{A}$ thousand steps. That was all the time he had to get it done. Twice now he had counted it out, watching them walking their rounds. Both times they went in the same direction. Gimbden only hoped they didn't change that, because if they did, he was royally screwed.

While he counted, the second time, he walked the distance between his hiding spot to the wall, one foot in front of the other, wobbling as if drunk, cautious and focused.

Each time it took about five hundred steps in his mind. More than enough time, he hoped.

The whole thing caused him no end of anxiety as it was, adding this additional danger to it wasn't exactly something he wanted. He couldn't just put it off and come back another time. They clearly did this regularly. He should have discovered this in advance, but there had been little time. It was today or never.

After they went by again, Gimbden grabbed what he needed out of his backpack. First, he covered his face with charcoal, something he knew he should have done immediately after he came above ground. He also put on the black gloves. Apart from his eyes he would be nearly invisible to everyone in this poor light.

He took out the rope he had brought with him. Not just any rope, this thin cord was made from the Kabel vine and was many times stronger than anything else. It was thin like twine and almost invisible to the naked eye, especially in the dark, but could hold several people easily with almost no flex.

Learning how to rope walk on Kabel took a lot of practice as it had much less give than a typical tightrope which threw off your balance. Many from the college struggled with it because they couldn't adjust to the different flexibility. He untied the rope so it was ready to use, making sure the pronged hooks at each end weren't going to nick him.

With his bag on his back, he waited until the guards passed again. As soon as they turned the corner and headed north Gimbden hurried across the road and slung one end of the rope up the twelve-foot wall. The hook grabbed on the first go, his well-practiced hand meant he didn't have to waste valuable time.

He hurried back across the road to the side of the shop he'd been hiding at. On the sides of the small roof that covered the entrance were wooden frames that supported it. They also made useful climbing ladders. He scaled up easily and onto the roof.

Once there he adjusted the hook on his end of the rope and locked it onto the edge of the building, the teeth biting firmly into the wood. He fed the rope through the loop in the hook until it was taut and used the clasp to lock it out.

Looking at the way the apparatus worked he was thankful for how clever the metalsmith was that made these for them. The ability to adjust and release only when needed was what made them perfect for this job.

Focusing back on the task at hand he peered down the road. He'd lost count while climbing up and didn't know when they'd show up again. He waited. And waited.

Something wasn't right, he knew he hadn't been counting but they should have shown by now, his instinct for time wasn't that far off. He started counting to see how long it would take for them to appear. He reached two thousand and still no one had come.

Whatever had changed wasn't helping his anxiety. There were only so many hours until dawn and he couldn't be here all night.

Then the sound of boots carried to him through the midnight silence coming from the same direction as before. Breathing more easily, he peered across the roof edge to see the guards. As they came closer, he understood the delay: they were different guards. He could tell by their builds and how they walked, even in the dim light.

It meant he would have to count them out several more times before he made his move, a necessary delay to avoid detection. It worked in his favor in the end, the new guards appeared to be slower than their predecessors, taking twelve hundred steps to do their loop.

He took the vial from his pocket and removed the stopper, waiting until the guards showed themselves again. Gimbden waited two more times to be sure. After their fourth loop he swallowed liquid from the vial as soon as they turned the corner on his left.

He stood and stepped confidently out onto the rope stretched across the road. The first few steps were always the riskiest. Despite having set the rope as taut as he could, he still had to gauge its flex and how he would disperse his weight.

He balanced briefly, maintaining the count in his head.

One hundred and forty-five.

He took a deep breath - not something he could normally do - and soaked up the air to fill his chest. Then he started walking the rope.

One hundred and ninety.

The rope beneath his feet didn't move and the air was still. The counting in his head worked to help him concentrate, and he didn't have to use one of his other techniques. He looked forward only, his focus on the compound and the roof he wanted to reach.

Three hundred and twelve.

Halfway across he took another deep breath, pausing to stabilize himself. Then he moved forward again, his arms spread wide, a perfect picture of balance, if anyone had been watching.

Five hundred and seventy-three.

Sweat was dripping down his brow now, the effort of maintaining this posture taking its toll on him. The warm evening wasn't helping. A drop tickled its way down his nose, distracting him a little. He wavered slightly before regaining his composure and balance.

Zucker, where was I?

He carried on the count even though he'd missed a few. Two thirds across now.

Seven hundred and forty-one.

His heart rate was picking up. Gimbden knew he had enough time but the pressure of the guards was something he'd not originally factored into this plan.

A quick blink helped him reset his focus without losing his balance.

One foot at a time. Nine thirty-two and done.

He placed both his feet on the wall edge and breathed easier. Instinctively he dropped to a crouch, hoping to make himself less visible.

There was still a little bit of time to get off the wall before the guards returned. He doubted they'd miss a figure perched on top of the wall.

He scanned the western wall to his left, all the way up toward the gate. Thankfully it was obscured by a building. He rose a little and scurried along to his right in line with the roof he wanted to be on.

One thousand and nine.

He leaped and landed on the roof with a dull thud. Dropping down into a crouch he then lay flat on the roof and let his racing heart settle.

No one called out.

He heard the sound of footsteps over the wall on his left.

One thousand eleven hundred and forty-two.

He'd made it albeit with only just enough time to spare. He had thought the thousand would be enough, but it had taken him longer. Most likely he would have been spotted if the earlier guards were still on duty.

As soon as the sound of their steps had faded, he slid right to the edge of the roof and slid over it, hanging perilously. He was just offset to the ledge below him that he wanted to use. He had to move sideways hand over hand until he was in line with it, then he dropped onto it and braced himself using a ledge above.

No one would have thought the horizontal ledges that ran along the sides of this building were a security issue, behind such high walls, but they made a perfect walkway for him. The window he reached had only a simple latch and he bypassed it quickly.

He slid into the room and surveyed where he was. His luck was in. He'd found a perfect display room. Glass-top cases filled the space, and even with little light he could see they contained many gems.

Gimbden knew he had to remain cautious. While he had made it in here safely it didn't mean there weren't other types of security. He checked several of the cases for booby traps just in case. Vendren was an astute trader and very protective of his wealth, it wouldn't have surprised Gimbden if he didn't trust anyone that worked for him.

Part of the plan was to make sure Vendren knew he'd been robbed, but Gimbden didn't need anything to complicate the plot. Once he was certain that he was safe to open the cases he removed a total of six mid-sized gems, and one large gem, putting them in a pouch which he tucked inside his tunic.

He closed the cases but left a small tear of cloth on the edge of one, hopefully enough to alert someone to pay more attention to that case. Retracing his movements, Gimbden made it back to the roof without incident.

He waited until the guards had made two more rounds and then leaped onto the outer wall, wobbling slightly before regaining his balance. He detached the rope from the wall and leaped down with it in hand, landing heavily on the road below.

Even after bracing for it, the landing forced air out of his lungs. His knees weren't happy either, but he forced himself to stand up and hurry back over the road. The potion had almost worn off now and he was tiring.

The climb back up onto the shop roof felt much harder than earlier. He hid behind the edge just before the guards returned. After coiling the rope back up and securing it in his bag, he took out a knife and made the bite holes in the woodwork from the prongs bigger and less even.

Gimbden doubted anyone would work out how he'd entered the compound, but if they did, he didn't want them to work out the exact equipment used. The court's secret apparatus didn't need to be discovered by others.

The journey back into his compound took twice as long as earlier. His lantern had run out and he had to stumble back through the tunnels in complete darkness. He considered placing the gems now while it was dark, but he knew if he was caught dressed this way there'd be no explaining it away.

Besides it would be much easier to place the pouch in the morning when he was going about his usual business. And he was exhausted. The potion had long since worn off, and not only was he feeling his lack of air, like normal, but it was if his body was making him pay for the previous exertion.

The stairs up to his room were the worst of it and it took multiple rests before he got there. His clothing was soaked in sweat and his breathing was very labored by the time he was able to secure the door behind him. He hid the tools of his work and collapsed on his bed. The rest would have to wait for the morning.

18

KARPENMOR

Karpenmor had hoped being out on the balcony would fix what was bothering him, but it hadn't helped at all. He felt on edge, like there was something crawling under his skin which he couldn't reach no matter how hard he scratched. There was nothing on or under his skin. He'd checked.

If nothing else it had brought him some peace and quiet. The servants stayed well away from him after he yelled at one of them over nothing in particular. Something about his servants was bothering him, and he couldn't put his finger on it.

There had been an event several days before, it must have been on the day of gifts. That was the only day that anything unusual happened.

Why is my mind so foggy?

Someone had said something about servants, about a price, or cost of what was said. The memory was right at the edge of his mind but he couldn't grasp hold of it.

He shook his head and paced around the outside balcony.

Perhaps it was that he had woken thinking to visit his father today, then realized he couldn't. He had always visited on his birthday, though not that it mattered, his father had never shown any recognition. It was important to Karpenmor. If nothing else he had wished for the feeling of a birthday with his family, like others did.

Today was a significant day, or so Uksod kept telling him. Uksod was no longer Regent now that Karpenmor had come of age.

It meant he was the ruler of Enderk as heir, although not absolute until the ceremonies and processes had been completed. Karpenmor wasn't sure what exactly would be different, as Uksod still seemed to want to tell him what to do. More father than advisor.

There was reluctance there, which he understood. Uksod had been the only real father he'd known for his entire life. Karpenmor was sure that Schevenal, his father, had been capable at some point, otherwise he had no idea how on Enderk he would have come into being.

But for as long as he could remember, his father had lived within the Amber Room. He was mostly catatonic and rarely had anything to say to Karpenmor. What he did say was usually the mutterings of a madman, and he'd long since stopped paying any attention to them.

His father only left the Amber Room several times a year, when it was necessary to parade him to the masses. Usually it was at a distance from the central balcony overhanging the front of the palace. There he would wave and speak to an audience who couldn't hear a word.

Which was probably just as well, as he'd normally be ranting like a crazed fool. Which meant Karpenmor had to visit him in the Amber Room. He didn't like being in there any more than sitting with his lost father.

On entering the room Karpenmor always felt like his skin was being peeled back and something was looking inside every part of him. That really did make his skin crawl, and it made it easy for him to justify to himself not going very often.

A wind whipped over the edge of the balcony and brushed through his hair, bringing his attention back to the present moment.

I just wish…

Wishing wasn't going to change anything. He needed to grow up, it was just him, him alone, and that was that.

The idea of ruling had never appealed to him at all. He couldn't see why anyone would want to rule. Whatever power it granted you was offset by the endless ceremonies, meetings and issues to be dealt with. It left little time for peace, or enjoyment.

Karpenmor would occasionally get to view young children out in the streets below the palace, playing amongst themselves, laughing and having what appeared to be fun. He envied them, it looked like what they did meant something, but he had no reference point for it.

He didn't laugh. There was nothing he wanted to really do, or that he got such enjoyment out of. Except perhaps the more recent desire to annoy Uksod. He did enjoy that. Just arguing about something with the older man, pleased him. He didn't show it, but inside, and afterward it would make him smile thinking about the color of the priest's face changing.

There was a quiet sound coming from his room. Someone not wanting to be heard, but they weren't like the Vrah, there were still steps. Karpenmor turned quickly, unusually alert, and rushed to the doors. He startled Hurf, the only servant who had been allowed to attend his father.

"Hurf, what are you doing?"

The elderly man was bent over, about to place something onto the table at the end of Karpenmor's bed. His eyes opened wide in shock and he froze where he stood.

"Your Highness, I'm sorry."

"It's okay, Hurf, what is that?"

"I was just trying to leave it here, I didn't know you were around."

He had stood back up but his eyes had dropped downward. His face looked scared to Karpenmor.

"Bring it to me."

The man shuffled his way around the furniture to Karpenmor and handed him what appeared to be a scroll tube.

"What is this, Hurf?"

"He told me to give it to you on your birthday, or if anything ever happened to him."

"What do you mean by 'happened to him'?"

"If he died..." The old man looked downward again, and seemed wary. "When he died, I was sent away, and couldn't get it to you. I forgot, but then I heard it is your birthday, so I bring it for you."

Karpenmor could see the man was nervous being there. If he had been sent away then his presence in the palace was probably not allowed. He wasn't sure why the man had been sent away; he could find that out later. Right now he was grateful for what he had done.

"Thank you for bringing it to me, Hurf. You served my father for a long time, did you not?"

"Yes, Highness." He looked up at Karpenmor. "All my time here, since I was a young man."

"Did he ever speak much to you?"

"Rarely, Highness. At the beginning, but mostly his words they were…"

"It's okay, I understand, Hurf. He was wrong in the head."

The old man look down again and nodded.

"What will happen for you now?"

"I will go home now, spend my days at my people's place."

"Where is that, Hurf?"

"Oh, way to the west, Highness, a small town near the coast."

"I should have liked to have spoken more with you about your time with my father, you would know more than me."

The man was hesitant in his reply, an awkwardness. "There's nothing much to tell, Highness."

"Is there anything I can do for you, Hurf? For all your service?"

"It was my job, Highness. I was his servant, that was enough."

"Thank you, Hurf."

Karpenmor watched the servant leave the room, another connection to his father now gone. He turned and headed back out onto the balcony, opening the tube as he went.

He pulled out the paper rolled up inside and something fell out to the ground as he did so. Bending down he picked up a pendant on a thin silver chain. The setting, also silver, appeared to have been crafted by someone with skill, strands of metal intertwined on each other as if twisted together while liquid.

More than that, the stone in the pendant was a deep blue. The palm of his hand seemed to tingle as he placed it there to inspect. It was like the stone was alight as well, just slightly, but the glow disappeared as quickly as Karpenmor looked at it.

His father sending him a gift was unusual on its own. The man couldn't string multiple words together. This was so unusual for a Derk piece of jewelry, it intrigued Karpenmor even more. It was possibly the first gift he could remember he had been given by his father.

Opening the scroll he began to read. The words were scrawled roughly, which was better than he expected from someone who Karpenmor had only ever seen strapped into a chair or lying flat on a bed.

~

My son
> *The times my mind still works are tiny.*
> *Today I have a moment not waste words.*
> *So hard hard to do*
> *Hurf get this to you*

~

It will get me now. No more protection
> *But so tired*
> *Gift for birthday from me*
> *Now you can be better than me*
> *Watch out for them*

~

The words became swirls of ink, totally unreadable. Karpenmor was stunned. Not only was his father lucid enough to have written this but he had known his birthday was coming, it wasn't just a random gift. It was all surprising. And what had he meant when he said, *It will get me now*? What would get him now?

Uksod had told him that Schevenal had passed away in his sleep, so this made little sense. And the pendant, he had said it protected him, but from what? Or who? Maybe it was just the ravings of a madman after all.

Karpenmor was thankful his head seemed so clear, but now it was filled with questions, and he wasn't sure who he could ask. He pulled the pendant out of his pocket and looked at it again. *Maybe Uksod would have answers?*

It wasn't a voice, or words. It was a feeling, a very faint feeling, that he shouldn't ask Uksod about it. That he shouldn't mention the old man to Uksod. He didn't know why, but it was there none the less. It wasn't the first time that he worried about Uksod and what he did behind the scenes.

Maybe he needed to pay more attention to him. He tried to recall the times when he'd thought this way before, but he couldn't reach them. Karpenmor needed to think more about this note, about the pendant. Something felt different, and he didn't know what, but he knew he'd work it out.

19

KARPENMOR

Back in his room, Karpenmor tried to think through what had just happened. The fact his father had known it was his birthday surprised him more than what he had scrawled onto the paper.

How had he known? He always seemed so completely catatonic, it never occurred to Karpenmor that there was a man living inside the shell. Of course there had to be, but he had ignored that fact and had only seen what was on the surface.

He looked at the pendant again, this time inspecting it. Tiny pulses of light could be seen when he held it in his palm and stared into it. Something felt different but it was hard to understand what it was.

The clarity in his head was still there, as if he could see clearly and not in the fog that seemed to encapsulate him most of the time. He reached out for his drink with his left hand and stopped.

Karpenmor wasn't sure why, but his hand didn't want to pick up the drink. He concentrated on his hand and reached harder for it. Slowly he grasped it, but inside his head it was if he was telling himself not to.

What is wrong with me? Am I going mad like my father did?

One of his worries was whether whatever had broken his father was something he would get as well. Was it passed from parent to child? Was he just making up what he thought his father's words meant?

But the pendant was real and he looked at it again, before putting it away in his pocket. He still wasn't certain enough to consume his drink and placed it back on the table. He called a servant to get him some plain wine.

Today was his actual birthday, which meant he had to parade himself in front of the people and eat his cake. The traditions that existed around their rulers seemed ridiculous to him. He had no concept of why the people thought it even relevant to watch their rulers eat birthday cake in public, but ever since he was a small boy the annual event had occurred.

Uksod had made him. Always Uksod telling him what to do, when to do it, and how to do it.

I'm tired of his direction. I can think for myself!

The other thing that changed today was that Uksod was no longer his Regent. He was the true heir now, and in due course he would become High Prince. Karpenmor wasn't actually sure when that would be, not that it mattered. From today it would be as if he was anyway. Uksod's power was no longer there, it all fell on him now.

Who was it his father was warning him about? He had written to watch out for them but Karpenmor had no idea who that might be. Was it Uksod? Is that what he had been sensing all along, why he had been feeling at odds with the priest?

It would be reasonable to expect there would be some issues with Uksod and this changeover. He'd not really spent much time thinking about it.

Up until now it had seemed part of a foggy dream.

My head is still clear. This is good.

What position would Uksod have then? How would this all work? Karpenmor knew it was not going to be smooth. One thing he had always done was read. Having so much time to himself he read a lot. Much of the materials he found were books on war and fighting, and yet he'd never known a war to ever happen here in Enderk. Certainly not one he'd ever been told of.

One of the histories he had read multiple times was about the loss of face that his father had suffered at the hands of the barbarians. He had gone to their Great Fair as a guest, but returned chased by the foreigners and his entourage completely slaughtered.

That had been when Schevenal had become broken, or so the books suggested. The land bridge had been destroyed in massive storms that followed him, and some obscure texts he found suggested the gods had caused them. Karpenmor only knew of the one god that all Derks worshipped, Yantarnaya.

Why she would destroy it he couldn't fathom, but he also knew not everything written in these old books was fact, some of it wasn't much better than the tales of bards.

Bards were considered no better than vagabonds in Enderk, and their type were banned from performing. The only storytellers allowed were the official Reciters who trained under Uksod's priests. Not that Karpenmor learned much from them either.

He'd learned that Schevenal had been threatened by the Imperial Families when he returned, as each had also lost their leaders who had traveled with his father to Dharatan. When none returned, the Families had caused a small uprising, which had been quashed by the Vrah.

There wasn't much else about that time written, not in the books Karpenmor could find, but it was enough to know that for a long time no one questioned the rule of the High Prince. Not publicly anyway.

With the land bridge destroyed, contact with Dharatan had initially been limited. Both sides had little trust for the other, and travel by boat around the remaining islands between them was precarious. The craft Enderk had back then weren't suited to the rapid-like seas and it was some time before they built boats capable of traveling around them.

Once the barbarians needed tin from Enderk their attitude had changed, and over time trade had begun again, although limited and hampered by the lack of road transport. Still Derks were treated with contempt over there, by all the accounts Karpenmor had read and what Uksod had told him. Perhaps when he was High Prince he could change that and seek revenge for his father's humiliation.

Now this note from his father it triggered an upsurge of anger deep in his stomach. He had been robbed of a relationship with his father because of whatever the barbarians did to him. He was angry about that, more than he had ever realized before. With no mother, a catatonic father and no siblings his life had been empty.

Uksod had been responsible for his birth, or so the old priest had explained. When there was no heir, and his father had become bound to the Amber Room, the priest had set about finding him a wife, to bear him a son. Eventually it had happened, but his mother had died shortly after.

He knew nothing of note about her, nor anything to remember her by, just that she had borne him and died of a mysterious illness. Karpenmor shook his head. Thinking through it now, the whole thing seemed a strange tale. How old in fact was his father? As he thought about it now, the years didn't seem to match up.

A loud knocking on his door caught his attention. He tucked the scroll under a blanket on his bed before walking over, knowing full well it would be Uksod. His only surprise when he opened the door was how red his face was.

"Why is your door barred?"

"Because I wanted it barred." He didn't move out of the way to let the priest in.

"What are you hiding, Karpenmor?"

"Hiding? Nothing." Karpenmor laughed, which enraged Uksod even further. "I just don't need people barging in here without my approval."

"Since when has that been a problem?"

"Since forever, Uksod. People come and go as if I'm just a painting on the wall."

"You exaggerate, Karpenmor. This is nonsense really."

"Not to me. And today, if I'm not mistaken, am I not in charge of everything around here?"

A cold look crossed the old man's face. Behind him the two guards each seemed to ease away just ever so slightly.

"You are, Highness," he said through gritted teeth. "I wasn't aware you were going to thrust yourself against me so suddenly."

"I'm not, Uksod. I simply barred my door, it was you who got all uptight about it. Why don't you come in?"

The old man couldn't see the grin on Karpenmor's face when he turned and walked back into the room.

I really do enjoy this don't I?

He could hear the man follow him in. "What has come over you, Karpenmor? You know I'm just here to help you."

Karpenmor sat down in his armchair by the table and watched Uksod standing there, his face still red.

"Are you not thirsty?"

"Not particularly, why?"

"I see you haven't had your regular amber brandy. I was just curious. Perhaps some of that might put you more at ease?" He quickly added, "Highness."

"Perhaps."

The man picked up the tall skinny vessel and handed it to him.

Karpenmor sipped it, to ease the man's anger if nothing else. He was tired of fighting with him anyway, for now at least. The drink seeped down his throat, and he sighed, as if welcoming back a lost friend. He felt warm, and pleased.

He didn't notice the fog gently slipping back in. His thinking eased and he sat back in his chair.

"What is so urgent, Uksod?"

"The cake ceremony, Karpenmor. You need to be ready."

"When is it?"

Uksod sighed and rolled his eyes, although the red color in his cheeks had passed now. "Within the hour."

"I'll be ready."

"I should hope so, especially now that you're the head of state. It wouldn't do to keep people waiting." The tone in his voice dripped in sarcasm, but Karpenmor was too busy enjoying his drink to be too concerned.

"Of course."

"I'll send in your servants. Please try to refrain from saying things they shouldn't hear today, if Your Highness could manage that."

The old man turned and walked out of the room, leaving the door open. Karpenmor felt like that was a slight on him and that he should be bothered. But he wasn't. He should go and close it, but he couldn't be bothered with that either.

What does he mean about the servants? I recall something happened, a few days ago, what was it?

GORAN

While he had only held the responsibility for just over a day, Goran felt reluctant to hand over the key to Slava. It felt wrong that while Henri lay dying, they were already replacing him.

It's only until he recovers.

The words sounded hollow even in his own head, worse if he had to say them out loud.

Last night, he slept alone in the downstairs area of the Safe House. He could neither sleep in Henri's room, nor the room that Ash had used when he was here. His neck felt tight, and he had tried his best to free the muscles but could sense it was going to cause him grief all day.

Slava was a Kystenite. Like most of their race she was broad enough that Goran wasn't going to pick a fight with her.

"You know the way to test the tokens? You will need to do it for all that want to visit, until you know them."

"As you've told me more than four times now, Master Goran."

"I'm nobody's master."

"Is it always so quiet in this place?" she asked.

"At times yes. The role of the Safe House Keeper is not the same as an innkeeper or anything else in our network. The fewer people that you have here the better. Only let one group in at a time. You must ensure the integrity of the safe and this building."

She nodded, her eyes almost rolling upward.

Goran realized he was just going back over everything again, and it was time he set off on his own task. "I know you'll be fine with it. It's not you, it's me."

"What do you mean?"

"I mean I'm not ready to hand over what belongs to Henri. I've known him for so long, me leaving now and not knowing he will be all right is what's causing me the angst."

"Sorry," she shrugged. "I'm not a hugger so…"

Goran headed to the door, looked back at the table area, and then stepped out. "Remember to lock it after me."

This time he could see her roll her eyes and she made a point of loudly barring the door with the bolts as it closed behind him.

When he reached Follies Inn, Brando was in the yard out back preparing their rides.

"Brando."

The keeper turned to look at him. "There you are. I'd hoped you hadn't found yourself a drinking hole to avoid what we have to do."

"I was just handing over the reins to Henri's replacement."

"Temporary replacement, Goran. I have faith."

"I have wishes, but my heart feels grim."

"There's nothing we can do to help standing here talking about him. He'll recover or he won't, but we need to be on our way. We're already several days behind the girl if she is where Beantic told you."

Brando had loaded both the spare horses with saddle bags of supplies. They needed the extra horses to speed up their chase of Lani, and they could lose less time if they only stopped for simple breaks. Having the extra food and drink with them would mean they could sleep rough and push further instead of stopping at the most convenient lodge or inn.

Leaving through the south gate, they turned quickly east and headed for the road that followed the outside of the forest that bordered Ngahere. The border itself was somewhere between the outer edge of the forest and the road. No one contested the relatively narrow strip of open land between, but it also housed nothing and nobody.

Much of the forest was hidden from view but Goran could see changes in the type of forest the further southeast they went.

"The Tombs?" Brando asked.

Goran nodded. "It always amazes me how big they are."

As far as they could see off to the south there was a thick forest which allowed little view inside.

"I know enough to never go in there," Brando added.

"From the story I've heard I wouldn't either. Although it does sound more like superstition."

"Keep your eyes on the tallest of the trees and you'll be able to see hanging pods."

"Pods?"

"It's the best way I can describe it. They will look like wrapped bodies."

"Oh Thenis, I can see where this is going."

"Have you not noticed them before?"

"To be honest I've not paid it much attention. I was warned no one that goes in there ever comes out again, and just treat it as sacred."

Goran laughed. "That's a limited view of it. When Ngaherians die, they are brought to the Tombs and laid to rest high up in the trees. Hence the name. No one is able to enter the forest except their Protectors."

"Protectors?"

"Ngaherian warriors that choose to live in there and guard it. There are no religions in Ngahere, they put a lot of their belief into respecting their ancestors."

Brando shook his head. "Don't know why someone would choose to live in there, when there's perfectly good cities around."

"It's considered a great honor."

"They can keep it. You wouldn't see me in there, that's for sure."

They rode in silence for a while, and Goran tried to think through what it must be like for the men living inside the Tombs. Now that they were so close, he tried to look inside, but the density of the foliage seemed to block any attempt to see into the lower areas. Occasionally he could have sworn he saw movement, but that could just be his mind playing tricks on him.

He did sight several of the pods in the upper trees deep into the canopy, long body-shaped objects wrapped in what appeared to be leaves or other foliage. It had always seemed an odd way to honor your dead to him, but as he thought about it, burying them in dirt wasn't such a brilliant idea either.

"Hold up, what's that ahead?"

"Horses, by the look of it," Brando answered.

They slowed their mounts and approached more cautiously. Goran noticed Brando had shifted his sword and rode with one hand on the handle.

There was little need for caution as the horses were on their own. They startled as the men approached.

"Belongings and horses but no people. What does that mean?"

"Someone made a mistake, I suspect."

"They went in?"

"This stuff has been tossed out of there by the look of it. There should be bodies, they never leave other dead in there." Brando's voice was quiet, but Goran could hear the concern in it.

"If this was our group, then…" He didn't need to say any more.

Goran dismounted and approached the small pile of bags. As he knelt down to look at them, he sensed someone nearby and looked to the forest.

Two tall and very broad men stood just inside the outer edge of the forest. Goran had not heard them make a sound. They wore long pants and soft boots but no shirts. Their torsos were covered in extensive tattoos as were their faces. In the shade of the trees, they looked fierce and dangerous.

He stood and held his hands up palms toward them. "Tekan Ma," he called out. "We do not wish to enter the Tombs; we are hunting people who took a friend of ours."

The warrior on the left placed his hands on his hips and stared out at them for what seemed an age. "Tekan Ma. You know of our sacred grounds."

"I do."

"Those who enter shall never come forth alive again, that is the rule of the Tombs."

"We have no need or desire to enter. We only seek our friend."

"Those things you see belong to these men." He raised his right hand and signaled behind him. Three other warriors walked out of the darkness carrying large objects and approached the edge of the forest. As they reached the outer boundary each effortlessly flung what they carried out past the line of scrub.

Goran flinched at the thud of what were three male bodies as they landed before them. His stomach turned and he breathed slowly and deeply through his nose, choosing not to look at the badly disfigured men.

"These men were foolish. We have not seen any like them before. Dangerous men, very strong, they fought much harder than we could believe. Strong men but still foolish. They leave dead, just like any others who come into the Tombs."

"These are their things?" Brando spoke for the first time.

The warrior nodded; his colleagues disappeared back into the dark. "Your friend?"

Brando shook his head, "No. Our friend is a woman."

Again, the warrior stared at him for a long period of time without moving. "A woman came with them, she looked like a prisoner. We have not found this woman. One horse and one woman are missing."

"She escaped?" Goran couldn't help himself.

The warrior turned to look directly at him, making Goran's spine shiver. "No one who enters can leave the Tombs. She should not have left. We have hunted inside the Tombs, but so far we have not found her here."

The man took several steps away from the boundary and stood with his lone companion watching them.

Brando turned to Goran and whispered, "What do we do?"

"I'm not entirely sure, Brando. I think we're best to take all of this and get away from here. They are not pleased by what has happened."

Brando nodded to him.

"We are sorry for what has happened to you. These men are from

Enderk and have hurt many people since they arrived. You have done a great favor to all in disposing of them."

The man said nothing and simply stood guard.

"What will happen next?" Goran asked.

"Our elders will be the judge of that." This time it was the other warrior who spoke.

"What would you have us do with all of this?" Goran pointed at the bodies and the gear that lay beside him.

"It matters not to us. We will watch until you are gone." With that they stepped backward again, and Goran could see nothing of them, although he knew there were still eyes watching them.

"Let's drag everything closer to the road, Brando, and we can sort through it all."

By the time they had settled the horses and moved all the gear the sun was beginning to set on the horizon.

"I suggest we think about making camp here tonight. No one will stumble onto us here in the night. And there's a few things to go through." Goran was absentmindedly rubbing several of the beads in his hair as he surveyed the area around them. "Yeah, this will do as good as anywhere."

LEO

*L*eo stood transfixed by the closed door that the strange woman had just gone through. He had never had a one-on-one conversation with one of the leaders here in Anderwell, and he was stunned by what had happened.

He cautiously went outside into the late morning sunshine, and looked across the massive forecourt. She was long gone from view, clearly able to move fast despite being no bigger than him.

What was she doing in my head? And what did she find? It didn't seem to bother her. She seemed intrigued.

The thought of being different felt good for a change, for the first time since arriving here. It hit him like a brick that he'd been his own worst enemy. He'd been resisting everything here, as a way to be different, when he was already different anyway.

The irony of it wasn't lost on him. All of his life he'd been trying to not be different, and yet here, he'd done everything possible to not fit in. As if he wanted to sabotage his safety here.

How very strange.

Leo wasn't sure what to do next. Normally his days would be filled with classes, but he had the afternoon to himself. One thing he hadn't done, was have a good look around the city. The only time he ventured outside the college grounds was late at night. It happened whenever his anger got too much. He'd be outraged at his treatment, or annoyed about something and unable to let it rest.

Many nights he would slip out of the accommodation while most people were asleep or studying and run along the river's edge, slipping under the wall, and running until his legs burned. Then he'd hobble back, falling into bed hours later and when he woke the burning need to attack someone, or something, had abated.

It was a strange thing, mostly he couldn't even remember the run itself. Part way through the run he would lose his focus, and only realize he was back when he woke. He would have a distant memory of the run, of bounding along like an animal, which made no sense given his body form, and he'd be exhausted from it.

That tiredness would last for several days, which he didn't mind. He always felt cleansed after it, like whatever was burning within him had briefly gone out. It never went away for long, but those days after he seemed more at ease, inside anyway.

When he was cleansed like that he felt less inclined to argue about things. That was one of his problems, he couldn't leave an argument alone. If something made no sense, he'd spurt it out, mostly to his own disadvantage.

Now he thought about it, he hadn't been on a run in some time, which explained why he'd exploded today. He'd been holding in his opinions for too many weeks, and then he'd let it all out on Miss Wenthern.

It wasn't really about her, but because he hadn't let it out more constructively. Maybe he could ask Toolet about that, whether she understood why he needed to do that. She'd been in his head, maybe she could see the reason.

That's if she'd share with him what she'd learned. Leo didn't know if he trusted her or not, he was more intrigued than anything. Given time she'd probably get annoyed at him, like most people did after he was honest all the time with them.

His attitude had been the main cause of him being such an outcast back in Thabeng, where he'd grown up. The people there weren't the biggest anyway, so being a dwarf didn't make him so different that he was naturally outcast. His attitude did though. The few dwarves that lived in Thabeng were generally accepted and lived amongst everyone else. He'd been told that his size was considered a variation of their race, and it was just something he'd need to live with.

His mouth was something else though, and he constantly told 'it how it was' whenever he had cause. Over time people started to shun him. Few people like to have hard truths told to them on a daily basis, and his anger coupled with it just made him a pariah.

In the end he upped and left, setting off to find a new world to live in. He made his way across the border into Rohumaa. He wasn't quite sure why he thought that would work out so well. Humaas were like a gazillion feet tall, which made him quite the contrast.

Leo had talked his way into helping a building project, far outside the city of Okeans. He didn't like that place, it smelt like too many fish had been shoved into the carcass of a rotting horse. At first he'd just done his bit, and they liked him because of his size.

He got dropped down into holes to dig out things others couldn't get to. The pay was good enough, and he was fed and had his own tent, which was better than living on the streets of some city or town. He did his best to ignore all the jokes, especially when they had him strung up to some gantry lowering him into a dark hole full of muck, to help dig.

But over time, even the physical labour didn't get rid of the fire within. He chose to start orally jousting with one of what they called the first hands. Even that made little sense to Leo. If they were in charge of the other workers, then they did the least amount of work, so their hands weren't the first being used. They were the last.

Most people just looked at him like he was crazed, but the man, called Onot, who'd been his supervisor, took against him.

"Shouldn't you be the last hands?"

"What do you mean, dirty runt?"

"First hands would be people like me, who actually do the work first up. You don't do anything with your hands, it's your mouth that does all the work."

That explanation had cost him several hours stuck down in the muck at the bottom of the hole, in the pitch dark of night, before other workers had lifted him out.

From that point on he'd ended up with worse treatment, and often a thumping or kicking out the back of the building site, which ended up making everything worse. Leo responded by sending verbal barbs at his attackers, which was easy enough given most weren't the smartest thinkers.

One late afternoon he'd hidden from several of the diggers who had sought to give him a kicking, and had snuck behind a large marquee that filled a section of the compound that workers weren't meant to be in. He had chosen that area as he doubted his pursuers would follow him there.

He'd lain down between the marquee and another large tent beside it. After waiting for nearly an hour he'd been ready to get up and sneak out when the sound of men talking from within the marquee stopped him. Afraid of being discovered, he froze still.

He'd drifted off, that's how it had felt, and the rest felt like he had dreamed it, as if he had slid under the edge of the tent, like a snake. He could hear what the men were saying, most of it.

Words like 'chapel' and 'walls' came to him. Something about horses and the nights. He wasn't really sure what it all meant, and he never did find out.

A voice had woken him. "Hey what are you doing?"

As Leo turned over, rubbing at his head to wake up, the guard had hoisted him to his feet and marched with him round to the front of the marquee, where two men had rushed out.

One of them Leo couldn't forget, his face was pointed to his chin. He had a full head of hair but many creases in his face. He wore a dark blue robe, and stared at Leo with malice.

"What's going on here?"

"Eminence, I caught him sleeping between the tents."

"Sleeping? Why on Daskare would you be sleeping here, midget?'

Leo looked at the man but for some reason held his tongue.

"Does he speak?"

"I don't know, Eminence."

"I don't like people not knowing their place. Have him gone from here."

"Of course."

"And make sure none of the other workers are near my quarters!"

"Yes, Eminence."

He'd been trussed up like an animal and carted off into Okeans, and left there with the city guards for several weeks in one of their cells. One evening, when he'd thought he'd rot to death in there, he was dragged out of his cell and loaded into a caged wagon, with other people.

At the time he'd not known it was the Fool's Cart. Once they'd gotten across the river back into Thabeng he'd learned his fate.

What had looked like a terrible event turned out to be something else completely. While the wagon was caged, that was for the outsiders, to supposedly make them feel safe. Each evening on the trip they were let out and made camp and the wagon master explained what was happening.

On that journey he'd made friends with several people who were now his best friends at the college. He was almost back there now, and the setting sun was a sign to go and eat.

The evening meal was filled with his friends grilling him about what his punishment was and what had happened. Many roared with laughter as they mimicked him and how he'd spoken to Miss Wenthern. Part of him felt bad by the time they were all done. He had been pretty rude to her. Then the other part of him scoffed internally and he forgot about it; she was boring, and he'd been right.

By the time everyone had left, amazed he wasn't being punished, his head was spinning.

There was no way he could sleep. They'd all asked so many questions and he'd had to repeat his story so many times, his brain had taken on a life of its own.

In the dining room he warmed up some water and brewed up one of the floral teas he liked the most. Cupping the mug, he sat up on one of the soft bench seats and thought about what it would mean to be working with this lady. He wondered how long he'd last before he annoyed her and was too 'truthful' for her liking.

A heavy thumping was moving toward him from one of the hallways. Looking up, he saw Roifreaz coming toward him, the wooden crutch under his left armpit aiding his walk, replacing the leg he didn't have.

Roi was the first friend he'd made in the Fool's Cart. He'd been grabbed in Lletem and had been very upset about it. Leo had been able to make him feel better, strangely by telling him the hard truth, and they'd developed a close friendship ever since.

"If it isn't his lady's servant," Roi mockingly taunted him.

"Yeah yeah, hoppy, you're just jealous."

"Too right I am, little one, I'm just trying to work out what I can do to get thrown out of that boring class." He dropped down onto the seat, almost causing Leo to spill his tea.

"The pot over there's still got warm water if you want it."

"No thanks, if I have any more now, I'll end up peeing my bed."

"Not sure I'll sleep tonight."

"Why's that?"

"Don't know. I'm just not sure what this all means. I don't even know what I'll be doing."

"You're going to be her lackey, like I told you."

"Maybe you're right, I'll just be doing her chores."

"Could be, but even that's better than sitting through Wenthern isn't it?"

"Yeah."

Roifreaz hadn't lingered long, he needed all the sleep he could get. Leo never understood how the boy could sleep so much, and always be yawning. Especially when he didn't even feel remotely tired.

Looking around the dining room, Leo felt something. Not his usual burning anger, it was calm, and almost pleasant. Despite the way Wenthern had made him feel, he didn't want to run away as he usually did. He liked having friends who didn't judge him, and he was excited about what was coming next.

2 2

LEO

The sun came up early in Sahro. Their whole lives revolved around the sun, and the harsh land around them. From any floor, except the ground one, you could see the desert outside.

Leo hadn't waited until the dawn. Despite only grabbing several hours' sleep, he was already standing in the foyer when the first rays of daylight arrived.

Yesterday standing in the same spot, he had thought it quiet, but it was nothing like it was now. The foyer and halls leading off it were still and without any sound at all. When the heavy door squeaked open on its noisy hinges, he jumped in surprise.

A young woman walked through and closed the door as quietly as she could.

"You must be Leo?"

He looked up at her, unable to speak. She had long black hair, and the darkest eyes he had ever seen, and she was as beautiful to him as anyone had ever seemed.

"What's wrong? Can't you speak?" she asked with a hint of annoyance.

"I... I can speak. Yes."

"Good. And yes you are Leo, or yes you can speak?"

"Both," he grinned, but she didn't reciprocate.

"Miss Toolet sent me to find you. She instructed me to have you come with me."

"Why do you call her Miss Toolet?" Leo's words were back in full flight now.

"Because she's one of the leaders, and one of our teachers." The girl rolled her eyes and shook her head a little at him.

"She told me to just call her Toolet, that she was no miss."

"That wouldn't be proper. You mustn't do that."

Leo shrugged. This girl might be pretty but she was already beginning to annoy him with her tone.

"What's your name?"

"My name is Sabant. Now come along."

"Where are we going?"

"Do you always ask so many questions?"

"Yes."

"You're coming to our training. Although I don't know why."

"What type of training?"

"We do advanced things that general students don't do. You have to be selected as part of your preparation."

"Preparation for what?"

She stopped walking and looked at him.

"How long have you been at the college, Leo?"

"Just about a year or so I think."

"And you haven't heard my name or Aakesh's name mentioned before?"

"No." Leo shook his head.

"I'm not sure I should be telling you, perhaps Miss Toolet should be the one to do that. Let's get going, I don't want you making me late."

They left the main building and entered a wing of the college that Leo had never been in before. It was relatively small in comparison to the main halls and accommodation wings. There was a silence within it, similar to the way churches always held a silence that was more than just from the lack of people.

In the middle of the building was a large open room, filled with equipment and weapons off to one side. A young man, about the same age as Sabant, stood beside a bench filled with objects. He turned to the sound of them arriving.

Leo nearly gasped. The boy's neck was about three times as long as other people's and he could see that his hands were much bigger than normal as well. His fingers looked swollen and distorted.

"Who's this?"

"Apparently he's meant to be training with us." Sabant's voice had all the haughtiness back from when she'd first met Leo.

"Why's that? I thought it was just the two of us!'

"I couldn't tell you, Aakesh."

The young man looked down at Leo, his eyes staring hard at him, but unlike Toolet he wasn't actually getting in Leo's head.

"Hello, do you have a name?"

"Yes. Leo. Leo Peggle."

"I'm Aakesh, as you probably guessed. What are you going to be practicing?"

Leo was about to reply when the sound of someone else entering the large room, caused them all to turn. Toolet was hustling toward them. The woman seemed to cover more ground than possible given the size of her legs.

"Excellent, you have him. Good morning, Peggle!"

"And you too, Toolet."

The other two students both turned to look at him.

"Don't worry about those two, Leo. They refuse to drop the 'miss' silliness. I should have got to them earlier. I assume you've all been introduced?"

"We have, Miss Toolet." Sabant emphasized the 'miss' as she said it. "Leo asked who we were, I wasn't sure it was my place to tell him."

"Okay, thank you, Sabant. Perhaps that's the best place to start. Why don't you two begin your practice and I'll speak with him."

Without speaking Aakesh and Sabant moved away from them and Toolet shepherded Leo over to a bench off to the side.

"What you'll learn here, Peggle, is quite different to what you were learning in the other classes."

"In what way, Toolet?"

"Perhaps I should give you a little more insight into what's going on here in the college, and Anderwell."

Leo sat waiting for her to continue.

"You've probably worked out the basics, from how you came to be here. We give safety, a home and training to those people across Dharatan that aren't normys. Especially to those who have been persecuted, abandoned or who might struggle to survive on their own."

Toolet folded her legs under her.

"Doing all that takes a lot of money and resources, which we have to generate. Anderwell of itself isn't the most prosperous of cities. Being in a desert doesn't help. You following me so far?"

Leo nodded.

"A large number of the people that belong to Anderwell, do so as part of the one thing we do have in abundance."

"What's that?"

"Entertainers, and skilled servants."

"I don't understand."

"Have you ever seen the troupes traveling the lands?"

"Yes."

"Did you not notice how many of those performing are different?"

Leo had to think about it. "Now you mention it, I do. Well I didn't so much then, but I can now."

Toolet laughed. "Well that's good in a way."

"How so?"

"Part of their training is to be able to stand out for their performing, and much less for their differences. Many of them were rejected by the very places they now entertain."

"How does that relate?"

"All of those troupes were trained here. They're all part of what we call the Circuit. The monies they make, enable us to do what we do."

"Oh. Why don't they just do it for themselves?"

"We're all part of a very large family here, Leo. A very large family. Unlike their own families that abandoned them, or tried to have them killed, we take care of our own. They do what they do, to make sure we can do what we do."

"How do they survive out on the road?"

"We have a network of inns and lodges in many places, where food and board is covered. Else they use portions of what they make to survive."

"I still don't get what this has to do with why you brought me into here?"

"The classes you were in before, they are to educate everyone that comes here on basics. We're making everyone in our family get the standards of learning, so they can read and write. All of that is power. If you can't lift or do heavy work, but can do mental work, you're even more important out in the world, Leo."

"I guess."

"But after that we move students into different categories. Some become cooks or the like, others become entertainers and so on. We find a place for everyone, and then they start doing the more advanced training. For a bard, they have to learn to not just be a bard, but a great bard. Make sense?"

"Kind of." Leo was still not linking all the pieces together as to how this affected him, and what Sabant and Aakesh were training for.

"Then there are those who have skills that others don't have."

"What type of skills?"

Toolet turned to face the others. "Sabant, a demonstration please."

"Yes, Miss Toolet."

Toolet turned back to Leo. "Leo, I want you to cover your mouth with your hands, and whisper, and I mean whisper almost so I can't hear, into my ear."

"What do you want me to say?"

"Anything, Leo."

He leaned over and whispered, "I still have no idea what on Dharatan is going on."

Across the room, Sabant spoke up, "I still have no idea what on Dharatan is going on."

"What?"

"She can hear you, Leo. Sabant has the most extraordinary hearing."

"And Aakesh?"

"Watch."

Leo saw Sabant pick up a staff from the bench of tools and swing it without warning at Aakesh. He didn't move, or even attempt to move, and the staff cracked him across the head. Nothing moved on him. Leo had expected his head to rock backward if it didn't knock him out. She did it again and Aakesh just smiled.

"What the…"

"His body doesn't work like ours. It's like he has armor on."

Leo was stunned. "It's like magic?"

"Not like, Leo. It is. There's a magic in some of us, which serves our other purpose."

"… Other purpose?" Leo was actually having trouble speaking, something he wasn't used to.

"There's a level of us, Leo, that do more than just entertain on the streets. We have counsellors, aides, guards and others who work right across the realms." Toolet explained how they influenced decisions and got information to help resolve issues before they happened.

"And there's a level of us called the Court, of which I am one, Leo. But there are others. Twelve in total. Usually."

"Usually?"

"That's a story for another day. The Court is particularly special, we… we can do things others can't and our role is to oversee everything. Of course over time we lose members of the Court. When that happens we have to replace them. Which requires those who have been trained in things at a higher level. Those who have shown particular promise, both in ability and aptitude. We call those people the Prospects. Meet the current Prospects, Sabant and Aakesh."

The two across the room bowed. Leo could see where the confident smirk on Sabant's face came from. He could see something similar on Aakesh's.

"And now there are three."

"Three?"

"Yes, Leo. You."

23

KARPENMOR

He woke and tried to remember what had been happening for the last couple of days, but it was the usual blur. He could recall some things, a vague idea of what he had done, just not in any detail.

That was how the last few years had felt, as if all of the detail had been removed, and he was simply passing through blurry images.

Sometimes the voice accompanied him, other times it didn't. Something scratched at the back of his mind, about the voice. He wasn't sure what it was or who it was.

Karpenmor rose and wrapped himself in a woolen robe and tied it with cloth around the middle. He opened the two doors to his balcony and stepped outside, the first light of the day beginning to appear in the sky.

He enjoyed the fresh air, breathing it in deeply, letting it flush his head clear. The contrast felt good, seeing and smelling everything with more clarity. There'd been no more insight from his father's note. Karpenmor had read it a hundred times, but he got nothing else from it. He only wished he could have spoken with his father, for real, even just one time.

In the end he'd hidden scroll and tube so no one would find them.

Part of him knew he should burn it, but it was the last thing, the only thing, his father had ever written him. It was something to remember him by. That, and the pendant.

Karpenmor went back into his bedroom and fetched the pendant from a box beside his bed. He marveled at the blue color of the stone, such a contrast to all the orange stones around En Carta. All orange and black. This blue added a spark of life.

He held it in his palm and wrapped the thin silver chain around his hand, walking back out on the balcony until he stood overlooking the vast courtyard below.

Stop the drinks.

They weren't really spoken words in his head, not like the voice. It was more a sense of the words, an idea that just appeared there. It was that same idea, the feeling of not wanting to touch the amber brandy from days before. The same day he had received the message from his father. And the pendant!

Karpenmor looked at the stone again, wondering what it was. Was it speaking to him? He shook his head and stuffed the pendant in the pocket of his robe. He didn't need to daydream about magic in pendants.

He needed to think about his father. It was as if a veil had been lifted from his mind, and he had begun to think more about his father, and the time he had spent locked away in the Amber Room. Why had he lived so long?

How long had it been? How long could he survive like that in there? Again Karpenmor began to think about Schevenal's age when he had died. He thought back through the histories, trying to recall the dates. Each time he shook his head, it couldn't be right.

He would be hundreds of years old! Something didn't add up. Changing into clothes, he hurried down the left one of two broad staircases to the second level. So early in the day the only people he passed were servants, all of whom quickly cleared out of his way, either in deference to him or due to the fact that a member of the Vrah was several steps behind him.

He strode into the main chamber known as the High Prince's Office and found it completely empty. In truth it had always been Uksod's office, which is why Karpenmor had come here now. He wanted to find the priest and thought this would be as good a place as any to start looking.

The room was lifeless, not just in the absence of Uksod. It was so tidy that it appeared as if no one occupied it at all. He walked around the room, taking in everything about it in more detail.

Usually, he was in here to be lectured by Uksod. He had never taken much notice of its contents. Today it all appeared different. He still had his hand on the pendant in his pocket and looked around as if seeing the details for the first time.

Many times he had been in this room but taken no notice of anything specific. He couldn't have described it with any detail if asked, but now he could see everything. Shelves and shelves of books covered all the walls, many of which were accounts from across Enderk.

Strangely the desk was completely bare of any papers. He was tempted to open the drawers and start inspecting everything. In theory everything belonged to him, if he wanted he could look at anything he liked, but he knew it would create even more friction with Uksod.

Word would be out that he was in this room, that was a certainty. Karpenmor moved to sit on one of the small sofas in the middle of the room, facing the door. He wasn't disappointed. It was only a short while before Uksod walked in.

"Good morning, Karpenmor. It's early for you to be up and about."

"Good morning, Uksod. It is, but then I guess things are changing, are they not?"

"True." Karpenmor could see the wariness in Uksod's eyes.

"I wanted to apologize for my manners of late. The changes… they are taking some getting used to."

Uksod looked at him a while before replying. "No need, Highness." It seemed as if the older man was swallowing gravel as he said Karpenmor's title. "May I join you?"

"Of course, it is your room."

Uksod sat and his mouth formed into a small smile. "It is the ruler's chamber, and it was only mine while I was Regent. It would now be yours."

"Oh. That makes sense." Karpenmor tried to sound as if the idea was new to him as well. "The other day... I was most ungrateful to you."

The priest waved his hand in dismissal.

Karpenmor continued. "No, it's true. You have given so much of your life in service of Enderk. To my father, and to raising me. I am sure that wasn't what you had in mind when you became a priest?"

"Not entirely, Highness, but one does what one is called on to do."

"I can't imagine I was easy to raise. And I haven't always been the most willing student, but I have been learning, I know there are so many things you do, have been doing, to keep things running. After more than twenty years I understand this change is going to be as difficult for you as it is for me."

"Much more than that."

"Really?"

"Yes, Karpenmor, much, much longer. I've been with him since he returned from Dharatan."

"Oh?" Karpenmor was surprised by the reply, and it must have shown on his face.

"You were not my first try, Highness."

"What do you mean?"

"Meaning, that we tried to create an heir many times before you came to be."

"I did not know that. Tell me more."

"Are you sure that's wise?"

"I have to know, Uksod. I know so little about him, he lived in that horrid room my entire life."

"What do you want to know?"

Karpenmor could see the priest wasn't entirely comfortable with where the conversation was going.

"Why was he in that room?"

Uksod shifted in his sofa and began the tale. "After your father returned from Dharatan, it became clear he was no longer himself. It happened so quickly and took all of us by surprise."

"What did?"

"The loss of his mind. Before long he became hysterical all the time.

I tried the brandy and other things to calm him, but it was all useless. In the end the Amber Room became the only solution. He was only ever calm in there. So, we moved him into it, and he's been there ever since."

"I don't understand how he could be calm in there, there's something about that room that unnerves me."

"Really?"

"Yes."

"Have you spoken to her about it?"

"Who?"

Uksod smiled, and sat back. "You've not spoken to her in that room?"

"Who?" Karpenmor's voice had become a little agitated.

"Our goddess, Yantarnaya. That room is like the ultimate temple to her."

"Oh, I didn't know. No one has ever spoken to me in there."

"Perhaps you should try?"

Something clicked into place in Karpenmor's head, about the 'they' in his father's letter.

"Was it her, is that why he stayed in there?"

"Mostly. We found that he couldn't survive outside of it for long, as if his only sustenance came from being surrounded by her."

"Why is that?"

"We're not sure, Karpenmor. It's always seemed to be linked to his madness. It of course created a problem for us."

"What was that?"

"There was no heir to rule, and your father was not in the best of states. She and I discussed what would happen here in Enderk if he died and one of the numbered Families took control. Our goddess said that could not happen. It is one thing that she has not explained to me, so I can't explain it further."

"Really?"

"Yes. I am but her servant."

Karpenmor looked at the older man, and decided to file that for later, and not press it now. "Okay."

"It became my task to find suitable women and bring them to him, and reward them for performing their act on him."

Karpenmor cringed as he thought about how catatonic his father was, and what Uksod's story meant.

"As forced as it was, Karpenmor, there was no other way. It took many tries but over the years several women fell with child."

"Several?"

"Yes, but they all birthed girls."

"I don't understand?"

"Women cannot rule here in Enderk. It is not the way. If a girl was to be heir, then the throne would have passed to another family."

"But the girls?"

"I had to end them."

"What! Why on Enderk? My sisters?" The knot of anger in his stomach tightened.

"No, Your Highness. None of these were from your mother."

"So, these were different women?"

"Yes. It was why it took so long, for some unexplained reason every child your father begat was female. Until you."

"What happened to the mothers?"

Uksod shrugged his shoulders and Karpenmor understood, not liking it at all.

"So should I ask how many times it took?"

"I wouldn't, Highness. I try not to think of what I had to do, if I can."

He said nothing for a short while. It took willpower to not bite back.

"Of course. I apologize, I shouldn't forget the sacrifices you've had to make."

An awkward silence fell between them.

"My mother?"

"She died shortly after giving birth to you, as you know."

"What caused it?"

"I cannot say, Karpenmor. These things often happen, we know so little of their causes."

"Thank you."

"For what?"

"For the explanation. It was bothering me about father's age." He looked at the priest, realizing how old he must also be.

Uksod smiled. "Yes, Highness, my age as well. One of the benefits of my position. Our goddess has bestowed a long life on me, to serve her."

"What of my father?"

"What do you mean?"

"How did he die?"

Uksod seemed taken back by the question.

"I told you when it happened. He passed away in his sleep, Karpenmor. I am not a physick and I doubt there was much one could tell. We just agreed how very old he was, did we not?"

"We did, Uksod. Sorry, I just wanted to ask. In case… in case you felt like you had to protect me from anything. Hold anything back? I'm not a child anymore."

Uksod stared at him for a few moments before answering. "No, nothing, Highness. You know it all."

24

UKSOD

Something about Karpenmor's tone bothered Uksod, but he couldn't put his finger on it at that moment. Back in his private underground study he paced, seeking to understand what was causing him to be so unsettled.

He knew the transition was causing him angst. He had told himself he'd be able to handle it but ruling for hundreds of years wasn't something you simply forgot. All in all he had enjoyed the power and best of all, he wasn't culpable for it.

As Regent he'd been able to say it was the will of the High Prince and leave it at that. No one could question Schevenal, he was never accessible, which made it very convenient. Now, though, it was all changing too fast.

The people had someone they could access, if the young man made the mistake of being too available. Uksod would have to manage that, explain to the lad the harsh realities of handling the people. A sword worked far better than kind words, fear kept people in order, not pleasantries.

Too much time was being taken up handling the boy. He seemed to be having more independent thoughts than he had in a very long time. Uksod would need to check that he was still getting his loaded brandy.

It was such a simple way to keep him under control, no one ever took notice. Slipping the tiniest slithers of amber into the brandy was the job of only one person, and that servant knew very well where their bed was made. Holding a blade over the head of their nearest and dearest was an easy way to get compliance. They knew if they let it slip, they'd lose what was most important to them.

The brandy kept Karpenmor subdued, and accessible to Yantarnaya. That was the main goal as, for whatever reason, the boy had resisted wearing any jewelry his whole life. Uksod had fashioned necklaces, brooches and rings for the boy but he wouldn't wear any of them. Or they'd be found somewhere around the palace a few days later, as if a common toy.

Him not wearing amber restricted her direct access to him, something she'd been most upset over. That was when he'd come up with the idea of putting tiny amounts into the drink. Karpenmor had taken to the drink quickly, and even better, it seemed to control his childish urges to charge about the palace causing mayhem.

In the end the boy had become a quiet, sullen child who simply did as he was told. Up until recently. Uksod struggled to pinpoint exactly when it had been, but there was something definitely different about him. It was worth checking in on the servant to make sure the drinks were being made correctly, if nothing else.

He could do with some of the brandy himself. Taking a break from everything racing around in his head would be a relief.

Not that he could though. His strength had returned, enough for him to find out more about the amulets. It had taken all of his willpower to not tell Yantarnaya about the developments. After what had happened when that slave had stolen it on its way here, he was never going to subject himself to that again.

He would tell her the good news when he knew enough to guarantee it was in fact good news.

She'd requested he update her as soon as he had information, which he hadn't done yet, but he would need to give her something, and soon. It was she who held the power over him, not the fledgling High Prince, he would never forget that.

The boy would need to keep doing as he was told, for now at least.

Maybe Uksod needed to double the doses? Or would that render the lad incapable? It wouldn't do if people thought he was losing his mind. Enough rumors about Schevenal had spread over time; if it appeared his son was crazy as well, that would undo all their work.

He found Pasqal, the skinny little servant, hiding in the back of the kitchens.

He nodded his head for the man to follow him out into the hall.

"Highness?"

"Eminence, now. The boy is Your Highness." Uksod couldn't mask the sneer in his voice.

"Of course. How may I help?"

"His drinks." Uksod peered down the hall, ensuring there was no one else around. "You're still dosing them?"

"Of course, Eminence," he said a little too hesitantly for Uksod's liking.

"Really?"

"Yes. I am! But…"

"But what?"

"He's not always drinking them."

"What do you mean?"

"Some days they aren't drunk, he just drinks wine or ale."

"Why didn't you tell me?"

The servant looked to his feet, saying nothing.

"How long? How long has this been going on?"

"Only a week or so, Eminence," he said feebly.

"Or so?" Uksod raised his eyebrows. "This won't do. You're to advise me every day if he's taking them or not! Understand?"

"Yes, Eminence."

"Don't let me down, or you know what will happen!"

The man said nothing.

"Now go."

More fools. It's as if I have to do everything myself.

Uksod stormed off toward his room in the palace, and found one of his guards.

"Prepare my workroom, I need it urgently."

"Of course, master."

"Two, like the other day."

The man, all in black, bowed his head ever so slightly and slipped away without a sound, even his footsteps on the stone floor were silent.

Why isn't he taking the drink? Is that what I've noticed in his behavior? The boy is becoming too smart for his own good. For our own good. It won't do for him to think for himself.

Uksod went and refreshed his face and head with a wet cloth before heading to the workroom. As he made his way there a solution to the Karpenmor problem became apparent to him. The young lad was so keen to take over, perhaps he should have it all. At once!

He smiled, a tight snarky smile.

That will keep him tied up in minutiae and annoying details and allow me to do what matters most. But then he'll be in full control.

That thought bothered him more than anything else.

When he reached his workroom, two subjects had already been strapped to the benches. A calm fell over him, as he contemplated what he was about to do. As much as it strained him, he loved the feeling of power it gave him.

No one truly knew what he did in here, even the guards. He stood beside the table and looked at the man before him, looking at the state of him. Unshaven, dirty and lean. Whatever crime he had committed he was about to have his sentence delivered. Uksod cared nothing for what it was, and there was no court that heard the cases. In Enderk the High Prince, and by extension, his Regent, ruled supreme.

Taking a deep breath to ready himself, he checked the placement of the headdress on his head and without thinking adjusted the rings on his finger, so the amber stones were centered on top of his fingers. He felt a rising down below, as the complete power he had over this being emboldened him.

Placing one hand on the man's chest and the other on his forehead, he waited until the first attempts at resistance were over. The light on the rings now shone strong and coupled with the one on his forehead. Under their influence, he entered the darkness.

Uksod's calm wavered as he sensed that there was no Ninety-three, not any more. The ring was attached to a man who was as dead as his two companions. All three of the men who had captured the woman, and the amulet, were dead.

He couldn't understand how that could be. These men were meant to be the best of the best, they'd been trained all their lives for this work. Nintey-three hadn't indicated any threats, just that they had found the amulet on a girl.

Clearly the man wasn't as capable as he'd believed himself to be. Uksod focused in trying to establish if all of the rings were there. The original team had been seven, and he could detect seven rings close to each other — none of them on anyone living.

Uksod didn't think this could get any worse. He could feel his chest tighten, knowing what Yantarnaya would say if she knew.

Who did this?

His mind nearly lost the connection to the blackness, and he had to concentrate to search out his next contact. He wavered a little on his feet but didn't move his hands. The method for alerting the man he sought was somewhat similar to the tapping Yantarnaya did to him. He pushed against the man's ring and then waited for him to connect to him.

"Uksod?" the voice came faintly at first.

"About time, Fuling."

"I wasn't alone, master. I needed to clear my room. How can I help?"

"I am chasing news about the amulet."

"It is most amazing, master. Truly."

"How so?"

"It is like it is connected to the King. He seems more alive."

"That's a good thing?"

"Yes, he seems more open to suggestion that he was, at least for now."

"So our plans?"

"We're on the move. He's demanded forces be put in position, ready for us to start the hunt."

"Excellent news, Fuling. There's more though."

"Tell me, master."

"It needs to come back here."

"What, the amulet?"

"Yes. You need to get him back here with it, for a visit. Come up with a reason, some sort of state visit for trade, or better relations. I don't care. Just make it happen."

A silence hung between them.

"Fuling?"

"Sorry, master, I was just trying to think how best to make that happen."

"Solve it later, I can't be here long."

"Of course."

"There's another matter."

"What's that?"

Uksod was uncertain before he started how much to tell Fuling, but he knew more than anyone else as it was. He explained about the missing amulet and his predicament.

"I can help with that. I have to head north anyway, I can put some people on her trail. We can retrieve it. Can you tell me where?"

"I'll see what I can do. Our mistress can sense it at times. There's magic involved, shielding it, so it's problematic."

"I have a crew of men who can find this girl, but I will need directions, something to point the way. I will meet with them when I am in Rohumaa, so they can hand anyone or anything they capture directly to me."

"Who will guide the King while you are away?"

"One of my priests fills in when I am away. Ahn is set on this path. I think he'll be fine for now."

"Be wary, Fuling. Do not touch that amulet when you find it. You'll need to handle the woman carefully. I have no idea who she is, or how she can carry it, but I have lost too many men on its trail for me to think it a coincidence."

"Of course, master."

"Do not fail, Fuling. It is as important as getting the King here." He ended the connection.

Uksod didn't have problems working with barbarians like Fuling. Maybe that was why he was best suited for his role. Ultimately they would all be under his control, his flock.

He could feel the last of the life force draining from his second subject, and Uksod's head was swimming.

As he came back into the room he grabbed at the edge of the bench. Sucking in deep breaths, he stumbled his way to a chair and got himself a drink. The wine tasted sour, the air in the room fetid, and he could hardly breathe. He sat, his muscles trembling, as he waited for some of his strength to return.

UKSOD

The back of Uksod's head throbbed, every so often sending out pulses of pain. If that wasn't bad enough, he was sure that when Yantarnaya found out, she would punish him. The sour taste in his mouth mirrored his mood.

It always took him several days to recover from connecting like he had, but he didn't have that luxury. He needed to take action as there was too much happening. Dealing with the new ruler was just the final piece for him to have to suck up.

Except he wasn't in the mood to accept it, not today. It would have been much easier if the fool boy just drank his drink and hid somewhere, leaving Uksod to continue as he had.

But no, not only was he needing to chaperone him, the boy wanted to think for himself. They'd never seen that coming, or he hadn't at least. If Yantarnaya had then she'd kept it to herself.

He knew being jealous was ridiculous. He'd known what he was doing all those years ago when he'd brought the lad into the world, but it had seemed too far-fetched back then. For more than a normal person's lifespan, he'd run this realm, and it was doing just fine.

If I must say so myself. No one else will!

If it hadn't been for Uksod, the snotty little infant would never have even survived.

He sipped one of his favorite wines, hoping the taste of rot that always lingered in his mouth after using people would go away more quickly. It didn't and he spat the mouthful out on the floor.

Someone else can clean that mess up.

Telling Yantarnaya was the thing really making his stomach sick. If he could just keep her focused on the amulet King Ahn had, and what it meant, that would do, but she had a way of sensing what it was you didn't want to discuss.

Every day he avoided having to discuss that with her, the closer he was to having it solved. Or so he told himself. It was always much better to provide her with solutions to any problems. He'd had more than enough experience of her anger to know not to turn up empty-handed.

Either Fuling was going to have to capture this girl for him, or the last shipment of Vrah they'd dispatched several weeks ago would do the job. He couldn't sense them when he looked, which meant they must still be on the water, a place he could never reach no matter what he tried.

It would be much easier if the rebuilding of the land bridge had been completed. The dangers and delays on the water from Enderk caused him to lose far too much time. It would be much easier if they could cross by land.

Just another problem.

He held little optimism about the teams working on it and the progress they were making, but there was no way to achieve what Yantarnaya wanted without it being restored in some shape or form. It had been so many years now and last he heard, they weren't more than a third of the way across.

So many things to manage. How on Enderk am I meant to keep a handle on this? Yes, the boy has turned the corner just in time, but I can't just hand it over all at once, he has no idea what to do. I'll just have to keep adding more to his plate.

Uksod rubbed at his scalp. The stress of everything coming together at once was suddenly causing him to doubt himself. For now he needed to speak to the head of the Vrah, and it wouldn't hurt to bring the lad with him. He'd find out about it all soon enough.

He knew that if Karpenmor was up early again he would go to the office. That would be the place to find him. Uksod had guessed correctly and found the heir to Enderk sitting on the sofas eating his morning meal.

"Your Highness." He dipped his head as he spoke, partly to hide his frown.

"Uksod, good morning. I'm glad you're here."

"Why is that, Highness?"

"I'm kind of at a loss what to do. I can sit in this office all day if I want but I have absolutely no idea what I am meant to do."

"Which is exactly why I am here. I think we will need to break you into it, slowly at first, while you get used to the duties required."

Very slowly, hopefully.

"What did you have in mind?"

"Ironically, today of all days is the one that I like the least."

"What is it?"

"People's day, Highness."

"You're lumbering me with that?"

"Well as tradition would have it, we allow the... " he paused and took a breath "... common people an opportunity to petition the High Prince. And as your now Regent I feel it should be you!"

"But it's the most tedious thing I've ever sat through."

"At least it will be you making the choices this year, not just watching on."

"I never really paid much attention to what you said or did. How will I know what to do?"

"I'll accompany you for much of the day. What you have to remember is that we don't have a never-ending supply of money or resources. We have other goals beyond just keeping the commoners grateful."

"Surely there are exceptions to that, Uksod? What if they just need guidance?"

"I've made it my goal to keep things simple. Initially I gave people solutions and they expected more. More and more people turned up and the expectations grew. I put an end to it."

"How?"

"By giving away nothing. Mostly."

"Mostly?"

"That and a few beheadings."

"What on Enderk did you do that for?" Karpenmor's pitch went high.

"One doesn't rule without harsh judgments, Highness. It's something you'll need to understand. Wait until you've spent hours and hours listening to people complaining about the most mundane problems."

"When does this begin?"

"They'll be queuing outside already, no doubt."

"Already?"

"Yes, but they can wait. That wasn't what I wanted to see you about. I imagine you would like to attend my next meeting?"

"Where are we going?"

"To see the leader of the Vrah."

"The Vrah? What about?"

"Come with me, Highness, and you will see."

Behind the palace, up against the mountains that wrapped behind En Carta, lay the quarters for the soldiers of the Vrah. Their leader lived in his own rooms that were part of this structure. The single-level building lay behind a wall that separated it from the main palace's rear grounds. A training courtyard filled in the space between the wall and the quarters.

Guards opened the gates and they crossed the courtyard filled with Vrah training around them as they walked. Uksod pushed the main entrance door open and pointed out parts of the building to Karpenmor. "Down that corridor is the main quarters for the force stationed here."

"There's more?"

"Many more, Karpenmor. This force is essentially your own guard. They protect the ruler, his family and the palace itself."

"Where are the others based?"

"There are several main camps and many smaller ones all over Enderk. We'll get into the specifics at another time, if that suits?"

Karpenmor nodded to him.

"These are all the training rooms and equipment we're passing now, and there's a series of studies which hold information about many subjects throughout the realm, as well as on Dharatan."

"We have information from over there?"

"Plenty."

"How?"

"I've been sending soldiers of the Vrah over there for a long time. I tried to discover the cause of your father's condition, if there was anything from Dharatan behind it. Mostly we seek knowledge. Everything we learn gets added to the journals in these rooms."

"I would be most interested in learning more."

"As you wish, Highness."

At the very end of the complex, Uksod rapped his knuckles on the door they stood before. Without waiting he opened it and entered, Karpenmor following right behind him.

"Good, Number One, I'm glad you're here."

A lone man sat behind the simple desk opposite the door. When he looked up and saw who had entered, he stood up and bowed.

"Highnesses."

"There's only one Highness in here, One. That is our Regent. My title, now that I am no longer Regent of Enderk, is Eminence." It took all of Uksod's will to say it without scorn in his voice, but there was little he could do about it. If One was bothered by Uksod's tone he showed no sign of it.

"Yes, Eminence. What brings you here this morning?"

"May we sit?"

"Yes, of course." The elder man waved his lean arm and hand in front of his body toward the seats before the desk. "My apologies."

"Thank you. Your Highness." Uksod gestured to the chair to his right and stopped himself sitting before Karpenmor. "One, I have bad news."

"Oh?"

"Ninety-three and his colleagues have all perished."

The older man closed his eyes briefly once and let out a deep sigh. "What happened?"

"Who is Ninety-three?" Karpenmor asked before Uksod could answer.

One looked at Uksod who nodded slightly back at him. "He was the leader of one of our teams, on a mission, Highness."

"What mission?"

"Ah…"

Uksod spoke up. "Something I haven't yet brought you up to date on, Highness. Can I suggest, Highness, that I give you all the details afterward, to save explaining what One already knows?"

"I guess that will be okay."

"So they all failed?" One asked Uksod.

"Yes, One. Sadly it seems your men aren't living up to their reputation. How hard can this be?"

"I am unable to provide you any more information than you have, Eminence. I do not… cannot see what you see. I would need to speak to those over there, but of course I cannot."

"I cannot reach the latest teams either. I'm beginning to lose my faith, One. Perhaps they too are lost, out on the water."

"We send more?"

"Immediately! But not just one, you need to throw more resources at this. Whoever is thwarting our plans, needs to be eliminated."

"Word will go out immediately. There are those stationed near the bridge, best suited to cross that way. It will be quicker."

"But they will be far from our target."

"Where is the target?"

Uksod got up and walked over to a side table as One and Karpenmor followed him. He pointed at the crude map. "Heading south, a long way south and already well past that place they call Callet."

"Then we have little choice. I must send more of the boats."

"Do we have many more?"

"Enough, perhaps."

"Then we send them all. If we have some luck then perhaps those already on their way will reach land and I can give them new instructions. At least one of your boats must push much further south."

"How much further?"

"Here." Uksod pointed to the place on the map marked as Rohumaa.

"But..."

"No buts, One. We have no choice. If the prize is already moving away from us, crossing land will take too long. Someone needs to be sent to the south quickly."

The leader of the Vrah showed no emotion to Uksod. You didn't get to his position by being hotheaded. "Of course. Is that all, Your Eminence?"

"I think you need to plan to have some stationed permanently in that compound I've told you about. So we have resources more readily available."

One looked up at him, and nodded. Uksod would have to tell Fuling about that, in time. First they had to get this amulet back.

26

KARPENMOR

The whole exchange had caught Karpenmor by surprise. He knew that the interactions between himself and Uksod would feel strange at times, and at others they would have to argue.

And there was a feeling, lingering deep in the back of his head, that Uksod hadn't given him all the information. He just couldn't quite grasp control of that feeling or why. Not yet at least.

The operations of the Vrah was not something he'd put his mind to before. As the young prince, for the most part he had lived within the palace ignoring many of the people around him. He was conscious of the guards of course, but had given little thought to who they were, where they came from and who was in charge of them.

Like most things about his life, he just knew Uksod had it covered. Which he did, but he also had a lot more going on than just overseeing them. It was another stark reminder of how spoilt and privileged he had been for years.

No wonder Uksod found him annoying and was constantly frustrated at him. He would need to learn a lot more now to rule properly. No longer could he keep going through the motions like an observer as he had done previously.

It was all going to fall on him. For now, he knew he would have to rely on Uksod's knowledge and advice. As much as he had a burning feeling inside to take control, he needed to temper that.

No matter how annoying the old man can be.

Karpenmor had so many questions about the conversation with the man Uksod had called One, but he was smart enough to know that they shouldn't be discussed in the open. He kept quiet and walked alongside Uksod as they returned to the main palace building.

Once back in his office, he couldn't hold it in any longer. "I have a lot of questions, Uksod."

"I am sure you do, Karpenmor. I'm surprised you didn't ask me the moment we left One's office."

"Well, I wanted to, but I recognized that this is one of those things we wouldn't want discussed in the open."

"Ah, wisdom already. Perhaps this will come along quicker than expected."

"What will?"

"You being ready, Karpenmor. That might sound impertinent, but you've not been particularly interested or willing up until now. There are many things about being the ruler you haven't been exposed to, or interested in. I was… unsure how you'd adapt."

Karpenmor chose not to reply immediately. He knew Uksod was right, but part of him still wanted to put the old man in his place and let him know he was the ruler, despite feeling all at sea now that he actually was.

"I think it's going to be a lot of learning, quickly, to make up for what I should have been doing earlier."

He watched as Uksod nodded slightly and clasped his hands on his lap.

"Where would you like me to start?"

"I don't really know. Maybe you can tell me what is happening in Dharatan that requires so many men at the cost of so many lives?"

"How much of the history of what happened to your father do you remember?"

Karpenmor paused to think about what he had learned over the years, which wasn't a lot. Mostly, people didn't want to discuss that period.

"I know he went over to meet with their rulers. I believe there was some sort of mass gathering. There was a major disagreement which saw father leave and rush back here. When he reached the Stepping Isles something major happened, a massive storm or such and the bridge was destroyed? After that he came back and was holed up in the Amber Room. That's about it."

"That is the bones of it, but you're missing a lot of detail. The gathering you referred to was an event that used to happen on Dharatan every four years. It was known as the Great Council and the Dharatan rulers met and made decisions that affected everyone. Back then Enderk was connected to Dharatan by a solid road bridge across the Stepping Isles. The islands were bigger, and they connected over the top in a wide road bridge that multiple carts and many riders could cross. We traded freely with Ngahere and Malamig, for the most part."

Uksod paused and took a breath.

"Your father considered the two land masses connected as one, but the rulers over there viewed things differently. They always treated us as outsiders. In one way it used to drive him… mad. He would lose his temper easily over such matters. That all changed when they needed our tin."

"How so?"

"Well, your father realized that he could use that leverage to become included in the bigger 'world' view. To be honest I never know why he wanted it so much, well not then, but he did. I offered him a different solution, but he wouldn't take it."

"Which was what?"

"I told him if it bothered him so much why not just take it by force?"

"What was his reaction to that?"

"He hated the idea. He didn't want to be part of any fighting. He wanted them to recognize him as a worthy peer, and that if anything we were the largest partner of them all, Enderk being more than double even the largest realm they have over there."

"Could we have invaded?"

"Back then, who knows? Most likely. They didn't have the same military focus as we do, most of theirs is for show. We'd been building our forces the whole time, and ours have always been more ruthless, in my opinion. But none of that matters anymore."

"Why not?"

"Without the land bridge we can't get enough soldiers over there to make any attempt. Not until it's rebuilt or we can build bigger, safer ships."

Karpenmor considered what he was saying. "Go on."

"As it turned out, once he started limiting access to our tin and other goods the other rulers recognized that they needed to play nicer with us. Your father was invited to attend the Great Council as a guest. He believed that it would lead to a formal invitation to the council, or at the least major trading agreements."

"Did it?"

"No. In fact, things went badly."

"How?"

"Schevenal wanted to present Enderk in the friendliest way he could, and he struggled to find the perfect gift. It was our goddess, Yantarnaya, that came up with the solution ultimately. She advised him to make each of the rulers a very special amulet of amber as a gift. A specialist gem carver and jeweler was brought in to carve the eight amulets from our best source of amber. Each one was blessed by Yantarnaya and packaged beautifully. Except for your father's, which he wore."

"Where does he keep it? I have never seen an amulet like that."

Uksod held up his hand to stop him.

"If I can, it will all become clear. He took a large entourage over there, including the heads of each of our Imperial Families. The Council was held as part of what they called the Great Fair. As I understand it, when the leaders gathered for their Council, they brought representatives from their realms and a mighty fair was held. It involved trading negotiations, entertainment and even sporting events. Your father took a suitable traveling party, including advisors for trade matters, his attendants, and a guard force, and of course his own servants."

Uksod took a small break.

"The whole trip was wrapped in bad omens, if you listen to the few who knew the story. There were many delays getting there. The weather was dreadful, even crossing the land bridge was dangerous, they had obstacles all the way south through Dharatan. They reached the border of two realms, Sahro and ... Lletem it was. That's where the event was being held. Apparently, there was much wide-open space suitable for such an event."

The old man rolled his shoulders a little and ran a hand across his skull.

"I was never able to find out what happened next at the event."

"You weren't there?"

Uksod laughed. "No, Karpenmor, that was the first time I acted on his behalf. I was left behind. Your father had chosen to not take his religious advisors with him. Perhaps that was a bad idea, or maybe I was lucky."

"How so?"

"We got little out of him when he returned. I've pieced it together from fragments we've learned from Dharatan. The amulets were too well received, fighting broke out, some jealousy or rivalries. It is very difficult to know for sure, almost all their records have been wiped out from that period. Your father still had his wits about him at that point, or so it seemed, and he pulled our people out of the event quickly. They fought their way free of the location and headed north at pace. They left everything behind, only people and horses fled.

"Blame was put on your father's shoulder for it all, that much I got from him. Word spread quickly throughout the surrounding country, and they were attacked by others as they sped through Lletem and Ngahere. They had to fight for food and their survival, no one willing to help them. And they were pursued from the Fair.

"By the time they reached the land bridge their numbers had been thinned dramatically. There were only several Vrah left to bring him back. I was told that he threw his amulet into the water below."

"Why did he throw the amulet?"

"A good question. He never said."

Karpenmor noticed Uksod look away as he answered the question. There was something more to do with that which wasn't being said.

"Perhaps he didn't want his pursuers to get it, or perhaps something else. We'll never know now, but there was a sizable gathering of soldiers that reached the land bridge ready to pursue him across. It would have been the first attack on Enderk that I'm aware of."

"It didn't happen?"

"A massive storm hit the land bridge. And by all accounts it was huge. Even here in the palace the weather was dreadful. En Carta suffered enough damage of its own. On the land bridge it was ferocious. It was if the weather was attacking the men from Dharatan, and even your father. The few remaining Vrah that were with him, dragged him over the crumbling land bridge."

"What do you mean crumbling?"

"The storm was so bad that it was breaking down the edges of the bridges and the sides of the islands, at their tops. No one but your father and two guards survived. The bridge was destroyed and even parts of the islands sank into the ocean leaving what we now know as the Stepping Isles."

Karpenmor got up and walked about the office. "He blamed the amulets or the people of Dharatan?"

"Both, I think."

"But how does this relate to what you were discussing with One today?"

"We believe we have found his amulet."

"What?"

"We think his amulet resurfaced from the ocean."

"Why does that matter?"

"It belongs to your father. It was blessed by Yantarnaya and connected to your family. Not only does she consider it an important relic of hers, but it now belongs to you. It is worth some sizable fortune, Karpenmor. It's bad enough the other amulets are still somewhere in Dharatan, but this one is yours now."

"Shouldn't they all be returned?"

"What do you mean?"

"They were meant as gifts, but father was attacked for them. They don't deserve them."

Karpenmor saw Uksod smile, for the first time today.

"If we recovered them all, Highness, Yantarnaya would be very pleased indeed."

"Why?"

"They are very special, Highness. She blessed them, as I mentioned, and they are connected to her directly. She did not expect this outcome to occur, and she's been most upset ever since."

Karpenmor senses Uksod wasn't telling him everything, there had to be more to it than that.

"That's all?"

"Is it not enough for her to wish it?"

"Where did this one surface?"

"A woman found the amulet washed up on the Ngahere coastline. It was being brought back here when it was stolen by a barbarian on the Stepping Isles and taken back to Dharatan."

"A spy? And on the Stepping Isles again. It's like that land was a curse for Father!"

"Perhaps for us all. With the bridge destroyed we've been very limited in what we can do to recover them. This is what the Vrah have been doing. Teams of them have been following its trail, and getting very close."

Something about the way Uksod answered left Karpenmor unsure he was being told the full truth, but even so he felt angry about the past, in ways he wasn't even sure he fully understood.

"They must be stopped! It is ours and must be returned."

Uksod smiled again. "I'm glad you agree, Highness. Perhaps we can discuss it again later, but we need to get to the main hall for the people."

27

CARNUS

The guard post on the outside of the forest was not much more than a message relay, a conduit of information from Manawa and other parts of Ngahere to the Protectors, and on rare occasions in reverse.

Carnus had stayed at his post just inside the forest edge since he had delivered the news about the incursion into the Tombs by the Derks. Part of him had debated hiding the fact that there was a fourth person, but he couldn't do it.

Since he had learned more about the Wooden Path, it had become part of his being, much more than it ever had outside. Many spoke of it but few in the cities actually followed it. Many appeared to do so, but their actions were not from the place of a calm heart.

His heart was calm, he had found his place here in the Tombs, and even the turmoil that had bubbled up amongst his men from this event, hadn't affected him much at all. He had become reconciled to the Wooden Path. There were things outsiders would be bothered about, but the trees looked after his people.

The sacrifices were repaid many times over. The spirits of the trees fed his people, provided them with resources, and helped create barriers to their land. The good fortunes of the Ngaherian people were tied directly to the way of the Wooden Path, and if that was ever broken, only harm could come to his country.

Many wouldn't see or understand it, but those in power did. They would be concerned about the foreigners being in the Tombs, and about a woman escaping. He would be asked what knowledge she would have gained from being in there.

Carnus didn't know what the woman knew, but he suspected very little. She had only been in the outer edge of the forest for a brief time. She'd been a captive of the Derks and he didn't think there was much anyone could learn there, but it bothered him that he couldn't read her.

Since he had learned the touch, he had been able to get a reading from anyone. At first it had overwhelmed him, as the readings came without him seeking them, as soon as he touched someone. With guidance from a wood woman, he'd learned to control it, and to request it if he wanted it. The girl who had escaped had nothing to read, he had tried.

Many days had passed and the only word back was that someone was coming to discuss what had happened. Carnus assumed it would be the Dame of Manawa. As the nearest city, Manawa always held jurisdiction over the Tombs, and it was from there that many of the Protectors came.

The proximity meant the Tombs were ever in people's minds in that city, much more so than the capital Laumua. He was surprised it had taken so long for someone to come: it would have been the most urgent topic, he would have thought. *Surely things hadn't changed that much since he'd been in here?*

Almost on cue, a horse rode into view and hurried down the path to the guard post outside. The rider dismounted quickly and went inside. It wasn't more than several minutes before one of the guards came out, watched the messenger mount and leave, before walking down to the forest edge.

Carnus stood from his perch and walked over to the treeline.

"Carnus."

"Irran, what is the news?"

"It seems you lot have rattled many branches. The Queen herself is on her way here."

"Queen Vika?"

"None other, Carnus. She's in Manawa, and they will be here within hours."

Carnus stood still, thinking through what that meant. He knew they had taken it very seriously, and it explained the delay. He shrugged. There was no knowing what was in the mind of the Queen or anyone else.

"Any instructions for me?"

"No, except to advise you she comes."

"I'll alert my men, so we can prepare what we can."

He turned and walked away, heading toward the heart of the forest. He found the others of team four not so far away, as they had waited near him to hear what would be done.

"That can't be a good thing." Zelf spoke what was probably in the others' minds.

"Nothing can be done, Zelf. What's done is done. Spread the word and then meet at the Father Tree. I expect that's where the Queen will want us to be."

The other men hurried away, leaving Carnus to his own thoughts. He was calm, he could feel it. It wasn't just him telling himself that, he was very settled. He'd accepted who he was in here, and he would accept whatever judgment there would be.

Protecting the Tombs was their responsibility. That's why they took on the role, and why their families were honored and revered in normal society. They sacrificed their lives to protect, and the society protected their own in kind.

To the people of Ngahere, the Tombs was part of their beliefs from when they were born. This was where the ancestors were left in peace. Never to be disturbed by the living, except those who protected their peace. It was why little noise or sound was ever made by the Protectors.

Carnus knew people wouldn't accept what they saw if they came in, and so the narrative of respect and rule of law kept them sacred and untouched. Ngaherians believed that when you died it was the end of your journey and you had earned your great rest. That you could enter the Tombs and rest there for eternity. No other people but Ngaherians were allowed to rest in the Tombs.

Each of the Protectors had sworn to live there for the rest of their lives and protect the sanctity of the Tombs from the occasional treasure hunter seeking to raid what they hoped were graves or lost travelers. It was rare these days that anyone dared risk entering the sanctity of the Tombs as word had spread in the other realms. Leaving bodies outside as reminders was a good deterrent to those who might think otherwise. Word was always sent back to Manawa, but usually all they received back was a message to do better.

Whatever that meant.

That someone had got away was different. They had failed in their duty. They couldn't leave and hunt that person, not without permission of the Dame, and as that person wasn't a Ngaherian it made everything more problematical.

His team knew they had failed, and even Zelf had much less to say than normal. Those others in the Tombs that Carnus had crossed paths with also knew it. He could see it in their faces. After all this time, one girl had ruined his record of service. No one said anything but it was clear they were all concerned about what was going to happen.

Back at the forest edge he waited, sat on his haunches, breathing slowly and staring down the pathway outside. He had expected that the Queen might arrive with a massive entourage, but he was mistaken. Two women rode slowly on horses surrounded by no more than a dozen warriors.

The procession was quiet and did not rush, which eased Carnus's mind. They honored the peace and quiet of the Tombs even outside, as it should be. The two guards from the post were stood outside and bowed as the Queen rode up.

She got down from her horse and walked toward the border of the Tombs. There was strength and power in the way she walked. Queen Vika ruled with a strong fist and was known to have a fiery temperament. Carnus had only met her one other time when he had won the tournament.

The woman wore a skirt of multi-colored reeds sewn together, a harsh fabric that only the elder nostalgics continued to wear. There was not an ounce of visible fat on her frame and her shoulders rippled with muscle despite her longer years.

Around her neck a halter top covered her breasts and upper chest. Her exposed skin was tattooed in intricate detail depicting her age and seniority.

He stood and clasped his hands together in front of his body, a signal that he meant no harm. She acknowledged the gesture with a small blink of her eyes.

"You're Carnus?"

"Yes, Your Highness."

"Please lead us to the tree," she commanded.

"Of course." Carnus bowed slightly then turned and led the way. He had no need to look back and check on them, he knew the two women would be able to maintain the pace with him.

When they entered the clearing around the massive tree deep in the forest, many of the Tomb's Protectors were stood just outside it, encircling it. What was happening affected them all, they would want to be present to learn what was to happen.

The Queen said nothing but walked past Carnus and up to the Father Tree. She stood almost against it and placed her hands on it, while everyone waited. Many minutes passed before she stepped back and turned to face them all.

"Come forward, Carnus."

He walked forward.

"Please kneel."

He dropped to his knee and lowered his head.

Her voice seemed to fill the wide space. "This is not what is expected here in the Tombs. Each of you were given great honor by being nominated as a Protector. Your role is as your name suggests. To protect."

She took a small step, closing the gap between her and Carnus. The tone of her voice and the power she exuded had broken through his inner calm. He could feel his heart beating faster than normal and his hands felt clammy even palm-down on the ground.

"From time to time, those with ill will venture into the forests seeking what you are here to protect, the very heart and soul of our people. Each of them has always been dealt with. Until now."

Her words seemed to echo about the clearing, silence hanging heavily when they finally settled.

"Carnus, as the leader of the Tombs, you are responsible for what happened here. What of the woman that escaped? Tell me what you know."

He explained how little time the woman had been in the forest, and what had occurred. She queried him several times about her and what she might have seen.

"Thank you for your truth, Carnus."

She paused.

"We cannot abide such failures. The Protectors' name has been sullied by letting an outsider leave even if she may not know much of what the Tombs holds. Any knowledge is too much knowledge, especially for someone from another realm. As leader, Carnus, you have failed us."

His chest tightened as he waited for what she had decided.

"Normally when one of us leaves the Tombs you are allowed to hunt them down to ensure such knowledge is protected. But to do so of one that is not Ngaherian would be most unusual. Who knows how other realms might react? If she was here, that would be different, but she is not."

Again the Queen paused.

"Never before has such a thing happened here. This failure undermines the entire role of the Protectors. I cannot abide it. And thus, from this day forth, Carnus, you will leave the Tombs, and Ngahere, never to return on pain of death. You have failed in your duty, and you no longer deserve the honor bestowed on you."

Everything seemed to become dark for Carnus. He looked up slowly, and could only see the face of the Queen. Her dark eyes stared down at him.

"He will be escorted from here to the closest border as soon as we have left the Tombs."

The Queen turned and walked back the way they had come, leaving him where he was.

Carnus wobbled on his knee before stopping himself from falling. Everything seemed to be spinning around him.

This can't be happening.

28

TILLANDRA

Getting from Anderwell to Jarv had been simple enough, but having to sit in a boat and wait for it to arrive was frustrating for Tillandra. She was happier when she was in control of her own movement as she was now, being back on foot.

It only took her about an hour to settle into a comfortable rhythm. Her ability to cover ground quickly was enhanced as she traveled along an easy road through open plains and gently rolling hills.

Much easier going than Death Road.

Being back on the road again so quickly after making that trip back from Midderbuilt was entirely unexpected.

Rohumaa was a country of agriculture. The largest production of Dharatan's meats came from here, and her journey took her through vast pastures filled with cattle and sheep. Ironically, they also farmed horses, which the Rohumaa had little use for, but their land suited breeding animals.

Seeing all the life spread out around her and the grass pastures was calming, and at times allowed her to forget some of her concerns. No one paid her any attention except for the occasional extra-long look at her face, before the person turned away.

As much as she could, she wore a shawl to mask her disfigurement from general view, even though she resented it. In Anderwell she was able to just be herself, but the reaction and undue attention her affliction caused was simply not worth the hassle.

There was no knowing when one of the others might try to make contact, but the knocking feeling was quite distinctive. Thankfully for Tillandra she felt it just as she was finishing off an impromptu meal under the shade of a large fig tree beside a slow-running creek.

She sat and let herself slip into the Void.

"In All Jest, Mother."

"In All Jest, Bea."

"How's your journey?"

"I'm through Jarv and on the road to Okeans, it's easy going."

"I'm glad to hear that. I have news."

"Go ahead, I have some time."

"First, we've had word from Gimbden. He's been able to implement replacing Mayor Pravat."

"That happened quickly."

"Yes, but it seems to have been very effective. When word of the jewel theft got out the hunt began immediately. One of Pravat's maids found the jewels and reported it to the council guards. It took on a life of its own after that."

"What happens next?"

"He's being held by the city guards, but Gimbden said there was an issue with how to proceed."

"How so?"

"Normally the council itself would handle any judgment but given it's one of their own, they're reluctant. We discussed it here. It seems the captain of the guards should be the one in this instance. What do you think?"

"I agree with you. The sooner it's dealt with, the better."

"There's more to it. You and Gimbden were right to be concerned about him. Once he was arrested, Gimbden went through his office and found a letter from Envoy Reyes, which made out there was a bigger agreement being discussed between them than just what you were told."

"Oh?"

"The Skarians were looking to set up much more of an embassy in Watersend and wanted to be able to get someone on the council."

"What on Dharatan?"

"The letter was a little generalized in how it was written but the overall feeling Gimbden got was they were aiming much higher with Watersend, and that Pravat was aiding them."

"We didn't make a good choice with him, did we?"

"It seems not. He's gone now at least."

"What of his replacement?"

"A man called Huster, who Gimbden said is a pretty straight arrow."

"We'll want to let him know that we are going to be a bit more direct with our guidance for the foreseeable future."

"Understood. There's more news from Goran."

"Good news I hope?"

"No. The girl, she's been captured by the Vrah."

"Captured?"

"Yes. There's more. They headed south with her, but took shelter in the forest along the border. They went into the section known as the Tombs. By luck she escaped from there, while her captors didn't. All of them were killed by the warriors in there, and their bodies put outside."

"What a mess."

"The only thing of interest on them was their rings. Goran's taken them and is going to get them to us. All he said was, they are all identical and are set with amber stones."

"I'm not sure what that means?"

"Me neither, but they mean something to them, given they all have them."

"Where's Goran now?"

"He and Brando are following south. Ash's ring is still blue, and still moving, so they're trying to catch up."

"Any word on Henri?"

"No. And we'll not hear anything quickly on that front either. With Goran heading south, Hallendell in a difficult spot, and Clannack busy in Ngahere, we have no eyes or ears in the north that can communicate back to the Court in this manner."

"Okay."

"I think I should head to Callet and base myself there. Getting any messages from Malamig or elsewhere south by courier to Callet is a lot quicker than all the way here."

"You're right. We do need more timely information with all of this. What of your other work?"

"My classes anyone can do, but most of my work is handling oversight of the Circuit. I think it would do me good to get out."

"Okay. So when?"

"I'll need to plan, but I think within days. It will take me some time to get there, and I'll take someone to help me."

"Travel safe, Bea. These are interesting times."

"Yes. Yes, they are. And you."

Beantic broke off the connection. Even not being the originator of it, it still took its toll on Tillandra. When she stood up her legs felt weak and she had a small headache. She was pretty certain the next town wasn't too far away. She hadn't planned to stay there, but it was probably the best option now.

AFTER AN EARLY NIGHT AND A BED TO SLEEP IN, TILLANDRA WAS BACK ON the road early. She knew she was only one more day from Okeans if she kept this pace up. The weather was perfect for such a trip, neither too hot nor cold.

Tillandra swatted away a fly that had been following her for several miles now as she mulled over what was going on around them. King Ahn was clearly moving forward on wanting something from Watersend.

As valuable a city as it was, with it being by far the biggest gem trading centre in all of Dharatan, there was something she was missing. No one had shown that much interest in the city before, nor Midderbuilt.

In her mind an image of Mount Qum flashed across her eyes, almost in answer to her unspoken question.

Surely not?

The fly buzzed around her eyes again and Tillandra waved her hand across her face, trying to shoo it away.

What had the Lady in the Stone said to her? *Have faith in the messages.* Was that a message? A warning?

In Tillandra's mind it felt like several more pieces fell into place in the puzzle. She could almost picture everything but still part of it evaded her. The gems and jewelers in Midderbuilt still didn't seem a prize big enough to invade for. Unless.

The Citadel Stone? Surely not, no one knows of where it lives. No.

That didn't seem feasible either. How would King Ahn know about it? Tillandra was sure that the knights could never get access to it, the magic that surrounded it was too strong. She rubbed her temples and took a break from trying to solve that issue.

Trusting her visions was still not easy for her, no matter what she'd been told, but the goddess… She had to be a goddess, surely? Tillandra knew she needed to ask more of her next time she was there, including who she was. It wasn't something she could resolve right now.

She had to blink to block out a bright light. Raising her hand to her brow to shield it, Tillandra saw it was the sun reflecting off some walls surrounding a large property ahead. The light seemed too bright to just be a reflection and she slowed up to study it.

The walls were made of a light-colored stone that was reflecting some light, but not enough to cause that effect. There was something more to it, the brightness wasn't natural.

"That sense, coupled with the light, that's how you know our messages, Tillandra." Her recollection of what the Lady of the Stone had told her, jumped to the front of her mind. As soon as it did, the extra light above the property ahead, disappeared from her sight and it all looked more normal.

As she got nearer to it she could see the walls were at least double her height and made from the light-colored stone commonly found in the mountains of Thabeng. A queue of people lined the road leading from iron gates set in the walls, all the way back out to the road she was on, and then some.

As curious as it was, she might not have stopped to investigate had it not been for what had just happened. She walked down toward the compound, several of the people lined up in the queue calling out either abuse, as if she was skipping the line, or what they thought was helpful advice.

"You'll only get told to get to the back of the line."

Nearer to the gate was a marquee where several vendors were selling drinks and small parcels of dried food or nuts. Tillandra approached the tent and headed to an older man smoking a pipe around the back of it.

"Looks like a busy trade?"

"That it is. Just taking myself a break."

"I'm on my way from Jarv to Okeans and had to stop to see what all this was about."

"It's a new church." He held his pipe out toward the people queued up. "They're all wanting to be blessed by the priests that are in there."

"It's a big compound for a church, and why all the walls?"

"True that, can't say I really know. Maybe it's to hold their men?"

"Men?"

"Yeah, there's been a steady stream of knights arriving since the walls were finished. Anytime one of their priests shows up they're accompanied by a group of their knights. All very serious they look."

"From Daskare then?"

"Yeah. I guess their church wants to reach more people. Never heard of it until they started building this, although I heard there's a small one in the city."

"A small church?"

"Yes. The Children of Jolothos, or so I'm told."

Tillandra looked back at the walls. "How long has this been getting built?"

"Best part of the last year, lady. I'm happy about it. We set up this tent here from almost the beginning, once I saw the crowd they were attracting."

"Smart thinking."

"My sons are in there." He jerked his hand to the tent wall. "They do as much as me. Another one is on a run back from Okeans with more supplies. It's the best trade we've ever had."

"Do they let many people in at once?"

"Only one or two at a time. These people queue up most of the day sometimes, just for their blessings. I don't mind though, they all get thirsty." He grinned as he banged his pipe empty against the palm of his hand.

Tillandra shook her head. She knew how easily common folk would fall for any ruse promising better fortunes. "No doubt they get blessed shortly after a small donation."

The man chuckled. "I see you've come across such a scheme before, have you?"

"Seen a few, yes."

"Well, nice chatting but I need to get back to it." He moved around Tillandra and back into the tent.

"Thanks for the chat."

Tillandra walked back to the line of people and peered as best she could through the gates. She caught sight of several knights walking around in the background, and a chill ran down her back.

Nothing good can be coming from this. Not only Sahro but here as well.

Okeans was not so far away, and while she was keen to get there for the library, she was also interested in what lay beyond the walls. The more she thought about it the more the compound had the feel of a garrison, not just a church.

How many knights are here now? And how many will it hold when it's completed?

She looked back at the queue behind her, which seemed to have grown and not shrunk. It would take the rest of the day to get inside if she even made it.

In the end Tillandra decided she had learned enough for now, and not much more would be gained by getting inside, so she headed back up the road, away from the compound. Once she got back to the main road, she increased her stride and hurried toward Okeans.

LANI

The small room Lani was in should have been completely dark. It wasn't. In the darkness you shouldn't be able to see anything, but she could. There always seemed to be light coming from somewhere, even the tiniest trickle, but enough that Lani could make out shapes or lines.

There was a feeling she got when in the darkness that she'd felt back in Nkuku, when she had been in Watcher's base, and underneath when she escaped with that insufferable boy.

What was his name?

Her warren under Barnen was the same. At first Lani thought it was the same for everyone, but she had learned it wasn't. That was what made her feel so safe under there, because anyone else coming down that way would have had to use torches. The flames would have alerted her to their presence.

It gave her an advantage, especially on the few occasions she did rob people. She could do it in the darkest part of night or in the dingiest rooms, and she could always find what she hunted for and escape without problems. Remembering Barnen made her sad. Whether she liked it or not, that place was her home.

She'd left the Kin behind, she'd left Bragg the clothier as well, her job. Where did it leave her now? Holed up in a dank-smelling room, with a bed that appeared ridden with bugs, in a strange city, looking for a man with no eyes.

This isn't my life! This is someone else's life that I've been pushed into.

Lani didn't want any part of it. She still couldn't get over knowing that people were dying around her. She'd even seen Captain Kyro, from Barnen, cut down in the street, just from trying to catch her. Too many people either wanted to harm her, or came to harm because of her.

Why me? This is so silly. I'm no one!

Earlier she'd tried finding any mention of the seers in Ashantha's journal by using the mask. It was too hard. If there was a way to find topics using it, she didn't know how. All she could do was flick through the pages and read what was there.

Just the process of reading dumbfounded her. That she could do it with his mask on, and it seemed so easy, was crazy for her. She couldn't read anything normally. She got by from symbols or by asking. And she'd done okay that way.

When she'd asked the priest back in Callet about the seer it would have been smarter if she had gotten more specifics from him. Now she had to ask someone else, which was fine on a normal day, but without knowing who might be behind her, she knew she had to remain cautious.

Too many times she'd fallen into complacency and ended up in someone else's hands. Never in a good way either.

She tried to think who else, other than another priest, would be able to guide her to one of The Eyes. Watcher had known one, so maybe one of the street folk here in Union would be able to help. Except that was too risky, she was on her own, and they'd as likely rob her as help her. Or worse.

With no obvious solutions, she huddled up on the floor, using her satchel as a pillow and hunted some sleep.

It didn't take much to wake her. Sleep had been difficult as she couldn't get comfortable on the floorboards. The shutters on the window had enough holes to make them redundant as a light blocker, and the first light of the day had Lani's eyes open.

The innkeeper happily pointed her in the direction of the Church of Thenis, down toward the river. It looked much more like she expected a church to look than the one in Callet. Standing alone and proud as a little over two stories tall, the steeple was highlighted by the rising sun behind it.

Out the front, small rows of flowers lined the walkway to the main doors, with small paths heading off north and south, lined with more narrow gardens full of flowers, the brightness of the colors in contrast to the dark stone building.

Unsure whether the church was open so early, she tried the door. It opened almost without sound, and effortlessly despite its size. A lot more care went into this church, that much she could tell. The main hall was lined with benches in neat rows, a straight path down the middle.

At the far end, a massive glass window filled more than half of the top of the wall, filled with colored glass, depicting what Lani assumed was Thenis, standing on a mountain. Now that she knew Thenis was female, such images made more sense to her.

She quickly looked around to see if there was a statue like the one in Callet, but couldn't see one. Lani walked to the front, expecting someone to notice her, but the place was empty except for her. Up toward the small stage where the priest's pulpit stood, a table full of candles sat, none of them alight.

"Hello."

Lani nearly fell over in fright, turning to her right and stepping back.

A man maybe thirty in years, dressed in a grey cassock, stood off to the side, his hands held out in apology.

"Sorry, lass. I didn't mean to scare you so."

"It's okay," she lied. Her heart was pounding in her chest.

"What brings you here so early in the day?"

She looked closely at him, he was walking slowly toward her. His face look kind and he wore a simple smile.

"I need help and I thought this might be the right place to ask."

His smile broadened. "That is why most people come here to pray. They want to ask Thenis for help."

"Oh. Not like that." Lani could feel her face redden a little.

"What then?"

"I was recently in Callet and met your priest up there."

"Novak."

"Sorry?"

"You met Novak, the priest in Callet?"

"Oh, sorry, he never told me his name."

"Did he try to get you to drink that strange-tasting wine of his?"

That brought a small grin to her face. "He did, it had all these odd flavors in it."

"He keeps telling me it's quite the trend in the south."

"He said I could find what I was looking for here in Union."

"Okay, what's that?"

She was a little hesitant. "You'll probably disapprove as did he, but I seek one of The Eyes."

"Ah." He walked past her and up to the table of candles, and fidgeted about before lighting one. He closed his eyes and mumbled for a few moments.

"That is an odd request. I'll help you but I'd like to ask a favor in return, if you would humor me?"

Lani didn't like where this was heading but had little choice.

"It's quite simple, I want you to light a candle and pray to Thenis, asking her to help you with what you're going there to find out."

She looked at him, thinking he wasn't going to tell her.

"The person you seek is easy enough to find, there's no reason not to tell you, but as you guessed, I'm not a fan of their kind. So my favor is simply that you ask my goddess for help as well. Perhaps you'll get twice the insights you need, or maybe hers will be better."

Lani shrugged her shoulders. It was harmless. "Sure, but I've never really done any praying before."

"It's easy. Light one of those candles, and then close your eyes and speak to her in your mind. Ask her your question. Then wait a moment and open them again."

"That's it?"

"It is."

"How will I know her answer?"

"You'll know. When you get it, or something happens to show you, then you'll know."

"Okay."

"When you leave here, turn right, follow the road almost to the outer walls to the north. Maybe two roads back from the walls you'll turn right again, and you'll find your seer easily enough. It's quite unique."

"Thank you."

"Be wary of them, they are not all they seem."

Lani didn't answer and walked up to the table. There were candles of all thicknesses, and heights, some almost completely melted and some new. She chose a new one and used a taper there to light it from the one the priest had lit.

She stared up to where the glass window was and closed her eyes, thinking of the image of the woman she'd seen in the chapel in Callet. The face of the market lady in Barnen filled her vision, a broad smile on her face as if she was welcoming her.

Could you please help me get safe from all these people?

It wasn't a very good question she knew, the whole thing felt uncomfortable to Lani, but she'd played along as he'd asked. She opened her eyes and turned around. The priest was nowhere to be seen. She headed back toward the doors, off to find her seer.

30

LANI

The building was a simple wooden hut, but the space around it was definitely unique. Lani stood before a large, square open garden. Everything about it was perfectly even: if a plant was on the left it was mirrored on the right.

Each path had another shooting off in the other direction. In the middle of the space was a large pond of water. A small bridge arched up over it from the path she stood on, to the other side and another path ran from it to the wooden hut on the far side.

Lani walked down the path, the tiny stones crunching under her feet. If anyone was home, they'd know she was here. She stopped at the pond and looked into the clear water. Orange fish swam casually around in the water, small bubbles occasionally bursting on the surface.

She walked over the bridge and approached the hut.

"Hello, Lani."

She froze, and twisted her head in all directions checking to see if anyone was around. The garden was empty, but the sound of the voice had seemed to come from near her.

"I am in here."

"Who are you?"

"Such a good question. Who are you?"

"You already seem to know my name."

"A name is just a word given to someone or something so that others can recognize them. It means no more than that. Nor is it who you are."

"I am just a girl from a place in the north, looking for some help."

"That isn't who you are either, that's what you are seeking."

She wasn't sure what the man wanted her to say, so she said nothing else. This was much stranger than when she met Cideep, a lot stranger.

She heard him chuckle. "Maybe that question is too hard for you today, Lani of the North. Would you like to come in?"

"Yes." She quickly added, "Please."

"Place all of your things outside, including that which you hide on your chest. Such a thing I do not want so close to me."

Lani was surprised by what he said, but laughed internally. This was exactly why she wanted to find a seer, to get insight into her problem. After placing the amulet and brooch into the satchel she left them on the ground outside the hut, and walked inside.

To the right a thin bald man, with the darkest skin she'd seen, sat on some cushions. His legs were folded under him and his hands rested easily on his knees. Like Cideep he had only holes where eyes would normally be. She shivered even though she knew what to expect.

"Take a seat here in front of me."

As she stepped forward a cushion appeared as if out of nowhere. Lani sat down on it feeling awkward, trying to fold her legs comfortably like he did.

"You have come a long way, Lani of the North." He seemed to smirk whenever he said the word 'north', accentuating it for his own pleasure.

"I have. Not by choice."

"That is where you are wrong, my girl. There is always a choice."

"But..."

"There is always a choice. If you had stayed with Cideep, then you would have had different occurrences, but you chose not to."

"You know?"

"I know."

"But how?"

"How doesn't matter. What you must know is that you always have a choice. You might not like what you must choose between so you can explain it as not having a choice, as if someone or something has forced you to do it, but you always choose. Everyone chooses."

"Do you choose to have no eyes?"

His face stayed calm but he paused for a moment.

"I am not sure you need to know the way we come to be, Lani, but the simplest answer is yes. I choose everything. I chose to let you come to see me, and to answer your questions. You chose to take up the amulet you carry."

"I did not, it is attached to me."

"Was it always attached to you?"

Lani thought back and recalled the time when Yerat had died from it and when it had linked to her. She was able to see the exact image of it in her mind, frozen in time.

"No."

"So you chose to take it, and now it is linked to you."

"Yes."

"So you did choose this."

"I chose to take it from the dead man, that was all. He asked me to."

"At some point, Lani, you will need to accept your choice."

She sat still, feeling annoyed with the skinny old man. This wasn't why she was here, she wanted help to know what to do. Suddenly she felt as if nothing was going to work to help her. Her breath caught in her chest and she felt tears beginning to form.

"Tell me why you came."

His voice seemed to have a different tone to it and her sadness slipped into the background.

"Cideep mentioned something to me, which I was hoping you might be able to help with."

"What is that?"

"He said there is a lock on my mind, that he didn't understand it but that he needed to speak to his mistress about it."

"Oh, that. Yes, that has been quite the talk amongst us, such a thing has not been seen for so long. May I?"

Lani felt like a pet, the way he asked. A toy to play with, but he was her best bet at getting answers. She slid forward so he could reach her hand. He said nothing but it felt as if there was a tingling running through her fingers where it lay.

Several minutes went by before he spoke. "My, my, that is something quite interesting."

"What do you mean?"

"There is a lock, that's what it seems to be. I can sense no other way to describe it. Normally I would know who you are, Lani of the North, if I held your hand, but not you. No, you are special, Lani, someone has done something quite incredible to your head."

"It doesn't feel incredible to me."

"What does it feel like?"

"I don't know, but there's things locked away from me too. I cannot remember things, not even of my parents. And I get the worst headaches. I cannot move."

His hand moved over hers, and she could see him feeling the ring. "Oh, I will look some more."

This time he took a lot longer and she was beginning to feel very uncomfortable stuck on the floor. When he did speak she startled.

"This is not right, Lani."

"What?"

"This," and he pulled his hand back, taking the ring with it, holding it up for her to see.

"How did you do that? I couldn't get it off."

"No, it was behaving most strangely, it should not have been on you. Something quite strange happened to it, to you."

"What do you mean?"

"I know little of the magic that makes such things, Lani, but of magic itself I understand its sense. This belonged to that man, and when he died, it should have done its thing. But you got in the way."

"What?"

"That's the sense of it, what I could feel in it. I had to ask it off."

"You did what?"

"That's as easy as I can explain it. But what it was doing was wrong, I do not know why but you are freed from it now."

"Thank you. What shall I do with it?"

"I have nothing to say about that."

"Will it do that again if I put it back on my finger?" She pulled her hand back and rubbed at the finger it had been on, glad to be rid of it.

The seer closed his hand and then reopened it and the ring was no more. In his hand was a coin, made of silver. It still carried the same jester's face, but instead of being a ring, it was now a coin.

"How in Thenis's name…?"

"You may not be wrong in that, Lani of the North. I believe a god has been up to no good with you."

"I'm confused."

"That thing locking your mind, no person could do that. The magic or skill it would take to do such a thing… I have never met anyone that could do that."

"So you can't undo it?"

He laughed, a laugh of a man much more than twice his size. "Oh dear me no, Lani. No one I know could do such a thing, perhaps even the person that did it may struggle."

She shook her head.

"What of that amulet then?"

"Now that thing is something I don't want to hold. I know not what it really is or why it is as it is. It has power, a lot of power, and somehow it's connected to you."

Lani instinctively rubbed at her wrist.

"Perhaps you should leave it behind you."

"I can't, and there are people chasing me for it that I'm keeping it away from."

"See, another choice. You need not worry about those men, Lani."

"What do you mean?"

"Those who were hunting you, the Derks, they are no more."

So they hadn't survived. At least some good news for Lani. It meant she didn't have to keep looking over her shoulder all the time.

"The amulet, that's outside, maybe you could take it from me? Like you did to that ring."

The old man shook his head vigorously. "That I will not do, nor do I think I could. Our mistress, she forbade any of us to touch such a thing, after Cideep shared news of it."

"So I have no choice, no one seems to be able to help."

"Someone can."

"The woman they call Mother?"

"See, you already know what you need to know, Lani. Now you have to make a choice."

"I don't feel like it's much of a choice."

"Go, don't go. It's a choice. Speak to me, don't speak to me. Each thing you do is a choice. Your choices are somewhat more interesting."

"Hardly interesting."

"Oh, but they are. Much has been foretold of what is coming, but you, nothing was told about you, and yet you walk through the middle of the storm, with everything focused on what choices you make."

"I don't understand."

"I cannot tell you any more. You carry news with you, both bad and good news. You are the bearer of the news. That is all I can see."

"So I must keep going?"

"That, Lani of the North, is your choice."

She huffed at him, and he chuckled in answer.

"One piece of advice."

"Yes?"

"If you do choose to seek out the woman they call Mother, to the south as you know, there are ways you can be seen less. There are still those who seek you, and more will come. I cannot see if they seek to harm or not, but you must still take care. If your choice takes you south, use the way of those who wish to not be seen."

"What do you mean?"

"There are those who work the river, that know how to smuggle someone, or something, out of sight. The less you are seen, the better for you. Look for them in Diwedd, or thereabouts."

"Thank you."

"Here, Lani of the North, take your coin."

"You should keep it, as a payment."

"What we do, Lani, is not for money. I have all I need, what would a silly coin give me?. Travel smart, and be well."

She stood up, her knees groaning from the way she had been sitting, and walked out into the bright light of the day.

31

KOOKA

There were times when Kooka couldn't help feeling sorry for his condition. Despite the pleasure he took out of his work and the way his life had ended up, it just came upon him sometimes.

Kooka had come to accept the missing part of his leg many years before and had adapted to how he lived with the help of his friends in Anderwell. And they were his friends. Or in truth they were family.

That's what he was trying to help the young lass understand.

"Why should I leave? This is my home!" she sobbed.

"Is it, Purple? Truly?"

"Yes."

"You're living out here with the pigs, having to feed yourself, while your so-called parents and your brother live in that big house."

"That's just how it is." Her red eyes were almost cried out, but her face still wore her determination on it.

"It doesn't have to be, that's what I'm trying to tell you."

"I don't want to die!"

There it was, Kooka thought. The underlying issue that was his biggest problem saving these children from themselves. Everyone had always threatened kids with the Fool's Cart, ever since they were little.

If you don't behave, you'll get sent away on the Fool's Cart, or other similar threats.

"Why would you die?"

"You're the Fool's Cart. Aren't you?"

"I am, but not quite as you know it, lass."

"Whaddaya mean?"

"Can I sit down there?" Kooka pointed to the trough she was perched on the edge of.

Purple nodded to him.

He used his crutch to test the ground before he put his other leg in the mud and, satisfied he wouldn't lose the stump in it, moved to the trough and sat beside her.

"See that leg of mine?"

"Yeah." She rubbed her runny nose on her grubby sleeve.

"Been gone since I was about your age. Nine, aren't you?"

"Yea. How did you know?"

"I know these things, I've been helping people like us for more than half my life, Purple. It's what I do. Want to know why?"

She shrugged as if she didn't care. Kooka didn't smile externally but inside he knew she wanted to know, and she was slowly coming around.

"Because I lived worse than this." He spread his arms out to encompass the pen and back of the property. "My ma had died from birthing me, and my pa, well, he considered me the cause. He left me with a wet nurse and eventually just kicked me out."

"Out where?"

"Out on the street. I can still recall him kicking me with his boots, in the side and chest, as I tried to crawl away from him. He even kicked the side of my head one of the times, he never stopped until I was outside the small house I'd been brought up in."

"That's horrible."

"It did feel bad, and like I said, telling it to you still makes my heart tear a little."

"What did you do?"

"I crawled away. I didn't have no crutch like I have now. I could either hop, which was very difficult to do, or crawl. At first, I found somewhere in a nearby stable to hide, and I cried until my eyes felt like the desert. I got moved on, and sometimes beaten or kicked until I found a place on the outskirts of town that was an old animal hutch. I lived there."

"How did you eat?"

"I didn't much. What I could I scavenged, or I hunted rats and rabbits. I got good at trapping them, but my health wasn't real good and I was getting weaker."

Kooka took a moment to pause, leaving Purple to feel the depth of what he was telling her, but also because every time he had to tell it he was pulled back into the memory.

"One day I was sitting outside my hutch, it was right beside the road into town, when an old man driving this very cart stopped right in front of me. His name was Ruport, and back then he was the Driver."

"The what?"

"The Driver. That's my job title, what my people call me."

"Your people? I thought you said your pa kicked you out."

"You're a smart one aren't you, Purple?" Kooka let his face fill with a wide smile and could see the girl's eyes brighten a little. It turned his heart every time to see his kind, who had never had a good word said to them, respond to the simplest of praises. While it was true what he said, he was well practiced at pacing the tale and telling it in a way that encouraged the listener to see things his way.

"My birth people kicked me out, but I found a new family, and it was because of Ruport."

"How?"

"He told me his story, a bit like I'm telling you my story, and he persuaded me to travel with him back to the place where we live. Where my new family lives."

"Where's that then?"

"Have you ever heard of a city called Anderwell?"

She shook her head firmly. "Never."

"It's a marvel, Purple. Walls of sandstone, yellow like the sands of the desert."

"It's in the desert? I hate the desert."

"It borders the desert and the rest of the world. Have you ever been to the desert?"

Purple shook her head again. "No."

"Don't hate what you don't know. There's enough to hate from what you do know. The desert is like a land ocean, with waves and plains of sand. Did you know the sand isn't all the same color? There's hundreds of shades of sand, and the pretty pictures you can see are amazing."

"Really?"

"Really. But Anderwell isn't full of sand, it's a city like others. Except it is different."

"What different?"

"Most of the people that live there, they're like us."

"Bad legs?"

"Some, yes. But it's a special place for people like us that are special."

"We're not special, everyone tells me I'm evil born. Just bad."

"That's the thing, see. Small-minded people think things like that, because they don't like things that are different. They want everyone to be the same. Not me though."

He waited to see if she was curious as to what he meant. When she didn't say anything, he continued.

"I love differences. I don't want everyone to be like me. The idea of it sounds good but imagine how boring that would be. In my city, there's people from all over Dharatan. Mals and Dotokiens, Morskans and Bengs."

"What's a Beng? What's wrong with them?"

"A Beng is someone from a place called Thabeng. And there's nothing wrong with them as a race of people, Purple. But they're different. And each one of them has something else that makes them special."

"What?"

"Oh, it's different for them all. Have you ever met someone missing an arm?"

"No!"

"Well, how about someone who can't see?"

"No. That would be terrible, how could they...?" She didn't finish what she was saying but Kooka could see her thinking about it.

"See, there's many ways people can be different, but out here, in Normy world, people don't like different. They fight to not be different. We're different, Purple. We are all different and that's what brings us together. That's what makes us the same."

"That doesn't make sense."

"I know. It doesn't when you say it like this. Think about us, we're kind of similar, aren't we? Like I have no leg from here down, and you, you've got both legs, but they don't work really at all do they?"

She shook her head, and a frown filled her face.

"But we're much more alike than your family, right? We're bad leg people."

"Ha!" She did laugh at that.

"I'm man, you're woman, but we're both bad leg people."

The sound of her laughing brought a tear to Kooka's eye.

"Purple, the question for you is, do you want to believe the silly old parents' tales about the Fool's Cart where you disappear and die, or do you want to understand that, yes you disappear, from this place, but you end up living normally in a place where you're loved and can have friends?"

"But I have no money, how can I?"

"In our family we have ways to look after ourselves. And we teach everyone to read and write and learn things and you get proper food every single day."

"Really?"

"Really. Look at me, do I look like I'm not eating?"

"Haha. No, you don't. You look kind of fat."

Kooka poked his tongue out at her. "Mean but true." Her face dropped at his words. "It's okay, I'm not bothered. Truth is I am getting a bit fat but I'm not so young anymore and you know, who cares?" He laughed and watched as her face brightened again. Kooka had a special laugh, once it started it wanted to run forever, cackling.

"It has been lovely meeting you, Purple, and I'd like you to come to Anderwell with me, but I won't force you. Once I leave, I might not be back here for years, my journey takes me all over the world, but I'm heading back to Anderwell now. If you want to come that's up to you, but I have others on the cart, and we need to keep moving."

"Um." She had stuck her fingers into her mouth and was sucking on the ends of them. "Um. Can I?"

"Yes, you can, Purple. But only if *you* want to."

"I should say goodbye."

"To whom, Purple? They said goodbye to you a long time ago."

She thought about it quietly for a long time. Kooka just sat and waited for her to come up with her answer.

"Yes."

"Yes?"

"Yes, I want to come. I want to see the ocean of sand."

Kooka smiled and he reached out and very gently patted her on the back. "You're going to love it, Purple. I just know it."

32

GORAN

The black cloud had been creeping closer ever since they had discovered the dead Vrah back at the Tombs. He hadn't felt like talking to Brando much at all. Thankfully the keeper was just as happy saying nothing as he was being a host in the inn that he normally managed.

Goran disliked these feelings, and never understood where they came from. While he could still see normally it was like the outer ring of his vision was shrouded in grey. Inside his head, everything felt negative. It was why he preferred traveling alone.

By now he would have had something to smoke, something to calm himself, to block his thoughts. He always felt better when it passed. Sometimes it was days before he came back to himself, often without any memory of what had passed.

Usually that was for the best, but it was why he had to stay away from his peers when he did it. Now he felt different. It had been so long since he had endured it through the full cycle. He snuck a look at Brando, wishing the man would head off on his own.

"What's up, Goran?"

"What do you mean?"

"You've been quiet for almost two whole days. More than I ever known you, and your face looks darker than the night."

"Nothing's up, Brando."

"Have it your way."

Goran's chest tightened. He was even more conscious of his companion now that he was commenting on his mood.

Just leave me alone, let me deal with this.

But he didn't say it out loud, he just looked ahead, keen to arrive in Union, now that he could see it on the horizon. They had no inn of their own in this city, not yet anyway, which was better for Goran. Less of their own type around him would give him a chance to find some form of relief.

Again he pressed a knuckle on his right hand into his temple until it hurt. The pain gave him something else to focus on and not just his worries.

Thenis help us find this girl and be done with this task.

"I'll leave you to find us somewhere to stay, my head hurts enough as it is, Brando."

"As you wish. I'm tired of sleeping rough, so anywhere with a half decent bed and ale will do for me."

"Agreed."

The keeper sorted them somewhere on the western side of the city, and ensured they had separate rooms, which suited Goran perfectly.

"I'm going to wet my tongue on some ale, I'll be in the main room if you want to join me."

Goran had said he'd rest a while and headed to his room to lie down. Once in there, he fumbled through his bag until he had his pipe and weed in hand, then pushed the window open, and hurried through packing and lighting it.

It didn't take long for the first bite to hit the inside of his head, and he could feel his lips turning up in a grin. The relief felt so good to him, he closed his eyes and let it all soak in.

～

Better, much better!

Zoran stood up and stretched out his body. It felt oddly sore, but he wasn't so sure from what. Soft-head had been riding somewhere or something. It didn't matter at all, he was out and it was evening, only early evening, which meant there was plenty of fun to be had.

Looking down at himself he felt disgusted. He was dirty and had on such plain dull clothing, he'd have no luck finding himself a lady looking like that. *I need to wash and sort meself out, that's what I need.* When he went looking for a washroom he spotted the keeper, Brando, sitting in the main room of this inn.

This ain't his inn though, so where is we? Best I stay away from him, he's never been one for fun.

After cleaning up, Zoran slipped out the back of the inn, and set out looking for somewhere he could enjoy himself. There were always good places to be found, no matter what city you were in. You didn't need to know the place, just the type of people to look for.

After several alehouses that didn't do much for his desires he got lucky in a den that had all sorts of weird and wonderful drinks, but more importantly people who were keen to play the dice. He'd have preferred somewhere with a game of cards, that was his specialty, no matter what game it was.

It only ever took him a hand or two to learn the core of it, and he was able to read people, as easy as the face of their cards. True, his charm was the thing that made it almost too easy, just a suggestion here, a look there, and they would throw in their hand, despite it being good.

Dice weren't quite the same, too much chance, but last time he'd found there was a way he could play people off against each other that still let him win. That's all that mattered — him winning and watching them lose. He loved that.

"Your roll," the grizzly-looking horseman on the other side of the table mumbled.

"How 'bout we make it more interesting, like?" Zoran replied, a smirk on his face.

"More interesting for who? You already taken enough coin, no one else will play with you now."

"They just not up to it, me old mate. Not like you, you're the right challenge you are. How about we double the stakes but on a certain roll?"

The man shook his head, partly rolling his eyes at Zoran. "Go on then, tell me what you mean."

"If the roll is under six, I win, anything else you win. What do you think about that?"

The horseman's eyes lit up at the suggestion. "You gone mad or you up to something?"

Zoran sat suddenly upright. "Don't be calling me mad!"

Concern rushed into the face of the man opposite, which delighted Zoran even more, deep inside. "Sorry, sorry, I'm just saying that's an odd bet."

Zoran relaxed his posture and eyed the man, ready to hook him in. "But you gotta roll, that's the deal. You roll, six or under it's all mine, anything else you get it. That way you can't be blaming me, right?"

"Ha, I've no problem with that, better odds all round." He scooped up the dice and blew on them in his hands, looking at Zoran.

Zoran never took his eyes off the older man and breathed calmly, focusing all his will on him. It wasn't like wishing, or hoping, that the person would respond to his thoughts, Zoran just knew he would. The challenge with dice was that it still took a roll, and you never could fully control the dice, well not that he knew.

Now that would be the thing.

The horseman lowered his hand and rolled the dice, Zoran transferring his eyes to them and seeing the result he wanted. The first die hardly rolled and stopped on a four, funnily enough exactly as he'd seen in his mind. The other bounced around several times, heading for the edge of the table.

He needed the two he had pictured and it was all his. He could see out of the corner of his eye the old man getting excited, his chances were much higher.

The die stopped on an edge, a six showing.

"That's it!" his opponent shouted.

Then the die flipped over that edge onto the two and stopped still.

"What did you do?"

Zoran sensed trouble, and his senses became even more alert. His left hand moved down to the knife in his belt, not unnoticed by the other player

"Wasn't my roll, me old mate, that's what you rolled. You accusing me of something?"

The older man raised his hands palms out. "No, I'm not. Just the shock of it, is all, pal. Looks like Thenis is on your side today, or maybe it's Okiheck. That one, he's always up to no good."

"Luck, me old mate, that's all it was. It was a slim chance, but I'll take it." Zoran picked up his jug of ale and drank it all in one go, letting out a loud belch as he did. "Now let's get all those winnings."

The horseman emptied out his pouch on the table and split what was left in it, in two. He slid one half over to Zoran and put the rest back.

"Too rich for me, traveler, I'm out. Thanks for your company, but don't be looking to play with me again, I know when I'm beat." He stood up and pushed his way through the crowded bar toward the door.

Zoran was very happy. Tonight he'd filled the best part of two pouches with coin, and had a good fill of drink. His head was buzzing just nicely, now all he needed was to find himself the right type of lady to charm and it'd be the perfect night.

He carefully picked at the coins on the table, holding the pouch with his right hand, and dropping the winnings into it. Part way through he stopped, his head beginning to swim. Lying in front of him was a silver coin, higher value than he'd expected for sure, but it wasn't the type that stopped him, it was what was on the face.

His head went all giddy, and he placed his hand down on the table to stabilize himself.

Not now, this is too much fun.

❧

THE FIRST THING HE NOTICED WAS THE SMELL OF SMOKE, THEN ALL THE noise. Last thing Goran could recall he'd been in his room, quietly at the window.

As Goran opened his eyes he saw the crowded alehouse and the table in front of him.

"You alright?"

A serving maid was standing by the table, eyeing up all the coins in front of him.

"Yes, I'm fine."

"You don't look it, let me tell you. You have some sort of turn? I was just asking if you wanted another ale, and you went all funny like in the face."

"I'm fine, I told you!" He wanted her gone. "Here, have a coin for your help but I don't want another drink."

He saw the silver coin with the Jester's face on the table and gasped. Picking up another he gave her that, and she turned, walking away without another word.

His stomach felt in knots, and he wasn't particularly sober, that he did know. Before anyone else paid too much attention to him he put the coins in the pouch and pocketed it. It was then he felt the other pouch, and gently shook his head.

What happened?

Goran wasn't sure if it was the same night, or another. When it happened, he never knew. Sometimes he would lose an hour, other times a week. However long it was, he needed to find his way back to the room he was staying in, and safely.

If he'd taken these winnings off people then there was an equal chance someone would be waiting outside to relive him of them. He stood up, and made sure he had everything he'd come with, which was just a coat, before making his way toward the front door.

Before he stepped outside he detoured and found his way to the back of the venue, and waited a good while before slipping out the back door. No one was out there waiting, and he hurried off, looking for a familiar landmark to guide him back to his inn

33

TILLANDRA

Tillandra hurried through the gates into the capital of Rohumaa. The smell of the ocean had been teasing her for most of the day and now the salty air drew her toward their inn down near the docks.

It took another hour or so to work her way through the crowded streets and all the twists and turns before she was able to find the Three Jolly Whales. The outside of the inn wouldn't attract many fancy travelers — its wooden sidings were bleached and worn, the shutters hung ragged over the second-floor windows, and not a flower nor plant could be seen on the open ground near the entrance.

Tillandra carefully stepped onto the front porch and opened the front door. The door stuck a little in its jamb, all part of the ruse that kept the normal traveler away, and allowed their troupes and couriers a place to stay.

A tall but scarily thin man poked his head around the opening into the main room.

"How can I be helping you, ma'am?"

"Shanty?"

"That's my name, true it is, how do you know it?"

Tillandra was taken aback. She could see the keeper had aged a lot since she'd last seen him, but he truly didn't seem to remember her.

"I've been here before, Shanty. Several times."

"How is it I don't know your name then?"

"It's Tillandra."

"Tillandra. That name rings a bell, sure as them gulls outside will shriek half the day. Where's me manners, come inside."

Shanty shuffled across the hall into the main room. Tillandra followed, wondering how bad his memory loss was.

"Now where have I heard that name before, that's mighty rude of me it is. Especially if you've been Shanty's guest before."

Tillandra held up her ring and showed it to him. "Does this mean anything to you, Shanty?"

It was like a veil was pulled from his eyes. "Tillandra! You're here, so good to see you. You don't need to show me your ring, as if I'd forget you."

She had seen it with many of their elderly, a time when everything either became jumbled together or was simply lost. It saddened her to see him like this, but what annoyed her the most was why hadn't one of their teams alerted them to it?

Most likely they were protecting him. Shanty had always been a favorite on the Circuit. If you stayed too long here, your clothes would become much tighter and you'd not want to leave. Being close to the ocean, there was something about this inn that made everyone feel better.

"How long will you be staying?"

"Only for a few days, Shanty. I don't want to trouble you."

"No trouble. What else would I be doing? It's my role to look after all you lot when you come visit."

He made her some food, and sat while she ate it. On occasion he went back into the kitchen and worked on the meal he was pulling together for the troupes in the city, that would be back when their day's work was done.

Shanty had a few moments where he almost forgot who she was, and she could see his time was up. This wasn't early in the process; he needed to be replaced, the role of managing the inns on the Circuit was too important. Another thing that they needed to resolve.

"I'm beat, Shanty, and I have work to do tomorrow. A bath and a room, and I'll be asleep before you know it."

Watching him climb the stairs and help prepare things for her made Tillandra feel bad. She could take care of this for herself. By the time she'd bathed, her eyes could hardly stay open and she was asleep within minutes.

~

SHE WAS RUNNING THROUGH A DARK FOREST. THE TREES FELT ALIVE AND like they were trying to trap her. Limbs seemed to reach out to grab her as she pushed through, but none were quite able to hold onto her. Tillandra felt like she had been running for hours, her legs were heavy, and her lungs were burning but she couldn't stop moving.

Some of the trees we so big it took her minutes to run around them while others were saplings she could almost run through. She didn't know what it was that was chasing her, but something drove her onwards. Her fear was real, she knew that.

Ahead to her right she heard voices, but only just. They were so soft, she wasn't even sure they were really there. Then she'd hear them again. They sounded like voices she knew, but she couldn't quite reach them. Every few steps she thought she could hear them better but then they seemed to move, sliding sideways or further away. They were like mist you could not grab hold of, slipping out of the grasp of her ears.

A tree seemed to spring up right in front of her and she ran head-long into it.

~

TILLANDRA SAT UP WITH A START, GRUNTING OUT LOUD.

Her room was still dark, and she shook off the dream. She didn't know if it was a dream or a vision.

What had the Lady of the Stone said? Stop fighting the visions, look for the light and the senses.

Tillandra wasn't sure if there was anything about that dream that made it more than a nightmare. And yet it had the hallmarks of one of the visions. If there was a message there, she didn't know what it was.

Her mind was fully awake now and she got up from the bed and stretched out. She could still smell the ocean and took time to appreciate it, something Anderwell could never provide.

Today she would be heading to the library here in Okeans where she'd discovered the first book. If the vision she had was correct there was another book, or maybe even more, that had additional information. She needed to find it, and learn what she could.

It was a simple task, and she'd set aside two days in her mind for it. Once done she could head home, the idea of going to Daskare, to the Carver, made no sense. She needed to get home, and get back to overseeing the college and their work.

By the time the sun came up over the ocean she was itching to get moving, and slipped out without waiting for Shanty to prepare her anything. She was excited and her heart seemed to beat quicker because of it.

The feeling of anticipation was making her feel like a young girl. Tillandra did her best to walk slowly away from the inn and into the city. The city library where she was heading wouldn't open until dawn had passed but she intended to be one of the first there.

On the southern edge of the city only a street back from the wall the Library of Modern History stood surrounded by space on three sides. Behind it, and closest to the wall, the building that backed up to it was the accommodation for historians who maintained the library and all it held.

Tillandra had been here several times, not so often in the last ten years though. In her early years she tried to get here once a year if she could.

After what had happened in Midderbuilt with Ting's books she had hoped that something else might show up here she'd never noticed before. Ideally it would be that easy.

As she made her way toward the grey stone stairs in front of the building one of the wooden doors began to open, its hinges groaning.

An elderly man with only small tufts of silver hair on his head just above his ears was straining to push it open.

As she made her way up the stairs she reached out and helped him with the second one.

"Thank you, my dear. It's not as easy as it once was. Whatever trees these come from must be the hardest wood there is. They weigh more than several men."

"Surely there must be others to help you?"

"Not so much anymore, dear. Our numbers are thinning. Like my hair." His chuckle was weak and half-hearted. "Youngsters aren't interested in the past like they once were."

"To their detriment."

"Well, you'd be a rare one, if you agree with me. Come in, come in. I need to go and set some fires."

"How many librarians are there now, if you don't mind me asking?"

"Only four of us. And I'm not sure how long we'll last. If you want to keep chatting you best walk with me, these fires they won't light themselves."

Tillandra had to slow-step to walk alongside him. They went to three sides of the floor they were on and he stoked or re-lit fires that were there, bringing the heat back into the cool stone building. She knew the fires were to ensure moisture stayed out to protect the books. The building had always had a coolness to it and seemed to attract moisture out of the ocean air. The combination of the fires and the stones seemed to work best to keep the air inside perfect for the library.

"Something about you, dear. You've been here before I think?"

"Many times over the years, but it's been too long since my last visit. The librarian who I saw last time was a woman, Reillian."

"Oh. She passed away several years ago now, sorry dear."

"I'm so sorry."

"No need, she lived her life the way she wanted. She'd have preferred to be a book, I swear. That's what she always said. Then you live on forever." He let out another weak laugh. "Do you need my help?"

"Only if you could point me to the earliest records you have."

"Easy enough. You'll need to go upstairs though. On the southern side in the far corner, there's the beginnings of the works. They move around the floor against the sun until you reach the stairs then come down here and they follow the same path around this floor."

"Thanks again. Sorry, I didn't get your name?"

"Wren."

"Thanks, Wren. I'll let you be."

Tillandra headed to the stairs and went up them to the floor above. The air up here was mustier than down below, most likely due to not having a door or any open windows. There was still residual warmth up here from the day before and she quickly found the section he mentioned.

She stepped back from it and took a few deep breaths before letting her eyes drift over the books, looking for anything that might stand out as different. Like a glow that might highlight what she was meant to find.

The expectation that something would just jump out at her, as Tingfurlew's books had, didn't happen. The shelves all just seemed full of dusty old journals and books, with a few rolled parchments stuffed on top.

Her guess was that the book would be similar to the one she already had, but back then it had been in a section of recently discovered books, not sorted, so she had no idea where its partner would be. Tillandra decided it would be best to start with the very first book and reached for the brown cover.

34

TILLANDRA

othing she opened offered her any insight into the time period she wanted. She randomly pulled books from all over the shelf Wren had told her was the beginning of the collection, but they were all for time periods after the Great Fair of 4100.

The best she came up with was a faded and crumbling map, rolled up and pushed into a corner on top of some books. It was a crude outline of the seven realms and where they lay. She could recall enough of her own maps to see the differences.

Seeing how large the combined Vodotok and Daskare realm would have been and how small Sahro was back then, she was glad to not have just one threatening King below her. Sahro was a significantly smaller realm which had clearly grown with the storm that Tingfurlew had told her about.

She was about to roll it back up when she saw something else that caught her eye. Whoever had drawn this map had carefully included a significant portion of Enderk. It wasn't that which stood out the most but the solid connection between the two land masses.

If she interpreted it correctly, this was what was meant by the land bridge. As drawn, it looked like the land connected all the way across.

Now that is interesting.

Tillandra returned the map to the shelf and wandered about the room looking at other shelves and pulling out books at will in case she had misunderstood Wren as to where everything was. Unfortunately, it seemed she was correctly at the beginning and there was nothing close to what she wanted.

The one book she had found here all those years ago was better than anything here that she could find. Her heart sank. She was sure the vision she had had meant there was another book. Tillandra had trusted that vision but nothing was validating it, she was coming up empty-handed.

She had tried to temper her expectation on the journey to Okeans, but deep down she fostered a hope for new knowledge. Everything was linked to the amulets, but she didn't know how. Whatever they were, meant something.

Her hope was, someone had recorded words that would offer more insight about the world before the Occultation. That they knew nothing from before that time was concerning; there was much that could be learned from the past.

She spent another half an hour or so trying to find anything about events surrounding 4100 or before. In the end she decided this floor would offer her nothing and that her best chance now was downstairs, hoping to find something shelved in the wrong place.

"How's your search going?" She was shaken from her reverie by Wren's voice as she walked out onto the bottom floor.

"Not so good, Wren. I'm struggling to find anything much to help me."

"Oh, I'm sorry to hear that. It can be hard to find things amongst so many old books."

"Yes, that's true. Although I was hoping to find even older books, I'm curious to see the earliest scribes' works."

"Well, there's a lot of history up there that's for sure. Definitely all of the oldest books we have are up there."

"How do you date them?"

"Mostly by the content, sometimes by when we found them."

"Oh?"

"Well truth be told, we don't get time immediately to go through every book, there's so many to classify. Everything upstairs has been classified but some down here I'm still trying to get to. With so few of us now it's becoming harder and harder."

"How often does new material come in?"

"It's very intermittent, dear. We can go a year with nothing, then receive a wagon's load. Though it's rare to get much anymore."

"Why's that?"

"Could be people are hanging on to what they have, or it's being destroyed. Can't say I know. All we can do is look after what we have. While we can."

"You don't share with other libraries?"

"We used to, especially to the south. The Library of History in Bundok used to help, but not anymore. There were others but we're all getting too old."

"Too old for sharing?"

He laughed, weakly. "Traveling, dear. Sharing is easy, but there's too much travel involved, and all the librarians are old like me. I fear soon we'll be an extinct species."

Tillandra had an idea pop into her head, that she'd need to discuss with the others. Perhaps they could put some of their people here, and any other libraries. Spread their historians out into other places, not only for their own benefit but to protect the history.

"What happens when you get new books?"

"Depends on how they come. If it's just a few they end up in the carts over there." He pointed off to the side wall where several wooden carts were loaded high with books.

"What if there's a wagon load?"

"Oh that's different, too hard to carry all of them up the stairs. Back when I was your age I did it a bit, but then we changed that. We have a basement and there's a door on the outside of it. Much easier to load them down that way."

"A basement?"

He looked at her with a glaze across his eyes. Tillandra wasn't quite sure what was happening, but he seemed to go off into his own thoughts for a minute or two.

"What's your name? I'm Wren."

"Yes, Wren, you told me already. I'm Tillandra."

"Oh did I? Silly me, at my age things tend to slip away some times. I'd stop doing this if I could, but there's just no one to help anymore."

"Maybe I can speak to some people, see if there's others that can help?"

"You'd do that, Tillandra? That's your name isn't it?"

"Yes, Wren, you got it right."

"Good, good. I feel better now. What were we talking about?"

"You were telling me about the basement."

"Oh yes, the basement. There's so many books down there that we haven't even got to. When big loads would come in, we'd load them through the trapdoors outside. Then we'd get to them later, or that's what we'd tell ourselves."

"What do you mean?"

"I'm not sure when was the last time anyone went down there to bring books up, dear. Still so many up here in the carts."

Tillandra smiled kindly, she could sense he was going to be repeating himself a lot.

"Maybe I could look in the basement, there might be things for me down there?"

"Where?"

"In the basement."

"It's not very pleasant down there, but there's a lot of books, for sure. They're not unpacked, whatever is down there will be held in the cases we store them in."

"There's a lot then?"

"Yes, it's quite big as a matter of fact. And we have cases down there probably been there twenty years. There used to be no end to the new books that we got delivered here, it was so hard to keep up. Now we're just getting by."

"Perhaps my day didn't turn out so bad after all. I might start down there. I'm guessing I'll probably need a light."

35

TILLANDRA

*W*ren guided Tillandra down the old stairs, pointing out the crumbling edges and missing sections as they went.

"Mind your step, I've taken a tumble here once or twice in the past."

The lantern in his hand shook as he stepped down and Tillandra could see the truth of his age and diminishing function.

"Now why don't you wait here, and I'll go get you some more light. I thought one might be enough, but I don't think it will be."

"Thank you, I'll start looking if you don't mind?"

"Of course, dear. Those chests are full of books." He pointed with his right hand as he held the lantern out to her with his other.

Tillandra wasn't unfamiliar with dark places like this, and she knew that it was smarter to take cautious steps and not rush across what appeared to be empty spaces. She felt nothing strange under her feet as she moved and the light was strong enough for her to see there were no holes or other dangers to avoid.

When she got to the first of the large leather chests that Wren had mentioned she heard the sound and realized that something was wrong. She turned and hurried back to the staircase as another bolt was slid into place above. The door at the top was closed and if the sound she just heard was correct she was now locked down here.

She climbed the staircase to check and even banged on the door to no effect. Wren neither answered her nor opened the door.

How could I have been so stupid?

Tillandra retraced her steps back down to the chest and then set about inspecting the prison she now found herself in. She first wanted to know where she was and what dangers she faced here, before she considered the reasoning behind what had just happened.

She couldn't see what on Dharatan the old man gained from locking her down here. She was no threat to him, and he hadn't shown any recognition of her. Even if he had, this was a bit extreme as punishment for her taking a book from them. Worst of all, there wasn't anyone likely to be looking for her.

Wren had at least been honest about what was stored down in this basement. There were five large chests down here, as well as several shelves that held packages and some books. She doubted the contents of them would be very well maintained given the damp atmosphere of the dark space. A small wobbly table and several stools, clearly not made for Humaas, and other broken or discarded items of furniture lay about the rest of the basement.

There were several candles and she lit one and killed her lantern to conserve it. Several times she heard scurrying feet in the pockets of darkness that the light couldn't reach. Not that critters bothered her, at least there had to be somewhere for them to get in, providing some air if nothing else.

When she opened the first of the chests the rising dust and dank smell caused her to cough and sneeze. There were piles of books, stacked tight into the chest filling it to the lip. The chest itself was lined with some sort of cloth which no doubt absorbed what little moisture might get inside.

She lifted several of the books and reviewed them. The accounts of an estate of some lord, instructions for running a manor house, something that resembled a collection of cooking recipes and the most interesting of them was the words of a bard.

Tillandra didn't exactly know how she could go through all these books without putting them on the floor. She laughed. Here she was concerned about mistreating the books and what the librarians would think, when it was them that had imprisoned her down here.

Her heart sank at what was happening around her. She was still clueless about how to use her skill properly. If any one of them was meant to be in control it should be her, and yet she never was able to get a handle on the visions.

What was she doing wrong? And her leadership of the Jesters network wasn't working out so well either. On her watch King Ahn was looking to invade Sahro, she had lost Ashantha because of her bloody mindedness and belief that her visions were correct, a strange woman was roaming around wearing one of their rings carrying an amulet that was causing harm everywhere it went. And then there was the Derks on Dharatan as well.

She and her colleagues were meant to be the ones on top of what was happening across Dharatan, but Tillandra was beginning to feel like they were losing their grip. Getting information about King Ahn now was good, but they should have known what he was thinking long before it got to this.

Too many of her team were sitting in Anderwell running things. Their best people in one place, when they needed them out in the world, taking control of things.

She slid herself down the nearby wall and slumped to the floor. Things were not going well at all and her lack of faith in her ability was almost choking her. She cradled her head, her self-pity swamping her, and rocked against the wall.

Stop it, Tillandra! No one is coming to get you out of this, it's up to you.

It was true, sobbing on the floor would do nothing to either find the book she'd seen in her vision or get out of the basement. She tried to focus back on what she'd seen, the picture of the book. It was clearly different to most of these books, as was the one she had back in her office.

Where in general many of the book covers were brown, the one back in her study and the ones she'd imagined were black. Even more than that, while the one she had was plain, the one in her vision had a gold inset around the cover. It was quite distinctive.

She leaped up, knowing that instead of just looking at every book she could just move all of those that didn't match, and hunt for the one she'd seen.

While the first of the chests had been easy to open, the second one was much more difficult. The dampness of the room and its likely length of stay down in this basement meant the leather and buckles had fused somewhat.

Tillandra used the task to keep herself busy and had to pull and twist at each strap, finding tiny amounts of give and working on them. The exertion helped her stay focused in the here and now.

When the second buckle finally let go of its grip Tillandra managed to remove the strap with a final tug. Breaking the seal of the lid took more effort and she cursed her lack of tools. She had rarely ever carried a knife and here was a perfect case of one being handy — not only for the work on the cases but her own self-defense.

More dust and old air seeped out of the now open chest, making her sneeze. The smell wasn't pleasant either. The chest contained plenty of books and as she thumbed through them, she saw they were mostly about places in Kysten. Tillandra emptied the chest, placing the books on the floor on the other side of the room.

By the time she had emptied that chest, her arms and back ached. None of the books matched what she sought, and her spirits flagged a little.

The next chest smelled very moldy. Even the feel of the leather was different. She had to wrestle with the straps and when she opened the lid, a different sort of air escaped. Tillandra coughed and found it hard to breathe. She stepped away from the chest and waved her arms frantically to clear the air.

Her coughing continued for several minutes before it began to ease. By the time she'd finished, her chest and throat hurt. It took her another ten minutes before she was game to go back to the chest to see what was inside, this time pulling her tunic up over her mouth and nose. All the effort was wasted.

The books inside were very damp and covered in mold. She didn't try to open any, they were unusable, and if they'd held anything of value it was long gone now. She closed the lid, hoping the mold would stay where it was.

This is pointless.

Without any success her enthusiasm had waned. The smell in the basement seemed much worse from that last chest, and she was feeling thirsty. Something to wash the taste from her mouth would have helped. Out of nothing more than frustration she went back up to the door and banged on it, calling out Wrens name.

No one came, nor had she expected anyone to. Tillandra sat on the bottom step. She knew she needed to figure out how to get out of here, but she wanted to prove herself right. If she was to get a grip on her talent, she needed to know how the visions worked.

What did they mean? The words from the Lady in the Stone came back to her. That she should pay attention for a light or symbol that would shine the way for her. Like when she'd first met Ashantha.

She let her eyes drift over the dark room, trying to sense additional light, as difficult as that was with only two candles burning. Nothing stood out, there was nothing that gleamed or appeared to be colored differently.

She went back across everything and felt it, something she'd ignored on her first pass. It was as if her mind hit a bump when she passed over one of the chests. Like something being dropped and thumping on a surface, or when you had to step up and over something that lay in your way.

Tillandra would have struggled to explain the feeling to anyone else, but if she had to bet on it, that was as good an indicator as any about what she'd been told to look for. She walked over to the chest. The leather was just as worn as the others but it didn't appear damp, which she was thankful for.

The first buckle and strap hadn't taken much to work free, but the second wasn't so easy. It took her what felt like the best part of an hour. She'd lifted part of one of her nails, which stung, and her fingers ached, but finally she broke whatever was sealing the strap in place.

Finally!

Stretching forward, she flipped the lid over and let it thump down behind the chest, standing back in case there was more bad air. This chest wasn't as full as the previous ones; from where she stood it seemed only about half full.

Tillandra picked up the candle and held it inside the chest, and she laughed out loud.

Thank you!

In the pile in the left back corner, the books matched the image in her vision perfectly. There wasn't just one but several books identical in color and style.

36

KOOKA

The squeaking of the axle and wheels, as his cart rolled along the road, was part of Kooka's happy place. He could never have imagined that such simple things would be where he found his greatest peace.

His new recruits were all quiet in the back and he knew some of them were tired of being on the road. Altrab had been with him the longest, all the way from Malamig in the far north. At one stage he had felt like the boy would leap off and leave him, but now it appeared he had just accepted that he was part of the wagon.

They rarely stopped at inns. The reason these individuals were rejected from their own towns and cities was the same reason that no one wanted them around now. Each night they made camp outside a village or town and Kooka would buy food and drink and bring it back for them.

He carried a flute with him and many nights he would play for the group, and for himself. It wasn't unusual for people from the villages to come and listen, often hiding in the bushes near where they camped.

Kooka knew it, but he never minded. Many times, he would find something left for them in the morning. Food, or skins of wine, or even blankets. He didn't care, it meant that someone, in these places, had their heart softened, just a little, for a moment in time. That gave him hope and helped him get over the times when they were chased away.

Most towns let him be as they knew he was doing the work they wanted of him. They just didn't realize he was doing the opposite of what they wanted. Normies thought the children, or even adults he took, were being taken away to die, or be imprisoned.

If that's what they wanted to believe, Kooka let them believe it. The last thing Anderwell needed was people knowing too much about how his world operated.

Purple had touched a raw nerve with him, out of all the nine children he had collected. Maybe it was his old age, or it was related to her condition, but he felt a special connection to her. He didn't understand it, nor let it bother him, but just accepted it.

"Where we heading, Kooka?"

The sound of Altrab's voice from behind him brought him out of his daydream.

"Okeans, Altrab."

"That's the city by the sea you been telling me about?"

"It is, glad to see you remembered."

"How long is it till we get there?"

"Another night or two, if nothing delays us. But I need to check the towns on the way. If we find anyone that needs our help I have to stop."

"I know. I could do with a pee."

"Alright, we've been going for a while and to be honest I'm sick of sitting up here, I'll find us a place to stop and have a break."

Kooka steered the two horses that pulled his large wagon off the compacted road and over some wild grass to a shady spot beside a small running stream.

"How about you lot help water these horses? I think we could wait here for a few hours. I don't know about you but I'm sick of being on this wagon."

Most of his collection weren't talkers. They rarely were when they were first gathered. He knew why, he'd been through it all himself. When you lived rough, or even under the roof of your abusers, you could justify the way you were treated one way or another. 'They didn't understand,' 'It wasn't their fault.' But once you had been in the wagon for a few days and realized you were never going back, all of the hurt surfaced.

Not that any of them fought each other, but he could read the stages of it on their faces. As the denial broke and eventually the grief arrived some cried until their heads hurt, and others when given the chance bashed something.

Purple was still fighting the denial aspect. He could see that if she was able, she'd possibly walk away and try to go back.

"Help each other out, don't be like a normy," he called as they clambered or dropped out of the back of the cart.

Kooka knew that much of what he did was to act like a teacher and a counsellor. He also knew they didn't need to be coddled and they all needed a place, a purpose to hang on to. He had taken away the only connection to staying alive that they had, which was what they called home and family.

The irony wasn't lost on him as he left them all to water and feed the horses and sat beside the stream under the fig tree that draped high over the other side of the water.

Gizen was a prime example. She was blind and as thin as a twig. He had found her near Cuvar, a border town in Morska. She seemed to live part between the southern edge of the great forest and the town. Cuvar was so big she could easily avoid seeing the same people every day, but she struggled to scrape even a meagre living together.

At her age she should be filling out and heading toward womanhood, but she looked like a skeleton and even after the last month or so with him she had only put on a small amount of weight.

Like most of the Broken, those around her in Cuvar treated her as if she was dead already. Kooka couldn't tell if the injuries she carried had been from other people or from her lack of sight and trying to survive.

The other children had almost rejected her as well. She was a solo through and through and she didn't interact with anyone. Kooka had struggled to find a connection with her, but she had come with him nonetheless. It had seemed like it was inevitable to her, or almost that she had expected him, but not that she was pleased.

Kooka hadn't seen her show any form of joy or pleasure from

anything, and that concerned him, deeply. He sipped on a skin of water and let his eyes drift over the plains across the stream. As far as his eyes could see tall grasses bent gently in the breeze. They looked ready for the horse herds to be moved into and the grazing to begin, and no doubt they would come soon enough.

Rohumaa's herds were enormous, and they all fetched healthy prices on the open markets around Dharatan. Days like this were reasons why he didn't want to stop being the Driver. He'd always said he'd do it until he was too old to make it up onto his wagon. He knew what he did mattered, and the open country and all the people he met were a special kind of joy.

The collection had finished caring for the horses and had spread out along the bank of the stream, some in pairs, others on their own. He understood how strange they all felt, but he also knew he couldn't force them upon each other.

He was surprised when he heard Gizen behind him. He had fashioned a stick for her from a long branch. It wasn't a cane for helping her walk, but she could sweep it in front of her and avoid bumping into things. The sound it made as she dragged it from side to side was unmistakable.

Kooka waited. Her stick brushed up against his back and she then moved to his right before dropping down near him. She laid her stick beside her right leg and faced toward the stream as if she was admiring the view like him.

She sat in silence for minutes and Kooka let her. He didn't have the key to unlock her and wasn't sure if there was one to be found. It didn't really matter; his job was to protect, and he would protect her the best he could.

"Kooka?"

He turned to look at her, "Yes, Gizen?"

"Who is the lady?"

"What lady?"

"The tall lady with the twisted face."

Kooka was surprised by her question. This was the first open conversation they had had since he had found her, and even that had been more about him talking than a conversation.

"I'm not sure I understand, Gizen. Have you been dreaming of something?"

"Yes."

"Is it when you sleep at night?"

"I don't sleep at night."

"You don't? I see you lie down with everyone else."

"I do that because that's what people do. I never sleep though."

"Never?"

"No. I cannot remember sleeping. I trance but I'm still awake."

"Trance?"

"Um... I close my eyes and focus on the dark, and then I see things."

"What sort of things?"

"Sometimes just pictures of things - or what I think must be things - what things look like. Other times of people."

"And this is one of those people dreams?"

"Yes. I saw you coming."

"What do you mean?"

"When you found me, I was there on purpose. I saw you days before, coming with the wagon, and I just knew I had to wait there for you."

Kooka scratched his grey beard, which was as wide as his mouth but twice as long as his nose, which wasn't short compared to many. "Now that, Gizen, is very interesting. Back to this lady, can you tell me more? This could be important."

"She's very tall. Tall like a big tree. She has the box of books, lots of books. But her face, it's all twisted like someone broke it."

"Is there anything else you can tell me about it?"

"She wears a ring, with a face on it? It's strange, it's not a real face, but like a ..., I'm unsure what you would call it. Something you cover your face with to look different."

"A mask?"

"Yes, a mask. And it has a hat, with two sides."

"I think I know what you mean, I have seen this ring."

"She is trapped."

"Her face, is it like it has all been twisted off to the side?"

"Yes. Do you know her?"

"I do, it's the person who looks after us all. It's important, Gizen. What do you mean she is trapped?"

"She is underground, and the door is locked. She cannot get out and she has found these books. She's very excited about them, but she's stuck where she is."

"Do you know where, Gizen?" Kooka's heart had picked up and he was very concerned now for the woman he knew to be Tillandra.

"Underground. Somewhere that way." She pointed south the way they were heading. "A city. Many buildings but I cannot tell where."

"You've done well, Gizen. We might be able to help her with what you've told me. Let's get the others, we need to hurry."

37

KARPENMOR

*I*t was as if his whole body itched but from under the skin not outside it. Karpenmor felt like he was losing his mind.

Maybe it's true, I will go as crazy as my father.

He paced around the open balcony, trying to distract himself, but nothing would stop the feeling. He needed a drink, it was that simple. Over the last two weeks he'd been trying to stop them. He wasn't even sure why, but he had an urge to stop them.

That was easier said than done. He could last three days before this started. Sometimes it came in two, but he hadn't made it past three. He always gave in at three. What was worse was that in the first two days his head was clear, clearer than ever.

But once the itching started he couldn't think straight. It was too much. Whatever was in the drink, his body liked it, he needed it. He wasn't even sure why he was fighting it. He just needed a drink.

Just to ease my nerves. To stop this cursed itching.

He knew it wouldn't be that simple and now there was far too much that he needed to think on. Every day there was some minor crisis or piece of knowledge he needed to understand. Uksod was able to make decisions simply from the weight of experience and knowledge that came with it.

Many saw the young Regent as an opportunity to better their situation and tried to manipulate him. His lack of care for their aspirations was one thing that saved him from simply acquiescing to requests.

In all honesty he had little desire to rule these people. In the short time he had fulfilled the role, he had quickly realized why Uksod held many in contempt. At first, he thought it was Uksod's arrogance.

Karpenmor was fully aware of the man's arrogance, and previously cared little about it. Now the arrogance only bothered him if directed toward him. He had quickly learned to swallow his feelings about it while he learned what he could from the man.

He was torn between being thankful to Uksod for bringing him up and ensuring his safety, and a dislike at the way he had been conceived. At night when he was alone the anger about it came out. His blood seemed to boil, and he festered on the thoughts. It was a strange set of feelings and Karpenmor truly didn't understand them.

Part of him wanted to be kind to the man and the other parts wanted to remove him from any form of power. Deep down, Karpenmor didn't fully trust *his Eminence*.

The sun was close to dropping behind the western range and soon the Great Field would be dark. From his balcony high in the palace, he could look past the city and its walls and see the great square space that lay within the surrounding mountains.

He often stared out at the open area, wondering if it had been man-made or not. The mountains ran north to south with the Gharbi Pass breaking the range on the western side. More mountains lined the northern side to form the far wall. On the eastern side they were broken by the Alshar Pass that was almost in line with the city.

En Carta itself backed up to the rear wall of the mountains, which were over a hundred miles deep before they met the ocean. Karpenmor didn't know enough about Enderk, something else that had been itching inside him over the last few weeks.

Then there was the pendant with the blue stone his father had sent him. He'd tried to find the servant, Hurf, but he had left the palace and no one knew where he was. If he had gone back to his family home he was far from the city now.

Surely the man must have known more? The note was incomplete, and Karpenmor needed more answers. Was it that pendant that made him feel like this? Ever since he'd received it he'd started getting the craziness in his head.

If it was craziness? But it was like a voice, or a compulsion. And it was trying to stop him drinking the brandy. Was it the pendant also influencing how he felt toward the priest?

What was causing him the most discomfort were his thoughts about Schevenal, his father. The sadness had not left him since he'd received the note. It had almost become overwhelming when he thought about it. Which was why he thought about taking the amber drink again.

He turned to the west and looked at the wall of mountains that lay before him, through which lay the path to Dharatan. While he knew that whoever was responsible was long since dead, he held a growing animosity to the entire continent.

There had always been an us and them mentality that he had learned growing up. It never meant much to him, but now, even he felt it, and the more he learned about their past the more it bothered him. Enderk was isolated and treated with contempt by the barbarians in Dharatan.

Perhaps that was what his father had meant, about being better than him. If Schevenal didn't have the stomach to be ruthless toward others, maybe he brought his demise on himself, and punished them all in the process.

Karpenmor could be better than that. If that's what he meant, he'd happily turn the tables, and get revenge. He needed to learn more. Perhaps the Vrah library would hold more useful information about those across the water?

It was time he started to learn more about Enderk, corner to corner. An idea formed in his mind which he played with as he watched twilight fall over En Carta. He faced back to the north and watched the twinkling lights throughout the city as street lamps were lit, or residents lit lanterns in rooms with open windows.

And what about Uksod? He walked back into his room and closed the balcony doors. The priest knew much and was being rewarded with his long life by Yantarnaya. Karpenmor wondered what it was Uksod gave the goddess in return, or what she wanted from himself.

Uksod had said the Amber Room was where she could speak to you. Why had she not spoken to him? He had always felt alone in there, even with his father. Was that the feeling of being watched he'd sensed whenever he was in there? Maybe it was time to find out.

He drank a glass of wine from a jug which servants had left on the sitting table near his preferred chair and gathered his will. When he felt he was composed enough he left his room and walked through the palace corridors toward the Amber Room. Just the thought of the place made him shiver but it was time to go back in there.

Behind him two Vrah walked as silently as only they could. He didn't need to hear them to know they were there. Previously it had only been one who would follow him inside the complex, but now he was ruler it was always two.

As he stood before the ornate doors, etched with gold leaf and embedded with amber and other jewels, blue, green and red, Karpenmor took a deep breath. He pushed the door open and stepped inside. Like his own quarters this was one place the guards would never follow.

With the doors closed he looked around, soaking in the orange light. Everything was either rich wood, gold or amber. From ceiling to floor the most intricate of patterns were carved and layered. Even the lanterns were made with gold with embedded amber inside them so the light they emitted had an orange tinge to it.

The room had been emptied of his father's things, the bed and chairs where Karpenmor had always sat with him were gone. He felt sad, everything about the man was erased now. Like he had never been there in the first place.

Sadness, is that necessary?

"Who is that?"

"You don't have to speak out loud, Karpenmor, you can simply think at me."

"At who?"

"Do you need to ask?"

Karpenmor stayed silent. The interaction made him feel strange, as if the craziness was actually with him.

"You are not crazy."

"Now you can read my mind?"

"In a way, while you are in here at least."

"What does that mean?"

"Like I said, in here, I can sense your thoughts. Why are you sad?"

"Father, he's no longer here. That's why."

"But when he was he didn't even know you were there."

Karpenmor reached into his pocket and felt the stone in there. He tried to not think about the note or it, but he couldn't. He released it after a moment.

"You went away? How strange."

"What do you mean?"

"It was like you were not in the room. I could sense you there, but not your mind."

Karpenmor shrugged.

"I would have liked to have known my father, he was all I had."

"That is not true."

"What do you mean?"

She didn't answer for a few moments.

"Look around you, Karpenmor. You are now the ruler of an entire nation, a great nation. You can do anything you want; have anyone you want. And you have Uksod. And me."

Karpenmor felt uncomfortable at the way she said the last of it. There was almost a smirk in her voice.

"But he was my father. He's all I had of my family."

"Family, family. All people seem to worry about is family. Most of the families out in your city, Karpenmor, fight and hate each other. Many have become so estranged that they never talk to each other. You don't need a family like that when you have a family of hundreds, thousands even."

"Who?"

"All your servants, the Vrah, and more than that, your subjects. They span this mighty nation. Maybe it's time you saw how big your family is, instead of pining for an empty old man."

"Don't say that. He's still my father."

Karpenmor felt her sigh.

"*Was, Karpenmor. He's dead now. You can be sad all you want but it won't bring him back.*"

"Why did you keep him alive?"

"*He lived of his own accord, Karpenmor. It wasn't me, not directly. While he was in this room, he had enough sustenance to live, outside of it he couldn't.*"

"Why would he want to live like he did?"

"*I do not know. His mind was empty to me, but he gave you to us, Karpenmor. That is good. Good for us all.*"

"I don't know why. This all seems pointless, why did you even have me born?"

She was quiet for some time and Karpenmor thought she had left him.

"*Not gone, Karpenmor, just thinking. I'll strike a deal with you. Get your amulet back, and I'll tell you more. I want it back, Karpenmor, all of them!*"

Her voice had changed, and Karpenmor noticed she wasn't really asking. It was more a command than anything else. She said nothing more, and he put his hand into his pocket and held the pendant. He didn't want her to know he'd become uncomfortable with her presence.

He turned and left her presence, hurrying back to his room. He at least had answers as to why he'd never liked the Amber Room. He doubted he'd be back in there anytime soon. More importantly he also knew who the voice was that took over him when he drank the amber brandy. It was her.

38

TILLANDRA

She couldn't believe it, fully. As much as Tillandra ached to understand her visions, she still doubted herself more than the opposite. But it worked, she'd found what she had seen. As much as the books had made her heart jump, what had just happened was important.

Looking down into the chest she picked up the top black book and sat down to look through it. She held her breath and opened it. The words on the page, if they were words, looked like scribble; they were a mash of letters, if they ever were letters, and made no sense.

Tillandra turned more pages, flicked to the back of the book and started going backward before randomly selecting pages. Every page within it was the same. Whatever it was written in she couldn't read it. It was writing, there was a pattern to it, and it had structure, just not one she was familiar with.

Frustrated, she put it down and went to the next on the pile. There were ten of them, and every one of them was the same. Nothing in them was readable, even the drawings seemed strange, like they were all mixed up. She couldn't interpret anything she saw.

She sat down again and stared at the pile now standing at her feet.

All of the excitement she had felt had gone. Now she felt as useless as she had before she'd found the books. They offered her nothing. All of the effort to get here, being stuck in this basement, none of it was worth anything.

Tillandra was beginning to feel very tired. She had been down here long enough and wanted out but had no clue how to make her escape. She needed food, drink and fresh air. She still felt a little queasy from the air she'd inhaled earlier but there was nothing she could do.

In the end she made a place she could wedge into against one of the chests and the wall and tried to sleep as best she could. On and off for several hours she dozed, waking with a start each time her consciousness came back to the room. She had no idea if it was still night or the next day as there was no light from outside down here.

While she lay still, she sensed something sniffing around her feet. If she was right, it was a rat and she remained frozen, letting the creature build up a false sense of courage. It took time but it moved over her lower leg and started to cautiously sniff its way up her calf.

Tillandra's reflexes were still very sharp, and her extra-long arms gave the rodent no chance to escape. She snatched out at it and dragged it in. At least now she could talk to someone, if nothing else. While darkness never bothered her, being down in this basement, trapped and defeated, was causing her to feel extremely anxious.

She held the rat firmly in both hands, knowing it would calm once she tapped into it. With years of practice, she was able to drop into the Void quickly and waited for Junther to respond.

When he arrived at the space her conscious was in, she spoke first. "In All Jest, Junther."

"Mother. In All Jest, what fortuitous timing."

"How so?"

"All manner of things, Mother. But I'm in the map room with Toolet. She was quite animated about something and made me come and see."

"What is it?"

"We're not entirely sure. But... the other ring seems to have changed into a coin."

Tillandra was fully awake now. "What do you mean?"

"There's a purple light now, not two blue ones."

"Where?"

"If our guess is right, somewhere below Diwedd, on the River Roilaren."

"It's moving?"

"Yes."

Tillandra was feeling concerned now. "What did Goran say?"

"We haven't been able to reach him."

"What do you mean? That's not good."

"We've both tried, but he's not responding. It's like he's there, but not. That didn't come out right, but I just can't reach him."

"I think I know what you mean, I've had that happen before. So it's her then?"

"It must be. What we wanted your opinion on was whether it means... whether she's dead?"

"Dead?"

"Think about it, Mother. The light only turns purple once one of us dies and the ring changes into the coin. That lets them find their way back to Tingfurlew. Logic would say that's true here as well."

"Logic would say she shouldn't have been wearing it in the first place!" Tillandra snapped back. "Sorry, that wasn't called for."

"Are you okay?"

"Well, things are complicated."

"How so?"

"I've been locked in a basement under the library here. I'm still a little confused by what happened. It seems the librarian has locked me down here, and no one has come to let me out."

"By accident?"

"I don't think so, he'd only just left me to go get extra light when I heard the door being bolted."

"This will not do. We'll have to get you out of there."

"How exactly, Junther? There's no one within weeks of here, I'll have to find my own way out."

"Or?"

"Or you'll know where to find my things if you get another purple light."

"That's horrible, don't say that. Oh Thenis!"

Tillandra chuckled. "Don't stress yourself, Junther."

"You're taking it rather well, all things considered."

"I'm not ready to check out just yet, and there's plenty of time before I need to be worried about not making it. Besides, a rat has just offered itself up for my meal."

"Ewww, that's disgusting."

"It is what it is. What else have you gathered?"

"The situation is resolved in Watersend, and there's troops of ours moving down to the border. I think the new chap, Huster, is working well with Gimbden, they seem to be hurrying to put measures in place to protect the southern borders."

"Good. Talk it through amongst yourselves but it's probably time Gimbden went to a real posting."

"Such as?"

"Maybe Bundok, we clearly need to get more insight into what's happening in King Ahn's palace."

"Isn't that risky?"

"Why?"

"His face is known, that envoy you met, he'd recognize him in an instant."

"You're assuming that man spends much time near the King. He could be getting his instructions further down the line. But even so, Gimbden could spin that in his favor. Once Pravat was thrown out, he was also let go, and has lots of knowledge to share."

"Interesting idea. Still very dangerous."

"Having the King lining up his knights to invade Sahro is dangerous too. There's lots that's dangerous, but we're behind on news. We need to be back on top of things."

"Agreed."

"On that note, maybe Orwarn should be here, in Okeans."

"Why's that?"

"I think the Skarians aren't just looking at Sahro, there's a compound we'd heard about being built on the outskirts, which looks much more like a fortress to me. They're calling it a church, but there's knights there too, and it would be a handy way to set up bases, start moving soldiers into a church compound."

"That's concerning."

"I doubt Queen Marchier is seeing what I saw, it was only by chance I looked in a little more detail, and knowing what we know about his other movements, this seems a little too coincidental. Having someone closer to things here in Okeans would be much more useful."

"What of his current role?"

"Is it bearing much fruit? It's good to have people in place, but we need them where we can influence what's happening. The alternative is one of you."

Junther didn't reply.

"Then there's the numbers issue."

"What do you mean?"

"The Audition. If the ring has changed it means the clock has started, I have no choice but to get to the Carver. I have to get a mask, and somehow get to Tingfurlew and back in time."

"Didn't we say that was too dangerous a journey right now? You'd be heading right into Ahn's hands."

"I don't have a choice, Junther. No one else can do it, and we're not losing one of us, just because he's got his mind set on taking control of Watersend for his profit."

"Is that what you think it's all about?"

"Mostly…" She paused.

"What is it?"

Tillandra could feel the animal in her grasp was almost used up, she had little time left.

"A feeling, I can't explain, but maybe they're seeking the Citadel Stone."

"Sweet Seth, how on Dharatan?"

"I don't know, Junther, but you need to make sure they don't get across the border. I need to get out of this basement and get moving."

"I feel helpless, Mother."

"Don't we all right now?"

He faded from her view and she returned to the dark room. The foul taste from earlier was now mixed in with full nausea from using the animal. Tillandra crawled across the floor and slung the limp creature into the dark. Her stomach reacted and emptied what little it held.

When she had finished vomiting, she crawled back to her resting spot and drifted off into a restless sleep.

39

LEO

A week had passed and Leo was none the wiser about what he was meant to be doing. Every day he turned up to train with Sabant and Aakesh. And they treated him with the contempt he was used to in the outside world, but was probably deserving of here too.

They were much older than him, and had been students in Anderwell for a long time. Sabant was somewhere in her teenage years, so he wasn't going to ask her, it would give her too much pleasure to taunt him with something she knew he didn't.

Aakesh was twenty-one. The man had nothing to hide from Leo, and was the easiest to talk to, but both were suspicious of why he was now a Prospect.

"Another day, Leo, another day without any magic from you. How unsurprising." The drawling voice of Aakesh grated on him.

Leo had no idea what he was supposed to do, he had no magic. There was nothing special about him at all. He was tiny, only as strong as his wits allowed him to be, and well used to being kicked around by normies.

He was smart, even he knew that. But that was it. Smart wasn't magic, it just was. He'd tried to talk to Toolet about it, and she'd brushed him off.

"If I knew the answer to it, Peggle, I'd give it to you, but magic presents when it presents. It's there, I can sense it in you. Now it's up to you."

That was about as helpful as telling him there's water in the desert if you know where to look, now go look. He was beginning to think she was making fun of him, and using him to unsettle the others. Overnight he'd lie in his bed, planning to leave again.

But a tiny part of him wanted to believe it was true. He'd always wanted to be considered special. In a good way.

What if I am?

"So what's it going to be do you think, Sabant? Perhaps he'll be able to grow tall when he gets angry," the man laughed.

"Leave him be, why waste your breath? He'd just want to make sure he doesn't take up the mask first, or it won't matter."

"What mask?" Leo was back to caring what was being said.

"You don't know?" she asked with a condescending tone in her voice.

"Clearly, or I wouldn't have asked."

"Do you know anything about the Audition?"

"No, as I've said all week. I don't even know what being a Prospect means."

"A Prospect is one of the people that are allowed to do the Audition. Miss Toolet told you that when they have to replace one of the Court, they do that. The mask is part of the Audition."

"So you put a mask on, big deal."

"It is a big deal! The mask chooses you or it doesn't. If it doesn't you end up in the care facility at the other end of the college."

"Care facility?"

"Yes, where all the crazies are."

"Why, what does it do?"

"Wipes your mind, or so we were told."

"What on Dharatan would make you want to do that?"

"No one wants to do that, Leo. But you have to, if you want to become a member of the Court."

"That's stupid. I'm not doing that."

"Then why are you a Prospect?"

"You tell me, because I don't know. No one can tell me why. I'm not doing it, doesn't matter what anyone says, how stupid would you have to be?"

A door to the room swung open and one of the male teachers walked in. Leo didn't know his name, but before he could ask, the man spoke: "Too much noise going on in here. I want silence. You're meant to be training on the Kabel, so let's get to it."

The other two got up and walked over to the short ladder across the room. It led up to a small platform, with a thin rope of some sort attached to it linked across thirty or so feet to a copy of itself and another ladder.

"You too, Peggle. Stop moping about over there."

"But…"

"I said silence, and I mean it. Get over there."

Leo reluctantly walked over there, and watched as Sabant took the lead.

The girl had clearly practiced it a lot and after preparing herself, walked confidently across the rope. Now that he was close, Leo could see it was very thin, and yet didn't seem to bow under her weight at all. As she reached the midpoint she faltered and fell, letting out a cry as she landed hard on her knee.

There was no soft landing below, and Leo's lack of care for heights was now making him very anxious. He'd have normally laughed at her fall, but he was more worried about his own turn. His hands were sweating profusely and he wiped them on his tights.

Aakesh made light work of it, reaching the other side, without much concern at all. Sabant had recovered and stood behind him. Leo felt her hand in his back pushing him forward. He hardly moved as this wasn't something he wanted to do.

He didn't want to walk on anything high, especially not something thinner than his finger. Nor did he want to be a stupid Prospect, or wipe his mind with some mask. This was stupid, and he wasn't having any part of it.

"*Get up, Peggle!* Stop being a coward and walk it."

Anger boiled inside him. He wanted so throw something at the teacher, but he had nothing to throw. Slowly he walked up and climbed the ladder, and stood on the platform. He could hear the quietest of sniggers from below.

He didn't look but guessed it was Sabant, she was so annoying. Leo knew he was going to fall, that was obvious, he'd never done anything like this before, so it was ridiculous for them to make him do it now.

"*Now*, Peggle, are you scared? It's only a few feet up, you won't die."

Something flicked in his head, he wasn't sure what, but it was like a cord broke. Or a latch clicked. He went all dizzy and he could have sworn he was wobbling on the platform, about to fall off that. He expected someone to run over and catch him before he did.

Or he hoped, but no one did, and then he straightened up. Something felt very odd, and he must have dropped to his knees, because the rope was right in front of his nose. His nose was very twitchy for some reason, but he looked at the rope.

He could crawl across the rope, they hadn't said he couldn't. He just had to cross it, that's what they had said. So he did. Leo was extremely surprised how easy it was. He didn't even hardly wobble, just one foot in front of the other.

Something about his feet bothered him, but he couldn't figure out what it was. And what was that smell? Eww, it was bad whatever it was, coming down from behind him. Like Sabant and Aakesh needed to bathe.

How strange.

And then he was over and he went to stand up to celebrate, except he couldn't. He was already standing, but on....

That feeling happened again, his head went all dizzy and he heard that snapping sound. It seemed much louder now, and made his ears hurt, and then everything seemed normal, and the smell had gone.

He stood up, and looked down at the ground, and wobbled.

"Peggle, are you all right?"

"I... I think so."

He dropped to his knees, not wanting to look over the edge again and backed his way down the ladder.

"Well aren't you the surprise then, Peggle?" The teacher's eyes were wide open and he had a grin on his face.

"Doesn't surprise me he was a rat!" Sabant seemed quite put out about him.

"What are you all going on about?"

"Couldn't you tell, Peggle?"

"Tell what? I crossed it didn't I?"

"You did, sure as I witnessed, Leo. But not quite as expected."

"What do you mean?"

"Well, if you didn't know, it's best I just tell you. You turned into a rat, and walked across."

"I did what?"

Then it all clicked into place for Leo. He could see the rope just in front of his nose, his twitching nose... And then he passed out, and fell backward.

KOOKA

Normally he wouldn't spend much time inside a city with his wagon full. Typically, Kooka would stay on the outside of the city and do day trips in to speak to whomever it was he needed to see, or to hunt for any candidates for the Fool's Cart.

If Tillandra truly was in trouble then he had a duty to seek her out, full cart or not. His biggest issue was getting into the city. The guards on the northern gates had initially not wanted to let him past but with a bit of wrangling, and a contribution to their drinking fund, he managed to get through the gates. Now he needed to locate Tillandra without causing a fuss.

Okeans spread out from the ocean docks in the east, along the riverbanks that ran from Jarv, and was as big as any city he had visited. Its original walls had been moved several times in his lifetime and if you were a stone mason you had pretty much a full-time job here just working the walls.

The inn he wanted was closer to the docks than anywhere else in the city, and the lane it was on was only just wide enough for his cart to fit down. He went inside to learn what he could.

"Hello, young man." Kooka could see the keeper Shanty shuffling through from the back of the inn, noticing how much he seemed to have aged since he was last here.

"Shanty, how are you?"

"You know my name, how's that then?"

Kooka didn't have time to play any games. "What are you playing at, Shanty?"

"Playing, I'm not playing at anything. Have we met?"

"Several times, you don't remember?"

The man got agitated. "How am I supposed to remember everyone I ever see? No, I don't remember you."

"My name's Kooka." He could see that the man was more than just old, and he felt sad for him. He really couldn't remember.

"I'd remember that, fellow, that's a very unique name. You need a room?"

"No, Shanty. I'm looking for someone, I wanted to know if they had been to see you."

"Who's that then?"

"Tillandra, do you know her?"

"Of course I know her. You know her too, do you?"

"I do, Shanty. Is she in Okeans?"

The old man's eyes seemed to glaze over a little and he rubbed the side of his head. "Not that I know of, no."

"She's not been here at all?"

"I don't think so, son. Although sometimes it gets hard to remember, not as good as I used to be. But I'd remember her, I would."

"Okay, that's all I was after. I'll keep on my way then."

"Right you are."

Kooka went back out to the lane. He didn't want to attract attention to his wards, and the longer they stayed out in the open, that's exactly what would happen.

He asked Gizen to come sit with him on the bench at the front of the wagon while he steered the horses northward.

"Any chance you have anything else to guide me with?"

She said nothing but he saw her shake her head. Kooka kept moving, hoping he'd come up with a decent idea or something would lead him to Mother.

"I would know it if I was near it."

He turned to look at Gizen. "What do you mean?"

"I can't tell you how to get there, but I would know the building if we passed it."

"So, you know what it looks like?"

"Somewhat. More I know how it feels. I would feel it."

Kooka wasn't entirely sure he understood what she meant. All he could do was drive around and hope she could tell him what it was she was describing.

"No."

"No, what?"

"This is the wrong way."

"How do you mean, Gizen?"

"It feels colder. I don't know but cold seems wrong."

"Okay, I'll change direction." Kooka was more intrigued than he was annoyed at her. She had as much chance as anyone at guiding him, but what interested him was how little she knew about her skill. He was even more glad she was with him and heading to Anderwell.

"Yes, this is better," she said a few minutes later once they'd moved in a different direction.

"Do you think you'll be able to feel it out better using the temperature?"

"I'm not sure."

They traveled back toward the middle of the city and in the direction of the river that ran outside the southern wall. Kooka changed direction only a little when he had to divert around closed paths.

"That way," Gizen called out and pointed to their left. "It's much warmer - closer."

They had entered an older part of the city and Kooka could see several large historic buildings surrounded by small parks and outdoor spaces.

"There." Gizen pointed to his right. The building was tall like she had said, and stairs led up to the entrance.

It looked to Kooka like a library or school of some sort. While he couldn't understand why it would be that Tillandra would be trapped in there, he had nothing else to go on. He pulled the wagon over and handed the reins to Gizen.

"Just hold them still, don't do anything with them and the horses will do nothing. I'll go inside and see if anyone knows about Tillandra."

"She's here. I can tell."

Kooka smiled, not that she could see it. "Thanks, Gizen. Let's hope I can find her."

"Just go to the basement."

"Yes. But first I have to find out who runs this place. I'll be back soon. Just hold those reins firm but don't do anything with them."

"So you already said." Despite the attitude in her voice, she clutched onto them like they were the most important thing in her life.

When he climbed down, Kooka went around the horses and hobbled them, nonetheless. He couldn't afford someone spooking Gizen and for the cart to take off without him. He would have tied it up to something, but this was quite an unusual place for him to stop.

"And don't let the rest of them leave here. This is no place for them to be wandering around."

At the top of the stairs, he found one of the two doors open and stepped inside.

"We're almost closed, young man." Kooka could see the man looking at his cane and the stump under his leg.

"I hope not to take too much of your time then."

"Good, because my time is precious. What do you need?"

"I'm looking for a friend."

"I don't need any friends."

Kooka smiled at the doddery old man. "No. I don't mean I need a new friend; I mean I am looking for a friend of mine that I think came here."

"Not many people come here, young man. Dusty old books are all we have. Mind you, we did have a new visitor some days ago. Lovely young lady she was. Upped and left in a hurry she did, never even said goodbye."

"How young?"

"Young, like you."

"What did she look like?"

"I'm not going to tell you everything about her, I don't know if I can trust you."

"Trust me? I'm looking for someone I can't find."

"Why don't you tell me then?"

"Tell you what?"

"What she looks like."

"How would I know what your visitor looks like, if I wasn't here?"

"No, fool. What does your friend look like, then I can tell you if she was the same person?"

"Right. She's tall, Humaas tall…"

The old man interrupted him. "All of us Humaas are tall. Speaking of which, where are you from?"

"Elsewhere, let's stick with my friend."

"Okay, what's her name?"

"Tillandra. She has a distinctive scar on her face."

"Oh really?"

"Yes, almost as if half of her face is twisted sideways."

"How horrid. Now you come to mention it, this visitor, she had a shawl on, covering a lot of her face. But there was some sort of scar, running from her eye. Maybe they were the same."

"When did you say she was here?"

"Oh…" He rubbed his hand up from his chin and over his eyes as he thought about it. "A couple of days, youngster. At least. I'm sure. Very rude she was."

"How so?"

"She was all pleasant to me, and I offered to help her. I gave her access to some of our older books and then she just left without even a word."

"On that same day?"

"Yes!" He seemed to be getting impatient with Kooka.

"Do you mind if I ask where these older books were exactly?"

"I do mind, you're very nosey. I don't like all these questions."

Another older gentleman, not quite as tall as the one Kooka was talking to, wandered into the main hall. "What's the problem, Wren? Why are you getting so upset?"

The man he had been speaking to, Wren, waved his arms indicating Kooka. "This young man, he's asking me all these questions about the visitor we had the other day."

"What visitor?"

"I told you. I'm sure I told you."

"I'd remember if we had a visitor, Wren. You didn't tell me about anyone."

"I did, Hepold. I did."

"I think I'd remember."

"You forget everything, Hepold. I told you. Don't you remember me telling you that I showed her down into the basement to look at all the old books?"

"I'd certainly remember that, Wren. You never told me a word of it."

Wren was getting visibly agitated. "I can't believe you'd forget. Fancy blaming me that I never told you."

Kooka couldn't believe what he was watching. It was almost comical if it hadn't been for the urgency of what he needed to know. He was just about to ask about the basement when Hepold started back at Wren.

"When was this, Wren? When did you let someone down in the basement?"

"I already told you. Days ago. Maybe two. I told you it was very rude of her to go down there and then never say goodbye when she left. I don't even know if she found anything useful. Rude, you young people are so rude." He had squared back onto Kooka now.

"Oh lord, Thenis. You didn't."

"What?" Wren exclaimed.

"You never told me." Hepold turned and started hurrying away.

"What's wrong, Hepold?"

"I locked and bolted the door two days ago, thinking you'd left it open by mistake. Like you always do. What have I done?"

Kooka hurried past Wren who was still working out exactly what he'd just heard and caught up with Hepold.

"Here, help me with these bolts."

Kooka flung the door open once they were free. "Tillandra! Tillandra, are you there?"

He heard the sound of feet shuffling down in the dark. "Who is that?"

"It's Kooka, Mother. Are you alright?"

"Oh thank Thenis. How did you…?"

She stopped as she saw Wren coming up behind Kooka. "Watch out!"

Kooka turned sharply and saw Wren and turned back to Tillandra who had halted at the bottom of the stairs. "What's the matter?"

"He locked me in here, he's not what he seems."

Hepold cleared his throat. "Tillandra, is it? There appears to be a mistake made, I'm sorry." He coughed into his hand. "It seems I locked the door on you thinking Wren had left it open by mistake, and he never told me he had let anyone down."

"I told you, Hepold. I did!"

"It's okay, Wren. Never mind." He turned back to Tillandra. "It's safe to come up, dear. I am ever so sorry. You must be starving."

Tillandra had the most confused look on her face that Kooka had ever seen, but she cautiously climbed the stairs. Her hands and face were covered in soot and dirt, and her lips looked dry and cracked.

"You alright?" he asked her.

"I am now, Kooka. I am now. But I'm very interested in how on Dharatan you knew I was here."

41

LANI

*L*ani had felt mixed emotions about losing the ring. She had worn it from almost the very beginning, and had formed an attachment to it, even though she was glad it was off. That it had turned into a coin in the seer's hand confirmed that everything to do with Ashantha and his jesters was unnatural.

It was one less thing she had to worry about, and she had only wished the strange man could have freed her from the amulet as well. She wasn't sure exactly what she would do if that happened. There would be little reason to push on, she could leave it somewhere, and dump the mask and journal, and be free.

Free to do what?

The more she thought about it, the more she knew Barnen wasn't an option. Kyro had followed her, which meant they knew she was involved, or blamed her for what had happened. Even without him the guards up there wouldn't be kind. Especially if they blamed her.

That meant she would need to start new somewhere else. She had coin, at least for a while, but she would need to find work, and set herself up somehow. Maybe she could start her own clothier business, not that she really knew how.

It was all just fancy daydreaming. Whether she liked it or not, heading south was only the option she had. It wasn't a choice, no matter what The Eyes had said.

I have no choice.

Despite how she felt, Lani had made sure to spend the jester's coin in Union before she left. It was a small thing to her, but leaving that behind at least felt like a choice she could make. It got her a simple boat ride down the river to the city of Diwedd.

True to what the seer had told her there were people who ferried passengers and cargo out of sight from there. Lani shook her head and wriggled around in the nook she occupied on the boat. It had cost her, more than she'd liked to pay, but being out of sight and unknown to anyone hunting her seemed the best idea.

Anyway she knew nothing of the place she was traveling through — Lletem — and didn't care too much to find out. The captain on this boat was a woman, who'd cared nothing about Lani except for the amount of coin she had. Having paid, Lani had been smuggled on board in the night, wearing a hooded coat, amongst several of the crew.

Since then she'd sat in the spot where they'd told her, a makeshift seat in a nook on the outside of the cabin. It wasn't comfortable but she was completely hidden from view by anyone on either side of the river, or when they docked to change supplies.

One portion of the cargo was never unloaded, it lay covered completely with a heavy cloth that seemed to repel any water splashing on it. Lani assumed that was cargo similar to her, being smuggled to another location out of the sight of whoever might object to it.

The days were dull for her, and she often drifted off, sleeping away the time, trying to avoid thinking about anything. Now and again she would recall the words of the seer, about the lock on her mind, and that it was something he'd never seen before.

Why would any god care a whit for her or what was in her mind? It made no sense to her. She was no one of consequence, and if it hadn't been for Ashantha, she'd be standing in vats of urine, stomping on cloth.

Except the lock was there before that. Why didn't I ask how long it had been there?

Lani thought about the memories she could access, and they were only ones from when she was in Barnen, her early years. There was something she needed to know about, something that was blocked from her.

But what?

Every so often she'd watch the crew at work, rowing through the day. There were enough of them for almost two sets of rowers, with people swapping out every hour or so, allowing many to get a break.

The river cut the only usable pass through the gorge. Sheer cliffs rose on both sides and there was at best a tiny track on one side of it that a person might be able to follow. Now that the sun had risen enough to light the gorge, she could see how impressive it was.

The sides towered over them, a mix of sharp rock faces and massive boulders that looked ready to fall at any time. The sun reflected in deep oranges off the uppermost rocks and toward the bottom she could see low-lying shrubs and grasses.

It was pretty clear now why the boat trade was so important to Diwedd, as there was no direct path through the gorge south unless you were on the river. It was a monotonous view, and she could only see out through a narrow section of the boat.

As evening approached they entered a section of the river that was much wider than what they'd been on all day. Wooden jetties were built along the banks and their captain steered them to the one furthest south.

The crew seemed to be in fine spirits, and she could hear them talking about going ashore. Lani stood up to look at what they were up to, and poked her head around the screen shielding her from view. A wagon was being pulled up to the side of the boat, and the crew dragged back the cloth cover of goods they hadn't touched yet.

"Not yet." The voice of the captain came from further up the boat. "Wait until the sun's all down, you fools."

Then the stern-looking woman came into view and headed straight for Lani.

"Soon as it's dark, we'll be going about our business. You stay put, and best get yourself an early night. One of the leave-behinds will get you food."

"You're going ashore?"

"Crew needs some fun, and this city, Galon, it's a good place for it. We'll be back late tonight, and no matter how sorry their heads, we'll leave at first light."

"Can't I slip ashore when it's dark."

"No. You wanted to be hidden, so you stay hidden. I don't know what you're about, nor do I care, but if people are after you, you can get found here as easy as back in Diwedd. And that's the sort of attention I don't need."

The woman turned to look at something back up the boat.

"I've left a couple of crew behind with instructions you're to stay put, so don't get any clever ideas."

"Alright."

The captain walked off, barking instructions to her crew, and Lani went back to her nook. Suddenly she felt like a prisoner, not someone paying for passage. She was bored senseless sitting on the boat, and the thought of them going into the town, while she couldn't, angered her.

The sun slipped behind the mountains, enough to cover the work the crew were about to do. They were remarkably quiet about what they did, no one talking, none of the usual yelling or banter. Lani poked her head back around to see what they were moving.

Where the heavy cloth had been covering the cargo she could see the crew throwing large sacks up to others on the dock. She couldn't tell what they were, except each one of them was tied with a familiar red cloth. She'd seen similar sacks before.

Once they were all off the deck the rest of the crew walked over the gangway, all except for two burly men, who were clearly the guards for the boat while the others went into town. Neither looked particular happy about it either, and one of them scowled at her before she slipped back to her spot.

Lani rubbed the finger that the ring had been on, confirming it was no longer there. It was one less thing she had to worry about, and hoped that if the jesters were able to locate her through it, they now were chasing that coin.

She checked that the guards couldn't see her, and reached into her tunic, pulling out both of the jewels. The brooch was dull in the dark and she placed it back in her tunic, but rolled the pouch containing the amulet around in her hands.

It might not be the smartest idea, but she had begun to have ideas about seeing how the amulet worked. Perhaps she could unlink it from her, herself, if she just understood what it was doing. Before, she'd kept it hidden because the Vrah were always following her.

There was something there, something they understood about it, that led them to her. But the seer had told her they were all gone now.

That will mean it's safe to get out, or kind of.

Lani had nothing better to do so slipped the pouch off of the amulet. There was little light around the deck, but it seemed to draw in what it could find, and gleamed at her. The tendrils were there, faint but still there.

One reached out to the underside of her forearm, the link, while others drifted off away, the largest of them heading upstream. She stared at it, part of her worried about what she was doing but the other, like a second voice, was happy.

As she stared at it, she felt drawn into it, as her mind seemed to drift into the stone through the middle of her forehead. It was a strange feeling, one she felt only slightly in control of. A strange thought came into her head.

It wasn't her thought, it was a man's thought. Not just any man either, it was one of the guards on the other side of the deck. Lani pulled herself back out of the stone, the thoughts disappearing and her head clear from whatever the stone was doing.

What happened? It was like I could hear his thoughts.

Lani didn't know what was happening. Whatever it was she wasn't controlling, but she also felt the feeling of wanting to go into town growing, as if it was the most important thing to her. She wanted off the boat, but she needed to get past the guards. They were blocking the gangway, they needed to go somewhere else.

She focused more on that thought, of the men leaving their post, of leaving the gangway unattended.

The men moved. She sensed it, and pulled her mind back to where she was sat against the cabin. She could hear them talking and footsteps. Lani quickly put the amulet back in the pouch and tucked it away, but they didn't come her way.

She stood up, and saw they'd moved forward on the boat, prodding at cargo as they went. They'd moved liked she'd wanted them to do. As surprised as she was at what had just happened, she knew she could now make it if off the boat if she hurried, as long as she was silent. Lani didn't know if it was worth it, but what was the worst that could happen?

42

LANI

Getting off the boat had been easy enough, what she hadn't factored in was how to cross the jetty without them seeing her. Lani squatted down behind some barrels that were waiting to be loaded on the other side of the jetty, peeking around, watching the guards search the front of the boat.

It took them easily a half hour before they were done with whatever it was they had gone hunting for, and they returned back to their seats beside the gangway. As best she could tell, if she stayed low their view of her was limited, and they weren't expecting anyone.

She was unsure what had happened with the amulet, or even if it had done anything, but the guards had moved, and that gave her a chance. Being able to hear the man's thoughts was very strange, but maybe she could learn to do that again.

Any help to learn something could be useful. Maybe the amulet wasn't as bad as the seers had made it out to be. She didn't know what they believed or if she should be trusting everything they told her.

If anything this journey had taught her to be suspicious of everyone, and what their motivations were. Ashantha had called it evil, but she didn't know him either, or more correctly, his motivations. She'd learned more about him from his journal, and he seemed to be a good person, but he wasn't perfect either.

He'd been involved in manipulating people to do what he or his friends wanted. So maybe they wanted this amulet for their own use, and it wasn't so bad after all.

Concentrate, Lani!

She reached the street without anyone noticing her, and stood up, looking around. She'd grown up living rough, and couldn't see how the docks here would be much different to life in Barnen. The city was lit by a large moon. Any clouds that had followed them south had lifted tonight and she could easily find her way as she wandered casually away from the docks.

Several times she'd spotted lookouts and other junior workers who she carefully avoided. Her satchel would be of interest to those looking to make an easy profit for the night and leaving her money on the boat hadn't been an option.

While no one had harmed her she couldn't trust that her things wouldn't be rifled through. While there were only two crew left on the boat, they weren't honest sailors, they all knew what their main work was. Going through her things would have been second nature, if they had found her gone.

Her main interest was the cargo that the captain had unloaded. It consisted of quite a few sacks, and Lani couldn't shake the feeling they were the same as the ones she'd found in that wagon in Riverbend. It made her very curious.

All she planned to do was watch and see what they did with it. It was better than sitting on the blasted boat for the rest of the night, and already she felt better for being able to stretch her legs. There was only so much you could do when sat in one spot for days on end.

Thankfully the wagon hadn't gone far before she'd left the boat. They seemed to be waiting for someone. She wasn't wrong and a man approached them before waving them down a road heading further away from the boat.

They turned down several different roads, not rushing, but taking their time. Lani crept as slowly as she could, using the darkness to shelter her from view, following them from a distance. The wagon stopped at a warehouse with several men standing outside on guard.

After a brief exchange the men slid the doors open and the wagon turned into it. Everyone went inside and she could hear the clunk as the doors closed hard against each other. Lani waited to make sure no one came back outside before creeping up to the doors.

They were barred from the inside and she couldn't see through them. She walked a little further along and turned into a narrow back lane. The roofline above blocked most of the evening moonlight and she moved very slowly until her eyes adjusted.

Halfway down she found a side door that wasn't locked. Lani placed her right hand between the frame and the door and pushed very slowly. It moved without any noticeable sound, so Lani pushed at it until it was open enough for her to slip inside.

She could hear voices back toward the front of the warehouse and slowly weaved her way between rows of double-stacked barrels and sacks. When she was close enough to see between a row of shelves and more barrels, Lani crouched down to listen.

The wagon was about ten feet inside the closed doors and the captain was speaking to a man whose back was to Lani. One of the deckhands, who went by the name Koan, and another were busy unloading sacks and carrying them over toward where Lani was hidden.

"Twenty-four of them as promised." Lani recognized the captain's voice.

"The priest will be happy."

"What he wants all this wheat seed for, I've no idea, but we're happy to keep bringing it."

"I don't care what his reasoning is, not my concern, he just pays me to make sure it gets where he needs it."

"As long as we don't get caught with it, doesn't matter to me. Word is, to the north they're getting mighty upset about the lack of wheat."

"Just keep delivering what he asks and you'll get your coin. That's all you need to know."

"Speaking of which."

A sack was dumped almost right in front of the shelves Lani was hidden behind, and she let out a small gasp of surprise.

"What was that?" She could hear Koan's voice.

"What?" the other deckhand said.

"I thought I heard something."

"Probably the sound of your own body saying how much you smell."

"Shut up. I'm serious."

The men stopped and stayed still. Lani held her breath and squatted where she was. Her leg muscles burned from exhaustion and trying to hold the position. She closed her eyes and focused on staying absolutely still.

"Gah, nothing."

"Like I told you, all in your mind, or some filthy vermin scrounging around back there."

"You two finished carrying on like scullery maids?" Lani heard the captain call out.

"Yes, boss." They turned and walked back over to the wagon. Koan closed the tailgate and they walked around to the other side out of Lani's view.

Lani could see the last sacks that had been put down in front of her. All of them had the red cloth around them, and now she knew they had wheat seed in them. That didn't mean much to her, except what she already knew. Wheat was becoming a problem, that's what Arbery and Dedrick had been all worried about.

What a priest was bothered with it for meant nothing to her. She wished she'd stayed on the boat now, this was not much more interesting than that. The priests were probably just trying to protect themselves, although this seemed a pretty extravagant way to ensure you had bread.

It didn't matter to her, and she needed to get safely back to the boat. As she stood, her knees and thighs ached in pain and it took all of her will not to let out a big breath. Step by step she crept back to the door she had come in through. It was now closed. She put her hand on it and pushed against it. It didn't move.

Someone had closed it and she couldn't see where it was locked or barred in the darkness. Lani began to run her hands over the surface to see if she could find a latch when a hand grabbed the back of her tunic.

"Told you I heard something!" Koan shouted.

She tried to wriggle free but his hands, tough from years of manual work, held firm.

"Give it up, woman. You're coming with me."

"What did you say, Koan?"

"I said look what I found!"

She was dragged and pushed around the stacks of items until she was in the main staging area near the wagon. The captain looked around in surprise.

"What are you doing here?"

"She was hiding out the back watching us."

The man who had been receiving the sacks turned to look at her. Lani almost gasped when she saw his face. A scar ran across his face from the right top temple, over where his right eye and part of his nose should have been down the side of his left chin. "Who is this?"

"She's someone I took on in Diwedd."

"What does she know?"

"I don't know, she seemed harmless enough, but now I'm not so sure."

"I don't know anything," Lani burst out. "I was just curious when I saw you come in here."

"Well, curiosity killed plenty of cats, didn't you know? Bundle her up, Koan. We'll sort this out back on the boat."

"This better not be a problem, or this will be your last load."

"It won't be. Trust me!"

Someone covered her head with an empty sack, and she felt rope being tied around her. She was hoisted up off the ground and dumped into what she had to assume was the back of the wagon.

"Let's get back and sort this out quickly." The captain's words were the last ones she heard before the wagon started rolling out.

UKSOD

*P*atience wasn't one of Uksod's best attributes, and of late he was having to practice it more and more. Karpenmor was testing it in so many ways, none of them major, but enough that he constantly felt agitated.

The brooding had grown worse, and he sensed it was the way he was reducing the amount of the brandy he was drinking.

Fool boy, what you don't know is there's more than just amber in there. Good luck giving that up.

For all Yantarnaya lectured him about bringing up the boy over the years, the simplest solution had been adding a sedative with the mixture. Just a little, not enough to wipe him out, but combined with the effect of the amber it had made Uksod's life much more bearable.

As if he'd wanted to be father to a little boy! Of course not. He didn't enter the priesthood to be a parent, and yet for all these years he'd either been little better than a brothel owner, securing the right breeding wench for Schevenal, or looking after the little brat.

Now, he was a large brat, at times, and having to listen to his instructions was wearing very thin on Uksod. There was a pleasing side to the clearer mind Karpenmor was showing without the drink, he was certainly smarter than Uksod had realized. But that was only a good thing if it was helping them get the amulets back or to take control of Dharatan. The rest was immaterial to Uksod. The lack of influence he had when the boy was free of the drink was his bigger concern.

There were things that were just easier to do when he was ingesting some of the amber. If he wouldn't wear any then there was little other option. In the last week or so, it was if the boy was pushing back, even blocking his attempts to suggest what he should be doing.

That wouldn't do. It was why the amulet was a much better fix. Once it was leashed to him, then he couldn't be free of it, whether he wanted to or not. It was why the amulets were the best option for the barbarian leaders too.

It would be too hard to ensure they take the liquid like Karpenmor had. It was difficult enough here with servants who would do whatever he commanded, not so easy in a foreign court. The amount anyone could ingest was tiny, so it needed to be done every day, or more days than not, to allow the influence over them.

"Uksod!"

Yantarnaya's voice took him by surprise. He was concerned that she was talking to him directly and not requesting his presence in the cave. That couldn't be good. He sat down and answered her without talking out loud.

"Mistress?"

"The amulet was just used, Uksod."

"By the King?"

"What? No, the other one. The one you've been chasing. Unsuccessfully."

"I don't understand, how can it be used?"

"A very good question, Uksod. But it has been used just recently. I could sense it, it's very faint, so far away but a woman was connected to it."

"I thought..."

"This is wrong, very wrong. Who is this woman?"

"I have no idea, mistress. You know more than me."

"There's only one thing that makes sense, Uksod. I know this amulet is

Schevenal's. That I am clear on, not one of the others. If it was one of the others maybe that might make sense, but not this. If she used it, she'd either able to do what few can do, or..."

"Or what?"

"Or you lied to me, Uksod."

Pressure built up through the amber stone set on his forehead, in the circlet, crushing the inside of his head. He closed his eyes, gritting his teeth in pain.

"You said he was the only child!"

"He is! Please, mistress..."

She eased the pressure off.

"If this is the right amulet, then this girl, she has to be one of Schevenal's children, there is no other way. It felt like she was bonded to it, she was linked to the amulet, Uksod! You lied!"

"I did not, mistress. We kept none of the others, each of the girls, the ones from before Karpenmor's mother, were removed. I promise."

Yantarnaya was silent. The pressure was there, just a little, but Uksod knew she hadn't left him.

"Something isn't right, Uksod, this is all wrong. Very wrong. If it is the one then it will not come back to him of its own accord. Not if it's bonded to another."

"If, mistress. If it is the one."

"You were sure before, Uksod."

"Only because of where it was found, mistress. It made sense it was the Schevenal's but maybe I was wrong."

"Find out, Uksod. And quickly."

"Yes, mistress." And she was gone.

Uksod rubbed his scalp with his hand. Previous experience told him he would have to bear a nasty headache for the rest of the day, but that was the least of his problems. Who on Enderk was this woman bonded to the amulet?

Someone able to do that might be more resourceful than he had planned for. That might explain why she was able to avoid his teams. She would have help.

Who is she?

He stormed back to his underground office, fuming about what he had just learned. Something had gone wrong, and someone would know what. He just had to find out who that was, and he had an idea where to start.

Trorn was the first to suffer his wrath. He sent his second priest off to retrieve all of those who had any knowledge from their past endeavors making Schevenal's heir. Of the early attempts he doubted anyone would still be alive, but he had to be sure.

He even sent for One. The Vrah had been responsible for the actual deeds, of killing any of the children and mothers. All done at birth, and their remains destroyed. It was a simple thing, if a girl was born then they had to try again.

Uksod knew the only weak link was Karpenmor's mother. They had kept her alive and after the first year sent her away to live for a few years on a remote property on the western coast. It was as good an option as any for her. She'd been part barbarian, and after so many tries had delivered up the boy they needed.

Yantarnaya and he had decided to keep her alive just in case the boy had any issues. Their reasoning was that if she could deliver one boy, she could deliver another. That had all gone very wrong when they'd found she'd left Enderk.

Somehow she'd managed to get across the water and to a place called RaMar. By luck she had been spotted leaving on a tiny boat. A team of Vrah had been sent to fix it. They'd pursued her and caught up to her outside of that city, in the countryside.

Everyone had been killed. The cost had been high, they'd lost several of their own Vrah, but the returning team members had sworn that the woman and everyone accompanying her were dead.

Could it be a different amulet? Now that a second had appeared, it was possible. And yet he had been certain. The woman that had found it, the box, where it had been washed up. All of that fitted with what was known about when Schevenal had slung it into the sea.

As much as it had eased the pressure from Yantarnaya, Uksod did not believe what he had told her. He was still certain the amulet was the one. The one Schevenal had bonded to his family line. Which is why they couldn't just kill Karpenmor off, and anoint another family to rule.

No other family line could bond to the amulet, not even distant relatives of Schevenal's. Only his direct descendants. Perhaps that was why he had thrown the amulet into the sea. He knew that his time was short, that no one else could use it, as he was childless. And the stone would only harm people if it was left for others.

Who could have seen how badly that glitch in his bonding would play out? Uksod was sure that the old High Prince had done it for greed, back when he was still sane, when he accepted the amulet, and the bond. Linking it to only his family line was clever, to ensure no one else could ever hold the jewel.

For one who had always been relatively timid it was a bold move. What he thought would bind his family to rule Enderk. And ensure their power lasted forever.

Which meant this woman had to be a child of his. How had she survived? Where had she grown up? He needed answers. Someone knew something. Whoever had kept this from him would pay, and pay dearly.

The rest of his day was spent interrogating one person after another. Priests, servants and Vrah. Few could tell him anything of value, until he found an elderly servant who had been cooking for Schevenal for most of her years in the palace.

She sat before him in his study, two Vrah behind her within easy reach.

"Tell me again, what do you know of the mother?"

Tears ran down her face. "What mother, sire?"

"You know who I mean! Karpenmor's mother!"

"She not here, sire. She not been here for a long time."

Uksod rolled his eyes and could feel his neck throbbing, his patience a distant memory. A knock at the door annoyed him further.

"I'm not to be disturbed, go away."

He turned back to the woman and looked up at the guards.

"We'll need to take her back there." He nodded to his workshop off to the side. "She'll tell me what she knows, one way or another."

"Sire, no. I know nothing. Not me who helped his mother. I just cook." She was wailing now.

He held up his hand to halt the Vrah who had taken an arm each. "What do you mean, not you who helped?"

The door to his study opened without warning.

"I said I was not to be disturbed!" he shouted, turning to see Karpenmor walking through it.

"Really, Uksod?"

"Highness, my apologies. We're just in the middle of something here."

"I can see, Uksod. What exactly is going on?"

"Nothing of import for you to worry about, Highness. Just someone not telling me what I need to know."

Karpenmor looked at the two guards holding the woman. "Let her go! This is all too much, she's very old, why are you bullying her? Isn't she one of the cooks? What could she know about anything important?"

Uksod was furious. The heir should never have gotten anywhere near this office without someone getting to him first. The boy couldn't learn what he was seeking information on, not now, not ever.

Karpenmor turned to the old woman and leaned down near her. "It's okay. I'm sorry about all this. Are you alright?"

"Yes. It hurf."

"We hadn't touched her, Highness, you can see she's exaggerating, nothing hurts."

"She didn't say hurt, Uksod. She said Hurf, father's servant. Why do you want to know about Hurf?"

"I… I was trying to find out something from some time ago, something that came up."

"About my father? Didn't Hurf just tend to my father, Uksod?"

"Mostly, Your Highness." Uksod could feel the sweat beginning to run down his back. "Sometimes he worked on other things. It's not such a big deal."

"Not such a big deal? You're terrorizing this poor woman to find out something not so important, not such a big deal? I don't believe you, Uksod, not one bit."

Karpenmor turned to the two Vrah. "Guide this woman back to her work, and ensure she is not harmed. Not a finger on her. Do you hear me?"

"Highness." The two men in black nodded, and gestured to the woman to stand and leave the office.

When they were gone, Uksod tried to gain his control back. "Was that necessary, Karpenmor? When you embarrass me in front of the servants, you undermine me."

"I'm not worried about your pride, Uksod. I want to find this Hurf as well. He's the last connection to my father and I wish to speak to him. Find him, Uksod, and keep him safe. I want to question him myself."

"Of course, Highness."

The headache in Uksod's head was nothing compared to the sick feeling that had formed in his stomach. Today was not going well at all.

CARNUS

It all felt like a dream, or more specifically what people called nightmares. Carnus hadn't ever had a dream that was scary or bad. Nothing ever scared him, or bothered him that he would need to dream of it.

Until now.

He hadn't moved in seven days. His legs would probably cramp if he tried to move too quickly. All he could do was watch the forest, waiting for someone to come out and tell him it was all a mistake and he was to come back to his post.

But they hadn't.

No one else would come near him, not that he cared. Behind him was a wooden building, without a back entrance, and he had sat there, beside the border to Ngahere, watching for one of his kind.

Day had turned to night and back to day. It didn't matter, there was nothing else for him to do. He had reached the pinnacle of his goals, the Protectors, and it had been taken from him.

Exile? Why exile? It was the worst punishment, not one he would have expected. He struggled to accept why that had been chosen above anything else.

Yes, he was in charge of them when the invaders had come, and he had let the woman out of his grasp. But he didn't want to let her escape, he was fighting to protect the Tombs. That she had got away was more her luck than anything else.

He'd expected to be punished, and had already accepted that he would be removed as leader, but this... this was something else. His disgrace was insurmountable. The very thing he had worked to achieve, to remove the shame from his family name.

And now he had made it worse.

Carnus didn't cry, he had never cried, but in his chest he could feel his heart as if it was ripped through at the thought of his mother being removed from her home and left to fend for herself. She would be shunned.

First her daughter and now him, it would be too much for her. He dipped his head and shook it, finding it too hard to accept. There was nowhere for him to go, no one who would have him. He was an exile, worse even than a Runner.

Had a Protector ever been exiled before? Carnus didn't know. He had never heard of one before. There was almost no discussion of anyone that had been exiled, except to highlight the ultimate punishment for a Ngaherian.

Life within Ngahere was simple, if you followed the Wooden Path. Each part of life was governed by simple principles, that outlined how to be in sync with everyone else. Living with Honor was the highest aspiration, the formula on how to belong.

In his family the loss of honor after his sister had abandoned the Path left them as outsiders. A family was an aggregation of the people within it. If one displayed no honor it lowered the honor of the family.

There could be no recourse for his family now. When his sister had taken up her religion and sought to corrupt those around her, she had become an exile. Now Carnus had been subject to his own fate. Not even the sacrifice of his father could undo that fact. Two exiles, in one family. Was that the reason for his own exile, that his family had no honor?

Who was he now, if he was not a Protector? A warrior?

Everything about him had been removed all at once. He had seen the look of shock on the faces of the other Protectors, no one wanted to look him in the eye, not now. He was no longer one of them, they carried his shame as their shame. Their family was dishonored by him and they now had to make up for that.

Carnus didn't know how his mother would be able to endure this, whether she would take her life rather than live her remaining years as an outcast from society. She would no longer be buried in the Tombs, no matter what.

He could hardly bear the thought that he had failed her. In his chest all he could feel was emptiness. There was nothing left for him now, unless it was a mistake.

~

As THE DAY WORE ON, HE COULD FEEL THE SUN BAKING HIM, THE SHADOW from the morning gone. Carnus knew he needed food and drink but found no reason to move. Feeling sorry for himself had never been something he had experienced, but it was drowning him now.

He had no desire to move, no will to move. He no longer cared if he lived or died, why would he? Without his people, his mother and the Wooden Path there was nothing.

If it was to be soon, from starvation, he believed he could live with that. Who was he to not suffer, to not struggle as his body began to shut down?. Any suffering would help him to forget that which was gone forever.

On the first day he had clung to the idea that he knew who the woman that had escaped him was, what she looked like. He could have hunted her and brought her back, begged for his status to be returned. She could be offered up as his sacrifice.

But he knew that was ridiculous. There had been no offer of redemption from Queen Vika, no challenge to return the girl. He was exiled on pain of death, should he return to Ngahere. Bringing back the girl would do nothing for his position, it would only guarantee what he could do himself, without the effort of trying.

Nor did he know where to look anyway. It didn't matter, not now. Spots appeared in front of his eyes, and he struggled to see in the distance. Sweat ran down his nose, and his cheeks. He wobbled where he sat, knowing that he was close to losing consciousness.

It doesn't matter.

SOMETHING WAS VERY DIFFERENT, EVERYTHING SMELLED DIFFERENT, AND HE was cool and lying on something soft. And there was a humming noise coming from somewhere nearby. His head felt wet, and he raised his arm to feel why.

A wet piece of cloth was laid across it, which Carnus pulled back. He took stock of how he felt, trying to remember what had happened. All he could remember was passing out, that he had been outside looking across the border.

Now he felt very tired, and weak. There was no other pain than what was inside his head. He was thirsty, very thirsty which in the end was enough to get him moving.

He rolled to his side. He was in some sort of room and he saw light on the other side of it.

"Big Man is awake!" An excited voice came from somewhere near the light. "Slowly, slowly, Big Man, you were almost dried out. Silly Big Man."

Carnus couldn't see who the voice belonged to and it took him quite an effort to get himself upright. The light came from candles at the other end of the room. Beside him was a large wooden jug.

"Drink, Big Man. You need much liquid."

Carnus wanted to talk, but he was struggling to move his tongue. Everything seemed twice as hard, and he leaned toward the jug, making it easier to pick it up. Inside was a thin ale, but it was the best thing he had ever tasted.

He gulped at it and drank as much as he could before his stomach stretched and he began to ache.

"Where am I?"

"Alive, is where you are, Big Man."

Carnus was annoyed by the strange old man sat across the room.

The candles behind him gave him a shroud of light, making his face hard to see.

"Union, in my hut."

"I was by the border, how did I get here?"

"In the back of a wagon, like most sacks of useless things. Wandering Moon found you, she came and screamed at me to help. Look at me, how much help can a man with no eyes be? I sent others, they put you in the wagon and brought you here."

Now that the old man mentioned his eyes, Carnus could see they were missing. Empty sockets was all that remained. He was thankful that the light was dim. He had heard of these people, but had never seen one. He wished it was still that way.

"Why?"

"It stopped Wandering Moon from screaming at me."

"Who is Wandering Moon?"

The old man looked toward him with a strange look on his face as if he didn't understand the question. "Who is Father Sun? Who is Mother Land? Such silly questions, Big Man."

Carnus closed his eyes and tried to gather his thinking. He still felt woozy and nauseous.

"What do you want with me?"

"Me? I want nothing with you. It is you who turned up here demanding to see me!"

"You just told me others brought me here."

"Did I ask you to come here?"

"No."

"Were you at death's door, without food or drink, ready to throw your life to the dirt on which you lay?"

Carnus dropped his head in shame.

"So you did come looking for me. One way or another, Big Man, you found your way here. No one comes here by chance. Not you, nor the girl from the north that you seek."

"I seek no one."

"Words are so easy to say, Big Man. But if death you seek, outside in the stones you can find many weapons. Go pick one, do the job you are so sure you want. Just grant me one thing."

"What?"

"Do it somewhere else, blood makes me feel very bad." The old man laughed, a wicked laugh.

"What do you know of this girl?"

"She too came to see me, full of questions, like you. Everyone wants answers, no one answers my questions."

Carnus wasn't keeping up with the old man.

"What you seek you cannot find staring at the trees, Big Man. Nor will you get back the way you came. There are many things you can choose, Big Man, and choose to be, but you cannot go backward."

Carnus wished he hadn't woken up. This man was making his head feel worse, and he had no desire to hear nonsense.

"I have no wish to go anywhere."

"Ha, this is not true, Big Man. You try to want to leave this world, but it is not the choice you want to make. Two women you want to find. One will free you from your shame, the other will not."

"What two women?"

"Somethings you do not need to be answered."

"You make no sense, there is no getting back from my shame."

"I did not say that, Big Man. You want to return to the past, that path has no stones. You can only get lost trying to retrace that path. You must find the stones of your new path, Big Man. Then you will have a future."

"I do not understand."

"Nor will you, Big Man, not until you understand."

Carnus felt weak, and his head was hurting a lot. The words of the old man were making it worse.

"Sleep again, Big Man, when daylight comes you will go south. Each night ask Wandering Moon and she will give you answers. You have work to do, Big Man."

45

LANI

hen the wagon finally rolled to a stop Lani had worn herself out imagining all the things that would happen next. Even though she had been expecting hands to grab her, she still jumped when they touched her legs and dragged her out of the wagon.

She was stood up with her back against the tailgate.

"Put her on the boat." The captain's voice sounded cold. "Tie her to the side of the cabin for now."

A strong hand locked around her left bicep, and she was turned and marched forward. Lani could feel the gangway flexing under her and felt the boat move as she was pushed onto it. She was shoved to the floor, and she could sense her captor tying rope through the loop securing her hands.

When she heard their footsteps walking away, she tested her bindings. There wasn't much give in them and she couldn't really move from where she was. Her heart was beating too fast and the hood over her head was making her anxiety worse.

No one came and spoke to her, and as the night progressed, she heard people coming and going on the boat, but not many. She was too uptight to sleep and sat propped up against the cabin waiting for her fate. Eventually she could see a change in the light through the weave

280

in the hood. Then came the sound of the rest of the crew arriving back on the boat.

Her mouth was parched and she felt nauseous, but mostly she hated being without her sight. She had no way to prepare for anything that might happen, and her mind couldn't stop focusing on what that might be.

The boat dipped and swayed as Lani sensed new cargo being loaded. Her time on the boat had only been short, but even so she had begun to feel the differences in how it responded to people and objects.

Heavy footsteps sounded like they were heading her way. They stopped right beside her. "Don't try anything." It was Koan's voice.

Without much care for how he did it, the hood was untied and removed. Lani had to close her eyes as the bright morning light caused her pain. He leaned down holding out a skin.

"Drink." He tipped it toward her mouth, and she gulped down what she could, the rest spilling down her chin and onto her chest. He moved away with it before she could get enough to truly satisfy her thirst, but it felt good, nonetheless.

With a burst of activity, the crew freed the boat from its tethers and pushed it away from the dock. Before long it was back out into the river and continuing south. Lani sat and waited, happier she could at least watch the countryside passing by without wearing the hood.

An hour or more into the trip Lani could see the captain walking her way. Whatever was going to happen she would find out now.

"I'm not sure you're going to tell me the truth, but I'll ask anyway. What were you doing spying on us?"

"I wasn't spying. Not really."

"What would you call it?"

"I just saw you going into that building and I followed to see what was going on. Like I said, I was just curious."

"That was probably the biggest mistake of your life."

Lani felt her chest tighten. She had no way to defend herself and they were now so far away out on the river that there was no one around to help her.

"You're a problem I didn't need. The question is what will I do about you?"

"I didn't really see anything. You unloaded some cargo and that was that. I don't get why this is such a problem."

"Curious people tend to stay curious and my partners and I don't need anyone poking their nose into our business."

"I'm heading a long way away from here, and most likely won't ever be back this way again. How am I going to poke my nose into your business?"

"Easy to say, girl. But we don't need any loose ends hanging around." The woman turned to the man behind her. "Leave me with her for now, she can't harm anyone. Keep an eye on the crew, I want to make good progress to Mugan."

Lani watched the woman look out across the side of the boat for what seemed like five minutes.

"You might not know how serious this is, but you better realize it quickly. You didn't tell me what you're doing out here all alone before, but you better had now."

"I'm heading south, I told you that. I have to get to Statiiv."

"That's what you said last time, but I'm not sure you told me all of it."

"Why does it matter?"

"Trust me, right now it all matters. Or you won't be getting to anywhere, except down there." She pointed into the river."

Lani shivered. "I have to head much further south, to a place I've never been before."

"Where?" the captain's said forcefully.

"It's called Anderwell."

"Anderwell? Why there?"

"I … I have to deliver a message." Lani didn't want to have to tell the whole truth.

"A message? Right. You expect me to believe that you're out here all alone, without any protection, on some huge journey, to deliver a message."

"Yes." Lani stared back into the woman's eyes.

"I don't think you're telling me the whole truth."

"The man who got me to deliver the message, he'd taken some

things. People were after him, so he wanted to make sure the message got south."

"What's in it for you?"

Lani paused, she knew she was on shaky ground. "Coin, what else? He promised they'd pay me well for the message."

The captain chuckled. "So you're not much different after all, lass. But that's the thing isn't it, if you'll sell information to one person, why not another?"

"What do you mean?"

"Who's to say you couldn't find someone wanting to know what we were doing."

The captain turned around and looked out over the river again. Lani waited until she had finished thinking.

"What is so important about this message?

"I can't tell you."

"You better." Her tone dropped the friendliness and cut through the morning air like a blade.

"I can't."

"I'm not sure you're not working for our opponents. The best way to test that would be to send your body back to them as a sign."

Lani felt her chest tighten again and her voice cracked. "I'm not working for anyone. I'm telling you the truth. I've had trouble following me wherever I go, and I wish I'd never set off on it now, but it's all I've got."

"I don't believe you. Something about your story smells like rotten carp and that worries me."

She turned and walked away leaving Lani just as concerned as she had been before. The only difference now was she could see who was coming for her when they came. Once no one was looking at her she tested out her bindings again, trying to see if there was any freedom she could use to work at.

Koan, or whoever it was, had done a good job of tying them. There was no room in the bindings around her wrist and hardly any slack in the rope tying her to the rusty steel ring attached to the cabin wall.

She rested back against the cabin wall and looked out into the distance. Days before it had been the rocky gorge, now it was all plains that stretched far off to the dusty horizon.

How does this keep happening to me?

Each hour they progressed, the better she felt. She didn't know why but hoped that the further from the threat of the captain's colleagues in Galon she was, the less likely they would be to kill her. As the middle day came and went Lani noticed there was a lot less sunlight around and a wind had been building from the south. The boat's progress had slowed dramatically as they fought against it.

The captain and crew on the deck were regularly looking to the east, which was blocked to her by the cabin. Occasionally she could hear the word 'storm' mentioned by the crew and they worked even harder on the oars. The river was becoming rougher, and the boat rolled and bucked as they inched their way along.

In the distance the crack of thunder could be heard, and the captain yelled out, "It's coming our way, check everything is tied down, *now!*"

46

LANI

The first gust that hit the boat rocked it so hard, Lani was thrown sideways toward the gunwale. She screamed in pain as her body leaped forward but her arms stayed behind, twisting upward awkwardly.

Rain drops the size of coins began to thump on the wooden deck and roof of the cabin and more thunder cracked overhead. The day had turned to night, so dark were the clouds, and she could hear the crew rushing from side to side, trying to protect the cargo.

Lani twisted herself around and made sure her hands were in front of her so she could at least protect herself if she was flung around again. The river felt like an open sea, rollicking underneath them. Waves crashed onto the deck and soaked everything.

A flash of lightning lit the sky and showed Lani the rest of the boat. Some of the cargo was rolling about on the deck and it looked like several of the crew had been injured. More thunder boomed overhead and then a massive gust of wind threw the front of their flat-bottomed boat up before dropping it again to crash on the surface of the river.

With all its cargo, the front dipped under the water and only just lifted back out again. Lani could see it coming and had braced herself. She slid backward and then forward as it happened and was partly thankful she was secured to the cabin. Other people were being flung about like pieces on a Trigger board with nothing to hold onto.

River water covered the deck, and some raced down past Lani and seeped out wherever it could find an exit. Another flash of lightning and she was able to see over the side of the boat. The vessel was heading directly for the far bank. Except it wasn't a bank, it was a rock wall.

If they drove into it, the rocks would punch holes right through the side of the boat. All it would take was another gust of wind and they'd be done for. Lani desperately tried to work on the ropes binding her wrists. She didn't want to drown in the river if the boat sank and clearly she was the last thing on anyone's mind right now.

The wind eased back again, and the crew tried again to recover what they could. She heard someone yelling on the foredeck.

"Row! Row now! We have to push away from here!"

Some of the crew rushed to their benches and tried to free oars that hadn't been damaged. At first their work seemed pointless, but then they began to get the boat under control and pointing downriver the way they had been heading before.

There was hardly enough space between them and the river wall, especially if another gust came, but they rowed with all their might.

The captain made her way around the edge of the cabin, leaning awkwardly against the rolling waves. She carried a knife in her hand and a scowl across her face.

"Don't do anything stupid, girl. We need everyone we can get if we're going to get out of this in one piece." She leaned over and pulled Lani's ropes toward her.

It took an effort to cut through the wet ropes securing Lani to the cabin. Just as she was cut free another wave crashed against the far side of the boat, throwing her off her knees. Lani hit the side of the boat hard and grunted as the wind was forced out of her.

She got up on her knees and held her hands out to the captain who carefully placed the knife between the bindings and slide the blade back and forth. Lani prayed that there wouldn't be another wave or gust while the knife was so close to her.

Once the ropes were gone the captain stood, sliding the blade into her belt, and grabbed Lani by the arm. "Come on, help the rowers. We need to get away from the side."

She found an open bench and made sure to wrap the leather thong from the top of the oar around her wrists, like she'd seen the others do. The wood was slippery and she didn't want to lose it. The water was fighting against her as she pulled on the oar, and it took every ounce of strength she had to move it.

"Push! Pull!" the voices around her called in unison.

Together they worked against the weather, inch by inch turning the boat toward the middle of the river.

"Watch out!" the captain screamed from the middle of the foredeck. "Boat coming."

A small vessel, about a third of their size, was rushing down the river almost directly at them. In the dark light and heavy rain Lani paid little attention to it.

"Port oars *up now!*"

On the left-hand side of the boat all the rowers hurriedly lifted their oars, just before Lani felt a thud coming from that side.

The sound of splintering wood filled the air, followed by a flash of lightning. All the rowers had stopped, and she looked to the rear of the boat. The smaller boat has crashed into them but side on and it appeared little damage had occurred on their boat.

Three of the rowers on the left leaped up from their benches and grabbing poles, hurried back toward the other boat. They pushed at it, trying to uncouple it from their hull.

Thunder cracked followed by more lightning. Lani waited for a massive gust of wind, but it didn't follow. Finally, the smaller boat separated from their side and the river pulled it away from them, its bow pointing slightly downward.

As the crew rushed back to their benches Lani could hear the captain.

"That'll sink soon enough. We need to follow it down and get around it, we don't want to hit it when it's underwater."

Everyone pulled harder on their oars, dragging the boat back toward the center of the river. The current was stronger than ever, and they hurried along behind the smaller boat. Another crash of thunder and this time a huge series of wind gusts followed it. They rocked sideways and Lani felt like her side would dip under the water as they were lifted in the air.

The boat smashed back down again but the distance to the rocky bank had been halved again. More lighting cut through the darkness and they all watched as the smaller boat was flung into the bank ahead of them.

The speed it hit broke the boat up into hundreds of pieces. The sound didn't carry but as the light faded, they all knew parts of that boat were now directly in their path.

"Port side, pull back!"

The two teams worked against each other as they desperately tried to get the boat pointing away from the debris.

"All ahead!"

They started making some progress. Then another gust blew at them and threw waves at the bow, and the boat started pushing to starboard. Lani's team pulled against their oars while the others eased up. Again, they turned it and then both teams worked trying to drag the boat against the weather and toward the middle of the river.

Lani could feel the occasional thud against the hull but couldn't hear much, her concentration entirely on trying to do her part. She could sense the desperation all around. It occurred to her that their concern was for the cargo not themselves. It was unlikely even if the boat sunk that they all couldn't get free. Unlike the ocean, even if the river was wide and deep, it was something you could swim through.

What you couldn't do was save cargo that sank, and that meant coin. Their wages were dependent on having a boat that delivered its cargo. That's why they were so desperate to make it through.

More thunder boomed overhead, and the rain got heavier. Lani couldn't see beyond the ends of her arms. Whether they were heading in the right direction or not she couldn't tell, and she struggled to hear the chants from the crew.

The boat rammed into something solid, and the sound of crunching wood rang out through the heavy rain. Lani, distracted by her thoughts, was flung off the bench and skidded to her knees in water on the deck.

Suddenly aware she had a chance to escape, she crawled across the deck leaving the oar to its own. She headed back past other crew all too focused on rowing to even see her shape in the darkness.

She stayed low and hurried around the side of the cabin where she'd been tied up before. Now hidden from view of anyone she made her way to the back of the boat. There was little she could see past the edge of the boat, but she knew they were still likely closer to the western shore than the other.

Another wave lifted the boat up and without even putting in any effort, she was lifted over the edge. Lani pushed with her feet at the side rail and dove into the cold water, sinking under the turbulent swell. Her clothing and the bag filled with water and dragged at her. She could sense herself sinking and frantically pulled at the water above her. When her head broke free, she gasped for breath and tried to see what was around her.

A wave rushed at her, and she was picked up and carried sideways. She slammed into something hard, and her vision swam in front of her. As she had braced for the impact, she had turned her body and her back took the full brunt. Her breath was driven from her, and she began to sink again.

47

LANI

Whatever it was that Lani had been driven into hadn't had any sharp protrusions which was about the only thing she could be thankful for. She was pretty certain she had blacked out briefly which meant a headache would follow.

Not that she had time to worry about that right at the moment. Her body had been spun around and around and she was being tossed downriver by the current. She was only able to grab small gulps of air at a time in order not to swallow gob-fulls of river water.

She was slung into something else and stopped in her tracks. A solid horizontal object flat drove into her across her stomach, emptying her lungs of air again. She grunted in pain. Water splashed constantly over her head, but she was wedged against whatever it was she had hit and wasn't being dragged downstream.

Lightning flashed giving her time to look at her surroundings. The boat she had leaped from was closer to the middle of the river, far enough away that no one would see her. She seemed to be trapped against a tangle of tree roots. With relief she could see she was at the river's edge. The bank appeared to have partly crumbled into the river, exposing the roots, and Lani hung on, thankful for it.

The light went away, and her eyes could hardly see, but her ears heard the booming thunderclap that followed. Right now, this was the safest spot she could be, hidden from view and going nowhere, despite the tug on her legs from the passing current.

Once her eyes adjusted to the dim light, she looked at the root system she was hanging onto. The main twist of roots looked more than strong enough to hold her weight and the trunk of the tree was still on solid land. The bank around it was being ripped away in small amounts by the raging river and Lani knew the tree might end up being sucked in once enough of it was exposed.

She needed to make a move now and hope she could cling onto the roots against the rushing water. The bag strapped over her back was pulling against her under the water and she had to fight with what strength she had left to drag herself onto the top part of the twisted root stem.

Her arms wrapped around the biggest root she could manage, and she locked her hands. The river swept her legs downward and she started to slide off before dragging them back onto the slimy roots. By unlocking her hands and treating it like she was climbing a rope she pulled herself closer to the base of the tree.

The further up she got the slimier the roots became. The mud coating them made it harder for her to get a decent grip, but she kept pulling the best she could. Two thirds of the way to the trunk she stopped and locked her hands again. Her feet were now mostly out of the river flow, and she felt much more stable on the roots.

Lani closed her eyes for half a minute, turning her head away from the rushing water, and focused on catching as much breath as she could. Her shoulders were burning, and her forearms ached from all the work they'd been doing, both on the oars and keeping her afloat.

Turning back to her task she pulled forward, but her lack of concentration meant she didn't pay enough attention to her grip. Her right hand slipped on the greasy root, and she nearly toppled sideways back down into the river.

Lani righted herself and froze.

Keep your mind on the task, girl!

Again, she started up the root and this time took each hand grab slowly and very deliberately. When she got to the trunk, she wasn't sure exactly how she was going to get onto the land behind it. Most of the bank on the side she was on had been eroded by the water. The root system was heavily intertwined back into the ground above but most of the roots were small and unlikely to take her weight.

She knew crawling wasn't going to be an option and needed to stand up. Inch by inch she moved her legs up under her chest, her knees straining to bend that tightly after being in the cold water so long. The trunk of the tree was much bigger than Lani could reach around and the best she could do was press her face and chest hard up against it and stretch her arms out and around as far as she could.

While the bark was wet it wasn't muddy and Lani was able to grasp against some rough grips and force herself upright. She clung desperately to the tree trunk and gathered her wits again. The rain continued to pelt down into her face if she turned upriver, but she needed to try and see how to get to the river bank.

That was the only direction she could go; the southern side of the tree was just a straight plunge back into the river. A loud tearing sound broke her out of her rest, and she started to feel the trunk leaning toward her. She hung onto the grips, expecting to go backward into the river at any moment, but whatever had just happened it stopped as quickly as it started.

Lani knew she had no time to waste, and just hoped that her only option didn't see her end up tangled in roots waiting to drown. She took three steadying breaths then moved to her right, bringing her left arm over her head and down alongside her right arm which was wrapped awkwardly around the tree.

She moved her right foot forward, right up against the base of the tree and onto the thinner root system ahead of her. It seemed to take the partial weight she put on it and she moved her body around, so she was in a more natural position. As she did so the roots sank under her full weight.

Without hesitation she leaped forward hoping the natural springiness of the roots would propel her forward. As she pushed down and up into the web of roots her other foot started to sink, and she drove forward as fast as she could, no longer able to use the trunk to help her.

Then the roots became thick mud, and she was able to feel a more solid surface underneath her feet. She pushed forward a few more steps until she could drop to her knees on what was left of the riverbank.

Everything was thick with mud, the rain constantly pelting everything around her. Too tired to even bother trying to stand, she started to crawl up the last part of the riverbank. As she pushed down with her feet, she felt them give way. Nothing was below them. She scrambled with her hands and pulled upward; another massive ripping sound surrounded her.

On her left the ground started pulling open and a root as thick as her leg lifted out of the ground. Lani looked over her shoulder and saw the tree toppling toward the river. The root strained against the weight of the tree below it, then snapped just below Lani.

She pulled frantically at the slippery dirt above her and dragged her body over the crest. She turned and watched as the bank below her sank into the river, the massive tree now being battered by the water as it was pulled downriver.

Lani didn't wait any longer, she turned away from the river and kept crawling inland. After a short distance she forced herself upright and, even though she wobbled, managed to trudge through the mud and stones, bouncing off the few smaller trees that lined this part of the river's edge, using the momentum to propel her away from the angry waterway.

The storm continued to rage above and around her, but Lani kept moving, one step after another, until she felt safe from the river. She was drenched, cold and exhausted. Now that she wasn't fearing for her life, she could feel the pressure building in her head and knew she needed shelter before she blacked out completely.

Another flash of lightning showed her a clump of bushland to her right. She turned in that direction and blindly headed toward it. Once she was inside the edge of it, she felt a little safer. The rain was deflected by the trees and other bushes, and if nothing else she could take a break.

Unable to see much, she burrowed into some scrub and lay down, unsure if she should be thankful or not for what had just happened.

TILLANDRA

Tillandra had gone with Kooka and spent the night outside the city in the camp with him and those he had with him in the Fool's Cart. She rarely met new recruits so raw these days, and it was something she kicked herself about. Seeing them as they were before they became part of Anderwell and their society, helped her recall what most of their family had been through before.

Mostly they all wanted to hear the story of what had happened, and how she'd been imprisoned in the basement of a library. She indulged them with what she could tell them and embellished it enough to make it entertaining.

Of all the wagon riders there were two that she noticed almost immediately, and Kooka's description of them only confirmed what she already sensed. Gizen and Purple were more than just the others. They each had something to them that needed nurturing. But first, they needed to get settled and trust the way of life in Anderwell.

Next time she spoke to Junther or Toolet she needed to make sure they were given special treatment. Tillandra didn't know how long it might take to polish the rough gems they were, but she couldn't believe that two of them had arrived in one cartload like this.

Those with extra talent didn't normally stand out for quite some time.

Things are definitely changing. Is it the Occultation or something else?

She drank more than anyone else, her thirst very hard to quench, and she was happy to eat the simple bread and cheese that Kooka had. He had seemed embarrassed to only have such simple fare for her, but she was thankful to just have food.

When all the group but Kooka had settled in for the night, the pair spoke about his journey.

"You've been gone a long while, Kooka, we were getting worried about you."

"I took a slow route, Mother. There are places I've just never been. Too many roads I take I've been down the year before, this time I decided I needed to go a different route. It's been a hard year, though."

Tillandra just waited for him to continue, she didn't need to probe him.

"The cold in Malamig was brutal. I ended up as far as the road will go and got stuck there for a month or more, waiting for the road to clear enough to get out. That was where I heard rumors from the east."

"Rumors about what?"

"About the land bridge to Enderk. Did you not get the message?"

"I do not recall one, tell me."

"Just the odd person mentioning that the Derks are connecting the Stepping Isles, some story about how it used to be a land bridge, and now they're fixing it."

That peaked Tillandra's interest. If word of it had reached Anderwell she hadn't heard it. She filed it away for later."

"Then I ventured into Morska."

"How did that go?"

"Well, I wasn't welcome anywhere in the heartlands, but on the outside, it was the same as anywhere. I did nearly get into some trouble passing through the great forest, but it was that journey that brought me to Gizen. Strangest thing it was."

"What was?"

"She was sat there waiting for me. Like she knew I was coming."

"Well... given her talents."

"Yes, I know that now, but at the time she said almost nothing. Just stood up and climbed into the wagon essentially."

"Don't lose her, Kooka. She needs us, and we need her."

"I know, Mother. She's just hard to get through to."

"I'm not sure you ever would. She just needs to be with us, nothing else will matter to her."

"You seem to understand her better than me."

"I've seen her type before. You did good, Kooka. Very good."

"Thanks, but anyone I can save is good to me. Each of them needed me when I showed up."

"You deserve a good rest when you get home."

"It never lasts though, Mother. When I get there, I'm itching to head back out and find more. The thought of them all suffering just cuts me."

Tillandra reached over and put her hand on his shoulder. He smiled at her. "I think I'm going to turn in, you need anything else?"

"No, Kooka. I'm so glad you rescued me. It was becoming quite grim."

"I only hope it was worth it."

"Those books, keep them safe and get them back to Anderwell for me."

He laughed his infectious laugh. "Now, sneaking back down there and getting them for you, that was fun."

She smiled. "And I'm grateful to you as well. I don't think they'd have let me take them if I'd asked. I'm going to be heading across the river tomorrow, I have a long journey south."

"How early will you leave?"

"We'll eat together then I'll be gone."

~

WHEN SHE HEADED OFF THE NEXT DAY THE WEATHER HAD TAKEN A TURN for the worse. By the time she was on the road south to Havenby the sun was up but little of it filtered through the darker clouds.

Several times as she hurried along the road, she shook her head at the ludicrousness of what had just happened to her. Despite all the real troubles she was facing, two doddery old men had almost done her in. Part of her felt bad that they'd deceived the librarians, but she needed time to study the books, and the best place for her to do that was Anderwell.

When she settled into a roadside camp for the evening, she felt tired and several times an annoying tickle in her throat caused her to cough.

That's all I need right now, getting sick.

The next few days passed quickly as she hurried down the ocean road, not even stopping to check on local contacts. She had one purpose right now, getting to the Carver as quickly as possible. Now that Ashantha's ring had turned, she was on a deadline.

When she reached Verloren nestled in the mid-Kysten coastal mountains she was weary and still hadn't fully shaken off the minor illness she had picked up. While she would have passed through without stopping, her desire for a bath and a solid meal and some conversation tipped her over into staying at an inn.

She chose the first one she could see that looked clean enough and took a room.

"You'll be wanting a bath by the look of you, I'd say?" the keeper asked.

"Without a doubt. It's been a long road here."

"No doubt twice as fast as the rest of us."

"How long until the water might be ready?"

"You're in luck, someone else has only just finished, the fires are still running. Bathrooms are on the first floor, end of the hall. Left one is for women."

By the time Tillandra had scrubbed and soaked herself she was glad to change into the only spare clothing she had. When she returned downstairs a woman was waiting at the counter.

"Is it possible I could have these washed?"

"Hand them here, I'll see to them now."

"Thank you."

"Not a concern. You should get into the main room, there's fresh meals coming out any moment. We've got goat, freshly butchered and all. New supplies came in just yesterday."

Tillandra masked her lack of excitement. She'd never been one to see anything but grease in goat, but it was the delicacy in Kysten, and it was rude to not go along with them. "That sounds perfect. Thanks again."

There were only a handful of patrons in the main room when she entered, and the keeper seemed in better spirits than he had been earlier. He even surprised her when he personally brought her trencher over and placed it down in front of her.

"My mother's special sauce in that. And fresh meat only came in last night. You lucked out you did."

"Well as it stands, I feel like I could eat a whole goat."

He chuckled at the joke. "You said you were heading south, is that right?"

"It is."

"You'll not have heard about the pass then?"

"The pass?"

"Greppon's Pass, that's the road that cuts around the coast about thirty miles south of here. Right on the cliffs."

"Yes, I know it, I've been down there a couple of times."

"Not this trip you won't."

She looked up sharply. "Why's that?"

"Collapsed on itself it did. About a month or so ago. Whole road's gone."

Tillandra couldn't believe her luck. If she had to go west around the mountains it would take her the best part of a month just to get to the Carver.

"Don't be all worried though. It's turned into something of a boon."

"How so?"

"The King has been experimenting with different sea craft, and we've all ended up with a fleet of trader vessels carrying people up and down the coast. You'll get one almost every other day and it's a third of the journey than it is on foot. Even for one like you."

"That sounds like a nice way to travel. It's not too rough?"

"No, the coasters hug the coastline pretty tight and just skip all the road. You can go all the way to Grote from here now."

"Oh really? So where do I go to get a boat ride then?"

"So glad you asked." He smirked as he replied. "It just turns out my cousin has one of those vessels and would you know it, he's leaving tomorrow."

Tillandra rolled her eyes, now she knew why he was being so helpful. No doubt he would make a nice clip of the coin she'd need to pay.

"Aren't I lucky to have picked your inn then?"

GORAN

*B*rando rode ahead of him, not a word said in more than a day. When Goran had arrived back at their inn in Union, struggling to even stand straight, the two men had argued about him going out and not telling the keeper.

"You can't be going off on one of your benders! I'm not here to chaperone you."

"You've no idea what you're talking about. Leave me be."

They'd combed the city seeking news of the girl. For all Goran knew, if the ring had come off then she would have had to have died. That's if she was like them, which he knew she wasn't, but there was no other logical way he could understand it.

No one knew of any strange girl that had been killed or suffered any injury, which didn't help him resolve what to do. He'd tried to reach out to Anderwell, but he couldn't. It wasn't the first time he'd been affected like this, where the magic didn't work.

When he had minor episodes it didn't seem to matter too much, but after going dark like what had just happened it took days before he could get back to his normal abilities.

It didn't help them working together that Brando would hardly speak to him, but then the peace and quiet suited his dark mood. There wasn't a lot more he could do to find out if she was alive, so he made a decision to assume the worst. If that was the case then he'd failed.

He had been walking roads throughout the city in a pattern trying to cover as much as he could and looking for anything that might help; even a hungry urchin who might have seen something a coin would prize loose, but nothing had jumped out at him.

By the time he returned to their inn, his mood was so black he went to his room and slept. He wasn't even interested in having a smoke, the thought of that turned his stomach like everything else. After one of these turns, he just had to ride it out, and wait for it all to pass.

The next day he'd decided they should head to Diwedd, where at least they had resources. There was one of their inns there, and couriers. Goran hoped by the time they arrived his head would be clear and he could reach out, but sitting around in Union was not getting them anywhere.

He'd have to get word to the Court, and let them know she was probably dead. There could be no other reason for the ring coming off. She'd had it on since the beginning: if she could have taken it off before, why hadn't she?

And it had turned into a coin, which was the damning fact for Goran. It was no longer Ashantha's ring, or her ring, it was a coin, and would need to be returned to Tingfurlew. He'd never know how that all worked, but now he had it he guessed he needed to get it sent on so it could get there.

That means an Audition!

It was the first clear thought he'd had in days. Even more reason for him to reach out. Tillandra needed to know, everyone needed to know, the clock would be starting. They'd know then how he'd failed, and that he hadn't even found the mask.

You really are useless, Goran.

That wasn't even Zoran talking, it was his own voice. Then it hit him that they'd know already, or soon enough. The light would have changed colors, and they'd know. They'd be trying to contact him.

Less than a few hours' ride ahead sat the massive wall of rock that made up the Luze mountains. They were harsh and impassable except for the few breaks in the range. The city of Diwedd sat guard over one of those places, the River Roilaren.

Neither people or horses could travel any distance through the gorge that river ran in, you traveled through there by boat or not at all. Otherwise you headed east a day's ride and through the pass that led to Pasio. Goran had been that way once, it was not a pleasant ride. Whichever route you took, everyone ended up in Galon so it made more sense to pay the ferrymen and take a boat, besides which it was quicker.

Diwedd could have been part of the mountains for the way they'd constructed it. The square city jutted out from the mountains, wrapped in a dark solid stone wall that struggled to reflect the late afternoon sunlight.

On their right, open plains were being farmed. Further back they'd been fields of wild grasses, but this close to a major city, and transport centre, all types of produce were being grown. The land either flat or with gentle undulating rises was a visual respite before you met the huge wall of stone that lay ahead.

Brando had stopped his horse, and as Goran rode up, he turned to him.

"You ready to talk?"

"I've been ready the whole time, it's you who's been wordless."

"Is that right?" The man's eyes showed he was still angry with Goran, it didn't matter how pleasant he tried to be. "What's your big plan then? If we can't track her without the ring, we're clueless."

"I don't have a plan, Brando. I told you that. Other than getting to our inn here in Diwedd, and getting access to couriers. If she's even alive, which I doubt."

"I still don't understand why you can't… speak… to someone."

Goran shook his head.

"When I'm not feeling right, I can't do it. It doesn't work. Simple as that. I don't know why, it just doesn't."

"This is useless. We're traveling blind."

The keeper was right and Goran had no idea how to fix it. The truth was, he hoped to send Brando back home to Callet once they reached

Diwedd. Goran didn't need company, if anything he needed to be alone, very alone.

Maybe now was the time to go off on his own, seeking out someone to help him. He wasn't being used by the Court in any useful way, not now that he'd messed up this task. Maybe he could seek out a healer, someone to help fix him. Or he could just find a place away from everyone, and live alone.

~

GORAN'S WISH FOR AN EASY NIGHT'S REST HADN'T MATERIALIZED. No sooner had he lain down ready to fall asleep than there had been a banging on his room door. He shook off the fuzziness in his head and scrambled to his feet, approaching the door cautiously.

"Who is it?"

"Me, Goran. You better come downstairs."

Goran pulled his tunic over his head and pushed his feet into his boots. He'd tie them up later if needed. Brando was waiting outside the door for him.

When they got down into the main room there were two others already there. Yeta, the keeper, and one of their couriers, Dongan. "What's all this then? You just get here?"

Dongan nodded. He had the look of a man who had been riding for days. "I did."

"But it's late night, what on Dharatan were you doing riding in the dark? What's so important?"

"Henri died, Goran."

"What?"

Goran could feel Brando grab him as his body seemed to fall from beneath him.

"Sit down, Goran."

"I'll get us something to drink." Yeta hurried out to the back of the kitchen.

"Tell me." Goran looked at Dongan.

"He just got worse and worse, Goran. Zeresse and Yenrk tried but there was nothing for him."

It was too much for him to take, he could feel himself wobbling in the chair as if he'd pass out. Goran leaned forward and cupped his head in his hands.

"Take your time, Goran. It's a shock."

More than five minutes passed before he was able to gather himself and sit up straight, without feeling sick.

"What of the other man?"

"The Mal? He lived."

"Did he have anything worthwhile to tell?"

"Nothing that I was told. At some point he slipped out of the inn, not a word of thanks, and just disappeared. He can't have been that well, but no one was of a mind to go looking."

"Why him, and not Henri?" Goran couldn't believe Henri was no more.

Dongan shrugged his shoulders. "I'm just the messenger."

"You've done a fine thing, pushing yourself so hard."

"I'll rest up the night, but I best keep going. There's no one to pass the message on to so I'll have to keep traveling south."

"No need, Dongan. Go back via Union though, the keeper up there at least needs to know. They've been at it almost as long as each other. I'll see news of it gets back to Anderwell."

"Thanks, Goran. I'm glad to not have to ride this all the way south."

Yeta brought out a jug of strong brandy and poured all four of them a shot. By the time they were done, the jug sat empty, and Goran's head was a blur. He couldn't imagine life in Callet without Henri, nor never seeing his old friend again.

ZORAN

*S*ometimes it was like climbing out of a sack that was not quite big enough. Trying to get one leg out, then the next, and pushing yourself through awkwardly until your head was free. At other times, it was more like walking into a mist, and when you came through you could see clearly.

This time it was like someone had rung a bell, and everything changed. Zoran felt like it was just him, not Goran holding onto the box and only letting him out enough to see the daylight and take in some fresh air.

He could have done without the hangover though.

What in Seth's name were they all up to last night? All that moodiness and sadness, enough to dry up your laugh muscles for good.

Oh, I recall now. It was that old hunchback from the Safe in Callet. He'd moved on over to the other world. The dead one. Zoran didn't appreciate all the sentimentality, it wasn't like the dead person could feel a blasted thing.

Gone. Poof! Here today, gone tomorrow.

And as for the grumpy old hunchback, didn't matter at all to Zoran. One less person to have to listen to them grumbling about rules or ways of doing things.

Who was left in charge up there? *I have some vague recollection of a woman, but no idea who. They'd be still getting used to things, we could slip back there and help ourselves to a good amount of play money.*

Someone was knocking on the door, which made him sit up. His head wasn't as bad as he'd thought, and he sprang to his feet to go see who it was. Unfortunately it was the brute Brando.

"What do you want?"

The innkeeper's face turned sour at the question. "I came to check on you. How are you doing?"

"Perfectly fine, thank you. And you?"

Zoran didn't move from blocking the door and had nothing else to say to the man, which seemed to confuse him.

"Right. So no plans about Henri or anything else?"

"Henri's dead, isn't he?"

"Yes. That's what Dongan told us last night."

"And you're thinking that I'm going to magic him undead or something are you?"

Brando's face appeared shocked to Zoran.

"What in Thenis's name has gotten into you?"

"Too much cheap Lletem brandy is what's gotten into me. Surely we're able to afford something that doesn't taste like barrel sludge when we drink, can we not? This is tiresome, I'm in need of some food, if you'd be so kind as to move your broadness, I'll see what they've got on offer downstairs."

Brando reluctantly moved and let Zoran lead the way, but he could sense the man behind him all the way down the stairs.

I can see why Goran wanted to get rid of the bore. I'll need to drop him as soon as I can.

The food wasn't much better than the brandy, in his opinion, anyway, but he chose to make all the pleasantries to the serving wench that brought it to him. He eyed her several times. She might do for some activity later on, if he wasn't able to do better.

"You're looking pleased with yourself, does that mean you've heard from the others?"

"Others, what others?"

Zoran stared into the other man's eyes. He was tired of the man's conversation and wanted peace and quiet for now, so he turned on the thing he'd developed. That ability to get people to see things your way.

It was a little like nudging someone, ever so gently. They didn't notice it, not really, and Brando had that look. Ripe for a suggestion. "The others are all fine, Brando, just need you to go find us a boat south, why don't you do that?"

Zoran wrapped the words with his power, letting the suggestion travel with his soft voice. Zoran could see it work, the angst that was there before slipped out of the man's eyes.

"I'll leave you to it, and go find us a ride down the river. When do you think we'll be going?"

"A day or two at least. Why don't you see what's available and I'll have a better idea later on."

"Sure, Goran." The thickset keeper got up and walked out of the inn, his mind set on his task.

I hate having to be called that name, but it's safer with all of this lot. I need to go find some people who'll not care who I am.

The feeling pressed at him right between the eyes, like something was trying to poke right through there. That was it, one of the other Jesters was trying to reach Goran, except they couldn't. Not like this.

Zoran could feel them trying, but he had no interest in trying to see if he could do it or not. They'd only go on and on about something Goran was supposed to be doing. Or whatever he'd done wrong this time.

Which was why it was better he was out. Zoran was much more accomplished at doing the hard things, unlike the soft one, who was locked away grieving about the hunchback. He was safer there, out of the way.

But the pressure it caused in his head was too much. He couldn't stand up just now, he needed to let it all pass, they'd give up soon enough. Then Zoran would need to consider his options. Getting away from Brando long-term was a key priority, but he wasn't going to stay here in Diwedd.

Rocks bored him, and people that lived around lots of rocks seemed to be as stoic and boring as rocks. He was much more of a fluid guy, he needed palaces, and parties, nobles and celebration. And gambling. Lots of gambling. Particular cards, that was it.

He'd need some money, even if he did decide to go and help himself to the stash back in Callet. It would cost to get back there, he wasn't putting up with this nonsense of sleeping rough most nights.

That was another problem with Goran, he didn't understand the finer things in life. Zoran shook his head, thinking about some of the things Goran would accept. The pressure in his head left and he went walking through the city, hunting down somewhere he'd be likely to find a game going on, despite it being mid-morning.

In the right parts of any city, there was always a game going on. And where there was a game, there were those to profit from.

~

STANDING IN THE SHADOWS OF A SIDE LANE, BRANDO WAITED UNTIL Goran was far enough ahead that he could easily follow him without being seen. While he hadn't been in the city in many years, the bones of it hadn't changed.

And cities didn't change their aspects much at all. Goran was heading to the parts of town that only meant trouble. Brando wasn't sure what was up with him, but he'd seen this attitude once before.

It was like he behaved completely differently. It was confirmed when they had sat down to eat and he'd used his left hand for everything, as naturally as if it was his normal hand. The thing was, even late last night when they were all brandied up, Brando could remember him using his right hand.

His speech, and the complete lack of care about Henri, meant something wasn't right. There'd been no smell of weed from his room, he'd lingered long enough to see if the smell was there. Not that he couldn't have slipped out after they all went to bed, but it didn't feel the same.

When Goran was on weed, he was docile and sluggish, and this was completely different. If he hadn't seen it from him before, he'd think the man was playing a joke on him. All he could do was follow him and see what sort of trouble he was about to start.

SOMETHING WASN'T QUITE RIGHT. HE'D DRUNK PLENTY OF WINE TODAY, that was for sure, but his head was swooshing around like water in a swinging barrel. It was taking all of his will to keep it together, which meant he was having trouble pushing his will out to the men around the table.

Up until a half hour ago, he'd built up quite a stack of coin, and was very pleased with himself, unlike his opponents, who had all gone quite sour as their piles disappeared. Then they'd changed up the game and their attitudes had altered.

As had his fortunes. He blinked slowly again. His eyelids were getting heavier and heavier.

It's not that late, what's got into me?

"Play, Zoran. Let's have your cards, man." Directly over from him a nuggety boatman with a full black beard stared at him.

I need to stare at him, that's how I do it. But I can't seem to...

"He's lost his touch he has, lads. Doesn't like it much when the boot's on another leg, does he?" A voice to his left. Zoran couldn't focus on what he looked like.

Their patience was getting thin. He put his cards down and looked at them. They weren't good at all. And the other cards were put down as well.

Blackbeard laughed hard. "It's mine again then!" He waited for each of the others to pay up their loss.

"And you, Zoran," he barked.

Zoran looked down at his cards again, not believing how bad they were, his head wobbling a little.

"Looks like our pal here's had too much to drink. Pay up now, and you best be on your way."

Zoran went for his pocket, where his pouch of coins was, and pulled it out. He fumbled with it, struggling to get into it, his eyes almost completely out of focus now.

The wine, that's what it was. They changed it when we changed games. They gave me my own, said I deserved it. What have they done?

"Here, let me help you with that." Blackbeard grabbed at the pouch and tipped it up. "Hang on, this is empty. You owe me, Zoran."

There was nothing likely to get your attention more than an angry man wanting money from a gambling debt. Zoran was able to focus more on what was happening, and reached into the deeper pocket in his tunic.

He felt something there. There were multiple objects deep in the pocket, and he grabbed one and pulled it out. It was some sort of ring, a black band with an orange stone set in it. Something about it pulled at Zoran's head, but he couldn't think.

"Well look at what you've got there."

Zoran tossed it on the table. "There… paid."

One of the others pushed their stool back. "Sweet Seth, you can't take that!"

"Why on the rocks not?"

"That's amber, it is. You'd best leave that well alone."

The last thing Zoran saw was Blackbeard's hand snatch up the ring, before everything went black. He heard something bang loudly, right near his ear as he toppled but it didn't matter at that point.

UKSOD

It was rare that he chose to go see her without being summoned, but Uksod's concerns had not abated. As much as he hated the climb back up, at least the darkness was familiar and quiet. Since Schevenal's death things had become much more complex for him.

Uksod had hoped that it would simplify what he had to manage, but the boy had stepped into the role of ruler quicker than he had envisaged. Now he was changing and too quickly for Uksod's liking. It wasn't just about him trying to stop drinking the amber brandy, there was more.

He had spent countless hours focused on trying to isolate what it was, but there was nothing Uksod could pinpoint. He doubted it was as simple as him growing up, his birthday was just another day.

All of his work on the boy growing up had mostly paid dividends. In many ways Karpenmor was fitting into the role they needed him to fill. It was the other things that were causing all Uksod's angst. Especially his interference in the search for Hurf.

Uksod had no idea what the old man might know, but he didn't want the boy getting to him first.

No, that won't do at all.

Ever since the incident with the cook, Karpenmor had made it a point to visit with Uksod more regularly and without notice, making his work to discover the truth about whoever the woman was that held the amulet much harder.

It didn't help that the Vrah had been so efficient in their work eliminating Karpenmor's mother. Anyone that had traveled with her had been executed, which at the time seemed sensible. There was no expectation that in the future he would need to discover what they might know.

~

"This is most unusual, Uksod." He could almost hear a smile in her voice.

"Mistress."

"Does you coming to me without me requesting it mean you have good news for me?"

"The only news I have of a good note comes from Fuling, the priest in Daskare. The King still moves his forces into place, and the first of the major compounds they have built, in Rohumaa, is near to completion."

"Trivial, Uksod, unless they have found the stone. When will the King come back here with his amulet?"

"I have not been told, mistress."

"It must happen, Uksod!"

"Of course, mistress, and I have stressed it to Fuling. I have little to force the timeline with."

She did not reply for several minutes.

"I am getting frustrated, Uksod. Things are not happening the way I want. It is all taking too long."

"I understand."

"Do you? I am not sure you do, Uksod. The amulet is no closer to being retrieved, the boy is not bonded to it which means I cannot control him. And he's hiding something from me."

"What do you mean?"

"Something is different about him. I cannot reach him like I could. It seems he has something similar to his father in him."

"I don't understand."

"Without the amulet, Schevenal was not always accessible. He was able to hide his mind from me, for brief periods, or shut me out. I don't know how, but Karpenmor did the same to me."

"He still is avoiding the drink some of the time. Is it that?"

"No, he was in the Amber Room when he did it. In there I don't need anything to aid me, but he blocked me."

"What can I do?"

"Get him back on the brandy. Why is he avoiding it?"

"He won't tell me. He has developed quite an independent streak."

"Which is not to be unexpected, Uksod. Not only is he no longer a boy, but it's all his now, or it will be soon. Which is why the amulet must be returned!"

"I am working on it, mistress."

"So you keep saying. What do you know about the girl?"

"Little, although it won't matter either way."

"Why?"

"She can never rule in Enderk, so she serves no real purpose. The chance that Karpenmor discovered her is too risky. And getting the amulet back will be difficult enough without needing to drag someone along as well."

"And she needs to die for him to bond to the amulet."

"Exactly. When she dies, it will seek him out, will it not?"

"Yes, it should. But it is growing weaker, Uksod. Another reason for you to hurry! I will not lose it again."

"I'm going to the coast, to uncover the truth of his mother, if there's any left to be found."

"Why waste time going to the coast if you intend to have the girl killed anyway?"

"I don't like loose ends, and if there's anyone left that knew of such a thing, then I want it cleaned up. Someone must have known more than was discovered before. For a child to live there and word to never get back to us, and to leave with the mother, that required assistance. I need to know it all. We cannot have such people hiding in our midst."

"If the mother had been dealt with properly in the beginning none of this would have happened."

"We both agreed to keep her alive, just in case."

"That was foolish of us."

"Easy in hindsight, mistress, but after such a wait for a boy, keeping her alive just in case he didn't surive that first year or two seemed prudent."

"What of the boy?"

"His independent streak includes interfering in my daily affairs."

"Amulet."

"I know, I know."

"Is he safe to leave unattended? If I cannot control him, what will happen while you are gone?"

"There are many processes that govern who can decide on things. While he is the heir, he does not have absolute power yet. It is a fine line, but those left behind will hold him to that. At least until the ceremony is completed."

"I had wanted him bonded before the final ceremony."

"Before the amulet surfaced, we still intended to have him rule."

"Before we found it, yes. But now if we get it, then there won't be any issues, Uksod."

"I am doing all I can, to distract him and delay it."

"I hope it's more successful than your efforts to being the amulet back."

"For now he hasn't raised the issue, which is making it easier, but if he discovers the limits to what he can do, then I would think he will want to force my hand."

"Delay him, Uksod."

"I have plans, mistress. Remember he has to be anointed by me, and before that can happen he has to complete the rituals. They have been known to take some time."

"Good."

"In the meantime I will get some answers, one way or another, and put this problem to rest, before it grows. And I'm handing him over to others to teach him what he needs to know for the ceremony."

"Get that amulet, Uksod, and the other one as well. They need to be back

here. Then maybe we can find the rest. One was a start, two is better. Get them!"

"Yes, mistress."

Uksod turned and began the climb back to the top, annoyed at the inconvenience of this trip he needed to make. None of it should be needed. Someone had lied to him, and he'd find out who. They would pay, and anyone close to them.

At the time it had been a disaster to have found she had escaped, but it appeared to have all been solved. Never would he have thought that would reach forward and cause such problems now. And of course it was left to him to fix all the problems.

While Yantarnaya could reach anyone's mind within a short range of amber, and influence them, put ideas into their heads, it didn't guarantee results. She still needed boots on the ground to do what she could not. Or the special gems that had been carved from the Debrua stone.

The eight that had been used to create the amulets, and the one in Uksod's circlet. There had been numerous experiments where she had tried to use them to create more control. Her lack of patience with people tended to cause unexpected results.

Giving them out as gifts to the barbarian rulers had been a perfect example. She had not realized how they would react all so close together, binding to their owners. What had happened had been completely unexpected, although she still blamed the Citadel Stone for what ended up happening.

One story always made Uksod laugh. An ice bear in the north of Malamig had eaten someone carrying the first piece carved from the stone. Ice bears are a tricky beast to deal with even at the best of times. They are powerful and strong-willed animals best kept well away from.

In the early days of Vrah training there had been a test that trainees went through, having to enter an ice bear cave and bring back something significant from it. That stopped after too many never returned, despite their training.

Yantarnaya had tried to influence the animal after it had ingested the gem but the distance weakened her capabilities. The animal appeared to be upset by what it had swallowed and felt eating more things would quench the pain it thought it was suffering.

By all accounts it destroyed several villages on its rampage, before it ended up in a town and turned to liquids, consuming many barrels of ale. Having passed out trying to burrow into a large rock, it was speared to death by locals while it lay there drunk.

From what Uksod had heard, bards still sang the tale through Malamig to this day, or some variation of it. It was after that she had sought someone to help her achieve her goals. His very first task had been to retrieve the small stone that the beer had swallowed, before it was discovered by others.

That stone now sat in the circlet on his forehead.

In the early days she had held resentment toward him, at being able to do things in the real world, while she was trapped in the stone. As they achieved some of their goals over time, that had gone away. Up until the amulet was discovered. Now her short temper was causing him to feel more threatened than ever before.

The thought of leaving the palace didn't inspire Uksod, the idea of having to sleep rough made him cringe. But there was little choice, it was not a task he could leave just to One. Uksod didn't even know if anyone was still alive out there who would know.

He needed to dig carefully and sort through what people knew, and spot any lies. One way or another, he needed answers.

CARNUS

Throughout that night, Carnus had dreamed, something he didn't normally do. Images of a moon with a mouth, shouting at him, but he couldn't hear what it said. Every night he tried to listen but never could he hear the sounds. In the end he came to terms with the fact he had gone mad, and that everything was a dream. He was dead.

Except the ringing of the bell echoed through his head, forcing him awake.

"Dawn, Big Man, time for you to go. You make my hut smell."

It wasn't the normal way Carnus would wake, nor the most pleasant of things to be told when you wake, but if he was dreaming it was now a complete vision in all detail.

Carnus felt stronger than he knew he should. He pushed himself to his feet, and his head almost brushed the thatching on the underside of the roof. The hut that had seemed large last night now felt very small.

He looked around the hut for the old man, but there was no one else in there. Shaking his head in confusion, he walked out the open door to a massive courtyard full of small gardens all lined up in paths. Out of the corner of his eye he thought he saw the man moving but when he turned there was no one there.

Was it all a dream?

It couldn't be; the hut where he had slept, the empty jug, they were all real. He was alive, and looking at the city outside the courtyard, it appeared very real as well. He walked through the gardens, onto a small bridge over a pond, and then out onto the main road.

He had to decide what to do. He was without coin or anything else. He wore the pants that were typical of his people and no top or footwear.

Maybe I should go back to my post, and watch?

Was he actually in Union, like the man said? Surely they wouldn't have taken him far from where he had been? That meant he could easily go back to where he was and watch.

The old man had seemed real last night, his words had seemed real enough. Carnus knew the myth that went alongside these people called The Eyes. They could see the truth of things, not just the future, but of now, and even of things past.

Much as religion was not allowed within Ngahere, nor were seers. He wasn't sure how much of it was just ravings and if any was real. It seemed to make sense to him before he slept, but then he had been weak and unwell.

Carnus returned to the spot near the border and sat watching the forest, contemplating what had just happened. He tried to sit it out, to let himself give in and just die there, but he found he couldn't.

Whatever had let him get to the point of collapse before, was gone, he was too afraid to let himself die. As if the shame from his people wasn't enough, now he knew he was too much of a coward to even take his own life.

That old man had challenged him to do it, but Carnus wasn't even able to think of it anymore. It didn't bother him to die while fighting but to commit such an act was even below who he was now.

He had nowhere to belong, no honor, and not even enough courage to put an end to it. Before the first day ended he turned and walked back into the city of Union. One way or another he would find food, and a place to sleep.

No one he knew had ever spoken much of Union, or other Lletem cities. He had heard their names, and occasionally something about an event near one or other of them, but no detail. Few Ngaherians lived outside of Ngahere. He was told it was because it was nigh on impossible to live the way of the Path in the outside world, and everyone eventually returned.

The call of the Path was too strong, and even the most lost would eventually find their way home. That's what he had been told, it was what they were all told. Carnus had no idea what that meant for him now. There was no way home, no way to return to where he belonged.

Could he still follow the Path out here? Did it even matter?

He would have to get help from others, not those of his kind. It would be a new thing for him, but he had no choice. It didn't matter what that stupid old man said, he had no choice. His choices had been taken from him.

For two more days and nights he went without food or drink, before he began to feel weak again. It was getting to the point where he would have to steal something soon.

There had never been a time when Carnus hadn't been in a position to provide for himself. This city wasn't like anything he was used to, and by the third day he began to follow some of the street beggars to see where they lived.

He knew he could overpower them easily if he had to, and take what they had. Carnus was past caring about the lack of honor in the thought, he knew he'd take the action if he had to. If he needed to steal, he would.

Union spanned the merging of two rivers, and arced in a half-circle from those rivers toward the west. Given its proximity to the Ngaherian border, it appeared the churches had all been set up as far away as possible on the southeastern edge near the South River gates.

The two beggars had limped their way almost to the largest of the church buildings. It was the largest in this city by far and Carnus stopped before he got too close. He had never been in a church or even this close to one before.

If the beggars were going to go inside he wasn't going to follow them, he couldn't do that. That was one of the primary rules of the Path, to never partake in any religious practices or beliefs. It was something that he could feel grating on his very being.

Thankfully the beggars veered across the grass in front of the church and headed toward the side, where a large tent was set up. Carnus felt very uncomfortable being so close to the church but he wanted to see where the men went, and forced himself to follow.

What he found was a large gathering of those who appeared to be from the streets. Old and young, injured or not, most dirty, and looking unkempt. They were all gathered because of the men, whom Carnus guessed were priests by their robes, who stood behind a table handing out wooden bowls filled with steaming food.

Everyone was stood in a queue, with those who knew each other engaged in lively discussion while they waited their turn. Off to the sides, those who were already served, sat with their food and ate.

When Carnus approached the long line went silent, causing the priests to look up at the cause. Compared to the majority of the people here, Carnus was much bigger than anyone else. He would have appeared threatening to those waiting.

"Back of the line, friend. Everyone is welcome, as long as you all take your turn," one of the priests called out from the table.

Carnus turned and walked down the queue and took his place in the line.

If he thought his shame was already at its lowest he wasn't ready for how he felt when he accepted the bowl from the priest and nodded his thanks. After so many days without food, he was truly grateful, but inside he struggled with taking it from these men who went against everything he had been raised with.

Was the food poisoned, or would it convert him?

He shook his head at the silliness of his thinking and almost spilled some of the food, the bowl filled right to the brim. Carnus slid down against a tree, his attention totally absorbed on the food he had been given.

The spot he had chosen was away from others and no one came to join him. He was happy with that, as he had no desire to speak to anyone here. They only highlighted how far he had been lowered.

His bowl contained a fine soup, rich and dark but full of meat and vegetables, and a spice in it that was different to anything he had tried before. He knew anything would have tasted good at this point but it was the best thing he could have asked for.

Carnus looked up at the sounds of sandals slapping on the ground near him. One of the priests was approaching with a jug and wooden cups, offering a drink to those who wanted it. When he got to Carnus he paused and looked him over for a long time.

"Unusual to see one of your kind here. You've got all of my brothers chattering you have. Doesn't matter who you are, all are welcome here in the Church of Bleth. I have some thin ale if you'd like to wash that down?"

This was all very uncomfortable to Carnus, but he could fault nothing of what was happening. These people were feeding those who had trouble feeding themselves, and seemed to care not for what anyone believed.

"Thank you." He held up his hand to take a cup, while the man filled it with the jug.

"You are most welcome, son of Ngahere."

The words caused Carnus to shiver. Not that he was about to explain how wrong the man was. "What is the Church of Bleth?"

"It is for those of us that follow the path of Hembleth, our God."

"What is that path?"

"Ours is to provide for those less fortunate in this world. No matter from what design, Hembleth favors charity above all else."

"That is most honorable."

"Thank you, we do what we can. Tell me, if you would humor me, why does one so able-bodied as yourself, and not so far from home, need our charity?"

Carnus looked up. There was something disarming about the man. Much as he wanted to get up and leave, he felt welcomed.

"My home is estranged to me now. I am seeking my own way."

"Oh."

The man seemed to think for some time.

"From what I know of your people, taking food from us must be hard for you."

Carnus simply nodded, and looked at the ground between his legs.

"Some advice if I may. You still have much strength about you. The longer you stay in the company of these who have little, you will see yours fade too. That would be a shame. There are those who are in need of someone like you. Strong and capable."

"To do what?"

"Merchants that ship their goods in caravans or boats down the rivers, are being attacked more often. Guards get paid well to protect them, as well as food and a bed, by all the accounts I have heard."

Carnus wasn't sure what to say. He'd never considered what he would do next, but this was something that made some sense, if only until he had time to find his feet in this strange place.

"Where would I find such men?"

"When we have finished up feeding all the people, and cleaned everything up, then come back to me. It will be several hours, at least, but before the sun is down I will take you to someone who might be able to help."

"You are right."

"About what?" The priest looked confused.

"This is very strange for me, about you. But I am grateful."

The priest waved him away. "Let me get this ale to the others." He turned and walked away, leaving Carnus sitting there confused about the simple kindness the man had shown.

What is so harmful about him and his religion?

UKSOD

As if anything with the boy was easy anymore. When Karpenmor learned Uksod was leaving to go to the coast, he determined he would come as well. The boy wanted to find his father's servant, which was the last thing Uksod needed.

For the best part of a day he had argued with him about the importance of the ceremony, and that the travel would be unpleasant. Uksod had sworn he could interview Hurf, or even bring him back to meet with the heir, if he was indeed over there.

Not that Uksod would let that happen. He was going to interview the man, along with anyone else that might have had contact with Schevenal, the mother, or any who cared for her. And he would get the answers he needed, one way or another.

In the end, Uksod could not refuse. It had become Karpenmor's stock response to the things he wanted — to remind Uksod he was the soon to be High Prince. And so he had reluctantly agreed to them traveling together, but had One send off some men ahead to prepare the ground for his arrival.

The only positive in the trip was it added delays to the final ceremony needed for Karpenmor to take over the realm. Now he was old enough there were several rituals to be completed before his enthronement ceremony could take place. And Uksod hadn't yet shared that with him.

Karpenmor wasn't interested in the details of the preparations for their journey either, which allowed Uksod to take several more days in readying their entourage, one large enough to ensure the heir's comfort, and of course make their progress slow.

Uksod had tried to glean what the boy wanted with the manservant of his father's but he wouldn't say. He just explained he was interested in learning what he could about his father before the old man died.

The only concession he had been able to make was that Karpenmor would travel past Ponte to inspect the progress of the land bridge, his hope being that it would be enough distraction to give Uksod the time he needed.

In front of the royal palace an orderly procession of people, horses and wagons waited for the last few travelers to arrive. Those that had started the gathering had been stood or sat outside in the courtyard for nearly four hours, baking in the sun. Uksod had no desire to join them, and while he waited for Karpenmor he sheltered in the shade of the covered entrance to the palace.

"Uksod, is everyone ready?"

Uksod rolled his eyes while he still faced outwards before turning. "Yes, Highness. Are you?"

"I am now. Shall we be on our way?"

"As you wish, Highness."

Their procession was led out into the city by twenty mounted guards, all dressed in orange and white. Their armor and weapons gleamed in the sunlight. Uksod had always thought white was a ridiculous color for military men, as by the end of any campaign the uniforms could never be worn again.

Behind the formal guard rode twelve Vrah, then Karpenmor and Uksod, followed by four more Vrah and the rest of the procession. It took several hours for the entire cavalcade to snake its way through the streets and out through the main city gates.

Residents of the city lined the streets and hung out of buildings to get a glimpse of the first procession of its kind in many decades. Uksod was sure it would be a story told in the city and out into the country-side for years to come.

The resplendent High Prince-to-be and his guards, visiting the people. Not that the boy really seemed to care too much past what it was he wanted to do. Uksod had brought plenty of the brandy with him, now he needed to see about getting Karpenmor to take it.

Perhaps when Yantarnaya had him bonded and under his control there might be time for the boy to see Enderk, although Uksod doubted it. As soon as they had that one amulet, the hunt for the others would become even more important.

The road they followed went directly north from En Carta before a hard left-hand turn in the exact middle of the Great Square. Now they were riding due west with the Gharbi Pass before them. It was as if a mighty hand had swept down and with two fingers carved a straight line through the mountain range.

If they were lucky, they might make the other side of the pass by the time they needed to stop for the night, but Uksod didn't like their chances. Karpenmor had been strangely silent since they had left the palace and rode alongside him looking from side to side, taking in the vast open plain.

When he did speak, Uksod nearly fell from his saddle in surprise. "Surely this is not the pace we will go the whole time?"

Uksod chuckled. "Unfortunately, Highness, it is. Traveling with royalty requires an entourage of retainers and supplies."

"This isn't how I envisaged this happening. How long will it take us to get to Ponte?"

"Like this? Twenty days or more."

"No!"

"Indeed, Highness. The journey is long, and we will at best travel only five hours or so each day by the time we pack down and prepare for what we need to do."

"That is ridiculous."

"There are things we need to cater for, Highness, like food and places to sleep."

"In the books I've read of battles, and great wars, in eons past, the soldiers seemed to move much quicker than this. How on Enderk could they achieve anything moving so slowly?"

"We aren't soldiers, Highness. And in such circumstance the soldiers and horsemen tend to move at their own pace and camp fast. Logistics follow behind and they ferry supplies forward as they need them. Periodically they may wait for the supply train to catch up."

"So we could do something similar and speed up our journey?"

"That would be most unusual, Highness."

"That wasn't what I asked, Uksod. If we do that how long will it take then?"

Uksod had to think on the question. He definitely didn't like where this was heading.

"Eight to ten days most likely."

"Then that is what we will do."

"Are you sure, Highness? It will not be easy for you; you've never traveled on the road like this."

"Difficult as it may be, I don't intend to die of old age or boredom before I get to Ponte. After today, we will hurry on, let the rest make their own way. No doubt we'll be in and out of Ponte before they even get close."

"And what about your staff, and camp, Highness?" Uksod wondered whether he could change the boy's mind with some brandy.

"I'll camp like our soldiers. I don't need to have a moving palace where I'm going."

"You might regret that after a night sleeping on the ground."

"There's only one way to find out."

The Regent's mind was set and with all of these people surrounding them there was no way for Uksod to berate the young man.

"As you wish, Highness. I will talk to the captain in charge this very moment and let him know the plans have changed."

Uksod steered his horse out of the line they were in and trotted forward to the man leading the guards. After several minutes of heated discussion, it was decided that a courier would return to the palace to draw more guards who would race to meet those they would leave behind.

It wasn't that there was any particular threat to them, but protocol demanded they be protected and the captain was having no argument otherwise. They decided that they would direct the rest of the procession to the midway point between Ponte and Taras, so that when the Regent and soldiers headed north, they would meet the cavalcade there.

He pulled out of the line again and returned to ride alongside Karpenmor.

"It is arranged?"

"Yes, Highness."

"Good. I want to get to Hurf as soon as we can, Uksod, so the sooner we're through Ponte the better."

Uksod held his anger in check until he was on his own. This wasn't what he wanted at all. He was glad he'd sent men on ahead, to at least scout out the farm. He needed to keep Karpenmor away from Hurf, and anyone else, until he'd resolved it all.

He wanted news of the amulet as well. Dealing with the newly empowered ruler wasn't enjoyable at all.

LANI

After several days of trudging through open countryside Lani had reached Pohja, a river town on the border between Rohumaa and Lletem.

The walk had been hard for her; she was sore from being smashed around in the river. Getting to Pohja was just about survival but it had given her plenty of time to think. She struggled to understand why she kept putting herself into dangerous situations.

She had no reason to stick her nose into the business of the smugglers. Lani wasn't sure why she had, and why she kept making things harder for herself. She needed to change that.

The storm on the river had been more frightening than Lani could have imagined. She wasn't sure if her leaping off the boat was the smartest thing either, except now she was free of the smugglers.

What might have happened if she had stayed? She would never know. Maybe they ended up wrecked further along the river. If that had happened, she might not have survived the crash.

In the end worrying about the past wasn't going to change what happened next. Her instinct to leap free had probably saved her life. What she needed to do in the future was stop getting herself in those positions in the first place.

Pohja offered her little but somewhere to sleep, clean herself and her clothes, and eat. Even the satchel she carried was mud-riddled and took an effort to clean as best she could.

She didn't linger more than the one night, and caught a boat south to Statiiv, this time keeping to herself, and wrapping a shawl around her head to hide, just in case she came across the boat she'd escaped from.

It gave her time to think. The words of the seer had made it seem like she had a choice. He told her that she was making choices, but he as good as confirmed what Ashantha had put in his journal, that the only person who could help her was the woman called Mother.

After a single night's rest in Pohja, Lani caught a boat south to Statiiv, too mentally worn out to think about much more than getting there, and staying out of harm's way.

When she arrived in Statiiv it was close to sunset, and she needed somewhere to stay. She walked away from the docks a good way on the off chance her captors were in the city, staying near the docks. After all of this the last thing she needed was to bump into them.

Lani's tiny room, near the centre of the city, was hot, and the small window didn't open making the space stuffy and stale. Lingering smells from the many people who'd slept in it before left a sour dirty tang in her nose, but it was better than sleeping out in the mud and she fell asleep without effort as soon as she lay down.

SHE HAD BEEN DREAMING, A DREAM SHE HADN'T HAD IN YEARS. WHEN SHE had been smaller the dream would haunt her almost weekly. She would be hunting all over Barnen looking for her mother, going up to every woman she came across asking *'Are you, my mother?'* The answer was always no and as the dream got longer the women became more annoyed and pushed her away.

Only a few times had she pursued the dream further and each time she had caught sight of a woman trying to avoid her. The woman had a shawl over her head and kept moving away from Lani. Once or twice, she caught sight of the woman's face, or what should have been her face, but inside the blue shawl was always nothing. There was just emptiness.

Lani got up out of the bed and wiped sweat off her forehead. The dream annoyed her.

Why now?

Everything she'd learned recently had pointed to the woman in Anderwell called Mother. Maybe that had triggered the dream again, after so long. Despite on the surface everything being about the amulet, deep down inside Lani it was about her mother.

She didn't care for the amulet at all, all she wanted was to be free of it. These Jesters seemed the most likely to help with that, more so than the Derks. Just before she had escaped it appeared Goatee had been ready to kill her for it.

What Lani really wanted was answers. If Ashantha's note in the back of his journal was accurate, her mother had died trying to save her. But save her from what?

She banged on her head several times with the balls of her palms.

"I want to know," she cried out to no one in particular.

The walls of her room in this shabby inn felt like they were pressing in on her. A feeling of gloom had put its hooks into her ever since Callet. It was there, under the surface, ready to spring on her if she wasn't careful. Normally Lani could keep it at bay by being positive or keeping busy, but at the moment she just felt it building.

This room wouldn't do, she knew that. Without outside air and with little light, she would descend into her own despair, and she had no time to allow that to happen. But what next? Changing inns was only temporary. Lani had to decide on her next step. If she was to continue south then a boat would be best.

What other choice did she have?

Lani took out the blue brooch and ran her fingers over it, seeking the familiar sense of calm it normally brought. It helped a little. Enough to push the gloom back a little, for now anyway. It was a constant thing in her life, now the only thing that remained from her previous existence.

She stared into the stone. The blue was always so attractive to look at and drew her in. The poor brooch had survived so much; looking at the thin strands of silver, she wondered how they could have with-stood what she'd put it through. It had fallen from height, been lost in drains for days, and generally knocked around.

At no point had it ever looked damaged and as she studied it in the limited light of her room, she couldn't help but be amazed at the quality of it, and how it still looked like it was new. Her only connection to her mother. She didn't even know why it was hers, why Kyro had been so serious about it.

The thought of Kyro brought tears to her eyes. Her resolve disappeared and she cried not just for him, but for Henri too. And Yerat. So many people had died, all because of her and the stupid amulet.

The brooch seemed valueless against their lives. It was just sentimental, not anything of value and unlike the amulet she could get rid of it if she wanted.

Maybe I could sell it. It would be worth a lot, and no one would die from touching it.

Even as she said it, she knew she'd never follow through with it. All her life she'd wanted to have a family and the silly brooch was all the family she had.

Lani looked at the stone. She'd noticed the blue seemed to be getting darker every time she looked. What lightness there had been was almost non-existent now. A tiny flicker of lightning flashed through it. Even that was duller than it had ever been.

She didn't know what that meant, if anything, but holding it was still comforting to Lani. As she stared at the stone, she began to drift off, not quite to sleep but almost. Her eyelids felt heavy and she became very relaxed.

It sounded as though a faint voice was coming from inside it. As much as she tried she couldn't hear the words, if there were any. Maybe it was just a sound like wind. It seemed to fade away and she became more awake again.

Lani wished she knew what the brooch was. It was more than just a piece of jewelry. Her experiment with it and the amulet in Callet had shown that. Somehow it seemed to block the amulet from her, but not completely.

Or maybe she'd imagined that. She felt totally blind to what it was doing. Fumbling around in the darkness of no knowledge, guessing at what it might be. It was the one thing she kept hidden; she couldn't chance someone trying to steal it from her.

Unlike the amulet, that they could come for all they liked. She knew that was impossible to lose. Lani put the brooch down and pulled the pouch out of her tunic. She put it on the floor in front of her and just looked at the gray fabric.

Since she'd used it on the boat at Galon, Lani had become more aware of the amulet than usual. There was always the tiniest sense of it, and she'd been able to shut that off when she held the brooch or kept the brooch near, but now that seemed to have changed.

She had to put the brooch on her skin to stop it and then it was almost like it wavered somehow, as if the amulet was winning the battle. When she connected to the amulet fully it hadn't felt like other times, not totally.

If she was honest with herself, being able to sense the men had excited her and she wasn't as afraid to try it again. None of the Derks had shown up, so her fear of attracting them had gone. Now it was only the warnings of Ashantha and the seer that held her back.

Taking it out of the pouch she held it in her palm and looked at the orange gem. It was odd that amber wasn't allowed to be traded on Dharatan, it was such a gorgeous color. Lani could imagine many people would want to have jewelry made with it.

The more she looked at the amulet, the more she felt at ease with it, as the tendrils snaked out from it. The thickest one always headed off, this time sneaking under the door and away. A tiny one crawled up her wrist and seemed to wrap around her forearm.

Lani had always been too afraid of it before as she hadn't looked in such detail at what it was doing. The other tendrils crept toward the small window in her room and pushed their way through as if the glass never existed. Everything seemed much slower than usual, but she couldn't say why.

Voices filled her head, people talking and what seemed like thoughts. Lani squinted her eyes trying to block them out as the tendrils drifted through the streets. It was as if her mind was partly following them, sniffing at people as it went by.

As she let it run she began to feel a draw on the amulet, as if something was pulling at it. Instinctively she pulled back against it but the stone was still in her hand. Again she could feel something pulling at it, trying to get her to follow it.

Her resistance to it slowly reduced and she stood up, slipping the amulet in her pocket, still in her hand, and left her room. Outside on the street, Lani followed the way it pulled her. She turned east onto a major road, mingling with the people rushing about their work.

While she stood out as a foreigner, being so short compared to all the Humaas, no one bothered her. She crossed intersection after intersection, and could see the outer walls of the city approaching. Still the pull on her kept heading to the east, or slightly north, it was hard to tell.

It was only the words of a guard at the gate that broke her out of the trance she was in.

"No shoes? It's a long walk to Kirje from here." He laughed to the guard beside him.

Lani removed her hand from the amulet and stopped in her tracks. She looked down. Her feet bare, and she didn't have her satchel. She'd been walking without thinking, following that pull. The pull was still there, almost as strong as ever, and she put her hand up to her chest to feel for the brooch.

She gasped when it wasn't there, and the guards laughed at her again. Lani turned and ran back the way she had come, fighting against the feeling that had brought her out here, but needing to get back to her room.

When she reached it, she barred the door behind her and forced the amulet back in the pouch. It was only then the pulling sensation went away. She picked up the brooch and, rubbing it frantically, stood with her back to the door, looking at the pouch on the floor.

5 5

LANI

*L*ani's heart hadn't stopped pounding in her chest since she had run back to the room. Holding the brooch tightly in her hand helped to block most of the amulet, but it wasn't calming her down. She had been completely out of her own control.

That was the only way she could explain it. The whole time she had been aware of what was happening but only as an observer, not actively participating in it. The pull she felt had been very real, she wasn't imagining that.

And it was trying to get her to head north east, away from the city.

Why?

Once she was feeling calmer, she tried to think what had happened when she'd been using it. The whole goal of getting it out was to understand it better, but it had almost taken over her, rather than her using it. She didn't like that, and it worried her that it could happen again.

Was that what the brooch helps stop? I should never have taken that off!

Leaving the room without any of her things had been foolish, she couldn't let herself lose control like that. If she was going to try to figure it out she needed to be more careful. There had been almost a sense of desperation threaded into the feeling of the pull, a strange sense she didn't understand.

There were too many things she didn't understand, but she needed to choose a path. While the amulet seemed to have its own direction it wanted to go in, there was nothing about that direction that attracted Lani. From the vague images she had learned in Ashantha's journal, she would have been heading toward a massive mountain range with a pass that led back north to Ngahere.

There was nothing for her up that way. If she wanted to go back home she might as well turn around and go back up the river. South was the only way that led to new possibilities, a chance that in this place called Anderwell she could get some answers.

Inside she could sense a small part of her that was attached to the amulet, that didn't want to undo what had happened. Lani shook her head as if to get rid of the feeling

No, I need to get it away from me, especially after what just happened.

Her mind was made up, for now at least. She stood and gathered up all her belongings. It was time to get moving.

Statiiv seemed brighter today than when she'd arrived, light bouncing off the stone buildings. Lani wrapped her shawl around her head with a peak draping down across her forehead, slightly shading her eyes. Mindful of the sailors she needed to avoid, she made sure her appearance didn't match anything they would remember and set off toward the harbor.

It was a vibrant city, and the tall stone buildings seemed to trap the sounds and let them bounce around continuously for as long as they could before they escaped into the open sky. The closer she got to the harbor the more people there were. She had to fight her way through carts and horses, large wagons and hundreds of busy people all rushing to get their work done.

Passing through the wide harbor gates, Lani stayed close to the wall to avoid being run down by the traders. She casually wandered the length of the jetties using her time to take in everything she could and to confirm the smugglers' boat wasn't docked there.

Lani breathed a little easier and unwrapped her head before walking the length of the busy harbor again.

Traffic came and went constantly, with the occasional high-pitched screeching when boats got too close and their sides grated against each other. Apart from numerous curses and shouting not much else seemed to come of it. Lani saw city guards prowling along the jetties letting everyone know to keep within the law.

Lani had no idea how to find the type of boat she was looking for. She couldn't tell if they were going north, west or south until they were well out into the river. On the widest jetty of them all Lani approached what appeared to be an office.

That was where the customs officers operated from, rushing to and from the different vessels as they arrived. When they came back, they carried either scrolls or pouches of coin. Unsurprisingly there were plenty of guards on this part of the jetty.

Lani walked up to one. "Where would I find out about getting passage to the south?"

The tall Humaas guard looked sideways at her, deciding she was definitely not from here, and he softened his stance. "Over there in the front office, the harbormaster will answer that. Stay away from the back office though, if you know what's good for you."

"Thank you." Lani moved on quickly to avoid any further scrutiny.

Inside the harbormaster's office was absolute bedlam, a constant flow of people coming and going with papers and coin pouches. Men and woman were yelling to be heard over everyone else, and at one end, two young men stood beside what looked like a hand-drawn copy of the layout of the jetties.

Each jetty had multiple hooks along it and the lads were constantly removing or hanging colored boats onto different hooks in response to someone yelling. She stood to one side and watched in amazement, letting it all wash over her. With a little bit of patience, she was able to focus on the people calling out and work out a pattern.

"It's not a gallery in here, girl. What you need?"

Lani was startled by the man's voice and turned to look at who was talking to her. "S-sorry. I wanted to find out some information," she said, her face blushing a bright red.

"What do you need?"

"How do I find passage south? Everything is so confusing."

"South? Jarv, or further?"

"Is Jarv toward the big lake?"

"Jarv's right on Lake Phyrgian. You sure that's where you're going?"

"Yes, it is."

The man turned and pointed to the wall with all the hooks and wooden boats on it. "See the left side?"

Lani nodded and he turned back to it.

"All those boats, mostly, are heading that way. Best way to tell is to look for a Skarian or Kysten flag. They won't normally go any further north than here, so you can bet your money on them heading back south again."

"What do their flags look like?"

The man rolled his eyes at her but answered anyway. "Daskare has a bear on it, normally white for their ice bears. Kysten one has a picture of a berserk fighter on it. You'll know it when you see it. Now, is that all?"

"Yes, thank you."

"On your way, girl. Not enough space in here for spectators."

With that information to help her, Lani went back to the main dock area and headed to the section the man had pointed out to her. Sure enough most of the boats there flew one of the two flags he had mentioned. It was easy enough then to work out who was just recently arrived versus those looking to head out.

A wide boat halfway down the southernmost jetty looked as though the crews were loading it with cargo. A flag on its mast bore the symbol of a white bear sat up on its hind legs snarling. It appeared to be the one referred to as the Skarian flag.

There were so many porters coming and going with sacks and carts of goods, she wasn't sure how to get close enough to seek passage.

A lean, wiry man walked down the jetty, his eyes roving all over the boat and all who brought goods to it. He had a thin black mustache, the hairs of it twisted and drooping either side of his mouth. The skin on his exposed arms looked leathery from much time exposed to the southern sun. Lani could see he was fit despite his age.

The top he wore had no sleeves and hung loose to his knees, tied at his waist with a thick brown belt held by a bronze clasp upon it. As slight as he appeared at first glance, Lani could see he was strong and carried the wariness of a cat, always ready to pounce.

He eyed her cautiously as she walked up to him, the planks of the jetty creaking under her.

"You're the captain of this boat?" she asked.

He continued to eye her up and down, not rushing his response. "That's me, who's asking?"

"I am looking for passage to Jarv, are you heading that way?"

He wiped his hands against the backs of his pants and turned to properly face her before reaching out his hand. "That I am, miss. Minook is my name."

Lani shook his hand, watching him carefully. "Do you have room for a passenger?"

"That's a long way from here for a woman to be going on her own who isn't one of these hustling Humaas."

"I am not one of them, that's for sure, but alone or not, Jarv is where I need to get to."

"Normally passengers have to share with the crew, but I can't have that with you being one woman alone. As much as I like my crew, that might be one temptation too much for them."

Lani was ready for the rejection, and in a way she was glad. She didn't need that sort of attention.

"If you've the right coin I have a very small spare cabin at the back behind mine. It's not much, but you can bar the door for the night."

"How much?"

"One silver coin. Do you have so much?"

Lani knew it was a good chunk of what she had left, but after her last experience working her passage, she just wanted a ride south. If it meant locking herself in for the whole trip, so be it.

"I do."

Minook looked her over again. Something concerned him but he wasn't telling her what.

"You're sure now then? The ride will be simple, and the room is very plain. It's no princess's ride."

"Do I look like a princess to you?" Lani couldn't keep the sneer from her tone.

He didn't seem to mind, and seemed to prefer her talking that way. With a laugh, "No, lass, that you don't. There's probably an hour more here then we're done. We don't lie around these docks at night. As soon as we're done loading, we'll push across the river and tie up on the south side for the night at the docks over there."

"Docks?"

"Not from around here I guess, so you wouldn't know. This river twists and turns in all directions, with the different rivers all coming together it's not the easiest passage to cross. We prefer to park up, once we're loaded, over on the far side of the river, as do most heading south. It's hard work getting across this current so it's best we do it now and not tire ourselves out first thing in the morning."

"Okay."

"If you're not here when we leave, I'll leave without you. Now I'll need payment up front."

Lani wasn't handing it all over and gave him half of what he wanted but only when he showed her to the cabin, which was as he told her not much bigger than a closet. It would do, and she settled down while she waited for the boat to leave.

56

LANI

*W*ith not more than an hour or so until sunset their boat pulled out of the harbor. As they did so the usual chorus of yells and curses, orders and jest filled the air, both from the crew on the boat and those on the jetty.

Lani had chosen to sit on the back rail of the boat for the latter part of the afternoon, taking in all she could see of Statiiv. She had not paid much attention to the city and she wanted to at least see what she could.

From her position she found many different hues coming from the city which she'd not noticed when she'd arrived at dusk the day before. The buildings were all of different types of stone. It was a patchwork of construction types and colors that gave it a lively vibe. Perhaps in the future she might get to explore it more.

The crew on her boat were all similar in size to Minook, just as wiry and sun-baked. No one paid her any attention the couple of times she moved around the cabins to watch them at work, and she felt safe when she perched up on the rail.

The Roilaren and Boctok rivers merged into a swirling open area of water that created its own issues for boat captains. When they entered the churning current the boat twisted back and forth, unsure which direction it wanted to go, and the ride was bumpier than an old wagon on a rutted road.

She moved forward to watch the crew and captain at work. Minook stood at the wheel issuing commands as they nosed through the waters. Once clear of the most turbulent water they caught the south-flowing current that easily pushed the boat over to the eastern banks. They oared their way around the bend ready to drift south and then tied up alongside another half dozen vessels.

There was a small makeshift jetty they linked up to as well as throwing out anchors. The boats were all close enough together to throw conversation back and forth, but far enough from the center of the river to avoid any boats that might travel in the night.

Minook had told her they would be here until first light. Once they were all sorted, he and his crew settled into an open area afore of the cabin and bridge area. One of them used a special brazier on the deck to grill up meats and charred vegetables which they ate and partook in ale from a barrel beside the captain's cabin.

Minook brought her a plate and a drink and advised her it would be best to stay back out of the way, which she was happy to comply with. As the evening drew on the crew got more boisterous and Lani could hear similar hilarity drifting across from the neighboring boats. She hoped their heads wouldn't be too heavy in the morning as she was keen to be underway.

Lani retired to her cabin and as instructed barred the door from the inside. She also pushed a small chest which doubled as a little table across the door. It wouldn't stop anyone but the noise it made would alert her long before anyone came in.

What she had for a bed was not much more than a cot only long enough for a large child. She needed to lie with her knees up close to her chest to keep on the mattress. It was lumpy and had a strange sour odor to it, which she chose to ignore. She lay on top of her cloak which was thick enough to keep whatever it was in the mattress away from her.

Slowly, as she reviewed the events of the last day, she found herself thinking more about the amulet. It was hard not to. Lani looked again at the door which was securely barred, and figured she could take another look at the stone without getting into much trouble.

There wasn't anywhere she could really go, not without going past Minook's crew, which made it very unlikely she could leave the boat. Knowing that made her feel a little more confident. What had happened intrigued her and she took the pouch out again.

Aware of the need to be able to control it, Lani kept the pouch alongside it in one hand, and the brooch in her other. The familiar tendrils crept from the stone and out through the door as if it wasn't there.

She began to sense minds, something that had become familiar. Most likely it was the boat crew from the light-hearted exchanges she could hear. The pull didn't seem to be there, which she was happy about, and apart from the thoughts or voices it helped her hear, there was nothing else she could sense from it.

Laughter outside broke her concentration, and Lani put the amulet away in the pouch and settled back on the bed. If nothing else she felt more at ease that the brooch seemed to help her with the amulet. One day she might find out why, but for now it was enough.

It took only an hour before the noises outside began to stop and not long after, the only sounds she could hear were the lapping of the water against the hull and a variety of creaks, either from the boat itself or the ropes and ties that held it in place.

When she drifted off to sleep Lani tried to put the last week behind her and think of what she could learn when she got to her destination.

It was pitch black when she woke, startled by something, but unsure what. Her room was empty except for herself, and while she listened it didn't appear that anyone was at her door. She lay nervously wondering what it was that had brought her awake. There was a little bit of shuffling distantly and then a couple of thuds on the deck but then nothing but more silence.

Suddenly there was shouting, and people were rushing about the boat. She could hear the crew yelling, not just close at hand but across the water as well.

Lani dragged the chest away from the door, wanting to know more about what was happening but still conscious of how many times she'd been in danger from being too curious. She'd also learned to never leave anywhere without all of her things and slung her satchel over her head before creeping out onto the back of the boat.

As she walked around the back of the cabins, she could see what all the commotion was about. The boat next to them was on fire and her crew and the others were all desperately throwing buckets of water onto it trying to quell the flames.

Everyone's focus was on the threat that boat made to all of them. They couldn't get out of their berth quickly without crashing into the boat next to them, and like brothers they wanted to save the other vessel. The crew of her boat were rushing frantically back and forth, some loading buckets and passing them to those who were throwing the water onto this side of the boat.

She stayed back, watching all the drama. It looked like they were winning, on this side at least, then something inside exploded and more flames burst out of the cabin.

With such noise she never heard the feet behind her until it was too late. Nothing alerted her to any other danger, her senses were focused on the threat of the fire. A gloved hand reached around and covered her mouth while a second quickly placed a knife right on her throat.

She was pulled back by the gloved hand until they were hidden behind the cabins. Her assailant had a companion, and both appeared covered completely in black. Even their faces seemed black and only the whites of their eyes were visible to her. The second man pulled a small sack over her head and tied it around her neck.

She felt the man behind her lean in close to her ear. "Make a sound and I'll cut your throat and feed you to the fish." His voice was deep and low, and full of menace. Her hands were wrenched behind her back, and she could feel a rope being tightly tied around them, cutting into her wrists.

Lani knew none of the crew would even see them, distracted by the fire most likely started as the perfect distraction. She was lifted like a doll and thrown onto a shoulder by someone clearly very strong. She was passed to more hands, her feet pointing downward, and she could hear the water closer. Whoever took her held her despite the rocking of the boat he must have been standing in.

The boat rocked again, as someone jumped into it. Then they were moving and Lani could hear their boat cutting through the water before abruptly coming to a stop as it drove into what she guessed was the bank.

Two quick splashes sounded before she was being passed again. More splashes and they were moving out of the water and uphill. Whoever's shoulder she was perched on dug awkwardly into her hip and with her head now pointing downward she felt woozy.

She wanted to get free and started trying to wiggle, before a sharp jab hit her side and she cried out.

"Stay still," the menacing voice growled at her.

Her eyes filled with tears, and she let them come, not caring. She was trapped again, and no one could see them anyway. Once onto the flat the men must have started running. She was constantly bobbing up and down and she gave up her crying and concentrated on breathing. She tried to guess how many paces they were taking and when they abruptly stopped, she guessed maybe a few hundred yards.

Despite his strength the man carrying her was breathing heavily and he dropped her like a sack on the ground. There were more voices here and if she wasn't mistaken, she could hear horses as well.

Not again!

57

GORAN

*H*is head throbbed and the effort required to open his eyes seemed far too much. Goran lay still, trying to think through what was happening.

That's right, he had heard about Henri, and they'd started drinking. So he was hungover, and that explained the wooziness and sick feeling in his stomach. His left eye felt heavy as well, and it didn't want to open. He went to lift his arm but discovered both his arms were tied down.

Slowly he opened his right eye, carefully checking to see what was going on. Something wasn't right, the room he was in was different.

"You're awake then?"

The familiar sound of Brando's voice eased Goran's concern.

"What happened to my eye?"

The keeper laughed, not pleasantly, "That was me."

"What do you mean?"

"It was the only way to stop you."

"Stop me from what?"

"Trying to escape."

"Escape? Escape from what? Why am I tied down?"

"You don't remember?"

What happened?

As much as he tried to remember, he couldn't. The last thing he could recall was the news about Henri and then they had all sat around drinking with Yeta. Until he had passed out. Then nothing.

"What did I do?" His tone was less confrontational.

"What didn't you do, fool. Which bit don't you remember? The part where you lost all your money, or when you tried to pawn one of those Derk rings? Or how about trying to jump off the boat, or the best one, trying to attack me with your knife?"

Oh no!

"Where are we?"

"Mugan."

"What? Why here?"

"When you went crazy I had no idea what we were meant to do. We can't find that girl, so that was useless, and you kept doing crazy things, so I chose to head back home."

"Home?"

"Your home. Anderwell. I figured if you can't cope maybe they can sort you out. If I left you in Diwedd, you'd have got your throat cut. As it was you nearly did."

"Tell me. I can't remember anything."

"I'm not surprised about that. They drugged your drink good and proper they did, only way I can explain it. You'd all but lost everything to them but they were well ripe with you. When you passed out they dragged you out back. Can't say they looked like they were of the mind to care for you."

Brando gently patted his own left arm.

"Tis how I got this nice wee cut. They didn't figure on me showing up, and they'd had their own fill of drink, which helped me. Four against one never the best of odds. End of it, I dragged you back to Yeta's inn and we waited till you came good."

"How long?"

"A good day and a half before that poison wore off, but you weren't right. I had to hunt you down again, you were doing crazy things, trying to get yourself killed I'm sure of it."

Goran closed his good eye.

"And my eye?"

"Couple of days back when you tried to get off the boat and nearly had both of us thrown off it. Raving you were, and I couldn't get any of the special drink in you."

"Special drink?"

He didn't answer for a minute.

"Yeah. Zeresse gave me some powder before we left. She said if I needed it, it would knock you out. Must be a bit like what those sailors put in your drink I guess. I don't know how she knew I'd need it but I'm glad for it."

Goran didn't care for the attention Zeresse had shown him, giving that to Brando, but he couldn't do anything about it here. "My eye?"

"Simple, Goran. I punched you good and proper. You dropped like a sack of rocks and left me be for the best part of yesterday. Since then you've not tried to get away."

Goran tugged at his wrists. "Not exactly easy like this."

Brando walked over. "I'll do it again if you act up."

He didn't reply, and when his hands were free he slowly sat up on the edge of the bed. His head spun and he wanted to lie back down, but sat there until it settled. By the time he was able to properly open his eye another couple of minutes had passed.

"Drink?"

Brando brought a skin over to him. The thin ale helped somewhat to wash the sick taste from his mouth and settle his stomach. Not much but enough. Goran wished he could open his other eye, but he couldn't.

"Thank you."

"For what?"

"Looking out for me. I'm all good now."

"We'll see."

Goran didn't like the tone in the keeper's voice. He didn't need someone to watch over him, he was fine just as he was. Somehow he needed to get Brando off back where he came from and work out his own path. While he couldn't recall anything since the night at Yeta's when news of Henri's death had arrived, he could remember every-thing before that.

Thinking about the news cut him inside again, as if it was just yesterday. Which it was to him. And the girl, she'd been lost too. He'd failed, that was the truth, and he was of no value to the Jesters. He'd been thinking about going off and finding somewhere to hide.

Hide from himself, and to hide from his failures. He couldn't do that with Brando looking over his shoulder. He needed to leave the man where he was, and head off. Brando could get back to Callet and return to his normal life. That option made no sense anymore for Goran.

He'd been on the outside anyway and now he'd messed up trying to catch the girl. It was too much, he'd lost Ashantha and Henri, two people that he cared about. Apart from Tillandra in the Court, none of them cared much for him. He'd been away from Anderwell so long now, it didn't feel like home. He needed to find his own way.

Not knowing what had happened the last few days actually felt good. It felt much like it did when he smoked the weed.

That's what I need right now.

Goran slowly looked around the room. Brando was sat on the edge of the other bed, staring at him. "What now?"

"That's what I was going to ask you. I'm meant to be helping you, not making the decisions."

"I need to get my head clear." He looked at his clothes and the state of them. "And clean up."

"I'll get water seen to, there's a wash room left down the hall. No doubt you'll be hungry. You've hardly eaten a thing in days. Don't do anything daft, you hear?"

Goran nodded slowly. "I'll be fine. I just need some time."

Washing seemed to take him twice as long. He hurt all over, and his head still wasn't settled. Brando had brought a bag for him, which at least had a change of tunic, and his things. Tucked in his leather roll that held his pipe and bac was a pouch of weed that he hid there.

Good thing Brando never looked, he'd have thrown that out.

Once he was all done, he joined Brando downstairs and ate two servings of a greasy beef stew and chunks of hard bread. It wouldn't have mattered at that point what it was, once he recognized his hunger he needed to fill it.

His head was clearer from the effects of whatever Brando had used on him but he was still no closer to knowing what he was going to do. He brought his pipe out and filled it with bac, puffing away on it once he'd lit it, looking out the window of the inn at a muddy street, and the slow wispy rain that was falling.

"I think I need some more rest."

Brando nodded but didn't reply. The keeper had been sullen the whole time he'd been in the main room.

Instead of going back up to his room, Goran snuck out the back of the inn and found himself a spot under cover in the horses' stable. He dug out the zongleweed from his pocket and filled his pipe, lighting it and breathing in the sweet smoke. The ache in his head eased immediately and he lost any concern about what Brando was thinking.

The keeper could do what he wanted, except for keeping Goran captive. That wasn't right.

He didn't notice the last words didn't really come from him. As the weed slowly relaxed his head, he sunk into himself, sliding down the wall and staring out the back of the stable.

Like opening the door for me. Now that you helped get me free, I can slip away. Just one more smoke.

The switch had happened, but the weed remained. Even Zoran was too relaxed to do anything much at all, he just took another puff and slowly let his eyes close.

~

BEANTIC WANDERED INTO THE MAIN ROOM OF THE INN, SHAKING WATER OFF her coat, relieved to be out of the weather. The last few days hadn't been pleasant at all; no matter how well you covered yourself, water seemed to find a way inside.

A face across the room seemed familiar to her, and when he looked around at her, he too seemed to recognize her.

"I know you."

"And I you, but I'm not sure from where."

She saw him look down at her hands, and she pulled the glove off her left, her ring showing so if it was that he would know.

He saw it, and seemed pleased for some unknown reason. "I'm Brando, formerly of Follies in Callet."

"Of course, Brando. Beantic, we have met before although only once or twice. If you're here, then where's Goran?"

Almost on cue, she heard heavy footsteps behind and turned to see her guard, Cwefen, struggling into the inn, carrying a man in his arms.

"I think he needs some help."

Brando jumped up and hurried to him, helping support the man, who she recognized as Goran once he was unravelled.

"Weed."

"What?" she asked.

"He's been smoking that weed again. I best get him upstairs, and safe. I thought he was better."

Beantic was a little confused, but left him to it. She took up a seat at the table he'd been using and waited for him to come back down.

"He doesn't look so well," she said when Brando returned.

"That he isn't. I don't know what it is but he's been unlike himself ever since he heard about Henri."

"Oh."

Brando filled her in on recent events. "He's always been one to use the weed from time to time, but something else happened. Only earlier he seemed back to being him again."

"What do you mean?"

"Just like I said. I'd swear I've been traveling with someone else, not Goran, right up until this morning."

Beantic looked at the keeper and pondered what he said. Something wasn't right. She had no idea what, but it didn't look like she was hurrying off to Callet right away. She would need to find out what was wrong with Goran.

LANI

They didn't rest for long, only enough for whoever her captors had met to reorganize themselves. Lani was hoisted onto a reluctant horse, and her hands were tied to a rope, which felt as if it wrapped around her horse's chest.

She wasn't given any reins and assumed her horse was being led by someone else. Lani tried to listen to hear how many people or animals there were but inside the sack it was almost impossible to discern any real details.

When her horse jerked forward Lani nearly fell off and only managed to right herself by digging her knees into its sides. For the next few hours, she rode in a constant battle of never knowing when the next change in direction was coming and trying to balance herself without sight.

Even if she wanted to, there was no way she could fall asleep in the saddle, her nerves on edge waiting for the next movement that might topple her. It sounded like someone rode alongside, but how long it would take them to bring her horse to a stop if she fell, Lani had no idea. It could all be too late by then.

When tiny filaments of light squeezed through the weave of her head sack, Lani knew morning had arrived. She heard a muted conversation ahead of her and moments later the horses slowed. Lani waited on top of the horse, unsure if they were dismounting.

Her question was answered when she felt rough hands untying the rope that bound her wrists to her horse. Strong hands grabbed either side of her hips and she was dragged off the saddle, sideways. As soon as her legs were clear she was righted and stood on the ground.

Even though Lani knew it was coming she still wasn't prepared enough for it. She almost collapsed and wobbled about drunkenly as she gained her balance.

"Stay still!" a male voice barked.

"I would if I could, idiot," Lani barked back. She was sick and tired of this and with little left to lose, she decided to take a chance. If they wanted her dead she would already be so, but they didn't and while they were treating her poorly, she had a chance to leverage it.

She never saw the punch coming, but she felt the impact in her side as whoever it was threw their body weight into the attack. She collapsed in pain and surprise, tears flooding her eyes as she gasped for breath.

There was nothing said, but Lani climbed onto her knees. "Go again, coward. Hit a defenseless woman, show everyone what sort of warrior you are."

She waited for another hit or a kick, but none came.

"What's happening here?" Another male voice.

When no one answered, Lani took another chance. "Your men like to beat defenseless women, that's what's happening, cowards."

"What does she mean?"

Lani could hear a few steps being taken, as if whoever else was there were stepping away.

"Touch her again, and you'll all be dealt with. If she needs to be disciplined, then it will be myself and no one else. Understood?"

Footsteps approached her and she braced for what might happen next. Fingers around her neck played with the cord tying the sack over her head, and then it was pulled off. The brightness of the daylight caused Lani to squint and instinctively she pulled her tied hands up to cover her eyes.

A man not much taller than herself stood before her. He held out his hand and when she placed her hands toward his, he grabbed her forearm and pulled her up.

"They can be... over-enthusiastic. They won't do it again."

That would be all the apology she would get, she knew. The dark-haired man walked her under the shade of the copse of trees they had stopped beside and gently pushed her downward to sit. She complied, not wanting any more trouble, especially as this man had helped her. Her side was already burning from the punch and Lani knew it would bruise badly.

Another guard came toward the man and untied Lani's hands, before retying one of them to a rope behind the tree. There was enough movement that when they brought her a skin of water and food, she was able to feed herself by leaning forward on her knees.

When she had eaten, she spent the rest of the time sipping the water slowly. It was warm and tasted leathery, as if it had been in the skin for weeks. Lani was grateful for it anyway. She looked around the makeshift campsite, collecting images in her mind.

One thing she knew was, they were highly organized and weren't planning on hanging around. This was only a rest for the horses and men, not an ending point. Not long after, the team of men quickly repacked their kit and gathered the horses.

This time Lani was led to her horse and lifted on somewhat more graciously. She had to bite her tongue when the man lifting her placed his hands on the bruise. There was no way she would give him or any of them the satisfaction of knowing they had hurt her. She'd learned enough from bullies amongst the elder kin in Barnen, not to ever show them your weakness. They would only ever play on it if they knew.

Now that she could see while they rode, the journey was much easier. They passed through rolling countryside dotted with small undulating hills that they rode over. The land was hidden from view for minutes before they burst over the top of their crests, gaining a view of the entire terrain.

Plains of grass spread out in all directions, dappled with small herds of free-running horses. When they neared villages or towns, they found fenced and guarded horse farms. Her team never strayed too close to any settlements and often left the road to travel over open country.

Whenever they did stop, it was under some form of shade, whether trees or sometimes a rocky outcrop in a hillside. That night they camped beside what was the first waterway they'd seen since they'd left the Boctok River.

Dinner was simple, as had been each of the meals. Dried meats, flat bread and a strong-flavored cheese. Lani watched everything, trying to work out what the pecking order was, who it had been that punched her, and what opportunities might arise for her.

While she didn't want to be anyone's prisoner, the one thing she could tell was they were still heading to the south, even if it wasn't directly where she wanted to go. She also knew that if circumstances changed, she needed to be ready in case a chance to escape came.

That night she slept poorly but it gave her another opportunity to watch the people holding her prisoner. They spoke little amongst themselves, but she was beginning to make out who were the people of power and who were the workers.

There were five of them altogether, enough to share the load but not too many that they'd stand out as a threat to anyone they passed. The next day they followed a similar routine, rising at dawn and eating before packing up quickly and setting off through the open fields.

It was slower going but they soon rejoined the road they had left late the day before and the pace of the horses improved. Occasionally Lani tried to get someone to speak to her, but she was ignored. Even the leader of the group, the man who had saved her on the first day, didn't engage in any further conversation.

All Lani could do was ride and wait. Their journey continued on like this for several more days. Lani's butt was sore from the constant riding, her back ached from sitting upright all day and sleeping rough on the ground, and despite the food and water, her lips were cracked and sore from constant sun exposure.

Her face had burned the day before and while the others wore head scarves or caps, they hadn't bothered to cover her face at all. With the seriousness of their work, Lani guessed it was probably the least of her worries.

As far as she knew, none of them had gone through her belongings, her satchel she still wore on her back, unmoved since the first night. She was pretty certain that they were just the foot soldiers, and they were going to deliver her to someone. Who, she had no idea.

Not once had they varied from a strict routine, and she still hadn't seen any way she could try to escape. With so much open country around them, getting away would be almost impossible. She would be seen for miles in any direction.

The sense of helplessness she hated had been growing within her. She didn't like feeling helpless, but there was little to be positive about. The only thing that kept her spirits slightly balanced was knowing that whoever was behind this most likely wanted the amulet. And they were in for a surprise when they came to take it from her.

59

BEANTIC

Mugan wasn't a place Beantic had planned to spend any time in, nor to find Goran as she had. Out of all of the members of the Court she knew her colleague the least. What she knew of him was mostly from discussions between the other members.

She'd been face to face with him only twice or perhaps three times, but he was well known amongst students. The teachers often described the way he could captivate an audience and deliver a story with so much power that you could believe you were there.

One of the times she had seen him was not long before she'd passed the Audition. He'd been in Anderwell and presented to a class about performances. Just as they'd been told, he seemed to turn the room into a real world setting.

The entire group of students came away in awe, and groups met and discussed his performance for hours, and days afterward. There was something special about him when he performed, but then what she heard amongst her colleagues told of his other side.

Goran had always been a bit of a rogue, against the rules and processes. Toolet and Junther had always been the most outspoken about him, and didn't care for his approach to what they did. Beantic could understand that, but she didn't have the same view in regards to how things were done.

Maybe that was her age. She was the youngest of them all, and had been in the Court the shortest time. She always considered that a good thing, that new ideas and energy helped to keep things up to date, and not stale.

She could see how some of their old ways of thinking might not be serving them so well. There seemed to be a lack of timely information getting back to Anderwell, and that could only be helped by more of them out in the world.

Perhaps the Court had become too comfortable sitting around the table in the map room, making decisions. Maybe her older counterparts were too comfortable and had forgotten what one of their major functions was: to manage the peace across Dharatan.

To do that you needed to be close to the source of problems.

Beantic felt her head twitch several times. Mostly she just pushed it back in her thoughts, but the tic had forced its way to the surface as she watched over Goran. Stress always made it worse, that and when she didn't get enough rest.

Her plan was to be closer to Callet, and base herself there. She was enjoying being away from Anderwell and part of the world again. It only confirmed her feelings. But Beantic knew she couldn't just leave Goran. Something was not right with him, and she needed to see what she could do to help.

Brando had said to her it was as if he was traveling with someone else. The more she had queried him about that, the stranger it seemed, and she wasn't sure if it wasn't just him creating something out of nothing. The keeper was a serious individual, that became obvious within a few moments of speaking with him.

He had a solid reputation for his role in Callet, but this was different. Brando had told her how he knew Goran tended to abuse drink and weed, and not always take things as seriously as he should. Well, not in the keeper's opinion anyway. He'd also said this seemed different.

Goran caught her attention as he passed wind in his sleep, and grunted.

Nice!

She hoped the fool would wake soon. She had half a mind to throw water over him. He grunted again and turned from one side to the other. It was another half an hour before he finally roused from his sleep.

He groaned from the bed, and began muttering to himself.

"You're awake?"

Goran rolled onto his back and turned his head to see her, his eyes slowly opening. Then he woke with a start and sat upright in a hurry.

"Who are you and what are you doing in my room?"

"It's me, Goran. Beantic."

He shook his head, and she saw his eyes narrow. There was only faint recognition there.

"Beantic, of course. Why are you here? How rude to be in my room without my permission."

She struggled to respond, and her twitch went into overdrive. This wasn't the response she'd expected. While they weren't that close, they had always been friendly. She recognized what Brando had said, his speech did seem different.

"I'm here because I'm on my way to Callet, and you turned up stoned off your face. I was concerned."

"Stoned? Me? How ridiculous."

Despite his words she saw the man retreat a little into himself, albeit briefly. She thought he mumbled something to himself as well. She couldn't be sure but one of the words sounded like his own name.

"So you were just comatose for over a day from tiredness? Is that what you'd have me believe?"

"I don't think it's any of your business what I am, thank you kindly." His tone was very stern and laced with superiority, which began to annoy Beantic. "If I needed rest then that's my business. Now I would have you kindly leave me be, Beantic. I'd like my privacy."

Usually she controlled her skill, only using it deliberately, but his tone, and a feeling she had about him, brought it out. While she wasn't the biggest of individuals, she'd never worried for her own safety, especially after the Audition, when the skill had come fully into its own.

She was able to intimidate anyone she set her mind to, and have them do her will, albeit only for a short while. Today it broke free on its own and filled her angry words with a power of their own.

"You rude little man! Leave you be, as if I didn't have my own things to do. But I've been sat her for over a day tending to you, caring for your wellbeing, just to have you be so impudent?"

She'd been told that from the other side it appeared as if she doubled in size and width, and blocked the other person's view. "No wonder the others think you're wrong for this job, look at you. Full of your own self-importance but not even able to see how pathetic you are!"

Beantic pulled it back and gathered herself, knowing it wasn't right to use her power on one of her own. In front of her Goran had frozen on the edge of the bed, and his eyes seemed to be looking elsewhere. He hadn't said a word, and the aggressive posture he'd held moments earlier was gone.

Goran's body appeared almost deflated, like she'd pushed all of the will out of it. He blinked rapidly and his eyes seemed to roll back in his head before he collapsed back on the bed. Then he started to thrash around, his feet kicking up and his head flicking from side to side.

Frightened by what was happening, she ran to the door and hurried down to find Brando in the main room. "Come quickly."

By the time they'd got back to the room, Goran was still and appeared to be just sleeping. Beantic told the keeper what had happened.

"See, like I told you, it's as if there's someone else in there. Like something evil has taken over his body. Except it's like him. I don't understand."

"Me neither. But we can't leave him alone. I think I might need to go and see if there's a healer that can help. Will you be okay to watch over him?"

"Of course. I'll not let him go anywhere if he wakes. Let's hope there's someone useful around."

Beantic knew how to ask the right questions to find the type of healer she was looking for. There were those that tended to things on the surface or an illness that was obvious, more a physick than anything else.

And then there were those that had a different approach. They experimented with mixtures and things that helped in ways that were special. She'd heard about the woman Zeresse in Callet, who was one of these unique individuals. She'd felt like they accessed a form of magic but no one knew exactly what.

It was one reason why she had no problem moving up to Callet. In her mind she'd hoped to form a relationship with Zeresse and learn more about her and where her skills came from.

The woman she found now wouldn't have stood out to anyone as anything unusual. Her home was wedged amongst others and if anything her neighbors looked out for her, protecting her from those who weren't welcome. Negezen agreed to come with Beantic and see if there was something amiss with Goran.

When they arrived, and she explained who Negezen was, Brando only shook his head. He left the room using hunger as his reason to be elsewhere.

"He seems withered." The deepness of the woman's voice still surprised Beantic.

If she wasn't looking at her, she'd swear it was a man speaking.

"How do you mean?"

"Like he's withdrawn in on himself."

Beantic knew she was probably partly responsible for that, but she couldn't explain that easily to the woman, nor did she want to.

"I'm going to sit with him, I'll need to touch him."

"Do as you wish. I need to know if he's unwell, whatever the cause."

While Negezen sat and placed one hand on Goran's head and another on his chest, Beantic sat in a chair and watched. Apart from the occasional grunt or breath from Goran the room was soundless. From time to time the woman would shake her head or nod, but she said nothing.

Then with a loud sigh she stood up and shook her hands vigorously, turning around to Beantic.

"I need a drink, let's go downstairs and talk."

Beantic sent Brando back up and the two woman sat in the far corner of the main room. The healer emptied her first mug of ale in one go, and asked immediately for another.

"Thirsty work, that is. Always makes me feel like I've been lying in the desert sand for a week."

"What did you sense?"

"Your man, he's not right. He'd be behaving like a different person you said, well that be the truth of it."

"I don't understand. I've heard that people can have something bad possess them, is that what you mean?"

"It is and it isn't. I've not seen the like before so at best I'll explain what I felt and you'll have to make of it what you can."

Her second mug turned up and she took a good swig of it before plonking it on the table between them.

"It be similar in that I felt two men in there, and they be quite different. One of them felt like it has been the dominant one, which most likely be the one you're familiar with. The other, though, seems to be getting free."

"Free?"

"Getting out over the top of the other. Inside they're fighting a battle. He must be in a lot of pain in his head. It's no doubt why he takes the weed. It would help him in one way and harm him in another."

"How so?"

"It would block out the pain, the fight in the short term. Might even be how the poor lad gets to sleep. But it also takes down the defense he's put up for so long. The more he uses it the easier it is for the other one to get out."

Negezen emptied her mug and let out a belch, wiping her mouth with her forearm.

"What can I do?"

"That's above my knowledge. Don't be alarmed but I see you and he both wear the same ring, and I felt something about his mind that was mighty strange. He wears something I cannot see, and he's got his own power, that was very clear. I might be a simple healer, but I'm no fool, so I imagine you and he are something more than just passing travelers."

Beantic wasn't going to confirm what the women was saying. It was always a risk when she asked the woman to look over Goran that she'd be able to sense more than just what was up with him.

"So all I'm saying is, whoever you two are, you're more likely to know a fix than I are. There's nothing a simple healer like me can do. And if you can't, then best you pray for who you want to win the battle. Maybe it's up to Mukazi now."

"That's not a name you hear very often anymore."

"Much is the shame. She's the god of health and wellbeing, if anyone can save your friend from himself it'd be her. Those of us that heal, it's her we follow. I'll be saying my prayers for your man, I will."

Beantic paid the woman for her help and watched her leave. She had to make a choice about what to do next, and didn't know where to start.

60

ODAJEEN

While she could sort of see shapes, Odajeen couldn't really see things. It was strange and up until recently it had been the only thing she had ever known. Up until the injury.

Odajeen was still struggling with what she was beginning to see in her mind, images and recollections of things that must have meant she could see at some point. It had been roughly four months, give or take, since some memories had returned and she had spent most of it trying to find the solution in the bottom of a wine jug.

Or a brandy jug. Even ale if it was strong enough.

Before that she hardly drank, as not having sight made it difficult enough. Getting drunk wasn't a good way to look after yourself.

Right now, she didn't care so much. Now that she knew there were things she couldn't remember, it bothered her. If she had never been able to see, then these pictures were visions of some kind, or she was going crazy.

But if they were real memories, it meant she had once had eyesight, but she had no recollection of ever being able to see, or when she lost her vision.

Now that she thought on it, she should have been able to remember more than she did. She knew she was physically old, and up until the injury, she'd not questioned why she had no memories of her earlier life.

Of the life she did remember, Odajeen had begged to survive. She was smarter than a typical beggar, and she knew more than just sitting on the street, but all that she needed to live by, she took from her bowl.

In the places she traveled to she made contacts, friends she guessed, and learned to do better than she should. She always had a good place to sleep and eat and safety when she needed it. She had been in Vidus now for almost six years and there was plenty to like about it for her.

No one typically bothered her, and she even recognized those who regularly gave her coins when they had no cause. Maybe it was because of her age, or maybe because she knew how to play the game.

She kept an eye out for the locals as well. As funny as that sounded, it was true. She couldn't see long distances in any detail, but she could see changes. She could see a blob of a horse moving against the background but only sound let her know it was a horse. Up close she could see black and white outlines of some things.

She couldn't really tell much about people. Her smell and hearing filled in some of the blanks, and she would draw images of sorts in her mind when she could touch things. So many shades of black, gray and white in her head, helped her differentiate the few outlines she saw.

On the day of the injury, she had been positioned opposite a merchant's shop, someone who often left her something to eat, or a small coin or two. He sounded to her like an older man, and often he missed a day of trade. Odajeen could hear in his voice he was unwell, and she had noticed the days he missed were getting more frequent.

That afternoon she was tucked in against the building opposite when she saw the shapes of three people approach where the door of his store would have been. One of them tried the door but it was locked.

Suddenly they smashed through the door and disappeared into the store. Odajeen knew they were up to no good and started yelling for help and ringing her bell. Before she knew what happened one of the shapes came out of the door and straight at her.

Whatever it was they hit her with cracked her across her temple.

Odajeen had passed out and woke later with others standing over her. Guards had taken her to the shop of a healer, known as Morjery. She had stayed there for almost a week while Morjery tended to her head wound.

The club she had been hit with had made a severe indent on the left side of her skull and cut it. She'd worn a bandage while Morjery kept her at her place to help her rest. At first all she had felt was pain, headaches she couldn't get control of no matter what foul-tasting brew Morjery gave her.

When the wound had healed Odajeen had thanked the other woman for her care and paid her some coins, even though the healer had been reluctant to take them. Her appearance helped her fit the character she played; little did they know she had collected more than enough coin to live better than she appeared.

Her men had been worried when she hadn't returned to her secret accommodation. They had to hunt down where she was and luckily learned about it from a guard.

After that she had to tell them where she was going each day. At first they had tried to protect her by being around her, but Odajeen knew it wouldn't work. A beggar doesn't have guards.

When she had settled back into her small home, the pain still bothered her, and she had begun to drink it away. It passed after another week and initially she had stopped using drink to ease her pain.

That was until the first images had appeared.

At first Odajeen thought she was going mad. She had a pretty good idea what mad sounded like. Having worked on the streets for so long she knew those whose minds were gone and what they spoke of.

She had seen colors, something she had not understood at first. But with it came the thoughts that accompanied the images. Images of places and people. Her head struggled to recall who they were, and for many of them she couldn't find their names in her head. What she did remember was how she felt when she saw the pictures.

That was when she realized they were memories. Memories she had been blocked from. Memories of her, when she was younger. Much younger, and when she could see.

It was that which caused her the greatest anguish. She had never felt sorry for herself before, her only memories were of her without sight, and nothing else. But that had changed, and she couldn't control how it felt, it just happened. Now she was grieving for her previous life with sight.

Odajeen didn't know what the images meant, or the places they were. She couldn't actually remember things contained within them. Faces, or people, others who smiled or laughed with her. Others who seemed dangerous or not on her side.

Mostly she longed for the return of her sight. And the knowledge about how she had lost it.

What had happened? When did it happen? How was it she had all those people she knew and yet she was wandering the world alone? Where were the memories that showed what happened?

Day after day she had drunk herself into a haze trying to forget as well as to remember more. At one point she had taken to banging her head, trying to free up more of the memories in it. It seemed the injury had freed some of them, but not all of them.

After knocking herself unconscious one day she had visited with Morjery again and discussed with her what had happened. The old healer had little experience to help but had told her that maybe it was head damage that caused it and she needed to be very careful she didn't cause herself any more harm by taking more knocks to the head.

From that point forward, Odajeen stopped the heavy drinking and sought to let whatever she was now seeing work itself out in its own time. Sometimes she dreamed of her past, and woke amazed at the colors she could remember, only to be disappointed when she couldn't see the world she now lived in.

It pained her more not knowing. More than not being able to see. She knew she was lucky to have lived as long as she had, much longer than most of her kind, and that she had experienced so many great things, even with her lost sight, that she should give up playing a victim.

There was something that she needed to understand, and she knew she had more than enough time and smarts to let it show itself. Of late she was trying to make sense of an image that she had seen in some of her dreams.

The dream itself was one she saw regularly, a scene of her sitting with some others talking and enjoying each other's company. Because she was seeing it over and over eventually, she started paying more attention to the detail of it. Being able to pick out each piece of detail had become a task for her, almost a hobby.

It was her way of seeing what she could no longer see. It became significant, because she could see that almost everyone in the dream wore the same thing. On her left hand there was a silver ring. Carved into the top of the ring was a mask with a two-pronged hat on it.

The image was distinctive, and when she stared at it Odajeen felt connected and whole. It belonged there. She had always played with that finger, but there was no ring on it. She knew that. Now though there was a feeling of loss attached to the finger, from the deep dark pockets of her mind where the memory of that ring had arisen from.

It belonged on her hand, and she missed it. The others in her dream also wore them, yet she didn't know what they meant. Who were these people, what did this ring mean?

Odajeen wasn't sure where she would get the answers and she could feel inside a discomfort. That same discomfort that had been like an insight of a change to come. Something was about to change in her life, but she had no idea what. Normally when she felt it she resolved it by changing where she was.

But she liked Vidus, there was a comfort here that she'd not had anywhere else, and a way of life that worked for her. She didn't want to leave here, not unless... not unless it would provide her with answers to the memories she was seeing.

61

UKSOD

The sight of Ponte was not usually something that inspired Uksod, but today it meant a bed, bath and real food. The last week, riding hard and camping light, had not been something he enjoyed. Unfortunately for him, Karpenmor seemed to thrive on it.

The overgrown town was now referred to as a city, but Uksod could still recall its beginnings. When the land bridge existed it was the toll booth and customs point that monitored who came and went.

The land bridge had always been a fragile construction that required management. Limited numbers of people could travel it at any one time, and at each end the gates ensured control. Ponte grew from the demand to cross the bridge. Back then it was mostly made up of inns and services for all the travelers.

Now it was a bastion of hope and dreams. People had stayed when the storms had passed and never left, hoping one day the road would reopen. It had no defences to speak of, the only wall was the one that gated the cliffs facing Step One.

Each of the six islands had been named as numbers. Step One, Step Two and so on from this side over to Kuwaha. Uksod always thought it was the dumbest idea he had ever heard but he cared nothing to change it. His only interest was how to get a lot of people across to Dharatan.

The wall was maintained as if it would be used again. The gates were polished steel and stood twenty feet tall, tall enough for the biggest load that the original bridges could carry to get through. They were impressive to see, especially for the first time.

It would take them another hour to reach the outskirts of the city, where countryside changed to ramshackle buildings. The deltas around the forked rivers that ran from the western ranges down to the sea had created lush farming land. Much of the best produce for En Carta was grown here in Ponte, especially their rice.

People worked the fields and looked up as their group rode by. They would have been noticed for miles with the amount of dust they were producing. The lack of rain was one thing Uksod was grateful for, as he doubted he could have coped with being soaked to his core for days on end.

As they approached the city, the wall was clearly visible behind it. Nothing had been built to compete with it height-wise, instead the council had chosen to spread the city wide and far. Buildings covered land as far south as Uksod could see. One constant here in Ponte was building.

"What is that compound to the south, Uksod?"

He turned to look where Karpenmor was pointing. "That, Highness, would be the Western Barracks."

"It is massive!"

"It is indeed, and it's only half-built."

"What on Enderk?"

"Preparation, Highness. One must have the forces ready for any eventuality. Perhaps it's best we speak of this elsewhere?"

Karpenmor looked at him, and then back at the distant compound. "Yes, of course."

Uksod marveled at the scope of the compound. By itself it was likely one third the size of the city, possibly more. It had been one of his more memorable achievements. One day soon he knew they would need a force able to battle those on Dharatan.

If anyone ever came to attempt to fight them it would be here across the stepping isles or in the bays south of Taras. He had created barracks in each place and constantly recruited young men from across Enderk to fill them.

But this barracks was actually for the main goal, and it could house the largest numbers of soldiers of anywhere in Enderk. As units of soldiers crossed the bridges into Dharatan, more waves of them would arrive from around the country and prepare to follow. It was still a work in progress but getting much closer to completion than ever before.

Their group slowed to a walk and as the dust around them settled, Uksod could see a similar-sized group of horsemen approaching from the city. They had sent word ahead about their arrival and this formality from the Captain of Ponte and the Governor was for show alone.

Both groups came together and stopped so that the Ponte Captain could greet his superior. He then rode forward to the pair of them.

"Your Highness and Eminence, I am most pleased to welcome you all to our humble city."

"And your name, Captain?" Karpenmor asked.

"Cincen, Highness."

"Thank you for greeting us, Captain Cincen. Now, if we may, it's been a long week and I believe we'd all be better for being off these horses."

"Of course, Highness." The man quickly turned his horse and rode back to his men, issuing a quick command. The merged group started back at a trot toward the city.

Uksod couldn't have imagined the chaos that would have ensued after the first courier alerted the Governor to the impending arrival of their group. The appearance of the Regent was a big enough deal as it was, but as the very first visit anywhere, no one knew what to expect of him. While they had seen Uksod before, he tended to leave the Governors mostly to themselves if the cities ran well and spent his time mostly with the Vrah.

While the main armies had barracks that were obvious and conspicuous, the Vrah worked more covertly. They had locations within cities that held a small working number of their people.

Between cities and other remote locations all over the country training compounds were maintained.

They were never visited by normal people and anyone stumbling on them by accident would not live to tell of them. The Families within whose territories they resided knew better than to attempt to interfere with them.

Uksod had maintained a constant rotation of seniors throughout the compounds and city houses so that no one was able to be easily bought by any of the Families. Only he knew where anyone would be next, and he instructed One of the next directives only on the day he issued them.

It was this that Karpenmor had no understanding of. The need for absolute control, and how little he should be trusting those around him. It was what posed the greatest problem for Uksod. He had trusted no one, not even Karpenmor himself when he was young.

Now he served the young man, and there was so much he wasn't sure of about him. The soon to be ruler needed to make sure he understood how weak and corruptible most people were. Uksod had seen it through his use of the amber. When he broke people using it, he could see how weak their will was, how easily he could get them to do what he needed. He trusted no one.

Somehow, he would need to find a way to trust Karpenmor, if they were to succeed. He had given his life to this goal, he wanted to be there when the success came.

When they reached the royal complex within the city, Uksod breathed a sigh of relief. It was not a big compound, but it would be clean and well supplied. Captain Cincen dismounted and issued commands to the guards in front of the complex as the gates were closed behind the last of their group. A flurry of servants rushed out to meet the Regent.

"What is this building, Uksod?"

"It is yours, Kar..." he caught himself before he went too far. "Highness. Each city maintains a complex to house the High Prince or his family."

"Really?"

"Yes, Highness. They are always functional and well kept. I would suggest we will need to meet the Governor tonight; most likely he will have arranged for a dinner to be served. You might spend the next few hours settling into your rooms and preparing for it."

Karpenmor looked at him with a curious stare.

"If that's suitable to Your Highness, that is. I only make suggestions, Highness."

"Relax, Uksod. Thank you, I will do exactly that. Will you not do the same?"

"I will once I have taken care of some business. No doubt there's those here that expect me to answer their questions which in time you should deal with."

Karpenmor waved a hand at him. "Yes, you take care of that. I need some peace and quiet."

Uksod was pleased to see that Karpenmor's enthusiasm for the ride might have at last dwindled a little. It was the first time he'd even hinted he wasn't enjoying the trip.

With everyone busy Uksod hurried into the building and found his way to his own rooms. Waiting in there was the head of the local Vrah, known as Seventeen.

"Highness." he bowed as Uksod entered.

"Not anymore, Seventeen. Eminence is my title again now. The heir is Highness. Understood?"

"Yes, Your Eminence."

"What do you have for me?"

"News that you sought, Eminence."

"Of the farm or the man?"

"Both. The farm still exists, and there seems to be those who may have been there at the time you asked about. The man, the servant to the past High Prince, lives quite close to here."

Uksod smiled, this was good news.

"How far?"

"A few hours by horse, Eminence."

Uksod had to think about how best to handle this.

"What about the farm?"

"It is not in the same direction, Eminence, but it is a similar distance. It is to the north."

"I will need to visit them both, quickly. Without anyone else knowing. Perhaps tomorrow. I will need to work out a way to be away from His Highness for part of the day. I will advise you when, but be warned it will be at short notice."

"We will be ready."

Uksod didn't dismiss him, there was more he needed.

"I will need your discreet assistance."

"As always, Eminence."

"Are my chambers in the basement still intact?"

"As far as I am aware, yes."

"After the dinner tonight, when everyone retires to their rooms, I will make my way down there. I will need one or perhaps two slaves. Dispensable slaves. Do you understand?"

"I think I do, Eminence."

"And after I am finished with them, someone will need to clean up without anyone else knowing."

The man bowed his head and said nothing more.

"Good work, Seventeen. As always, I can count on you."

"We are here to serve, Eminence. May I ask a question?

Uksod looked at the man. For the first time there was a small doubt in the man's eyes.

"I am intrigued now, Seventeen. Ask away."

"The new High Prince, how is he disposed?"

Uksod laughed. "You mean how is he disposed to the things we do?"

Seventeen nodded his head quickly.

"He is green, but he is one of us."

If Seventeen ever smiled, Uksod thought he saw it then. A small twitch on his lips. And then it passed.

"Is that all?"

The man nodded and left the room. Uksod rubbed at his temple, trying to massage out the headache that was there. Two days out from En Carta Yantarnaya has again hounded him. She'd sensed the first amulet in use again, and was annoyed that she didn't have the information she needed.

Uksod didn't know how it would change what happened, knowing if the woman with the amulet was Karpenmor's sibling or not, but she was worried about it. In his mind it was a simple problem: kill her and bring the amulet back. Albeit bringing it back had become harder than he had planned, but the girl was nothing, either way.

She couldn't rule in Enderk, so she offered nothing of value to them, and if she was bonded to the amulet then it was simply a matter of severing that link. Karpenmor definitely need know nothing about it, he just needed to be bonded and that would solve multiple issues all at once.

Again he rubbed at his temples, and could feel the grime in his skin.

I need a bath, a very, very long bath.

ODAJEEN

Today Odajeen sat on the roadside in the dust. Her head was twisted so she was looking skyward showing off her all-white eyes, the mark of a blind woman.

Few people would look deeply into them, most chose not to look at such afflictions. Those that did would automatically flinch when they saw they were in fact rippled with a purple tone, almost like a bruise within the eyes.

She had heard many talk of them, people were so stupid. Because they believed she couldn't see they also thought she was either deaf or dumb, and they spoke around her as if she didn't exist. 'It's an evil mark,' was the most common. Especially in Rohumaa, the color purple had often been associated with those things people would prefer not to face.

Some days she deliberately stared out at people enticing them to look at her, and when she sensed their discomfort, she laughed inside. Not so they could tell, but deep down inside, she laughed.

To most she was a horrible old blind woman. She dressed in scruffy and dirty baggy pants and a man's tunic that was tied with rope around her waist.

Her feet were hard and cracked and her hair knotted, matted and dirty. None of this bothered her. She had no smell, that was something different about her from other beggars. In truth she should smell of the streets, of herself. She was careful not to smell of anything, particularly not of soaps of perfumes, that would tell others that maybe she wasn't all she seemed.

Vidus had been her home for the last half dozen years and like any good beggar she had been living off the coin of those who felt guilt. Particularly the wealthy and noble, those she was able to bother enough so they were generous in what they threw her way.

Playing ill and afflicted was easy, and she used her condition without remorse, maintaining a regular vigil around certain parts of the city. In her first year in Vidus, one or two less than scrupulous individuals had tried to steal from her.

When her men visited them shortly after to reclaim what they'd stolen plus an additional tax, word spread quickly to leave the old woman alone. She had learned that paying for her protection was worthwhile and the two who looked after her now had become more than just paid help.

When people saw you as blind and an invalid, many times they ignored you completely. Odajeen used that knowledge and played on it, enabling her to loiter in places where she could see and hear things that others tried to keep private.

Over the years she collected more than a healthy sum both from her begging but also from leveraging what she learned. That's where her boys came into the picture. Sometimes she'd hear about something valuable that she could set her boys to steal. Other times she'd hear some knowledge so that they could then lean on whoever was vulnerable to it.

The money she collected from that meant she had her own stockpile as well as being able to give money to the real homeless or street children throughout Vidus. It didn't matter which city you were in, there were always those that lived rough.

In some places the churches helped out but none of that happened here in Vidus. It was one of the things that had kept her here so long, feeling like she made a difference. Before she had settled here in Vidus, she had wandered the roads of

Dharatan, seeking something she couldn't explain and didn't understand.

Deep down there was something she could sense, something she tried to grasp, but it always stayed out of her reach. Eventually she had reached Vidus, and she had been drawn to stay here.

Of late she had an inkling that time was almost over, even though she had no understanding why.

Today her attention had been drawn into the dark quarter of Vidus. This section of the city was a place most would avoid at all costs, and even for Odajeen it wasn't exactly safe.

She was watching a warehouse that had been vacant for a long time up until roughly a week ago. Then people had begun visiting it. Anything out of the ordinary was useful to her, it meant possibly something of value she could learn.

Her ability to sniff out things she could benefit from was what enabled her to live the way she did. Things that happened in this part of the city were done here, so few would know about them. And that was what interested Odajeen.

The things others wanted hidden were exactly the things that her and her men could profit from. It all depended on what exactly was going to move through here, and who was behind it. And why priests were involved was even more interesting.

If what her men had told her was correct it wasn't local priests either. They weren't from round here, and neither from elsewhere in Rohumaa. Their description didn't help Odajeen much, but her interest had been piqued.

What had been abandoned up until last week was now locked up and someone came there every day, staying until dark, then leaving and returning the next morning. Yesterday she'd left it to one of her men, but today it was her turn to be there.

Odajeen had positioned herself up against a small wall protruding from an abandoned shop so she could monitor down one direction of the main road but mostly down the side lane to the warehouse. The change in shapes Odajeen saw wasn't enough to tell her anything about people or buildings that far away, all she could do was be alert for a possible delivery.

She made out she was sleeping or resting in her spot and did her best to remain insignificant to the few people that passed by. In this part of the city begging would have been an alert that something wasn't right. You didn't beg in the dark quarter.

Her tatty cloak was wrapped around her, covering all but her head, with her knees tucked up under her chin. Apart from the activity in the building, nothing else had caught her interest. Odajeen was considering whether she should spend the night watching or come back tomorrow, when distant footfalls caught her attention.

The last remnants of daylight were being squashed by the growing twilight and no one else was on the street. She focused in on the sounds as they carried through the city streets, the horses being ridden faster than was probably necessary inside the walls.

Dark made no different to her minimal sight, she could see the same shapes and outlines irrespective of the light around them.

Six shapes sounding like horses turned into the main road heading toward her. They were all packed closely together, surrounding one in the middle, almost as if trapping it there. Whoever was on that horse was not there voluntarily.

It wasn't that which caught Odajeen's attention. Somewhere on the shape of the rider in the middle was a color. A blue color. Odajeen nearly gasped out loud. It was the first time she'd seen a color outside of her memories.

The horses slowed before turning into the lane. The back of the last riders blocked her view of the blue color or anything else. She wasn't sure if it was a mistake — had she imagined it? After all these years why would she mistake something like that now?

It was real, I know it was!

The sound of the wooden barn door being slid open echoed down the lane, making it seem louder than it really was. No one else moved, only the horses. Once they were inside the warehouse the door was dragged closed by the two young boys being paid for the upkeep of it. Then they left and hurried away.

Her mind wandered back to the blue shape she had seen. It was glowing, like a light, to her eyes. She was sure it was blue, not purple.

She smiled and inside her chest her heart beat faster. After so many years, so many years lost wandering, there was still color in her life.

She had to know more about what it was. A shiver ran down her spine, and she knew this was where she was meant to be. Right here, today, right now. She was called to see that color, that person.

Odajeen didn't know what it meant, but she did know she was tied to it somehow. The tune serendipity played in her life had sounded again, and this time she was ready to dance with it.

There was no way now she could leave this building. She needed to know more about what was happening there, and who wore the color. One of her men would be along soon. She could sense daylight was gone now, and they'd come for her.

Sure enough she could hear the near silent footfalls of Vefed before he got to her.

"You were right, wise one." He had a tone of humor in his voice.

She scoffed at him. "Wise, cheeky lad? I'm not wise, just old enough to notice things. What did you see?"

"Six horses, six riders. Five men all looked like paid men, circled around a young woman on the middle horse. Her hands were tied to the saddle, she wasn't there by choice."

"Good."

"Good?"

"I mean good information. There's something about her, Vefed, I saw a blue light on her chest."

"You saw color?"

"I did." Even she could hear the excitement in her voice.

"That is a first!"

"I was meant to see her, Vefed. Get your brother. We're going to find out more about what's happening in there, and who this woman is that I can see color on her."

"You alright here on your own?"

She turned her head to him and stared with her white eyeballs at him, trying to put a scowl on her face.

He laughed and walked away.

There's definitely something about to change, that's for sure.

63

KARPENMOR

*E*very part of his body ached. He had done his best to not show it to Uksod or any of the soldiers but his first long horse trip and sleeping rough, was as uncomfortable as anything he'd ever experienced.

Karpenmor knew he had lived a luxurious, privileged life, as son to the High Prince, and now wasn't so sure if this idea of his was particularly smart. The residence here in Ponte was more than comfortable and he'd enjoyed a bath, a more than decent meal and eventually a good sleep.

The evening dinner hosted by the Governor of Ponte had been tedious, long and he'd needed Uksod to remind him of his proper role. The gathering was not large, and only contained key personnel to the Governor and the senior men within Karpenmor's guard.

Thankfully invitations hadn't been extended to the prominent families in and around Ponte, mostly due to the lack of notice. As he'd learned in conversation, the leading family in Ponte chose to reside in their estates on the northern coast, only coming into the city when trade required it.

Even as new to this as he was, he knew posturing, and he didn't doubt that today invitations would arrive from all the players throughout the region. He sighed as he stood, pulling his coat on and stamping his feet more comfortably into his boots.

He had woken early; the unusual sounds echoing up the cliffs from the ocean below had disturbed him several times through the night. The last time he had decided to get up and get some exercise on his own.

On his own meant accompanied by a dozen guards, all Vrah, but it was on foot. Despite the protest of the head member of his guard, he hurried out of the residence before any of them went off to wake Uksod.

There was no doubt someone would still do that, but he wanted the peace of just his own company for a while. Arriving at the outer gates to the compound caused a stir in and of itself. The guards were as reluctant to open the gates as his guards were to exercise.

"I'm happy to have them removed permanently, if they can't follow my orders," he said to his primary guard, loud enough so that everyone present could hear. It was delivered with what he felt was just enough bite to cause discomfort.

Suddenly everyone seemed to be on the same page and men moved in haste to haul the large gates open. Karpenmor noticed the ornate curved patterns, symbolizing what looked like waves, fashioned within the gates.

The gates clanged behind them as they moved away from the compound. While he had nowhere specific he wanted to be, just outside, Karpenmor decided a look at the Stepping Isles would be as good as anywhere to head.

What he knew about them both intrigued him and angered him. The Stepping Isles were the barrier to them being able to reach Dharatan easily, but also the place that had ended his father's sanity. Or so Uksod and the books declared. Being so close he wanted to see for himself.

His guards surrounded him in a circle as they walked through the streets, despite there being only limited numbers of people about.

There were only single-story residences close to the compound and mostly built from stone. Half a dozen blocks or so from his compound they entered what was more of a trading area. His nose twitched at the aromas of freshly baking bread and his stomach grumbled at him.

Workers hurried between buildings, and the smell of cooking meats and other fires wafted along the winding street they were following. Inns lined the street every third or fourth building. Some had visible courtyards separating them from the next building, with stables built to the back of them, abutting shops of all types looking to service the patrons housed within.

Many of the buildings down here looked in poor repair, and some of the inns didn't really look as if they housed anyone.

They walked out into an open square that seemed to expand before his eyes. It was simply an illusion having left the tightly packed street by turning a corner and then stepping out onto the edge of the open space.

The square was easily two hundred yards across, the entirety of it cobbled although much of it looked old, dirty and cracked. At the far right-hand side stood the wall of Ponte and in the middle of that stood the massive gates.

Karpenmor stopped where he was and took in the surrounding view. He marveled at how grand the wall was and how impressive the gates in comparison to the cobbles and buildings around him. Either side of the gates even larger guard towers reached upward, with ramparts spanning out either side of them.

Even when not at war guards manned the walls and towers watching to the west.

As the first beams of light from the east climbed over the mountains their rays reflected off the polished steel of the gates. At twenty feet high the steel sheets in themselves were as impressive as anything he had seen. He would need to ask Uksod how they had been made, as he had never seen anything of their nature, and from so long ago.

The sound of crashing waves booming below was loud here and he started walking in the direction of the gates. He approached the right-hand gatehouse, a stone structure built into the wall. An elderly man stepped forward before they got there, leaning forward in a sweeping bow before Karpenmor.

"Your Highness, you honor the gate guard with your presence."

"Stand. What is your name?"

"Machal, Your Highness."

"Tell me, Machal, when do the gates open?"

"These gates only open when needed, Highness. If there's a convoy heading over or coming back."

"I wish to see the other side." Karpenmor wanted them open, he wanted to see what progress had been made.

"There are the man gates, Highness. Our gatehouses open out to the other side. If you would follow me?" Machal had asked it more as a question, unsure if that would be enough to satisfy Karpenmor.

Karpenmor merely nodded and waited for the first of the Vrah to precede him into the gatehouse. The building was made up of two rooms, the first like a mixed office and kitchen, the other room was blocked by a door. Karpenmor thought maybe this man lived here, the other being where he slept.

They passed through another door on the backside of the room into a small outside viewing area, where a gate was built into the back wall. Karpenmor was surprised by how thick the wall was. It hadn't occurred to him that it would be so wide.

The sound of the crashing water was louder out here, without the main wall to buffer it. Machal looked at him and his guards as he stood at the gate, the lock in his hand. One of the Vrah nodded and the man fumbled into his pocket for a key.

Nervously he opened the lock after several goes and then swung the gate open, stepping through to hold it open for them to pass through.

There was only ten to twelve feet of land ahead of them before it fell away. Karpenmor could feel the spray of seawater rushing through the air, carried by the blustery wind. He looked across the span to the island directly in front of him.

"Step One." Machal spoke up.

The Vrah spread out. Three of them moved to the cliff edge and turned back to face Karpenmor. Their duty to protect him clearly included not allowing him to fall over the edge.

"It seems so close."

"Looks can be deceiving, Highness. There's more than forty feet between the lips. Perhaps you would like to use the viewing platform?"

The man held his hand out to the right where a curious stone structure stood. Like a parapet it rose a few feet before arching outward, so that it was slightly further out than the edge of the cliff.

Karpenmor raised his eyebrows at it. "This is a strange shape, Machal."

"It was the first design, Highness, made by one of our engineers. When they needed to solve the problem of the bridges." He turned back to face Step One.

"How stable is it?"

"Very, Highness." He almost laughed. "I would not let you on there if it was not tested. It has been here for many years and is used most days, we have had more than ten people on it at one time."

Karpenmor started toward it. He could almost see the panic written on the face of his nearest guard. Two of the Vrah hurried forward and cautiously climbed the steps into the structure.

The other guards blocked Karpenmor's way until they were sure it wasn't going to collapse. When he climbed the steps and stood out on the stone platform, he understood their trepidation. While there was a small wall around the half circle shape that was the platform, he lurched a little from the view below.

The drop was massive, and he could see all the way to the ocean below, and the huge rocks on either side of the gap between Enderk and Step One. He wobbled with vertigo and one of his guards quickly grasped his arm.

He took a couple of deep breaths before giving the man a look. The grip on his arm quickly removed.

"It is hard to believe."

"It is, Highness, there are no words that even a bard could tell that would do such a sight justice." Machal wore a small smile on his face, as if he was the proud parent.

"I see now how challenging this has been. How many are there now?"

"Bridges, Highness?"

"Yes, Machal."

"The fourth is almost done. That's been the biggest one so far."

The wind swirled around them on the platform, and it didn't take much of a reason for Karpenmor to want to be safely back on land. He had stood there as long as he could bear it, his stomach lurching several times as he looked down, but he hid it as best he could.

As he stepped back on land he looked up and saw Uksod striding toward him, a scowl on his face.

64

UKSOD

The gloominess of the weather did nothing for his mood, or how dreadful he felt inside. Given his own way he would still be in bed, not standing out by the bridge to Step One. A fresh gust of wind whipped through his cassock and made his knees ache. Standing so close to the cliffs meant coping with the constant wind that was tunneled between the island and the mainland.

Why anyone would want to live in this cursed city is beyond me.

The only good news he had heard was that the bridges were now almost completed across to Step Four. That was the biggest island and his plans were to ensure a large base of operations there. Finally they were making decent progress.

It was an ungodly slow process, having to haul rock up from the water below, on the far side of each bridge, in order to complete the span. They'd made as good a method as they could, but Uksod still wasn't sure how that would work when it came to the last of the bridges.

They would need the barbarians' help to let them finish it. As of yet, that hadn't been broached with anyone. Not at least until they were close enough to make it matter. He had spent months thinking

386

about his options for the last stage, and found few choices available to him. If need be they'd have to land boats from Step Six onto the mainland and fight it out until they could secure the point outside Kuwaha.

He didn't need to be worrying about that now, he needed to see what the heir was up to.

Karpenmor had moved alongside him. "I am glad to be here, Uksod. Everything makes more sense seeing it for myself."

"What's that, Highness?"

"The scope of the problem. Getting bridges built across these gaps. How long has this taken?"

"Nearly fifty years, Highness. It wasn't until they were able to get the arch bridges working that they made any progress. Everything before that was unable to handle the weather or any form of load."

"Really? How long until we reach the other side?"

"If they've almost secured Step Four, then they might only be a half-year from completion. But."

"But?"

"There's a lot more to be achieved than just the bridges. And we do not know what the reaction on the other side will be."

Karpenmor didn't say any more, he just stared across the bridge through the now open gates. Workers and wagons were making their way over it.

"I want to go and see."

"See what?"

"I want to see where we are up to."

Uksod felt happy inside. This was the perfect distraction, he just needed to let the lad go on his own. Then he'd have several days to take care of the business he was really here for.

"It's a hard few days' ride, Highness. Unless they've made other progress there's not much in the way of services on the islands."

"That doesn't bother me, Uksod. It's important I see it."

"Of course." Uksod frowned and forced several coughs.

"You're not well are you? I noticed when you came out before. You best stay here if it's as rough as you say."

"But Highness…"

"No, Uksod, I'll be fine. I'll be surrounded by guards. It will be good to see it for myself."

"Only if you're sure, Highness?"

"I am. Let's return and make arrangements, now that my mind is set I want to set off today."

Uksod could see the boy heir was very excited to be exploring, and it didn't bother him in the slightest, but he needed to play along. "But, the Governor, surely he'll have made plans?"

"He can unmake them. Perhaps it would do him good to escort me even."

Uksod nearly choked on laughter. He couldn't imagine anything the Governor would hate to do more.

"I'll let him know as soon as we are back and then, if you'll allow me to, I'll retire for a while."

~

BACK INSIDE THEIR ACCOMMODATION, UKSOD ARRANGED FOR THE majority of the guards to go with Karpenmor on his trip across the islands. He didn't need anyone to observe what he was up to, and the local Vrah were all that he required.

Their discretion was guaranteed, at least for now. Once the heir was truly High Prince he would need to exercise more caution. While he had their loyalty, or it seemed such, most of that was because he had been Regent. He wasn't stupid enough to think they were more loyal to him than the throne.

Eventually they would belong to Karpenmor, so he might need to consider building his own group of people to do this work.

I should have thought of that earlier.

Not only would they be there to protect him, but once he had religious control on Dharatan he would need his enforcers. The Vrah would always be based here on Enderk.

Seventeen arrived within minutes of Uksod sending for him.

"We'll leave an hour after the party leaves here. Enough time for people to get back to their normal business. I do not want to be seen, Seventeen."

"I'll arrange it. It would be easier at night."

"I want to be off today. I'd have you bring the people from the farm here, but there's too many opportunities for someone else to see them. It will be easier if we set up camp somewhere isolated and then I can conduct my questioning."

"We've already sent men out to set up, Eminence. I'll be back an hour after."

"Good."

~

THE VRAH HAD DRESSED UKSOD IN AN INNOCUOUS ROBE, AND PLACED HIM amongst their numbers as they rode quickly out of the city. He'd left word not to be disturbed while he slept from whatever was ailing him. True to seventeen's prediction they only rode for several hours before they approached a small camp set up hard against a growth of bush.

Not that they needed cover, the weather was calm, and it was far enough away from the main road out of Ponte that someone would have to deliberately seek them out to find where they were. The ride had been fast and hard on his older body, but the thought of his interrogations eased the aches in Uksod's back and legs.

He went to the tent set up for him to rest in and was glad for the wine left there for him. The efficiency of the Vrah was something he'd need to emulate when he formed his own division. He didn't have long to wait until the sound of horses approaching caught his attention.

The flap to his tent opened and Seventeen stepped in.

"We have the first of them, Eminence."

"What do they know?"

"Nothing. This woman was the main housekeeper on the farm at the time you advised me of."

"Where is she?"

"I've set up a tent at the back of the camp, she's being held there."

"Take me to her." Uksod gathered up his knife, something he used only when people were most unhelpful. It had been a long time since he'd needed it, usually the power from the stone he wore was more than enough to get what he needed.

She was an old woman, and Uksod doubted he'd need the knife on this one. He waved the guards out. There was no threat to him here, and he preferred no one else saw what he did.

"What do you want with me? I'm a simple old woman."

Uksod didn't answer immediately, he sat beside her and held her hand. She flinched at first but once he let the amber stone begin its work she relaxed under his touch and he looked her in the eyes.

"What's your name?"

"Finark."

"Do you know who I am?"

She shook her head. "No."

"That doesn't matter. What matters, Finark, is what you know, about a time not that long ago. Back on the farm you were the housekeeper on."

"What do you mean?"

"Who did you housekeep for?"

"A woman, a noble of some sort. Lonely darling she was."

"What was her name?"

"Verlani. That's what she said."

Uksod smiled. So far she appeared to be telling him the truth.

"What do you want to know about her for, she's been gone a long time now."

"Has she?"

"A real long time, easy fifteen years, I'd say. I thought she'd stay there forever, we were all happy there, especially after she had the little one."

"Little one?"

"Yes. The girl. She was already pregnant when she turned up there, never did see the father none though. He must have been a right brute."

"Why do you say that?"

"She always told us never to tell anyone about the little girl. Or even her much. Let outsiders know nothing, it was safest for her, she said."

"Safer from what?"

"She never said. Just keep it to ourselves. Never said a word I have. Kept it all to myself."

Uksod smiled. *Shame you kept your word so long old woman. It would have helped if I had known.*

"Why did she leave?"

"That was very strange that was. One day she got all in a fluster. Some traveler or the like had been around the farm. Oddest old man I've ever seen."

"In what way?"

"He had the longest beard, and he wasn't particularly tall. But his beard should have been white, what with the age he looked. Instead it was like a rainbow of color."

"Color?"

"Yeah, all sorts of it. Strangest thing. After he was there, she left. Never said a word to any of us. They all left, and we never saw her or the little one again."

Uksod sat back in his chair and released her mind from his. She'd been easier to manipulate than he hoped. So it was true, somehow the woman had become pregnant again, so it must have been Schevenal's. If her daughter could link the amulet then she had to be Karpenmor's sister.

He wasn't looking forward to letting Yantarnaya know, but at least he had answers.

"I must have fallen asleep, I'm sorry." The old woman looked at him confused.

"That's alright, one of the men will look after you."

Uksod stood up and walked out of the tent. He turned to the guard on his right and swiped his thumb across his own throat. The man nodded in recognition. Uksod went and found Seventeen.

"How was that, Eminence?"

"It got me what I needed to know from the farm. Did anyone see you bring her away from her home?"

"Not that I know of."

"You aren't sure? This is important, Seventeen."

"It is hard to tell, Eminence. We are not invisible, if someone was watching that we didn't see."

"There can be no chances. Leave no traces there either."

If the Vrah leader was disturbed by the command he didn't show it.

"We don't need to stay here. I will take some men and return to Ponte, tomorrow I'll want to go see Hurf." He turned and walked back to his tent.

6 5

LANI

No one had said a word to her since they had arrived yesterday. Lani's captors had pushed hard to arrive there before nightfall and she had been pinned between them as they rode through the city streets.

They didn't seem afraid of attracting attention and the few people on the streets they passed through to reach where they were now, seemed intent on not getting involved in anything that didn't bother them.

With five armed men holding her, any attempts to escape would have been futile. Lani had hoped to see some guards to yell to, but they seemed to have snuck in a back way and had avoided any populated parts of wherever they were.

Their accommodation was an empty warehouse, in an equally empty pocket of the city. She had hardly slept all night and apart from their own noises, Lani had heard almost nothing coming from outside. Compared to all the cities she had visited recently, that surprised her.

She was cold and had no way to know if there was anything she could do about it. They had covered her head with the sack again as soon as they took her from her horse. Lani hated the feeling and her mood had grown darker throughout the night.

When they had first captured her, the covering had bothered her but it had only been temporary. For the bulk of the trip, they had removed the covering and if nothing else she felt as if she had opportunities.

Now with the sack back on her head she felt a victim, hopeless and helpless. Lani had exhausted any thoughts of escape, and her wrists were raw from trying to find a way loose from her bindings. If she could have, she'd have pulled the amulet out of her tunic but she couldn't do that either.

Her stomach grumbled and her lips felt cracked. No one had fed her last night nor offered her a drink. Lani had been dragged off her horse, walked to a corner of the big open space and shoved down to the ground before they covered her head and tied it off again.

Throughout the night she had tried to get comfortable but the lack of warmth in the building made it difficult. She dozed occasionally while huddled on the floor, but it didn't do enough to relieve the worry she felt.

Lani was now sitting with her back against a wall, watching tiny slithers of light through the weave of the sack. She had no idea who these people were. They weren't Derks, that was obvious. All but one of them was shorter than her and that one was only just her height. Even though they were slight of frame, each of them carried lean muscle that looked as if they had trained for many years.

Their size didn't match their strength. She didn't know which one it was that had been lifting her onto and down from her horse, but they did that easily. Lani had been wary of taking the men lightly. While they had traveled from the boat she had tried to see if any of them wore a tattoo like Goatee and his colleagues. She had seen none and nor did they wear that strange black clothing.

If she had to guess, she thought they were a team of mercenaries, but that made no sense to her. They had come for her, she was sure of that, their attack on the boat was far too specific. They wanted her, or what she carried, but it was the fact that none of them had searched her which informed her.

They were doing what someone else wanted them to do. They weren't after what she carried; they were after her.

She'd accepted she was bound to the amulet somehow and she had to deliver it to Anderwell, hoping someone there could undo whatever had happened to her. Lani didn't want to think what would happen if she was stuck with it for the rest of her life.

Would people like these be forever chasing her? When would someone figure out if they killed her maybe then they could take it? That was the thing Lani couldn't understand. If they wanted the amulet so badly, why did they not kill her?

None of it made any sense.

Not that she wanted them to kill her. She was just over this whole twisted saga that involved the Derks and Jesters. It didn't matter what the seer said, or Ashantha, this wasn't any of her business. She didn't ask for it, and she would be glad to be out of it. Safe, somewhere safe.

Someone coughed and Lani could hear movement across the room. Her captors were now awake and starting to move about.

"Can I have a drink?"

No one answered and no one came near her. Her lips were cracked and licking them with an almost dry tongue did nothing to help. As the day wore on, she struggled to swallow, her throat was sore, and her stomach had given up trying to ask for food.

With nothing to do she had wriggled about trying to get more comfortable, but any change only lasted a short while before her butt hurt in that spot as well. The only noises she heard were muted conversations across the warehouse and little outside noise. There were no birds chirping or sounds of a working city, everything was subdued and quiet.

It was hard to judge the time of day with the hood over her head, but it seemed to be heading toward evening when a door opened across the other side of the warehouse.

Lani heard the murmur of voices and then footsteps slowly coming closer to her.

"There in the corner, this is the one. The one you sent us for." The voice timid and subservient to whomever he spoke.

No reply came. Only silence.

Timid Voice could not leave the silence sit. "We came from the boat, no stopping. None to follow us, no trouble."

A deeper, older voice spoke. "Take off the bag."

Someone stepped quickly to her and fumbled with the tie around her chin, before pulling the hood off quickly. Her head jerked back as it was pulled free of the cover.

Another man similar in look to the others, but much older, stood before her. He wore a dark blue robe that went almost to the ground covering everything except for his leather sandals. The hood had a white edge sewn on it.

"It is her?" the man who she thought of as Timid Voice said.

"That is what I am trying to determine but for your incessant talk." The man wore a square pendant around his neck on a gold chain. The inner bars in the pendant crossed over each other making eight segments within it, all of it made from gold.

He was clearly someone religious, some form of priest. While he was a similar race to the guards, he was different. His clothing was crisp and clean, the white edge around the hood was too white for someone who spent a lot of time outside or on the road. He even smelled clean, a mixture of soap but also smoky. She recognized the smell the more she thought about it, like the incense Despring burned inside his chapel back in Barnen.

He stared at Lani for a long time, unconcerned when she looked back into his dark brown eyes. He pulled a chain from under his robe, which threaded through a ring with a small amber stone. A shiver ran through her when she saw it. He closed his eyes and gripped the stone in his hand.

She sensed something that she couldn't really explain. Like a tiny wisp of wind brushing across her, but on the inside of her head, not outside. Instinctively she pushed pack at it. His eyes opened in surprise. There seemed to be a gleam to them, and while he wore no smile, Lani could sense he was pleased with himself.

"You have done well; she is who I seek. Did anyone see you take her?"

"None, Your Highness. We set fire to another boat to distract everyone. They were all looking at that and trying to help save it from burning. We did it in the dark and were gone in the dark. We were not seen."

The priest wasn't one to answer quickly, Lani observed. "Good. You have done well for the first part of this journey."

"First part, Your Eminence? I thought this was our journey." He sounded disappointed.

Again, another pause. "Just the start, I could not share with you all the details before. I needed you focused on what you had to do. But now you have done so well, I am sure you wish to earn double what you have so far?"

The priest pulled out a coin pouch from his robe and shook it in front of Timid Voice. "I do believe I promised you all this."

Timid Voice's eyes lit up and Lani could see his hand wanting to grab the pouch. It was bulging and sounded to be full of a lot of coins. The other guards had approached the group now, moving in closer, at the sight of the money they had all been promised.

Lani had been right about them. This lot were really just paid hires, in it for the money and had no idea why it was her they were paid to catch.

"Who would like to earn the same again for a few more days' travel?"

Murmurs of affirmation sprang forth from the group. "Where would we be going before we agree?" Timid Voice was trying to sound like he was in control of the situation, but Lani was sure if he rejected the offer, he would most likely be gutted by his own crew.

"Outside Okeans."

"Okeans, and the same payment again?"

The silence while they waited for the priest to respond hung tense in the air, such that Lani held her breath as well.

"Yes, the same again. You'll turn to the east before the city and skirt it and head to my chapel where you will hand her over. I will be there to receive her, and it will be safe then to have her in my care. That will be the last of your work for me, for now at least. You will receive this much again for a much easier task." He held the pouch up so all could see and shook it again.

No one spoke but the other guards all looked at Timid Voice and waited for him to speak.

"When do we leave?"

"Tomorrow will be good enough. Wait until middle day, we don't need to be seen on the road together. You'll be moving much slower with the wagon. Most importantly she's not to be seen. Is that clear?"

"Yes, Your Eminence."

At that he put the pouch back in his robe, turned and strode toward the far wall.

"But…" Timid Voice tried to say, quickly hurrying after him.

"Keep her well, better than she is now, or there will be punishment. Feed her, and make sure she is healthy when she reaches there. And bring all of her things."

Then she couldn't hear the rest of their conversation. Once the priest reached the door on the far wall, he stopped and turned, bringing the pouch back out of his pocket and lobbing it up in the air toward Timid Voice.

As he watched the man desperately grasp at it in the air the priest laughed. Lani couldn't hear it, but she could see the dark sneer that accompanied it.

Lani didn't like him and sensed he would be done with these mercenaries when they reached Okeans. She doubted they were smart enough to recognize that, but that wasn't her concern, unless she could use it to her advantage.

She had almost two weeks before they would reach this chapel, at least that she knew. They had to keep her fed and with drink, so she wouldn't lose her strength, but somehow, she needed to use what she knew to help get away.

Whoever this priest was she had no desire to end up his prisoner, at the chapel or anywhere else. He looked nothing like Despring and carried himself with a greater air of authority. Lani didn't know what he wanted with her, or why.

She didn't understand any of it.

Not that it matters, I just need to get away.

The guards were arguing over near the door, and Timid Voice had been forced to share out some of the coins with his men before he started ordering them about again.

He sent one of them to fetch her food and water and for now at least they left the hood off. Lani knew she should have felt more despondent, but being able to see and know what she faced somehow made her feel better, not worse.

66

UKSOD

Morning was no more pleasant than the night before. Uksod had ridden back to Ponte with his guard through heavy rain that had come in from the coast. When they'd finally reached Ponte near on nightfall he'd needed a hot bath just to drive the aches from his legs.

It had taken all his will to go to the basement there and seek out the rings on Dharatan. They had moved south but were still all together, and finally he had a team near enough to send after them. But the toll it took on him left him completely exhausted.

He had slept through the first part of the day and once he was up and about he discovered it was closer to middle day than not. Seventeen should be back by now, but he wasn't so keen to go back out in the weather to find Hurf.

Maybe I should have him brought here or close by?

Uksod stood at the window of the small study he used during the day and tried to list out all the things that would be needed to get the bridges complete. The issue of the final stage he'd filed away as something for another day, which turned out to be now.

With the progress being made, that day was quickly approaching and it would require him to have answers. Their relations with

Ngahere were cordial, at best. There was an impasse of sorts that allowed for only limited trade to go ahead.

The sabotage of the wheat crops hadn't worked to their advantage yet. It had been a long play that Uksod and One had put in motion, the idea being that they could offer wheat at a reasonable price, but they'd need to have the bridges working to make it feasible.

Which was why they hadn't just ruined one crop but poisoned the seed as well. It would take time to build the bridges and they'd have to use boats in the short term. It had always been a long shot, which at the moment wasn't working.

Tin was the main commodity the barbarians wanted, and Enderk had plenty of it. Once again it was only movable in small amounts, and the antagonism between Dharatan and Enderk meant the Ngaherians would only do small trades.

If needed they'd have to use force. It wouldn't be easy, but they'd have to do what they needed. It would come down to timing. Ferrying large numbers of soldiers there quickly enough to secure a base on the top of the cliffs would be hard.

They'd need constant reinforcements and supplies, but if they were already on Step Six, then it was only one stage by boat. Staging resources and supplies on the last island would make that easier. That was something they should start now. Make sure there were not just camps for men, but storage houses for anything they might need.

They would need buildings made of stone that could withstand the weather, and hold large quantities of supplies and arms. A smile crept across his face. He knew this was why he was in charge of all of this. Most men were incapable of solving these problems, but look where they were at already.

Not quick enough for his goddess (though nothing ever was), but now they had solid bridges that wouldn't be blown away easily. They just needed to complete it, and everything would change. It felt good to have something he could see a positive end to.

Uksod turned at the knock on his door. "Come!"

Seventeen closed the door behind him.

"Everything handled at the farm?"

"Yes, Eminence."

"Good."

"There is a problem with the other plan."

"What is it?"

"While we were gone, His Highness returned to the city."

"He did?" Uksod was bothered, it meant he may know that he wasn't here.

"The weather met them much quicker than us, so my men advised him it was best to return for his safety. As we know it can be treacherous on the Stepping Isles in bad weather."

"Of course."

"When they returned, he dispatched some of my men to find the manservant and bring him back to Ponte."

"How…"

"It seems he was already aware of the man's whereabouts. I must assume that it was well known who Hurf was amongst the servants, he did serve the High Prince for a very long time."

"So where is he?"

"Hurf or His Highness?"

"Both."

"They are in a meeting in His Highness's chambers."

"I must attend immediately."

"The guards were left with strict instructions that no one was to disturb them, including you."

"He wouldn't!"

"He did."

Uksod was furious. He knew he could override that instruction, but to what point? He didn't want to alert the boy to what he wasn't aware of, not when it was already too late. They were talking now, what the manservant had to tell him could already be out.

He was still angry, though. And afraid. If he knew everything that Hurf knew he could judge for himself what the risks were, what Karpenmor might learn. But he didn't know. That had been why he was so happy for the Prince to go across the bridges. It bought him time to find out.

"Leave me, but I want to know when they are done. And the

servant is to be mine after, one way or another, he's not to leave Ponte without me seeing him. Understood?"

"Understood."

Once he was alone Uksod cursed out loud. He hadn't thought that the boy would be so proactive. He knew the lad was smart, he'd trained him to think like a ruler. That was the point. Of course he hadn't expected it would be used against his own wishes. Not now, anyway.

He needed to be ready for whatever came from it. The worst possible information would be that Karpenmor had a sibling. Underneath it all the boy longed for family, Uksod knew that. He'd used it against him where he could. But Hurf had never left Schevenal, how would he have found out?

How much did the servants talk? What else might he know? Nothing else would have reached the old man. Only the Vrah, Yantarnaya and himself knew the full story of Karpenmor's mother's death. Which meant the worst of it all would be what Uksod had only just found out about the girl.

Anything less than that was manageable. He could talk his way out of not telling the truth about how long his mother lived. The boy might not like it, but it would be salvageable. At least Uksod hoped.

What else could the man know?

His door opened, catching him by surprise. Karpenmor entered.

"Uksod, you're up, good. You still look a little pale, are you feeling any better?"

"Some, Highness. You're back and safe. I was concerned when the weather took the turn it did."

"Yes, much as I wanted to see more, the men guarding me gave me sage advice. I would have seen you but you had left instructions you were resting. I guessed you wanted it that way."

"Thank you for your kindness, Highness."

"I found other ways to fill in my time. Most interesting."

"What was that?"

"You recall Hurf, my father's manservant?"

"Yes, of course."

"Well it turns out his family village isn't that far from Ponte, so I sent men to collect him. I wanted to speak with him."

"Oh!" Uksod made sure to act surprised. "What about?"

"My father mostly. I guess he probably knew him better than anyone, even you. He was always around him."

"True. Did he tell you much?"

"Mostly little details. What he liked to eat or wouldn't touch. What he remembered of him from before he went to Dharatan."

"He wasn't his servant then."

"No, but he was in the palace, his mother worked there, or so he said. Which is why he was chosen. So he saw father a lot in passing."

"Do you feel better for it?"

"Yes. As much as I wish I had seen more of him that wasn't the empty shell, it helped. There was one thing though."

Uksod's heart skipped several beats. So far it had been easy, but now the boy was pausing and had his eyes firmly fixed on Uksod.

"What is that?"

"Hurf seemed to think my mother lived not far to the north from here, after I was born."

Uksod didn't know what to say. It was partially a trap; if he admitted it he had to explain it, if he denied it he could be caught in a bigger lie. Hurf might have given him more than just the knowledge, he might have had proof.

"He said that?"

"Yes, Uksod, he did. He also said she didn't die soon after my death, that she was in the palace for at least another year."

Uksod needed to hear everything the boy knew. Of course he was upset, that was understandable, but he had to wait it out and make sure what he told him next fitted the story.

"Nothing to say, old man? That surprises me because you told me, not even that long ago, that she died after my birth. Why did you lie to me?"

"Highness, I understand why this would be upsetting."

"Upsetting? I want the truth!"

Karpenmor stood in front of him, waiting. Uksod wasn't going to learn anything more from the Prince so he had to take his chances, with the least he could.

"It is true that she didn't die straight away, but the rest is similar. She wasn't well, and we sent her out to a farm in the hopes she would recover, but she didn't."

"Why didn't you tell me this before? What's the big secret?"

"It seemed a minor discrepancy, Highness. I wanted to keep it simple, especially when you were younger. She died, and it was before you ever really knew her, so what was there to tell?"

"The fact that she didn't die so quickly mattered. To me at least."

Uksod stood silently. Of all the things he could have learned this was the least important of them all. That she was from Dharatan, and only half Derk, would have been much harder to explain. He waited to see what happened next.

"I want to go there, Uksod. To where she lived. If it's near here then I want to see it."

"Of course, Highness. Can we wait until the weather clears?"

"Yes, but then I want to see it. And no more lies, Uksod!" Karpenmor turned and left the room.

Uksod went to the window and looked out. He knew he should feel relieved that he'd solved that problem already and the visit there would do nothing, but like everything with the boy of late, he wasn't sure things hadn't gotten harder.

67

LANI

*L*ani had expected an open wagon, something she would be tied into and have to endure for the trip from Vidus toward this place called Okeans. She was wrong.

It really was a carriage, just not the type she envisaged riding in. There was no seating or side windows within it. The back door, which was only wide enough to load goods, had a small viewing window barred from the outside.

The roof and walls were solid wood, and she couldn't stand within the carriage. At best she could be upright if she kneeled. Inside were three blankets and several sacks of feed for the horses.

She was grateful for them, while they were still full. They gave her a seat of sorts that protected her as the carriage lumbered along the roads. Every rut or bump the wheels bounced over threw her around in the back of the carriage, and without the sacks she would have bruised her back long before now.

The window was her only view of where they were and the world around her. She made sure to look out of it every few hours to try and remember anything important. It was possible she would need to come back this way when she got free.

If I get free.

Two of the armed men rode behind the carriage blocking some of what she hoped to see, and so she viewed the narrow angles either side of them from her small viewing window. The men paid her no attention at all, and never once looked her way while she was peering out the portal.

It had been three days since they had left the last city. The only time she was allowed out of the carriage was at night, when it was dark, and then only briefly to relieve herself and to eat. Despite only being allowed to walk a short distance and being tied firmly to a tree, it was preferable to being locked in the carriage.

While Lani knew they wouldn't harm her, they never left her alone long enough to find any way to escape. One of the five men seemed to always have his eyes on her, and if it wasn't for the words of the priest, she would have felt much less safe around him.

The carriage stopped abruptly, and Lani fell sideways into the sacks to her left. She sat herself up and waited, expecting that soon they would drag her out for the routine. She had noticed the sun was beginning to wane to her left, which meant it was time to camp and make food.

They left her inside for the better part of half an hour before the bolts slid across the back door and it opened.

"Out!"

Lani slid herself over the floor closer, and the guard grabbed one of her ankles and dragged her the rest of the way until both feet were clear of the door. He then reached in and grabbed the back of her tunic and stood her up outside the carriage.

They might be keeping her alive and fed but they showed no care for her at all. Now would be the most embarrassing part of the process as the guard would take her somewhere she could empty her bladder.

He might turn his eyes away but there was no mistaking what she was doing, and even without anyone watching Lani felt her face redden every time. She had no choice and had learned to manage the process of toileting even with her hands loosely tied together.

The routine each evening was the same. The camp was always positioned away from the road, typically behind some rocky outcrop or in some woods. The fire wouldn't be lit until it was too dark for other travelers to be on the road, and then they'd cook and once everyone had eaten the fire would be covered over.

They always had at least one guard on duty throughout the night, not that Lani could envisage anyone causing them trouble.

Maybe bandits think the carriage contains valuable cargo.

Lani didn't know if that would be better or worse. If bandits attacked them, they wouldn't care one iota about keeping her alive.

As the night progressed her mood darkened. Until now she'd been more anxious than anything else. She had felt in a hopeless situation, being their prisoner, but still held out hope that she would be able to get free somwhow.

That was changing bit by bit. Lani was beginning to think that she was stuck properly this time and any luck she had received so far had run out. She knew she was brooding but she couldn't seem to shake it. Being cooped up in the carriage didn't help. All she could do in there was think.

Why me?

None of it made sense. Lani had no idea why she was in the middle of this. She still couldn't work out the meaning of what Ashantha had written in his journal. He had said he knew her mother, and that she had family. But the way he wrote it meant her mother was dead, so what did he mean? Surely her father had been part of the people in that fight scene? He had to have been killed as well, hadn't he? He wouldn't have left her alone and in danger.

Maybe he was already dead? If he wasn't then why hadn't he come for her? Or did he think her dead as well?

The way Ashantha wrote made it sound like he is still alive.

Lani thought about using his mask again to look at the journal. But there was hardly enough light during the day, and almost none at night. There was still so much she hadn't read. Maybe somewhere in there was more, something that would make sense of it.

It was mostly boring information about what he was doing, or things to do with events in large cities. The only mention he had about her was in the sections to the end, and she'd read them over and over.

The helplessness came back even heavier.

Maybe Ashantha didn't actually know much at all. He never

mentioned her father directly and hadn't exactly explained what happened to her mother. Perhaps he hadn't really known much at all, like she first suspected, and it was all a ruse.

None of what Ashantha said made any sense. She was sure if it wasn't for the amulet, and her inability to put it down, she would have abandoned this journey already.

As one of the guards kicked dirt over the fire, Lani couldn't help but think about how the amulet might be able to get her out of this mess. If she mentioned it to them, especially the creepy one, who even now sat across the camp staring at her, they would definitely want to look at it. She recalled how greedy for the coins they had been.

All it would take would be for one of them to pick it up, and that would be the end of that person. But would that help? One less wasn't enough for her to escape. It would have to be several of them, and she'd need them to be close. Very close, so she could use a weapon of theirs to get free, after they died.

It was all too complicated, and she shivered, thinking about how casually she was considering using the amulet to kill people. That wasn't right. She would be no better than the Derks.

She could still see Yerat's dead eyes looking back at her, the first time she had seen someone die from touching it.

She shook her head thinking about it.

No, I can't do that purposefully.

If she was willing to do that then she was no different to any of the others. Up until a few weeks ago she wouldn't even have thought about killing anyone. But then up until a few weeks ago she hadn't any reason to be captured and threatened.

Lani looked off into the darkness, thinking about how she was going to escape, what opportunities there would be. No matter how much she tried to talk herself around, the only solution she could think of was to use the amulet.

The shadow of someone walking toward her brought her back to the reality of where she was. It turned out to be Creepy Man. He reached behind her and undid the rope tethering her to the tree.

"Up!"

He dragged her up by the arm and manhandled her to the carriage.

The back door was already open, but he held her upright longer than normal and leaned in close to her. His lips brushed against her left ear, making her shiver, as he whispered into it, "Maybe I should keep you warm tonight!"

Lani closed her eyes and was shocked when he shoved her forward into the carriage, and lifted her feet, pushing her in. He laughed, a sick deep forced laugh, as he did so, and the door slammed closed behind him.

She heard the bolts slide across as she slid back over into the corner. Tears ran down her cheeks as she took shallow breaths and thought about protecting herself. The priest had told them to look after her, but he probably just meant to feed her.

Her thoughts came back to the amulet in her tunic, and she placed her hands on it, trying not to think about what she would need to do.

TILLANDRA

Kahoy was a small village two days south of Terletak. It was a pass-through village that was surrounded by woods on all sides. Over the years the villagers carefully cleared space for what they needed while retaining the connection to the surrounding wood.

City people didn't understand their connection, nor liked the proximity of something they feared, but the villagers were more than comfortable with their way of life.

Tillandra slowed her walk as she neared the clearing where the village lay. She had been on the same road since she had left Terletak, and all of the last day under the canopy of the trees. The roads were well maintained, and a small distance left either side of them allowed the traveler to not feel like the woods were completely on top of you.

For her it was a nice respite from her time in Okeans. The boat trip she had taken from Verloren to Grote had given her time to digest everything and relax a little. The journey from Grote to Terletak was hectic and noisy and she had found herself back on edge again, without reason. She had let her colleagues know where she was and that she was safe and then had set off on her walk south.

The quietness of it was the most important part of the walk. The rhythm of her stride, the ability to blank out the world around her and just 'see' the world as she hurried by without needing to be in it.

As she broke free of the trees into the village proper, she walked into a light drizzle of rain. She had been dry the whole journey through the woods and hadn't even known the weather had turned.

The village was no more than twenty houses spread around the large clearing. Individual constructions stood between some of the houses. Some were like small sheds, others were fixed canopies to provide cover for the benches or workspaces below.

Tillandra had been here only once before but knew it was wetter here than in other parts of the realm. The canopies allowed the villagers places to meet, work and dry their clothes for much of the year.

The clearing was like a long egg-shaped oval and in the very center was a large peaked covered area, their commons. Here the villagers spent much of their time, eating together, drinking, talking and paying games. Work was never done in the commons, that was always done elsewhere.

Today it looked like the entire village was gathered and Tillandra could smell meat cooking as she approached.

"Ho, traveler. What brings you to Kahoy?"

"Greetings, Kahoy. It has been many a year since my last trip here. I wish to pay Vindisil a visit."

At her words a woman turned her head to look at Tillandra. She was seated in the opposite corner to where Tillandra had approached the commons, and the woman had been facing the other way. She gave Tillandra only the slightest recognition, a tiny nod and subtle look with her eyes.

"Well, Vindisil, it's rare you have a visitor," the man who had greeted Tillandra replied.

"Rare it might be, Tibok, but visitor she is, and she's welcome here on my behalf."

"Good, good. What is your name?"

"Tillandra, Tibok."

"Welcome to Kahoy, Tillandra. Please come sit with Vindisil and enjoy our hospitality. We eat our evening meal while there is daylight here. Why, I couldn't tell you, but it's what we do." With that he broke out into laughter and rubbed his round belly with both hands before patting his chest and sitting down.

Tillandra walked through the large, covered area, moving around each of the tables and smiling at those who were looking at her. Many of the village seemed unmoved by a visitor and carried on their conversations or eating their food.

Vindisil had risen from her seat and made some space for Tillandra to sit with her. A young boy hurried over with a thin wooden square plate laden with bread chunks, steaming meat and green vegetables.

"Thank you."

The boy nodded to her and handed over a pair of wooden tools. Tillandra took them and studied them curiously.

"They are to eat with, Tillandra," Vindisil said to her.

As she awkwardly got her long legs under the table and sat beside Vindisil, Tillandra watched how the others used the wooden tools. The pronged tool they used to pick up pieces of food and ate from it, rather than using fingers. The other had a sharpened edge to it and a handle, making it like a small paring knife, but wooden. She saw Vindisil use it to break up the food she held with the pronged item.

"Clever."

"You know we like to use wood. These have become our way now."

"These would be a hit all over the world, Vindisil. People would pay a lot for them."

"Yes, but then we'd be bombarded by city people, and others. No, better we just use them for ourselves."

Tillandra smiled. She could appreciate a place where they had no interest in the progress of time or things. Unfortunately, she had no option to live that way, and even less so now with the way the world was spinning.

"It's been quite some time, Tillandra. Is it that time?"

The older woman looked at her cautiously out of the corners of her eyes.

"Unfortunately yes, Vin, and I had hoped to hear your advice on some things."

She chuckled, her chest crackling a little as she did. "At my age I have lots of advice for everyone. Isn't that right, Purdu?"

Across the table from her a young man, about half Tillandra's age, looked up from his plate. She knew that he was listening to their conversation, it would be impossible not to, but he appeared adept at looking like he wasn't.

"It is, Grandmother. I never cease to be amazed by how much you have to tell me." He smirked as he finished the sentence. Vindisil cackled again.

"Eat, Tillandra. Then we can go and drink some berry wine in my cabin and talk about things."

There seemed to be no rush to their eating, everyone happily taking their time. Even Vindisil was in no rush to finish, and seemed to concentrate on every bite she took, savoring it like it was her last.

When it came time to leave, Tillandra struggled to walk alongside the old woman. Vindisil shuffled very slowly and relied on Purdu's arm for stability as he stepped gently beside her. It had been a few years since Tillandra had last seen the Carver, back then she had been full of energy and still very spritely.

They entered Vindisil's cabin and Purdu made his grandmother comfortable before getting them all something to drink. Tillandra was surprised how tasty the wine was, and how fresh and bright it zinged on her tongue.

"Something special, isn't it?"

"It's lovely and very unique."

The old woman nodded her head sideways at Purdu. "It's his specialty. Must have gotten the skills from his father, bless his soul. No one else here knows how to make it, and don't you go telling any outsiders about it neither."

Tillandra smiled and looked at the woman. She didn't want to discuss what was happening with her grandson in the room.

As if she understood, Vindisil nodded to her grandson, who got up and walked over to the door, closing it. He then returned to sit beside his grandmother. Tillandra must have looked perplexed.

"He's to hear what you have to say, Tillandra. Purdu is the next Carver."

"Next?"

"You can see how I have aged, Tillandra. You know we are tree people, people of wood. Like a tree, my time has finally come. My limbs are hollow and weak, my trunk has dried out and my roots are all but dead. I shan't be here for that much longer, and Purdu has been chosen by the woods to be my replacement."

"Really?"

"I won't go into how that happens, but it has, and he will be the one moving forward."

Purdu had a soft smile on his face. Tillandra could tell he was proud of being chosen, but his humility showed through in his posture and respect for the process unfolding.

"Perhaps it is a good thing. My senses must be slipping, I was not expecting you."

"That's why I am here. There's been a few surprises." Tillandra told the pair about the loss of Ashantha and the emergence of Lani. She spoke of her visit to Tingfurlew for the ring, and how the girl had been able to wear the ring up until just recently.

"This would explain the false shoot."

"False shoot?"

"There is a plant, in the woods, that is how I know when I need to carve a new mask, Tillandra. Around the time you are talking about, a new shoot appeared on it, which informs me of the need. But it died off within days and nothing new has appeared."

They all sat in silence for a long time before Tillandra spoke again.

"Purdu, do me a favor, go and check the shoots."

He looked at her, perplexed, but left them alone all the same.

"He will do well, Tillandra. He has youth and energy, which has all but drained from me. There are those here that are happy my time is nearly up."

"What? Why?"

"They do not like what it is I have to say anymore."

"About what?"

"Recently I see things of darkness, things others wish to hear nothing of. I have seen men fighting, Tillandra, death everywhere. "

"You have visions?"

The old woman nodded and looked at her. "But I know not what they mean. Perhaps your talk of this veil lifting is similar. I do not know. I think I will be happy to be gone if such a thing is to come. You will have much to handle, Tillandra."

"And I struggle with the thought every day."

"You have been chosen, Tillandra. There's nothing else to be concerned about. The choice was made knowing you would be ready and the right person for the next age. Do not be afraid, you will succeed."

Tillandra smiled back at Vindisil but in her heart she wasn't as convinced as the old woman.

They sat in silence for some time before the door swung open quickly and Purdu hurried into the room. "There's a new shoot, Grandmother."

She smiled and nodded her head back and forth a few times. "Then your clock, as you refer to it, Tillandra, is in play. It seems I have work to do."

Tillandra realized what she was saying and rubbed her temples. Now she had to wait for the mask and get back to Midderbuilt for a new ring. The only way to do it in time was to head directly across Daskare and the desert to Watersend. Right through the likely location of King Ahn's forces.

"It looks like you will be our guest until the mask has been made."

"So it seems."

"Purdu, you will need to make room for her to stay with us. Get to that. I will need to prepare my things and then we'll go to the woods. I think we'll take her with us, so she can see the beauty that the masks come from. There's more she needs to know."

69

TILLANDRA

Tillandra felt uncomfortable asking it, but she knew she had to. "Vindisil, I have another favor to ask."

The older lady looked at Tillandra with warm eyes that let the awkwardness melt away. "Yes, my dear?"

"As strange as it may sound, how easily could I get hold of a couple of live rats, or…" she stumbled a little over her words. "… Chickens?"

"What on Scurra would you want live rats for?" The surprise showed all over her face.

"That's the thing." Tillandra had been debating how much to tell the woman. In the end she realized this woman knew so much about the magic in their world anyway, she couldn't see telling more would harm anyone. "There's a way that I can communicate with those that wear the masks, and it means using the… life force, I think you might call it, of a small animal."

Vindisil laughed at her which made Tillandra blush furiously.

"Why are you laughing? It's true."

"I'm not laughing about what you're saying, Tillandra. Just that you don't need to use a rat, well not here anyway."

"I don't understand."

"You forget, Mother, that I am well aware of the power of the masks, and our role in them. You seem to think you're the only people with knowledge about the magic. That isn't true. The mask's ability to communicate has been explained to our line since the beginning, but the masks themselves are a conduit."

"Ummm."

Vindisil smiled and held up her hand. "Let me finish. The thing that helps you communicate is the power of the wood. As you know, we use the wood of a special type of tree. What makes it special is how it's connected to the forces we can't see."

"Forces?"

"I too struggle for the words to explain it. You used life force, so I am using that part of the word as well. There is a life force in more than just animals and people."

"People?"

"You really don't know do you? Anything that breathes can be used to access that power."

"You mean…?"

"Yes, you could use a person as well."

"But…"

"You don't need to say it, Tillandra. Yes, if you used that much of their life force they too would die, but keep in mind they are a much bigger life force, so they don't have to be used up. You could use them partially."

"Wouldn't that harm them?"

"I have never tried but I don't think it will permanently, unless you drained them too much. It would be like you were extremely tired and then recovered. The life force recharges within you."

Tillandra was having trouble thinking about how that would work.

"There is a cost though," Vindisil went on. "You cannot use the same person continually, as there is a finite number of times they can be used. Like a counter."

"What happens after the counter runs out?"

"Then they are no more. Before that they would be very weak."

"How many times?"

"I do not have that knowledge. It's not something we've ever tried."

"You've communicated using the method?"

"Sort of, Tillandra, but not the way you think. We don't wear a mask, like you do. For you it allows you special ability and access to your kind all the time. For us, we have another way. It's the trees."

"The trees?"

"More specifically the sycamore fig. There is a network of these trees, and they allow us to communicate."

Tillandra stared at Vindisil, trying to grasp what she was telling her.

"Who communicates?"

"Those of us of the woods." She laughed as she said it. "I am sorry, I'm not used to explaining this to anyone outside of the people."

"Your people?"

"Yes. Our people of the woods. There is a group of us that are connected deeply to these trees. It is our role to protect them."

"More than this village?"

Vindisil laughed again. "Yes, Mother. More than this village. They live across the realms, wherever there are these figs. Wherever we have been called."

"Called. I guess that's how we feel about what we do. We were called to it."

"Certainly, the early ones were called. Now much of the calling is done within our families. Like Purdu, I knew it was him that would be the one, he is being called to it, whether he can sense that or not."

"How does all this help me?"

"Firstly, you too can use the tree. Your mask lets you do it, you can reach the life force within the trees and speak to your mask wearers. I suspect also you could speak with us as well."

"Your people?"

"Yes. Although they might not understand."

"Can you help explain that more to me? This is all a little new and I'm struggling to see how we all fit together like this."

"I understand what you do and who you are, and I understand my people of the wood. I do not tell them about you, and this is the first time I've told anyone else about them."

"And why have you?"

"Because I was told. The voice behind the trees – I suppose it's a god – told me it was time."

"Like Tingfurlew."

"Tingfurlew?"

"Sorry, the Ring Maker. He was told to explain his story as well when I was last there. When there was no new ring after Ashantha's passing."

"You've never used his name before, only ever Ring Master. It feels as if there will be much change ahead for you and Purdu, I sense that. I am glad that my time is nearly done, I am not sure I care to be part of what might happen."

Tillandra shivered at the old woman's words, a chill much like a premonition, and she didn't like the sensation at all.

If Vindisil noticed it, she didn't say a word. They sat in silence for a few minutes disturbed only when Purdu returned to them.

"We shall go now, Grandson. I think it is time to visit the great fig."

"Yes, Grandmother." He dipped his head in a respectful bow. Tillandra felt a little strange knowing that next time she was here it would be him she dealt with and not Vindisil. A tinge of sadness swept through her.

The trio left the cabin and walked around to the back of it, where a well-trodden path headed into the woods. Tillandra walked at the back and watched as the others walked almost reverently through the trees and shrubs underneath. Every branch they brushed they did so gently, and she could almost feel them sighing with love as they brushed their fingers over them.

They didn't place their feet blindly on the ground either, every step within the woods seemed deliberate. It was a conscious form of movement, of mindfulness, where they were experiencing everything around them as if for the first time, and yet as if they had been there forever.

A sweet spicy smell pinched at the inside of Tillandra's nose, drawing her attention away from watching the others. She didn't recognize it but adored the aroma. Her mind drifted to thinking about what it was, how she wanted some, where was it coming from.

Vindisil's voice seemed to be subdued, as if under water. "That's the first test."

Tillandra looked forward to see both Vindisil and Purdu stopped on the track and facing her. The hold over her thoughts fell away as she stared at them.

"You can smell the lilies?"

"Is that what it is?"

"Yes, the Stargazer lily is the first test."

"What do you mean a test?"

"In order for the figs to be protected they don't just use us, there are several ways that nature protects them. The scent of the lily is one. If you follow it, you'll find yourself in a field of them, completely over-whelmed by their smell. Sadly, those who do often die, they become so infatuated with the flowers that they are unable to leave and die from starvation and thirst."

"Oh."

"Sometimes we know someone is near and can rescue them, but often they will fight to stay."

"That's a little scary. What other tests are there?"

"Soon you will see the most beautiful orange plant. It looks like a hand of orange fingers, and it draws you into wanting to touch it. We call it poison fire because you'll burn from the inside out if you touch it."

"And you live near this place?"

They all chuckled at her words. "Yes, but then we are not affected like others are."

When they passed through the part of the woods where the strange orange plant grew Tillandra could see why it would be so attractive. Purdu walked behind her through this part and when she started to head off the path, he grabbed her arm and kept her moving forward.

"It's actually a fungus not a flower," he told her as they passed a clump of dozens of the vibrant orange fingers.

Tillandra wasn't ready for the feeling she experienced when they broke free of the outer woods and reached the huge sycamore fig that was their destination. There were other figs behind this one in a grove that appeared to shine with a translucent shimmer.

"Welcome to Kahoy Wood, Mother Folly."

Tillandra almost felt like the trees themselves spoke to her, and not just Vindisil.

70

TILLANDRA

*U*nder the cover of the massive tree Tillandra felt as if she was in another world. The air had a cleaner feel to it, not that she even understood how she could tell the difference. The sounds of nature were there, alive but muted in a beautiful way so that even the buzz of a bee seemed in harmony with the way things were.

Kahoy Wood was the closest thing Tillandra could compare to how it felt when she was under Mount Qum at the Citadel Stone.

She perceived at that moment that they were connected, one way or another.

Yes, we are, Tillandra.

The voice was the same but different. She recognized it from her last visit to the stone. Rather than seeking more answers, Tillandra closed her eyes and took in three very deep breaths. They felt cleansing and she relaxed, although on the last one her chest tickled, and she coughed.

Clearly it had been a while since she had allowed herself to fully breathe. When she opened her eyes, she soaked in the depth of color in everything that was near to her. It was like seeing the world for the first time.

"Wow."

"Wow, indeed." Vindisil's voice had a smoother sound to it here under the tree. "This is the tree at the center of our world, Tillandra. It is this one we will seek a new mask from."

"Seek?"

"Come and sit under the tree and I'll let you know a little more before it's time to go to work."

A huge limb lay out from the tree, as if it was offering itself up to be sat upon. Tillandra could see part of it had been cut and smoothed and the pair of them sat there, while Purdu casually walked around the area under the canopy looking at what lay on the ground.

"We are servants of the woods, not their master, Tillandra. This is the difference that many fail to understand. When others come to trees, they cut them down or burst through the undergrowth believing that people dominate nature."

"Instead of nature being dominant?"

"In truth it's much different from that. There's a natural order to things. Why does anything need to be dominant? That's such a human concept."

"But aren't there dominant creatures or plants?"

"Not in the way you think. When a wolf eats a rabbit, you imagine that the wolf is dominant. What then if a bear eats a wolf? Is the bear dominating the rabbit through the wolf? In nature the animals give themselves up as prey when they feel their time has come. Much like I explained, my time is nearly over."

Tillandra couldn't help herself. Tears formed in her eyes, and one rolled down her cheek.

"You cry because of our relationship but also because to you I am lost when I am gone. But to the tree I am still there, I return to where I belong, and my being-ness is absorbed back into the ground. The trees can still find what was me there."

"I'm sorry."

"Don't be. I've come to understand that the way we think is different to many people. You're so busy in your world doing, always doing. That's why you feel so special when you come to Kahoy. It's so opposite to your world outside. You get to reconnect to what is."

"You are correct. I've only been twice but this time I wondered why I don't come back more often."

"It would be better if you did, Tillandra, but you don't have to come here. There are places much closer to you."

"Really?"

"I will show you, come with me."

Vindisil took Tillandra by the hand and walked up to the massive trunk of the sycamore tree. She guided her to sit in front of it and placed their hands on the trunk.

"And your other one. Once you have them there, close your eyes."

Tillandra did as she told her. At first, she pulled her hands away quickly – the tree seemed to be moving.

Vindisil chuckled, warmly. "You can feel its pulse?"

"Oh, is that what it was? It moves."

"It does. There is nothing to fear. Start again."

Tillandra placed both hands on the trunk and let herself become accustomed to the feeling of motion under her hands. It felt to her as if the bark on the tree was rippling, like waves on the ocean. It was gentle but very obvious. The longer she held them there the more natural it felt, and she found herself being pulled into the tree.

"Don't resist that feeling, you aren't actually moving. Think of it like you do when you communicate, your mind goes inside but your body stays where it is."

At once Tillandra understood. She thought of the tree like the Void and allowed her conscious mind to step inside. The feeling was similar but different. There was something there, unlike the Void, and it was as if she passed through honey to get to the center of it. Once inside she had trouble standing up, if that's what she could call it.

Vindisil's voice came to her in her mind. "Breathe. It's the Flow that you're feeling. It can be overwhelming. Picture me."

Tillandra did, just like she would normally do, and everything else dropped back into the background. Beside her stood Vindisil.

"Welcome to the World of Wood, Tillandra."

"World of Wood?"

"I know no other name for it, that's how we describe it. What do you call it when you communicate using your masks?"

"The Void."

"Is it different?"

"There doesn't appear to be a 'Flow' as you called it. Not the same. There's like tufts of clouds that pass by, but you have to be more deliberate to find what you're looking for. This is something else."

"Interesting. Maybe it's because you are using another's life unwillingly for it. Here the tree welcomes those who wish to travel."

"Travel?"

"In your mind, Tillandra."

"Oh, of course."

"I want you to do an exercise. I want you to ask the Flow to show you its family of trees. All you have to do is think it, and when it starts you can 'squeeze' your mind to speed it up or slow it down. Understand?"

"I think so."

"Have a go, I'll ride along so I know what you're experiencing."

The idea of someone riding along felt strange. She then recognized this feeling was more like the way she accessed the Majamig of a passed Jester, without needing a living being to do so. It piqued her curiosity, but for now she wanted to do as Vindisil had told her.

She reached out to the Flow and was immediately swept up in a torrent of images. As Vindisil has advised her, she squeezed at her mind and slowed it down, letting the images come to her singly. She was able to go back to the beginning and followed the trail. At first it showed her all the figs around her, and related trees, she then steered it north, and found she was able to visualize a kind of map in her head, pushing toward Kysten.

Images of single trees and small groves of trees were shown to her. Some she had passed or recognized their location, others she didn't know where they were. She turned the direction and pushed further north and was surprised when she felt her mind approaching Anderwell. She came across the old gardens at the back of the college section of the city, a rambling section of land they had planned to build on one day but somehow had always left alone.

There amongst the different trees, shrubs and weeds was a fledgling tree that was connected to the Flow.

"What on Dharatan?"

She sensed Vindisil watching over her. "That was planted there by one of our people back when your kind were first given their power to do your work. But the instructions of its care haven't been followed. It struggles to breathe, choked by weeds and unfed, especially with love."

"How do I...?"

"Keep looking. We can speak of this later."

Tillandra spent the next few hours traveling parts of the realm finding pockets of 'special' trees, each in various states of health and care. At times she felt sadness for those telling her of lost kin that had been cut or burned, other times the pure joy of a thriving grove.

When she felt overwhelmed, she felt what seemed like a tug on her arm, and then Vindisil was in front of her again.

"Enough for now. Sit back there and recover. You've used a lot of energy doing that for the first time. I need to ask for a mask. I'd like you to be present."

Tillandra took a step back and imagined herself sitting. She saw Vindisil approach the center of the space they were in and kneel down, placing her head on the ground. She could hear her chanting. It went on for some time before the old woman's voice could be heard.

Center of our world,
Mistress of the woods,
I come as your servant,
Servant to all who would serve you.
Our friends the Court need the mask for a new beginning,
A new member of their family.
I would ask you to shed for us part of yourself so they too can serve you.

She lay there for several more minutes then she stood and walked to Tillandra. "When you leave, be sure to express your gratitude for what you have been able to do. And ask that you may return in the future."

As she exited the space Tillandra almost fell backward as if she had to step back from it. As she recovered herself, she looked at Vindisil, who sat beside her. In her hands she held a small sheet of wood, and where it had lived on the outside of the tree was obvious by its absence.

"The tree provides it to us when we ask, our skill is to carve it."

Tillandra had many questions she wanted to ask, but her head was also quite woozy, and she wasn't sure exactly what to do next.

"Purdu will help you walk back, the first time you do this is quite draining. Tomorrow, before you go, I will tell you more of the lore. For now, I need to carve this mask. You have so few days to do all that you need to do."

71

TILLANDRA

For the first time in ages Tillandra's sleep felt as though it was deep and calm. When she woke, she couldn't remember any thoughts or dreams, as if her own mind had been wiped by a mask.

When she rose from her makeshift bed, Tillandra expected to feel groggy and sluggish. She felt anything but that, and her mind seemed the clearest it had been in a long time. Even the things she worried about seemed to have a space of their own, like a small box that she was able to close the lid on and leave them there to consider later.

"How do you feel?" Vindisil asked as she walked into the open main room of the cabin.

"More awake than I have in a long time."

"I used to explain it as if someone had tipped your head to its side and poured water through your ear, flushing your head out through the other ear. It always feels like everything has been scrubbed clean and all the unnecessary thoughts have been removed."

"Yes, that's exactly what it feels like. All of my energy seems restored. I can hardly believe I've been on the road for weeks, I feel so fresh."

"You're going to need all that energy if you have to reach

Tingfurlew and be back in Anderwell. How long has it been since you were told the ring changed?"

"Maybe twenty days or so, Vindisil."

"Blasted splinters indeed. We must get you away."

"While I didn't spend time thinking on things last night, I have a solution to how I need to approach my next task. I'd like to communicate with some of my colleagues, if you would show me how, before I go."

Vindisil looked at her intently. "I can see why it makes sense, but you'll be worn out afterward. It will delay you until tomorrow if we do."

Tillandra shrugged. "I believe doing it will save me time in the long run. I intend to ask to get some things done in advance so I can travel fast without seeking resources."

"Only as long as you're sure. While I carved last night, it came to me that I should teach you more of it, but it's not for me to force you. I think you will need it more as time goes on. I can't say what or why, but I feel that your challenges have only just begun, Mother."

"Don't worry, I know it myself. I'm not ready for whatever it is, but all I can do is try to keep up."

Vindisil said nothing for close to ten minutes. If Tillandra hadn't seen her eyes open she would have sworn she was asleep. When she spoke she was again full of wisdom. "No one will be ready for what is coming, Tillandra. That's the impression I just received. It would not matter who was in charge, you are as capable as anyone."

Tillandra cocked her head to the side about to ask what she meant, when she spoke again.

"I can't explain it. Sometimes I just get a feeling."

And there it was for Tillandra, the one person who could perhaps help her understand her gift, and this would be the last time she would see her. It was as if she was never meant to understand her gifts.

Tillandra discussed what she could with Vindisil, including the lack of confidence she had in her visions. Purdu brought them some warm tea and toasted bread with butter while they shared the way they experienced these premonitions.

While there were no clear answers to it, Tillandra felt more at ease about the messages she received and how she could interpret them after the conversation. While she knew she had to make the journey here for the mask, these precious few moments with Vin were of more value to her.

The clarity of her mind here helped her understand how much was still missing from their own court. Each of them was struggling with their own skill, they had no one to guide them on how to use it. If she was struggling, what of the others? Were they not speaking of their own challenges?

Close to the middle of the day the two of them returned to the grove, where Vindisil instructed Tillandra in the way she communicated with other people of the wood. The knowledge she shared gave her insights that helped her understand now why Ngaherians were so respectful of the forests they protected.

Not dissimilar to the way the Court had its network, so too a small network of people of the wood existed, helping each other maintain the ways of their people, handed down over generations.

"Many people look for knowledge in books, Tillandra, when all they have to do is look to the source. The trees themselves carry much of the knowledge passed on through time. The only library you need is the tree in Anderwell."

"But it looked so sick. How long will it survive?"

"Before you go, I have a favor to ask you. I think I know the answer to help with that."

"If there is so much knowledge within, can we find the answers to what I have been seeking here?"

"What answers are those, Tillandra?"

"I have been seeking books, history, about the past, but there has been that block that I described to you. What would the trees know? What would your people know?"

"That is something else that you have helped explain to me. This veil that is falling away, we have been blocked by it as well. There's a point where we can see no further, where access is not open to us. We can share our ways but the past has been hidden from us as well."

Tillandra felt disappointed. "It was worth asking."

"If what you say is true, then that door will open to us as well.

Perhaps this is why I felt the instruction to show you the way of the wood. To help you restore your tree. So you can find guidance when you need it."

"I only hope so."

"For now, let's get you talking to your people."

Tillandra again entered the space. This time it felt more normal, and she focused more on her traditional way of speaking than seeking out the visual information she had received last time.

"In All Jest, Toolet."

"Mother, In All Jest to you as well. You're with the carver?"

"I am, but not for long. I have the mask and I have to reach Midder-built, quickly. What of the coin?"

"I can see it on the map, slowly making its way back there."

"Tell Gimbden I will need people to meet me at the border. I have no choice but to cut through Daskare direct to Watersend."

"What about the forces gathering there?"

"I'll have to chance it, any other way will be too slow. I've already been gone long enough."

"I'll tell him."

"What of your work there?"

"There's been a development."

"What sort of development?"

"We have a new Prospect."

"How in Seth's name did that happen? We don't need more complications with an upcoming Audition. They can't be ready in time?"

"There was little choice, Mother. He kind of chose himself."

Toolet relayed the story about how she had discovered him, and what had happened when he was put to training with the others.

"My, he is unique then. What is his name?"

"Leo, Leo Peggle."

"Look after him, Toolet, that's a skill worth protecting."

"He's more than capable of looking after himself, although his new nickname isn't making him very happy."

"Let me guess: Rat?"

"Close enough. Rodent. It's shaken up the other two Prospects though, they had thought themselves quite special to have been chosen. That he has come in, much younger and with little training, has definitely put a rat in the henhouse."

Tillandra laughed. "How apt. I can't remain here much longer, I need to start my travel. There's one more thing."

"Tell me."

"You know the overgrown gardens behind the college, toward the back wall?"

"Yes."

"In the middle of them there is a tree that is struggling. Get someone to start taking care of it. Water it every day, and keep the area around it clear. It needs to be someone sensitive to caring for plants."

"Okay, for any particular reason?"

"I'll explain when I'm back. Just get them to tend to it like they would a tiny animal, nurture it to health."

"Yes, Mother."

Tillandra felt tired from the conversation, but less so than the day before. What she liked more than anything was that there was no sickness with it. She definitely could get used to this way of communicating.

72

KARPENMOR

Waiting to leave the compound had taken more days than Karpenmor had wanted, the rain and winds had only increased. He did not intend to stay stuck in this place forever and had woken resolved that they would set out today no matter what.

It wasn't as if the farm was even that far away, but he also knew he was chasing after something that didn't exist. His mother wasn't alive and he wasn't going to find anything of her there, after all this time. So there wasn't that much of a rush. Not enough to leave the comfort of the compound.

He wanted to fill in the gaps of what he knew. It was his history and he resented the fact that Uksod had not been honest with him. He was annoyed at everything he didn't have, what he had missed. And Uksod was the easiest target.

That had only become worse on this trip away from En Carta. Karpenmor had stretched the time between when he drank the brandy, and now he was able to go almost seven days before his desire for it grew. Today was the end of that count, and the pounding in his head had come back.

Nothing helped it, except more of the drink Uksod made. The headaches started around the third day and grew in intensity until they were all he could think of. Today he wanted to push past the seventh day. That was another reason to get out of the city and see the farm.

Karpenmor hoped it would distract him from what he was fighting with. He grasped the pendant in his palm and squeezed it tight, wishing it could make the pain in his head go away. It didn't, but it reminded him of why he was enduring this.

The pendant helped him think more clearly, that he knew but it didn't stop the pains from not having the drink. That clearness of thinking was helping him take note of what was happening around him, even through the pain. He knew that would be even more important now that he was High Prince.

When he was High Prince. That was another thing he needed to confirm with Uksod, exactly when that was to happen. He was aware of the need to conduct the ceremony and there were some formalities in coordinating that, but there had been no discussion of when.

And for whatever reason, it seemed Uksod did not appear to be pushing that along with his usual vigor. It was understandable the priest was reluctant to finish the reign of his own power, but he had to get used to it.

Every day the feel of it began to sit more comfortably within Karpenmor. Where not so long ago he was apathetic about it, even completely antagonistic toward the idea, now he was comfortable with it.

He had been trained for it, albeit by Uksod, his whole life. There had been little else for him to do, he had no siblings, no family. At the time it had been tiresome, all the learning and processes he had been through, especially while still young.

Now his head was clearer he found those memories served him well. The training was there, he did know what he was meant to be doing, and he had a sense of purpose to it. The more he paid attention to the world he lived in, he saw things he didn't like, things he could change.

A chuckle burst out of him.

Now that will upset the old priest.

Even though he hadn't made it all the way out across the Steps, it had triggered a desire in him to finish them. He wanted to see Dharatan, the land of the barbarians. There was an anger there, a wish for some redemption in his father's memory.

If he could undo the harm of the loss of the land bridge many would forget what had caused it. And then there was the amulet.

Something about the jewel had captured his attention. Karpenmor didn't know why, but it felt like another missing piece, something connected to his father that bound it to him. He wanted it back, which was a reasonable reaction, he felt.

Except it had become more than that. He found himself thinking about how to get it back, almost obsessing on getting it back. And he had no idea why. It was worse than that though. He had begun to think about getting them all back. It had begun as a daydream and now he found himself coming up with imaginary stories of finding them and taking them from whoever had them.

That wasn't likely to make him popular on Dharatan, not that he cared. Maybe it wouldn't make him popular here either. But then he was soon to be High Prince, he could do what he wanted.

If he wanted them, he would make it happen.

It was that sense of purpose that was building within him, and this trip to Ponte had helped him feel more capable. Making his own decisions seemed easier here, away from the capital, En Carta, and he liked it. It was another thing pushing him to outlast the headache and sweats.

I can get off that blasted drink!

By mid-morning he had forced his will on everyone and the party set out in light rain to the north. The road they followed was sodden and rutted and progress was slow. It took until early afternoon before they crossed a narrow bridge and followed a path up a small hillside to a farmhouse.

No one was around, and no smoke rose from the chimney.

"Do we know who lives here now, Uksod?"

The priest shook his head. "I have no knowledge of the place, not since your mother was here, Highness."

Karpenmor found it hard to fully believe him. The fact he had lied once meant he could do it again, or could be doing it now.

Several of the guards returned from inspecting the farmhouse and surrounding outbuildings. "There's nothing living around here, Highness. It appears no one lives here at all."

"It is strangely in very good condition for an abandoned farm, don't you think?"

He didn't expect an answer and dismounted, stepping through the mud, to inspect the farmhouse himself. The house was cold and damp, the fireplace empty. But it was clean, and excepting the recent foot marks of the guards, everything else looked as if it had been used not so long ago.

Everything looked in working order too, as if the occupants had simply gone on a journey and would be back soon. Karpenmor tried to imagine what his mother had been like, how her life here had been. It still seemed strange that the mother of the heir would have been hidden away.

Someone must have lived here with her, known her. Uksod was hopeless at providing anything resembling an image of what she was like. What she looked like, or her nature. For a religious type he was quite cold as far as human nature went.

All Karpenmor wanted was to speak to someone that might have known her. Not that he'd assumed they would still be living here, but one of the occupants, had there been any, might have remembered who was there. And where they were now.

Back outside the sight of Uksod dripping in the rain, atop his horse, almost made him smile. The old man looked extremely uncomfortable, and for whatever reason it eased the angst he felt about this place being empty.

"Nothing, Highness?" It almost sounded to Karpenmor as if the priest was happy about it.

"Strangely, Uksod, nothing. And yet it seems someone was here not very long ago. Perhaps they have had to visit family elsewhere. I would have thought at least one person would have remained to protect the property and tend to things."

"I cannot say, Highness. The ways of farmers are not common knowledge to me. Would you like me to try and find out more?"

"No, Uksod, I can take care of that. I'm still very interested in finding out more, and no doubt there'll be someone who has memories to share."

He climbed up on his horse, and stared into the old man's eyes. "I'll start with Hurf, when we return. Perhaps there are some things he hasn't told me yet."

"Oh…"

"What, Uksod?"

"Ah, well, you see I thought you were done with the poor servant, so I had him sent back to his property."

"In this weather? What on Enderk was the rush? Are you trying to kill the man?"

Uksod's face seemed to glow red. "Highness, I only thought…"

"And that's well and good in the past, Uksod. But we aren't in the past anymore are we? The man was my guest, and you should not have sent him away without… You just shouldn't have!"

"I'm sorry ,Highness. I will try to do better." The tone in his voice was harsh now, Karpenmor could sense the resistance in him.

"I want him back, make it happen."

"Yes, Highness." Uksod began to turn his horse.

"And Uksod."

"Yes, Highness?"

"Make sure he makes it back healthily would you? He can be a formal guest of mine in the compound."

The priest pulled his horse around and rode toward the local leader of the Vrah, and talked to him quietly. Seventeen nodded several times and turned to the guards. Within minutes two of them raced off on their steeds, back down the way they'd come.

Karpenmor turned his head away and a grin came across his face.

Another thing I need to handle. The Vrah should be reporting to me, not him.

73

LANI

The tree Lani was tied up against seemed particularly rough. The bark poked through her tunic and scratched at her back. Maybe she was simply tired of being captive, and of being leered at.

Since the second night when the creepy guard had threatened her, he'd been making her feel even more uncomfortable. Lani wanted to fight back against him, but she was helpless, and they never let up their vigil of her.

If he was going to try something she didn't know how she'd defend herself apart from screaming. Maybe one of the others might defend her. The thought she'd have to rely on one of them to help her didn't make her feel any better.

She wished she could run but there still hadn't been any opportunity to escape. They had at first seemed like a rough bunch of mercenaries but her opinion of them had changed.

Lani doubted any of them would be on her side, they were a tight group. Most nights while there was still light, three of them would practice their skills with sword or staff, while the others tended the horses and took turns cooking a meal. One of them had a bow and he could use it as well as anyone Lani had ever seen. Not that she had seen many, but he would hit his target every time.

It was rare that they let anything slip. Mostly they spoke out of earshot of her, not that they had much to say in general. While they had appeared subservient to the priest, on their own they were anything but.

That frightened Lani. She was even more certain she didn't want to end up in the hands of the priest. If he was willing to use men like these to do his work, she wasn't sure she wanted to be near him at all.

At least they had done as he asked and made sure she had food and water. There was nothing feast-like about it, but it was enough to satisfy her hunger and not leave her tired and weak.

Right now, they were camped in a group of trees that were spread six feet or more apart. It was a strange grouping; there was little undergrowth, and the trees provided little real cover. They stretched tall above the group camped below, but each limb, while strong, was sparse, and had little leaf.

Anyone traveling down the road would be able to spot them if they looked hard enough west, certainly in daylight. Come night only a fire would highlight them, but it would be unlikely for anyone to be on the road at night.

There were few sheltered places to camp amongst the wide-open plains. The countryside around rolled with low undulating hills, plains full of grasses and the occasional clump of trees like these. An early evening breeze helped cool Lani down.

The weather was becoming cooler the further south they rode. It was subtle but Lani had enough time to notice it, cooped up in the carriage. She wasn't cool enough to want to put on her coat, although if she hadn't slept in the carriage each night, she imagined she would need it now.

Creepy Guard had cooking duty tonight, which meant he was the only one close by, while the others were off practicing. As he went about preparing the fire and food, he kept looking her way. She did her best to not look back and stared out across the plains.

He was still there; Lani could see him out of the corner of her eye. It made her skin crawl, but she was in no place to do anything about it. She tried to focus on other thoughts.

There was something she couldn't work out about the priest. Why hadn't he checked her for the amulet, if that's what he wanted? Maybe he hadn't needed to, that's why he used the amber stone.

If it was the amulet they wanted then why keep her? That made little sense at all to her. There was no reason she was important, so it had to be the amulet. No one knew what she knew about how it had bonded to her, so why was he spending so much money to get her to Okeans? There seemed little logic in it.

And how had they found her? Could he sense when she used it like the Derks had? Was he in bed with them? She looked out across the plains, trying to find any other reason for what was happening.

Footsteps to her right made her turn quickly. Creepy Guard was walking toward her, a sneer on his face.

"Just you and me right now, maybe I should have some pre-dinner fun."

"You're a good talker. You've always been saying what you're going to do, I bet you don't even know what you're talking about." Lani wanted to slap herself. She knew she shouldn't say a thing, but she was sick of being captive and this creep leering at her. He was like Harsop but worse, picking on her only while she was unable to do anything.

His sneer turned into clear anger. "You've got a smart mouth for someone tied to a tree."

Lani shrugged; she'd already done enough with what she had said.

He walked forward and stood over her, looking down. She refused to look up at him and turned back to the plains. There was little she could do while her leg was tied up and he stood far enough away so her hands couldn't reach.

None of the other guards were close by and she doubted they'd care too much about what he was doing, not while he was just trying to intimidate her anyway.

He stepped in closer now and she could sense he was unsure what he was doing.

"You think I won't have my fun with you, girl? Just you wait. It's been a few days out of the city now, me and the boys, we're all a little edgy. Maybe tonight's the night?"

"Your priest told you clearly not to harm me, don't think I wouldn't tell him if you dare to touch me."

The guard moved in closer and started bending toward her. "What did you say?"

Lani took the only chance she could see. She twisted her body quickly and swept her free leg around at ankle height, connecting with his leg. As they collided a sharp pain ran up from her shin, but she had generated enough momentum to rip his leg from under him.

He wasn't stable from bending over, and she was able to sweep both his legs from under him. He fell sideways landing heavily right in front of her. Before he had a chance to push up from the ground, she wrapped her hands around his head, pulling the short length of rope around his throat, and yanked his head toward her, so she was behind it.

The man thrashed on the ground, and finally got his hands up, one trying to grasp the rope and the other trying to swing at her. She had him just out of reach, so that the best he could do was slap against her left arm and shoulder while keeping her head out of his way.

She pulled with all her strength and felt the rope biting into his neck. His face began to darken and his movements started to slow.

"What's going on here?"

Lani looked up startled as another of the guards ran over. Inadvertently she eased the pressure on her grip. The man on the ground regained some of his strength and thrashed more vigorously just as the other guard reached her.

She saw the guard's fist coming toward her and felt the impact and a burst of pain briefly before she passed out.

When she came to, little time had passed. Creepy Guard was kneeling several feet away, coughing as he recovered his breath. The guard who had punched her was shouting at him.

"What was happening here? How did you get so close to her?" Creepy Guard never answered. "You're a fool, if you touch her and he finds out, we'll all be flayed. Is that what you want?"

Finally Creepy Guard stood up, his voice still a little croaky. "What would he do? I was just having some fun. What does it matter to him if she's been used a little? Look at her. Now, she'll have a bruise on her face. That's more than anyone would have seen from what I was going to do."

"Listen real good, Shigerand, leave her alone."

Creepy Guard looked alarmed as the other said his name. They both realized at the same time what had happened. It was the first time any of their names had been spoken aloud.

"Come away, see what you've started."

It was the first time in the trip they had made a mistake, and she didn't know if it would help or cause her more trouble. The other guard had confirmed, though, that protecting her was important. She just had to hope Shigerand wasn't up for taking revenge.

74

LANI

$\mathcal{T}$he side of her head ached. Lani had only passed out for a short while, but it was enough. Soon a headache would turn up, and she'd be defenseless. What had she been thinking? Even if she'd been able to disable Shigerand, what then?

Even if she'd gotten free of her ropes, and started to run, it was light enough that the others would be able to follow. It wouldn't take them long to catch her, on her own. She didn't move, not wanting to attract any attention.

The men sat around a lit fire, the last of the daylight almost gone, eating a meal, but this time they brought her nothing. It would be a long night locked away on an empty stomach.

It was the first time they had kept an open fire longer than they needed to cook food. She noticed they had also brought out skins of wine and seemed to be settling in for a session of drinking.

Lani didn't know if it was the events of earlier that had spawned it, but there seemed to have been several discussions between them, with occasional looks her way before the wine was brought out and they settled near the fire.

The guard who had punched her rose reluctantly and walked over to her. He cautiously knelt behind her and untied her from the tree.

She waited nervously to see what he was going to do with her as she didn't want to be taken to the fire amongst them.

"Up," he growled, prodding her in the back.

She stood slowly, before he grabbed her left arm and walked her toward the wagon. Lani was relieved that was where he was taking her. He roughly pushed her in and barely waited while she dragged her feet in before slamming the door closed.

Lani heard the bolts slide across. The sound of his footsteps let her know he had moved away, and she got onto her knees and moved over to the door, looking out. She could just see the fire and she watched the guard sit back down with his men and take up a skin.

Something had definitely changed, and it was the first time since she'd been captured that they'd let down their guard. After a few hours they became louder and less worried about what they were doing. They spoke out loud and laughed a lot.

Maybe it was because they were so far from any village or city that they didn't care as much. Or perhaps what had happened today forced a change in their routine. What had Shigerand said? Something about needing to take the edge off.

Lani's main concern was what would happen if they decided she was fair game now their inhibitions were removed.

Her view of Shigerand was obstructed by another guard, but she knew he would not have forgotten what she did. There was nothing to be done while she was in the carriage. They couldn't sneak up on her, and she'd not get any rest worrying about them.

She moved to the back of the carriage and leaned back onto the sacks while stretching her legs out toward the door. Still, she couldn't stop fretting about what they might do. She had no weapons, only her feet and the rope between her hands, that she'd used earlier.

No doubt they wouldn't fall for that twice. They'd be watching her even more closely now, which meant she would have even more trouble trying to escape. She couldn't get away by harming just one of them, she needed something more.

Lani thought about the boat near Galon, and how she'd seemed to have guided the guards away from the gangway. She still wasn't sure that was what had happened. Maybe it was just her wishful thinking, and she'd been lucky?

She'd need more than luck now. The only other way was to put the amulet out and let them touch it. But that would only work once. The others wouldn't be stupid enough to touch it if one of them died. That was just as foolish as what she'd done today.

How can I even be considering using it like that? Before were accidents, not deliberate.

A roar of laughter came from the fire, and the conversation and song rose and fell as more wine was consumed. Lani heard people moving and shuffled to the door again to look out. Several of the men were kneeling over one of the large tree logs that they used to sit on, their arms locked together by their hands.

The other three guards jeered and chanted as the two men fought each other in an arm wrestle. Eventually the one on the right slammed the other's arm down to cheers from the others. They continued swapping out with each other with much pushing and laughter.

After a handful of bouts, they all sat back around the fire and went back to their drinking. Lani returned to her sitting position and tried not to fret about what would happen later. She reached into her tunic and felt the brooch and amulet. Her fingers seemed to tingle slightly as she brushed across them.

No.

A thud against the back of the carriage broke her reverie. The sound was frighteningly loud to her, as if they were throwing things at it. Another thud slammed into the back of the carriage.

Cautiously she crept over to peer out the small window. The guard who carried the bow was wobbling on his feet near the fire, being cheered by the other guards as he struggled to nock an arrow.

When he seemed to have it ready, he steadied himself as best he could, and sighted the carriage before firing. Lani instinctively dropped to the floor. The arrow coming through the small window would have been only dumb luck, but she had no mind to be skewered by it.

No sound came. The arrow must have sailed clear, given the jeering from the campfire. She slid herself back to the far wall of the carriage, pushing with her feet as she went. Their focus on her didn't bode well for what would happen later and her already racing heart was making her sweat.

Another thud made her heart jump. She was huddled up by the remaining sacks, wondering when they'd come closer.

Lani reached into her tunic and struggled to pull the amulet pouch out, her hand catching on her top several times.

Another thud.

She shook her head but untied the pouch anyway. As she slid the jewel out onto her palm her hand and forearm tingled and she could sense the stone connecting with her.

Instead of dropping it or pushing it back into the pouch she held it out in front of her. With her eyes partly closed, her vision slightly out of focus, she could see the tendril creeping away from the stone. It was like a thin trail of smoke, there but not there. It snaked off out the small window and away to the north.

She stared at the stone, as if she could feel it. There was a connection there, it wasn't just her imagination. Her skin crawled at what the feeling did to her, and she pulled the pouch closed again.

Another thud hit the carriage, and the jeering seemed even louder. Lani put the pouch down and kept hold of the amulet. If nothing else she could tempt them with it.

Suddenly her mind filled with pictures and sounds. She could see the area outside the carriage almost as if she was out there. The pictures moved toward the group of men, as if it was one of the tendrils snaking its way through the air.

She could almost direct it and moved toward the man holding the bow. She could sense emotions coming off him. He was struggling with conflict, the alcohol wreaking havoc on his control. He was fighting between heading to the carriage or doing what they had been paid to do.

The raw animal sense of power the man believed he had was sickening to Lani. Anger flared in her and she directed it toward him, envisaging she could strangle him like she had with Shigerand. Suddenly he dropped his bow and reached for his neck.

He seemed to be struggling to breathe and dropped to his knees.

The others rushed toward him, and Lani's thoughts changed from focusing on him to the confusion of thoughts that flooded her from the other men.

It was if their thoughts were all pouring into her head, and she struggled with the woozy feeling that came with it. She dropped the amulet on the floor and gasped for breath herself. She shrank back from the amulet, unsure exactly what had just happened.

Once she had regained her own self-control she grabbed the amulet and pushed it back into the pouch before drawing the string tightly closed. Lani put the pouch away and then crawled back to the window.

The mood by the campfire had changed. There was no laughter anymore and they had regathered on the other side of the fire, occasionally looking her way but only briefly. Maybe they had an inkling it was her, or purely superstition, but they didn't appear to have any further interest in her.

All of the men seemed to be taking big swills from the wine skins as they passed them back and forth, their conversation now muted, almost inaudible over the distance. Lani wasn't comfortable about what had just happened but she was grateful for the change in their behavior.

She settled in against the remaining sacks, staring at the door, listening for any sound that one of them had changed their mind. Once her heart had calmed down, she found it harder and harder to keep her eyes open. When she did drift off, she fell asleep to a dream of an orange room, filled with the thoughts of thousands of people, her brain cringing at the cacophony of sounds.

75

LANI

It was a scratching noise that woke her. Outside it was still night but a strong moon helped throw light into her carriage. There were none of the sounds the guards had been making earlier, so she wasn't sure what it was that had disturbed her. Lani slowly pushed herself backward away from the door and more upright, trying to wake her sluggish mind.

Her heart was racing from the disturbance, and she heard it again, something or someone scratching or playing with the lock.

"Hurry," a woman's voice said quietly, but more than audible in the confines of the small wooden carriage.

"Who is it?" Lani spoke up. "I'll call the guards."

The noise outside stopped. A shape moved across the small, barred window in the door. The woman's voice again, "We are here to help you. To get you out. Do you not want that?"

Lani stammered, "I… do, but…" She didn't know what to say. "Who are you?"

"Enough for now, let us get you out, then later many questions."

The scratching sound continued followed by the click of the lock. Then nothing. After what seemed minutes Lani could hear the sound of the metal bar being slid back as slowly as it could be. Inside the carriage it seemed very loud, she just hoped it wasn't enough to wake any of her captors.

Whoever was outside was just as concerning as what had happened earlier. Why would anyone be out here in the middle of Rohumaa supposedly trying to help her escape? Lani hadn't seen anyone following them. She knew this was likely a trap and braced herself for what might be coming. Without even thinking about it she placed her hand on her chest and felt the amulet there.

Maybe she should use it like she had earlier? There was definitely a way she could do things to people; it wasn't just chance. She'd proved that earlier. Lani hadn't liked the way it had felt, but if these people were here to harm her, she wasn't so sure she wouldn't do it again.

These strangers must have only been able to get so close because her captors had drunk themselves into a stupor. It was the only time they had altered their routine.

Maybe my luck has changed after all?

The door swung open and in the moonlight, Lani could see two people outside the carriage.

The woman stood on the left, a hood up covering most of her face. She held out a hand. "Come, we must be quick."

The man stepped away and created space for her. In the dim light she could make out his bulky physique, much larger than the lean guards who had held her captive, and he appeared to wear a sword on his hip.

Lani cautiously slid over to the door and let her legs hang over the edge. As she touched the ground, she released a breath. Was she escaping or just changing captors?

When she took the woman's hand, she felt a chill run through her. Not that the woman's hands were cold but something about her set off a charge through Lani's body. The woman quickly pulled her hand away – she must have felt it too.

As she turned to the man with her, Lani caught sight of her face in the hood. While her eyes were open, all that was there were whites, and thin dark lines that ran through them like the way lightning struck the ground.

She gasped, and the woman turned back to her. A thin smile formed on her face. "Fear not, child, I am blind, that is all."

Lani felt embarrassed for her reaction. She noticed there was another man with them. He had stepped forward dragging what appeared to be a body.

"Quick, be out of your clothes. We have more for you here."

"What...?"

"There is no time to explain, this body will buy us some time." She pointed at the shape that Lani could now see was a woman about her size.

"Who is she?"

"Was. And there's not time to explain. They could wake anytime!" Her voice crackled and Lani looked between her and the men, even more uncertain than she had been before.

"The clothes?"

One of the men threw a bundle at her feet, and the two of them turned away from her.

"Quickly now, there is no time," the woman repeated, then stepped away from her.

Lani wasn't so worried about the clothing change but needed to keep what was stowed in the special pocket in her tunic out of sight of any of them.

In the bundle was a set of tights and baggy over-trousers which she put on. She felt the pockets and they were deep, running a long way down her leg. Carefully she moved the brooch and amulet and stuffed them in one of the pockets before changing tunics and putting on the coat that came with it.

Almost as soon as she put the tunic on the ground one of the men hurried over and grabbed her things, taking them to the body. A cough and movement came from near where the fire had been earlier in the night.

All three of their little group froze, then the two men very slowly moved a hand onto their swords, waiting to see if anyone called out. Another cough sounded, some more movement, as if someone was rolling on the ground, then nothing except the occasional snore.

They finished dressing the body before hoisting her up and

carrying her to the carriage, pushing past Lani as they did so. With a bit of pushing and cursing they got her into the carriage.

One of the men climbed in and they dragged her to the back and rolled her to face away from the door. He got out and closed the door.

"Done?"

"Good enough for a few hours," he replied to the blind woman.

"That will have to do. We need to get away as far as we can by then."

It took more minutes than Lani wanted to count before the bar had been slid back across the door and the lock closed. As it clicked into place, they all froze again, waiting to see if the sound alerted the sleeping men.

"Leave no trace, let them think she is in there for as long as possible." The woman took Lani by the arm and shuffled away from the carriage. She could hear the sounds of boots scraping dirt, and thought they were making far too much noise for people trying to be stealthy.

Again, none of her guards stirred, and when the two men caught up to them, one took the old woman by the arm, while the other took Lani.

"This way," Lani's man said and they veered to the left, not running but moving quicker than they had before.

It took them the better part of ten minutes to reach a small thicket where four horses were tied up.

"Up, up. Quickly," the blind woman said to them all. Her helper guided the blind woman into the stirrups and up onto the horse with an easy push. As Lani went to climb up the man holding her hoisted her easily. His strong hands plopped her into her saddle, in a single motion.

Being lifted so casually and dropped into place was a little disconcerting, but Lani had little time to be offended. The horses set off, away from the camp site.

"Vidus?" one of the men called to the woman.

"Ssh, Vefed, you shout too loud." She moved closed to him. "Back just a bit, there's a road west. We take that." The hushed speech still carried to Lani over the sounds of the horses' hooves clicking on the dirt road.

All Lani could hope was that she hadn't just leaped from the pot into the fire and that the guards left behind didn't wake while they rode away.

Who was that dead woman?

Another dead body in her story. Lani's stomach turned a little. As glad as she was to be out of the carriage, the number of dead people that had fallen around her was unsettling her. Why her, kept running through her mind.

Who are these people? Have they really saved me? But why? Why am I so more important than that dead woman?

She shivered and tried to check out her riding companions without being too obvious. The fresh air blowing through her hair and across her face was a pleasant benefit to being free, but she'd been in too many situations of late to trust this was as simple as it seemed. Holding the reins with her left hand she casually reached down and patted her leg, feeling for the two items in her pocket.

She could feel the larger of the two at least, the amulet. For now, that would have to do. She was free of the priest and heading away from Okeans.

As soon as they stopped, she would be asking this woman questions. Lots of questions. As it was, she enjoyed the freedom she felt, letting her eyes take in the distant shapes as they picked up speed and hurried along the road.

After a short while the leading horsemen slowed and looked back at the woman before calling out to her, "Here?"

"Yes," was all she replied.

They took the road to their left, a path between tall grasses on either side, not more than a carriage width apart, and rode single file, with Lani second in the line. They weren't going back the way they she had come, nor toward Okeans.

Maybe this wasn't such a bad thing after all, she thought.

Time will tell.

76

LANI

A breeze drifted through the fields of grass, the heads of the stalks only giving way a little as it brushed over them. It carried no smell and was hardly felt by the group of four people who were taking a break from their mad dash on horseback through the night.

Lani stood, trying to stretch out the kinks in her back and the backs of her legs. After being stuck in the carriage for so long and not having walked more than a few steps each day she was enjoying the apparent freedom.

As the breeze touched her face she looked back to the east where the sun was only half visible over the distant mountains.

"They might know by now." The woman's voice was nearer than she expected.

When she turned the blind woman had walked from the horses to stand beside her.

"Perhaps now we should talk a little. Soon we will need to push the horses again, to create as much distance as we can."

Lani didn't respond immediately. Something about the woman caused her alarm, but she didn't know what. She wasn't sure if it was the look of her eyes. When she had been forced to look at Cideep's eye sockets she had been more uncomfortable than this, but still the whites of her eyes laced with purple lines didn't put her at ease.

She didn't know if it was something else, or simply the woman's condition, but Lani knew all too well she couldn't trust anyone. Even something as simple as a boat trip had twice now ended up with her in jeopardy.

"That would be good."

The woman turned to where the men were standing. She seemed to know exactly where everyone was. "Boil us something to drink, Vefed, if you would." She moved over to the small bank on the side of the creek they had stopped alongside.

What water flowed through it was hardly more than a trickle, but it allowed the horses to drink, and for them to fill their skins.

Lani sat down beside her, not willing to start the conversation. She was very interested in why they had come for her, but she wasn't going to give anything away.

"Perhaps you have many questions? I would if I was in your shoes. Maybe I can answer a few for you."

"Okay."

"My name is Odajeen. Not that my name matters much, but names, they matter when we talk. You know Vefed," she pointed to the man filling a small pot in the creek, "the other is his brother, Irdan. They help me with things."

"Things?"

"Let me say that a blind woman alone, she might not always have the best of times. My boys make sure I am not bothered."

Lani shrugged. It made sense, but their names weren't what concerned her.

"I have traveled many places, I am not sure why, always on the road, seeing things." She laughed. "Maybe not seeing, but many places I have been. Until Vidus."

"That was the city where I was before here, right?"

"Yes. You were brought there on horseback but left in that carriage. I have been in Vidus for most of five years, maybe less, maybe more. It is not so exact. But never could I leave. Don't think me daft, but many times I planned to leave, but never could I."

"I don't understand?"

"Do you know about a..." she rubbed the left side of her face as she considered what she was saying. "A compulsion? Have you ever had a compulsion to do something? Or not do something?"

Lani looked at the strange woman. "Yes, I have. I think everyone has."

"No, no. People don't often know what they do. But if you have felt that compulsion, you know what I mean. No matter what I did, I needed to stay in Vidus. I thought it was just to help those who could not help themselves."

"Okay." Lani didn't really understand what she was being told, except she too knew that feeling of being compelled. This whole journey had that feeling to it.

"Until you came."

"What do you mean?" Lani sat up a little straighter. This was the point of this conversation.

Why exactly had they helped her?

"I knew we had to help you."

"How? What do you mean?"

"I always keep my eye out for things, where the information might be useful to us. There's always knowledge you can sell or make a profit from if you have help."

The woman turned her head toward the two brothers.

"I was in such a place, watching that warehouse, which hadn't been used for a long time. But someone was visiting it. So we waited, and watched. I was sensing something important was about to happen. These were signs."

Lani felt like her eyes rolled up in her head. Thankfully the woman couldn't see it.

"You don't believe me?"

Her face flushed. How could this woman know what she was thinking when she couldn't see her facial expressions?

"I'm still not sure what you're telling me," she deflected quickly.

"I say that you were the reason I had to stay in Vidus. And then you came, and I had to follow. We were sure you were a prisoner, but it wasn't so obvious what to do about it, or where to go. We kept an eye on you for the traveling, making sure the men didn't mean to do anything to you."

"I never saw you."

"My boys, they are very good. We kept our distance. Until last night."

"But why?"

The blind woman was facing her directly. Her eyes looked down across Lani's chest and then to the pocket on her right leg. Lani felt very self-conscious about what it was she was focused on. Could she sense the amulet?

Her eyes came back up and it was like her eye whites were staring straight through Lani.

"The truth might seem stranger than a story."

"I've had many strange truths recently; one more won't worry me."

Again, the woman paused and considered her. "Then this is what I know. All of my life, as much as I can remember, I was blind. That's what I thought I knew."

"What do you mean by that, Odajeen?"

"I mean what I said. Up until just recently I could only remember being blind. Not before."

"You weren't always blind?"

"Listen, girl!" Odajeen snapped. "I'm trying to tell you and we have little time. Yes, I thought that was all. Then some months ago I was attacked by thieves and my head was hit very hard."

Lani bristled at the woman's tone as she listened.

"When I recovered, my memories were different. Now I see things, memories, I didn't before. I know now I was not always blind."

Odajeen seemed to withdraw inside herself a little as she had said it, and took a few deep breaths.

"Now I know I used to see things, colors, people, places. I can recall things, but I do not know what they mean. Then you came along."

"I still don't know what that means."

Odajeen pointed to Lani's pocket. "I can see that blue object."

Lani pulled back instinctively. "What do you mean?"

"When you rode in, I saw color for the first time with these eyes. On your chest, back then, the blue shone like a light. An oval of blue. I can see odd shapes, not clearly, but shapes. I could see a moving shape of you and the horse, dark, blurry, but on your chest the blue shone clearly. Now I see it is by your leg."

Lani didn't know what to say. This woman and her men could easily overpower her, if she wanted the brooch. There was no way she was giving that up. She would definitely use the amulet here if she had to, but that brooch was not being taken by anyone. Lani knew she needed to be cautious with this woman and her guards.

"Easy, girl. I do not want it. Easy." She held up both of her hands, the palms faced toward Lani, in a sign of peace. "I just saw it and I needed to know why. Maybe you can answer my questions, why I can see color, what happened to me."

This all seemed too fanciful to Lani, but there was no other obvious reason for why the woman had followed and helped her. And she knew she had the brooch, that was obvious, even though she was blind. Lani didn't know what the connection was, but somehow it meant this odd woman was linked to her.

"Never mind, for now," Odajeen said. "You needed to know. This is why we followed you, this is why we needed to help you. It was a sign, and somehow you and I, we are connected. But let us drink and get moving, we can talk more, we have a long way to go."

"Where are you taking me?"

"Toward Jarv."

"Jarv?"

"Yes, the big city down by the big lake water."

"Why are you taking me there? I still don't understand why you're helping me."

"We freed you, that's what. And you're not safe yet, whoever it was that had you may still come after you. For me, I'm hoping that you will know something I don't. It's selfish I know, but a fair trade for your freedom, is it not? We will get time to talk more, there's a long way to go. Come, drink."

Lani was more confused than ever now. She didn't know what to make of this woman and her instincts were also confused. She flittered between wanting to run and wanting to know the connection herself.

Like herself this old woman sought answers to her past, to the brooch that had been given to her by her mother.

Did she know my mother? But she doesn't remember her past, how can I find out?

Too many questions and still no answers. Lani was glad to be free, but just as wary of what this woman and her guards wanted. For now, they were heading to Jarv, which is where Lani had been heading for when she had left Statiiv.

She was free of those men, that counted for something, and she should be thankful for that. After everything that had happened since leaving Barnen, Lani just wasn't ready to accept what seemed good luck at face value. Not yet anyway.

77

TILLANDRA

The morning was grey, a very dark grey, and Tillandra could have easily turned back to face the wall and slept longer, except today she had to be on the road. She couldn't laze about, nor lose any more time here in Kahoy.

With the mask stowed in her satchel she had a deadline that she had to make. It was going to be a hard journey and she had given up part of yesterday which she hoped would pay off in the long run.

If Gimbden got her camels to the border station, then she could push herself hard over land to get there and know she would be fine the rest of the way. It hurt her Humaas pride to request an animal to carry her, but knowing when to get help was one of the things she had to be better at if she was going to be an effective leader.

Leader, ha! I guess I'm finally accepting it.

There were no sore muscles or aches in her body, the connection with the tree and the rest she'd here in Kahoy had left her feeling like she was back in Anderwell. She stood and quickly stowed her meager belongings, keen to get a quick breakfast and drink before heading off.

Vindisil had told her Purdu would lead her through the forest, to a tiny village at the end of the Gumala river. From there she would be carried over water by their canoeists across Lake Mata and back onto land.

Tillandra didn't want to go anywhere near Linaw and certainly nowhere near Bundok, but Vindisil had told her this was her quickest route. She could use the cover of trees for much of her journey, and then make the last dash to the border where she would find her camp.

Something was still left unsaid and Tillandra wanted to know what the favor was that Vindisil had mentioned. Perhaps it wasn't going to be asked anymore, she had difficulty reading the elder woman.

In the central eating area, Vindisil was already making hot drinks and food for them.

"Good morning, Tillandra."

"And to you, Vindisil. You are up early."

"Old bones need little rest. Here, drink this while I finish stirring these oats."

Tillandra was surprised they had oats here, tucked away in the deep forest, but chose not to ask. It had been some time since she had eaten them herself and the hearty meal would set her up for the walk ahead.

Once Vindisil was finished and sat with her, they ate in silence. Tillandra was scraping the bowl clean when the elder lady finally spoke.

"There is still the favor I would ask of you."

Tillandra looked up at Vindisil. It was the first time that she saw a lack of confidence in the old woman. Whatever it was she was requesting was unusual.

"Ask away, Vindisil. If it's mine to give I will aid in any way I can."

"This is not an easy thing to ask, Tillandra. I am ashamed to have to…"

Tillandra reached across the table and laid her hand on top of the other woman's. "It's okay."

"We have one of us who was born…" The woman paused. "…with a difference. Even explaining it we have so few suitable words. You think our people are relaxed and at peace, tending to the trees as we do. But we still suffer from the follies of outsiders, when it comes to one of us."

Tillandra was conscious of what the woman was trying to say. This story was true across all parts of Dharatan, and while she hadn't expected to hear it here, she understood. She didn't like it, but she understood.

"He cannot hear. Not even the loudest of noises. He has no hearing at all."

Vindisil lifted her mug and blew steam off the top off it, slurping at the spiced tea. Tillandra had been smelling hers and was keen to taste it as well. It was thin compared to the chai she had back in Anderwell, but the taste was pleasant.

"Our people are not kind, in this regard. Purdu and I have been protecting him, but I fear that he will not survive when I am gone."

"You keep talking about your passing, Vindisil, but you still look full of life."

"When it comes, Tillandra, it comes immediately. Like an uprooted tree, when the time is right, then my time to pass will be swift. I can feel it coming."

Tillandra had to trust what the elder woman said but could feel a sadness inside to lose someone she had only truly just connected with. This woman could have taught her much about the visions, but if what she said was true, Tillandra would not get to see her again.

"Don't look sad, it is what must be. All of us must return to the earth, Tillandra. It's just that my time is near."

"Purdu?"

"He is a good lad and will tend the trees well. But he is young, and there are still many elders here who will not allow him to dictate to them, not for some years to come."

"They will not harm the child?"

Tillandra was surprised when Vindisil tried to avoid answering and looked down at her drink. When she finally spoke, it was but a whisper. "We would not harm a soul, and never a tree, but it has happened before, once when I was much younger and I still, to this day, do not know what happened to the child."

The news shocked Tillandra. "But..."

"I know. You would think, but we are all at best simply people. And people carry with them their superstitions and prejudices, Tillandra.

Our people believe that those who have such problems will poison the forest. I can only hope that they are banished, but I cannot truly say what might happen."

"You know we will take him in Anderwell. It's not a favor, that is part of who we are."

"There is rumor that you care for many there, but I have never asked the truth of it."

"We don't speak of it, but we do more than care for our people, Vindisil. Anderwell is a safe haven for anyone that the rest of Dharatan rejects, for any reason. There they learn to live healthy, important lives."

Tillandra could see some of the weight she had been carrying lift off of the older woman, but not all of it. She could sense there was more. "Who will bring him to us?"

Vindisil breathed deeply, and slowly raised her eyes back to look at Tillandra. "This is the favor. I fear he will not survive the next month if he remains here. My time is so close Tillandra, and there are already those planning for it. I heard of a meeting they held but two nights ago without me."

"What is it you're asking, Vindisil?" Tillandra's voice had become sharper.

"You need to take him with you, Tillandra. Or I do not know what will happen to him."

"But, you... can't be..." Tillandra for once was speechless.

A child, she wants me to take a child with me.

"I will not last the next week, it is that close. If it happens while Purdu walks you to the river, then I fear he will not be here when Purdu returns. I cannot let this happen."

Tillandra was still speechless. She was concerned at the loss of Vindisil, but the thought of her caring for a small child on this trip was too much to even consider.

"He would tend your tree."

"What?"

"In Anderwell, the sick tree, he will be the one to tend it. If you take him, he will live a long life and bring your tree back to health. You will then have the access you need."

Her words touched something in the back of Tillandra's mind. She closed her eyes as her head felt heavy. A vision came to her, something that rarely happened when she was awake. She was back in Anderwell looking out across the back of the college. The gardens there flourished, and people were sitting out there, basking in the beauty of them, and all facing the center, where a massive fig tree flourished.

The image stuck with her even once the vision crumbled. She opened her eyes and shook her head.

"What is it?"

"It would appear that the decision has already been made for me."

"How so?"

"A vision just came to me, of the tree in Anderwell. I rarely get visions like this, but it speaks of me needing to do what you ask. I have no idea how I will care for him, but it seems I must."

"He will be no trouble. He is small, but he is also held deep within himself. He doesn't speak except in the trees."

"Yes, but a small child." Tillandra shook her head, unbelieving of what she was agreeing to.

"Let me bring him, he is already packed. Just in case." She raised her two hands pleading as she said it.

When she returned carrying the boy, Tillandra realized it wasn't just that he would be traveling with her, he was only a toddler, and she would be carrying him the whole trip.

"How will I feed him?"

Vindisil placed a bag on the table. "Here is food for him, and clothing. It is the best I can do. I am sorry, but so grateful."

"Does he have a name?"

"We call him Peka."

Tillandra looked at the boy as he waddled over to her. He raised one of his tiny hands and reached up to her face, his green eyes staring deep into hers. He ran his chubby little fingers down the scar on her face, a little smile forming on his face as he did so. Then he reached out his other arm as well. Tillandra had no choice but to take him and he nestled into her long arms without any struggle.

"This sling will make it much easier." Vindisil lifted it over her neck and shoulder and then wrapped it under Peka.

Tillandra felt more out of control than she had in a long time. This wasn't what she needed right now, and yet the vision seemed clear. This boy was part of her story and she had to bring him back to Anderwell. All she could think of was handing him to Gimbden to get him back to Anderwell while she traveled on, but even that was several weeks' travel.

With a toddler!

78

TILLANDRA

The rest of the morning, Tillandra walked almost in a daze as she followed Purdu through the forest. It was rare that she was talked into anything she didn't want to do, and yet here she was carrying a small child in a sling over her shoulder, as she journeyed west.

It was, as the Lady of the Stone had said, one of those things where she just knew it to be true. Whatever purpose Peka had, it was in Anderwell. But she had never wanted a child of her own, and while they collected and raised hundreds of children of all ages, she had never been personally involved in that process.

Much of her discomfort was from a lack of confidence. Here she was, the head of their society, and the ruler of Sahro, and yet she feared this young boy, or what it was she would need to do to help him, more than anything.

Purdu stayed silent the whole walk, leading her as fast as they could go through the depths of the forest to the north of Kahoy. There was no path that Tillandra could see, certainly not worn into the ground where they went, but Purdu was clearly following some form of track.

It was almost as if the forest opened itself to him as they walked, and he just followed the direction it led him in. What she did know was, there was no way she could have done this herself.

As for Peka, he hardly moved. When he did, it was to lean back in the sling and look up at Tillandra. Occasionally he would raise his small arm and brush his hand against her chin, which was all he could reach from where he was cocooned.

He was fascinated with the scar and damage to her face, and given any chance ran his fingers over it. Tillandra wasn't sure how she felt about that. Normally she didn't think about the scarring herself. She had lived with it so long, it just was. The only time it surfaced was when people stared at her face and brought it back into focus.

With Peka stroking it, it meant she also thought about it. It held uncomfortable memories, not about the scar itself but the treatment she'd received because of it. Perhaps it was Peka's way of connecting with that part of her that had been rejected, like he was being rejected from his village.

Tillandra couldn't understand how a mother could give her child away. And yet she could. She too had been rejected and abandoned by her family. It had only been the care of an old woman, who thought nothing about the conventions of their Humaas world, that took her in and housed her.

When the Fool's Cart had come through all those years ago, it had been a difficult decision to leave. Ultimately it was the truth that her carer was soon to die that made Tillandra leave. The similarities to Peka's situation struck her in the heart, and her eyes watered. The memories of that day still ran deep inside her.

She had felt so lonely and lost when she left her second family, it took her quite some time to trust that those in Anderwell weren't going to do the same again. She had been nearly nine, which was different to Peka.

Will he even understand? Or will it all be a distant memory once he has grown?

Tillandra swapped the side he hung from while she kept walking. One thing she was certain about was that her shoulders already ached, and they had only been walking a few hours. Once every so often she paused to catch her breath. Despite the rest she had received from the trees, her chest was still sore, and she coughed once or twice – a timely reminder to make sure she didn't push herself too much. It had not been that long since she had been ill.

It took them the best part of six hours to reach the village at the end of the Gumala River, as they had to stop and clean Peka several times. The first time he fouled his swaddle had nearly dropped Tillandra in her step. One minute they walked as they had for hours, the next she was overcome with the smell of him. The suddenness and unexpectedness of it was what caught her out.

She would need to wash those things now there was water available. The village was not more than a dozen small huts each built on stilts as high as Tillandra's chest. Looking at the ground around the end of the river, she could see where little vegetation grew further out from the riverbank.

"It floods many times a year," Purdu said pointing at the area she was studying.

"But they live so close to it?"

"They will not cut down more trees. They only use what the forest grants them."

Tillandra wasn't sure where they would grow anything to eat. The canopy of the forest separated only slightly along the river path, but little direct sunlight reached the ground.

Everything smelled of mud to her. No doubt the residents didn't notice but she did. At the sound of their talk, several people came out of their huts. Each of the huts seemed only big enough for basic sleeping and storage. The walls were all logs strapped together, and the roofs were thatched with grasses.

Purdu went and spoke with one of the men who had sleepily come down the rickety stairs from his hut. He nodded several times and walked away from them toward the furthest huts. He banged on the stilts of several of the huts and a few minutes later more men came out and joined their group.

"These people will not speak to an outsider, Tillandra, not even you."

She nodded as he spoke.

"But they know your purpose, and what you do for Peka. They will carry you swiftly north to the lake and beyond so your journey can continue. They honor you, you will have two paddlers and their fastest canoe. Perhaps you will travel quicker than you planned."

"Thank you, Purdu, for all your help."

"It is what we do, Tillandra."

"I am sorry for your loss, I wish it was not to happen, I wish I could spend more time with Vindisil."

The young man shrugged and despite the sadness in his eyes replied, "We cannot control the trees, nor when our time will come. I have always been raised this way. Yes, I will miss her, but her time is her time. It is not something we can change, so I shall not resist it. That is where most pain comes from, resisting what is."

Tillandra looked at him, recognizing he was already much more than she had realized. She judged him for his age, not what was within, a mistake that she hated from others, but still she behaved the same way.

"I do not know when I will next see you, Purdu, or if I will. I know not when my time will come either, but I will take special care of this one." She patted Peka on the back.

A woman had come forward now and Purdu turned and talked quietly with her. She came forward toward Tillandra with a smile on her face.

"She will help clean up his things and him with you, but she will not speak. I ask you not to speak to her."

"Of course."

The woman held out her arms and Tillandra handed Peka to her. She seemed unbothered by his condition and beckoned Tillandra to follow her. Out the back of the village there was a small fire with a cauldron hanging on branches over it.

Inside was warm water and the woman filled a pail, made from a hollowed-out chunk of tree, with water. Tillandra helped her wash the cloths and the woman used some bark which cleansed the cloths as she rubbed at them. She wanted to ask what tree it came from but remembered Purdu's words. By the time everything was cleaned and dried over the fire, the light had faded in the small clearing around the river's end.

Purdu brought her back to a circle of fallen trees where the villagers were gathered, drinking from wooden cups.

"They will take you now, and I will return back to my grandmother."

"In the night?"

"These villagers have no need of daylight to travel the river. You will travel through the night; it will save you much time."

Tillandra was glad it wasn't her that had to guide them in the dark, but she was happy to keep moving. She was very aware of the deadline she had.

79

KARPENMOR

It had taken two days before they had brought Hurf back to his compound in Ponte and Karpenmor had been angry the whole time. He knew that much of how he felt was because he still refused the amber brandy.

This was the longest he had ever gone without it, and he felt dreadful. The shaking had stopped, which had helped him be with others. For one of the days he had stayed in his room, they were so severe. The physick that had been sent for told him it was just fevers, but Uksod and he knew that it was not.

Several times, the priest had suggested it was an easy fix, but now that he had survived this long, Karpenmor was determined to keep going. He didn't want to rely on the drink at all, and he wanted the clearness of his thinking to remain.

He just didn't want the headaches and nausea that came with it. Sitting across from the manservant he simply wanted to be back in his room, the curtains pulled, until the pounding at the back of his head eased.

The anger inside of him came from the constant headache, but it was something else as well. Karpenmor didn't understand it, but he wanted to lash out at everyone, Uksod included. Or maybe especially Uksod.

How many more lies were there? He didn't know, and he had wanted to see if Hurf could help him with that, but the man was offering him nothing new. He seemed afraid, of Karpnemor, what he was asking. Or maybe it was Uksod, who stood silently at the back of the room.

The high priest of Enderk had insisted he be present. Karpenmor had given in this time around – the man had been very firm in his request, much firmer than normal, and there was a hint of the old Regent in it.

He found himself agreeing without even realizing it. So Uksod and several Vrah stood in the background of the room. He had to make sure the pendant wasn't brought up by Hurf as he had no desire to share knowledge of that with Uksod, or anyone else.

"So you know nothing of the farm where my mother lived?"

The old servant held his head downward and only looked up enough to speak.

"No, Highness. I was always just with your father."

"No one from the palace knew the people out here?"

"As I said, if they did, I was not aware of it. My time was almost always with the High Prince, I did not have time to gossip with others."

Karpenmor wasn't convinced, but he had no evidence otherwise. Maybe he was just hoping the servant could help because of the dead end at the farm. He wanted to know more about his mother, and no one else had any connection to that time.

Except Uksod, and he never shared anything. Had Uksod gotten to Hurf beforehand and told him to say nothing? In his previous conversation the man had been much more open. He moved his chair much closer to the man, startling him.

He leaned across and whispered to him, "Is there anything you would say if it was just me here, Hurf? I can get rid of the others."

Hurf shook his head, "No, Highness."

"You're sure?"

"Yes."

Karpenmor pushed his chair back aggressively, frightening the old man. He held out his hand. "Sorry, Hurf. Thank you for your time, you can go."

Uksod came forward and guided the manservant to one of the guards and watched while he was ushered out.

"Are you satisfied now, Highness?"

"No," Karpenmor snapped back.

"I'm not sure why you're angry at me."

Karpenmor looked at the man, wanting to yell at him, but it wasn't him he was angry at. He had hit a dead end, there was nothing more to be learned about his mother. Now he would never know who she was, what she had been like.

"I'm not, Uksod. I'm just angry."

"Can I suggest…"

"No, don't bother. I've told you, I don't want that anymore."

"As you wish, Highness."

Karpenmor started toward the door, unsure of where he wanted to be, just that he didn't want to be in this room. The remaining guard opened the door for him as he approached. Karpenmor stopped and turned back to look at Uksod.

"Highness?"

He stared at the old man.

"I want to go back, Uksod."

"To the farm, Highness?" The priest's eyebrows rose as he spoke.

"No. To En Carta, Uksod. I'm done here."

"You don't want to wait and see the bridges? The weather has all but blown over now."

"I've seen enough. I want to be back."

"As you wish, Highness."

Karpenmor turned and went back to his room. When he was alone, he pulled out the pendant that he had left in a drawer by mistake earlier, and examined it. He ran his forefinger over the small blue stone, and closed his eyes as he did.

It always seemed to help him relax more, even if it was just his imagination. The edge came off his anger, a touch, but enough that he didn't want to pick up a knife and start stabbing the bed. Or maybe it was that he was glad that he at least had this one thing from his father.

He still didn't really understand what the note had meant, who he was warning him about. It had to be someone from across the bridges, in Dharatan – whoever it was behind what had driven his father crazy. Karpenmor's focus had already begun to move toward that.

Finding out more about his mother had been important, but a long shot. He had seen where she had lived before she died, it would have to do. As for the people behind what his father had endured, that was a different matter altogether.

He was going to go to Dharatan, and he was going to find out, and he would get his answers. Someone would pay. He could do that at least. It wouldn't bring them back, but it would bring him peace. If he was High Prince it might as well be for something he cared about.

That needed to be solved. Another reason to be back in En Carta was so the final ceremonies could be completed. He couldn't do anything about that here, but once they were in the palace it was time to finish it. He was the heir and his birthday had passed.

Karpenmor wanted Uksod out of his way, he had his own plans now.

THE WIND THAT GUSTED UP FROM THE CITY BELOW AND WHIPPED AROUND Karpenmor on his balcony was tame compared to the storm wind on Step Two that had turned his group around when he'd been in Ponte. He enjoyed the coolness of it as he watched the sun rising across the mountains to the east.

He was ready, and he had been unable to think of anything else since they had left the west coast city. There were all sorts of things he had drawn up in his head, on what would be needed. If the weather in Ponte was always so horrid, he would need to expand his compound there.

Karpenmor needed space outside, like where he stood now, to think, and breathe. He had always felt trapped if he was stuck inside buildings for days on end. He would need to have someone make him a covered space, from his room upstairs, in the compound.

That was the closest place to Dharatan, and he could foresee himself spending more time there, making sure the bridges were completed. But much more would be needed. The books he had read always emphasized the importance of supplies and support.

He might never have fought a battle, or even wielded a weapon, but that didn't mean he couldn't lead. He had learned enough to prepare. Karpenmor knew he would also have to prepare better for battle. His training with weapons had always been something he hadn't taken seriously.

If he was going to face the barbarians he couldn't rely on others. He needed to be prepared. Much better prepared than he was now.

Being back in En Carta had eased the feelings he had felt in Ponte, and the headaches had receded so much now that Karpenmor felt like they had gone completely. At night when he lay down in the dark, he still sensed them, loitering at the back of his head, but they were manageable, and that was all that mattered.

Several times he had nearly drunk the brandy without even thinking. It had taken several stern words with his servants and Uksod before they stopped leaving goblets of it lying around his rooms. Why Uksod bothered, Karpenmor didn't know, but he had been less pushy about it since they had been back.

That could also have been because Karpenmor had deliberately gone out of his way to stop annoying the priest. Much of his attitude had come from the discomfort Karpenmor had felt after stopping the brandy, and the hurt from wanting to know more about his father.

But he still hadn't told Uksod anything about the pendant or note, and nor would he. He had no need. He also didn't need to spend so much time bothering the old man. Karpenmor had his own plans to worry about. The libraries of books had become his friends.

The Vrah library was where he was when Uksod came to him.

"Good morning, Highness."

"Uksod! Good morning to you."

"Your study continues, I see."

"One thing I have always enjoyed is reading history, Uksod, as you know. There is much here to learn about the barbarians."

"Why the sudden fascination, Highness?"

"Why not? We want these amulets back do we not? And they are over there." Karpenmor pointed to a wall, unsure even if it was in the right direction.

"If we're going to do that, then I need to know everything I can. It will matter, when I'm... That's something I wanted to discuss with you."

"What is that, Highness?"

"The enthronement ceremony, Uksod. It's been long enough, and you've not mentioned a date, or anything about it to me. This seems most unusual. Looking back through these books, it seems the time from the passing of the High Prince to the accession is never more than a month."

"Ah, yes. Well, there was your age, Highness."

"My birthday was months ago, Uksod. It needs to happen, it is time."

"Of course, Highness. I didn't want to rush you."

"Our people need their leader, Uksod. And that leader is me. When can we set it for?"

The priest stumbled over his response.

"W-well, there's a few things to prepare, Highness. It is not just a simple thing."

"How long, Uksod? Of course we need to prepare but surely you can give me an idea?"

"Well there's the announcements."

"The what?"

"The announcements. We have to formally announce it in each of the capitals of the Imperial Family lands."

"Why on Enderk?"

"It's the way it is done, Highness. Each of the Families must be advised and come. They all must be there for the ceremony or it cannot proceed. It has been a long time since the last one, Highness, so I am relying on what is laid out in the records."

"So we send out messengers."

"There is some suggestion that previous heirs visited each Family and made the announcement themselves."

"That's not going to happen, Uksod. It would take an eternity to do that."

"It was just a suggestion, Highness. But heralds must go, and we must get them back to confirm it was received."

"And?"

"As I said, each Family head must then come here to attend. Then we can begin proceedings."

"How long, Uksod?"

"It will be several months, Highness. At least."

"Then you better get started, Uksod. I expect the heralds to be sent by tomorrow."

"I will do my best, Highness."

Karpenmor turned back to the book in front of him. He was struggling with some of the names in it, but he was intrigued by the descriptions of the city called Nkuku. The walls sounded truly impressive. He looked forward to looking upon them.

80

LANI

They didn't linger in the first village they chose to stop at, not that it appeared they were very welcome. Maybe Humaas were more popular there, but foreigners definitely were not. The villagers were happy to sell them food for coin, and even some sort of apple brandy, but it was clear they weren't encouraged to linger.

Lani's group had bought what they could and ridden on several miles and stopped under a cluster of trees. She was happy for the break, the shade and the food. Her previous captors had fed her, but reluctantly and without any care.

Being able to feed herself, unbound and without restriction, was one freedom she was grateful for. She drank heavily from water skins as the brandy didn't sit well with her, and the taste soured her mouth.

She kept an eye on all of her traveling companions. Lani was warily grateful to them as they had helped her get away, but still she wasn't sure she hadn't just swapped her old captors, for new ones that appeared friendlier.

Could she believe the story Odajeen had told her? It seemed fanciful to say the least, but then so much of what had happened since she had left Barnen would sound that way to her previous self. There were two ways to find out more about the woman and her companions.

One was to talk to her and see if her story made sense. The other...

I can't do that again. I mustn't touch it.

Lani still struggled to accept using the amulet like she had, especially to harm the bowman. It wasn't by chance, unless it was controlling her and not the other way around. She wasn't sure if she really could sense what others thought, or if the amulet was putting those ideas in her mind. And when it was happening, she enjoyed what it felt like.

That was what concerned her more than anything else. She wanted to harm that man, she felt good about it, about hearing his thoughts. Even when it had made her wander through Statiiv, she'd not been bothered at all. While she was connected to it, she didn't care about anything else.

Their group remained quiet while they ate, and they didn't rest for long. The two brothers seemed keen to keep the group moving and Odajeen went along with them. That night they camped rough, off the road, in a gully between two hillocks behind a small rock mound.

The evening was cool, and a clear sky let Lani watch stars flitting and flickering above. She kept to herself, wanting to clear her head about what she had just experienced before she discussed what Odajeen wanted to know.

Lani was sure the woman would be disappointed she had little to tell her about the brooch. Odajeen hadn't mentioned the amulet, so Lani had to assume she didn't see that, and she wasn't going to offer that knowledge up either. As far as the brooch went, she only knew a little herself.

For now she was happy to follow along with them, until she had worked out Odajeen's story. There had to be another angle that she wasn't telling her. Maybe they were just going to steal the brooch from her – what was it she had said? 'Knowledge they could use for their own profit.'

Or would they sell her back to the priest for a reward? Lani could feel her suspicions growing, despite having nothing to base them on. Something was eating away in the far recesses of her mind, warning her about the woman. It didn't feel like her normal instincts, it was different, and it didn't help her feel any better.

Two more days they rode, heading west but slowly arcing to the south. She had thought to learn more from Odajeen, but there never seemed to be the right time, or the woman was avoiding her. Both options were beginning to bother Lani.

They crossed huge plains, some of which had flocks of wild horses roaming across them. Lani was able to follow the path where the horses had grazed in their huge numbers, where patches without long grass could be spotted across the prairie.

That evening, when they camped, Odajeen had the men light a fire, and they ate warm food for the first time.

"Fire?" Lani asked.

"I do not think we are being followed, Lani. The boys said they have seen nothing behind us, no dust, no signs of anyone following. It seems we are free of your captors."

It appeared now they were going to talk. Lani was feeling very wary of what might happen, but didn't want to sound it.

"Thank you, again."

"No need to thank us. Like I said, it was as much for me as for you."

"Still, you did free me. You might as well ask me what you've been waiting to, though I fear I won't have much to tell you."

The woman laughed. "You're direct, you are, girl. It's true I've been biting my tongue, but I saw no rush in it. We're still days from Jarv and unless you were going to leave us, there was always time to talk."

"What is it you'd have me tell you?"

"What is it?"

"The brooch?"

"A brooch is it? I can only see a blue shape, that's all I can see."

Lani instinctively reached into her pocket and pulled it out. She held it close, but there was the little sense of peace she felt when she rubbed her fingers over it.

"Where did you get it?"

"My mother, or so I'm told."

"You didn't know her?"

"No." Lani couldn't help but sound sad when she replied.

"So you don't know where it came from?"

"I don't. Like I said, I doubt I have much to tell you of value about it. It's just something that means a lot to me. I get comfort from it when I hold it but that's all."

"If you put it away from you and close your eyes, can you see it?"

Odajeen's question seemed strange to Lani, but then she'd never thought about it. It was almost always on her, so she wouldn't know.

"I don't think I've ever tried."

Lani closed her eyes and held her hand out in front of her body, but there was nothing there. She could see an image of the brooch in her head, but that was just from memory not a color.

"No, I see nothing. What is it you see?"

"Just a bright blue, shaped like an oval. I don't see any metal or anything."

Lani did her best to describe it. "It is an oval stone, and it's blue to look at. It's much as it appears to you but not a light. The blue has become darker over the years, but it still is a pretty blue to stare into."

"How strange. I wish I knew what it meant. I just can't seem to pull together the memories in my head. It's like they're locked and I don't have the key."

Lani understood what she meant. Ever since the seer had told her of the lock on her mind, she'd wanted to know what was behind it, if anything. Or was it just a lock to stop people like him seeing into her thoughts? Even that meant more questions than answers, it meant there were things to hide in there, and she had no idea what they were.

"I'm sorry, I wish there was more I could tell you."

"Where is it you're from then?" Odajeen asked.

"A town way north in the Malamig."

"That's a long way from here. You've not said where you were heading before you were caught."

She'd known there'd be questions, especially about her traveling alone. Lani just needed to be careful about what she shared. "South, down past Jarv."

"Anywhere in particular?"

Lani hesitated, but decided to tell her anyway. "A city called Anderwell."

"Anderwell?"

"Yes, why?"

"I know of this place, but it is not such a welcoming place. I was told I should go there; they look after those with… injuries like mine."

"They didn't take you?"

"No, no. But I've survived all this time from my instincts, and what I was pushed to do. Every time I thought about going there, I got a strong feeling not to. As if the compulsion I told you about wanted to keep me away. I always ended up heading away from it."

"Strange."

"Perhaps, but like I said, I've done alright up until now following where that feeling takes me. I'm not about to go against it easily. What takes you there?"

This was where Lani needed to be careful about what she said. "I have a message to deliver there for someone."

"Must be some message if you'd be traveling this far, and all alone. Is that what the bandits that had you wanted? Your message or the like?"

Lani didn't like where the questioning was going. "I don't know, to be honest. I've stumbled into trouble half of the journey, and I just want to get it done."

Before Odajeen could keep probing into her journey, Lani asked her own question to change the topic. "You said you had some things you could remember, you don't remember anything like this brooch?"

"No. That's the thing, they're all just pieces. Like a painting was all torn up and only some of the pieces were put back, and not in the right places. I can't make much sense of it all."

"You can't tell what any of it is?"

"I can see people and places, but I can't put names to any of them. That's maybe what's wrong with it, I can't link them up because the knowledge of who they are or where they are eludes me. Some days I bang my head to try and free it loose."

"How's that working for you?"

Odajeen laughed. "Not so well. There's one thing in them all that links them together, but I haven't worked out what it means."

"Maybe I can help?"

"I doubt it, there's no stone or brooch in it, it's just a strange ring."

"A ring?"

"Yes. A group of people in them all wear the same ring. It's silver, and there's an odd image on it, of a mask, with a two-pronged hat. Like they're entertainers or the like. But if I try too hard to focus on it, everything just gets blurry."

Lani almost gasped, and had to hold it in quickly. "How odd."

"It is. I wish you'd had more to tell me. But I'm tired, and you should get rest as well. We've still got plenty of riding ahead of us."

When Lani lay down, sleep was the last thing on her mind. The coincidence of this woman being able to see the brooch and knowing something of the Jester rings was too much. There was no way she'd found her by chance. There was definitely the touch of magic about how they'd come together, she was convinced of that now. She just didn't know if it was a good thing or not.

81

TILLANDRA

illandra's knees ached. Her back ached and the sooner they reached the far side of the lake wouldn't be quick enough for her.

After the better part of three days sat in the canoe, she could hardly move without something hurting. Humaas were built for walking, not sitting still. The only thing that had helped was that her mind was preoccupied with Peka.

The time on the water had given her plenty of time to reflect on what had happened, and the complication he presented. If it wasn't for her timeline she would push directly north and head for Anderwell.

She couldn't do that now, there was no time for a diversion. The best she could do would be to hand him over to Gimbden and either have him wait in Watersend for her or have Gimbden transport him to Anderwell.

Every time she thought about it she felt guilty. Vindisil had been explicit that Tillandra needed to look after the young boy. Tillandra felt a wave of sadness wash over her as she thought about the old woman. She'd seemed so certain that she only had a handful of days to go.

Imagine her having to look after a tiny toddler herself. It was ridiculous, and yet, here she was with the youngster sat between her legs in the canoe, leaning back against her. The boy said nothing, most likely due to his lack of hearing, but he also wanted for little.

If he became hungry, he would squeeze her thumb and look up into her eyes. When his green eyes stared up at her, she felt a deep tenderness toward him and in those moments, she knew there was nothing she wouldn't do for him.

Nothing seemed to upset the boy, it was if he knew his place as well as anyone, even one so small. She hoped this would stay true once they were moving across land. They had to avoid Bundok, that was for certain, with the news she'd received before leaving, even if some of it was just gossip.

A large gathering of forces near their border wasn't for no reason, and she had no plans to get caught by Skarians. Her carrying a Skarian native child would be difficult to explain as well, even if their Fool's Cart would do the same anyway.

She wondered why rejecting their envoy would have triggered such an escalation. Sure it was an irritation, but they were planning to enter Sahro and take control of a road, so what did they think would happen? There was more happening with what King Ahn was up to, and as much as she wanted to know what it was, she had no desire to meet him in person at this time.

The situation was getting out of hand and they would need to send someone to see him, but only once their presence was firmly noted at the border. Crossing the desert was the hardest of routes for anyone, especially without resources, so they had a distinct advantage there, one they needed to exploit.

Ultimately she needed to deescalate what was happening, as soon as she was done getting to Midderbuilt. Their job was to maintain the peace, not get caught up in the fighting themselves, but nor could they let anyone come probing into Sahro.

She was not going to travel on conventional paths this trip. Vindisil had given her a basic idea of a path between the fig trees, trees that she could connect to. There were only a couple on the northern side of the river, they couldn't survive in the desert-like conditions in the north of Daskare.

If she was able to, she would make her way quickly enough that it wouldn't matter. It was still a long walk once they got back onto land, and she had a child to carry.

The silence of this trip had been pleasant for Tillandra but with it being in the company of others, she had felt self-conscious. These people were going out of their way to help her and there was little chance to interact with them. The two men who paddled the long canoe hardly stopped. For hours upon hours they had paddled, even through the night, with occasional breaks for drinking and fewer for food.

The dark of evening was rapidly approaching again, and they were pushing to reach the far side of the lake. There had been little other traffic on the lake since twilight had begun which made it easier for them to head straight. Now as the bank came into sight, Tillandra was keen to reach it and be on her way.

Taking control of what she was doing appealed to her more than being a passenger, although she knew once she made the desert camp, she would be riding camels and not on her feet.

It must have taken them another hour before the men slowed their paddling before beaching the canoe on a small bay of sand, the sudden change in motion waking Peka just as it broke Tillandra from her contemplation.

The foremost of the two canoeists leaped out and dragged the boat a little further into the sand. By the time he was done, his companion was out as well. They approached her and one took the boy from her while the other grabbed her right arm and helped her stand.

That sounded easier than it was, both because he wasn't that tall, when compared to her, but also because her knees and legs were locked and unwilling to start moving easily. She grimaced at the stiffness in them and clumsily stepped from the canoe onto the beach.

All around was dark with only dapples of starlight helping them. The water of the lake lapped gently against the side of the canoe still in the water, and a gentle breeze brushed through her hair.

It felt good to be back standing, she knew that her legs would be fine once she had walked a little distance. She stretched out, pulling her back sideways and reaching above her head, letting her spine free itself.

One of the men surprised her by speaking, something she hadn't expected.

"We will not stay. As soon as you are ready, we will return."

"Of course. Thank you very much for your help."

The man from the front of the canoe bowed his head toward her and brought Peka over. Tillandra quickly grabbed her full satchel from the canoe and hung it over her back, arranging the sling again in front of her.

She took Peka and placed him in the sling. He had all but fallen asleep in the arms of the man and didn't stir as she settled him across her chest. As soon as she was set the men bowed their goodbyes and pushed back off from the shallows.

Tillandra watched them go until they were nothing but a dark lump in the distance, before she turned and walked up from the beach to look around the landscape. Her eyes were accustomed to the darkness and limited light, and she was able to make out a clump of trees close by. She couldn't hear anything to make her concerned for her safety, but her instinct told her to head to the trees, and she set off in that direction.

At first it was more a hobble than her usual walk as she hadn't realized the effect being sedentary while traveling over a body of water would have on her. But by the time she had reached the trees and shrubs her legs were back to normal and she was able to proceed at her usual pace. Each stride brought a smile to her face.

Her task now was to decide what she should do. She could set off in the dark and cover some ground, but with little to guide her and limited moonlight that was problematic. This clump of trees and scrub was more than enough cover for her to hide in for the night, then she could head off at the break of day.

The sound of horses caught her attention so she moved deeper into the bush and knelt down beside a tree, coddling Peka in his sling. Tillandra watched as a group of six horsemen approached from the left, coming from Bundok no doubt.

They carried torches and rode steadily but not fast. As they neared where she was hiding, they slowed to a walk and the sound of their voices carried to her.

"I see nothing, Captain."

"Me neither, Frishai. But we must look, the report came from a reliable source."

"Who is it that we seek?"

"There's a woman traveling over the lake, someone from Anderwell, I was told. The King would like them to be brought to him. That's all I know."

"How would we know what they look like?"

"The message said they were one of those tall Humaas, and this one bears a nasty scar across her face. They said you'd be able to tell, she's that ugly."

"I see nothing here."

"Me neither, nor can I believe they would travel at night, but our job is to check. We should travel slower I think now it's dark, who knows what we might hear or see."

Their speech slowly faded from her hearing, but Tillandra had felt a twinge of pain in her chest from their words. It was rare anyone made such hurtful comments about her appearance, not since she'd moved to Anderwell.

All the history of bullying she had experienced when she was young had flooded back into her body, and she felt defeated. She slumped down against the tree, using it to prop up her back, and decided to settle here until dawn. Her eyes had filled with tears, and she didn't wipe them as they rolled down her cheeks.

TILLANDRA

hy is King Ahn looking for me?

That question was the one that ended up consuming much of the night in Tillandra's mind. She needed rest but it never came until far too late.

After listening to the words of the soldiers it had taken her some time to pull herself away from her painful memories. She didn't know why after so many years such words caused her such pain, but they still did.

She ran a network of what were effectively spies all over Dharatan, and had resources and magic at her disposal, more than any of those small-minded people could imagine. And yet, such a simple phrase uttered from their mouths cut her deeply.

In a different context, she would likely just ignore it, but she was concerned now. Her stress was building, and she felt that what little control she thought she had was slipping away. This journey was enough to worry about in itself without all the other complications she and the Court faced.

The simple timeline she was on left her little room for complications. Had she been caught by the soldiers and hauled back to meet the King, there was little doubt she would have lost many days resolving whatever problem King Ahn had. That's assuming he didn't have more malicious intentions in mind.

Tillandra had no doubt it was related to what the envoy had been up to in Watersend, but that was an end product, not the whole game, and she didn't know what he was really planning. In many ways she wanted to hand herself over, turn up at the palace as if a foreign guest arriving to see the King and see what she could learn. But she couldn't afford the time.

If she wasn't back in Anderwell in time to conduct the Audition, then all of this would be in vain. They had to replace Ashantha, or they'd lose one of their number. That wasn't going to happen under her leadership.

She had little choice but to haul Peka and herself across the bottom of Dharatan in a mad race against time while others were wanting to get in her way. Tillandra also knew she needed to speak to the Court as well, at some point.

Then she ended up back on the question of what did King Ahn want with her? They'd concealed their greater purpose in the Court so far, and any role she had as one of the Court to the outside world wasn't well known. He would have more idea from his envoy that she had more sway in the decisions made, but this was something else.

Yes, they'd blocked any attempt for Daskare to build and control a road between their capital and Watersend. If nothing else it showed that their neighbors thought of Sahro as a collection of independent cities and towns, not a realm like others. It made sense they'd approach Watersend directly in that case.

No doubt the envoy would be back here by now. That would not bode well for her, back here where they had the power to detain her, and to exact revenge for her treatment of him. No, she couldn't afford to fall into their hands, not now. Not ever in truth. And who had let him know she was there in the first place? That was equally as concerning, they knew she was coming.

Tillandra stood up and stretched her arms above her head. The color of the night sky had changed, only slightly, but enough to signal to her that dawn was not far away. It was time to get moving.

Whatever King Ahn was up to, it was linked in with their church somehow. The Order of Jolothos had always been militant, but their compound near Okeans was significant. It could house a sizable number of knights, as protectors of the faith, which would be difficult to object to.

She'd seen no other similar compounds when she skirted down the Kysten coast, but that didn't mean they didn't exist. The Circuit would need to pay more attention to such constructions now. It was a clever method for the Skarians to expand their reach and prepare a military base.

Was the breaking of the veil causing this? As knowledge broke free, did old tensions or aspirations bubble up as well? It had to be related, there'd been no such efforts by anyone before, or none during her time.

I can't solve it all now. I just have to deal with what's in front of me.

Tillandra leaned down and picked up Peka, who had been lying tightly wrapped in a shawl against the tree. He squirmed a little, but his eyes remained closed, and he settled quickly once she had him back in the sling across her chest.

A small tinge of warmth spread through her body. After only a few days she was already connected to this child like she had never been to anyone. It wasn't quite happiness she felt, she couldn't explain it, but it was pleasant.

Once she had also placed her satchel on her back, Tillandra carefully stepped out of the clump of trees, looking left and right quickly to confirm no one else was visible, then headed north. The road the soldiers had been on was only a few strides away from the trees, which explained why she could hear them so easily.

If Peka had been a fussy child any noise he could have made would have carried to them easily in the still of the night. She kept moving, off the road and into the fields, her goal to be as far in-country as she could by the time the sun was fully risen in Daskare.

Her eyes managed the dim light well enough, but she had to tread carefully to make sure she didn't end up in a hole.

Picking her way through tall grass, bare patches and small clumps of scrub, she was grateful when the peak of the sun had broken above the horizon behind her. Now that she could actually see where she was walking Tillandra was able to pick up the pace and fully stride out, using her natural ability to cover as much ground as a horse, or more.

Vindisil had told her that she had to head directly toward the setting sun, and her first tree would be there. That was helpful except for the fact she had a whole day ahead of her before she'd be able to line up the setting sun.

With how much ground she could cover in a day, she might pass right over it. Once she was far enough away from the road, and the sun had risen enough, Tillandra stopped and guessed the likely path the sun would take.

It was the only real option she had, until at least later in the day. There were few landmarks to point herself toward, only some hills in the distance. She had never spent any time in the open lands of Daskare and had little idea of what she was in for.

Every hour, Tillandra stopped and rechecked her position in relation to the sun. Mostly she felt like she was heading in the right direction, but she would never really know. Vindisil had warned her that the trees she would find out here would be nothing like those in the grove she had been shown. She had told her that some of the live trees would be on their own or in small woods, but many would not appear anything other than a standard tree.

Over time many of their trees were cleared by man and some struggled for survival in harsh terrain or with little support. Tillandra was amazed that the trees themselves needed the contact with people as much as the people benefited from it.

The reason that the groves existed was because they had always had plenty of people to feed them energy and attention. She had hinted that's why the single tree in Anderwell was suffering despite being in a city, because no one nurtured it.

By the time the sun was ahead of her and beginning its downward route, Tillandra was worried she might have passed by the tree she sought. There had been little to spot as she walked, and if the tree was not that tall it was possible it was hidden in a valley out of sight as she climbed and dipped along the undulating land.

Every time she came across a creek or small river, she topped up her skins, not knowing when she would find the next one. Peka was awake and looking forward but rarely moved. He had taken to clapping his hands above his head if he wanted her attention, and that normally meant he needed cleaning or food.

She was crouching down filling a skin and absentmindedly looking along the riverbed, when she was drawn to following it. It wasn't a vision just a sensation, as if the land itself was talking to her.

Once the skin was sealed, Tillandra walked along the riverbank as it wound between several small hills and out onto a plateau. Not more than a quarter-mile ahead sat a small clump of thin trees that appeared to be almost saplings, lining the banks of the small river.

As quickly as she spotted it, she backtracked and ducked behind a small hill. A sole person was sheltering under the trees, not that it appeared there was much cover for them. Tillandra didn't think they had seen her and didn't want them to. She needed no interaction at all if she could avoid it.

Squatting down to rest, she hoped whoever it was would move on quickly. She had little time to waste.

TILLANDRA

The sound of horses running carried across the open land and caused Tillandra alarm. She lay down on the ground as flat as she could against the side of the small hill. She knew the sound as it came closer, heavy hoofbeats and the squeaking of steel armor.

If she looked, she was sure that on the other side of the hill more than one Skarian knight would be visible.

How have they found me?

She waited for them to come closer, but they didn't. The horses slowed and she was certain that they were nearer to the trees, not her. Sliding up on her side, so as not to squash Peka, she hid behind a clump of rocks. Looking around the edge of them she could see the backs of the knights.

They stopped near the trees surrounding the person who had been sheltering there. It looked tense and she could hear distant voices as the knights pointed at what looked like a woman. She was frantically trying to find a way out from the four knights that had her encircled.

As quickly as she stepped sideways or turned, the horsemen nudged their horses to move, closing any gaps that formed. One of the knights leant forward and Tillandra saw him knock the woman over the head with what looked like the hilt of his sword. She fell in a heap on the ground.

Gasping at the violence, Tillandra slid back behind the rocks. They could not find her, there would be little she could do to escape them, and who knows what they would do to the boy? She had promised Vindisil she would protect him. Losing him to the knights wasn't what either of them had meant in that agreement.

At the sound of the horses moving again, Tillandra briefly closed her eyes and took a deep breath. She looked out across the land before her and could see nothing that would help her if she had to run. She was a little tired from the day's travel, but she knew she could outrun any horse if she had to.

The knights must have been riding a long while as well, their horses, while trained for heavy loads, couldn't last forever. It would all be about surprise: if she had to run, she would need a head start that she could maintain so that none of their weapons would reach her.

They didn't appear to be approaching where she was hidden, it sounded more like they were returning the way they came. Tillandra slid to the other side of the rocks and poked her nose around the edge. She could see the woman slung over the back of one of the horses, and the knights heading back the way they had come.

Who was she? Did they think she was me, or are they normally out here patrolling?

Tillandra didn't move from her spot until it was dusk. She used the cover of fading light to creep along the side of the hill and down into the small creek that ran toward the trees. It was difficult for someone so tall to get low enough to avoid detection, but she hoped now that no one was around to see her anyway.

When she reached the trees, she remained low and tried to determine which of them was the one she could use. There was only one that seemed alive enough to have any potential, most were saplings that were struggling to take hold in the dry land.

As she stooped low and stepped carefully toward the tree, she tripped over something and fell heavily, only avoiding squashing Peka by twisting sideways at the last moment, landing hard on her shoulder.

"Shikes!"

The boy cried out as well, the first time he had made a sound for the whole day. Tillandra startled at the cry, and he began to sob. She sat herself upright, ignoring the pain in her shoulder and wrapped her other arm around him.

"Shush Peka, it's okay."

Tillandra rocked back and forth until he settled again. She looked back in the direction of her feet and saw what looked like a bag of some sort. Sliding along on her behind, she grabbed at the bag and pulled it with her as she moved toward the tree she needed.

What sunlight had been left was now all gone, and the trees gave her more than adequate cover. The moon and starlight didn't penetrate the wispy canopy of the trees and she felt a little safer. The bag had to have been the woman's, but the knights hadn't seemed to be bothered about her belongings.

There wasn't enough light to see what was inside, but Tillandra cared little for it. What she was here for was this fledgling fig tree, and the next step on her journey toward the border. She unstrapped Peka and sat him down beside the tree. He leaned forward to hug it, resting his small head against it like he did her.

Tillandra shrugged her shoulders, trying to free up the knots that had formed there and in her neck from carrying the toddler for so many days. Then she placed both her hands onto the tree and waited until she could feel it rippling beneath them.

Like she had done in Kahoy Wood she moved into the tree, the World of Wood, as Vindisil had called it. She didn't want to spend long in here, there was no way she could tire herself like she had before. What she was looking for was the best path across the north of Daskare.

Word had been sent out to the people of the wood, letting them know she was traveling this way, so she could get help. Tillandra wondered if that was who the woman captured by the knights was.

Was she one of the people that looked after the trees? Was she here for me, to help me? What have I done?

"There is no one that watches over those trees."

The voice was familiar, but she struggled to make sense of who it was.

"It is I, Tillandra. Vindisil."

Her thoughts were passing directly to the other woman, and probably everyone that was connected. She had to remember that.

"I am glad for that, although I don't know who she was."

"Not one of us, that is all I can tell you. How is the boy?"

"Can you not feel him?"

"No. He hasn't come into the trees, not yet anyway. "

"He is resting beside the tree, his head is against it, like he can hear."

"He probably can, he is a wonder, that boy. Keep him safe, Tillandra."

"I am trying, Vindisil. I need to know the next way to head."

There was a gap in time before a reply came, and this time it was a different voice, a male.

"You must head north, here let me show you," it said.

Images floated across her mind, first of the trees where she was, in daylight, then the path alongside a small range of steep hills, before heading out into plains of open ground. She knew she would be very exposed there.

"You might want to travel there in the dark. Men can see for many miles across these plains. There are camps of soldiers. Many soldiers, all across the north."

"Soldiers?"

"You will see once you pass the hills, the plains are littered with camps. There are no more trees. Not out here."

Tillandra thanked the man but realized too late she never knew his name. Before she left the power of the tree, she reached out to Gimbden, wanting to get a better idea of where the base was now she was closer to it.

He never answered her call, so she could only follow the direction north. That was as good as she had to go by. She stepped back out of the syrupy barrier in her mind and sucked in air as she landed back in her body.

Peka hadn't moved, he almost seemed asleep against the tree. Not wanting to move him, she lay down beside him, feeling tired and ready to sleep. She had hardly touched her head to the bag she lay it on before sleep took her.

TILLANDRA

Tillandra dreamed of land splitting apart creating great rifts, with people falling between. Men and woman wearing crowns, driving their people toward the fissures. The more that disappeared the more, they sent.

Speckles of orange flecked the heads of the so-called leaders. Great whips seemed to launch from their foreheads and crack over the heads of the hordes of people they drove into the gaping holes.

Far in the background she could see two men, chained to a tall woman, bathed in orange light. She toyed with them, and they bobbed and weaved at her feet. She looked beautiful to Tillandra, somehow all she could see was her beauty, but beneath it there was something terrifying.

The woman beckoned to Tillandra, her fingers longer than seemed humanly possible, reaching out across the length of the mass of land, over the fissures and falling people, toward her. It curled back toward her, calling her.

Alongside her a young woman wavered and began to walk toward the finger. A path – of nothing, but solid, like solid air – appeared before the young woman. She stepped up onto it, and Tillandra screamed "NOOOOOOOOO!".

She heard crying, a child crying, and the images around her dissolved. Then she heard it again and woke, realizing it was Peka. He was pushing her and tears rolled down his face.

"It's okay, Peka." She grabbed his tiny hands in hers and pulled him close. "I was just having a bad dream."

Tillandra sat up and cradled the toddler. Had she been calling out in her sleep? Was she tossing and turning? She wouldn't know, there seemed to be no way he could speak to her.

It was still dark, but only just. The sky had taken on a lighter hue more black-blue than the dark of night. Dawn would be here soon, Tillandra knew, and yet she felt like she had never slept. Between the tree and now the dream, her energy felt low.

She didn't understand what the dream meant, she rarely did when they first came. Maybe the walk today would help her make sense of it.

In the dream, before the land had started to split, she had a feeling of something behind her. She had been walking along a street that seemed familiar; it was in Anderwell, or almost. It felt like it was there, symbolically, if nothing else.

Someone or something was behind her, watching her, yet every time she turned, she saw nothing. Or she only saw people she knew, but no one strange. If she faced forward again, she got the same feeling. It was impossible to make any progress along the street — not that she had any idea where she was going, but as soon as she went forward a few steps the feeling came back.

She would turn and take a step back looking, but there was never anything to help her understand the feeling.

Peka clapped at her, and then moved his hands as if he was drinking. Tillandra fumbled around on the ground until she found her satchel and grabbed one of the skins from it. First she watered Peka, then herself before gathering everything, including the second bag, and setting off.

She knew where she had to go now; the issue wasn't which direction but how could she reach her destination and avoid the soldiers in her path. When the sun finally did crest the horizon on her right, she could see the ridge line that she had been told about. It wasn't that tall but it was all rock, running in an almost direct line north.

There were no shrubs or trees growing on it. In some hollows tufts of wild grasses or small plants clung to what life they could find, their seeds blown up there by some misfortune. She considered crossing over it to take shade from it but the words of the man in the trees worried her.

Were the soldiers on the other side of the hill? Is that where the knights had come from? If she was that close to them, the last thing she needed was for some stray man to spot her peering over the top. Tillandra stuck to the task of covering as much ground as she could, sheltered from sight by the range.

It was not until mid-afternoon that Tillandra finally had respite from the baking sun. There had been nowhere to shade, and she had used a tunic draped over her head to shelter her and Peka as they walked. Her biggest concern, apart from where the soldiers might be, was water.

Heading into Sahro on foot wasn't the smartest thing for anyone to do, she knew that, but her options were limited. If she couldn't make the new base camp she'd instructed Gimbden to arrange, she had no chance of getting to Tingfurlew and back to Anderwell in time.

Even then it was going to be close. It was why she couldn't afford any delays and wasn't traveling via normal roads. She pushed onwards, sipping water only when she needed to, and making sure Peka took his share.

They found no creeks or riverbeds near the rock range, and she pressed as hard as she could, enjoying the relative coolness without the sun on her. She had shed her outer tunic and wore only a sleeveless top under it that allowed her skin to feel the air brush across the sweat running down her arms.

It was enough to let her believe she was better off. She didn't stop when the sun dipped, instead choosing to push on until her body said it was done. The ground had been stable enough throughout the day, but she walked further away from the ridge in the darkness, hoping to avoid any unseen rocks that might cause her harm.

She only managed several more hours before she spotted a darker patch in the rock line. Her eyes had adjusted enough to use what limited light the stars and moon provided to see the makings of somewhere to rest up.

As it turned out it wasn't much more than a hole that spanned only a body width back into the rocks. It wasn't a cave, but it seemed the perfect place for her to wedge into and get some sleep.

Throughout the night Tillandra twisted and turned, never quite able to get comfortable, either sat against the rock or lying on the ground. Peka lay snug on the two bags at the back of the recess. Sometime in the night she crept out and sat looking out across the darkness.

The silence was complete. There was nothing she could hear, but she wanted to know more about the soldiers. She crept up the side of the hill, making every foot placement and hand hold secure before taking the next one.

Glad she hadn't tried this with Peka, she edged toward the crest until she could see over the top. It was as dark, or darker on the other side, but fear ran up her spine. Twinkling for miles across to the west all she could see were small campfires.

Shadows moved around the lights closest to her. She didn't need to be able to see properly to know what she was looking at: an army was spread across the broader area to the west of the ridge.

So the news was correct. This is not good.

Tillandra shivered. An army this size could march into Sahro across the expanse of land that lay between towns, without anyone being the wiser. Unless their own forces were in place. She could only hope.

The only thing in their favor was the desert. The knights would suffer in the relentless heat, and they would need supplies. Everything was harder than on hard land. More than anything they would need a lot of water.

To get a few dozen knights to Watersend was possible, even if you had to sacrifice a few animals or people to achieve it. Moving this many men was almost impossible. No wonder they wanted to secure a road to Watersend. With a fixed road and supply stations, they'd be able to arrive in large numbers and with an element of surprise.

But why now? What do they really want?

A drop of water hit her face and she jumped in surprise. Then another in the dust beside her. Looking up she saw why: it was so dark on this side, clouds filled the sky. A few more drops fell, and Tillandra knew she needed to get down to Peka, before it came down in earnest. Storms across these plains could be fierce.

LANI

There was something that bothered her about Odajeen, and Lani couldn't settle her mind on what it was. The woman had done nothing wrong. They had now been traveling together for five days and if she was faking it, Lani believed she would have found her out by now.

Even her look wasn't an issue. Lani had become more comfortable with the way her eyes appeared, the purple lines running over the whites with no iris. She wasn't completely at ease with it, but it didn't conjure up images of dead people when she looked at her now.

The last couple of days there had hardly been any talk between any of them. Maybe it was her reason for helping that caused Lani's instincts to itch, she just didn't know. They had ridden many miles, through wide-open country, all for Lani's benefit.

It didn't make sense that someone would do it without seeking something in return. Perhaps she'd just become cynical of everyone, but she just couldn't reconcile it. Odajeen wanting to know more did make sense.

Lani knew that if she were in her shoes, she would follow herself as well. There was just that thing that she couldn't grasp. It was a thought, or a warning, that her mind was trying to show her but it was behind a curtain, and she couldn't pull that curtain aside.

Maybe I'm making it into more than I need to.

The group slowed as they reached the crest of a hill and Odajeen rode up alongside her.

"There's a town ahead that I think we should stop at. I don't want to force you, but I for one could do with a bed and a bath. We have no followers, or none close. I think we will be safe in there."

Lani looked down the road they were on and could see the shapes of buildings and a wall off in the distance, partly obscured by the small rolling hills.

"They will welcome strangers more than the villages we've been through?"

Odajeen nodded. "Yes, it's a big town. Ostaba it is called. It's becoming a large waypoint from Jarv, so more outsiders pass through it. There are many of the big horse-breaking farms on the western side of the town."

"Horse-breaking?"

"Wild horses don't care for people to be on them, and certainly not saddles and bridles. They 'break their resistance' to these and teach them to accept people."

"Oh," Lani replied.

"It makes it one of the larger horse-trading towns in Rohumaa. That's why it keeps growing. Maybe it will become a city one day."

Finding somewhere to stay the night turned into more of a problem than they'd intended. The town was about to host a horse fair and all but two rooms were taken. They were in different inns, and after much arguing, it was agreed Lani and Odajeen would take one while the brothers the other.

The inn wasn't that big and the women's bath area only had a single bath, which she let Odajeen take first. When her time came, she eased herself down into the hot water, sighing in relief. Off the top of her head, she couldn't remember her last proper bath, and it had been perfumed with some oils which masked how she smelled.

It took her the best part of an hour to scrub herself clean and get her hair washed through. She dressed in the fresher of her clothes and went back to their room, wishing she had clean clothes. The ones she'd been wearing were from the dead woman, and she'd be glad to be rid of them. Maybe she could buy some in the morning before they moved on.

Her stomach was hungry but she knew she had to brush out her hair. Lani hated the way she had to do that, and wished to have it short like she used to. It was now longer than she'd ever had it.

For now.

Another knot caught on the brush and Lani threw it onto the bed in frustration.

"Here, let me help with that," Odajeen said as she shuffled over from her own bed. "Pass it to me."

Lani picked up the brush and put it in the woman's hands. Odajeen sat beside her on the bed, and at first felt her head and her hair. Then she started to gently brush through it. Initially Lani was uncomfortable at having someone else touch her like this, but as Odajeen began to work through the knots, she relaxed and it became more enjoyable.

"There, see? It's much easier for someone else to do."

"I'm not used to hair this long. It's never been this long before."

"The feeling of brushing out my hair is one of the things I enjoy the most. Especially at the end of a day, it helps to release tightness in my head."

"I can feel that."

"Much of this is new to you, isn't it?"

"What do you mean?"

"I sense you are not so used to traveling on your own."

Lani didn't answer.

"It must be important for you to leave your home and risk so much."

"I think it is."

"Can I ask you something? Do not be upset with me if I do, but I feel I must ask."

Lani felt anxious – what was it she wanted to know?

"Okay."

The woman stopped brushing and turned side-on to Lani. She seemed less confident than normal. "Can I touch it?"

Lani turned sharply to look at the woman. "Touch what?"

Odajeen seemed a little startled by her reaction and leaned back and away from Lani. "It's okay, I'm sorry I said anything. Don't be upset. I was just wanting to touch the brooch. To see what it feels like, if it feels like I see it."

Lani felt a little silly for her reaction. "I'm sorry." It made sense for the woman to want to feel the object she couldn't actually see.

What harm could it do? The brothers aren't here, she can't steal it and escape from me.

"It's alright, dear. I'm sorry for upsetting you."

"No, Odajeen, it's okay. I'm just very possessive of it as it's the only thing I've had for as long as I can remember. It's always been with me."

"I'm sorry."

"Don't be. Just forget it."

Odajeen held the brush up. "Can I continue?"

"Yes, thank you."

Now Lani did feel foolish. Here was this old blind woman that had only helped her, wanting to brush her hair, and all she'd asked for was to touch the brooch. She was overreacting she knew, but something was cautioning her, holding her back from it, and she didn't know why.

As the woman kept evenly stroking through her hair, Lani tried to understand what reason there was for her reluctance to open up to the woman. Of anyone she had met, outside of Henri, this lady was the most connected, the most likely to know something to help.

Was there something Lani could tell her to help her make sense of her memories? She had held back on telling her more about the ring, including that she had worn one up until recently. Lani couldn't imagine what might have happened if she still wore it.

Would it have triggered more memories for Odajeen? Maybe it would. Maybe her touching the brooch could do the same thing. If it did, wouldn't that be a good thing to do in return for the help they'd give her? What had the seer told her? She had to make choices.

She carried with her good news and bad news. Maybe the news for Odajeen wasn't so good, which is why she was holding back. Or she was just being paranoid, which she could understand after everything that had happened. Lani needed to choose.

"You can."

"I can?"

"You can touch it, Odajeen. I see no harm in it, as reluctant as I am to let anyone near it, I trust you."

The words seemed to break her apprehension and Lani felt more relaxed. She took the brooch out from the pocket on the inside of the chest of her tunic, and rubbed her fingers across the stone. The stone responded to her touch and a crackle of light flickered across the surface.

As she looked at the old woman her arms tingled as she saw the lines in Odajeen's eyes were the exact same pattern as the light she saw on the stone. It had been there in the back of her mind the whole time but she couldn't link them together until now.

Lani held the brooch in her open palm with the stone facing upward, and took Odajeen's in her other and gently placed it down on top.

ODAJEEN

The palm of her hand went cold, a sharp chill that almost hurt but made Odajeen gasp out loud. She could feel the girl instinctively pull back at her reaction but her fingers curled around the younger hand and held on.

Then it spread, slowly, a breath at a time, up through her wrist before creeping up her arm. The sensible part of her, the part she ignored as often as not, told her to let go, to step away from it, but she held on. Bit by bit the crawling cold reached her neck and then up into her head.

And as it did, what she'd had in her mind seemed to fuse together better. The broken pieces didn't really exist, only shapes did, with some tones of color washed over them. She could hear voices in the memories, and recalled holding someone's hand, or running her fingers over their face.

Parts of real images flitted across her mind, but they were distant, and she could feel they were from her youngest days. And the memory of when her sight went away, that too flowed back into her mind, the pain of it fresh as if it was only recent.

It was then she began to understand what she had been seeing. The fragments she thought she could see were only layers from her childhood, laid over the shapes and forms she'd created in her head. Her head injury had mixed up the two sets of memories and created distorted images.

Now they separated and the pain of that loss felt as real as the loss of her sight when she was only small. She remembered how her family abandoned her, leaving her to live whatever life she could. Odajeen felt like she could hear the words 'devils' shouted at her as she was rejected by all around her.

Tears ran down her face, but still she clung to the girl's hand. She knew she needed whatever she could get from this stone. She heard her conversations with people she was working with, who looked up to her and expected her to make decisions.

It was with them she got the shape of the ring, from being around them, from running her fingers over the ring hundreds of times a day. The ring she had worn, on her left hand. That ring was hers. Words rushed by, and with them feelings, and time.

Everything became jumbled as so much opened up in her head. She was trying to make sense of it, to understand what she was doing. One word kept running through it all, over and over: "Mother."

Odajeen didn't know her mother, she wasn't a mother, was she? Her body trembled at the thought of it. Then everything seemed to slow, almost as if she'd reached the end of the memories. The voices were loud and angry, but the same voices.

"Mother, how could you?"

"What have you done? This is not allowed."

And the feelings that she'd held at the time. She'd faced a choice, a conflict that she'd had to resolve. Something that went against everything she had believed in, but deep down inside she'd felt she had no choice. She'd had to do it.

On the inside of her mind, about where her forehead was, a brightness appeared, something she could actually see. Odajeen didn't know if she was imagining it but it seemed she could see the shape of a woman approaching her.

"This is a surprise!"

"What is?"

"You don't need to speak out loud, I can hear your thoughts."

"Who are you?"

"I do not have much time, what you are doing is draining the stone you are touching."

"I don't understand."

"Once you knew exactly who I was, back when you were the Mother Folly. Until you broke the rule."

"What rule?"

"The most important of them all. Never to kill another except in your own defense."

"What did I do? Why can't I remember?"

"That is the price of breaking the rule. Your mind was cleared and you were sent away, but something has shifted in your mind. And by finding this stone, a most unlikely occurrence, well... perhaps it wasn't just chance."

"I don't understand."

"Perhaps you will get your chance to find out. The path back for you, Odajeen, requires great sacrifice, but you have only one task at this time."

"What?"

"This girl, she must get this brooch back to Anderwell. It is almost completely drained. If that happens another thing which she holds will have no barrier to her mind. It is all that's keeping her safe. Do not touch the brooch again, or it will be all gone. She must get to Anderwell, and soon."

Odajeen could see the light fading, the image of the woman sliding backward.

"How do I learn more?"

"It will come in time. I must go."

Odajeen hung on greedily for more, but there was nothing. She tried to focus on the brooch under her palm but even the chill from that had faded. She had learned things, she could remember, but it wasn't enough. Why did she call her mother?

Uncurling her fingers and lifting her hand off was the hardest thing Odajeen had done in a long time. Inside she wanted to suck everything it might tell her out of it, but she felt a compulsion not to do it. Whatever it was, forced her to let go, to follow the instructions she'd been given.

"Are you alright, Odajeen?"

She could hear Lani's voice, as if through a heavy door. Her ears were ringing, a sharp high-pitched noise that made it hard to hear anything else.

Thenis, don't take my hearing!

"Odajeen?"

"I can hear you, just."

"What's wrong?"

Rubbing her ears didn't help. She took several deep breaths. "Is there a drink handy, girl?"

Odajeen felt Lani move from the bed, and then heard soft footsteps. Her hearing seemed to be returning quickly, which eased her anxiety.

"Here, take this."

She drained the whole goblet of thin ale which hardly quenched the thirst she had. Right now she wanted something much stronger.

"What happened, Odajeen? You were crying, did you remember something?"

"I did, girl, not all of it good. I'm trying to make sense of it."

They sat in silence for well over ten minutes, while Odajeen went over what had just happened.

"I wasn't always blind, Lani."

The girl didn't reply immediately. "What happened?"

"The memories were real. I used to be able to see, like normal people. I remembered when it went away..." She didn't want to explain it all, it was hard enough to think, even for something so long ago.

"I'm sorry."

"Hard enough to have it happen once, I feel like it just happened again."

"What about the memories?"

"Fragments, all mashed up, of what I normally see in my head, shapes and blobs, with some of those early memories mixed in. It all sorted itself out with that stone."

"So the brooch, it helped?"

"It did. You're right to want to hang onto that, girl, it's magic that jewel. Is there more of that drink?"

When Lani brought it back she drank all of that as well.

"Someone spoke to me."

"Who? When?"

"When I held the brooch, girl. She didn't say who she was, but I knew her before, or so she says."

"How?"

"There's a thing about it that I should know but I can't recall. She said my memories were taken away from me. I think she means blocked."

"Why would they do that?" Odajeen could sense an urgency in what the girl was asking her.

"She told me some of it, but not all. I did something I shouldn't have, and I was punished."

"By who, that lady who spoke to you?"

"Perhaps. She didn't have much time, she said. She warned me about the brooch."

"Warned you? Warned you about what?"

Odajeen knew she had to tell it all, but all she really wanted was to go to her bed and try to remember.

"She said that it is almost drained. That its power is helping you. She told me you have to get it to Anderwell, where it can fill up again. I don't know how, but she said something about another thing you carry. Hang on, I'll try to remember."

A headache was forming in her head, and everything seemed twice as hard. Odajeen suddenly felt like the life had been drained out of her, and she needed to sleep.

"If it gets empty then the other thing you carry will get to your mind. Something like that, it's hard to remember. I'm not feeling so well."

"Let's get you on your bed then. Stand up."

She almost collapsed into the girl's grip when she stood, and staggered her way across the space. The bed felt like heaven to her and as she lay down she could feel sleep racing up to her, unlike anything she'd felt before.

"The ring…"

"What about the ring, Odajeen?"

"I used to wear it."

"What?" She could hear the surprise in the girl's voice, which meant something but she was too tired to think.

"I was one of them, but I did something bad... It was taken from me."

And then the sleep came, and she felt it like a heavy weight, pressing down on her. As if she would never get up from it. But it felt peaceful.

87

TILLANDRA

Trying to climb down backward in equal parts haste and caution was no easy feat. In truth the hill wasn't a sheer face, but the loose shale and stones were possible traps to Tillandra getting to the ground without incident.

Several times a rock she placed a foot on fell away from her sending a small avalanche of stones and small rocks to the ground. She was glad she had not climbed directly above where she had left Peka.

Each time Tillandra slipped she pushed herself flat onto the side of the hill, getting a mouthful of dirt and grit. More drops smacked onto the stones around her, some on her back or head. She knew that the storm would be heavy simply by the size of the drops falling now.

This was no misty drizzle coming.

Touching the ground at the bottom with relief she pushed out from the hill, looking around. There was little to see as it was completely dark now, the clouds above blocking any light sources.

Tillandra walked back to the recess where she had left Peka. She knelt down into the space and her heart stopped. He was gone. She felt around frantically in the ground.

Where is he? Oh Thenis, what have I done?

"Peka," she called frantically, realizing as she did, that he could not hear her.

Lightning crackled overhead and lit the sky. Distraught, she looked left and right before the fleeting vision disappeared, leaving only the black night and the increasing drops of rain.

She walked forward.

Where would he have gone? Why?

Tillandra had never raised a child before so there was no context for her to understand what this child might do. Raindrops continued to fall. Heavily. She decided she had to act like him and got to her knees and crawled forward.

How far could he have gone?

She had been up the hill for some time so if he crawled non-stop, he could be anywhere. Her chest tightened. She knew she had promised to look after him, but it was more than that. He was unable to survive, he needed her, and she had left him in danger. What had she been thinking?

Now wasn't the time for her to dip into a gloomy mood, and she pushed on with her search. The rain got heavier. Not just drops now. Thunder boomed in the distance and Tillandra hoped now that there would be more lightning.

She crawled on, feeling out in front as she went, looking as best she could as her eyes adjusted back to the dark. The rain began to fall constantly now, her clothing would be soaked in no time.

When she put her hand onto his leg, she nearly crushed it, not realizing what it was. He was crawling just in front of her. Lightning lit the sky just as she reached him, and he looked back at her in surprise.

Tillandra had never felt more relief in her life. It had been as if she had held her breath the whole time.

"Peka," she shouted with joy, pulling him to her.

She wrapped him in her arms, and he reached up to touch her face. Her eyes could only make out his shape and the whites of his eyes. She pulled him close to her chest, the rain running off both of them as it fell in ever increasing streams.

Tillandra stood and buried him against her, the only protection she had, and tried to reverse her path until she found the rock hill. She had veered away from the recess when she crawled, but it didn't take long to find it.

The rain was getting into the recess as well, there would be no relief from it there. She placed Peka down into the most protected part and looked around. The sky was pitch black as it would be for hours.

Once her heart had calmed down an idea came to her. As crazy as it was, she knew this was her best chance of getting past the camps. She would be unseen by anyone in the storm, unless she physically bumped into them. No one would be able to see in the deluge and darkness, and most of the soldiers would be holed up inside their tents trying to stay dry.

She knew it was madness. She would be stumbling around in the dark without any guidance, but with some luck it would see her through. Reaching back at where Peka was sitting, she decided finally it was what she had to do. If she was going to get him to protection and herself back to Anderwell she couldn't be stuck here.

When the boy was settled against her tunic, she covered them both with the only cloak she had and started north. For now, she knew where that was, all she had to do was follow the ridge line.

Above them the storm continued to increase. Tillandra was grateful for the lightning when it came but resentful for the loss of sight that followed straight after. The thunder got closer, creeping always toward them like a tide from the west.

At the end of the ridge line she stopped and looked to the west. She could see nothing but a wall of rain. Any fires were all washed out now, and she had no direction pointer apart from her own nose.

Her feet were sloshing in her boots, every part of her was soaked. Water ran off her nose and down her cheeks, dripping onto the exposed part of Peka. He would stay warm against her, or warm enough, but it would now be many hours before they would get dry.

Trudging through what was quickly becoming mud, she kept moving. Each step was progress. Thunder crashed much closer to her, the gap between it and the lightning was getting less.

To her left Tillandra saw the shapes of many tents as lightning flashed across the sky. Lots and lots of tents. She couldn't worry about that now, she had to keep moving. One step, then another. Lifting the boot from the ground before it got stuck, constant motion.

The pace was nothing like her normal one, but her leg strength helped her keep moving, despite the exhaustion she felt inside from another night without sleep and a whole day carrying the boy. Tillandra wasn't sure how long she could keep it up. She was tired. Very tired.

Lightning flashed high above this time, and Tillandra froze. She had almost walked straight into a tent she hadn't seen. She had been so busy watching to her left she hadn't seen what was ahead of her.

Down the narrow channel between the tents she kept moving, forcing herself to breathe slowly. The shapes of the tents were all around her now, she could see them even in the dark. Thunder crashed. Shapes moved in the distance ahead of her, but none came near her.

Counting in her head, she dropped to her knees, earlier than she needed to. She waited until the lightning had flashed and took in what she could. She was right in the middle of rows of tents. There were guards walking around the outside of the campsite, but just single men and only a few of them. She doubted they expected any trouble out here, even less in the middle of a storm.

As soon as the flash disappeared, she stood and plodded forward, hoping to not trip on a rope or stake. Thunder. Tillandra dropped to her knees again, feeling them sink into the mud. She counted. This time the flash came right when she expected.

To her right she caught the shape of a guard walking across where she was heading. She stayed exactly where she was, feeling the wetness eat into her knees, cold chewing through her skin.

When the shape passed she stood quickly, lumbering forward, through that line and onwards. More thunder.

Tillandra dropped down again, her knees aching with the damp that had settled inside them.

One. Two. Three. Four.

Lightning crackled again. She kept her head down below the height of the surrounding tent ridge lines and waited for the light to pass.

There were only two more rows ahead of her. Tillandra moved up until she was beside the last row of tents.

She heard what sounded like someone to the right. This time she lay down on her side, her back to the tent on her right, and waited. Praying for no thunder. The squeaking of boots and mud was close now. Tillandra was grateful she had heard it over the pounding rain.

They were right next to her now.

Had they stopped?

Being caught and held captive was a delay she couldn't afford. If they were looking for her back closer to Bundok, it wouldn't take too much for word to get to the men here to hold onto her. Tillandra couldn't afford any delay, and she wouldn't have them take the boy from her either. She braced herself to fight if she needed to.

There was a sound of constant water. A stream of it. Then she heard the sound of a man grunting, and then footsteps passed her head.

Thunder crashed. Tillandra held her breath, unable to hear the footsteps while the thunder boomed above. This one was longer and louder.

One. Two. Thr…

A fork of lighting lit the sky. Tillandra waited to be found out, but the guard was walking away from her on his path.

Dark came back and with it the night blindness. She got to her feet as quickly as she could and hurried forward. Her feet sloshed through the water running across the ground, sticking to the deepening mud. As much as Tillandra wanted to make no noise, it wasn't possible.

She had to make as much distance as she could before the next lightning flash. Then she'd have to lie flat again; there were no more tents to hide between anymore. Poor Peka wouldn't know what was going on, being crushed into the mud.

All she could hope in this light was that she'd look like any other dark shape out in the distance.

Thunder boomed above her.

88

TILLANDRA

Tillandra didn't stop. Rain pelted her face, and she hugged her coat tightly around Peka, trying to protect him as best she could. When they had first broken free of the cover of the tents she had intended to lie down every time the thunder came, but after the first one she knew she couldn't keep that up.

Lying there in the mud and rain trying not to squash Peka and feeling her exhaustion, she understood she had no choice but to keep moving. By the time the storm passed she needed to be out of sight of any soldiers or patrols.

There was no way to tell when it would end so Tillandra just kept moving forward. Occasionally she would stumble over a hole in the ground or rocks in her path. She would stagger like a drunk until she could right herself and plod on.

Peka never moved, the small child either frightened out of his wits or content to stay wrapped up, knowing she had him covered.

Tillandra couldn't guess how long it had been as there was no way to judge time or distance. Nor did she know how she would find her way to the camp, or when she would cross into Sahro, not that she felt the soldiers would honor that border if they spotted her out here.

Once she tried to think about the dream about being chased, but then she nearly fell, tripping over herself in the dark. After that she just concentrated as best she could on placing one foot in front of the other and keeping up some momentum.

If she had to guess it would have been another hour before the thunder began to peter out. Explosions became crashes. The lightning fizzled out until there was no light at all. Small crevices formed in the clouds above and slithers of moonlight squeezed through giving Tillandra some sight lines.

Then gusts of wind would come, the clouds blocking the moon, leaving her blind again. The cloud cover was as much her protection as it was the cause of her difficulties. She doubted it would have been as easy to get through without the storm.

Easy! Ha, if this is easy, then Thenis don't bring me hard.

As the weather turned it brought an overnight chill on the back of what started as a gentle breeze. Out here on the border of the desert lands, days were hot and nights cold, even in the middle of summer.

Now mid-season, the temperature was dropping fast. The breeze made Tillandra shiver. Every part of her was wet, and if it hadn't been for the walk, she would have had no heat at all. The wind sucked at what warmth she had left, drawing it away from her.

Pulling her wet cloak around her she tried to shake off the shivers and just kept herself moving.

Forward, just keep moving.

She couldn't believe where she was. Walking through mud, in the middle of nowhere, approaching the border between Daskare and Sahro. And carrying a toddler and a new mask.

Not that long ago she was happily worrying about an annoying student or what Goran was up to. Everything had been turned on its head when Ashantha had died. Been killed, she corrected herself. The last few months had passed so quickly, Tillandra had hardly had the time to take stock of the changes befalling them.

Her foot rolled sideways as she stumbled over another small rock, catching her unaware. Tillandra fell to one knee, grimacing as it smacked against the ground. She forced herself back to her feet and straightened her back.

Pay attention!

Ahead she could see some tall dark shapes. As she approached, she could see they were a small copse of trees. Several of them were tall and wide enough to provide some shelter from the wind, even if the ground beneath was as wet as anywhere else.

She used one as a prop to lean back against as she caught her breath. Without the constant rain she opened the cloak to check on Peka. He appeared to be asleep, so she left him be, taking a drink from her bag and quenching part of her thirst. She pulled out some dried beef strips and packed some in a pocket, so she had something for them both to eat, before sealing everything up again and heading back into the rain.

Tillandra couldn't tell how long they'd been walking, but she watched as the remnants of the storm disappeared from the sky. Slowly clouds began to part, and thin yellow strands of light chased away the last of the night. Blue sky opened in the distance with a tinge of orange far off to her right, signalling dawn's arrival.

With daylight Tillandra was able to pick her path through the rough ground, grasses and small collections of rock or mounds of dirt, much more easily. She checked over her shoulder occasionally to ensure the camps were far out of sight. If she couldn't see them, then they couldn't see her either.

The knock she felt confused her at first. She thought it was just her own mind making noises, like she had talked to herself throughout the night. When it persisted, she knew what it was and smiled. There was no way she was stopping now, if she sat down she would never get back up again. Hopefully she could walk and talk at the same time.

"Hello?"

"Mother…?"

"Yes, who is that?" The connection was strained.

"In All Jest, Mother. Can you hear me?"

"Toolet! Oh wonderful. In All Jest. I'm … okay, yes."

"You sound weak, Mother. The connection is distorted."

"I'm walking, Toolet. We survived a massive storm, but I have to keep moving. I don't know who might be behind me."

"You sound exhausted. Let me be quick. You're not heading in the right direction."

"What?"

"Go west, Mother. Gimbden is waiting for you at their camp."

"West?"

"Yes, northwest but mostly west. It's not so precise looking at the map. I can't tell how far but if you turn you should be okay."

"That's good news. I've been walking through the night with no lights to guide me."

"I'm glad I called then. I will let Gimbden know."

"Thank you, Toolet."

Tillandra couldn't hold the connection and it fell away as quickly as it had arrived. With her energy flagging she needed nothing else to sap it. It was a risk connecting like that but she was thankful for it. Hopefully Gimbden could find her before her legs gave out.

She stopped and looked in the direction she felt Toolet had mentioned. With the rising sun as her guide, she turned and headed toward her best guess at west. Thankfully there was little ahead of her to cause her problems, only mounds of sand.

Even with her Humaas build and characteristics, her legs were sore and tired. Each stride was demanding every ounce of energy she could muster, and her back ached. Her body shivered with the coolness of the night, and it felt like a lifetime before the sun had risen enough to send warmth. Tillandra stripped off her cloak to let the sun bake her from behind, hoping for its warmth.

Close to mid-morning she stopped and cleaned up Peka, making sure he drank and ate. She sat him on her coat to keep him from the mushy sand and dirt, and he enjoyed the sun on his face, staring up at it and waving his hands across his eyes, like a game.

The sound of horses caught her by surprise. She hurried to put him back in the sling and gathered her bag and cloak and started to look for the threat. Coming from her left she could see a group of horses; they were heading directly for her.

She started walking the way she had been going, and let them do what they would. She was in no position to outrun them, or to fight. The closer they got, she could see the sunlight bouncing off their armor.

There were six of them and the bear on their shields on top of their armor identified them clearly as Skarian knights.

"Hold there!" the man at the front of the group yelled out as they slowed.

Tillandra stopped walking and struggled to stay upright.

"What are you doing out here on our borders, woman? What is that you carry?"

He had lifted the visor and Tillandra could see narrow eyes, a broad nose and what looked like a dark mustache.

"Is it not a free land to walk across, good knight?"

The man edged his horse a little closer. "Within the realm of Daskare, it is for us to decide what is free or not free. You are not one of our kind, you appear far from your own lands. I ask again, what are you doing here?"

She stared back at him as defiantly as she could, struggling to hold herself upright.

"I am making my way into Sahro, to visit friends."

"You expect me to believe such folly? You have no supplies, and are on foot, you'd never make it. What is that you're cradling?"

Tillandra wrapped her arms tightly around Peka. "Just my son."

Another of the knights caught the man's attention, and they all looked to their left. Tillandra looked in the same direction. More horses were approaching, a bigger group than this one.

The knights began turning their horses in the direction of the approaching riders. She could hear hands reaching for weapons and an uneasy shifting in their saddles. The first knight also turned to see who it was approaching.

"Knights of Daskare, what do you do here?" A soldier, also armored although nowhere as impressively as the knights, called out as his group of ten arrived.

"I answer not to you, whoever you may be. State your purpose or leave."

The new group were spreading out into a line, the nearest now close to Tillandra. He unwrapped the cloth tied around his face, and she could see Gimbden's eyes and nose underneath.

"Knight, I can see you wear the standard of Daskare, and will give you the courtesy of seeing your presence here a mistake. You must have mistaken where you were, because you have crossed into Sahro. If I were to think it more than a mistake, as the border guard we'd have to consider you a hostile force here. So again, what is your purpose here?"

Tillandra looked at the man, a smile forming on her face. He had courage, that was for sure. Even with his ten men, she knew, as he probably did too, the knights were no easy force to contend with. Both sides were tense, hands resting on swords, and holding their horses in position.

"We, like you, ride our borders. What's to say this isn't Daskare, and it's you that's the hostile force?"

"That is an easy answer. Ride to the top of that dune and look east and west, you'll see the stone way markers off in the distance. And the line between them falls behind you. This woman will be coming with us, and you need to turn about now, and return to your lands."

The knight appeared uninterested in riding up the dune or anywhere else. Horses snorted, and armor creaked in saddles, while both sides stared each other down. The knight to their leader's left murmured something to him.

Again they looked to see movement coming from the northwest. Tillandra watched the face of the Sahrian solider who'd done all the talking, and it formed into a smile. Within minutes a squad of men, riding camels and fully armed, climbed the dunes around them.

The lead knight said nothing, but looked at her, and the opposing men. Several times he shook his head, before turning his horse around and leading his men away.

"Are they always this impudent, Mother?"

"Yes, they are. There are a lot more of them camped less than a day's march from her, stretched out in large numbers."

"We've seen them as well."

She nodded. "Your name, Captain?"

"Lieutenant, Mother, and Duiller is my name."

"Thank you for your timely arrival, Lieutenant Duiller, and greetings, Gimbden."

"Mother." Her colleague nodded his head.

Tillandra unwrapped Peka's head so the soldier could see him. "Perhaps one of you could carry him, while I follow you back."

"I think we can do better than that, Mother." Gimbden turned and whistled to the men on the camels. One of them hurried their beast forward, trailing another creature behind it. "You can ride back with us."

LANI

*I*f the room could have gotten any smaller, Lani didn't know how. She sat on her own bed watching Odajeen sleep, trying to unravel in her mind everything that the woman had just told her.

Odajeen had worn a ring in her past. If that were true then she was one of their people, up until whatever bad thing it was she had done.

How bad must it be to wipe someone's mind?

Except she didn't say they had wiped it, but that they had locked it. Lani suddenly went all light-headed and had to prop herself up with her left arm, to stop herself toppling over.

Just like I have a lock!

The thought shouldn't have shocked her, but it did. The Jesters hadn't done it to her and Odajeen had they? She wasn't one of them, and she was too young. Who was that woman that Odajeen had spoken to? Was she some god?

What magic was at play with the brooch?

Lani had come to accept the amulet had some form of magic attached to it, she couldn't doubt that anymore after her recent experiences, so what was so different about the brooch? Why couldn't it be magical? Is that why she felt so good rubbing her hand over it?

Is that why it helped block the amulet?

The memory of when she'd tested the two things together and apart weeks ago had proven to her that it was more than just a brooch, but she'd kept denying it. She wanted it to just be a simple gift from her mother, something that was just between the two of them.

A lone connection to her past.

Sitting there she could feel the touch of the amulet, and if anything it seemed more prevalent than before. Lani knew that was probably just her mind playing tricks on her, but then…

What had Odajeen said about the brooch going empty?

If it was a barrier protecting her from the amulet, and it was weakening, then it would make sense to be able to feel the amulet more. She shivered at the thought. Mostly she felt like she was in control of her decisions, like she could choose to override the feeling of the amulet.

But what if that wasn't true, what if the brooch was the thing helping her do that? Would it eventually take complete control of her? There was the pouch though, she was still unsure what that did to help. It seemed to block most of the amulet from her, which was a good thing.

It had also allowed Ashantha to carry it, so there was magic in it as well. Lani just didn't know what or how much, and the idea of losing control over it began to scare her. What had happened in Statiiv when she'd been led by it to leave the city had shaken her a lot.

That did show she had some will over it. She'd been able to break its control over her, and return to her room putting the thing away in its pouch. How, Lani didn't know, but it was at least something.

It really is evil isn't it?

Yet the things she could do with it attracted Lani. She wanted to test it further, to see how to read others' thoughts, to see what it allowed her to do.

Imagine what I could do with that? No one could push me around then!

Lani knew that was wrong deep down, but the feeling kept growing inside her. It was only in the background, sneaking around behind her normal thinking, preying on her sense of helplessness. She could see it, what it was doing, but couldn't stop it.

And it was bigger than before, now that she focused on it and didn't ignore it, she was able to give it a size. It had grown, only a little, as if just a drop at a time, but instead of a small puddle now it was big enough to create a splash if you stood in it.

I won't use it!

The only way she knew was through her will. And the brooch. Lani's thoughts came back to the brooch. Sitting there in her hand it was lifeless. She never heard voices in it, it was a comfort for sure, but it hadn't spoken to her. No one had spoken through it to her.

Maybe Odajeen was just going crazy, and the voice was her imagination. Why trust her? Except everything seemed to make sense.

Odajeen had already known about the Jester's ring, she had been able to describe it like she'd seen it. And Lani knew it was real, she'd worn one. She had seen Ashantha and what had happened to him, she still had the likeness of his face in her satchel.

In addition, the old woman had seen the blue stone on Lani when it was a fact that she was blind. That was no act. All of it made sense, even if it didn't. None of it made sense to her old self, Lani the girl who'd been standing in piss, pressing cloth for a few coins a week.

Now, though, she was willing to accept almost anything. Too much had happened for her to be able to write it all off as nonsense or coincidence. Lani looked back at the old woman who was still very pale and hardly breathing.

The knocking on the door startled Lani and she jumped to her feet. As another knock sounded she heard the voice of Vefed through the door.

"Odajeen? Are you in there?"

Lani nervously walked to the door. She'd done nothing wrong but the old woman didn't look so good and her men were very protective of her. They'd not been happy about splitting up as it was, so now she wasn't sure how he would react.

She opened the door. "She's sleeping."

"Sleeping?" He pushed past her into the room and walked up to the old woman's bed.

"What did you do? She seems very weak."

"I didn't do anything!"

The man turned to her, scowling. "Then why is she asleep like this? She said we'd eat."

Lani wasn't sure she wanted to tell the man, but he was not going to let her go anywhere.

"Do you know about what she saw on me?"

"You mean the blue light?"

Lani nodded.

"What about it?"

"She asked me to hold it. It's a brooch I wear." Lani opened her hand to show him it.

"And?"

"She had a vision and said someone spoke to her when she held it. Then she said she was very tired and I had to help her lie down. She's been like that since."

"What did you do?"

"I did nothing. I just told you what happened."

"Sit down there," he said, pointing at her bed, "and don't move!"

Lani did as he said. She was as concerned about the woman as he was, especially now she had more knowledge about her past. Maybe she'd remember more of it when she woke up.

When Vefed didn't show up downstairs, his brother had come looking for him. Now the two of them stood guard, watching over Odajeen and Lani, saying nothing. The room stank of tension and too many bodies and Lani's anxiety grew.

What happened if Odajeen didn't wake up, or was sick? Maybe the brooch wasn't all good either, although saying it in her head didn't make sense at all. She doubted she'd be free to just walk away if the woman did not survive. Lani needed a plan to help her get away.

Again the thought of using the amulet crept forward from the back of her head. Sliding around her objections and will, it reminded her how she'd been able to escape before, how she'd used it to get off the boat, and to hurt the bowman.

Sitting on the bed, feeling the danger around her, the idea began to make perfect sense to her.

Just to get free, that's all. I don't have to keep using it, just control these men so I can get out.

Then what? Back and forth she bounced between telling herself it was alright to use the amulet and not. That she could control it and that she couldn't. Each hour that went by her mind became foggier as she became more tired, no one willing to sleep while they watched over the old lady on the bed.

It started as a wheeze in the old woman's chest, the breaths scraping in through her mouth and out again as if it hurt. They all woke from the doze they had been watching over her in, the dim light of morning casting a shadow across the bed.

Next came the coughs, bucking the woman as she lay, and still her eyes remained closed. Every so often Lani would see one of the brothers turn to look at her, accusation in their eyes. Then Odajeen opened her mouth and seemed to suck in enough air to fill two people before sitting upright in a sudden movement.

As she did so her eyelids opened, and her breathing returned to normal.

"Lani, are you there?"

"We all are, Odajeen," Vefed said.

"What on Dharatan are you boys doing in our room? What time is it?"

"Dawn, and you've been lying there at the entrance to death's cave all night. We came when you didn't show for dinner, and she told us what she'd done."

"What she'd done? Whatever do you mean?"

"The stone, she used it on you."

Odajeen laughed. "Dear Vefed, I love your concern, but Lani didn't do any such thing. I chose to touch it, and I'm so glad I did. It must have drained me to do what I did, is all. I must admit I did feel so very tired, but not now. Now I feel like I could eat a horse, or two. When's breakfast?"

Even Lani chuckled. The air in the room had changed, and seeing the brightness in the woman had relaxed the two men. She too was hungry and relieved that she could now push the thoughts she'd been having to the back of her mind.

LANI

The size of the wall was hard to imagine. Lani and her companions were still a long way from Jarv, but Vefed had told her that the blurred grey line she could see was the length of its northern wall. He'd told her it was miles long.

She could believe it, if she could see so much from this distance.

The weather had been kind to them, dry and not too hot, not yet anyway. For several days after Odajeen's session with the brooch, the group continued their journey. The old woman was still tired, Lani could see, but was trying to pretend otherwise.

It didn't look like the brothers were fooled either, and they rode alongside her, watching her very closely the whole time. Lani wanted to discuss it more with her, but knew she'd have to wait. As it was, the men were angry with her, despite the assurances Odajeen gave them about her wellbeing.

Lani knew it must have been hard for the older woman to have learned what she did. What little they had spoken, she'd told Lani she believed everything she'd heard. Finding out her punishment for the second time must have been harder.

Before, Odajeen had no memory of it. Of course she must have been aware of it at the time it happened, but since whenever her memories were locked, she'd not had to face up to it. In a way it was a merciful punishment.

With the opening of that lock, she had to face it again, and relive the feelings and pain of knowing that she wasn't blind before. That her sight had been taken from her.

Maybe in Jarv they'd get time to talk about it. Lani's mind had been running wild with thoughts and questions about the brooch, and was frustrated at not being able to discuss them with Odajeen. She'd have to force it when they got there, no matter what the men thought.

The city they approached was the last one she'd visit before Anderwell if she chose to finish what she'd begun months before. She was both drawn to it and repelled by it. The knowledge of what had happened to Odajeen hadn't eased her concerns about going there.

What type of people do this to their own? Who did it to me?

More concerning to her was what she might have to remember if someone could open the lock on her mind. What was it hiding from her, in the darkness she couldn't reach?

If the brooch was really protecting her and now growing weak, her time to decide was short. If it was true, it was almost as if she had no choice at all. That was what bothered her the most. It had begun with others giving her instructions, which she'd followed only to learn they were false. Now it was as if the two stones were pulling at her, in different directions.

She didn't like it, not one bit. But after all this time she still had no other path to follow. If she didn't find this Mother in Anderwell, and plead for her help, perhaps the amulet's pull would take over. What then? Was there someone in Enderk with answers?

The closer they got to the city walls, later in the afternoon, the stranger they appeared to Lani. This wall that from a distance had appeared to be a straight line, was actually a massive curve, spanning from east to west.

Great turrets rose from it and Lani had to tilt her head fully back to look up at them as they continued their ride slowly along a well-worn road of stone. Cities she had seen with defenses like this made her wonder why they were built this way.

Maybe some of what Arbery had told her on their trip from Little

Big Rock about wars was true, but then there had been nothing in recent times the she had heard of. Was this city that old, that the walls had been built to protect the inhabitants from invaders in another time? Why weren't there songs and tales from tellers about it?

After passing through the outer gate, Lani became lost in the dark tunnel under the wall. Their whole group was swallowed up by it, as were those they followed. The wall was easily sixty feet thick, which was at least double the span of Nkuku's.

What sparse lanterns there were lining the walls of the tunnel did little to brighten the gloomy passageway into the city. The slow clopping of horse hooves, creaking of wagon wheels and murmurs from everyone in the tunnel echoed off the curved stone walls and roadway, making everything more pronounced.

Lani couldn't have been happier than when they broke out of the tunnel into what could be loosely called daylight. Like Statiiv the city was constructed of many tall buildings, but the stone here was different. It was black and grey and seemed to rob the limited light that made it over the walls and through the buildings.

With the walls so close and the height of the neighboring buildings, shadows lay across everything. Lani pulled her coat tighter around her to fight off the chill inside the city.

"Strangest place, this," Vefed said quietly, leaning toward her. "Always dark and gloomy, and come the middle of winter it's draped in constant smoke."

"Smoke?"

"Yes, it gets so cold in here everyone burns wood fires to heat their houses. Even out on the streets there are usually big iron barrels that they light fires in. If you look at the street corners on major intersections, you'll see the blackened stones where they sit."

"I thought we were close to the desert, I expected it to be hot and dry."

"We are close, well, much closer than we were. It is off to the west, across the Boctok river, but over here, with this beast of a lake, the weather is as far from the desert as where you're from."

"Vefed?"

"Yes, Odajeen?"

"We're out of those horrid tunnels now aren't we?"

"Yes."

"Then let's get to an inn. I don't care for this horse anymore. I'm dirty, hungry and thirsty and if at least one of those doesn't change soon, I'm going to be cranky as well."

"We'll be there soon."

"Good."

No one spoke again while they led her through the city. As tall as every building was, the city was not very deep. Everything ran widthways along long streets that initially followed the line of the wall but then became straighter the closer to Lake Phyrgian they got.

Lani counted the number of roads between the northern and southern walls. They turned on the twelfth road, and she could only see two more ahead of them. The road they turned onto was lined with boarding houses and inns.

"There's a place we've stayed before," Odajeen said to her, without turning her way. "It's good we made it when we have, if what the guard at the gate said is true. We're in for a lake storm soon enough and no one wants to be out in those."

"A lake storm?"

"The lake is so big, it creates its own storms. When they come, they are worse than being stuck in a blizzard. So much water smashes against the walls and buildings, especially on this side of town, people get washed away."

"Really?"

Odajeen chuckled. "Yes, Lani."

They turned to their left down a narrower road and just before the next intersection turned the horses into the open gate beside an inn called The Captain's Anchor.

A sign out front had the painting of a large anchor on it, hanging from a beam by a rusty chain, that squeaked as it moved. A man at least as old as Odajeen stood up from a chair by the back door to the inn. He made his way over to meet them.

He limped badly, using his hips to help pull his legs through their motion, and Lani thought it looked painful even if his face showed no sign of it.

"You'd be wanting rooms as well then?"

"If you have them, we would."

"Best see my lad inside, he's the keeper and he'll sort you out. I'll sort these horses for you."

The back door of the inn opened inwards into a narrow hallway. The only light to help them see their way came from around a corner at the left end but Lani could see the height of the ceiling matched the typical height of buildings in Rohumaa.

"He's not Humaas?" Lani asked.

"No, he is not. He's from Kysten. You'll find plenty of Kystenites live here. There's a lot of trade through Jarv and it always brings people looking to profit."

They walked toward the light with Vefed at the front, leading Odajeen into the entranceway from the main street. A man taller than their group but only just, welcomed them as they came around the corner. Lani could see he had broad shoulders a good yardstick across, and muscular arms, with big hands.

He stopped and seemed to notice Odajeen's eyes. "Can I help?"

"I hope so, keeper. We'll be needing rooms, especially if there's a storm coming through."

"You're in luck, everywhere will be filling fast. Anyone that can make the city will be trying. I can do two rooms, all I have left."

Odajeen turned to Lani. "All right with you, lass?"

"Yes."

"Done then."

All Lani cared for right now was food and then talking to Odajeen. Having her in the same room would make that easier than having to bypass the brothers. She could see the two men talking quietly amongst themselves, but there wasn't much they could do. She wasn't sharing with one of them.

There'd be time if the storm really was as bad as they said. A day or two most likely. Lani just hoped that what was running out with the brooch could wait that long.

CARNUS

Why am I here?

Carnus stood in the middle of this strange city full of tall, dark buildings, watching the native Humaas people speeding down streets, rushing to finish their business. He had heard word that a large storm was approaching and it had everyone in a stew.

He had lived within the trees for so long, in tune with their natural flows, that weather did not bother him as it did these people. A storm was a storm, it would pass once it had blown through. What was more frightening for him was the building he watched.

It had been three days since he had arrived here, and still he couldn't approach it. A church was a church after all. Even if his people had rejected him, he still could not easily think about entering one.

Everything he believed was being challenged, started by the charity of the priest in Union. Nothing about the man had been challenging, he never even mentioned his religion to Carnus, except to name it, when asked.

They had fed him, and then the priest, as promised, had taken him to meet some merchants. Once the traders had seen him, he found himself in the middle of a frantic bidding war. The offers meant little to him, and he was grateful for the priest, who negotiated with him.

When it was all agreed, he had a room, meals, clothing and a sword, as well as work leaving on a caravan heading toward some city called Copia. At that point it mattered little to Carnus where he went. If he could not return to Ngahere, then any place was as good as another.

He'd only been paid for the leg of the journey south to that city, the merchant advising that if he didn't get the right cargo to bring back, or go elsewhere, then he'd not be needed. That didn't bother Carnus either, and the priest had made sure that what he received in payment was more than adequate for him to survive until he found another gig.

None of it meant anything much to Carnus. He rode with the caravan, and watched for any trouble, of which there was none. He felt like he had robbed the merchant, for he had done nothing and still received his money.

In Copia, he found a merchant with a longer journey. This caravan was made up by multiple merchants, and they were needing to cut through the Devor mountains and make for a place called Statiiv. He was warned it was a long ride, and he wasn't disappointed.

Day after day they rode, Carnus normally at the back ignoring anyone trying to make conversation. He did the task only for the money, and to take him away. He couldn't stop his mind thinking, but he didn't have to share it with anyone.

At night he often took the watch, rarely able to sleep more than a few hours. Near the town of Heke, wedged at the pass through the mountains, Carnus had spotted the outlanders. They were almost invisible, and would have been to most people, but for him, he could see them like outlines moving in the dark.

It was exactly the same as the night the Derks had entered the Tombs. The day that ended his life. There was a group of them resting in the shadow of a large outcrop from the mountains, using the shadow for cover. They had lit a small fire earlier right on the turn of the day, and he had spotted it just before they'd put it out.

While his caravan settled in and ate, he had snuck out and scoped the location where these men hid. It became obvious to him they weren't interested in the caravan. At a guess they were readying to head through the pass at night.

Carnus knew it was none of his business, if they weren't a danger to the caravan then he had no business there. It wasn't that easy though. Men just like these had changed the path of his life, and brought the woman into the Tombs.

Would they know where she is? Is that where they are going?

Not that it mattered whether they did or not. She had escaped and he was in exile. There was no way back for him, not even if he found the woman and took her back. The Queen had been resolute that if he returned he would be put to death.

And the seer, if he could believe anything from that strange man, had said his path was not backward. But Carnus wanted to go back, it was his life. He cared nothing for helping these weak people who were unable to defend themselves.

A warrior should be defending a purpose, not a paid bodyguard for men who traded things for profit.

But you aren't a warrior, are you?

Carnus hung his head, knowing it was true. Now he was simply a man from Ngahere who could fight. And that was all. His purpose now was to make enough money to eat.

The Derks had begun moving. They quickly mounted their horses and rode off toward the pass, now that all light was gone from the sky. Carnus made his way back to his camp and took up his watch again, knowing nothing would happen.

Either word had got out that this caravan had one like him guarding it, or simply these soft men worried for no reason, and there was no threat out here anyway. Throughout his watch he pondered what the Derks were doing.

Where were they going? Would he see them again? Where was that woman?

That was the most eventful thing that happened on their journey to Statiiv. He passed through more villages and towns than he had ever seen. Every day was something new to him, but none of it really mattered.

The merchant reluctantly settled up with him in Statiiv after trying to get him to return back the way they had come, but Carnus didn't think he could. It was only the fact that everything was new that prevented him descending into the gloom that lingered deep inside him.

It was in Statiiv that he heard the tale of the priestess from Ngahere. While on the road he ate by himself and avoided everyone, but in the cities and towns he ate in inns like everyone else. He didn't always get the chance to sit by himself; some would brave the scowls he would give them and sit across from him.

One man had been ripe with ale, and wouldn't stop talking.

"Not often your type show up here. Where you heading?"

Carnus was happy to say nothing. He didn't even look up.

"Like that, eh? Don't matter to me. Best thing is no one will bother me sitting next to you." He laughed to himself.

"Rare as amber you lot are. Last time I saw one of your type was down south near the lake. Strangest thing you ever did see, everyone always talking about her."

Carnus raised his eyes from his food.

"Oh, that caught your interest did it? Well what was even more interesting, she was a priestess."

"Where was this?"

"So you do talk?"

"Where?"

"Easy, pal. It was in Jarv, like I said, down by the lake."

"Where did you see her?"

"She was in the main square. She's always there, they say. Whenever there's anyone being sentenced or punished she's there. Tending to those in the stocks, or begging for mercy. She's one of them who follow that god."

"What god?"

"Seth, the Desert God, or that's what they call him. They are the seekers of justice, or something. That's all I know. Do I look like I spend a lot of time in a church?"

"When was this?"

"Month ago, easy. I worked a boat down and back. Easy a month, maybe more."

And now here he was, watching the building that was the church of Seth, in Jarv. He'd not seen any woman, entering or leaving. He'd seen no one going in at all. It appeared to be empty the whole time he had been there.

Now Carnus felt as if the story from the man in Statiiv was all designed to trick him, although he had no idea why.

This is pointless. Why would she even be here?

He headed off back toward what was known as the main square in the city. Word from the keeper in his accommodation was that there was a sentencing to happen today, so Carnus thought it was his best chance of finding her if the story was true. If not, he'd lost little. He was further away from Ngahere, and would find work here as easily as anywhere.

The square was the one bright part of the city, which didn't say much. With the swirling clouds and brewing storm there was still little light, but Carnus could imagine on a normal day how this square would be a relief from the darkness of the streets.

It was huge, and the buildings around it weren't as tall as the ones in the background. On the northern side, a large wooden platform was being prepared, with a caged wagon parked alongside. Guards surrounded it all and faced outwards to the meager crowd that had gathered.

Most of the city's residents were safely locked in their buildings, not even a sentencing interesting enough to bring them out into the weather.

In front of the platform a broad figure in a brown robe was talking to one of the guards. The guardsman noticed Carnus approaching across the shoulder of the robe and that person turned to look at what he saw.

Carnus stopped. It might have been years since he had seen her, but stood there, dressed in the simple robes, was his sister, Deenef. Her eyes showed her recognition and surprise.

"Sister," was all he could manage.

She said nothing, her eyes flickering side to side, as if she sought an escape from him.

He stopped and held his hands palm outwards to her. They were both Ngaherians, even if both in exile. She would understand. He offered no threat.

CARNUS

*U*p until the moment he had seen her, Carnus had no idea what he had hoped for. On seeing the fear in his sister's eyes, he knew this wasn't going to be a comfortable reunion. In truth he'd known that anyway, for up until recently he had tried to ignore she had even existed.

"I have work to do, leave me be."

"I would like to talk to you."

"You will have to wait, Carnus, today will be hard on me."

A bell rang on the platform and people began forming up on the platform. He turned away from Deenef and found a place to watch off to side of the square. She was right, it was a long day. The magistrates of the city argued about each case, allowing those who defended the accused to have their say.

Some of the punishments were enacted immediately. A separate area was guarded off from the small crowd and there the punishments that could be completed were carried out. Carnus was not squeamish, nor did he disagree with the harsh punishments some men needed to fix their ways.

Screams of pain followed the removing of hands or ears administered in that area. Each time he could see his sister appearing to be praying fervently. In almost every case she would speak on behalf of the accused. He didn't want to hear what it was she said, it didn't matter to him.

The weather degraded progressively through the day, and what light he'd celebrated in the square was long gone by the time everyone had been seen and punishments meted out. Deenef stood defiantly, staring at the stage, even when the majority of others had gone.

Carnus walked back over to her and waited until she was done.

"You're still here?"

"I am."

"What do you want, Carnus?"

"To talk."

"About what? We are not the same, once brother, neither your words nor your strength will take me from my path."

He wasn't surprised she thought he was here to bring her back to Ngahere, not that she'd be welcome. Perhaps her anger was because she knew if she did return, she would suffer a harsh punishment, not unlike what they'd witnessed today.

Deenef turned to face him. "I do wonder why now though."

"Why now?"

"Why, after all this time, you're here now?"

"Things aren't all that they seem, sister."

"Once sister, Carnus. You chose to abandon me as did our people. You cannot choose to undo that."

She bent over and began packing away her things.

"No doubt you probably enjoyed seeing the punishments dealt out today, oh great warrior."

He cringed at her words. She didn't know how they cut him more than blades could have.

"I take no joy in others' pain. If they broke the law, then they must pay the price."

"Always the follower of the rules, but do you ever question why?"

"Why what, Deenef?"

"Why those are the rules, who decided they were fairness, the correct justice."

"Such questions are not for one like me."

She let out a snide laugh. "Just a follower."

His sister slung the sack of her things over her shoulder, turned and began to walk across the square.

"Will you not talk to me?"

"Is that not what I have just been doing?"

Now Carnus remembered why he had always fought with his elder sister. She could infuriate a mosquito, or a gnat, such was her way. It seemed religion had not scrubbed that out of her.

A wind snapped its way across the square staggering even the two Ngaherians, such was its strength.

"Follow me. If you want to speak further you will have to do it where I work. It is time to get out of the weather, the storm is coming and it feels to be a big one."

Rain pelted Carnus as he followed her out of the square in a westerly direction. She said nothing more, just strode with the certainty of a Ngaherian. That also had not been diminished in her. They were a strong and proud people, and she carried her dignity even inside the robe of a priestess.

He had been walking with head down, avoiding the rain and wind, following the heels of her feet, and didn't see the yard she turned into. When he looked up he stopped in his tracks.

"A church. I cannot."

She turned from the landing at the top of the stairs to the doors. "Still hanging to your Path, I see."

"Why here? You know I cannot enter a church."

"What do I look like to you, Carnus? I am a priestess. I follow Seth's way, and give aid to those who need it in the name of justice. It is what I do. Where exactly did you think I live and work, if not in a church?"

Carnus stared downward, not wanting to tell her his own news, his own shame. He didn't think he could.

"Suit yourself, but this is where I will be. If you need to talk then in here is where it will be. Best of all, go back to where you're staying and do what you need to do before you go back to your home. Travel safe, Carnus."

He heard the door to the church open and then slam closed.

"I can't," was all he could say. He turned and walked back down the path to the road, looking about, trying to work out how far he was from his inn.

As it was, where he stayed was only several blocks across, back toward the center of the city. He stood opposite it, not wanting to be inside and confined by walls, nor the smells and sounds of people that would fill the building.

This was all new for him. He had never expected he would ever see Deenef again, and previously had not wanted to. By the Wooden Path, she was exiled and no longer part of the Ngaherian family. So he had cut her from his mind, mostly. Whenever he reflected on his past he could never not remember her, she had always been his elder sister.

But he had sought her out, and found her, but again his cowardice had come to the fore. He could not even tell her of his own shame, or enter a building that their Path rejected. What was he but a coward, able to take money to scare off would-be attackers but little more.

A woman came into view, stumbling along in the heavy gusts and bursts of rain. Not his sister, just some woman out on her own, walking the near-empty streets. He decided it was time to go inside and eat. The idea of being stuck in there for days when the storm hit did not appeal, but from what everyone said, you couldn't survive out in it.

Maybe that's my answer? Face the storm and get swept away!

Carnus shook his head. He knew he couldn't do that either.

The woman stopped across the roadway from him, terror in her eyes. Carnus didn't understand at first, then he struggled with what to do. He rushed across to her. She hadn't moved, and he could see her about to turn and run, but he reached her just in time.

She wasn't big like a Ngaherian woman, and he grabbed hold of her as easily this time as he had back in the Tombs.

"You!" They both said almost in unison.

"Let go of me!" She squirmed in his grip. "Help!"

"Stop!" He shook her vigorously and she stopped fighting him. "You, it's you who caused all of this."

"All of what?"

He couldn't tell her any more than he could tell his sister.

"What do you want with me? I've done nothing to you."

"Oi! What's going on here?"

Carnus turned to see two guards on their horses, closing in on them at a fast walk. He let go of the girl and turned to face them. "Nothing at all."

The woman looked at the guards, turned and ran off in the opposite direction. "I'm fine."

"Wait up!"

Neither of the guards chased after her, and Carnus could see they both had hands on weapons. "What was that all about?"

"I thought she was someone that had stolen something from me, is all."

"And was she?"

"No. I was mistaken."

"Then be on your way. You're not from here, but you should have heard, these storms aren't to be messed with. Get inside and stay in there if you've any wits about you."

The guards kicked their horses forward and passed him by. Carnus stood exactly where he was, looking at the door to his inn, but not going in. He wanted to pursue the woman, he wanted her to pay.

But he had no idea what that even meant. What sort of punishment could he give her that made sense? He didn't even know what he was thinking. Who was he to dish out punishment? He was no one, but he knew someone who might make sense of it.

Carnus turned and walked back to the church. His clothing was soaked through by the time he got there. He stood outside the doors of the church trying to will himself inside. Twice he raised his hand and went to grab the door handle.

Many times he turned and went to leave. But he was stuck here now, needing someone to help him. He had no idea who he was, what he was, or why he couldn't finish it. At least his father had been able to do that.

The door opened inward and his sister stood before him.

"For Seth's sake, you've either lost your mind or you're drunk but you can't stand there all night. If nothing else you'll scare away those seeking shelter. Get in here!"

Carnus looked into her eyes, and could see there was no fear there anymore. He was probably delusional but he thought he saw warmth, and right now he could do with that. He stepped forward through the door.

93

LANI

*L*ani had hoped that Odajeen would want to talk, but no sooner had they got into their room than the woman wanted to go and eat. Straight after the meal, the older woman had excused herself to go and sleep. It felt as if she was doing her best to avoid speaking about any of it to Lani.

Rather than disturb her, Lani chose to step outside and get some air, the main room of the inn felt too crowded for her. She could see it would likely be the last time in several days before she could do this as already the rain was coming heavier and the wind kept building.

She had mindlessly wandered down a road before swapping across to another and heading back the way she had come, keeping her inn close at hand. Lani had no care to look around the city, especially with night upon them and the weather as it was.

Almost every building she went past was shuttered and boarded closed, with limited light anywhere. It was her ability to see in dark places that allowed her to just wander without too much attention. She should have cared more, and when she did look up and saw the huge man, her heart almost stopped.

Perhaps it was just a trick of her mind, but he looked like the man who had been in the forest near Callet. Maybe she was just generalizing; she hadn't seen many Ngaherian men, so they probably all looked the same to her.

Until she saw the recognition in his eyes. He was no stranger, it was the same man. She'd turned to run, but he was quick, much quicker than his size would suggest. Everything felt like it was repeating — the darkness, the hand grabbing her across the shoulder, his strength, and her inability to free herself.

Then she heard the sound of horses and another man's voice. City guards were approaching and calling out to them. As soon as she felt his hand let go of her, she did what she had the time before, and ran.

Someone called out behind her, but Lani never looked back, not until she was several roads away and tucked into a dark alley. She could hardly breathe from running so hard, and her heart pounded in her chest. She dared peek back down the road she had just left, and saw no one there.

What luck!

Luck to have escaped but no luck to come across the Ngaherian. What was he doing here in Jarv? It felt like her life was repeating. Someone else following her, seeking to catch her for something not of her doing.

Lani had no idea why he would even want to find her. She had done nothing to harm him, simply run away. Any fool could see she was a prisoner of the Derks that had taken her into the forest. The seer had told her they were all gone, so what in Thenis's name was he doing?

When her breath settled, Lani realized that he probably wasn't after her at all. It was just a chance occurrence, to have crossed paths, again. Except the idea of chance seemed an odd thing to her now. Too many events had happened that didn't seem just chance. Like meeting Odajeen.

The sound of a thunder clap across the lake brought Lani back to the present. She retraced her steps in her mind, using images of where she'd been walking before. If she was right her inn was only a road away, and with the cover of the dark she should be fine to get back there.

In the safety of her room, Lani changed into dry clothes and hung her wet items across the back of the chair. She sat on her bed listening to the approaching storm, rain pelting against the shutters, and the breathing of her room mate.

On the second day cooped up in the room, with an unbelievable storm pounding the city outside, Odajeen finally chose to talk.

"I needed time, Lani. What I learned was not an easy thing to face."

"Of course."

"Who are you, Lani? What does all of this have to do with you? You are not one of them."

"I wish I could tell you, Odajeen."

Lani had already decided she would share more of her story with the woman. Every time she'd tried to handle everything herself she'd ended up worse off. Maybe this blind woman, who had also had memories blocked, was there to help her. The only way to find out was to trust her some more, and see what happened.

"If what has happened since I met you had not occurred, I am not sure I would believe you, young woman. But how can I not? You truly are something."

"What do you mean?"

"Do you not see what you have survived? One such a thing would have been too much for many to cope with. And yet here you are, saddled with a burden you did not ask for, far from your home, and still you push on."

Lani shrugged. To her it had only been one day at a time, she'd not chosen to be anything more than just alive. To survive. And so far she'd been able to.

The shutters rattled violently against the outside of the building and squealing wind forced its way through tiny gaps wherever it could. Lani shivered and wrapped her blanket tighter around her shoulders as they sat across from each other on their beds.

"Can I ask something?"

"Yes."

"You mentioned a mask, or the like. Can I feel it?"

Lani thought it a strange request, until she remembered that this was how the woman saw things. Through her fingers. She couldn't see any harm in it, and fetched it from her bag, placing the black wooden face into Odajeen's hands.

There was silence while the woman ran her fingers over it carefully, repeating her movements many times. Then she lifted her head.

"I knew this man, the face I have felt before. It is different carved from wood like this, but it is the same. Somewhere in here," she tapped the side of her head, "there is his name, but I cannot find it."

"Ashantha."

"Ashantha! Yes. Thank you, Lani."

A smile rested on the woman's face. Again she was quiet for a time.

"Now I remember him, the sound of his voice. And I miss him now, for he is gone. He was a good man, and it was him that put you on this path?"

"It was. Although he wasn't honest with me."

"He is not one to be trivial with such a thing. While I understand your anger at him, I sense it would have been for good reason. Let me think for a while, Lani. Every time I remember something it brings with it many more. I need to review them."

Lani took the mask back and propped herself up on the bed, facing the door. An idea formed in her mind as she held the mask. Something she'd had no time to consider before, and with Odajeen unable to see her, she was safe to do it.

She took Ashantha's journal out of her satchel, and then slowly brought the mask up to her face. As she pushed it on, she heard the click and felt the cool wash over her. Everything shifted as she became him.

Again like the last time she was still able to access the words in the journal despite the external damage, and this time she flicked through it looking for Odajeen in it. She couldn't find that name, no matter how she tried to spell it.

Back and forth she scanned, but could not find the woman's name.

What if her name was different? If her mind was blocked wouldn't she need a new name as well?

Instead of searching for a name, she looked for notes about what might have happened. Surely he, Ashantha, would have written something about an event so significant to them as this. Guessing how long ago it might have been, she hunted and hunted.

And then she found it, his notes about a woman called Burgendetta. Not only was she one of them, but she was the woman known as Mother, or in her time. Their leader, in charge of him and his kind. The words he wrote, and the feelings about her and what had happened, were strong.

Just as she felt about him, Ashantha had been fond of her, they had been close. He had been young when it happened, and it had caused him much turmoil. He provided a lot of detail. She had gone off to the north, which turned out to be Malamig, on later pages.

She was following the trail of a mass killing event, that had some significance, although Ashantha didn't write what that was. This Burgendetta, Odajeen, had reached a large town, and found someone who was being protected, a girl.

In the town she came across a man hunting this girl, whom she had killed. Not by her own hand but by getting another to do it, and in doing so she had sealed her fate.

Ashantha had written that she made a deliberate choice to do it. He discovered her after a Jester's coin found its way into his hands. Using the Void he had sought each of his colleagues and learned that Burgendetta was missing.

He had written of his anguish when he found her, and that both her sight and memory had been taken from her. She didn't know him, and was lost to their group. He couldn't leave her on her own, or at least not until she was able to fend for herself.

She refused to come with him to be cared for in Anderwell, and in the end he had to leave her to her own future. Before he did he had found a note in her belongings. Reading it had hurt as much as seeing her as she now was.

~

THERE WAS A SURVIVOR FROM THE RAMAR KILLINGS. I COULDN'T LET ONE of their hunters find her. I had to do this, for her safety. The blue stone marks her. I chose to do it.

WHEN SHE PULLED THE MASK FREE, LANI FOUND HERSELF HARDLY breathing. Her skin was cold and she stared at the old woman across the room from her.

"What is it, Lani?"

Tears ran down the Lani's face. This woman had been talking about her.

94

LANI

The room closed in on Lani. She wanted to step outside and think through what she'd just learned, what she knew about Odajeen, but she couldn't move. Things began to spin before her eyes and she had to plant her hands firmly on the bed to stay upright.

Breathe!

"Lani? Lani, are you okay?"

"Yes. I need a moment."

Lani closed her eyes and just let everything settle down. It took some time, and as soon as she felt a little better and what she had just learned came back into mind, she struggled again.

By the time she could control it, she could see Odajeen was sitting looking in her direction, concern on her face. Could she tell the woman? It was probably a step too far, she'd had a hard enough time facing her past as it was.

"Are you truly okay, girl? Things felt mighty strange in here before."

"What do you mean?"

"I could have sworn someone else was in the room, and you had gone."

"Oh." Lani was aware that without her eyes the woman relied on her other senses much more. "I am here, it's all okay."

"But something did happen, correct?"

Lani still couldn't decide what to tell her. The last thing she wanted was to cause her more pain. Was she aware even of what the 'bad' thing was she had done?

"You said you did something bad, which is why they locked your mind, Odajeen?"

"Yes," the older woman said quietly.

"What was it?"

Now it was Odajeen who was quiet. Lani didn't push her, but depending on how the woman answered would determine how much else she revealed to her.

"I killed someone. There, it's out!"

Her shoulders seemed to straighten up, as if she'd been carrying it like a weight.

"What happened?"

"I have very vague memories of it, but that is the one thing we were not allowed to do. We were only allowed to kill in self-defense, there was no other choice. Nor can we direct someone else to do it, that would be akin to doing it ourselves. Because of what I did, is why this happened to me."

She shook her head and leaned forward as if staring at the floor.

"I do not know why, or who, I killed. It is what has been eating at me since I learned all of these things. The not knowing is worse than knowing nothing at all. I cannot stand now to have missing parts to my memory."

"I know."

"What?"

"I know what you did."

Her response was harsh. "What are you talking about, girl? How could you know?"

Lani told her about the mask, and what she could do with it. When she revealed it to Odajeen the woman gasped out loud. By the time she was finished, tears were streaming down both of their faces.

"It was me, Odajeen, me, that's who you were protecting. It has to be. The blue stone, why you can see it. It all makes sense."

"So it seems."

"What do you mean?"

"It does seem to make sense, Lani, but I'm loath to jump to conclusions. It feels true, I will tell you that, but it hasn't unlocked that in my mind. Although I can glimpse a view of the blue stone in my memories. It was there."

"It has to be. You… you did what you did to protect me. I don't know why, but you did. Thank you."

Odajeen, or Burgendetta, just sat there, speechless. She was processing again. Lani could understand that.

"I cannot find an answer inside me, Lani, but I do not believe such a coincidence would happen without reason. That thing inside me that compels me, brought us together, *that* I am certain of. Such a thing is important to be aware of. When things appear like coincidence or a copy of what came before, they are the things I have learned to take much notice of."

Her words brought back the events of earlier. She told Odajeen about the warrior.

"Exactly like that. It was not by chance that someone like you met him again. Too many things are happening around you for it to be random chance. He was drawn here, like I was to you."

"But why?"

"That is not something I can answer, Lani."

"This is driving me mad!"

"What?"

"Not knowing. Not knowing why these things are happening to me. Why me? I didn't ask for any of this, nor do I want it."

"So you want to have a pity party to celebrate poor little Lani, is that it?"

Lani laughed, a much-needed break from the tension that filled the room. "No, crazy old woman."

Odajeen laughed back. "Then don't speak as if you do. There are some things you can control and there are those you cannot. Whether or not you asked for this, it is yours now. And no one else can do it. Or they would have been given the task."

"You seem quite certain."

"I told you before, there is that which others could not have done and you have done them. But it's not over. You were given a task, and it seems this feeling of woe you're wearing like a cloak is holding you back. Making you doubt yourself."

"What are you telling me to do?"

"I'm not telling you to do anything. I do not qualify to be such a person, after what I did."

"But you did it for good!"

"So you say, but who chooses what is good? Me? This compulsion? What if I'm just making that up in my mind?"

"What about the gods?"

"If it's them that punished me for this, why would they get me to do the very thing that requires such a result?"

"A sacrifice you mean?"

"Indeed. So you think they may require such a thing from me, but poor little Lani can just go where she likes, can do as she pleases."

"But...I don't know. I am no one."

"That's where you are most wrong. Did you not hear me? All of this, everything with me, with you, with this Ngaherian, it is because of you. Without you it doesn't happen."

Lani felt the weight of Odajeen's words hit her in her chest. Her heart felt squeezed and a headache formed in her head. She still couldn't believe it was her that this was all about, even if what the woman said seemed to make sense.

"What now then?"

"You need to choose."

"Choose what?"

"Choose between whatever it is you're wavering about. You wouldn't be asking me if you were sure about what you should be doing. I can't choose for you."

"You sound like the silly old man in Union."

"Who?"

"The seer I told you about."

"Maybe I'm not so ignorant after all."

"Why do you say that?"

"They are called The Eyes for a reason. What they see is true. What did he say?"

"That in everything in life we have a choice, and I need to actively make my choices, not just let them happen."

"Uh huh."

"What does me seeing the man mean though? It's not related to my choice about Anderwell."

"Everything is related, one way or another. It might not be directly, but one way or another he will be in your future. Your paths will cross, or he would not have appeared like he did. Whether it is connected to this choice, that is not for me to know."

"You're no help."

"What is it that you need to choose, Lani? That is what you're avoiding."

She sat there looking at Odajeen. That was the question wasn't it? She'd continued on her way, letting events happen, not actually choosing what it was she was doing. Even if by default she was choosing. She was so close to Anderwell now.

That was the choice, her ultimate choice. She'd avoided it for much of the journey here. It had become her assumed destination, the place Ashantha has told her she needed to come to, but all along she hadn't truly bought into it.

Lani had just run from thing to thing, avoiding that which she could, or running from what frightened her. She could see that actually getting there frightened her just as much, and she wasn't fully sure why.

Odajeen said it was because she was something unique. But inside she didn't feel special, she was afraid. She had nowhere to go back to, she was alone, and hardly wiser to what she had learned. The clues about her parents were just that — tiny clues but no answers. Instead she'd ended up following someone else's directions but to what end? And did it matter anymore? She was almost there anyway, she might as well complete it.

Or?

What were the choices the seer told her she had to make, or

Odajeen? Or herself, that's what this was about. Could she do it? Did she really want to know the answers? She got angry at not knowing, but that was easy.

Now she could see it was much harder to actually choose to do it. Up until now, she was able to put the decision off. Maybe she still could, at least until she was even closer, except for what had happened. Odajeen was challenging her, pushing Lani to challenge herself.

She did have a choice. But could she make it?

"Do you not know, girl?"

"I know. I choose to go to Anderwell, and find out what in Seth's name is going on."

"Perhaps you choose a good name to swear that under. If any god might help, perhaps he will. If you're going, girl, I'm coming with you. If you'll have me?"

"Of course. Are you sure?"

"I am. We'll just have to wait this cursed storm out."

95

CARNUS

The church was dry, and warm, and Carnus was not the only one in there taking shelter from the storm. His sister left him in the care of others, who gave him a cloth to dry himself and directed him to food and somewhere he could use for sleeping.

At least a hundred people were within the main hall of the church, finding nooks or pews to make their own. Some in small groups, others like him on their own. He had never thought about those who had nowhere to live in bad weather.

Ultimately he rarely thought about anyone other than those he had lived with. Since he had left Union, it was as if he was a youngster learning about a new world. Every day he saw something that made him review what he knew of the world.

Carnus's world had been small, and insular. It still hurt him deep inside when he thought of what had happened, the loss of his place, who he was. And here he was, mixed in with those of no consequence, those who survived only at the mercy of others.

Except he could have returned to his inn. He did have that choice, and he had some money, even if it was from easy work. He was different from these people. At least he had that.

By morning, Carnus was edgy. Sitting around doing nothing, trapped inside by the storm outside, made him feel like a caged animal. He wanted to be out of it, the smells irked him, and the noise as well. If he could speak with Deenef, he'd probably take his chances to get back to his inn, but until then he had to bear it.

Later that morning, she approached him. "Come with me."

He followed and she took him up to the front of the hall, where the stage and lectern were. Carnus struggled to think of her standing there, speaking to a room full of people.

"Do you use this?" He pointed to the lectern.

She laughed. "No, Carnus. I'm too low in the order to be one who preaches for such an audience. My work is to help, and speak for those who cannot."

"Oh."

"Why did you come here, once brother?"

"I don't like it when you call me that."

"But is it not true that for you, a proud Ngaherian warrior, I am no longer your sister?"

He knew he had to tell her. It was the very reason he was back, Carnus needed help to understand his life now, his shame. But his mouth would not work, he couldn't say it.

"What is it? I can see you want to answer me. Are you afraid?"

It was if she knew that he hurt and she was poking a hot stick into it. Was that what her role really was? Is that the justice she fought for, to make those in pain suffer?

"I thought you wanted to talk, but if you have nothing to say, then let me go about my work. You're welcome to ride out the storm here, but I ask of you, when it's run its course, to leave me be. I will not be coming back there with you."

She turned to leave him.

"I am not."

Deenef turned back to him. "You are not what?"

"I am not a Nagherian."

She laughed. "What in Seth's name are you talking about, once brother?"

"I am an exile."

To Carnus he thought the whole church went silent, even the noise from outside. All he could hear was the breath in his nose, and the beat of his heart. Her eyes opened wide.

"You are what?"

"I said it once, don't make me say it again."

"For what, for how long?"

"Forever. I can never go back, on pain of death. Which might be better than this."

"Better than what?"

"Better than being no one."

"No one? Is that what you think?"

He looked at his feet. Maybe he had been wrong to come here, to tell her. Sharing his shame didn't make him feel any better.

"Sit, Carnus."

She sat and waited for him to do the same.

"So that look in your eye now makes sense. I thought it was you seeking me, the shame of what I am, but it is you that is ashamed. Am I right?"

He couldn't answer.

"What happened?"

Carnus told her the story. Once he had begun he ended up telling her everything, including what had happened in the street and finding the woman again.

"Ah, so there's more at play here than just your shame."

"What do you mean?"

"Such things, brother." He looked at her, startled. "You are my brother, Carnus, and now, without the shackles of the Wooden Path, you might see me for who I am, not the who I once was. Such things as seeing this woman again are not chance."

She looked around the church, and swept her right hand over the view. "I'm here because it's what I am meant to be doing. For years I fought that inside me. I was torn inside, between what they told me I should be and what I knew I was. It was not easy to leave, knowing that they would judge you as well for what I did, but then that was not of my making. I was born there, but my needs were not met there. This work, this makes me sing, inside. And I matter here, I make a difference."

"It looks like a hard way to live."

"Was it not hard living in the Tombs? Everything can be hard or easy, Carnus. It isn't the thing you do that makes it hard or not. It's how you choose to think about it. To me this is the easiest thing I could be doing."

He had never thought much about what his elder sister was, outside of the label he and others had given her. He struggled to think even so much of who she had been when they were younger. But here he could see what she was and how wise she was.

"I am lost."

"No, brother, you are not lost. If you were lost you would not be here. You are seeking answers that before you have never sought to ask for."

"What answers?"

"What you stand for. Who you are. What you will do. These are deep questions that matter. Before, they were answered by others, you did their will."

"How do I get the answers?"

"You don't get the answers. You choose them."

He actually laughed, something he couldn't remember doing since he was a child.

"What's so funny?" Deenef looked confused.

"You sound just like the seer I told you of."

"How?" She had a small smile on her face now, and he liked how she wore it. He couldn't remember her smiling before.

"He kept telling me that I had to make choices. Everything was a choice. And that I would need to choose what path I took."

"I am still shocked you went to a seer, not that we have anything to do with their kind."

"You sound like you have rules of your own. How is that so different from our homeland?"

"Not my homeland, Carnus. Perhaps you're right, I must reflect on what you say. Rules are rules wherever they exist. I must think about those here which have no grounds to them."

"Besides, I didn't go to him, I was taken to him. He told me something else, I just remembered."

"What was that?"

Carnus wanted to get the words right in his head. They mattered. "Two women you want to find. One will free you from your shame, the other will not."

Deenef laughed this time. It lightened his mood.

"Well, I do not know if it is I that will free you from your shame, brother, but two women you have found."

"I did not set out to find you or her."

"Maybe not directly, but you did, or you would not be here. Nor would you and her have crossed paths. Let me tell you a story."

She told him of what had helped her decide to take up the way of Seth.

"I saw the strange man sitting beside the road several times. Each time I smiled, and he smiled back. One day I had a strong feeling that I had to stop. I spoke to him and it was as if someone put a whole new head on my shoulders. Everything looked differently."

"And?"

"And, when I thought back, I had seen this man years before. Every so often when I was at a certain point in my internal conflict he would appear, almost as if by magic. From that point forward I decided I would not ignore repeating things, or what seemed coincidence."

"Ah."

"Nor should you. If you seek answers, follow that path. Each thing will be like the next stepping stone to where you need to be. That is a choice you can make. What?"

Carnus had grinned when she'd said it.

"Another thing the man with no eyes said was about stepping stones and paths."

"Repeating things, Carnus. It is your choice. I know you are here seeking answers, more than this, but all I can say is don't ignore things that repeat."

"So I should seek out this woman?"

"Perhaps a little more delicately than you did."

They both smiled. Carnus felt quite different. None of this was what he had expected, but sitting here, with his sister, was something he had never foreseen. He could have lived his whole life and missed out on this.

He was glad that had not happened.

TILLANDRA

The gleaming walls of Watersend beckoned their fast-moving party. As the sun dropped to their left threatening to leave them in complete darkness, they pushed their mounts as hard as they would go— not that camels responded to their direction in any particular way.

With horses you knew what they responded to and what their feelings were toward what was being asked of them. Camels were something different altogether. The last time she had ridden them was not fully two months ago.

How is it only that long?

When she had pushed herself last time to get to see Tingfurlew, she had no idea that she would be returning so soon. Nor that the stakes would be just as high, or higher.

Every mile they covered gave her hope they would be inside the walls tonight. While she wanted to be away immediately, arriving at night meant it was safer to sleep here and leave at first light. Tillandra felt sorry for Peka; the lad had been cooped up on her chest for the last ten days, with little chance to crawl around or be a child.

He never seemed to complain though. Her biggest problem was he wouldn't leave her side without screaming. That was going to create complications she could do without. The plan was that she would leave him in Watersend while she traveled to Midderbuilt, and collect him on the way back, unless Gimbden could find a way to safely get him to Anderwell.

They'd discussed the options, and she knew that ultimately it would need to be her that carried him there, but she had hoped for an alternative. Not that she wanted rid of him, in fact she had become used to having his body tucked against hers.

She had felt feelings that she had never expected to. Not a desire for her own, but a connection that felt comfortable.

Maybe I need to spend more time being an aunty to the orphans back home.

Shaking her head, she kept her focus on her balance and their destination. There were six in their small group. It was as many of the animals that could be spared for this leg of the journey. The teamsters had split their team into two.

When they reached Watersend they would take the second group north to Midderbuilt, allowing this team a rest. Tillandra thought they could trot constantly the way they ran, nothing seemed to bother them, and even after a full day being ridden when they stopped each night, they still appeared to be fresh.

The speed difference they made traveling over the sand, compared to horses, was significant. It was a major advantage they had over the knights from Daskare.

As they approached the southeastern gate Tillandra felt herself relax a little bit, and sighed deeply. Despite having the companion guards, Gimbden and the teamster with her still she had worried about running into more knights that might have skirted the border patrols.

Over the previous days she had been ruminating on the many options to get King Ahn to pull back from whatever it was his soldiers were planning. Tillandra still struggled to believe they would actually try to take Watersend. Yet she'd passed through the massive gathering of soldiers, and they weren't there for a change of scenery. At this point she didn't have any answers, or none that were a clear best option.

Despite them being alert enough to the threat to get their own troops in position, she was rightly anxious about the military might

King Ahn had. He was weeks or months ahead in his preparations, whatever he planned. They, on the other hand, were behind on that, and needed many more troops in position to shore up their defenses. It would take time to get them all there.

Why was she even having to consider fighting? Previous Mothers had successfully managed things without force. Had she failed? Was it her fault that things were this precarious?

It bothered her even though she knew logically that argument didn't hold water. She had managed their society in exactly the same way as Ninarto, her predecessor, it was the world around them that had begun to change.

Everything appeared to have happened so suddenly. But had it? Tillandra stewed over any signals she might have missed. Was it her failure that all of this had occurred? She still couldn't shake the guilt about Ashantha, no matter how far she traveled, or distracted she was.

His death was tied directly to the mission she had sent him on. Her logical thoughts argued with her feelings, until she was exhausted. She knew that without him going to Enderk, they would have even less knowledge than they did now. There wouldn't be this girl wearing his ring and she would never have learned what she had from Tingfurlew.

"What's wrong, Mother?" Gimbden had ridden alongside her.

"Sorry?"

"You were shaking your head and have a very worried face."

"Sorry, Gimbden, just so many things on my mind, but nothing specific," she lied.

"I'll be glad to stand on the ground and take a bath."

"Me also. I am so grateful for everything you've done; I can't imagine what might have gone wrong if you hadn't been there to help."

He shrugged, the cheeky look on his face almost made her laugh. "It's what we are here to do, right?"

"Indeed."

"Besides, this was easy, except for dealing with these foul beasts." He patted the back of his camel as he complained.

"I'd rather them than horses. Let's get to the inn, that's where we're going isn't it?"

"Yes, it is. I warned Wessen before I left, although he wouldn't know about Peka. What's your plan with him?"

Tillandra looked down affectionately at the bundle asleep on her chest. "We'll discuss that later."

"Understood."

It didn't matter that he couldn't hear them, Tillandra was still conscious about him feeding off their emotions.

The city gates were closed when they slowed to a halt outside them. It was early evening now and the torches were burning on the tops of the walls. Gimbden signaled to the teamster who made his camel drop to its knees. He clambered off and walked to the locked door set into the gates.

Tillandra couldn't hear what was being said but could tell Gimbden's voice had risen and there was a terse discussion happening with someone on the inside. At one point Gimbden banged the palm of his right hand on the door.

It took another ten minutes or more before the door opened and Gimbden stepped back, letting three guards through. From her position on the camel, Tillandra thought it looked like the captain of the guards, Orgeth.

Everyone looked a little tense before Orgeth looked up at her. She nodded at him and suddenly everything moved quickly. He began directing his men and called out for the gates to be opened, his voice notably loud enough to carry to her.

She made a point of greeting him as they rode through the partially opened main gates, thanking him for coming out at night.

"Not at all, Mother. Everyone was a little surprised is all."

"Of course, Orgeth, and for good reason. Don't admonish your men, they did the right thing, and more than you know right now. We will speak, if not before I head north, then when I get back."

He dipped his head as they hurried past.

The slow trot to The Clown Prince seemed to take longer than any part of the previous day's riding. Knowing they were almost there tricked the mind that way. You could let hours upon hours blur into the background, but when you knew you only had a short distance to go, every second of it seemed painfully slow.

Word had clearly been sent ahead. Wessen stood out front of The Clown Prince, wearing a dark apron and with his hands on his hips as if set to tell off one of his workers.

When Tillandra was finally down from her camel he hurried over and wrapped his arm around her, stopping suddenly when he felt the lump between them.

"What on Dharatan?"

Peka had woken and was looking up at the man.

"His name is Peka."

"But...what on... I mean."

She laughed at the man unable to finish what he was saying. "Well, that is a first, Wessen. You speechless."

He scowled at her. "I'm guessing there is a good story behind you being back here so quickly. Let's get you all inside and cleaned up. Stories can come after food, drink and most definitely baths."

He turned, patting his broad stomach with both hands, and headed back toward the front door of the inn.

Tillandra took another deep breath, exhaling slowly and letting a little more tension drop from her shoulders.

It's good to be back, Wessen. You don't know how much.

TILLANDRA

This time there was no threat of being followed, only the Audition deadline Tillandra was chasing. In the end she couldn't stomach Peka's reaction to her trying to leave him and brought him with her. She wished she could speak with him, as it seemed he was adamant to be with her.

And to get his impressions of what he was seeing. The boy had been fascinated by the Spire of Sand once they were close enough to Midderbuilt to see it.

Even though he couldn't hear, Tillandra had begun talking to him as if he could. She would explain the world around him. It felt the right thing to do, not that she could explain why. Sometimes she found herself talking to him like others spoke to their pets, a being to help talk through what was bothering you.

It wasn't that she thought of him as a pet, and she knew he was far too young to hold a proper conversation, but the companionship was oddly comforting to her. She had never thought of having children. She had never wanted to bring anyone into the world that might suffer what she had, despite the safety of Anderwell and their world.

Maybe it was also from how she felt about herself. Tillandra knew she wasn't attractive; even without the distortion to her face, she couldn't imagine anyone wanting to mate with her, nor partner her.

Those types of thoughts rarely surfaced, and she had to shuffle her feet and shake out her body as a physical way to change her thinking. She said goodbye to the teamster and the other guide and walked toward the ledge road that would take her up to the town.

After so much time on camels, stretching her legs out felt good. Her upper back ached, and was tight from carrying the sling with Peka in it, but there was little she could do about that now. And he wasn't much trouble. Despite everything the pair of them had been through he had made little noise, or complaint.

It was only when she had tried to leave him behind in Watersend that he had made a scene. He might not have been able to hear in the normal sense, but he understood full well what was happening. At one point he turned to her, and his green eyes stared at her with such pain and indignation that Tillandra couldn't bear it.

They had tried several of the older women who had grandmothered plenty of little ones, men, and other children, but he would have nothing to do with any of them. And so, here she was, climbing the steep ledge road that switched back and forth toward the gate to Midderbuilt, with a young boy on her chest.

She marveled out loud at the people who must have cut the road into the side of the mountain and how much work it would have taken, but Peka stared upward, always looking to catch glimpses of the spinning Spire of Sand.

After arriving in the middle afternoon, she hadn't lingered in Traveler's Rest. There was no time to waste. Once she got up to the Midderbuilt gate she stopped to look back out across the desert. The sun was almost completely gone behind her, dropping west below the range she stood on.

A shadow spread out left and right from the base of the mountain range and was creeping eastward, the colors of the sands changing as it hauled them in. Soon the darkness would take it all, all the way to the horizon.

Taking a big breath she turned, smiling, and headed toward the house cut into the base of the spire.

I wonder what sort of mood he'll be in today?

At his door she raised the orb of stone in the brass knocker and swung it down to crack against the wooden door. Peka jumped in surprise, which confused her. Surely he couldn't hear anything? Perhaps it vibrated through her arm and into her body.

He must have felt that.

Tillandra waited, more than she expected to, but she knew Tingfurlew would come when he was good and ready. But there was no voice yelling to wait, and he never came to answer the door.

She waited a few minutes before trying the door knocker again, a little harder, and longer. Still he didn't come, and that concerned her. In all her plans none of them had factored in Ting not being here. He'd always been here when she came.

On her last visit, when he explained the history of how he came to be there, he had told her how he was unable to leave the town. Not even a little. Whatever magic granted him his power to make the rings, bound him to Midderbuilt as well.

He had never seemed a particularly social person. He would be best described as prickly, but to Tillandra she accepted him as he was. She doubted he had many friends at all. Not that she'd ever taken the time to ever get to know anything else about him.

When she came here it was always to get something or to recharge the stone. Afterward, she always left quickly, although on reflection he often was the one hurrying her out the door once their business was complete.

She tried the door handle but while it turned, the door had been locked and without the key, she wasn't getting in. A final time she tried the knocker and listened, even resorting to calling out his name. He never came to the door, and she could hear no sounds coming from within.

Picking the lock crossed her mind, except she assumed that with Tingfurlew being the craftsmen that he was, the lock would probably be a custom piece that only he could get past. And with the way the rules of Midderbuilt were, anyone that crossed them usually lost their pass to the city.

Tillandra walked around the side of his workshop–cum-house. The back was the edge of the mountain and there was no getting around there. On the two sides what few windows that existed were high up under the eaves and so small she wasn't even sure Peka could get through them.

She walked back to the front door and fruitlessly banged several more times on the knocker before giving up. Tillandra headed up the hill toward the guest house that she usually stayed in. Maybe he was up there. She banged on that again to no answer, but surprisingly the door was unlocked, unlike on her usual visits.

She peered in, to make sure it was empty, before going in and closing the door. The day was mostly gone anyway and she was tired. She and Peka could do without food, they'd had small things on the journey and as it was she felt sleep was more important.

Peka seemed very happy as she placed him on the bed, as if he too could feel the hum that she sensed as she sat down. He clapped and bounced on the bed and a sound not dissimilar to the feeling she got of the hum came from his mouth.

He moved to the edge of the bed, and Tillandra hurried to stop him falling, but he turned and slipped himself down carefully, before crawling over to the hidden doorway. She watched him and was surprised at how he could sense exactly the right spot.

Peka turned to look at her, and if his eyes could speak, she knew what he was saying. He wanted to go in, that was as plain as she was tall. Half of her wanted to lie down, go to sleep and wake up to find Tingfurlew back in his home. The other half was intrigued by Peka's reaction, and she knew visiting the stone would be worth it.

She placed her things on the bed, barred the door, then dragged the bed back over to blockade the door further, but mostly to allow the hidden room door to open. Picking up Peka, she wondered how she could open the door without the Mother Stone from Anderwell.

The only time she had been here that had been the key for her. Using one hand then the other she placed them on the door, feeing the vibration of the Citadel Stone and the mountain but nothing seemed to do what the Mother Stone did. Shaking her head in frustration, she was about to give up when Peka stuck out his little right hand.

He was too far from the wall to reach it and, intrigued, Tillandra moved closer. His tiny hand touched the door, in exactly the spot she usually touched the Mother Stone to it. There was the smallest indent there and his hand fit into it perfectly, something her hand couldn't do.

The click almost caused her to drop him. While she knew something was happening, she hadn't actually expected the door to open. She pulled it open and started walking down the long dark corridor.

TILLANDRA

The corridor was dark, an under-the-ground, inside-a-mountain kind of dark. No light eked its way from the guest house and there was none ahead either.

Tillandra walked as straight as her mind would let her, occasionally bumping off either wall when her distorted sense of location misled her. She knew once she had walked for long enough the light from the Citadel Stone would become visible, but how long that would take she could never tell.

On her last visit she had been in here for two whole days. She couldn't let that happen this time around, she needed every day she had. If it hadn't been for Peka being able to open the door, she doubted she would have come at all.

Her main concern was finding Tingfurlew. He had always been inside his home when she had come before, and him not being there left her on uncertain ground.

Without a new ring they couldn't run an Audition, and if that wasn't done on time and a new Jester chosen, they would be permanently one member less. It was always a strange time elevating a Prospect, who went from being part of the college to one of their Court.

They would bring new skills which hopefully might help her with the dangers posed to them. Perhaps they'd be suitable to plant in Daskare near King Ahn. Maybe that was the way to pull him back from whatever he had planned.

And this mysterious amulet that Lani was carrying, Tillandra needed that in Anderwell. They needed to keep it safe, and find out what they could about her.

She almost tripped over her own feet, it was so dark.

Concentrate, Tillandra.

Without the sling, her arms tired much more quickly from carrying Peka, and she was constantly having to move him around to ease her muscles and take a break from each position. He wanted to be forward facing as well, which limited the number of ways she could carry him.

If she turned him to drape on her shoulder, he promptly wriggled around until he had twisted enough to look forward, expectantly. She could hear him humming quietly in the back of his throat. He rarely made vocal sounds, but this was perfectly in sync with the hum from the Citadel Stone.

Tillandra had never really thought much about the hum, but the more she let it sink in, the more she could hear the musical tone to it. There was a vibration that seemed to fuel her energy the closer she got to matching the tune of it. That was the only word she could connect to it, a tune.

When she got in tune with it, everything changed. Now she understood what happened when she meditated here while the Mother Stone recharged. Her body instinctively got in tune with that resonance. As she let herself become one with it, her arms lost their tiredness but more importantly it was that which allowed her to see.

She had always thought it was the light of the stone, but she was still not able to see the stone, she could only feel it. The corridor suddenly seemed much wider, and she was able to reach her full stride.

When they did eventually reach the main cavern where the Citadel Stone resided, she felt wet on her hands. Looking down she could see Peka crying. He seemed happy enough and tears of bliss rolled down his cheeks as he stared at the stone.

He squirmed in her arms and Tillandra placed him on the ground. He stood, shakily, and waddled toward the stone. Every time he looked like he would topple, Tillandra was braced to rush over to him protectively.

His tiny arms reached out for the stone, and he tried to embrace it, his face pressed sideways against the shining surface. Tillandra could see a light seem to embrace and wrap him back in return, and she felt tears of her own roll down her cheeks.

"You are back much quicker than usual, Tillandra."

The voice took her by surprise. She looked around for the image of the woman that had come to her from the Citadel Stone last time, but she saw no one.

"There is no need to see me to be able to speak with me. All you have to do is connect with the stone and I can hear you."

"I am not here to recharge the Mother Stone, but to collect a new ring."

"Yes. The girl, she causes much to be different. Everywhere she goes, things happen that should not."

"Like wearing Ashantha's ring?"

"And other things. She should be in your care, Tillandra."

"But she is not one of us. What can I do for her?"

"She bears that which can cause us much harm. But her path is not clear. There are different roads she can take, one of which would be disastrous for us all. The girl is floating in a sea not of her understanding, and she needs a guide."

"We cannot even find her. Since the ring came off, we're playing a game of chance."

"You already know how to locate her. You did it once before."

"Even that isn't so exact. And she seems very adept at avoiding us."

"Fear not, Tillandra, for even now she is with one of your own."

"Who? No one has told me they have her!"

"Like I told you, she makes things change whereever she goes. She crossed paths with the one who should not remember."

"I don't understand."

"The woman once known as Burgendetta, they have been traveling together. The stone brought them together."

Tillandra felt her stomach go heavy, as if she'd eaten rocks.

BURGENDETTA HAD BEEN MOTHER FOLLY BEFORE NINARTO, TILLANDRA'S predecessor. She'd killed by choice, not in self-defense, and broken their most important rule. Her memory had been wiped as was the rule. The history of it was well known in their group. She had declared that she had willingly done it, a sacrifice to protect them all.

Tillandra wondered now if deeper down she was working against them even back then. If the amulet was what had brought her to Lani.

"She knows of the amulet?"

"No, Tillandra. The girl, Lani, carries with her a brooch set with a slice of this stone. It is one of the things protecting her from the amulet. Burgendetta was able to see this."

"See? Isn't she still blind?"

The voice chuckled. *"Come now, you know there are many ways to see. She has laid her hands upon the stone, and now she remembers."*

"Remembers? What does she remember?"

"Her past, about your combined past. She knows who she once was. I had to intervene."

"I thought her mind was wiped?"

"Perhaps it should have been. We locked away her memories from her. Let her start anew. Perhaps it was fortuitous, as she can now help the girl get to you."

"How?"

"I have explained to her the importance of getting her to you. I can only hope she will cooperate."

Tillandra shook her head. Just another thing that differed from how things were meant to be. So much was unraveling on her watch, she felt like she had no control over any of it.

"Everything feels out of control."

"You expect that nothing will change, and when it does you become disappointed. If you had no expectations, then you could not be disappointed, Tillandra. Change is part of the way this world is made. Accept that, and you will find your way easier."

"That's easier said than done."

"No matter what, the girl must get to you, or you to her. The amulet she carries must not be allowed to get into the hands of those from Enderk. I cannot stress this enough."

"I tried to find out more about it, but the vision I had led me to books I could not even read."

"The girl is the answer to that problem as to others. She can help you as much as you can help her. You must get her."

"So many things to solve. Her, the Audition, King Ahn."

"You can manage them all. A note of caution. The King is not operating on his own."

"Who else is involved?"

"He too has an amulet. And is aiding those who seek to harm us."

"An amulet? Another one?"

"Yes. The Occultation is lifting, it won't last forever. Be wary of what the King is trying to do. They seek this stone, Tillandra, your instinct was correct. Trust yourself and keep them at bay."

Tillandra didn't feel relaxed at all, this news had just increased her concern.

"This boy, he is special."

"He was given into my care by the Carver. I am taking him back to Anderwell to be looked after. He cannot hear."

"He hears but in his own way. When there are trees or the stones, he can hear this type of speech, you can communicate with him through the stone."

"Tandra." The voice that spoke to her grabbed at her heart and squeezed it until she felt she couldn't breathe.

"Peka?"

"Tandra! Tandra!" he squeaked in delight.

"Now Peka, do you understand she can only speak to you in this way?" the goddess said to him.

"Yes."

"Where she is taking you will be your home now. Do you understand?"

"Yes."

"I must go. Let him help you, Tillandra. You must let others help you."

"But…?"

Tillandra could feel that the presence was gone. She didn't know how much time had passed outside, it only felt like minutes in here, but her previous experience taught her otherwise. The time pressure seemed to have increased in her mind, not eased.

Before they could leave she needed to check in with Anderwell, but first she needed to find where the girl was. In the alcove she drank from the fountain before settling back in the cushions and reaching out to the Void.

Like she had done before, she tracked Ashantha's mask. She was still no better at it, and the process was very awkward, but she was able to place Lani on the road near Lakeside. The image shimmered and was more blurred than clear, but it was enough. Enough to pass on to those in Anderwell.

"In All Jest, Toolet."

"Mother, In All Jest. I saw you were in Midderbuilt, and wondered if I would hear from you."

"I am waiting for Tingfurlew."

"Waiting?"

"He wasn't at his place when I arrived, I hope he won't be far."

Toolet didn't answer; she never spoke when she had nothing to say.

"Are you prepared for the Audition?"

"There is little to do, Mother. The Mother Stone is recharged as you know, but I was worried about the numbers."

"What do you mean?"

"We need five of us to conduct the Audition, as you know, but when Beantic left, that meant there were only four of us here. I thought perhaps you would bring Gimbden back with you, but hopefully that won't be a problem."

Tillandra could feel her jaw tense in her body outside the Void at yet another mistake. She had not given any thought to the numbers of Jesters needed. But then this is exactly what she was being told to do, let others take care of things.

"What do you mean by not a problem?"

"I have other news."

"What is it?"

"Goran is unwell."

"Where is he?"

"He's with Beantic and Brando, on his way back here."

"What on Dharatan happened?"

"He has been acting very strangely, almost as if his mind has cracked. I didn't get much time with Bea to discuss it, but she has had to restrain him and he's sedated much of the time. It sounds very serious."

Tillandra didn't know what to say.

"When will they arrive?"

"They are in a wagon so the travel is slower, but Thenis willing they'll be back in time. Else we will need Beantic to rush ahead."

"What of the girl?"

"We followed your last guidance, but without knowing who she is it's almost impossible to track her. When she wore the ring we at least had some chance."

"Do you remember Burgendetta?"

The name clearly took Toolet by surprise and she didn't speak for a good while. "Yes."

"The girl is with her, or was. She is near Lakeside, hopefully heading our way. Seek out an old blind woman and you'll have a good chance of finding Lani."

"But how? I mean, how is Burgendetta with her?"

"We'll talk when I'm back. At least you know what she looks like. I hope it's enough. We need to get her home with us."

Tillandra stood and sought out Peka. Being here hadn't eased her anxiety, if anything she felt worse. Sometimes knowledge wasn't power at all, especially if you felt unable to use it. With a potential invasion about to happen, now two amulets, Burgendetta about to arrive back in Anderwell and Goran unwell, it seemed like her world was spinning out of control.

She had to focus on what she could control, and right now that was getting the ring, and getting back to Anderwell.

TILLANDRA

The door slid closed with a click. In the quiet room it sounded louder than it was, but in reality, only Tillandra could hear it. Maybe Peka felt it through the stone, she didn't know. It was another thing she would need to ask him when she had time.

The little boy sat on the bed where she had placed him. His face seemed more at ease than at any time since she had first met him. He was an enigma to her. She was unsure exactly where he fit into the puzzle of her life, but they were connected now, no matter what.

She slid the bed back into place with him on it, then made sure the room looked as normal as possible. Strong daylight forced its way under the door. How long they had been with the Citadel Stone she didn't know, but it was important she find out. Every day was important right now.

The best Tillandra could hope for was that it was only the next day, if not the day after. Any more than that and she was at risk of falling behind her schedule. The consequence of that would mean her entire trip would have been wasted.

Without spending any more time brooding she arranged Peka in the sling and tied it off around her neck. She gathered her bag, removed the bar from the door and stepped outside. Tillandra had to raise her free arm to shield her eyes from the mid-morning sun. In its current position it shone directly at the front door of the guest house, and right into their faces.

The large wooden door at Tingfurlew house showed no sign of change from the time before, only there was more light on it now. Once again Tillandra raised the knocker and let it swing to hammer on the wooden door, bouncing several times in the process.

No sound came from within, no scrape of a chair against a stone floor, no high-pitched voice yelling at her to stop. Again, she raised the knocker.

"Stop it, stop it already. So impatient."

Tillandra turned with a start, the knocker slipping from her fingers and banging against the door.

"I said stop it! Give a man a headache already."

"Ting, it's you!"

He looked up at her strangely as he hurried along the road, his arms full of books. "Who else would I be? Silly woman. You know who I am."

"Yes, but…"

"But, but… No buts. Quick, move and let me in."

He pulled a large key out of a long pocket in his baggy trousers. The hole for the lock was at his height, at the same height as Tillandra's knee. He wiggled it back and forth in both directions and several clicks could be heard before he pulled the key back out, thrusting it back into the pocket.

Tingfurlew turned the handle and leaned with his right shoulder against the big door. Tillandra was about to reach out with her arm when the door suddenly shifted and swung inwards quickly.

"Blast the thing. I need to get someone to shave the bottom off. It has swollen in the heat, man can't open his own door."

He hurried in, rushing over to the portion of his open-plan quarters where several sofas and a table were set up, dropping all the books on top of it.

"What are you waiting for? Don't loiter out there, get yourself in here and shut that door. Not going to talk to the whole street. Hurry up now!"

Tillandra did as he said and walked over to the sofa, a grin on her face. There was a pleasant familiarity in his manner. She took Peka out and placed him on the floor.

"Mighty sand devils! What is that?" Tingfurlew's voice was a loud shriek as he jumped back.

"It's a child, Ting. Careful, you'll scare him."

"You scared me, you did. When did you have time to have a child? You weren't big last trip."

For the first time in days Tillandra laughed. "He's not mine, Ting. I acquired him from a friend."

"What type of friend gives away their children?" He waved his hands frenetically over his head. "I don't want to know. I don't want to know."

He left her and Peka, who had stood with one hand on the table and one on a sofa and was trying to take in everything that was Tingfurlew's home and studio, to head over to the kitchen area. Tingfurlew came back with a large jug and several cups.

"Does he drink wine, or do I need to find him something childish?"

"He's hardly more than a babe, Ting. Do you have any water?"

"Water?" he squealed. "We're in a desert, we don't waste water."

"It's not a waste. He's a child!"

"Oh, alright then." The short man shuffled off back into the kitchen space before returning with a leather skin which he placed on the table.

Tillandra tipped some of it into one of the cups and offered it to Peka, who gladly took it and drained it all quickly, some of it spilling off his chin and onto his top. Tillandra filled two of the other cups with the wine, handing one to Tingfurlew who had clambered up onto his sofa and was rearranging the cushions.

"Wine, that is good. Why are you here, Mother?"

"You don't know, Tingfurlew?"

"Know what? Why speak in riddles, just tell Ting!"

"I need a new ring."

The little man shook his head and banged his temples with the base of his palms. "Didn't we do this before? No ring, the girl is wearing the ring."

"Not any more, Ting, she no longer has it."

"Did she have an accident?"

"It's off, Ting. It turned into a coin, that's all that matters."

He raised his hands and waved them at her. "Okay, okay, no need to bite me, I was just curious. Wait here."

"Wait, wait for what?"

"I didn't know about this, I need to go and check I can make the ring. If there's new silver I can make it, if not, I can't. Stop the questions and let me go, so I can see."

He jumped down from the sofa and went to his workstation and shelves. He took down a cup and some utensils and rushed off out the door without another word.

When he did return with the silver he needed, he ushered her out of his workshop so he could work on it. She spent the rest of the day wandering around the strange town of Midderbuilt. Everything here was either about mining gems from the mountain or turning them into pieces to be sold in Watersend.

Any other industry here was only to support the miners and lapidarists, which left the place feeling both busy and empty at the same time. Peka spent the time doing all he could to stare at the spinning circle of sand that surrounded Mount Qum.

By the time the sun passed over the back of the mountains she was back at Tingfurlew's, desperately hoping he was done.

"Good, about time you were back!"

"You're finished?"

"Yes, for ages. Come see."

Tillandra walked to his table where he was polishing the small silver ring. She marveled at how he was able to have fashioned this so quickly. It was identical to the one on her own hand. She put Peka down and pulled out the locket hung around her neck.

After placing it on the table and opening it, Tingfurlew placed it inside.

"Only the person with the mask can wear that."

"I know, Ting."

That was one of the things only the Mother could do. Only she could take the ring out of Midderbuilt, and only in the locket. Once closed, the locket would only open to the Prospect who had successfully taken up the mask. It was how it was done.

Tillandra snapped the locket shut and felt a small tingle in her hand as she did. She hung it back around her neck, not ready for the journey to come, but happy at least to have this part done.

100

TILLANDRA

She hadn't wasted any more time in Midderbuilt after taking the ring from Tingfurlew. He had no more answers, and she couldn't spare the time to chat. One day she needed to make a journey here to see him, without the pressure of time.

The team of camels was ready for her and Peka when they descended into Travelers Rest. The guide had been waiting for her return with food and water prepared. Tillandra knew he and the animals could travel through poor light, and she wasn't going to waste another night. By the time the sun had set over the desert their group was hours away from the strange town under the spinning mountain.

Peka had stood against her until the light had gone completely, his head on her shoulder as he watched the spinning sands around Mount Qum. Tillandra would have to ask him what it was that fascinated him about it the next time they were able to connect.

She wondered if the tree in Anderwell would facilitate that or not. Tillandra felt sad as she thought about Vindisil. Was the woman gone now? Vin had wanted the tree to live and flourish in Anderwell. As she'd explained to Tillandra, it would mean she could seek help from those of the trees. It would also help Peka stay connected to his people too, even if they didn't want him around.

Once the mountain was hidden by the night and distance, Peka nestled back into his sling, and she watched him until his eyes closed. Tillandra was amazed at how still and calm he could be. She would have been impossible, even at his age, bound up like this for so long.

The days went by in a blur, and she did her best to stay positive about what was happening. Her worries about King Ahn were not easily forgotten, and she still had no idea how to resolve that without conflict. Their usual method was to influence, not fight, but she couldn't ignore the man had other intentions.

He would know now that they weren't going to just lie down and hand Sahro over to him, but her biggest concern was finding a way inside his palace. She needed to get someone on the inside to help solve things longer term.

Or if not, to help bring about the man's end as ruler, if possible. She shuddered at even thinking such a thing. She didn't really mean to have him killed, but replaced. Not that it would be easy either, and without really knowing his motivations, the replacement could be exactly the same.

If the Derks were working with him, which was what Tillandra understood from what the goddess had told her, then they could do the same with the next King. Putting anyone there would be a massive risk. If they were found out, then their life would be at risk, as Ashantha's was.

Tillandra didn't know if she could willingly put someone in that much danger again. She still blamed herself for Ash's loss. Amulets, Derks, soldiers ready to attack, it all felt like a tale from a bard, not what she'd thought her role would be. And at the center of it all, a young woman from Malamig. That was something they did need to get right: find her, and get her to Anderwell.

The beacons of Watersend were a relief to see, but a reminder how far it was she had to travel. They all had to dismount to get through the small gate at the back of the city, and from that point she chose to walk.

"Thank you, Jilfer, I'll walk from here."

The guide bowed to her. "It's always my pleasure."

"Will you be traveling with me to Anderwell?"

He shook his head. "No, my brother will. He wishes to see the city."

Tillandra left the small team and headed in the direction of The Clown Prince. The streets were quiet, and even the inn didn't have much in the way of noise coming from it.

She was surprised to find the door locked when she arrived and banged on it with her fist several times.

"I'm coming. Ease up or you'll wake the whole building." The sound of Wessen's grumpy voice was still audible through the wooden door.

"Mother?" he rubbed his eyes. "My apologies, but it's the middle of the night."

"Sorry, Wessen, I only just arrived back."

"Clearly. Come in, come in." He gently tugged at her sleeve. "Let's get you inside and I'll wake someone to help me prepare you something to eat."

"I'm sorry to put you out."

"No issue, Mother. If you'd been some random traveler there'd have been trouble."

She laughed. "No doubt, Wessen."

Tillandra pulled Peka from the sling and put him down on the floor. He quickly wobbled to his feet, holding onto the leg of a table, and set off from table to chair, looking around the room.

"I see you've still got your friend?"

"What did you think I was going to do? Leave him in Midderbuilt?"

They both laughed weakly.

"I'm going to need Gimbden too, Wessen. Sorry, but someone will need to go get him."

"It can't wait until morning?"

"I aim to be gone by morning, or at worst leaving then. I think I'm going to be waking a few people tonight."

Wessen shrugged and walked over to the fire at the end of the room. He stirred up the coals and threw some more logs onto it and grabbed a wick, setting it to flame in the coals before heading around and lighting lanterns.

The main room of the inn sprung to life with the light. The man went out through the back into the kitchens and came back a few minutes later. Tillandra could hear someone else was working back there.

"We'll have you something to eat soon enough. I'm going to go and rouse Gimbden myself. It'll be the easiest way to get to him. I doubt the guards will be easy to deal with tonight."

~

TILLANDRA DIDN'T WANT TO WAIT UNTIL MORNING FOR HOT WATER, SO cleaned up as best she could using a washcloth in her room. She changed her clothing and packed everything else back into her bag, ready to leave as soon as her work was done.

Peka slept on a blanket in the main room near the crackling fire, and Tillandra watched him while she waited for the men to return.

"In All Jest, Mother."

She stood and hugged Gimbden. "In All Jest."

"How was Midderbuilt?"

"Good. I was able to complete my business, and now have to be back before the next full moon."

"You're not going to walk are you?"

"No, I can't carry him and risk not getting there in time." She pointed at the boy asleep by the fire.

Gimbden nodded. "Of course."

"How are things on the border?"

"Tense but so far controlled. I think we surprised them with the size of our army. It doesn't look like the envoy figured out there was any such force here. I'd suggest he wouldn't be very popular right now."

"Let's hope. I learned more while at Midderbuilt. There's more to this than just a simple land grab, or seeking to exploit the gem trade."

"Oh?"

She checked that Wessen wasn't back before continuing. "I was told that they were being helped by the Derks. I doubt it's over just because we have our forces there. Warn the mayor and captains there's still a high chance of them attacking."

"Still. Okay, I will. What can I do?"

"What you're doing. Keep us informed. If they can't get across here, they'll look for new ways. Which means coming closer to Anderwell or through Vodotok."

"They wouldn't."

"Who knows, Gimbden? I'd not have thought they'd be doing what they are now. Stay alert and watch this city closely. They'll seek to get others in here as well, work from the inside out."

"Spies?"

"At least. You need to be very careful, and watch for anything unusual. We'll need your eyes and ears more now than ever before."

"And here I thought I had the dullest posting in the group."

"Perhaps it was, but not anymore."

By the time she had finished with Gimbden, Tillandra's eyes were red and sore. Peka had woken with the first light of the day that began to peek through the shutters. They all ate, before Gimbden left her.

There was nothing else now but to get home. Tillandra patted the locket hanging under her tunic. Next, an Audition. She said her farewells and put Peka in his sling, before heading outside and down to the team she'd be riding back with.

BEANTIC

oday was an easier day for Beantic, as they'd subdued Goran before he wore them all out. The journey back to Anderwell had not been easy. No one would let them on a boat as every time they tried, whoever the other person inside Goran was would scream and carry on in such a way the captains would throw them off.

In the end she had to buy a wagon, and they tied him in it and started down the long road home. Every time he woke was a dice roll as to who they saw. Some days he seemed himself, annoyed and wanting to be free.

Progressively though he was becoming a shell of himself. That they had him tied up like a criminal was causing the Goran they knew a lot of emotional pain, but she had little choice.

The other one was the opposite. Aggressive and sharper than a blade, he would thrash and yell at them. Sometimes he would pretend he was Goran and plead for freedom, but there were a couple of tells Beantic had recognized and she ignored him.

Brando struggled with it, and she had to ease his concern as well. The keeper felt as though he was to blame, and when they needed to be physical with Goran it was him that did it. Their friendship made that as hard for him as it was for her to do what she did.

When the other one came out, then she had to battle him with her will. He would cast his charm around them. Once he actually caught her unawares and she nearly fell for it. Several times Brando or her guards were caught in it, and now she made sure they rode far enough away while he was awake, so that they were out of his reach.

He needed to see them to have his charm work. That meant Beantic was forced to drive the wagon, and when he was awake she used her own skill to push against him. The battle inside Goran made it easier for her to dominate him, but she took no pleasure in it.

To be using it on one of their own, felt wrong. When she did, she could sense it causing him as much harm as good. She was intimidating his goodness back as much as she was the bad of the other.

Brando had secured valerian root from one of the towns they had passed, and she'd had him make a tonic from it. Beantic would have used it constantly but it was often a physical battle to get enough into him. When they were able, it bought her time to recover from the exhaustion of using the skill.

Never before had she needed to use her skill so often, but if nothing else she had learned much more about her stamina with it. The negative was that the exhaustion left her unable to make or receive any connection from her colleagues.

The only time was before they set out, and she knew Toolet would see them on the map, so Beantic didn't give it too much thought. Whatever else was happening was not her concern, not while she had Goran to tend to.

Going to Callet had felt exciting to her, but that option was gone now. At least until they got Goran in care back in Anderwell.

Perhaps he wouldn't recover. It was something she had to concede the more she saw what was happening to him. The bubbly man that they loved, and sometimes hated, was missing, for now at least. If he never recovered then their colleague would spend the rest of his days in the care of others in Anderwell.

At least there was that, although the idea made her very sad.

"Lakeside, Beantic."

The keeper still would not call her Bea, he was quite the serious type. They had gotten to know each other well and she liked his company. If he had nothing to say he didn't speak, and was more than happy to ride in silence.

But he also was engaging when he wanted to talk, and over campfires and some wine at night, she found him a great traveling companion. His discomfort at her tics, and occasional outbursts, passed quickly, as though he never noticed them.

"So close and yet so far, Brando."

"I am yet to discover."

"Best part of two weeks to go. Unless we tie him to a horse and run it hard."

The keeper looked at her, trying to gauge if she was serious.

"It crossed my mind, don't look at me like that."

He grinned back at her. "There is something."

"What?"

He came closer, and almost whispered. "I've got a bad feeling about here."

"What do you mean, Brando?"

"I can't explain, but when I was in the army, I'd often get this feeling before trouble. I can't explain it, but it feels like the air is wrong. It's set my skin and hair on edge."

She half smiled. Beantic wasn't superstitious but she also knew when to trust someone's gut as well.

"What could it be?"

"I can't tell you, Beantic, but to be honest, I've felt like there were eyes on us for days."

"Why didn't you say something?"

"It sounds silly, that's why. I've no reason for it."

"Then why did you?"

"Because it hasn't gone away, and it seems stronger. I don't know."

"Best we pay attention then, be more cautious about who we see."

Brando pulled his horse forward again and went and spoke to her two guards. The three men led her on toward Lakeside. She could do with a meal from an inn, and some ale. It would make a change from what they'd been having.

As she drove, she kept her own eyes vigilant, but had no inkling of what to look for. There were so many people on the road, all trying to catch up after the major storms that had hit Jarv. The big ferries across the river had only just begun working again after being damaged.

Now wagons and horses as well as cargo were able to get across like normal and the merchants were hurrying to get on with their business. People and traffic of all kinds cluttered the road, only allowing them to travel in a line with everyone else.

That night they parked the wagon in the yard of an inn. It was safer for all, and Beantic and one or two of the men would take rooms inside while one stayed out and watched over Goran. They didn't set him free even at night, after he'd tried to get away several times.

The guards would change part way through the night, never leaving him alone. Tonight Beantic wanted a solid sleep, she was exhausted, and she retired as soon as she'd eaten. This would be the last proper bed before they got back to Anderwell, and she was going to enjoy it.

Shouting and the clash of weapons woke her from what had seemed a pleasant dream. The sounds were coming from the yard out the back of the inn. She threw her cloak around her and hurried down to the bottom level of the inn, where others were beginning to gather.

"Let me through."

Beantic used her will and people moved aside enough that she could squeeze through and out the back door. Several men were fighting, and she could see a body on the ground. One of the men across the yard looked like Brando but it was hard to tell. Two men, almost impossible to see, were moving with such speed that their curved swords were more visible than them.

She focused on the nearest one and threw out her will, trying to dominate his. He turned to face where this new threat came from, and began to move toward her. Beantic could sense he had a strong mind, and was very determined.

If she hadn't been weakened by what she had been doing for days it might have been easier, but she had to throw her whole concentration into it. The man floundered. Struggling to push forward, not used to being unable to move swiftly.

Beantic could sense his anger, his push to get to her. And she could sense what these Derks had come for. Rings, the bag of rings she had found in Goran's belongings. She pushed back against him. He was moving very slowly but still he came toward her.

Then suddenly he was cut down, a sword stabbed through him from behind, and he toppled forward. Behind him was a large man holding a bloodied sword, who turned and went toward the other sounds. With his back turned, he never saw another one of the Derks leap from the wagon, holding a pouch.

Moving quicker than Beantic could believe, he swooped down to his fallen comrade and removed the ring from the dead man's hand, not even giving him any more thought, before attacking the Ngaherian from behind.

Beantic had no more aid to give, but she could still shout. "Watch out!"

Whether he heard her over the noise in the yard, she didn't know. But the Derk cut him as he ran through, then the other men wearing black retreated out the gates behind him. Those who had been fighting them moments before stood in shock that it was over.

Several followed out the gates in pursuit, but returned shortly after. "They've gone."

She hurried out into the yard, "Someone get light, we need light."

As she checked on the men in the yard with what little light there was, she saw one of her guards lying still on his back beside the wagon. She clambered up into the wagon, its sides blocking any light from outside. Beantic crawled forward to Goran, her hands desperately trying to discover what her eyes couldn't see, checking if he lived.

Someone lifted a lantern over and he seemed fine. Fast asleep and unharmed. Beantic almost laughed, before sliding back and climbing out of the wagon. She found Brando slumped against a wall of the stable. He had a bad cut across his middle and was struggling to stay awake.

"You'll be fine, Brando, stay with me." She turned to the people arriving to help. "Water and cloths, over here, quick."

She saw the Ngaherian sitting against the wheel of the wagon, holding his arm. He looked much brighter than Brando, but he'd still need tending to. Beantic only hoped there was a physick or herb woman close by, they'd need all the help they could get.

102

KOOKA

*D*espite the time of year, the heat that surrounded Sahro could be felt even this close to the water. Neither the people of Lakeside, nor the villagers living in the many small groups of houses sprinkled along the road south to the bottom of the lake, realized how lucky they were to have both water and warmth.

There was no other large town or city between Lakeside and Anderwell or further south into Kysten. People had just spread themselves along the water's edge, forming villages where they could. None of them spread inland very far, the desert was a barrier all of its own.

Kooka was tired now. Mostly he knew that it was because of how close he was to home. He chuckled to himself.

Home, I don't really have a home, or if I do it's this blasted cart.

It had been some time since he had been back in Anderwell for any length of time, and he knew this time around he would stay a while. Parts of him were sore and overall he was just feeling tired. Maybe his time was coming to an end, like Ruport before him.

Days before, he he'd been adamant he would go back out, but he was beginning to think that was his ego not wanting to admit the truth. He did love the open road and the way of the cart. He had been feeling okay up until the storm had hit them. It took all his strength to protect them, stuck outside the city in the open. He'd collapsed all the tents before it hit, and they all just hid under the wagon as best they could.

Purple had been the most frightened, but she wasn't alone, all of them had been scared to one degree or another. Even himself, and he knew it would pass, but it was the first sign to him that his time on the road was probably nearly done.

He had faced plenty of obstacles and threats over the years. Looking like he did and driving the cart he often found himself in tricky situations, or simply on the receiving end of abuse or mistreatment.

It had not bothered him, as long as he was able to keep the kids away from harm. But something about the storm had unsettled him, and he knew that it was most likely simply age, and he had run out of energy for it all.

Persuading the outcasts to come to Anderwell was honorable in his mind, and almost always led to a much better life for them, but there was a toll. He had to convince them the best ways he could and every time he questioned his motives, his reasoning and methods.

Even after so long doing it he hadn't once found a situation where he felt he had done the wrong thing, but that level of self-scrutiny did wear on you. As they approached Lakeside after the storm had passed, he could feel that it was time.

A sense of sadness crept over him as he recognized it for what it was. His retirement. He'd need to think about how to hand over to someone new, but he also knew that, like Ruport had done for him, mostly you needed to let them take ownership of it.

Lakeside allowed them to stay much closer to town than was usual. The town had no walls, it just began as sporadic buildings, then slowly formed into a more typical town before the buildings thinned out again as you carried on south.

Over the years Kooka had often needed a smithy, the old wagon always needing some help, or help to reshoe the horses. On the south side of Lakeside, where there were fewer buildings, Berriam had his workshop and never objected to Kooka camping the night alongside.

He'd only stay the one night, never wanting to outstay their welcome. Berriam would never visit the people Kooka brought through, and never asked what Kooka did, but he didn't have anything bad to say either.

The men would sit inside the workshop drinking ale, while Kooka would share stories from the road. He'd often thought the smith was just enjoying life on the road through him, without having to do it himself. Kooka enjoyed the man's company, he spoke in a direct and plain way which suited the Driver.

Tonight had been typical. After the man had helped him repair one of the wheels on his wagon, they'd enjoyed many mugs of ale before Kooka had fallen asleep alongside the wagon, outside in the cool air.

Someone was shaking him, his head was confused. He could hear Gizen's voice.

"Kooka! Kooka, wake up."

It took him a few moments to clear his head and open his eyes. It was still dark and he could hear shouting and screaming not so far in the distance.

"What is it, Gizen?"

"There's fighting up the road."

"Are they coming near here?"

"No. I can't tell where it is but it hasn't come any closer. Some of the others are scared."

Kooka stood up and quickly checked on everyone. They were all awake, and had were mostly under the wagon, trying to stay out of sight.

"Let's hope it stays that way then. Altrab, come out lad, you'll be okay. Why don't you help me gather up everyone's blankets and stuff? We'll put them all in the wagon just in case."

He held the boy's hand as he reluctantly came out from under the wagon. The two of them made quick work of roughly throwing everything into the wagon. Kooka checked the horses and was confident enough they could be hooked up quickly enough if needed.

All going well, whatever trouble was back up the road would stay well away from them. His wishes were answered shortly after when any distant sounds of the fighting ended. He went out into the road and looked north toward where it had come from.

An inn not so far from them seemed to be the center of it. Whatever had happened had brought the occupants awake, and every window was lit with light now, and a group of people were moving around outside with lanterns and weapons.

Kooka turned and went back to his wards.

Best we stay well away from trouble. Even more reason to be on our way in the morning.

Gizen stood with one hand on the wagon, as if she was looking his way.

"Kooka, they need her help."

"Need whose help, Gizen?"

"Purple's."

"What do you mean, girl? What's Purple got to do with them?"

"There's men up there, she can fix them."

"Fix them?"

"That's what she is. She fixes hurt things."

"I don't understand what you're saying."

"Purple can heal things, Kooka."

He was totally confused. He'd not seen Purple do any such thing, but he had to at least hear Gizen out, she'd been the one that had helped them rescue Tillandra after all.

"She can save your friend."

"My friend? What friend?"

"The man who fixed the wheel, he's up there, he's been hurt."

"In Seth's name, not Berriam." Kooka scratched his head. He wanted to help the smith, but he didn't want to go anywhere near trouble, especially with little Purple. Nor did he want to leave the others here if there was danger about.

"What can you see?"

"The fighting is done now. There are several people hurt. They need her."

"Purple, where are you?"

The young girl poked her head out beside the front wheel. "Here, Kooka."

"Gizen here says you can help when people are hurt, is that true?"

The young girl didn't want to look him in the eye.

"It's important, Purple. Some men are hurt."

"I only helped animals. I don't know."

Kooka wasn't sure what he was doing was right, but if he could help the smith, he knew he had to try. And he'd seen stranger things in his time than someone being able to do more than what most folk could. He picked up Purple and grabbed Gizen's hand.

"You better come too, lass. The rest of you, get back under there and stay here. No one come out until we come back."

He hurried up the road toward the inn. There was definitely no sound of fighting coming from it, but plenty of people were standing around out in the road, looking into the yard, where people were hurrying about to help several injured men.

"Let us through, out the way." He used his size to bump their way through.

There was still only limited light but he saw Berriam standing propped against a wall, his arm bleeding, but a woman was wrapping it with a cloth.

"Berriam, you okay?"

"I'll live, Kooka. There's worse than me here." The smith nodded to his left, where a woman was crouched over a man who lay prone on the ground. He could partly hear her, and something sounded familiar about her voice.

He led Gizen that way. As he approached, the woman turned her head and looked up at him, her jaw and neck twitching violently as she did.

"Kooka?" she said in surprise.

"Beantic? What on Dharatan?"

"What are you doing here?"

"We're camped just down the road..." He nodded at Purple in his arms. "She might be able to help."

"What?" Bea looked at him confused.

Gizen stepped closer to Purple. "You can, Purple, you can, I know it. Just do it the same."

"Okay." The young girl's voice was quiet and uncertain but she nodded slowly at Gizen.

Kooka put her down beside Beantic and turned to Gizen. "What now?"

"Use your hands, Purple."

The young girl dragged herself right up to the man lying on the ground. Kooka could see he had been bleeding a lot and had a large cut across his chest and middle. Purple put her small hands on both sides of it, and began to hum.

It was a soft sound, but the tone of it affected Kooka, even amongst the other noises around them. He watched with amazement as her fingers seemed to get the tiniest glow of light outlining them. She sat there and hummed and the cut on the man's skin slowly began to close.

The bleeding stopped and before his eyes, what had been a large gash shrank until there was nothing but a long scar. She stopped humming and took her hands off him and the light around her hands disappeared.

"What in Seth's name?" Beantic exclaimed.

"Oh my," was all Kooka could say.

The man coughed several times and his eyes opened briefly before closing again, and he passed out. Beantic leaned down and listened to his breathing.

"He's alive, and breathing normally now. Dear girl, that was amazing." Her face beamed at Purple, and Kooka saw the girl sit up more and smile herself at the praise.

"Could you do that again?"

"I think so."

"Kooka, there's others. That one there, he came out of nowhere to help."

It took them an hour or more to tend to the injured, and at the end of it, he could see that there was a toll on Purple. The skin around her eyes had gone very dark, and she looked exhausted.

He went to Beantic. "I'll not let her do any more, Bea. Look at her, she doesn't look well herself."

"You're right. I should have thought there'd be a cost to what she can do. You've found a very special one there, Kooka."

He nodded. "What happened here, Beantic?"

"Not out here, Kooka. I need to check on Goran."

"Goran. I haven't seen him, is he all right?"

"That is a matter of opinion." She took Kooka around to the side of the wagon and lifted up the blanket he'd been covered with.

"What's wrong with him?"

"Later. Are you heading to Anderwell?"

"We are, and you?"

"Yes, Kooka. We can talk on the road, then. Away from other ears."

103

TILLANDRA

After so many days riding the camels, Tillandra had come up with a way to keep Peka secure but not loading up her back. He was sat upright in front of her, and the sling strapped him to her around her middle.

He was facing forward and raised his little right arm and pointed his fingers off in the distance.

"Yes, Peka, that's it," Tillandra said to him. She knew he couldn't hear her, but she knew she had to treat him like he could. It reminded her to also make physical contact with him to acknowledge what he was looking at.

His small round face tilted back and looked at her as she nodded her head. The smile that formed on it made her heart twinge a little. When he looked forward again, she shook her head. How on Dharatan had this happened?

As much as being back home excited her after the best part of two months on the road, she knew her tasks would deprive her of the time she had spent with him. How he handled it would be of much interest to her as well as how she would.

It would be good to be back in Anderwell, that was for sure. There were things she had to resolve, all of which seemed as important as one another, but one had its own time limit.

For the first time in a number of years they would need to hold an Audition. Auditions were always an anxious time. Having a deadline to them always raised the stakes, as did the consequences of the selection process.

All the students in the college that became Prospects had something special about them, something that marked them out as candidates for the Audition. It was usually a skill that bordered on the magical, if not clearly so. Those that didn't went out on the Circuit, or took up other key roles around Dharatan.

The Prospects always remained in Anderwell, in case they were needed. The Court never knew when one of theirs would pass, and the rules around when one had to be held meant it was safer to keep them close. Perhaps that was a folly they needed to change, so they could use the skills out on the Circuit.

An Audition was a unique event, though that made it sound more mysterious than it actually was. It was a simple way of selecting the next member of their group.

Tillandra followed the rules passed down to her from the Mothers before her:

- If no one was elevated then they lost that spot. Twelve would become eleven, and so on until there were no more.

- Four Jesters were needed to activate the stones for an Audition to take place. This meant if they got to less than four then they could never replace anyone.

- A Prospect taking up the mask had to do so of their own volition. They would be called to do it, and if they were true they would be elevated.

Tillandra remembered how it had felt on the day she passed. There were four in her cohort that had waited for their chance to be the one.

Once it had begun, each went to the tower to see if it was them that would be chosen. Tillandra was second and she had seen the disappointment in the face of her friend when they were unable to pass through the door that led to the very top where the Mother Stone was housed.

That was the first obstacle to get through. If you could not pass that doorway then you did not get the option to take up the mask, which was the next step. It seemed simple to pick up the mask, but when confronted with it, the process was very different.

Doubts, fears and threats whirled through your head. All the confidence you had before was stripped away, any logic that it was a simple thing, pick it up and put it on disappeared. Standing there, Tillandra hadn't seen the four senior members, or even the stones, lit up a vibrant blue and white.

All she saw was the dark wood mask, her hand, and what seemed an impassable gap between them. It took what seemed hours to her to fight against what held her from it. All of her will, to be confident enough to take it, to know she was worthy of it.

Tillandra laughed. She had been so certain in the end that she was worthy, but that confidence had disappeared since she had become Mother. It was that confidence she needed to recover, above all else. That sense of surety that she could lead her people, and solve what they faced.

As she walked through the gates into the city Tillandra felt a little more at ease than she had in some time. There was a smell to your hometown that triggered things within your body and mind. When you had been away for a time, the smell was noticeable. It only took hours or sometimes days before it became part of your nasal palette and disappeared from what you noticed.

Like the particular sounds they became part of the background, the familiar. All of these things signaled to your mind what home really meant. Tillandra breathed in the strange mix of aromas that were Anderwell.

The path from the western gate led you through a pocket of inns before you entered a space that could be defined as more residential. This late in the afternoon meant she could smell the sweat of a day's work but now over the top came the aroma of food being prepared.

Smoke from heating fires mixed in layers with stewing meats and vegetables. People moved in groups while some hurried to complete tasks before the evening came. It wouldn't be long until the lantern lighters were out.

That was one thing she had ensured stayed part of Anderwell. The oil lanterns that lined the main roads were lit every night and burned until the reserves ran dry. Many cities became dark enclaves when night fell, not so much here. They usually lasted until the early hours of the morning before all would run dry.

Tillandra wasn't entirely sure why but there was something about the deep dark of night that allowed those with ill intent extra freedoms. She'd never wanted that as part of her city.

Peka was back in the sling across the front of her body but turned so he could take in the city. Tillandra wished so much she could speak with him, tell him where he was. She would take him to the tree as soon as she could and discuss things with him there, if it worked.

It was so hard for her to adjust to dealing with someone you could not speak to in any way. Despite the difficulties of others, this was one of the hardest she could imagine. She felt sad that the boy's mother had wanted rid of him, that the burden was too much, even though she felt it intimately.

Perhaps they would have to visit the tree each day and she could learn from him as much as she taught him of the city. If her time allowed it. Another thing to resolve.

The decision now was where to go first. Her house or the college? She couldn't simply leave Peka at her house, he most likely would howl if she left him alone. But Milfred needed to know she was back. It would be good to have someone to look after her. Looking after herself for these last few months had been freeing in many ways, but now the tiredness couldn't be held back.

Having Milfred prepare her meals and keep things organized would be welcome.

Yes, it's there first. The others can wait.

~

SHE OPENED THE DOOR TO HER HOUSE AND STEPPED IN, FEELING THE warmth reach out and wrap around her. While the city might have its own smells, her place smelled exactly like it should. The old wood, layered with years of living, cooking and fires. The touches of incense that lingered in corners.

"M-m-mother!"

"Milfred!" Tillandra turned to her aide as he came from the hallway into the large kitchen and reception area.

He approached her and stopped when he saw Peka on her chest. "What is that?"

"He's a boy, Milfred." She laughed at the look on his face.

"But… but.." He looked up at her and down at the boy. "You've only been gone a few months."

"He's not mine, Milfred. He comes from a special place, but he cannot hear, they could not care for him there. I was asked to bring him here."

"So, he will be going to the school?"

"Right now, I have no idea what will be happening. What I do need is a bath, Milfred. A long hot bath."

"That I can take care of. Toolet warned me you would likely be back today, so I have made sure the house fires were lit and the kitchen has some food if you are hungry?"

"I've missed your care, Milfred. How long for the bath?"

"Some time, M-m-mother, to warm the water."

"Then once you've done that, I'll eat something. We've not eaten since an early middle-day meal. Or I haven't. This one eats all the time."

"Let me see to the water and then I'll get started. Here, take a seat."

"I can sit myself, Milfred. I want to put some things in my study first, then I'll come back here." She struggled to wipe the smile from her face. "It's good to be back."

"It's good to have you, M-m-mother. It's been very quiet around here without you." He turned and hurried out the back toward where he would have water waiting.

Tillandra went to her study with her bulging satchel on her shoulder. She was glad to place it on her desk. The room had a small fire burning which kept the chill out of it. She knew how cold it could get if it wasn't lit. This fire had probably been burning all day.

She put Peka down on the ground. "Don't go far, Peka."

Tillandra looked toward the shelf where the book was hidden away. *Hopefully Kooka won't be too far away and someone might be able to make sense of those I found.*

She unlatched the satchel and pulled out the dirty clothes and wrapped bundles. Taking the freshly minted mask wrapped in linen from it and the pouch that held the new ring, she placed them to one side of her desk.

Most of the items in the bag were ready either to wash or throw out. Some were so stained she wondered how she had ever worn them. Remembering Peka, she looked around quickly for him, her heart racing, only to see him sat on his haunches in front of the fire, staring into the flames.

While he was distracted Tillandra took her clothes toward the back of the house where she would usually leave the laundry. As expected, the basket was empty, and she felt a little bad for dumping all her things in there.

It felt strange being back and having someone to look after her needs.

I wasn't away that long. I shouldn't feel bad about it.

Grabbing Peka on the way back through, she carried him to the kitchen area and placed him on the ground where he promptly crawled closer to the fire in there. Maybe it was something he had not witnessed much before, inside fires.

Milfred came in and fussed about, making her a platter of some dried meats and fruits. He piled up her favorite, dates, and then a warm chai. Now this she had missed.

"You're incredible, Milfred. Even a warm drink for me."

"I do what I can, M-mother. Will this be enough?"

"For me, most likely, but he will need some bread and cheese. As well as goat's milk if you can?"

It wasn't often that Tillandra saw Milfred remark on anything other than her welfare, but he did raise his eyebrows at the request.

"I'll see to it shortly. Where will he sleep tonight?"

"Tonight, at least, in my room, Milfred. I'll want another cot for him. He'll sleep almost anywhere."

"I'll see to it once you've washed."

"There'll be plenty of time, I have to go to the Court once I'm washed."

"What will happen to him then?" The man looked almost horrified she would say he was staying here.

When she told him she would take him with her, he almost cried in relief.

By the time she and Peka were washed, dried and in fresh clothes, the sun was all but gone from the sky. Tillandra felt much better for the meal and wash. The oils and perfumes that she owned had made the water even nicer, and she had been able to scrub herself cleaner than she had been in months.

Peka wasn't as impressed with all the flowery smells and oily feel to the water, but she managed to wash him from head to toe. Clean clothes were a harder thing to achieve, and in the end she had to reuse a tunic he had used the day before which she retrieved from the laundry pile.

It would do for now. It would be most interesting to see what the others thought of her companion.

104

LANI

For days the storm in Jarv had continued. Lani had never experienced such a thing. It had taken five days to blow itself out and by then they were all keen to get outside. At first it was still raining but then that too passed and life in Jarv began again.

The quickest way to get south was across the lake to Lakeside, but Odajeen was adamant she would not go on the water. She neither explained why, nor relented in her complete refusal to travel that way. As it turned out no one was sailing for at least another week, while they waited to be sure the storm was gone.

That left the ferries across the Boctok river to reach the road that led to Lakeside. The storm had been so ferocious it had damaged or destroyed the largest of the ferries, and they were the ones that could carry animals and stock across.

After several heated discussions, and then a high price paid, they left their horses behind and secured a small boat across. Odajeen had been firm with the brothers, that they couldn't keep delaying, but wouldn't tell them why.

Lani knew, and the woman's concern only made hers worse. Once they got on the road, that concern only grew. If the brooch was helping her the way they'd been told and was weak, she had no idea when it might run out. Even if they could have afforded enough horses, there were none to be had over here.

The merchants who needed them had secured them on the first boatloads across after the storm. And so they plodded along, one foot after the other, on the well-worn road to Lakeside. On their left Lake Phyrgian spread as far as your eyes could see. They could still see Jarv back to the north, but there was no end to the water both east and south.

Lakeside was as different to Jarv as she was to a Humaas. Where Jarv was dark and gloomy, all stone and surrounded by a high barrier, Lakeside was wooden and open. There appeared to be no protection from the storms, nor the heat blowing from the desert.

Today the wind came from the desert, dry and hot, cracking your lips and draining you of your strength. Lani wondered how people lived out there, where it would be like that all the time. She had overheard other travelers hope for an evening breeze off the lake.

There was no wall around Lakeside, you just arrived at it. At first it was a few buildings, farmhouses or barns, spread thinly through the countryside, then it was lines of buildings. Once you entered the town proper it was like many other places, roads of buildings constructed together or close enough to each other to make up a constant row.

Roads spread out west from the lake, crossed with others north to south. There were butchers and farm grocers, blacksmiths and seamstresses, all mixed in with boarding houses and inns. The smells of many people congregated together en masse filled the air: waste, cooking, fires, smoke and sweat.

Once they left here, they would only pass small towns or villages before reaching Anderwell. It had felt right when she'd made that decision, as if something inside her had clicked into place. It was an odd sensation but that's what it had felt like.

Even so she could feel the amulet, in the background, like a voice pushing words that she could only just hear. She knew it was there, it never seemed to go away, or if it did, not for long, but she couldn't make out what it said.

If she put her concentration on that voice, that spot in her head, she could sense it like it was pulling at her, back the way she had come.

That, and a desire to get it back out of the pouch. She would get odd ideas in the back of her head.

She would look at someone and feel like they were a threat to her, before it would pass, and she would see just a passing stranger. If she looked at Odajeen it was a sense of dislike, or even more than that. Mostly she just shook her head and turned her attention ahead.

It never went away though.

South of the town center, Lakeside had a market, and a sizable one at that. There were porters running their handcarts full of supplies off in the general direction of the docks. The brothers bought what supplies they could all carry for their walk south, after they all agreed they would be better to carry food with them than rely on finding it along the road.

While they waited Odajeen turned to Lani. "How are you feeling?"

"I'm good. And you?"

"Once the decision was made it was made. Now I am just wondering what it will bring."

"I too am glad to have made the decision. I am anxious, but also keen."

When the men had finished, their group gathered at the side of the road to eat the lunch they had purchased, some balls, gritty like breadcrumbs, but more substantial and filled with spices. She took a handful of them and a little leaf with dipping sauce in it and devoured them. They were still a little warm and soft, but it was the unique spice mix to them which she liked the most.

There were so many different types of people here, but mostly they must have been Sahrians, those of the desert country. Which meant Lakeside must be in Sahro.

Most of the Humaas were based around the docks, probably managing the business back up into Rohumaa. The rest of the people dressed differently and were not at all like the Humaas. While they were taller than Lani in most cases, they were not Humaas tall.

Many of them had bright red hair, and even those that didn't seemed to have red tinges to their color. Blonde hair shone with an orange hue in the sunlight, and dark hair seemed to be highlighted with tints of bronze.

Their skin was pale, almost as pale as the Derks she had seen, but with a bit more color. She had noticed one of the ladies serving in the market didn't have her arms covered in the robes many of them wore, and she was freckled with spots all over her skin.

The little she had seen of Derks, their skin had been a ghostly white, almost blue in some light. The Sahrians were not colored that way, or not those she had seen.

Even this close to the water you could sense the vast desert that lay behind Lakeside, probing and creeping toward the water. Lani could see why many of them were draped the way they were in their long robes and head covers. The heat of the sun to the west would impact their lives a lot.

They left the town and kept to the busy road southward, heading closer to her goal. There were many people that took the road south, most in wagons, or with a mule train, and they passed those coming back with empty loads.

Lani learned from Vefed it was because Anderwell was so isolated and had limited water that many of their needs where carted in, or up the river that fed from the bottom of the lake. At night they took up open cot beds in makeshift shelters at roadside camps. They followed the same pattern endlessly down the south road. She wished they'd kept their horses now, doing this on foot was tedious.

About two days from Anderwell something felt new to Lani. She wasn't exactly sure what but her head felt different and she could sense the amulet more strongly than before. It was still in the pouch, tucked away inside her tunic, but that voice was stronger, more persistent.

Several times she looked behind her as if it was coming from someone back there, but there was no one. She didn't want to talk to her companions either and the further they walked, the worse the feeling became.

She felt as if her choice had been wrong, she was doing the wrong thing. Anderwell wasn't her choice, she'd not wanted to be there, it was others pushing her. This woman alongside her, Odajeen, she was one of them. She'd carefully concocted stories to make her believe.

Everyone wanted her to go there, but she didn't want to. She wasn't going to be safe there, she just knew it. She had to turn back, she had to get away from them.

"What's wrong, Lani?"

"What do you mean?" She stepped away from the old woman suspiciously.

"Is something bothering you?"

"No, I'm fine."

They kept walking but Lani put a little distance between herself and the woman. Then she decided she couldn't go any further. She just stopped. At first the others didn't notice, and Lani turned, ready to go the other way.

She heard footsteps behind her and both brothers and Odajeen came to her.

"Go away, what do you want from me?"

None of them said anything.

"I said leave me alone. I'm not going that way."

"Lani, you decided. You said this was what you wanted."

"You decided for me! I didn't want to, this wasn't my idea." Her voice was raised now, and others walking down the road turned their heads to them as they passed, but Lani didn't care. Maybe she could get help from one of them.

Odajeen was quiet. Lani wanted to leave, to go back. They could keep going, it didn't matter, she would survive. That's what the older woman had said, look how special she was. Look how she'd survived.

Lani felt confused. Now she was arguing in favor of the woman, not against her. That didn't make sense at all. What was going on?

"Lani?"

"What?"

"Where's the brooch?"

"The brooch, why do you want my brooch?"

"I don't want it, Lani, I asked you where it was."

Lani looked at the older woman. She didn't trust her, but her voice cut through the suspicions. She reached up and felt the outside of her tunic. She could feel two things under it.

"It's here, where it always is."

"Pull it out, Lani."

"Why, do you want to take it from me? That's what you're after isn't it? I knew it."

"No, Lani. It's for you. Just do it, please. You'll see."

Even though she thought the woman was lying to her, Lani still put her hand down inside her tunic and found the brooch, bringing it back out, with her fist clenched tightly around it.

"Good. Do you feel any different."

Lani was confused. Her head was foggy, but it was a little better. That voice, it was less clear, she couldn't quite hear it. It was like her ears were full of cloth. But she could hear the woman.

"Anything?"

Then suddenly she took another breath, and Lani felt the voice slip away to the back of her head.

"Oh my. What was that?"

"Don't let go of that, Lani. It must be almost done. The amulet, it was the amulet affecting you."

Lani knew she was right, but she could only just see through the thoughts she'd been having.

"Do you want to go on, Lani? It's important. You have to choose. Only you can choose that."

She looked at Odajeen. Lani felt very tired, tired of it all, tired of the battle in her head. When would it be over? The answer she knew was ahead of her. She had to get there, no matter what.

"I do."

Odajeen turned to the brothers. "We must hurry, she has little time left. Let's be off."

105

UKSOD

What else could go wrong?

Last night he had finally got word back from Fuling. And not the words he had wanted to hear. By now his curate should have advised him that he had secured Karpenmor's amulet. When Uksod had heard nothing from him he sought him out.

Several times the man avoided him, but when he was finally able to speak with him he learned that the woman had escaped his men. Uksod couldn't believe how incompetent everyone had been.

Do I have to go and do it myself?

Thankfully the man hadn't executed those who had held her captive, they and the curate were the only people that knew what this young woman looked like. With a little guidance Uksod had at least been able to determine a likely region she would have headed to.

Fuling had no answers from his men as to how she'd gotten free, except that she had to have had help. The details had bored Uksod, he only cared for a method to locate her. So much time had been lost, and every day this woman headed further away from Enderk.

Away from Uksod and his goddess.

He had been able to put her off so far, as he waited to hear back from Fuling, but this would go poorly for him. And yet he was here across the ocean trying to move pieces in a game of trigger, without seeing the board or who he was playing against.

The only bright spot, albeit a tiny one, had been the retrieval of the rings. After speaking with Fuling he had contacted one of the Vrah team chasing them, expecting to get more bad news, or excuses. Instead he was informed of their retrieval. Uksod had confirmed the location as best he could as well.

A random thought had interrupted him when he was speaking with the assassin. It was possible that the woman with the amulet could be heading in that direction, or had been near there in her travels.

He couldn't say exactly why but his understanding of the area they were in and where she was supposedly heading had given him that idea. Uksod told the Vrah to stay in the general location, find somewhere to hole up and wait for him to get more information.

Maybe it was a small bright spot, but compared to everything else it felt like a win. The rings and the possibility that maybe all wasn't lost. Now he just needed some luck. Wins had been hard to find of late, between trying to shepherd Karpenmor from pushing his accession, to Yantarnaya's demands.

The battle over the amber-laced brandy had been lost. Uksod had tried to get it into food and other drinks, but Karpenmor was always thinking ahead of him. He had given up trying now. The boy had broken the dependency he'd formed on it, and there was nothing Uksod could force on him.

Uksod thought of him as the boy, but he was a man, and he was going to be the High Prince soon enough. Unless Uksod could find other ways to distract him, or delay it. The messengers took long enough, with Beigartz being suitably far enough away to take the best part of a month to get there and back.

Undoubtedly their group would have set out not long after receiving the message, the distance only being part of what would confront them along the way. The land they had to cross, and then to seek permission to pass through other lands to avoid the longest delays, would require careful negotiation.

None of the Families played nicely together, all of which made

Uksod's delays easier to achieve. It wouldn't last forever though, and Karpenmor kept pressing him on it. Once all of the Families arrived the process would begin, and at that point there was little he could do to delay it no matter what Yantarnaya said.

He had sent a team of Vrah south to delay any of the parties they could by stealth, but they were last-ditch efforts and none of it would be major. Without any knowledge of the exact location of the amulet it wouldn't matter anyway.

Karpenmor would complete the enthronement ceremony and become High Prince. Uksod had shifted his work now to ensuring the boy was committed to getting the amulet back as well. Then they could work together on that objective.

Uksod wasn't sure if he'd just given up, or whether he thought it was a better ploy anyway, but he'd decided in the last few weeks that all the effort in delaying the accession just kept them away from what they needed to be doing.

Bridges had to be finished, a base had to be settled on the Ngaherian coast, and at the same time get King Ahn back to En Carta. Uksod growled to himself. Even that was heading nowhere at this point. Fuling was too far away from the King to impact his thinking, and hadn't yet come up with any reason for the old king to buy into making such a journey.

That amulet was not moving, and Karpenmor's had gone silent again. The woman carrying it, if she still had it, had not used it, or at least not in any significant way that Yantarnaya had detected. Her biggest concern had been it weakening to the point she couldn't sense it at all, then they would not have any way of finding it.

Back and forth they argued about how he might solve it. His only respite from her anger was that he could highlight how hopeless it was for him to find it, when she, his goddess, couldn't locate it. It had bought him a break from her constant demands, but it wouldn't last forever.

His stomach felt rotten, and he knew he was weak from the efforts last night, even the wine had tasted bitter. Just sitting at his desk was painful, but he needed to review the plans he'd had One draw up for the possible way to get the bridges finished. He didn't want to delay any decisions that would take months to implement.

❧

"UKSOD!"

He couldn't have thought of a worse time for her to call.

"Mistress?"

"Something significant changed I can sense the girl."

"Where is she?"

"The desert. I am able to sense thoughts about the size of the desert, how hot it is."

"That's not much to go on."

"Big red walls, a road leading up to a fortress, or a city."

"Is she using the amulet again?"

"No, but it's connected to her. It is as though something was blocking her. Like the boy, Uksod. Like Karpenmor, the same."

"What could be the same? They are continents apart. Nor have they met."

"I know they haven't met. It must be interference by the other stone. You need to find out, Uksod. Something is shielding the boy. If it's the stone then he must have a token, or something."

Several things began to fall into place in Uksod's sore head.

"Didn't you say that Schevenal just before the end no longer shielded himself from you? Before that I was unable to poison him like I did. I had tried before if you recall?"

"Yes. I see what you're thinking."

"This is too coincidental, that one stops and another begins."

"He might not even know what it is. Something from his father, in his father's belongings that he received when he died, or before."

"Maybe he took it from the old man and that's what left him exposed?"

"It is possible. It would not be big, or I would have been able to sense it. Something small, a jewel or small object. It would carry a stone."

"I will have to see what I can do. He's become very private in his own quarters."

622

"It all fits, Uksod. Whatever this woman has, or had, isn't shielding her."

"Then you can influence her? Bring her to us?"

"I am trying, but like I warned you, the amulet seems to be weak. Or the distance, or both. It is not strong enough to command her."

"Can you detect anything more about where she is? If we can get to her while she cannot block it..."

"A well? Something well. A city."

"Anderwell?"

"Yes, she is close to that, or heading to it. Do you know of it?"

"Yes, and there's a team not so far away. This is very good news."

UKSOD SAT UP AND FELT BRIGHTER ALREADY, UNTIL HE REALIZED WHAT HE would have to do now. To connect again was dangerous, two days in a row, the last time had been very hard on him. But he had no choice. This opportunity was too good to leave.

Could he direct Yantarnaya to do it? Her impatience with others was hard to control, and she had never spoken with members of the Vrah directly. No, it would take too long and take too much effort. He only needed a short time, he would be fine. It would make him sick but then it was worth it.

106

TILLANDRA

he early mornings had always been a good time for Tillandra to work in her main office in the college building. With no one around it helped her check over the few things that were outstanding for her, before beginning to put her mind to planning what needed to happen over the coming days.

She was glad for the quick time she'd made back to Anderwell, the extra days helped to take some of the pressure off getting prepared for the Audition and the impending arrival of the others.

The lights above the map in the basement showed that it would likely be today when Beantic arrived back with Goran. There had been no word from her in some time, and as uptight as the others were to find out how they fared, they knew there was little to be gained from going out to meet them.

Whatever they had to do for Goran would be done back here in Anderwell. Her thinking was disturbed by the arrival of Toolet.

"They're here, Mother."

"Outside?"

"Not yet, I had a messenger at the gates to run here and alert me. Shall we?"

The two women made their way downstairs, sending others to

fetch Lionel and Junther. Surprisingly a large number of students were hurrying outside as well.

"That's odd, Toolet."

"It is. I wouldn't have thought they'd be as interested in…"

She stopped as they reached the landing outside the main doors overlooking the great forecourt in front of the college.

"That might explain it." Tillandra had a smile on her face.

There wasn't just one wagon pulling up, but two. In front was what was known as the Fool's Cart, while Beantic drove the one behind. Several men rode on horseback alongside, while a large brute of a man rode on the bench beside Bea.

A mighty cheer went up from all the students gathered on the steps and in the forecourt. The arrival of the cart was a day they all celebrated. For most this was a reminder of when they first arrived here, and only a few never stayed.

Tillandra saw that the young woman that had helped find her in Okeans rode beside Kooka on the first wagon. She had talent that marked her as special. One day she would likely be marked as a Prospect, if she stayed.

It was rare for older students to come here. Leaving what they had grown used to was hard for older people. Sometimes too much. It was normally easier with the younger children, as they welcomed the new life, and were not too hardened to the world. Tillandra had to stretch her recent memories to recall the girl's name.

"Gizen, isn't it?" she asked as she reached the front of the wagon.

The girl turned her head to look at her. "Yes, Mother."

Tillandra was surprised she used that name. She didn't recall it being used when they briefly met in Okeans, although the young woman had traveled for some time with Kooka now, it probably came from there.

"Welcome to Anderwell. I hope you will enjoy living here, if that's what you choose?"

"It's where I must be." The young woman's voice was almost devoid of passion, very matter-of-fact. "It's what I knew I needed to do."

"And what is that?"

"The boy, I am here to look after the boy."

"What boy, Gizen?"

"Your baby. The one you carried across the desert."

"Peka?"

"Is that his name? I only know he cannot hear."

"Yes, that is him." There was a feeling of concern inside of Tillandra, her protectiveness for the boy had grown on the trip.

How does this girl know about him?

"What do you mean, you're here for him?"

"It's what I saw. I would be needed, and then I saw Kooka's cart and that was what I needed to do next. So, I came and now I'm here."

"That's a lot to take in. I sense we'll be talking some more about these things you have seen. Let me get you somewhere to stay for now. Okay?"

"Yes."

Tillandra reached out and touched Gizen gently on the forearm and waited for her to lift her hand before taking it. Gizen slid over toward her and she guided her down off the wagon.

Tillandra watched the young woman walk holding her guiding stick in her left hand. Her claim about Peka was intriguing. Tillandra recognized the small twinge of jealousy about the boy as soon as Gizen had mentioned him, but she also knew he was going to need care from someone else.

It was more the surprise of it, and the certainty of Gizen's claim. There was no ambiguity to it. She was certain that was why she was here. That meant Tillandra would see much more of this young woman than the other new arrivals. She had no intention of losing sight of Peka.

～

"MOTHER?"

She turned to see Kooka looking up at her. "Kooka, how are you?"

He looked around to see who else could hear him before he quietly answered. "Tired, Tillandra. Very tired."

She took a moment to take a proper look at him, and she could see it too. His whole form looked worn out. Not defeated, but exhausted. "It's over, Kooka. You deserve your rest."

"I know, but part of me feels like I'm letting them down."

"Who? This lot? You've just brought them to their new life."

"The ones I missed, Tillandra. Or those I have not yet found. There never seems to be an end. Every time I pass through somewhere and find one who is eight or nine, I feel gutted that I didn't find them when they were three or four. That they had to endure for all those years."

Tillandra felt tears well up in her eyes. Kooka's burden was much greater than she had even understood. The time on the cart meant he saw nothing but the pain of the children he brought here. She hadn't truly understood that he was always out on the road, searching, looking, thinking about who he might miss.

No wonder he looked so exhausted. "Perhaps that should be someone else's burden now, Kooka? Think of all the ones who live here now, or are on the Circuit, all because of you."

He closed his eyes briefly and nodded, before looking around at them. "Every story lives inside me. Like they are my own."

"In their own way they are, Kooka. No one forgets the Driver that brought them home the first time. You only have to ask the current students you brought here. They will never forget what you did for them."

"Ah well, I need to stop sounding like I'm dying. Part of me is, but I doubt I could survive another trip as it is. This last leg has been the best, surrounded by warm air. There were some nights in the north where I wasn't sure I'd be able to walk the next day for the cold."

"We can catch up later, I need to see how Goran is."

"And the others."

"The others?"

"We all met on the road here, not in the best of circumstances."

Tillandra hurried over to the second wagon and hugged Beantic.

"In All Jest, Bea. Are you okay?"

"In All Jest, Mother. I am but..."

The large Ngaherian man hadn't moved from the bench on the wagon. He watched everyone around the courtyard suspiciously.

Tillandra raised her eyebrows upward toward him but kept her eyes on Beantic.

"That's just a part of this story. I've no idea why but I convinced him to come with us. He's looking for the girl, but I don't think he means her harm. To be honest I'm not sure he knows what he means. He's just adamant on finding her. I figured better it was here than out there."

Tillandra's concern grew. The girl was still out there. What did this warrior want with her? It was rare to see a Ngaherian male anywhere outside of their homeland. He must have a very strong reason to be this far south.

"What about Goran?"

"He's back here, with Brando."

"Brando?"

"They were traveling together. It was Brando that brought him to me, and he's been hurt as well."

The two men were in the back of the wagon. Goran lay there as if asleep, curled up and peaceful, while Brando sat with his back up against a sack, a little pale, but alive.

"Mother."

"Brando! Are you okay?"

"I've been better, but I'll live. All thanks to that wee lass."

Tillandra looked from him to Beantic.

"That's another story, Mother. I think one for inside. I could do with a wash and something to eat."

"Of course."

She left the guards and others to help Bea get everything inside and walked back to Kooka, who was helping his children down and introducing them to the teachers who would take over their care.

He suddenly seemed concerned and hurried around to the back of the wagon, Tillandra following him.

"There you are, Purple. What's wrong?"

"I'm afraid."

Tillandra immediately saw the side of Kooka that had made him perfect for the cart. He didn't berate the young girl but pushed himself up onto the back of the cart to sit beside her.

"Afraid of what?"

"These people. What they'll do to me."

"You think they will harm you?" His voice was gentle and filled with care.

"Dunno." She shrugged her shoulders at him, before she edged a little to her left, so she was up against him.

"Do you trust me?"

"I guess."

"I didn't harm you, did I?"

She shook her head sideways.

"These people they are my people, Purple. Do you remember the story I told you about my people, on the day we met?"

"Yes."

"Well, this is where we're from. These are my people. I know there seems a lot of them. I know you can't really see from back here, but all the voices you hear out there, that's all the other children. Children like you, that came from other places. Places where their old people didn't look after them. Can you hear them?"

"Yes."

"Do they sound like they're happy?"

She nodded.

"Do they sound like they're being harmed to you?"

Purple shook her head.

"It's okay to be afraid of something new, Purple. Most people are, they just won't admit it. Most people put on a brave face, pretend they're all good, when deep down they are very scared. Makes them be silly at times. But you, you're very brave. You know you are afraid, and you spoke about it. That's one of the things that makes you special, Purple."

She looked up at him, and Tillandra's heart nearly melted. The look in her eyes, the adoration for this old man, who she had only known for such a short time, was so deep. His words had touched that part of the girl that needed them.

Tillandra was reminded how important what they did was, that no matter what else they had to do, this part of their role was more important than any. She hadn't spent any time with the Court deciding who the next Driver would be, but that had to change.

This was what they had been set up to do, as much as they had to keep Dharatan at peace and protect the stone, bringing the broken home to Anderwell was also their job.

"Can I carry you, Purple?"

She smiled up at him and lifted her arms out in front. He got down off the back of the wagon and hugged her into his chest, before turning and heading around to where the teachers were.

Tillandra saw the smile on his face and the pooling wetness in his eyes. She knew whoever took up the role would have a hard act to follow. She left them all and headed back to the college, adding the weight of yet another decision to those already there.

107

LANI

Ahead in the distance Lani could see the city of Anderwell. The tall red walls looked more like those of a fortress than a city. They spread to the scrawny river on the left and the desert sands on the right. It too seemed to call her.

For the last few days as she trudged along, the pendant squeezed in one hand while the other was held firm by one of Odajeen's, Lani felt a slither of hope. Or she hoped it was. Days before, when she'd felt the fever of despair flood over her, the only thing pulling her was behind her.

But over the last half day she began to feel something else. At least she hoped so, and not her imagination. Lani was more exhausted than she could have every imagined. Not from the constant walking but from something else.

She had hoped that making the decision in Jarv to come to Anderwell willingly would set her mind at ease. But it hadn't. She still doubted herself, she was upset with those that had used her to come here, but more than anything she was perturbed by not knowing.

There were things hidden from Lani which affected her, and she was tired of not knowing what they were. She hoped the feeling she had, that something was pulling at her hand, the one with the brooch in it, was real. That in this city, she could find the answers she sought.

Maybe it was a sense of uncertainty in Odajeen that had appeared as well. The older woman was putting on a brave face, Lani could sense that, but she wasn't sure about coming back to this place where she had once lived.

Lani had tried to ask her about it, but was met with a, "Don't worry about me, girl. Let's just get you safe." There was nothing more said about it.

Their group had hardly spoken at all over the last few days, making their arrival in Anderwell seem even more serious, as if they were all concerned about what would happen there. A half mile back from the gate they approached, Lani stopped in the middle of the road.

"What is it, Lani?" Odajeen stood beside her.

"I don't know. I just can't take another step."

"Can't, or won't?"

Lani considered the words her strange companion had said. She could move, if she wanted to. Whether or not she wanted to was the question. All of her thoughts, the battle in her mind, had come to this point.

She thought she had made the choice in Jarv, and several days before when she'd clung to the brooch, but they were all only part of the choice. It was now, or more importantly when they got to the gates, that she actually had to choose.

Once she went in there, and found the woman known as Mother, she couldn't turn back. Whatever happened then was something she couldn't see. One bit of her wanted to cry. She'd finally got here, and after everything she was not sure whether she'd done the right thing.

That part of her knew the whole idea was stupid. How could she do all this and turn back? What would that achieve? A distant voice in her head wanted her to turn back, to leave this place. To go far from it.

It had not returned as strong as it had been, but it was still there, just. Lani assumed it was as much the voice of her doubts, rather than actually being the amulet. It was easy to blame the thing tucked away in the pouch, but it couldn't really talk to her.

She didn't doubt it could affect how she thought. In Statiiv she had seen and felt that. But this was different, this was Lani choosing what was to happen next. Did she really believe in what she'd been told, what she read?

Many things had seemed to direct her here, but now she tried to pick the thread undone, to separate the strands from each other and weigh them up individually — Ashantha, his journal, Henri, the seer. Odajeen.

"What do you want to do, Lani?"

She'd forgotten she still held the woman's hand, that she stood beside her. The brothers stood off to the side, waiting patiently as other travelers and wagons bustled by.

Lani looked again at the city ahead, and then at the woman beside her. She looked back over her shoulder, at the road behind her. Maybe it was that which helped her make the final decision. The thought of having to walk all the way back.

Back to somewhere else. Not Barnen. She had nowhere to go, no one to go to. Maybe it was that. And the exhaustion she felt. And being so utterly tired of he questions about her past, about the amulet she couldn't leave behind, and now the brooch.

She needed answers. Thenis help this mother, if she couldn't provide her some.

"We go on."

Odajeen nodded her head, and the two of them began their walk in step together, toward the open gates in the tall red walls.

Lani held her breath as she passed through them. It was that final moment, when the choice was made completely, and it wasn't until they were out of the tunnel in the wall that she was able to take another deep breath.

Inside the walls she felt almost relief. And the complete lack of wind. Which meant it was even hotter than outside, if that was possible. Without the breeze outside the walls, the heat seemed to bounce up from the paved road, making it even more broiling.

Lani wiped her brow with her sleeve. They moved away from the gates and off to the side of the road.

"What now, Odajeen?"

"That's up to you, Lani."

"Is it? This is as much about your homecoming as it is me being here. We made it. I'm safe."

"Perhaps. I don't understand much about it, but there's so little blue left in that stone of yours, I want you in the hands of the people here. It needs to be boosted. Then I'll feel happier."

"So?"

"There's a place here where they are all based. A college, I think. We should go there."

"Do you know the way?"

"I can't say. A the moment everything seems so new to my ears, I can't be sure of anything."

Lani got Vefed to ask directions and the small party started off again, deep into the middle of the city. The whole place was very orderly and pleasant. While there were guards patrolling, they seemed less threatening than in other places.

Everyone was polite and the roads were the cleanest she'd seen in a long while. There were even people who seemed to spend their time sweeping up the excess sand and loading it into carts that took it away, back outside the walls, Lani guessed.

A thing that struck her as very different was the number of people here who had physical differences, the type that would normally have them thrown out or bullied in other towns or cities. You'd usually only see men and women with missing limbs or the like begging, in corners of the worst parts of the city.

Not here. It appeared on the surface that more than half the people she had seen were like that. She saw many other blind people, which explained why Odajeen would have been living here. She didn't understand why the place was this way, nor did it bother her. But she'd noticed it. Just one of the many differences this place seemed to have.

They'd been told the building they wanted was the tall dome that stood above many of the other buildings in the city. Every building had a similar red tinge to it, and beneath her feet she could feel the gritty sand not yet swept up.

Lani imagined it was a never-ending task. While there was no wind today, she could picture sand blowing in here from the north and west. The stain of it was everywhere.

When they turned toward the college, she could see that a large open area led to it. It had to be at least a hundred paces square and all of it was cobbled. In each corner stood large palm trees, as still as the air they walked through.

The square and domed building were impressive, and she stopped and took in the sight. Massive columns ran along the front of the college building supporting the roof that jutted out. Two large doors, much bigger than any person needed, were open.

"What's wrong?" Odajeen sounded concerned.

"Nothing. I was just taking in the college. It's amazing."

"Describe it to me, would you?"

Lani did her best, trying to explain the way it dominated the city.

"Thank you. It's something I don't think I ever asked anyone to tell me before. I know it was somewhere I lived in, or around, from what I can recall, but not what it looked like from the outside. To someone else."

"I guess we should get this over with then?"

Hand in hand the two travelers walked toward the college.

Everything seemed to move slowly. Lani reasoned it was probably her tiredness, and the anxiety about finally being in Anderwell. She was very nervous and also excited. There were possibilities here. She hoped at least.

What she hadn't counted on was seeing him here. Stepping out of the shadow of one of the tall columns at the top of the stairs was the warrior. The same one she'd run away from in Jarv, and back in that forest.

"It can't be!"

"What, Lani, what is it?" Odajeen had picked up on Lani's fear.

"A man, the one who I told you about, the Ngaherian."

"Be easy, Lani. Remember what I said to you before. When people cross your path several times, pay more attention, in case they have something to teach you."

"But..."

"The brothers will not let any harm come to you."

As if on cue one of the men behind her called out. "Easy pal, what do you want?"

"To speak to this one." The warrior pointed at Lani with his right arm.

She could see his left had a wound on it that was very purple and looked poorly and he carried the arm as if it was sore.

"What do you want with me?"

He had stopped on the steps looking down at her. He was already a large man, but with the extra height he towered over them. It didn't help her feel any more relaxed.

"It was you, in the Tombs. You got away."

"What Tombs?"

"The forest, you were brought there by those men in black. Don't you deny it."

"I was taken into the forest, I don't know what you mean by Tombs. You tried to grab me, I wasn't one of them, they had me prisoner."

"Because of you, now I have been sent away."

Lani had no idea what the man was talking about, but he was upset, she could see that. He didn't look well either.

"It's your fault!" His voice sounded angry but his face looked sad.

Vefed and Irdan and come forward and were in front of both her and Odajeen now. They were on edge, and Lani could see they both had one hand on their swords, waiting to see what the Ngaherian would do.

No one moved, and Lani could feel sweat running down her back, as the sun cooked her out in the open courtyard. The Ngaherian man stared at her, but he seemed elsewhere, his look not as focused as she thought it should be.

Then everything that had seemed to be going slowly sped up.

A group of people hurried out of the open doors at the top of the stairs, led by an extremely tall woman. She called out, but Lani didn't catch what she said.

The Ngaherian turned his head toward her voice, then wobbled and collapsed down the stairs and didn't move. What had been tense moments before had turned to feelings of concern. The people hurried down the stairs, the brothers stepped forward and knelt down to check the man.

"What is going on, Lani?"

"I wish I knew, Odajeen."

TILLANDRA

The five members of the Court sat in the meeting room next to Tillandra's office. She hadn't wanted to be down in the map room, not today. Overnight in a fitful sleep she'd had a small vision. In it someone was knocking on the door of the college.

Tillandra couldn't see who it was, and was hurrying to get there but she couldn't seem to find her way. It was one of those dreams that you woke from feeling agitated, as if you'd failed at something when all you wanted was to rest.

Beantic had explained everything that she'd experienced from Mugan back to here, including the appearance of the man called Carnus. They'd not had time yet to talk to him, and he had told Bea only a little of why he had been following them.

He had recognized Brando and Goran on their wagon. He'd told her that they had been hunting a woman when he'd last seen them, and he wanted to find that woman. She and Tillandra knew who he meant, but not why.

Brando was recovering but slowly, and what he might know could wait for now. Goran was their immediate concern and then the Audition.

"Does anyone have any idea what's wrong with him?"

"I'm not a physick, Mother," Lionel answered, "but it sounds like he's lost his mind."

"I think it's different from that," Bea said. "There's two people there, he's fighting within himself."

"Like good Goran and bad Goran?"

"Kind of. Much as we all have voices in our heads that veer different ways on different topics. It's as if one of his is bigger and meaner than just a voice. Goran changes into someone else, even his speech changes. It scared me the first time, I thought he was all gone."

"He's not?"

"Not yet, at least. Although the other one seems more dominant. I've had to will him back when he shows, it's hard to deal with. He'll cuss and thrash, then be as nice as a lover before going into a rage. Brando has seen him in full flight."

"We can't keep him asleep like this forever. We'll have to do something." Tillandra hated knowing how dire it was for her friend.

"We need a healer, or someone more able to help. But I think now we're here, he should be contained."

"What do you mean by contained, Bea?" Junther's voice sounded grim.

"Locked in a cell. Out of the way of others."

"What on Dharatan?"

"Yes, Junther, I know. Hear me out though. I think part of the problem at the moment is that I have to bully this other Goran back into his shell. Normal Goran feels that too, he feels me hammering at his will, one of his friends, colleagues. If he wasn't already feeling on the outer, he is now. It's not helping. When he comes out, he's timid, flaccid almost, like he's already given up. We need to stop that, and stop the potion that's knocking him out. As long as there's no one around him that he can charm, then maybe they can battle it out in safety."

The group sat there, contemplating what she said.

"Until we find someone that might be able to help, I agree." Tillandra didn't like the idea much, but she liked it more than seeing Goran as he was now.

Reluctantly the others agreed as well.

"The Audition then. I want to get it done, are we ready?"

Lionel shifted in his chair and sat up. "We're never ready, not really, but with Beantic back we have four of us, and we've got three Prospects. I don't see any reason we can't proceed."

Tillandra looked at Toolet, who had been strangely quiet. "Is your new lad ready?"

"I don't know. He's only young, but he's a spark, let me tell you. And his skill is very very distinct."

"That it is. If he's not ready to enter the doorway then no harm will come to him. But you chose him for a reason, so it counts for something. Tomorrow evening then?"

That had been much easier to decide than Tillandra had thought.

"What else do we need to cover?"

"Kooka?" Beantic asked.

"What about him?"

"He's done isn't he? I mean as Driver."

"Yes, I think he should be. He's done more than enough time on the road. We will have to appoint a new one. But I think that can wait a few weeks, there's no need to hurry someone back out just yet."

"He's bought one awfully special group with him this time." Lionel had started on his pipe and puffed as he spoke over it.

"That he has." Tillandra thought of the two females in it who both had special skills. "It's rare when he brings someone whose skill is already well out, but two?"

"Feels as if there's more magic breaking through, to me." Junther butted in.

"What do you mean?"

"This Occultation thing. Makes sense to me if whatever was covering everything over is slipping away, that all sorts of things will bubble up. Just seems almost obvious in a way. We usually have to coax out the skills from people, or after the Audition their magic comes out. What if it's able to come through much more easily?"

"You could be onto something, Junther." Tillandra hadn't considered that, she'd been so worried about the bad things that might be coming, she hadn't thought about the opposite.

Someone knocked on the door loudly.

Tillandra called them in. It was one of the senior students. "There's something happening down in the forecourt. Perhaps you should come and see."

When they reached the main doors, Tillandra could see a group of people looking up at the Ngaherian warrior who stood above them on the stairs. As she stepped through the doorway she yelled out, "Stop!" which caught the attention of Carnus.

He turned to look at her but as he did so he wobbled and fell forward, collapsing in a heap at the bottom of the stairs.

"Oh Fuzzelbutt," Beantic yelled out, rushing down toward him.

Of the group two men moved forward and started checking on Carnus. There were two women left standing in the open courtyard. One of them stopped Tillandra in her tracks.

It couldn't be.

And yet she knew it was, and she'd been told as well. The steps felt unstable under her feet and she had to slow herself until she was at the bottom.

"Burgendetta?"

The old woman turned her head, her white eyes different than Tillandra remembered them. Now several purple lines ran through them almost like lighting. But it was her.

"Who is that?"

The young woman beside her spoke up. "She doesn't remember all of it. Not yet anyway."

There was something about the young lady that captured Tillandra's attention, but she brushed it off initially. "I'm Tillandra, the current Mother here. You've been gone a long time."

The blind woman nodded her head slowly. "That name I do remember. I go by the name Odajeen now, Tillandra. I would prefer that to the other."

"Of course." Then it clicked for Tillandra who the younger woman was, and as she turned back to her she spoke up.

"You're Mother?"

"I am. And you must be Lani then?"

That seemed to surprise her.

"How do you know?"

"I was told you were with our lost friend. And we've been looking for you, young lady."

"Well, I'm here now."

Tillandra's colleagues had moved over and were standing looking at Burgendetta.

"It cannot be, Mother. I know you told us, but…"

"I'm blind, not deaf, whoever you are."

"Junther, she goes by the name Odajeen now. And yes, it is her."

"Junther, that I remember. Your voice I don't recall though. Sounds like some old cripple to me. Now I remember. One arm but don't let it touch you."

No one replied, as if she'd said something wrong, then Junther broke the silence.

"So you haven't lost your sharp tongue. Can't see but can cut you with her tongue, that's Burgen… Odajeen for you."

The woman chuckled. "So it's true?"

"What's that?" Tillandra asked.

"What is in my head. I wasn't sure it wasn't just madness. But I was from here? I did those things?"

"Yes, it's true."

Tillandra looked back at Lani. "You've a way of attracting the strangest people to you, Lani."

"Not by choice."

There was reluctance in the girl, that Tillandra could see, and even some anger.

"Maybe it's because I'm an old woman and maybe you young folk are immune, but this cursed sun is baking me dead. Can we go inside out of it?

"Of course." Tillandra looked at her colleagues. "Why don't we go back to the room we were in, and get our guests some food and drink?"

They all turned and started up the stairs. Beantic joined them.

"I've asked the men to get Carnus into a room in the college. I think we need to watch over him, that wound on his arm has bad blood in it. He's a fever and all."

"Didn't the girl help?"

"She tried, but what is wrong with him she doesn't have the skill for. She's only young, Mother."

"Come with me, ladies. Let's get you out of this sun as... Odajeen suggested, and something to drink."

"There's something she needs to do, urgently, when we are inside."

"What's that, Odajeen?"

"Why don't we get inside and we can discuss it?"

Tillandra watched Lani take the old woman with her spare hand. Her other one was clenched tight as if she was holding onto something for all her life.

LANI

*E*ven seated Lani could see how very tall Tillandra was. Her face was damaged badly but had healed or perhaps she had been born that way. They had gathered in a big room with a large dark wooden table, on an upstairs level of the college.

It gleamed in the lantern light, the surface polished smooth. There were no outside windows although some light came through the open doors at either end of the room.

Everything Lani has seen about this college, so far, was impressive. From the entrance they had walked her through, the foyer and massive staircase, and each room she had seen on this upper level. There was age to it, and quality.

These people had money, even if individually they wore simple things. It was what she imagined kings and queens had in their palaces, not that she had ever been in one. And yet the people seemed unlike what she expected of royalty.

Each of them were distinctly different. A strange group, most of them seemed to wear their physical challenges with pride. They were quite definitely in charge here. Tillandra had the most presence about her, coupled with a touch of awkwardness, which Lani understood. It was as if she wasn't sure where she should sit or doubted what she was doing.

Lani wanted to feel at ease, to feel safe, but she'd seen too much to trust that things would be as simple as she hoped. And the appearance of the man they called Carnus had rattled her more than she realized.

It had been hard enough to face whatever had been going on in her own mind, getting here. To have someone from before still following her, had undone any sense of comfort she had. Now that she had heard about how he had been wounded, that had doubled.

The men he had fought sounded like the Derks from before. Obviously, not the same ones, but more of them. If they were back here, could they sense her, or the amulet? If so, she wasn't safe. Not now. Not unless she really could get rid of it. A glimmer of hope still shone, but she was so used to things going wrong, she wasn't so sure what right looked like.

"Odajeen, what was it you were so concerned about outside?" Tillandra spoke to her friend.

Lani did now feel like Odajeen was a friend, even a temporary one. She had seen how scared the older woman was to be here, to cross the gateway herself. And yet when Lani had faltered it was she who stood beside her, and helped her gain her strength.

She had not forced her to come, she left her to make her own choice. But for someone she had only known for such a short time, a fondness had grown there, and Lani liked how it felt.

"There are stones here, somewhere up high." She said it as a fact, not really a question.

The table was silent. All of the others looked at Tillandra.

"There are. You remember?"

"I remember lots of it, not all of it, and as of yet, it's not all stitched together into one garment. It's like someone tore it all up and threw it in a pile and my job is to make it whole again."

"What of the stones?"

Odajeen turned to Lani. "Show them. It's okay."

Lani pulled her hand up onto the table, and even she was surprised how tightly it was closed. It had almost taken on a life of its own, the fingers locked that way. She eased it open and her small brooch lay in her palm.

"That's how I found her. I can see it on her, a blue light." Odajeen explained what had happened when she had held the stone. "I don't know how to do it, but the color has nearly gone from it. It needs to be fixed."

"How do you feel, Lani?" Tillandra was looking at her now.

"Tired. Very tired."

"About the brooch, and the amulet?"

"I can hardly feel the brooch. Maybe it's all in my mind but it used to soothe me, but not anymore. I didn't even need to hold it in the past. Just having it near me helped. Now, I'm not so sure."

"And the amulet?"

Lani felt her chest without thinking, before quickly dropping her hand. "It's there." She tapped the back of her head. "I can feel it, but it too has eased."

"Eased?"

"The last few days, almost like it's weakened too."

Tillandra looked at her for a while without speaking. No one else spoke, but one of the older men was puffing on a pipe, blowing clouds up above his head.

"Would you let one of us take it to the stones to see?"

Lani closed her hand protectively. "I'm… I'm not sure."

"The thing is, no one can go up there, unless the stones let them. It's a special thing."

"Magic?"

"What?"

"You mean magic, don't you? Why not just call it what it is?" Lani didn't need them to mince their words. She was here for answers, not to be treated as a fool.

"Yes, Lani. Magic."

"Why don't you let her try?" It was Odajeen that asked.

"It's not that simple, Burgendetta." The other of the older men spoke up, the one whose voice always seemed angry.

"My name is Odajeen. I've told you that, Junther."

"Sorry, but that place is a very special area, we don't let just anyone go up there."

"She's already worn the ring, and used a mask."

The group as a whole gasped as they said together, "A mask?"

"Oh, sorry, Lani. That wasn't my information to share."

"It's okay, Odajeen." Lani reached over and patted her hand.

Lani pulled her satchel across her shoulder and reached into it. She pulled out the tatty journal and threw it into the middle of the table. The thud as it landed made several in the room jump a little.

Then she pulled out the black mask. Her hand ran over it fondly, and she still couldn't believe it was as new as when she had first found it. "This mask of Ashantha."

Everyone was quiet in the room, and she slowly slid it forward toward them. Tillandra's long arm reached out and Lani could see her eyes glistening as she brought it closer.

"What does she mean when she says you used his mask, Lani?" The tiny little woman down the far end of the table was stood on her chair, glaring at her.

"I wore it."

Even Tillandra stopped looking at the mask in her hand and looked up at her. "What do you mean you wore it?"

"Don't you believe me?"

"Not really, no."

Lani could see in Tillandra's eyes that she truly did not believe her. There was complete disbelief as she looked back at her.

"I'll show you, if you want?"

Tillandra clutched at the mask.

"Go on, Mother, if she's so adamant, let's see it."

"But you know what will happen?"

"She said she's done it before, she's perfectly fine is she not?"

Tillandra shook her head.

"She did it one day in our room," Odajeen told them. "I could tell, although it wasn't until later she explained what it was. It felt to me like she had left the room and someone else was there. If you don't trust her, let her prove it to you."

They all sat in silence for several minutes. It seemed everyone was looking at Tillandra.

"Alright then, but I accept no responsibility if it goes wrong." She handed Lani Ashantha's mask.

Lani didn't know what all the fuss was about, even she forgot the other part of what would happen when she did it. She pulled the mask up onto her face, felt the coolness spread through her head and heard the clicking sound.

Tillandra shrieked, and the others all cried out, "Ashantha!"

"What?" It was then Lani realized the part even she had forgotten. When she wore it her appearance changed. She'd seen it all that time ago in the mirror, and it had frightened the ghouls out of her, as it was doing to them. She quickly pulled the mask off and dropped it in front of her.

"Sweet Lord Thenis, what on Dharatan was that?"

"Like I told you, I can put his mask on."

"But… but you changed into him." Even Junther's voice had lost its harshness.

"Like him, not him. You didn't know?"

"No, Lani, we didn't. No one normal can do that." Tillandra had composed herself now.

"I'm normal. Can't you do it?"

"No we cannot. I can't explain right now why. Perhaps when we know each other better I can, but what you just did, that is unique."

Lani enjoyed hearing that. She'd been angry for so long at what she'd been forced to do, but knowing that she could do something others couldn't felt good.

"What about the others?" Junther asked.

"I was thinking that myself. We'll save that for another day."

"What others, Tillandra?"

"I think for now we'll just catch our breath. Having seen that, I think perhaps I'm willing to take her to the stones."

"Why now?"

"As Odajeen says, she was able to put on his ring, and this… well, this is something else altogether. Let me say that she seems to have unique talents of her own, so I'd be interested to see if she can pass that threshold."

"Ah, I think I understand," the one with the pipe mumbled.

"Just you and I? Will that be okay with you, Odajeen?" Lani asked.

"Yes. Lani, you must get it renewed, that's what she told me."

"I know, Odajeen. I will."

Tillandra led her away from the others, and they climbed up another floor before turning down a hall that was quite dark. At the end of it stood an open doorway, but the frame around it was all carved stone. There were letters in it that Lani couldn't read.

"What does it say?"

"'To cross you must choose.'"

"What is it with everything about choices?"

"I'm not sure I get what you mean, Lani?"

"Don't worry, just something I heard recently."

"I am going to go through. When I do you won't be able to see me, but I will be on the steps on the other side. Like it says, it is for you to choose if you want to be on the other side. Normally when we bring people here they have to make a choice which will change their lives. If there's anything in your mind that you need to resolve, choose and step through."

"What happens if it doesn't let me?"

"You'll walk into the door and bang your head."

"But there's no door there."

Tillandra laughed and stepped through. As she said she would, she disappeared and the open doorway stood before Lani. She could see through it but only into darkness. There was nothing on the other side, or nothing she could see. Definitely not any steps.

Lani shrugged her shoulders. She'd had to build her resolve so much these last few weeks, what was one more effort? She'd already chosen, she'd chosen to come here, to meet this mother. To learn about herself.

She stepped through the doorway.

LANI

*H*er foot landed on solid ground. The stairwell Lani was in had plenty of light and an astonished Tillandra stood a few steps upward. Lani smiled up at her.

"Aren't you just a bundle of surprises, young lady?"

"I guess I am."

"Come with me, it appears you are meant to be here."

They climbed up the stairs, which appeared to be a turret. The staircase wound around in a circle and when they reached the top, Lani could see out across all of Anderwell and out into the desert. The view was breathtaking.

"Special isn't it?"

"It is."

"Come over here."

Tillandra stood in the centre of the round level they were on. A single pedestal came up from the floor and held a platform on which a circle of crystal-like stones were placed. Each one was square in shape but long with a point on their head.

In the middle of them all stood another one, twice as thick and about the same height.

"That one in the middle is known as the Mother Stone."

"It's yours?"

Tillandra laughed. "No, but there are some things I have to do with it."

Lani could feel the stones, as if they were vibrating, and her body could sense it. She held up the brooch which was still in her hand, and it seemed to glow brighter. The vibration was coming through that and up her arm.

"Can I put it there?"

"I guess so."

Lani laid it down next to the stone in the center, and saw it light up immediately. She felt strange having finally put it down. Then she could feel a pain in her chest, a burning feeling around her heart, and it kept growing. She felt as if she was going to burst into flames, her chest felt so hot.

She put her hand on the edge of the pedestal to support herself.

"Lani, what's wrong?"

That was all she heard before she blacked out.

She could hear people speaking but it was distant, like she was in another room.

"What happened?"

"I don't know, she was fine. We got up there…"

"She got through?"

"Yes, first time."

"Wow."

"I know. Up at the pedestal the brooch reacted to the stones. She placed it next to the mother stone and stepped back. Then she clutched at her chest and her face went all red, then she collapsed."

"She said nothing?"

"No."

"Is she going to be okay, Beantic?"

"I don't know, Lionel. I'm not a healer."

Lani could smell the wood of the room they'd been in before. And she couldn't feel the pain in her chest anymore. She opened her eyes.

"Thank Thenis." It was Beantic leaning over her. "Here, sit up, lass."

It took Lani several minutes to think through what was happening. She was given some ale to drink and it felt good, quenching a very dry throat. Then she looked around frantically. "My brooch?"

"It's still up at the stones, Lani. When you collapsed I brought you straight back here. Besides, if it needs to be recharged it will take some time."

She wasn't so sure she wanted to be separated from it, but right now she didn't feel like going anywhere.

"What happened? One second you were fine, then you clutched at your chest, and went all red before passing out."

"It burned, so hot. My chest. I couldn't breathe it was so hot."

Lani felt where the amulet was on her chest. She could still feel the jewel on the inside. She reached into her tunic and pulled out the pouch, and placed it down directly in front of her. She could still feel warmth radiating from the pouch.

"I think it was this."

"What's in there?" Tillandra asked.

"The amulet that Ashantha gave me, that Henri told me to bring to you."

"The stones would not have liked that. I'm surprised you got through the doorway with it."

"The pouch, it blocks it somehow, and the brooch. I don't understand what they do, but they matter."

"When you put the brooch down it would have exposed it to the stones. You're probably lucky that pouch protects it."

"It didn't feel lucky."

"Can I?" Tillandra held out her hand.

"I'm not sure you can." Lani went on to explain what she'd experienced around the amulet, or the key parts. "So far I'm the only one that can touch it without dying. And somehow it's connected to me. I can't get away from it, like I said."

"I'm not sure we should take it out of that pouch just yet either,

Mother, who knows what might happen? And if Lani is affected by it, she doesn't have her brooch, it might not go in a good way."

Tillandra got up. "Give me a minute, I just remembered something." She left the meeting room and went to her office. She banged around for a few minutes then Lani could hear her talking to someone.

She came back in and sat down. "We'll need to wait a little longer. I was given something that might help, but it must be in my office at home. I've sent someone to fetch it."

Lani had some hope that maybe this woman could help her after all. When she'd first got up to the stones, she had felt a wave of calm come over her. If it hadn't been for what had happened to the amulet, she would have wanted to stay up there, soaking it in.

When the messenger arrived back they handed Tillandra a black box. It was very plain and not particularly big, but big enough for the pouch.

"I was given this by the person who makes our rings. He was told it would be helpful to keep something in that needed to be kept locked away. When you explained about the amulet, I remembered it. I think it's meant to hold it."

She opened the box and placed it in front of Lani. "It's up to you."

Lani didn't see any reason not to try it. After what had just happened, she'd be glad to be rid of it. Where it had always felt wrong, or contrary in her mind, the blue stones up in the turret had almost sung to her through the brooch. Now she knew the difference between the two stones.

She picked up the pouch, dropped it into the box, and closed the lid. She closed the clasp, and as she did it felt as if she was closing a padlock on a large crate. Even the sound of it echoed in her mind, like a loud clanging sound.

And then it was gone. That spot in the back of her mind, was gone. For the first time since Little Big Rock, it was gone. Nothing. Just her head, her thoughts, not the lingering sense of something else. She slumped back in her chair, relieved.

Finally.

"How do you feel, Lani?" Odajeen had been silent up until now.

"Free."

"In your head?"

"Yes, Odajeen. That spot, it isn't there at the moment. For the first time, since... Little Big Rock."

"That is a good thing. Although it is not gone, just hidden, for now."

The woman's sense flattened Lani's spirits, but she was right. It was blocked which was a good thing, but it wasn't undone. Maybe it didn't matter. Lani was keen to see if she could leave it behind, and got up and walked out of the room.

She got to the bottom floor and a grin spread across her face. She was much further from it than she'd been able to get before, so the box was blocking it. Lani returned back to the room, to a table full of curious faces.

"I wanted to see if I could walk away from it, unlike before. And I could, I got all the way downstairs, before I chose to come back."

"I think you'd be safe back up at the stones now too, Lani."

So many things now that she could choose to do differently. Not that she really understood the amulet, or why it was connected to her in the first place, but it was something.

"Are you happy to stay with us for the time being, Lani?"

"I think so."

"There are some other things that we need to take care of, but I think you and I need to get to know each other. I have a sense that there's more to you than we've seen yet, amulet or no amulet. I'd like time to learn more from you."

"Okay."

"And you, Odajeen. I'm sure there are many things for us to discuss."

"Perhaps, Tillandra. I have questions, but more than anything I wanted to help Lani."

"Nonetheless, you are our guests for as long as you wish. I'll get someone to find you quarters, and if you don't mind, a guard or two."

"My men will do that no problem."

"Of course, I forgot them. I just want everyone to be cautious after what happened to Beantic and Goran on the road."

As they finished up the meeting, Lani's initial joy had turned to exhaustion. She knew she was tired, but the rush of the last few hours had masked it. Now that the amulet was gone, and she knew the brooch was safe, she wanted to sleep.

When they reached their rooms, she didn't even bother washing. She pulled off her outer wear and collapsed on the bed. Within seconds she was fast asleep.

111

TILLANDRA

After tossing and turning throughout the night, Tillandra gave in and sat up on the edge of her bed. Being back in her own room, here in Anderwell, had made her feel better after her journey. But with everything that had surfaced over the last few days she just couldn't settle.

Burgendetta's arrival was one of the reasons. It wasn't her presence that caused Tillandra angst but that her knowledge had returned, or at least some of it. Every day now she felt like something else changed in their world, and Tillandra wasn't sure how she could keep up.

Junther's suggestion that the slipping veil was exposing new things, made a lot of sense. Burgendetta/Odajeen, was another example of that. The arrival of not just one, but two, skilled youngsters on the cart, was unusual as well. Then there was the enigma, Lani.

That girl had turned their world upside down. Simply wearing Ashantha's ring had been enough, but the mask, that had shaken Tillandra. Seeing Ash sitting across the table reminded her of the role she had in his death.

Everything the girl touched highlighted she was special, but Tillandra didn't know what it meant for them. The power of the amulet had been of major concern to Ashantha, and yet he'd allowed her to bring it to them. She was amazed that from what little she'd learned so far, Lani had made it all the way here. The gods were definitely guiding her one way or another.

Another reason she couldn't settle was Peka. She had become so accustomed to his company that now she felt as if something was missing from her life. He had been happy to go into Gizen's care, which allowed Tillandra the freedom to do her work, but it also made her sad. She would need to find more time to spend with him.

But out of everything it was her excitement about the Audition that kept her awake. Today was the day that everything she had done these last few months was for. To make sure they replaced Ash in their group of twelve.

Tillandra stretched her arms above her head before standing and quietly heading down to her kitchen. She hadn't expected to see Milfred so early in the morning, but he was sitting at the table.

"Do you listen at my door all night long?"

"No, M-m-mother. I just do not sleep much at all."

"I'm sorry if it's my work that causes you that."

"Not at all. I've always been that way. I don't fight it, I just carry on."

He had already made her a chai and they sat together quietly sharing a warm drink, as if she'd never been away. It was a pleasant way to start what was going to be a tiring day.

One of the things she had pondered through the night was whether Lani should also try on the Audition mask, whether it was her that would take up the mantle. She'd already been able to pass the doorway test, and a ring had attached to her before as well.

But the memory of the way the stones had reacted to the amulet on her, and the knowledge that the girl was bonded to it, pushed that idea away. Deep down she knew it wasn't right. Whatever truth lay behind the amulet, it didn't belong here.

Ashantha has warned it was evil, and the goddess had warned them as well. If only she'd told her what to do with it. For now the box would keep Lani and them all safe from it. They'd tried to put it in the map room, but even in the box, it couldn't pass through the doorway.

So for now she had hidden it in her office. Tillandra had decided that once the Audition was done, she would put it up in the tower protected by the stones. It had been able to pass through with Lani, she hoped it would also pass through in that box.

If the stones were able to mask it, then she believed they'd shelter them all from it, but not until after the Audition. Superstitious that might be, but she didn't want anything unusual up in the tower while that was happening.

Even she was aware of how much excitement there was around the college. Throughout the day she saw groups of students passionately discussing it. Perhaps because they happened so rarely, the tales and myths surrounding them took on a life of their own.

One rumour that had been around longer than Tillandra concerned Prospects failing and losing their minds. Or more accurately, that the mask sent failing Prospects mad. That one had grown from an incident many, many years before and was never quite told correctly.

The truth of it was that a student had put on the mask outside of the Audition, and it had behaved like the masks from a dead Jester and wiped his mind. That was what made Lani's ability to use the mask so amazing, just being able to put it on was unique, the other part of it even more so.

No Prospect was ever harmed by the mask in the ceremony, but then it never hurt to leave some myths alive to protect others from being harmed. It was another reason why now, the unfitted mask always lived in the map room, until the Audition took place.

No one could enter that room without a ring, and ring bearers were never able to wear a second mask, so they too were protected from any harm. Not that she thought any would want to try to do what Lani had done.

By tradition the Audition — or what people referred to as the Audition, the final ceremony for the seletion — was conducted from sunset and into the night and was a private affair.

Before that happened, the Prospects marched through the student hall, cheered on by everyone, teachers included, before being led away. By the time they approached Tillandra on the stage, at the back of the hall, she could see the reality of the event was hitting them all. Especially Sabant and Aakesh. Young Leo seemed less impressed by everything and followed along behind the other two almost unnoticeable amongst the crowd.

Without speaking Tillandra led them upstairs to the entrance to the tower. Downstairs two guards blocked anyone else from being able to reach this level. From now on only the three students and her colleagues would be present.

Partway to the doorway to the tower, Tillandra stopped and turned to face the Prospects.

"And so it begins."

The three students stood side by side in front of her.

"Today one of you will be elevated from Prospect to Jester. There can be only one that fills this role. You have not been given specific criteria on what is required, because each time the person selected is different. The world around you changes every day. And so when a new Jester arrives, they must be the best person to fill the role needed at that time."

She paused and looked at each of them, not knowing who it would be. Even she never could tell who it was that would be chosen, nor did she ever get a vision.

Aakesh was bold but always polite. His skill would suit physical fighting, or tests of strength. Sabant was a lovely young woman, with a rigid sense of what was right and just, her confidence absolute. Her ability to hear would be useful in any court, or situation. And then young Leo, the late starter.

Tillandra wasn't sure how his ability to change shape might help them, but then every skill had its benefits, and often drawbacks. He was very young, the youngest ever to face the Audition.

"You would assume by the name of this ceremony that you must show us your skills, talents, and abilities, to deem you worthy. In a way this is correct, but much of that you have already completed. None of you could be here today if you did not already have the capability to enter the door behind me."

She could see curiosity on Sabant's face.

"Today is not a test of your physical skills, each of you has already passed. Yes, even you, Leo. Each of you know your skills, and has magic within them. That is the first test you had to pass. To pass the rest of the Audition you must have knowledge, certainty and courage. These are the selection criteria that each Jester before you has had to meet."

Behind her the glow around the doorframe grew.

"The next test you must pass is the doorway that you can see. Only those who have absolute certainty may pass through the doorway. The light you see also protects what is through there from those who should not be there.

"If you are to be worthy of selection you must be able to pass that door. You will have one hour to do so. After the hour has expired the light will dim and no one shall pass through. Not even myself could pass through until the ceremony is complete. Do you understand this instruction?"

"Yes, Mother," Sabant said.

Aakesh mumbled yes, and Leo nodded.

"Through the door you will follow the light to complete the selection. It is not a race, the first one there is no more likely than the last to be selected. I will leave you now. Wait until the light around the door flashes three times and then the hour begins. Good luck."

Tillandra turned and walked down the hall through the glowing doorframe and climbed the stairs to the top of the tower.

At the top of the turret, her four colleagues stood around the pedestal. Each wore a white servant's robe, as did she. It signified their role as servants to the stones and to the people of this land.

"Everyone ready?" she asked.

They all nodded. A minimum of four current Jesters had to be present to conduct an Audition, but none would miss it if they were in Anderwell. Tillandra placed her hand on the mother stone, while the other four each placed a hand on one of the surrounding eleven stones.

She could feel the power flowing into her, and the light increased until they were surrounded by it. The final selection was not made by them, despite what the students might think, but by the Citadel Stone through them. Only those deemed worthy would pass the final test.

The pedestal and those around it were shrouded in a bright white-blue light that reached from the floor to the top of the turret. Suspended within it was the mask from the Carver that Tillandra had brought back. Unlike the other masks, it had no defining features carved into it, only the eye and mouth holes. It hung there, the only thing that the Prospects would see, apart from the light, when they reached the top level.

～

LEO SAW THE GLOW AROUND THE DOOR FLASH THREE TIMES JUST LIKE Tillandra had said, and watched as the other two walked toward it. Even Sabant, normally so confident, moved with trepidation.

"It flashed, right?" Aakesh asked her.

"Yes."

It was all a little too bizarre for Leo to accept. He followed them along, but was only going to wait for them to go through before he turned and left. He had to real desire to complete this silly test. He had never signed up for this, he'd been told he was part of it.

That never sat well with Leo. He didn't like to be told what to do, ever since he had been small. He laughed, he was still small. He also didn't like failing at things, and he knew he'd fail at this. He was certain of it.

I'm very certain about that!

He laughed inside again.

～

SABANT WAS CERTAIN IT WAS GOING TO BE HER. IS THAT WHAT TILLANDRA meant? She was certain, she just knew it would be her. She knew it wasn't going to be Leo, she knew that. More certainty, or was that knowledge? Maybe it was both.

She had studied everything she could. She had knowledge. And she felt certain. Was she courageous? That she was less certain about. What would be the test of that? Would it be something dangerous?

She and Aakesh had practiced many dangerous things, both of them together for the last few years. While all the other kids here had done the basic classes, they had labored at much harder things. Taken risks.

Yes, she was courageous, she was sure of it. That was it then, she had all three.

How long has it been?

Sabant didn't think it had been more than a few minutes, but then she had no way of telling. It made her feel anxious that maybe she'd misjudged it. But then the light still glowed, and no one else had moved.

She relaxed a little and let her certainty grow again. Some words were carved into the doorframe. Strangely, she hadn't noticed them when she had first walked up.

To cross you must choose.

What did she have to choose? Choose to pass through, or choose to be a Jester?

Sabant was certain she wanted to be a Jester, one of the chosen. That she was very certain about. She breathed in deeply and stepped forward. The darkness enveloped her, and then she was in a stairwell with steps leading up. A blue glow came from above. She started climbing up toward it.

I KNEW IT.

Leo watched as Sabant disappeared into the black of the door. He'd known she was going to be it, so it was no surprise that she got through. He still stood slightly behind Aakesh who didn't appear as confident as he had previously.

It was just a doorway, Leo didn't understand why the boy didn't just follow his friend through. All he had to do was step through, it wasn't a big thing to do. He simply had to choose he wanted to.

Leo wasn't even sure where that idea had come from, but he knew inside with certainty that it was true. He stepped up alongside Aakesh and looked at him. The young man had his eyes closed.

"Your turn," Leo said.

"I can't."

"Why not?"

"I don't know, Leo. I... I don't know."

Leo looked back at the doorframe and for the first time saw words carved around the frame.

I was right, it's just a choice.

He waited for Aakesh to build up his courage to do it, even though he didn't understand what was so demoralising about it. "There's nothing to be afraid of."

Aakesh looked at him and shook his head as if wishing Leo would go away.

They stood there and Leo didn't know how much longer Aakesh had before the hour would be up. It must be getting close. Even though it was almost impossible to judge, stood here in the near darkness, he just felt that it must be almost up.

"Come on, Aakesh, before the time is up."

"Stop it, Leo. I can't, I told you."

"Do you want to miss out?"

"No."

"Then you better do it, before the hour is up. I mean how hard can it be? Look I'll show you, I'll do it, what's the worst that can happen? I don't get through? You know you will, I know I won't. But you just have to choose."

As Leo said it, he stepped forward, just to show Aakesh he was being silly and suddenly he was in a blackness. Then he was in a stairwell, with steps leading up toward a blue light.

What on Dharatan?

He wasn't meant to be here, where was Aakesh? He couldn't see through the door as it was black from this side as well.

I'll just go back and get him.

The light around the doorframe dimmed, flickered and then went out. Leo pushed back at the center of it but it was solid stone. There was no doorway there. The doorframe was gone as well.

Oh, Aakesh, what have you done?

With no other option, he turned and began to climb the twisting stairs.

~

The light grew the higher he climbed. No one had mentioned that he had to scale a mountain for this. He didn't even want it, but he couldn't go back out so he had no choice. His small legs made it difficult, and he lamented how his skill had been to turn into a rat, not wings or long legs.

What use was a rat? Maybe I could change into a bird? He had to stop himself thinking crazy thoughts. He didn't even want to believe them when they'd told him. He still didn't, and did his best to forget. Except none of the other students would let him.

At first they'd nicknamed him Rat, but then the teachers had stepped in, admonishing everyone for bullying. So they'd changed it up, and now everywhere he went he was called Dent, short for Rodent. That had slipped under the notice of the teachers, and it had become a big inside joke.

The light was almost blinding when he got up into the top of the tower. It filled the center of the space and would have been noticeable for miles around, Leo didn't doubt. Oddly, though, it didn't blind him; it was a bright column of light, but all around it he could see the floor, and outer walks of the turret.

Sabant stood to his right and he saw the surprise on her face.

"You?"

Leo smiled. Part of him enjoyed the fact that it was him here just to annoy her. She was always so confident and condescending to him.

"Yes, me."

His attention was drawn back to the light, and what hung inside it. At first it just looked like a circle of darkness, but he could see it wasn't, and that the mask they had spoken about was suspended in the light.

A voice came from the light, not one he had heard before, a female voice, soft but strong. Kind but powerful, and both of them turned to face it.

Your knowledge and certainty allowed you to make the choice that brought you here. Do you have the courage to proceed? Within everyone lies the truth of who they are, when you hold the stones, I can see within to that truth. We will know who you are, and so will you. Can you bear to look at yourself, to see deep within, to your truth?

And then it was gone. Leo wasn't even sure if it was a real voice or a voice in his head. Sabant hadn't moved, and wasn't looking at him. He didn't want to speak to her or anyone. He didn't know what this meant, ultimately he just wanted it over.

All Leo wanted was to understand what his skill was all about. Why could he change into an animal? Why him? Magic had always been something people talked about with whispers and threats. It wasn't something he had given much thought to.

But here he was in this place, standing in front of a light, with a floating mask, and thinking he'd heard some magical voice. Sure the doorway was unique, that was definitely magic, and Aakesh, Sabant and he could do things others couldn't.

No, this was all too bizarre. He just wanted Sabant to hurry up and get selected so it would be all over, and he could get down out of the tower and back with his friends. It was then he realized he didn't know what would happen to him after this. If there was no need for Prospects any more then what would he do?

Would Toolet just put him back in the normal classes? He'd have to ask her when it was all over. If Sabant would just hurry up and do it. Then she could be picked.

Finally she took a slow step forward, then another, until she was at the light. Then she reached out with her left hand and pushed into the light. He thought he heard her cry out, but he wasn't sure. Suddenly she disappeared into the light.

I'm not doing that, where did she go?

The mask hung there in the light, nothing else changed. He tried counting to pass the time but he kept losing track, unable to remember where he was at. He decided to walk around the tower to see what it looked like on the other side.

The light was a circle; it looked the same from behind as it did from the front. There was nothing else up there. Strangely, the mask seemed to turn so it was always facing him wherever he went, which creeped him out a little.

Why is this taking so long? Can't they just elevate her already?

The more he tried to avoid thinking about the light, the more it drew his attention. He could just walk up to it, like she had done. She wasn't really gone, it was just a trick of the light. There was no mention of them being taken away, so he was just being silly.

Is that what the question of courage was all about? Being too sacred to touch the light, or the stones inside? Leo hated people calling him a coward, he'd always reacted to that. He had courage, how else could someone his size survive with the way he'd been treated?

I'm not a coward!

He wanted to yell it out, scream it at the top of his voice. He braced himself and then walked straight at the light, and put his hand forward.

It touched something cold, and the coolness spread up his arm. He couldn't remove his hand from it now that he had touched it, and he could see he wasn't inside the light, but part of it. His hand sat on a crystal stone, a blue color with bright white light emanating from it.

And then he seemed to float into the light.

He had expected to see people, or something, but there was nothing here but light. He didn't know why they were here. Why was he here? No one ever picked Leo, he was always an outsider. Why were they making him do this?

Everywhere he had been he had always been rejected. His parents, his town, everywhere. He didn't want to be in this stupid Audition, he had already known they wouldn't choose him, and he hadn't wanted to have to face these feelings.

All his life he had been alone, fighting for his survival, until he had come here. But then…

He saw it then, and he could feel tears on his face. He pushed people away, so he never had to be rejected again. Getting thrown out of the class was just another example of how he made himself different, how he wouldn't let himself be in a position for others to reject him.

Leo struggled to breathe, his throat was sore and dry, and he felt trapped in the light. He could feel the stone on his hand but he felt like he was floating in the light, just like the mask.

In that moment he knew what his truth was: that he was so afraid of rejection he couldn't let others in. The way he always said what was on his mind, the way he fought with people was his defense. It was how he survived the real battle, the one within himself.

He had rejected himself by taking on the rejections he had faced. And he was afraid.

With the recognition of his truth a sense of peace flowed through him, as though he had shrugged off a huge burden.

It wasn't the courage to touch the stones. It was the courage to face myself. To accept what had been before and start anew.

Everything began to spin around him. It was either him or the light but everything was spinning, and getting faster. Leo began to feel dizzy. As it slowed and stopped Leo could sense what passing the Audition was about.

The Jesters weren't here just for the college, they were here to serve everyone across the land. They were here to protect what lay beyond this light and these small stones. Where the voice came from - the Citadel Stone. And his head began to fill with knowledge, of what that meant, of those who had come before him.

Until that moment he had not taken it very seriously. It had never been an option he had considered. He was an outsider, making up the numbers, but that wasn't true at all. He was being given a choice. And in that moment, it all came together.

The knowledge, the certainty and the courage.

Could he do it?

"I can."

And as the words came out the mask appeared in front of him. It all felt perfectly natural, although later he would look back on it with amazement, and he took the mask in his hand and brought it up to his face.

The light flashed brighter than he could have ever imagined, his head burned cold and he could feel immense pressure as it pushed onto his face.

Then everything went dark.

Leo realized he had his eyes closed tightly, and he slowly opened them, unsure what he would see. Five smiling faces were grouped around the pedestal he stood at. The faces of the senior Jesters.

The biggest smile was on Toolet's face, directly across from him. His hand was still on one of the stones that circled the pedestal. The light from them was dull in comparison to earlier, just a light glow.

Sabant stood off to the side, shock written across her face. Her eyes narrowed and stared at him. Then she shook her head and collapsed.

"Oh dear, I'm not sure that one was ready to accept not being accepted," Tillandra said.

The two men hurried over and picked Sabant up. "We'll get her taken care of."

Tillandra looked back at Leo. "Aren't you a surprise, Leo?"

He felt a smile form on his face. "I don't even know what just happened."

"You just elevated, Leo. And now you're one of us."

112

LANI

There was a buzz around the college today, as people chatted and discussed the exciting news and important event that had happened the night before. Lani hadn't been told what it was, and while she was a guest, she wasn't one of these people.

She, Odajeen and the two brothers were all staying in the college grounds, not far from where the students lived. It was pleasant enough, and Lani did feel safe there. And she had slept, longer and deeper than she could recall in some time.

She wanted to get the brooch back, that was the only thing that bothered her. It was the only thing between her and her mother. Lani had many questions about it, and perhaps Tillandra could help her with them. The stone in it was the same as those up in the tower. That had to mean something.

Lani was eating in a common area where all the students ate when Tillandra appeared walking toward her. The woman seemed a little lighter of step, even more relaxed than the day before.

"Good morning, Lani."

"And to you, Tillandra."

"Did you sleep well?"

"Better than I can remember, being free of the..." Lani looked around the room. "You know, I think it helped."

"I can only imagine."

"There's a lot of excitement and chatter around the room today."

"Yes, that thing I said we had to take care of caused a bit of excitement. All positive. Now that it's out of the way, I wanted to see if perhaps we could talk, just the two of us?"

"Okay."

"I imagine you'd like your brooch, why don't we start up there?"

Lani smiled. She liked that idea a lot.

Tillandra didn't speak to her while they walked, not until they were both at the top of the tower.

"I wondered what would happen today."

"What do you mean?"

"Yesterday you had the brooch on you, and the amulet. I did wonder if maybe the brooch let you pass."

"I guess not."

"I guess not."

Tillandra picked up the brooch and handed it to Lani.

"How do I know if it's full again?"

"Maybe Odajeen can tell when she looks? Or..."

"Or?"

"I have an idea. I've never done it before but I'm going to try something, give me a minute."

For several minutes Tillandra stood holding onto the mother stone, her eyes closed. At times Lani felt like she heard her muttering but wasn't sure. When she was done she turned to face Lani.

"It worked!"

"What did?"

Lani saw the woman weighing up what to tell her.

"You recall how Odajeen spoke of a voice in your brooch?"

"Yes."

"I think it's the same one that I can speak to. I've just not tried here before."

"And?"

"Yes, she said for now your brooch is charged, it will aid you."

"I sense there's something else."

"She wants to speak with you."

"With me, why?"

"She did not say, Lani."

"In for a toe, in for the whole foot I guess."

"That's an odd saying."

Lani laughed. "I used to work as a fuller, it was something we'd say. What do I do?"

"Just go and put your hands on them, I think she'll do the rest."

Lani took a big breath and placed her hands on the stones.

It wasn't like passing out, Lani knew how that felt. It was more like being in a dream, except she couldn't see anything other than the view. Though the view felt as if it was in the background, her eyes weren't really focused on it at all.

She began to feel drawn into the stones, not physically, but her mind.

Hello, Lani.

Ah hello.

You made it safely.

I did. Who are you?

Someone with a vested interest in your wellbeing.

That's not a straight answer.

No it's not. I can't be here for long, so let me tell you what I need you to know. I think it's safe now to unlock your mind.

That was you?

Sort of. We did it, and I think now it would help to remove it. But you may not like what you learn.

Why?

You will find your memories, and because of your skill, they will feel very real. I cannot shield you from that.

Do I have a choice?

I don't think so. This is too important, you're too important.

Why does everyone keep saying that? Why am I?

You stand between us and the other side, and what they wish to destroy.

How?

So many questions. You are a gift to us, one we did not see coming. Many people have sacrificed for you to be there now. You've met one already.

Odajeen?

And now you will see another.

Why me?

Why anyone, Lani?

What if I don't want to be it?

Then what you know will cease to be. Those behind the amulets and who was sent to harm you will win, they will destroy everything you know, all of what we've protected for so long. We cannot make you, Lani.... You must choose. I have only a little time left, I need to do this thing.

And then the voice was gone.

In its place she felt pressure building up in her head. Lani squeezed her eyes shut but a blinding light pierced her eyelids, and the pressure continued to build. Her legs buckled and she only stayed standing by hanging onto the stones.

She didn't think she could let go even if she wanted to, they seemed bonded to the stones. The sides of her head felt as though they were being crushed inwards. It went away as quickly as it had come. Lani stood up straight just before a loud sound like rocks cracking shuddered through her.

It is done.

What is done?

Everything went quiet. Her eyes were locked closed now, but she could feel the stone floor of the tower under her feet, and the stones under her hands.

Lani heard the sounds of hoofbeats on the ground and voices. Images began to move across her mind, exactly like the way she would replay them when she used her skill. They weren't images she had seen before or could remember seeing.

The memories the lady had said would come.

Everything seemed strange to her. The horses were massive, and all the people tall, even taller than Humaas. It took her a while to realize why. These were images coming from her memory, but they were from when she was very small. Everything she was seeing was from the viewpoint of a small child.

In the images she was riding on a horse, hanging onto the pommel at the front of the saddle, while a woman's arm wrapped around her stomach. She could feel in her memories the sensation of that woman and the security that arm gave her.

Now that she knew she was seeing memories Lani took control of the images, slowing them and playing them backward and forward. Knowing they were real caused her chest to tighten. She could sense being there, her emotions had traveled back to how she was feeling at that moment.

She found snapshots of herself looking up at the woman holding onto her and tears flowed down her face.

My mother!

Here were the images of her mother she had been unable to retrieve for so long. Within her chest pressure was building as the moment overtook her. Lani moved the images forward; there were big gaps between them.

The gaps were inconsistent and Lani couldn't truly tell how big they were. In some, the light helped her to see the differences. She was able to detect a change in the expressions and posture of the group she had been traveling with. Now she could see fear on their faces and the men were securing their armor and freeing their weapons.

Next the whole group looked to be riding hard, and Lani could feel her mother's arm tightly holding her. Then images of the group being attacked and both the men and women fighting for their lives.

Lani's whole body shook with fear and tears ran down her face, as if she was back there all that time ago. The numbers of her group falling were growing and the images became more and more frightening. Almost completely surrounded now, her group had dismounted, trying to protect each other. She was in the middle of them all, close behind her mother who also was brandishing a sword.

She could see bodies scattered around the open ground they had stopped to fight on. One of the men who had been protecting them lay injured on the ground, staring back at the group. An attacker stood above him and drove their curved sword into his chest, causing Lani to scream out.

Everything about the scenes caused Lani grief. She could feel emotions flooding out that she had bottled up for almost two decades. Each snapshot triggered mental and physical pain, her heart was racing, and she was on edge thinking she was under attack right now.

She wasn't sure she wanted to see any more, but she had come here for answers and they were here right now. She had to watch it all.

One of their group forced several of the attackers back. Those they fought all wore black clothing with hoods up over their heads, but no armor. Their movements were fast and lethal but the man on Lani's side, defending them, was almost as good.

A man in black came around him sideways, closer to where Lani and some of the last of their party stood, trying to attack their defender from another side. Their guard frantically turned and engaged the man, blades flying back and forth. Lani could hear the sound of their swords clashing seemingly ringing in her ears.

With a fast slash downward, their guard cut right through the left arm of his attacker. Lani nearly vomited as the image flashed through her eyes of the arm landing at her feet.

What she saw caused her to pause the images and what she was remembering. There, tattooed on the underside of his wrist, was the same mark that the Derks from Barnen had been wearing. The men that had been following her since Barnen and captured her in Callet, the Derks hunting the amulet.

They were the ones attacking her mother all those years ago. The Vrah, Ashantha had called them. None of it made sense to Lani. Why were they attacking her mother and the people they were traveling with? Where were they?

She felt giddy and nauseous as her body relived the terror and revulsion of what she was watching. One of these men in their group, maybe one of the already dead, was probably her father. And she didn't even know.

The scenes continued to get worse. Her mother had knocked Lani down to the ground amongst some bags and one of their horses that had perished. She was wedged partly in safety but could still see everything. Looking up, she saw her mother frantically trying to slash a swordsman away.

Lani wanted to yell, 'Leave her alone', But her throat seized in terror. Nothing came out and she knew nothing about what was happening made any sense. A Derk cut her mother across the stomach and Lani could see the will in her mother's eyes diminish.

Lani could feel herself try to reach out, to help, but her mother fell to her knees and with one hand pushed Lani down to the ground. Her mother undid the blue brooch from her belt, the one Lani now carried, and as she fell to cover Lani, she placed the brooch on Lani's chest. Just before she landed on top of Lani her mother grabbed Lani's left hand and wrapped it around the brooch. Lani could see the look in her mother's eyes which she knew she would never forget.

The anguish, the pain, the sense of failing her daughter was written on her face and in her green eyes, before her body crushed Lani as she fell across her.

Lani was struggling to breathe, gulping for air, and burst into tears in the present as she relived the painful moment that her mother died on top of her.

In her memories she saw herself struggle for breath, with the weight of a dead body on top of her. She couldn't move and the sounds around her faded until it was just her with the bloodied tunic of her mother smothering her face.

Lani could sense the terror her younger self had felt, alone, surrounded by dead bodies and scared for her own life. As she slowly let the memories retreat in her mind she struggled to release the feelings, her face wet with tears, and she had to gulp in air.

She let go of the stone, then turned and slid to the ground. Tillandra rushed to her.

"Are you okay?"

Lani couldn't speak. Her throat was burning, her chest felt tight, and inside she thought her heart was ripped in two. Now she knew, after all these years, what had been locked away from her. She hadn't been abandoned, her mother had fought to the very end to protect her.

More tears came, and sobs, rocking her whole body. Lani felt Tillandra lift her to her feet, her long arms wrapped around her, and being walked away from the stones and down the stairs. Somehow she got her to her room.

She had answers but inside now she knew there were more questions. Later, she could ask them later. Huddled in on herself she sobbed herself to sleep.

Somewhere in the back of her mind she thought she heard Tillandra's voice. "You poor child."

113

TILLANDRA

The meeting in the map room had been a formality, welcoming their newest member into the group of twelve, the Jesters. Afterwards Tillandra had returned to her office to think through what would come next.

The most urgent matter had been resolved. After Leo had taken the mask, he had put the ring on and he was one of them. The youngest person ever to be elevated. She laughed out loud.

"What did I miss?" Beantic was standing at the door.

"Come in. Nothing, I was just thinking about the other night, about it being Leo."

"I didn't know much about him, but he's so young, I hadn't considered it would be him."

"Change is coming from all directions."

"So it seems."

"How is Brando?"

"Getting better. Whatever the young lass did, she seemed to heal what needed healing then, the rest is just about time now."

"Another young one with special skills."

"Yes."

"What of Carnus, that's his name isn't it?"

"Yes. Not so good. He's strong, and trying to fight it, but he's got bad blood in it and it doesn't want to heal. He asks when he can see Lani again."

"I'm not sure that would be a good thing."

"He's very determined. To what end I don't know."

"I wish I knew what to do with her as well."

"Do we need to do anything?"

"What do you mean?"

"She needed help with the amulet, you helped her with that. She's got some skills, maybe she can aid us here, and that's enough."

"The thing with her brooch, it's the key. Her mother had it and gave it to her. She's had it all these years. It appears that it saved her from the amulet, but how would her mother know that, all that time ago? Who was she?"

"I have no answers, Mother. I've got my hands full."

"You don't have to solve Goran yourself, Bea."

"Who will otherwise? I can't bear to see him like he is, I feel I pushed too hard."

"If you hadn't, maybe he wouldn't be here now. You did what you thought was best. How is he?"

"It's hard to watch. Yesterday he was howling like a mad dog. Then sneering at me, and even trying his charm. None of it was Goran, I haven't seen him out in days. And he's not getting anything to help, not the tonic we had given him or anything else."

"Good."

"We'll just have to wait and see. I think I'll visit the church later, I want to pray he finds his way back to us."

"It's probably entirely in his hands now, Beantic. I thought about what you said though, about him being rejected by us, and how he'd take it personally. I believe you might be right. I'm going to visit him each day, get the others too as well. We need to talk to him as Goran, and welcome him home."

"You think that will work?"

"I've no idea, but I don't know what else we can do. If he's buried under this other person, maybe we can draw him out."

Tillandra had little faith it would work, but she hadn't been able to come up with any other ideas. Anything was better than ignoring him. He was one of their own, they needed to try harder.

After Beantic had left, Tillandra was thinking about going to see Peka when Lani appeared furtively outside her door.

"Can I come in?"

"Of course, how are you doing?"

"Up and down, Tillandra. It was a shock."

"I can imagine. She told me some of what you were about to learn and warned me you would be able to see it as if you were there. I can't imagine what that felt like."

Lani seemed to choke up a little.

"What did you want to see me about?"

"I don't really understand what's happening to me."

"What do you mean?"

"All of this. The amulet, all of you, everything. I thought I'd get some answers, that's what Ash told me, what the seer told me. It's why I came, and I've had some relief but no answers. I still don't know why it's me that's having to do this."

The girl took in several big breaths and Tillandra could see tears in her eyes.

"My mother died giving me this brooch, and I have no idea why. The woman up in the stones, she told me I'm important, that I have to be the one. I don't even know what she's talking about. The one to do what? To be what? And why me?"

Tillandra just sat and let her get it all out. She sensed that getting it off her chest was more important than soothing words. When she was all done, Tillandra moved out from behind her desk and went and sat beside her.

"I don't have all the answers you seek, Lani. Not yet at least. I can tell you, though, what you're in the middle of is very much my concern. And I'm going to find answers, I promise you."

"How?"

"That's a good question. So far I've not had much luck and the clues aren't adding up to a full answer."

"Clues?"

"I see things. That's my skill, I get visions, of things that might be."

"Like the seers?"

"I guess. Something like that. I'm not sure if they see any clearer than me, and while mine come to guide me, I just don't always understand them."

Lani nodded at her, but not as though she really understood.

Tillandra stood up and went to a stack of books on the side. She pulled one of those Kooka had brought back for her, and took it to Lani. It was a crazy idea, but maybe she could read it.

"Like this, for example. I went to a place because I thought the answers I sought were in some more books. That's what I dreamed. But when I got these books, they were unreadable to me. Maybe they might make sense to you?"

Lani took the book from her and opened it, but it was just all lines and shapes.

"I can't read."

"But, Ashantha's journal?"

"I'm reading it like him, as him. So I can read it. I wish I could read, but when the mask is off I lose any knowledge of how I do it."

"Oh. Hang on a minute."

Tillandra hurried away through the door behind her desk to the map room. She went to the wall of masks and lifted Ashantha's off the new spot where he'd been hung.

"Sorry, old friend, but I need to try."

When she arrived back in her office she asked Lani to try using it. As she did, Tillandra struggled with her emotions again as the young woman before her turned into a fair likeness of the man Ash had been.

She looked at the book, flicking through pages.

"Nothing."

Even the voice sounded like Ash; it sent chills down Tillandra's back.

Lani took the mask off, and handed it back to Tillandra. "Sorry."

"It was worth a try."

"What now?"

"I don't know. These books are very old, I know that, but none of our historians know the script. If the answers are here, they aren't leaping off the page at me. I need someone a few hundred years old."

Lani laughed. "I think Ashantha was too young for that."

"What do you mean?"

"Well if it's that old, then he wasn't that old. I met him, he's your age or similar, right?"

"Yes." Tillandra knew the girl was right, it was an old script. "I've got another idea."

She hurried back down to the map room and put Ash's mask back up on the wall. Then she went to the beginning of the line, to the first of their kind that had passed away. One of the original Jesters. Tillandra couldn't remember how long after they were formed he had died. Snibbo had been his name, and his chubby face had looked very clown-like all these years hung up on the wall.

She carried it into her office and sat back down.

"Now you don't have to do this, and there's a risk I need to explain, but this mask belonged to someone way back very close to when that book might have been written."

"Another mask?"

"Yes. It's specific to our kind. When we die..."

"I was there when it happened, I know."

"Of course."

"What's the risk?"

"Normally, if someone picked up one of our masks and put it on their face, it would wipe their minds."

"Wipe them?"

"Everything gone. They wouldn't even know how to eat a meal."

"Seriously?"

"Yes."

"So if I hadn't been able to do what I had with Ashantha, I'd have been mindless?"

"Yes. And there's a chance, I don't know, that maybe if you try this..."

"And you want me to take that risk?"

"Sort of, not really. I mean, I think you're safe. When the idea hit me, I didn't receive any bad vision, or warning, in fact the opposite."

"The thing you're not sure of, is the guide to how I decide?"

Tillandra shrugged. It had seemed okay inside her own head, but listening to herself explain it out loud, she knew it was crazy.

Lani reached into her tunic and pulled out the brooch, holding it in her left hand. "In for a toe, in for the whole foot. If this doesn't stop me, I'll do it."

"You're sure?"

"If you don't have the answers I need, and this might help, how can it be a worse risk than what I've already faced?"

Before Tillandra could say anything else, Lani swung the mask up onto her face. Tillandra wasn't ready to see the chubby bald man sitting in front of her, his lips puffy and puckered facing her.

"I'm fine, Tillandra."

His accent was very odd. Tillandra wasn't sure she knew exactly what it was. It was probably closest to a Beng accent than anything else.

"Can you see anything?"

Lani/Snibbo opened the book, his eyes scanning down the page.

"Who was King Unx?"

Tillandra scratched her head. "I think he was from Daskare, but I'd need to check, why?"

"This is all about him, at some gathering. A big gathering, and the deals he was doing."

"You can read it?"

"I can."

114

LANI

*H*er ability to read the books kept her and Tillandra up through a long night. Several of the others had come to visit, or bring drink and food, once they'd become used to Lani looking like Snibbo.

Initially they had worked systematically, especially once Tillandra had confirmed that King Unx had been from the period she wanted. He was the lost king of Daskare, from the Great Battle.

While the books all looked similar, they were of very different events. Each appeared to be accounts of things that fell into the time period that Tillandra had said was important. Lani began skimming, calling out random names or things, to see if they should investigate further.

Tillandra believed these books were copies of other writing, completed by one scribe, explaining why the covers and writing were all the same, and why the topics varied so much.

On the fourth book they found much more obscure writings, a lot of what seemed religious in nature. It was slower to get through, as the style was harder to understand.

"Listen to this: Orange, orange, everywhere orange. A wave shall come, flooding the land in orange… Watch… Something I can't read."

"Wait, that sounds important."

"I've heard something like this before." When Lani scratched her head she felt her bald scalp and struggled to get used to it. "Who was it?… The Watchers, back in… Big walls, huge walls."

"Nkuku?"

"Yes. They're called the Watchers. They talk about an orange wave. They're watching for it, training for it."

"Okay so maybe this is Morskan in origin. Let's read more of this."

Lani read some more. She came to what seemed to be prophecy rather than facts or figures.

"Two sides of the same coin must face each other. Either separate or combined they will change us all."

"That sounds like prophecy." Tillandra has stood up and was stretching her back. "What else does it say?"

Lani went back a few pages.

"One will emerge, who should never be. A stone is carried, a gift to see. Another binds and never leaves. Ahead a path, a choice to make."

She pulled the mask off, and put it down. Lani stood and shook off the feeling of the chubby old man.

"What's wrong, Lani?"

"Did that sound like it was talking about me?"

"I think so, Lani."

"Or are we just finding what we're looking for?"

"Only the rest of it will answer that. In pieces it could mean many things."

"What did it mean about the two faces of the same coin?"

"I'm just writing it all down, but it doesn't add up to much just yet. If you're tired, we can do this tomorrow?"

"No, I want to know if there's anything here."

Lani sat and returned into the character of Snibbo, and read on.

She read pages of what sounded like prophecy and Tillandra wrote it all out in her language. Some of it seemed to refer to Enderk, and their High Prince from the same time, and the gifts of poison. They weren't sure if this meant real poison or the amulets that Tillandra already knew about.

Then as dawn began to arrive, they got toward the end of the writings.

"If the eight become one, and surround the tower of light, so shall she be free, and the light will shatter before her. In those times the battle will finally be won. For the only one who could stop it all will have failed.

"But should any one be gone, then the eight cannot be. For without all, none shall succeed. And she shall stay bound for evermore.

"The hope of all rests in the hands of one. In those unwilling hands, will the choice reside. Each choice destroys, one hope, one desire."

Which was where the previous lines had come next.

"One will emerge, who should never be. Hidden from all, they will carry with them each of the stones. One a gift, the other without choice. And there will come a day when the choice must be made. Hope or desire. Each path will lead to despair, each to loss. And at the end, all will be decided."

Lani freed herself from the mask. She stood up. "I can't do any more, not now."

"That's the end of the book isn't it?"

"It is. What do you think?"

"I think we need to eat, sleep, and let our heads clear. Those are heavy words, prophecy or ramblings. Either way, they need careful consideration."

Lani didn't feel like eating so she'd returned to her room. When she did wake it was to loud knocking on her door. She struggled to get up and unbar it.

Tillandra and Odajeen were outside the door. Lani went back and lay on her bed.

"You look terrible, what's wrong?"

"Just tired, we were up so late. I'm just tired, and a little off in my stomach."

"That was nearly two days ago, Lani. We've been trying to get you up since this morning."

"Just tired."

Odajeen has sat down beside her, placing her hands on Lani's forehead.

"She has no fever. But there's something not right."

"What is it?"

"I don't know. But if she's sick it's not normal."

"I think some outside air, and something to drink might help."

Lani went with them reluctantly, but she had no desire to struggle. Once she was up and walking she felt a little better. Except for her head. At first she thought the amulet was back in her head, and she struggled to think.

When the box had been closed she'd felt it gone, like it had been removed. Not like it hadn't been there. At first she thought it was that, but it wasn't, it was removed. Now that feeling had grown. It was more gone.

They went outside, and the feeling seemed to grow. It was like one of her headaches coming on, little by little. But it was small, she could bear it. She knew it would go away. When they went for food, Lani struggled to eat much, and took little joy from her drink.

After Odajeen left them, Tillandra walked with Lani to her office.

"Perhaps the toll of wearing the mask has made you this way?"

"I've not suffered before."

"But this was someone new, and you wore it all night."

"Maybe. I'll be fine."

"You look terrible. Do you still have the brooch?"

Lani patted her chest and nodded.

"Here sit down, rest up, only talk if you want to."

"What have you figured out, Tillandra?"

"All of us discussed it, even with Odajeen, in case her memories knew anything of this."

"And?"

"We tried to make sense of it and the best we have is this. There were seven amulets gifted, plus the one the derk Prince had, which makes eight. If all eight are joined together, then it will free a force that can destroy the source of the stones you've seen."

"The tower of light?"

"Yes."

"But there's only two amulets?"

"That we know of."

"And my one is one of them?"

"Yes. It's likely the one that belonged to their High Prince, given Ashantha stole it from there."

"And the rest?"

"It seems to read like it's you, Lani, but you knew that."

Lani nodded. She still felt weak. "So it's simple."

"What is?"

"Destroy the amulet I brought here and then there can't be eight. End of prophecy."

Tillandra laughed. "That seems such an easy solution. Don't forget it's connected to you, we have no idea what would happen if we did that."

"Each path will lead to despair, each to loss."

"We won't rush into believing it all just yet, okay?"

Lani had returned to her room, and slept some more. The next day she woke again late, and struggled through a day of doing little. That feeling in her head, like there was a hole in it, seemed a little bigger. At times it ached, a dull pain, but unavoidable.

Each day a little worse. One morning she couldn't open her eyes. The pain had become more like something tearing constantly inside her. And she felt too sluggish to move. They wouldn't let her bar the door, and at times she thought there were people in her room.

Someone lifted her up, and she struggled free of the pain in her head. Lani knew headaches, she had survived them before. Tillandra was in there, and a young girl, a girl about the same age as Lani, but she seemed to be blind, and Odajeen.

Everyone was looking at the young girl holding Lani's hands.

The blind girl spoke. "What is it, Purple?"

"Something is missing. I can't tell what, she's missing something, up here." The little girl tapped her own head.

"There's a box."

"What, Gizen?"

"A box, you put her in the box."

Lani could see Tillandra looking at the blind girl, then she stepped out of the room, and summoned the brothers. "Bring Lani, quickly."

The pain dug in again and Lani let her eyes close. She wasn't walking. The men were walking her, she just followed what they did. She was sat down in a soft chair.

"Leave us now." Tillandra's voice. "Not you, Odajeen."

"I thought the box protected her from it?"

"I did too, but I have to try."

It was like someone lit a lantern and shoved it in Lani's face. She opened her eyes, and looked at the two women.

"What did you do?"

Tillandra held the pouch in her hand. On the desk beside her sat the box it had been in.

"Why?"

"How do you feel?"

"Good. Like the hole that's been there has been filled again."

"I'm glad you feel better, but that's not great news. If it being in that box caused you to feel that way, we have a big problem."

Lani laughed, not really a happy laugh. It was a sarcastic laugh, one that rattled that spot in her head where the hole had been.

"What's so funny?"

"I came all the way here to be rid of it, which I thought we'd done, but it turns out I can't actually do that. Not only that but now I have to find a way to destroy it, and maybe me in the process. That about sums it up, right?"

The two woman said nothing. Lani could see the answer in Tillandra's face.

At least Lani didn't feel exhausted like she had, and she suddenly felt very hungry.

She was done feeling sorry for herself, and fighting it. It wasn't that she felt courageous, or angry. She just knew it was what she had to do. All the running and trying to avoid it weren't going to help. Lani at least knew what she had to do and now she did have people to help her.

"What are you thinking, Lani?"

"In for a toe, in for the whole foot!"

115

KARPENMOR

Every minute of every day he was hounded by people. Servants, priests, advisors all needing answers to more questions than he had thought possible. Too many of them were about the enthronement ceremony than he cared to admit.

No wonder Uksod always looked so tired, and was constantly sniping at him whenever he brought up the ceremony. Maybe he'd pushed him too hard, and that's what caused his collapse, although the old man had seemed fine the last time Karpenmor had seen him before it happened.

The day before, they had met and Karpenmor had actually enjoyed talking to him. That was because it was all about the amulet and retrieving it, as well as a partial discussion about the bridges on the Stepping Isles.

When they talked about those sorts of things they had seemed aligned, and Karpenmor recognized how much Uksod had stored in his head that was useful to what Karpenmor wanted to do. It was on other matters where they clashed, and mostly in recent times it was about the accession.

His accession.

Once Karpenmor had decided he was ready, he wanted it over

with. He wanted to rule, to be able to determine what happened around here. It was the simplest path to him getting what he wanted. But Uksod had been taking forever in getting everything in order. Karpenmor had considered it was deliberate.

Standing here looking at the priest in his chambers, comatose, pale and fragile–looking, he couldn't put that thought aside.

I wouldn't put it past you that this is your last game to delay me, Uksod.

Karpenmor felt childish thinking such a thing. Here was the man who had raised him, and who had maintained the rule of his father so that Karpenmor could rule. And he lay here in a deathly state, the last person Karpenmor had any relationship with.

Today he had told everyone that they could all wait, he would not be answering any more questions about cloth, and flowers, and what type of incense they needed. He wouldn't be approving anything that needed doing, or being in attendance to receive appellants to attend the ceremony.

All of that was something Uksod did, was good at, knew much more about. Today he was going to wait here and hope that the old man would regain his strength. Karpenmor needed him.

It struck him like he had been hit by a stick.

He had no one else. And for all of that over the last few months, Karpenmor had been doing everything to distance himself from the man. There was no mother or father, he had never had any siblings. His servants changed yearly and he'd never even met a woman likely to be a future bride, it hadn't even been discussed.

The only person in his life that he had any relationship with was Uksod.

Karpenmor looked around the man's room and noticed for the first time how stark it was. There was little of anything opulent in the space, nothing to signify that for many years he had ruled the greatest country in this world.

This was the room of a priest, a man dedicated to serving his god, or goddess in this case. The circlet on his head, with the amber gem on his forehead, and the gold candelabra on his side table were the only two things that were of any value.

And he had been the only parent Karpenmor had ever had. They should be working together, the angst between father and son needed to be resolved. It was Karpenmor who was to be ruler, but there was no reason the two of them couldn't be allies.

If he recovered, Karpenmor swore to himself he would do more to make it work, and not simply resort to the false pleasantry that he had used recently to try and win him over. They could have different opinions, but they should be working together.

After several hours, Karpenmor dozed off in the chair beside Uksod's bed. At first he thought it was a dream, but then he heard a voice. Uksod was stirring in the bed. The priest was twisting under his covers, mumbling incoherently.

Karpenmor grabbed a cloth on the side table, wet it in a bowl of water and wiped the old man's brow. He didn't know anything else to do, even though the priest wasn't feverish. Slowly as the day wore on Karpenmor sensed the man was recovering, if only because the restlessness had grown and occasionally he could hear real words spoken.

The room felt stale to Karpenmor, and hot, and he was getting tired of being there. His resolve to stay here the whole day was wavering.

He paced about the room, flicked through some of the man's books from the large bookshelf opposite his bed, and harassed servants waiting outside to bring him food and drink. As every hour passed, he felt glad that soon he could go and know he had been here at his side tending him. Even if Uksod would never know.

"Get it, at all costs."

Karpenmor turned and hurried over to the bed. Uksod's eyes were still closed and he was mumbling now. It sounded like he had said 'girl' and 'desert', but it was hard to tell. It wasn't like that first sentence.

Get what, Uksod?

Then nothing, more tossing about. Once it sounded like he barked, but it was probably a growl of pain. Karpenmor slumped back in his chair, his back aching from being in the same position much of the day.

"Hurry, we need it back. Only the amulet. Get the amulet."

Now Karpenmor was interested. "What about the amulet, Uksod?"

He knew the man wasn't speaking to him, but he needed to ask anyway. Maybe it would keep him talking.

Uksod's breathing was louder, but he had settled down more now. Most of the twisting was gone. It even looked to Karpenmor as if some color had returned into his cheeks. As if he had more life in him.

Good, the old man will live.

He was happy about it, but he also wanted to know what the priest was saying.

"You must hurry. Before it disappears. At all costs. Do you understand?"

He was replaying a conversation, that's what it sounded like. Or having one in a dream.

"Near Anderwell, the city. Head south."

That name didn't mean anything to Karpenmor, he would look it up when he left here. It wasn't an Enderk name, so it had to be on Dharatan. South. South of what?

Karpenmor found it hard to leave. He waited another two hours or so but there was nothing else out of the man's mouth. He had heard it all, for now at least. He hurried over to the Vrah library and looked at the map on the wall.

Everything they had learned from their ventures into Dharatan was marked out there. Cities, towns, mountains and rivers. Anything that they could remember had been drawn up on this massive map on the wall. Karpenmor started from the bottom trying to sound out names he read, unfamiliar names, until he found a cross marked alone, except for a large lake to its northeast.

Anderwell.

It took him another few hours to find a mention of it in the notes that they had. And it was only a mention.

A remote city on the edge of the desert. Those with broken minds taken there. Sickly children collected from other cities and brought there to die. Rumored to be full of sickness and madness. Investigate later, with caution.

Karpenmor found it a strange concept that one city would exist to accept and handle all of the dead or dying, and those who had gone mad. It was the least amount of information he had read about any city.

Some towns got little mention, but it was strange no one had found out more. The Vrah weren't meant to be affected by superstitions and irrational fears. He would mention it to One, and ask if perhaps there was a better description of the place.

What connection would this city have to an amulet? It seemed unlikely that there was one if it was a city for invalids. Unless... unless. A place where others wouldn't go, wanted to avoid. What better place to hide something valuable?

Now that was an idea. Something to look further into, something to discuss with Uksod when he recovered. Once the ceremony was over and he was High Prince. Then there'd be nowhere that he wouldn't look, crazy fools or not.

THE END

ACKNOWLEDGMENTS

A huge thanks to everyone that read Book 1, A Fool's Errand, and pushed me to hurry up and finish this one. No doubt you'll be chasing Book 3 just as quickly.

That support and encouragement helps keep you going when the end of the book seems a million miles away, or when you are wrestling with an edit.

Again many thanks to my editor Fleetwood Robbins and proofing editor Robin Seavill. To Jane Dixon-Smith for the cover and Lauren Atkinson for the map.

My family continues to encourage and support me and I am forever grateful to them for putting up with me during the many phases of creating these works.

ACKNOWLEDGMENTS

FROM THE AUTHOR

In All Jest,

First of all, I wanted to say a huge thank you for choosing to read *Fool Me Twice*.

I'd be grateful if you could write a review. It doesn't have to be long, just a few words, but it's the best way for me to help new readers discover the book, and my series, for the first time.

If you'd like to stay up to date with my new releases, as well as exclusive competitions and giveaways, you're welcome to join my Reader Group at my website, www.kingdarryl.com.

You can also contact me via Twitter, Facebook or by email. I love hearing from readers - I read every message.

Thanks again for your support.

Best wishes,
Darryl King

ALSO BY D.E. KING

The In All Jest series

Fool Me Twice (Book 2)

Spire Of Fools (Book 3)

The In All Jest World

Cut In Half (Book A)